M. François Guizot

Life of Oliver Cromwell

M. François Guizot

Life of Oliver Cromwell

ISBN/EAN: 9783337415686

Printed in Europe, USA, Canada, Australia, Japan

Cover: Foto ©Raphael Reischuk / pixelio.de

More available books at **www.hansebooks.com**

LIFE

OF

OLIVER CROMWELL.

By F. GUIZOT,

AUTHOR OF "MEMOIRS OF MY TIME," ETC.

NINTH EDITION.

LONDON:
RICHARD BENTLEY AND SON,
Publishers in Ordinary to Her Majesty the Queen.
1887.

ADVERTISEMENT

THE history of the English Revolution, its origin and consequences, extends over a period of sixty-three years,—from the accession of Charles I., in 1625, to the fall of James II., in 1688; and is naturally divided, by the great events which it includes, into four periods. The first of these comprehends the reign of Charles I., his conflict with the Long Parliament, his defeat and death; the second contains the history of the Commonwealth, under the Long Parliament and Cromwell; the third is marked by the Restoration of the Monarchy, after the brief Protectorate of Richard Cromwell; and the fourth comprises the reigns of Charles II. and James II., and the final fall of the royal race of Stuart.

Each of these four periods will form the subject of a special work by M. Guizot. The first of these has already appeared; the second is now published; and the other two are in progress. Together, the four works will constitute a complete picture of the most important epoch in our history.

With regard to the present Volume, I need say nothing, except so far as my own share in it is concerned. I have endeavoured to make as literal a translation as was compatible with our English idiom; and, in all cases, I have carefully verified the references, and given the *ipsissima verba* of the authorities quoted by M. Guizot.

ANDREW R. SCOBLE.

LINCOLN'S INN,
    FEBRUARY, 1854.

CONTENTS.

BOOK I.

PAGE

Organisation of the Republican Government—Formation of the Council
of State—Resistance of the Country—Trial and Condemnation of
Five Royalist Leaders: Lords Hamilton, Holland, Capell, and Norwich, and Sir John Owen—Execution of Hamilton, Holland, and
Capell—Publication of the "Eikon Basilikè"—Royalist and Republican Polemics: Milton and Salmasius—Outbreak and Insurrection of the Levellers—John Lilburne—Defeat of the Levellers—
Trial and Acquittal of Lilburne—Tyranny of the Parliament—
Increasing Greatness of Cromwell   1

BOOK II.

State of Parties in Scotland and Ireland—Charles II. is Proclaimed
King—Scottish Commissioners at the Hague—War in Ireland—
Cromwell assumes the Command—His Cruelty and Successes—
Montrose's Expedition in Scotland—His Defeat, Arrest, Condemna-
tion, and Execution—Charles II. Lands in Scotland—Cromwell
returns from Ireland, and takes the Command of the War in Scotland
—His dangerous Position—Battle of Dunbar—Charles II. enters
England—Cromwell follows him—Battle of Worcester—Flight and
Adventures of Charles II.—He returns to France—Cromwell returns
to London—Triumphant success of the Commonwealth .   .   .   44

BOOK III.

Impression produced on the Continent by the Trial and Execution of
Charles I.—Assassination of Dorislaus at the Hague, and of Ascham
at Madrid—Attitude of the Continental States towards the Commonwealth of England—Development and Successes of the English Navy
—Foreign Policy of the Republican Parliament—Rivalry between

PAGE

France and Spain in their Relations with England—Recognition of the Commonwealth by Spain—Relations between England and the United Provinces—English Ambassadors at the Hague—Dutch Ambassadors in London—Their want of Success—Negotiations of Mazarin in London—Louis XIV. recognises the English Commonwealth—War between England and the United Provinces—Successes of Blake—Effects of the War in England 118

BOOK IV.

Conflict between Cromwell and the Parliament—Attempts to obtain a Reduction of the Army—Proposition of a General Amnesty and a New Electoral Law—Projects of Civil and Religious Reform—Conversation between Cromwell and the Principal Leaders of the Parliament and Army—Petition of the Army in favour of Reform, and for the Dissolution of the Parliament—Charges of Corruption against the Parliament—It attempts to perpetuate its Existence by sanctioning New Elections—Urgency of the Crisis—Cromwell dissolves the Parliament 180

BOOK V.

Public indifference to the Expulsion of the Long Parliament—Cromwell's Manifesto to justify his Conduct—He assumes Possession of the Government—Convocation of the Barebone Parliament—Cromwell's Opening Speech—Character and acts of the Barebone Parliament—Prevalence of the mystical Revolutionary Spirit among its Members—Its Inefficiency and Resignation—Cromwell is proclaimed Protector—Plots of the Republicans and Cavaliers—Lilburne, Gerard, and Vowell—Government of Cromwell; his Court; his Reforms—Scotland and Ireland are incorporated with England—Foreign Policy of Cromwell—Peace with Holland—Whitelocke's Embassy to Sweden—Cromwell's Treaties with Sweden, Denmark, and Portugal—Cromwell's Relations with Spain and France—Election of a New Parliament—Cromwell's Opening Speech—Hostility of the Parliament—Cromwell's Second Speech, and Secession of a number of Members—Renewal of Hostilities by the Parliament—Cromwell's Third Speech—Dissolution of the Parliament 214

BOOK VI.

Government of Cromwell without a Parliament—Royalist and Republican Conspiracies—Different attitude of Cromwell towards the two Parties—Insurrections in the West and North of England—Attempts at Legal Resistance—Appointments of Major-Generals—Taxation of the Royalists—Cromwell's Religious Toleration.—His Conduct towards the Jews, towards the Universities, and towards Literary Men—Government of Monk in Scotland, and of Henry Cromwell in Ireland—Cromwell's Conversations with Ludlow 285

BOOK VII.

Cromwell's Preparations for War against Spain—His projected Campaign in both Hemispheres—Blake's Expedition in the Mediterranean,—Before Leghorn, Tunis, Tripoli, and Algiers,—and off the Coast of Spain—Departure from Portsmouth of the Fleet under Penn and Venables—Secret of their Destination—Don Luis de Haro, Condé, and Mazarin push their Negotiations with Cromwell—Persecution of the Vaudois in Piedmont—Intervention of Cromwell on their behalf—Penn and Venables attack St. Domingo, unsuccessfully—Capture of Jamaica—Rupture between Cromwell and Spain—Treaty between Cromwell and France—The Court of Madrid promises Assistance to Charles II.—Cromwell sends Lockhart as his Ambassador to Paris—Cromwell's Greatness and Importance in Europe—He convokes another Parliament 321

BOOK VIII.

Prognostics of a New Parliament—Vane's Pamphlet—The Elections—Cromwell's Speech at the Opening of the Session—Exclusion of nearly a Hundred Members—Success of the English Fleet off Cadiz—Thorough Adherence of the Parliament to Cromwell—Propositions and Intrigues to make Cromwell King—The Humble Petition and Advice—Failure of the Attempt—New Constitution of the Protectorate—Close of the Session—Manœuvres of Cromwell—Death of Blake—Second Session of the Parliament in Two Houses—Quarrel between the Two Houses—Cromwell Dissolves the Parliament—Agitation of Parties—Royalist and Republican Plots—Cromwell's active Alliance with France—His Successes on the Continent—Capture of Mardyke and Dunkirk—Embassy of Lord Faulconbridge to Paris, and of the Duke de Créqui to London—Cromwell contemplates the Convocation of a New Parliament—Decline of his Health—His Family—His Mother, Wife, and Children—Death of his Daughter, Lady Claypole—Illness of Cromwell—State of his Mind—His Death—Conclusion . 358

HISTORY

OF

OLIVER CROMWELL

AND

THE ENGLISH COMMONWEALTH.

BOOK I.

ORGANISATION OF THE REPUBLICAN GOVERNMENT—FORMATION OF THE COUNCIL
OF STATE—RESISTANCE OF THE COUNTRY—TRIAL AND CONDEMNATION OF FIVE
ROYALIST LEADERS: LORDS HAMILTON, HOLLAND, CAPELL, AND NORWICH, AND
SIR JOHN OWEN—EXECUTION OF HAMILTON, HOLLAND, AND CAPELL—PUBLICA-
TION OF THE "EIKON BASILIKÈ"—ROYALIST AND REPUBLICAN POLEMICS :
MILTON AND SALMASIUS—OUTBREAK AND INSURRECTION OF THE LEVELLERS—
JOHN LILBURNE—DEFEAT OF THE LEVELLERS—TRIAL AND ACQUITTAL OF LIL-
BURNE—TYRANNY OF THE PARLIAMENT—INCREASING GREATNESS OF CROM-
WELL.

In the Life of King Charles I., I have related the downfall of
an ancient monarchy, and the violent death of a king who was
worthy of respect, although he governed his people badly and un-
justly. I have now to relate the vain efforts of a revolutionary
assembly to found a republic ; and to describe the ever-tottering,
but strong and glorious government of a revolutionary despot, whose
bold and prudent genius commands our admiration, although he
attacked and destroyed, first legal order, and then liberty, in his
native land. The men whom God chooses as the instruments of
his great designs are full of contradiction and of mystery : in them
are mingled and combined, in undiscoverable proportions, capabilities and failings, virtues and vices, enlightenment and error,
grandeur and weakness ; and after having filled the age in which

B

they lived with the splendour of their actions and the magnitude of
their destiny, they remain personally obscure in the midst of their
glory, alternately cursed and worshipped by the world which does
not know them.

At the opening of the Long Parliament, on the 3rd of November, 1640, the House of Commons consisted of five hundred
and six members. In 1649, after the execution of the King, when
it abolished kingship and proclaimed the Commonwealth, there
scarcely remained a hundred who took part in its sittings and acts.
During the month of February, the House divided ten times ; and
at the most numerous division, only seventy-seven members were
present to record their votes.[1]

Thus mutilated and reduced to the condition of a victorious
coterie, this assembly set to work, with an ardour full at once of
strong faith and deep anxiety, to organise the republican government. On the 7th of February, 1649, the same day on which it
abolished kingship by an express decree, it voted the creation of a
Council of State, " to be henceforth the executive power ; " and five
members, Scott, Ludlow, Lisle, Holland, and Robinson, chosen
from among the staunchest republicans, were ordered " to present to
the House instructions to be given to the Council of Estates ; and
likewise the names of such persons as they conceive fit to be of that
Council."[2]

Six days after, on the 13th of February, Scott presented his
report to the House. All the practical functions of the Government were vested in the Council of State. It received power to
dispose of the national forces and revenues ; to direct the police ;
to repress all rebellion ; to arrest, interrogate, and imprison all who
should resist its orders ; to conduct the relations of the State with
foreign powers ; to administer the colonies ; and to watch over the
interests of commerce : being thus invested with almost absolute
power, under the control and in obedience to the instructions of Parliament—the sole depositary of the national sovereignty.[3]

On the two following days, the House proceeded to appoint the

[1] Old Parliamentary History, vol. ix. p. 12; Journals of the House of
Commons, vol. vi. pp. 128, 130, 132, 140, 141, 143, 147.
[2] Commons' Journals, vol. vi. p. 133. I may here mention that, at this
period, England had not yet adopted the reformed Gregorian Calendar, and
that her chronology was ten days behind that of the Continent. The 7th of
February in England, in the seventeenth century, would therefore correspond
with the 17th of February on the Continent. For convenience of reference to
the English authorities which I quote, I have adopted the English date in
speaking of English events.
[3] Commons' Journals, vol. vi. pp. 138, 139.

forty-one Councillors of State, voting specially on each name. Five ex-peers of the realm,[1] the three chief judges,[2] the three leaders of the army, Fairfax, Cromwell, and Skippon, and thirty country gentlemen and citizens, nearly all of whom were members of the House, were elected. The nomination of the five peers met with objections; the democrats wished to exclude them, as well as the House of Lords itself, from all participation in the government of the Commonwealth; but the more prudent politicians, on the contrary, gave an eager welcome to these noblemen, who were still powerful by their wealth and name, and whom fanaticism or meanness had connected with the party which had destroyed their order. The entire list proposed by the Commissioners of the Parliament was adopted, with the exception of two names, Ireton and Harrison, who were probably thought too devotedly attached to Cromwell, and for whom two republicans were substituted, conspicuous for their uncompromising distrust of the army and its leaders. They were all appointed for a year.[3]

When they met for the first time, on the 17th of February, 1649, they were required to sign an engagement, expressing approbation of all that had been done in the King's trial, in the overthrow of kingship, and in the abolition of the House of Lords. Only fourteen Councillors of State were present at this meeting; thirteen signed the proposed declaration without hesitation, and a fresh meeting was convoked for the next day but one; thirty-four members then attended, and on the same day Cromwell gave a report to Parliament of what had occurred. Six other Councillors of State, making nineteen in all, had signed the engagement; but twenty-two persisted in refusing it. They stated that they were resolved, in future, faithfully to serve the government of the House of Commons, as it was the supreme power, the only one which remained in existence, and therefore necessary to the liberties and safety of the people; but, from various motives, and in terms more or less distinct, they refused to give their sanction to all the past. The House, in great excitement, proceeded at once to deliberate on this report, forbidding all the members present to leave the hall without express permission; but political good sense

---

[1] The Earls of Denbigh, Mulgrave, Pembroke, and Salisbury, and Lord Grey of Wark.

[2] Henry Rolle, Chief Justice of the Upper Bench; Oliver St. John, Chief Justice of the Common Bench; and John Wylde, Chief Baron of the Exchequer.

[3] Commons' Journals, vol. vi. pp. 140—143; Ludlow's Memoirs, p. 123; Godwin's History of the Commonwealth, vol. iii. p. 12.

acted as a check upon passion : to originate dissensions among the
republicans, in the first days of the Commonwealth, would, it was
felt, be madness ; the regicides knew that, if left alone, they would
not be strong enough to maintain their position ; and the House
merely ordained that the Councillors of State whom it had appointed
should all meet to confer together on what had best be done under
the circumstances, and should afterwards communicate their decision to Parliament. The matter was arranged without further difficulty : the pledge of fidelity which the dissidents offered for the
future was accepted, and they took their seats beside the regicides
in the republican Council of State.[1]

This compromise was to a very great extent the work, on the
one hand, of Cromwell, and on the other, of Sir Harry Vane, the
most eminent, the most sincere, the most able, and the most chimerical of the non-military republicans. He was an ardent
revolutionist, and he detested revolutionary violence. When, on
the 6th of November, 1648, the army expelled the entire Presbyterian party from the House of Commons, Vane boldly denounced
that act, and ceased to take part in the sittings of the mutilated
House. He protested still more strongly against the trial of the
King, and ever since that period he had resided at his country-seat
at Raby, completely unconnected with public affairs. But the
Commonwealth was the object at once of his faith and of his
aspirations ; as soon as it appeared, he belonged to it, heart and
soul. Cromwell, who cared little for the embarrassments which
might at a future time be occasioned him by the allies of whom he
had present need, immediately used every effort to induce Vane
once more to give the republican government the support of his
talents, his devotedness, and his influence. Vane resisted at first,
but in a way which showed he soon would yield. He it was, who,
setting aside the past, suggested the oath of fidelity for the future ;
and Cromwell, quite sure that this would be enough to secure
Vane to the service of the Council of State and to the Parliament,
was one of the most eager to express his entire approval of the
suggestion.[2]

Cromwell was right, for no sooner had they taken their seats
than this same Vane, and that same majority of the Council of
State who had refused to take any share in the responsibility of the

[1] Commons' Journals, vol. vi. pp. 139. 146 ; Whitelocke's Memorials, p. 382 ;
Cromwelliana, p. 52 ; Godwin's History of the Commonwealth, vol. iii.
pp. 28—31.
[2] Forster's Statesmen of the Commonwealth, vol. iii. pp. 125—127 ;
Godwin's History of the Commonwealth, vol. iii. p. 31.

regicides, elected[1] as their president, John Bradshaw, the President of the High Court which had condemned Charles I.; and three days after, Vane, with several of his colleagues, proceeded to "a small house in Holborn, which opens backwards into Lincoln's Inn Fields," to offer the post of Latin Secretary to the Council to a kinsman of Bradshaw's, who had recently maintained, in an eloquent pamphlet, "that it is lawful to call to account a tyrant, or wicked king, and after due conviction, to depose and put him to death!"[2] That man was Milton.

At the same time that it was engaged in the constitution of the Council of State, the House turned its attention also to the courts of law; an urgent question, for the day for the opening of their quarterly sessions was at hand, and no one for a moment admitted the possibility of interrupting the course of justice. Of the twelve principal judges, ten had been appointed by the Parliament itself since the outbreak of the civil war; and yet, on the 8th of February, 1649, six of them refused to give any oath of fidelity to the Commonwealth, and the other six would only consent to continue the discharge of their functions on condition that, by a formal declaration of the House, the ancient laws of the country should be maintained, and that the judges should continue to take them as the rule of their decisions. These demands were complied with, and the six judges who had tendered their resignation were not replaced until the following summer.[3]

The Earl of Warwick, the Lord High Admiral, lived on intimate terms with Cromwell; but he was a decided Presbyterian, who inspired the republicans with no confidence, and who himself preferred his own ease to their service. His office was taken from him on the 20th of February, 1649; the powers of the Admiralty were vested in the Council of State, which delegated them to a committee of three members, of whom Vane was the chief; and the command of the fleet passed into the hands of three officers, Edward Popham, Richard Dean, and Robert Blake—the last a literate and warlike Puritan, who had already given proof of his great qualities as a soldier, and who was destined to augment at sea the power and glory of the Commonwealth, which he served with austere and unflinching devotedness.[4]

---

[1] On the 10th of March, 1649.
[2] Todd's Life of Milton, pp. 63, 70; Carlyle, Cromwell's Letters and Speeches, vol. ii. p. 16; Godwin's History of the Commonwealth, vol. iii. p. 36
[3] Commons' Journals, vol. vi. pp. 134—136; Whitelocke's Memorials, pp. 378—380; Clarendon's History of the Rebellion, vol. vi. p. 247.
[4] Commons' Journals, vol. vi. pp. 147, 149, 150; Godwin's History of the Commonwealth, vol. iii. p. 35; Hepworth Dixon's Life of Blake, pp. 114—122.

The House had revised and arranged every department of the administration ; the legislation and diplomacy of the country, the courts of justice, the police, the finances, the army and the fleet, were all in its hands.   To appear as disinterested as it was active, it permitted those members who had separated from the conquering party, at the moment of its definitive rupture with the King, to resume their seats in its midst; but it required from them, at the same time, such a disavowal of their former votes that very few could persuade themselves to take advantage of this concession.   To fill up the vacancies thus created, it authorised some new elections, but in very small numbers—seven only in the space of six months—for it distrusted the electors ; and it even directed the formation of a committee for the purpose of framing a new electoral law, to regulate the assembling of a new Parliament.   But these were mere demonstrations, not *bonâ fide* and effectual resolutions. Henry Martyn told the House, "That he thought they might find the best advice from the Scripture : for when Moses was found upon the river, and brought to Pharaoh's daughter, she took care that the mother might be found out, to whose care he might be committed to be nursed ; which succeeded very happily." Applying this, he continued: "Our Commonwealth is yet an infant of a weak growth, and a very tender constitution : and therefore my opinion is, that nobody can be so fit to nurse it as the mother who brought it forth ; and that we should not think of putting it under any other hands, until it hath obtained more years and vigour."[1]

Henry Martyn did not say enough : not only was the Commonwealth unable to exist without the care of the Parliament which had given it birth, but when that all-powerful Parliament wished to impart full vigour to the Commonwealth, it found itself too weak to accomplish that work, and could only fluctuate between precipitation and postponement, hesitation and violence. The acts voted on the 7th of February, for abolishing the kingly office and taking away the House of Peers, were not definitively adopted until the 17th and 19th of March ; and when the House ordained their official proclamation in the City of London, the Lord Mayor, Reynoldson, positively refused to proclaim them. When summoned to the bar, ten days afterwards, he alleged the scruples of his conscience in justification of his conduct. The House condemned him to pay a fine of two thousand pounds, and to be imprisoned for two months ;

---

[1] Commons' Journals, vol. vi. pp. 129, 130, 133, 136, 210; Godwin's History of the Commonwealth, vol. iii. pp. 33—35 ; Forster's Statesmen of the Commonwealth, vol. iii. p. 324; Ludlow's Memoirs, p. 134.

and ordered the election of another Lord Mayor. Alderman Thomas Andrews, one of the King's judges, was elected; but though the House did not think it wise to require of him immediately that official proclamation of the Commonwealth which his predecessor had refused to make, it gave intimation of more rigorous intentions with regard to the City. "They believe they may make sure of the metropolis," wrote the President de Bellièvre, the French ambassador in England, to M. Servien, "either by causing the election of other magistrates who are devoted to their service, or by absolutely suppressing the form of government which has hitherto been observed, and establishing one of the officers of the army as Governor of the city—as it is believed they intend to do. But, according to all appearance, although it may be their intention to do this at some time or other, they will be contented for the present with establishing their authority therein, without any display of violence." On the 10th of May following, more than a month after the election of the new Lord Mayor, and more than three months after the death of Charles I., the authority of the House was not established in the city, for the Commonwealth had not yet been proclaimed there. Inquiry was made into the cause of this delay, and twenty days after, on the 30th of May, the proclamation at length took place, in the absence of several of the aldermen, who declined to take any part in the ceremonial, and amid the strongest manifestations of popular disapprobation. "It was desired," wrote M. de Croullé, the secretary of the President de Bellièvre, to Cardinal Mazarin, "that this act should be effected in the ordinary form of a simple publication, without the mayor and aldermen being supported by any soldiers, in order to show that no violent means had been resorted to; but a quantity of people having assembled around them with hootings and insults, compelled them to send for some troops, who first drove away all the bystanders, and thus they finished their publication."[1]

The aldermen who had absented themselves were called to the bar of the House, and they unhesitatingly confessed the motives of their absence. Sir Thomas Soames, who was also a member of the House, stated, "That it was against several oaths which he had taken as an alderman of London, and against his judgment and conscience." Alderman Chambers said, "That his heart did not go

---

[1] Commons' Journals, vol. vi. pp. 133, 166, 168, 177, 179, 206, 221; White-locke's Memorials, pp. 393, 394; Leicester's Journal, p. 73; Letters of the President de Bellièvre to M. Servien (12th April, 1649), and of M. de Croullé to Cardinal Mazarin (14th June, 1649), in the Archives des Affaires Étrangères de France.

along with the work, in that business." They were both deprived of their municipal functions, and declared incapable of holding any public office. Sir Thomas Soames was even expelled from the House. But when it became necessary to replace them, it was found very difficult to obtain persons willing to be their successors, and seven successive refusals attested the ill-will of the citizens. A dinner offered to the House, by that faction in the city which was devoted to its cause, was a poor compensation for these checks; and in order to put the municipal body in a position to discharge its functions, it was found necessary to give to forty, and even, in certain cases, to ten of its members, the right to act in its name.[1]

The same obstacles and the same resistance were met with everywhere. The Parliament ordained the destruction, in all public places, of the King's arms, and all other emblems of royalty; and this order, though renewed four times,[2] was so imperfectly obeyed that, two years after the establishment of the Commonwealth, Parliament was obliged to make the parochial authorities responsible for its execution, and to authorise them to pay the expenses out of the parish rates. A simple oath of fidelity to the Commonwealth was required of all the beneficed clergy, of the members of the Universities of Oxford and Cambridge, of all public functionaries, sheriffs, justices of peace, and others; and refusals arrived by thousands, publicly sanctioned by the gravest authorities, among others, by the Assembly of the Presbyterian Clergy in London, which met in May, 1650.[3] It was only in the month of January, 1650, a year after the death of the King, that they ventured to change the names of those vessels in the fleet which were suggestive of departed royalty.[4] In the spring of that same year, a new frigate was launched at London, in presence of the whole Council of State: it was proposed that it should be named *The Commonwealth of England*, " but it was thought," wrote M. de Croullé to Cardinal Mazarin, " that if the vessel were to perish, as all vessels are liable to do, it would be a bad omen; "[5] and so that hazardous satisfaction was dispensed with.

[1] Commons' Journals, vol. vii. pp. 221, 222; Whitelocke's Memorials, pp. 384, 404, 405; Godwin, vol. iii. p. 97.

[2] On the 15th of February and 9th of August, 1649, the 9th of April, 1650, and the 5th of February, 1651; Commons' Journals, vol. vi. pp. 142, 276, 394, 531.

[3] Commons' Journals, vol. vi. pp. 306, 427; Neal's History of the Puritans, vol. iv. pp. 8, 10; Reliquiæ Baxterianæ, book i. p. 61.

[4] Commons' Journals, vol. vi. p. 340.

[5] M. de Croullé to Cardinal Mazarin (2 May, 1650); Archives des Affaires Etrangères de France.

Nothing is more irritating to power, and especially to a conquering power, than the consciousness of its weakness; and when it experiences this feeling, it immediately seeks some opportunity of manifesting its strength, by way either of diversion or of revenge. The republican Government of England, thus hampered in its progress, had in its hands some of the most eminent of the royalist leaders: the Duke of Hamilton, the Earl of Holland, the Earl of Norwich, Lord Capell, and Sir John Owen—valiant survivors of the last struggles of the civil war, who had fallen, at different times, into the power of the Parliament, and had been its prisoners for many months. At one moment they almost believed themselves in safety. In November, 1648, the two Houses voted that the Duke of Hamilton should pay a fine of one hundred thousand pounds sterling, and that the other four should be banished from the country.[1] But before this vote had been carried into execution, the Presbyterians, by whose influence it had been passed, were expelled from the House of Commons, and the Independents, left sole masters of the field, formally revoked it, and detained the five leaders in prison, announcing, at the same time, their intention to bring them to trial.[2] Regardless of his perilous position, when, a few days after, a more important trial, that of the King, commenced, Lord Capell, with the enthusiasm of a high-minded gentleman and of a valiant soldier, wrote from his cell in the Tower, on the 15th of January, 1649, to Cromwell, to represent to him the enormity of such a crime, and to conjure him to save the King. "I frankly give you leave to think," he said, in this remarkable letter, " nor do I value the inconvenience it could draw along with it, that there is not that honest expedient in the world to serve him by, that I would not hazard myself in to employ for him; nor do I know what earthly felicity it is could be so welcome to me as to advance a step beyond any other in my duty towards him. But my present condition refuseth me the ability of anything else but that of invocating the favour of God for him, and making my addresses to you, whom I take to be the figure that gives the denomination to the sequence of a great many ciphers that follow you." He then set forth at great length, and in terms sometimes of reproach and sometimes of flattery, all the motives of religion, justice, policy, duty, honour, interest, pride, and personal ambition, which might combine to influence Cromwell's decision; and he concluded with these words: " Sir, my conclusion shall be very

---

[1] Commons' Journals, vol. vi. p. 72.
[2] On the 13th of December, 1648; Commons' Journals, vol. vi. p. 96.

plain, because you may thereby be the better assured of my sincerity
in all the rest. The ancient constitutions and present laws of this
kingdom are my inheritance and birthright; if any shall think to
impose upon me that which is worse than death, which is the
profane and dastardly parting from these laws, I will choose the
lesser evil, which is death. I have also a right in kingship, the
protector of those laws: this is also, by a necessity and conjunction
with that other, dearer to me than life. And lastly, in this king is
my present right, and also obligations of inestimable favours
received from him. I would to God my life could be a sacrifice to
preserve his! Could you make it an expedient to serve that end,
truly I would pay you more thanks for it than you will allow yourself from all your other merits from those you have most obliged,
and die your most affectionate friend, CAPELL."[1]

Cromwell returned no answer to this letter, but he did not
forget it. He possessed that pitiless sagacity which, while it
enabled him to recognise the value of an enemy, only convinced
him of the necessity of putting him out of the way. On the 1st of
February the House resolved on erecting a new High Court of
Justice, to consist of sixty members, of whom fifteen should form a
quorum. Bradshaw was appointed President of this Court. It
was commissioned to "hear, try, and adjudge divers delinquents,"
among whom the Duke of Hamilton, the Earls of Holland and
Norwich, Lord Capell, and Sir John Owen, were specially named;
and orders were given that their trial should immediately be
proceeded with.[2]

On the following day, the 2nd of February, as soon as night
had fallen, Lord Capell, whom one of his friends had provided with
a cord, let himself down from his room in the Tower into the ditch
below. He had been informed as to what part of the ditch he
would find it most easy to traverse; but he either mistook the
place to which he had been directed, or the water and mud were
deeper than his informant had expected, for he sank into the mire
to his chin, and was on the point of giving up his attempt and
shouting for assistance. His tall stature and undaunted courage,
however, saved him; he succeeded in reaching the other side,
where his friends were expecting him. He was conducted by them
to the Temple, where he remained concealed for two days. The
Government, enraged at his escape, used the utmost diligence for
his discovery. One of his most faithful friends thought that he

[1] Lady Theresa Lewis's Lives from the Clarendon Gallery, vol. ii.
pp. 102, 264.
[2] Commons' Journals, vol. vi. p. 128.

would be unable to remain in safety in a place of so much resort as the Temple, and that he would find a surer asylum in a small house in Lambeth Marsh. That same evening Lord Capell, accompanied by his friend alone, went out for the purpose of taking the first boat they should find at the Temple Stairs. It was so late that only one remained. They entered it, and told the boatman to row them to the other side of the river. Lord Capell was carefully disguised : but whether his companion inadvertently called him *My Lord*, as was generally reported, or whether some other circumstance awakened his suspicions, the boatman determined to follow his two passengers on landing: and having watched them into the house, went at once to an officer, and asked him " what he would give him to bring him to the place where the Lord Capell lay ? " The officer promised him ten pounds ; the boatman fulfilled his promise ; Lord Capell was seized, and the next day returned a prisoner to the Tower.[1]

On the 9th of February the Court began its sittings ; fifty of the Commissioners appointed to form it were present. The five prisoners were brought to the bar, as different in attitude and language as in condition and character. The Duke of Hamilton was a great nobleman, a court politician, sincerely attached to the king, whom he had always desired to serve, but still more anxious to maintain his influence and popularity in Scotland, his native land, where he was careful to keep on good terms with all parties, and cared little to aggravate the difficulties or dangers of his master, if he could diminish or delay those which threatened himself. Lord Holland was a frivolous and reckless courtier, fond of money and pleasure, and characterised by very little faith, ability, or morality ; he had curried and obtained favour, first with the Duke of Buckingham, then with Queen Henrietta Maria, then with the King himself, and finally with the Parliament, passing, as his necessities or fears dictated, from one party to another : decried by all who knew him ; maintaining relations of a suspicious nature with the Court of France ; and regarded with jealous enmity by Cromwell, either because of some slighting language he had used concerning him, or, as it is said, on some lady's account. The Earl of Norwich was a jovial and good-natured Cavalier, anxious to do his duty to the King and to serve his friends, and inspiring his enemies with neither fear nor resent-

[1] Lady Theresa Lewis's Lives from the Clarendon Gallery, vol. ii. pp. 105—107; Clarendon's History of the Rebellion, vol. vi. pp. 258—260; Whitelocke's Memorials, p. 377.

ment. Sir John Owen was a simple Welsh gentleman, honest and
courageous, without any thought of ambition or personal advantage,
an obscure martyr of the cause he had embraced, and utterly
unconscious that there was any merit in his devotedness. Lord
Capell came last, as noble in heart as in race, the worthy de-
scendant of a grandfather who had been celebrated in his county
for his eminent virtues and olden hospitality. " He kept a
bountiful house," said his grandson of him, " and showed forth
his faith by his works; extending his charity in such abundant
manner to the poor, that he was bread to the hungry, drink to the
thirsty, eyes to the blind, and legs to the lame, and might be
justly styled a great almoner to the King of kings." [1] Lord Capell
had worthily represented in Parliament, at court, and in the camp,
the solid virtues of his family ; and Charles I. had had experience,
as the necessities of the time required, both of his independence
and his loyalty. These five men, thus thrown together in misfortune, formed, by their union, an almost complete and faithful
type of the royalist party, in its noblest as well as in its least
honourable elements ; and that entire party seemed represented
and arraigned in their persons, before the Court which began to
sit in Westminster Hall, a few days after the dissolution of that
which had tried and judged the king. [2]

Hamilton maintained a severe countenance, and asked for time
to send to Scotland for certain papers which he required. The
Court granted him an insufficient delay, and when he prayed for
more time, he was told, " that it was for prisoners to prepare their
proofs against the trial, he having been in prison so long." After
his condemnation, he was urgently solicited to make certain revelations about the past. Cromwell even sent messengers to offer him
not only his life, but the restitution of his former fortune if he
would do so ; but he indignantly refused, saying, that " if he had as
many lives as hairs on his head, he would lay them all down rather
than redeem them by so base a means." [3] The effect of supreme
and irrevocable misfortune is to elevate those souls which it does
not deprive of all virtue.

The Earls of Holland and Norwich merely attempted to diminish
the gravity of the charges brought against them, and to produce a

---

[1] Lady Theresa Lewis's Lives from the Clarendon Gallery, vol. i. p. 252.
[2] State Trials, vol. iv. col. 1155; Clarendon's History of the Rebellion,
vol. vi. pp. 252—266.
[3] State Trials, vol. iv. cols. 1156, 1187, 1188, 1191, 1211; Whitelocke's
Memorials, p. 381.

favourable impression on the minds of their judges by the modesty of their demeanour.[1]

Lord Capell was not only dignified; he was haughty and undaunted. Without paying any attention to the Court, he gazed severely on the audience, as if to reproach them with the complicity of their presence. He maintained that by the terms of the capitulation of Colchester, and the explanations of the Lord General Fairfax himself, his life had been secured to him. "I am a prisoner of war," he said; "I had a fair quarter given me, and all the gowns in the world have nothing to do with me." In any case, he demanded to be tried by his peers: "Though king and lords be laid aside, yet the fundamental laws of the land are still in force." He called the attention of the Court to "Magna Charta and the Petition of Right; he desired to see his jury, and that they might see him, and said he believed that a precedent could not be given of a subject tried for his life, but either by Bill in Parliament, or by a jury." In reply, President Bradshaw told him "that he was tried before such judges as the Parliament thought fit to assign him; and who had judged a better man than himself."[2]

When the Attorney-General concluded by demanding that he should be hanged, drawn, and quartered, Lord Capell "seemed to startle;" but speedily recovering himself, he told the Court "that however he was dealt with here, he hoped for a better resurrection hereafter."[3]

They were all five condemned to be beheaded. When the president had pronounced this sentence, Sir John Owen made a low bow to the Court, and gave them humble thanks. On being asked by one of the bystanders what he meant, he said aloud, "it was a very great honour to a poor gentleman of Wales to lose his head with such noble lords," and added, with an oath, "that he was afraid they would have hanged him."[4]

The High Court, however, was irresolute; and either from a desire to act with clemency, or with a view to shift the responsibility of such rigorous proceedings, after having condemned the prisoners, it referred the execution of their sentence to the sovereign decision of Parliament.[5]

[1] State Trials, vol. iv. cols. 1195—1250; Whitelocke's Memorials, pp. 381, 385, 386.

[2] State Trials, vol. iv. cols. 1209—1211; Whitelocke, pp. 380, 381, 383; Lady Theresa Lewis's Lives from the Clarendon Gallery, vol. ii. pp. 108—115; Clarendon's History of the Rebellion, vol. vi. pp. 253—255.

[3] Whitelocke, p. 381.

[4] Clarendon's History of the Rebellion, vol. vi. pp. 255, 256.

[5] State Trials, vol. iv. col. 1188; Whitelocke, p. 386.

On the next day, the 7th of March, the Earl of Warwick, the brother of Lord Holland, with Lady Holland, Lady Capell, and several other relatives and friends of the prisoners, presented themselves at the door of the House of Commons, and requested permission to intercede personally for the lives of those against whom the High Court of Justice had pronounced sentence of death. They were admitted, and presented their petitions. But, after some hours' debate, the House resolved "not to proceed any further upon these petitions, but to leave them to the justice of the Court that sentenced them." The republican leaders would have preferred, without interfering further in this melancholy affair, to profit by the severity of the judges whom they had appointed; but the Court was resolved not to allow the whole weight to rest upon its shoulders; it granted the condemned a respite of two days, that they might again appeal to Parliament.[1]

Thus compelled to decide, the republican leaders consulted only their animosities and their fears. The Duke of Hamilton, as an individual and as a Scotchman, inspired no interest; his petition was unhesitatingly rejected. Lord Holland had many friends; his brother and his wife were there to plead his cause; he was naturally of an obliging and kindly disposition; in his passage through all parties he had in all formed connections and rendered services; but Cromwell and Ireton detested and despised him: his petition was rejected by a majority of one vote. With regard to the Earl of Norwich, the votes were equally divided; but Lenthall, the Speaker of the House, said, "that he had received many obligations from him; and that once, when he had been like to have incurred the King's displeasure, by some misinformation, which would have been very penal to him, Lord Norwich had by his credit preserved him, and removed the prejudice that was against him; and therefore he was obliged in gratitude to give his vote for the saving him." Lord Norwich was saved, as Lord Holland had just been condemned, by a majority of one vote. No one was there to defend Sir John Owen; but Colonel Hutchinson said to Ireton, who was sitting next to him: "It grieves me much to see that, while all are labouring to save the lords, a gentleman, that stands in the same condemnation, should not find one friend to ask his life; and so am I moved with compassion that, if you will second me, I am resolved to speak for him, who, I perceive, is a stranger and friendless." Ireton promised to do so: Hutchinson obtained the poor Welsh knight's petition, which had been left in the hands of the clerk of the House,

---

[1] Commons' Journals, vol. vi. p. 158; State Trials, vol. iv. col. 1216.

delivered it, spoke for him so nobly, and was so effectually seconded by Ireton, that Sir John Owen's life was saved by a majority of five votes.[1]

Lord Capell now remained—the object, on the part of his family and friends, of the most passionate solicitude and the most active efforts; every means was tried to save him; money was offered, and even given, to persons who promised the support of their influence. A long debate took place on his petition; some spoke in his favour, extolling his virtues, and saying "that he had never deceived them, or pretended to be of their party, but always resolutely declared himself for the King." Cromwell then rose, and in the opening of his speech manifested more esteem and kindness for Lord Capell than any previous speaker had done; "but my affection for the public," he continued, "so much weighs down my private friendship that I cannot but tell you, that the question now is, whether you will preserve the most bitter and the most implacable enemy you have? I know the Lord Capell very well, and I know that he would be the last man in England that would forsake the royal cause. He has great courage, industry, and generosity; he has many friends who would always adhere to him; and as long as he lived, what condition soever he was in, he would be a thorn in your sides. And, therefore, for the good of the Commonwealth, I shall give my vote against the petition;" and it was rejected, by what majority we cannot accurately ascertain.[2]

The execution was fixed for the following day, the 9th of March, 1649. During the night, Lord Capell requested his friend, Dr. Morley, who had visited him in his prison, to administer to him the sacrament. "I desire to receive it," he said, "from a minister of the King's party, and according to the liturgy of the Church of England. * * * * I think I cannot accuse myself of any great known sin, committed against the light of my conscience, but one only—and that is, the giving my vote in Parliament for the death of my Lord of Strafford; which I did against my conscience, not out of any malice to the person of the man, but out of a base fear, and carried away with the violence of a prevailing faction; for which I have been and am heartily sorry, and have often with tears begged, and, I hope, obtained pardon of Almighty God. If you think it necessary or fit, I will confess this great and scandalous sin

---

[1] Commons' Journals, vol. vi. pp. 159, 160; Whitelocke, p. 386; Memoir of Colonel Hutchinson, pp. 339, 340; Ludlow's Memoirs, p. 123; Clarendon's History of the Rebellion, vol. vi. p. 258.

[2] Lady Theresa Lewis's Lives from the Clarendon Gallery, vol. ii. p. 120; Clarendon's History of the Rebellion, vol. vi. p. 260.

of mine, together with the cause of it, openly upon the scaffold, to
God's glory, and my own shame." Dr. Morley encouraged him in
this virtuous intention The next morning, Lord Capell's family
visited him—his wife, his eldest son, two of his uncles, and his
nephew, all together, for they were not permitted to see him separately. He kept them with him an hour, lovingly but sadly endeavouring to sustain their courage, and to address to them his last
counsels. "I would not," he said to his son, "I would not have
you neglect any honourable and just occasion to serve your King
and country with the hazard of your life and fortune; yet I would
have you to engage yourself (as I, thanks be to God for it! have
done) neither out of desire of revenge, nor hope of reward, but out
of a conscience of your duty only. The best legacy I can leave you
is my prayers for you, and a verse of David's Psalms, which I command you, upon my blessing, to make a part of your daily prayers,
as I have always made it a part of mine, viz., 'Teach me thy way,
O Lord, and lead me in a plain path.' For I have always loved
plainness and clearness both in my words and actions, and abhorred
all doubling and dissimulation, and so I would have you to do also."
When the moment of parting arrived, Lady Capell's strength failed
her, and she was carried away in a fainting fit. "Well, doctor,"
said Lord Capell, as soon as he was left alone with his friend
Morley, "the hardest thing that I had to do here in this world is
now past, the parting with this poor woman. I believe I shall be
called upon presently to go to the place where I am to take my
leave of all the rest of the world, and, I thank my God, I find myself very well disposed to it, and prepared for it. I am in good
hope that, when I come to die, I shall have nothing else to do but
to die only." Yet he wrote twice to his wife during the short
interval between their separation and the scaffold. "Let me live
long here in thy dear memory. I beseech thee, sorrow not
unsoberly, unusually. God be unto thee better than an husband,
and to my children better than a father. I am sure He is able to
be so: I am confident He is graciously pleased to be so."[1]

The Duke of Hamilton was brought first to the scaffold, which
had been erected on an open space before Westminster Hall. He
died with dignified courage, after having addressed the bystanders
in simple and quiet language, modestly justifying his life, and
professing his steady attachment to the dead king whom he had
served, and to the absent king whose return he hoped for, although

he would not witness it. As he spoke, the rays of the sun fell full on his face ; he was advised to change his position : "No," he said, "I hope to see a brighter sun than that very speedily." On the previous evening, Lord Holland had manifested considerable anguish and weakness ; he was ill in body and uneasy in mind ; but at the last moment, supported by two Presbyterian ministers, who had accompanied him to the scaffold, he exhibited becoming firmness. Lord Capell appeared last, and alone, on the scaffold. "Sir," said the officer who commanded the execution, "is your chaplain here ?" "No," he replied, "I have taken leave of him ;" and perceiving that some of his servants were weeping, he said, "Restrain yourselves, gentlemen, restrain yourselves." Then, turning to the officer, he asked, "Did the Lords speak with their hats off, or no ?" "With their hats off," replied Colonel Beecher. Lord Capell then took off his hat, and spoke briefly and firmly, showing equal frankness and decision as a royalist and as a Christian. He did as he had promised Dr. Morley ; he accused himself of his vote against Lord Strafford. "I do here profess to you," he said, "that I did give my vote to that bill against the Earl of Strafford. Truly this I may say, I had not the least part nor degree of malice in doing of it. But I must confess again, to God's glory, and the accusation of mine own frailty, and the frailty of my nature, that truly it was unworthy cowardice not to resist so great a torrent as carried that business at that time."[1] People and soldiers, friends and strangers, all beheld him die with mingled feelings of admiration and respect.

It is one of the first duties of history to render full justice to those virtuous and courageous martyrs, whose deaths act so powerfully on the feelings of nations, and give fresh vitality in the hearts of men to those causes which have suffered defeat on the field of battle. With the exception of the republican party, the whole nation was inspired with indignation and sorrow by the death of Lord Capell. The war was at an end ; the blood of the King had been shed, in expiation, it was affirmed, of all the bloodshed which he had occasioned. Why, then, more victims ? Why these severities inflicted, on prisoners made in a war which had terminated, by judges whom the laws did not recognise, and whose authority could be defended only by scholastic subtleties ? The Parliament itself felt that it could not persevere in such a course. It had still to decide the fate of several royalist leaders, both ecclesiastical, civil, and military. Against fifteen of them it decreed

[1] State Trials, vol. iv. cols. 1188—1194, 1220—1235 ; Lady Theresa Lewis's Lives from the Clarendon Gallery, vol. ii. pp. 145—153.

perpetual banishment, and the confiscation of all their property ; it ordered that five should be proceeded against by court-martial for armed insurrection ; it determined that two others, the Marquis of Winchester and tne Bishop of Norwich, should be detained in prison as long as might be deemed necessary ; and it voted that two only, Sir John Stowel and Judge David Jenkins, should be brought to trial for their lives, not before any extraordinary tribunal, but before the regular courts of assize. But even this vote was not carried into effect ; for they both remained in prison, Jenkins until the year 1656, and Sir John Stowel until the Restoration. The Parliament became anxious to avoid publicity ; it forbade the publication of the debates and acts of the High Court which had condemned Lord Capell ; pamphlets were seized, journalists were gained over ; and a committee was appointed to prepare measures for repressing abuses of the liberty of the press.[1] Silent acts of severity were substituted for public prosecutions and the scaffold.

But the Parliament had not the sole disposal of publicity and fame. A few days after the death of the king appeared the " Eikon Basilikè, or Portraiture of his Sacred Majesty in his Solitudes and Sufferings," which was said to be the work of Charles I. himself, and which, under the form of pious meditations, revealed to England the reflections, feelings, impressions, hopes, and griefs— indeed, the whole soul of the King, during the course of his trials. Aware, even before the execution of Charles, that this book was being printed, the republican leaders, foreseeing the injury it could not fail to do them, made every effort to prevent its publication.[2] They did not succeed, however ; the work got rapidly into circula- tion ; forty-seven editions of it were printed, and more than forty- eight thousand copies distributed in England during the course of the year ; and it was immediately translated and read with avidity in France and throughout all Europe. The effect which it every- where produced was prodigious ; attachment for the memory of the King became passion, and respect, worship ; his enemies were regarded as the murderers of a saint. It is to the " Eikon Basilikè " that Charles I. is principally indebted for the name of the Royal Martyr.

The work was not by him ; external testimony and internal evidence both combine to remove all doubt on the matter. Dr. Gauden, Bishop, first of Exeter and afterwards of Worcester, under

[1] Commons' Journals, vol. vi. pp. 164, 165, 276, 298 ; Godwin's History of the Commonwealth, vol. iii. pp. 43, 44, 349—348.
[2] March 16th, 1649 ; Commons' Journals, vol. vi. p. 103.

the reign of Charles II., was its real author; but the manuscript
had probably been perused and approved, perhaps even corrected,
by Charles himself, during his residence in the Isle of Wight. In
any case, it was the real expression and true portraiture of his
position, character, and mind, as they had been formed by misfortune : it is remarkable for an elevation of thought which is at
once natural and strained ; a constant mingling of blind royal pride
and sincere Christian humility ; heart-impulses struggling against
habits of obstinate self-consciousness ; true piety in the midst of
misguided conduct ; invincible, though somewhat inert, devotion to
his faith, his honour, and his rank ; and as all these sentiments are
expressed in monotonous language, which, though often emphatic,
is always grave, tranquil, and even unctuous with serenity and sad-
ness, it is not surprising that such a work should have profoundly
affected all royalist hearts, and easily persuaded them that it was the ·
King himself who addressed them.[1]

The Parliament felt that it could not remain silent in presence
of so powerful a public emotion, and it directed Milton to answer
the Eikon.   That sublime and austere genius, who in his youth had
determined, in opposition to paternal authority, to devote himself
entirely to poetry and literature, was animated by an ardent passion
for liberty : not for that real and true liberty which results from respect for all rights and for the rights of all, but for an ideal and
absolute liberty, both religious, political, and domestic ; and his
mighty mind revelled, on this subject, in noble ideas, lofty sentiments, grand images, and eloquent words, without his troubling
himself to inquire whether, in the world around him, positive facts
and his own personal actions corresponded with his principles and
hopes.   He was able to serve, and he did in fact serve, the tyranny,
first of an assembly, and afterwards of a single man, so long as, in
the intellectual order of things, he could profess and defend liberty.
He was a glorious and melancholy instance of the blinding effect
which imagination, abstract reasoning, and eloquent language can
produce on a great, but passionately dreamy intellect, and a stern
but noble heart.

Milton quickly wrote and published his Eikonoklastes, a lengthy
and cold, although violent, refutation of the Eikon Basilikè. Milton
did not understand Charles I. and his feelings, nor could he appreciate the sentiments with which the King inspired the royalist
party : he reproduced against him, with the utmost Puritan and re-

---

[1] A separate treatise on the authenticity of the Eikon Basilikè will be found
in my *Etudes Biographiques sur la Révolution d'Angleterre.*

publican animosity, all the threadbare statements, all the true or
false accusations, which, during ten years, had been current throughout England, without taking into consideration the new ideas and
impressions which recent events had originated in men's hearts, and
without adorning this retrospective diatribe by any vigour or
elegance of language. It produced only a very slight effect in
England; but on the Continent, and in France especially, it excited
the liveliest resentment; and at the request of Charles II., the
celebrated Protestant scholar, Saumaise, better known by his Latin-
ised name of Salmasius, then an honorary professor at the University of Leyden, undertook to refute it. To express his indignation,
Salmasius had not waited to be retained by Charles, and paid for
his services : eight days after the execution of the King, he had, in
a sudden and spontaneous letter, passionately denounced his enemies
and judges.[1] The " Royal Defence for Charles I., addressed to
Charles II.," produced a great sensation, more even from the name
of its author than for the merit of the work itself. It was a scholarly,
clever, and occasionally eloquent, but immoderate and untasteful
panegyric of monarchy in general, an enthusiastic apology for
Charles I., and a violently-abusive attack of the English republicans and their defender. When the work of Salmasius reached
London, the Government took it into consideration; and at a sitting
of the Council of State, at which it is said Milton was present, it
was decided that he should reply to it. He did so without delay,
and with far more talent and success than he had exhibited and
obtained when attacking Charles I. himself. His first and second
" Defence of the People of England, in answer to Salmasius's Defence of the King," are models of passionate discussion, both of a
general and of a personal character; the Commonwealth is defended
in them, in its principles as well as in its actions, with unshrinking
firmness ; and Milton brings himself before his readers, alluding to
his personal history, his manner of life, and the blindness he had
contracted by his application to this very work, with an eloquence
by turns noble and touching; diffusing everywhere, even over false
ideas and blameworthy actions, that splendour of thought and language which attracts and charms, though it may not convince, and
sometimes even may irritate. The success of these republican re-
plies was great, on the Continent as well as in England; Queen
Christina of Sweden expressed her admiration of them to Salmasius
himself; and the States-General of Holland thought it advisable to

---

[1] This letter is dated February 17, 1649; Carte's Ormonde Letters, vol. i.
pp. 255—258.

suppress the Royal Defence of the Leyden professor. Indignant at this treatment, he fell ill and died, leaving an "Answer of Claude Saumaise to John Milton," which was published after his death. Other writers, both royalists and republicans, French and English, entered the arena : Milton joined once more in the controversy, from personal irritation rather than from political necessity; and this great discussion, which had begun with apologies for a despotic King and a revolutionary Parliament, ended obscurely in a coarse and vulgar quarrel between literary men, who insulted one another with persevering acrimony.[1] When it at length terminated, the republican government had long ceased to take any interest in it ; more pressing cares and more dangerous enemies had absorbed its attention.

On the 20th of January, 1649, the very day on which the King appeared for the first time before the High Court which had been appointed to try him, the Lord General Fairfax and the General Council of Officers of the army, had presented their plan of republican government to Parliament, under the title of "An Agreement of the People of England, and the places therewith incorporated, for a secure and present peace, upon grounds of common right, freedom, and safety." This plan, prepared, it is said, by Ireton, consisted of ten articles, the essential dispositions of which were as follow :—

1. That the present Parliament dissolve on the 30th of April, 1649.

2. That the Representative (they rejected the word Parliament) of the whole nation consist of 400 persons.

3. That the people choose themselves a Representative once in two years, and that the Representative continue its sessions during six months : That the electors and members of the Representative bo natives or denizens of England, assessed towards the relief of the poor, not servants to and receiving wages from any particular person, aged twenty-one years and upwards, and housekeepers dwelling within the division for which the election is : That none shall be electors for seven years, or eligible for fourteen years, who have sided with the King against the Parliament during the late wars, or who shall offer or support any forcible opposition to the present agreement : That no member of the Council of State, nor any officer of any salaried forces in army or garrison, nor any treasurer or re-ceiver of public money, shall, while such, be elected to be of a Representative ; and in case any lawyer be chosen into any Repre-

[1] Todd's Life of Milton, pp. 123—136 ; Mitford's Life of Milton, pp. 77—95 ; Milton's Prose Works, vol. iv. and vi. (London, 1851.)

sentative, or Council of State, he shall be incapable of practice as a
lawyer during that trust.

4. That 150 members at least be always present in each sitting
of the Representative at the passing of any law, or doing any act,
whereby the people are to be bound ; but that sixty may make a
House for debates or resolutions that are preparatory thereunto.

5. That each Representative shall, within twenty days after their
first meeting, appoint a Council of State for the managing of public
affairs, until the tenth day after the meeting of the next Representative.

6. That in each interval betwixt biennial Representatives, the
Council of State, in case of imminent danger or extreme necessity,
may summon a Representative to be forthwith chosen, and to meet
for a session of not above eighty days.

7. That no member of any Representative be made either re-
ceiver, treasurer, or other officer, during that employment, saving to
be a member of the Council of State.

8. That the Representative have the supreme trust, in order to
the preservation and government of the whole ; and that their power
extend to the erecting and abolishing of courts of justice and public
offices, and to the enacting, altering, repealing, and declaring ot
laws, and the highest and final judgment concerning all natural and
civil things ; but not concerning things spiritual or evangelical.—
Certain limitations to this sovereign power were here indicated for
the safeguard of civil liberties, the financial engagements of the
State, and the disabilities which lay on the royalist party.

9. That the Christian religion be held forth and recommended
as the public profession in this nation, which we desire may, by the
grace of God, be reformed to the greatest purity in doctrine, worship,
and discipline, according to the word of God ; the instructing of
the people thereunto in a public way, so it be not compulsive, as also
the maintaining of able teachers for that end, is allowed to be
provided for by our Representatives ; the maintenance of which
teachers may be out of the public treasury, and we desire not by
tithes : That Popery or Prelacy be not held forth as the public
way or profession in this nation : That to the public profession so
held forth none be compelled by penalties or otherwise, but only
may be endeavoured to be won by sound doctrine and the example
of a good conversation : That all such who profess faith in God by
Jesus Christ have equal liberty and protection, so as they abuse not
this liberty to the civil injury of others, or to actual disturbance of
the public peace.

10. That whosoever shall, by force of arms, resist the orders of

the Representative (except in case where such Representative shall evidently render up or take away the foundations of common right, liberty, and safety, contained in this agreement), shall lose the benefit and protection of the laws, and shall be punishable with death, as an enemy and traitor to the nation.[1]

These were the views of the politic republicans, of the moderate men, both military and civil, who had already managed or closely watched the affairs of the nation ; but they were far from satisfying the ideas and passions of all the party that had made war against the King, and overthrown monarchical rule. No sooner was it installed than the republican government found itself face to face with an ardent democratic and mystical opposition ; and a man presented himself who, with indomitable courage and devotedness, became, not the leader, for no one was leader in that camp, but the interpreter, defender, and popular martyr of all the disaffected. That man was John Lilburne.

Nor was this a new part for him to play; during the reign of Charles I. he had already braved sufferings and won popularity. Even against the Republican Parliament he had recently, on the occasion of the King's trial, commenced a violent opposition, denouncing the appointment of a High Court, and demanding that the King should be judged in conformity to the laws of the country, and by an independent jury. Not that he was possessed by the spirit of demagogic cynicism, and desired to humiliate fallen royalty, but he was animated by a strict respect for the common law, and for the legal safeguards which it secures to every Englishman. He attacked, with even more vehemence, the High Court which was erected to try Lord Capell and his companions, and he even offered them his services for their defence, so anxious was he to find opportunities for gratifying his love of disputation. In the city, where his youth had been passed, and in the army, where he had served with distinction, he had old connections and numerous friends—citizens and apprentices, officers and soldiers, mystical sectaries and fanatics—all passionately attached, as he was, to the most ultra-democratic ideas and opinions, all equally argumentative and disputatious, never making the slightest allowance for the conditions of social order, or the necessities of the ruling power, but always ready to criticise and attack the government whenever it ran counter to the instincts of their conscience, or the fantasies of their mind, or the recently-acquired habits of their revolutionary independence, or the pre-

---

[1] Old Parliamentary History, vol. xviii. pp. 51C—536.

tensions of their pride. Lilburne used every means to promote the
fermentation of all these humours; he was particularly anxious to
resuscitate among the inferior ranks of the army, the practice of
holding meetings and preparing petitions—in fact, all the apparatus
of agitators delegated by their regiments, of which Cromwell and
the Independents had made such effectual use to intimidate the
Parliament.   At a council of officers held at Whitehall, on the
22nd of February, 1649, it was resolved to take severe measures
against these intrigues; and Fairfax issued general orders to the
army, forbidding all meetings and deliberations as contrary to
discipline, but recognising the right of the soldiers to petition, provided
they first informed their officers of their intention to do so.[1]   Lilburne immediately published a pamphlet,[2] under the title of
" England's New Chains Discovered," in which he violently attacked
this abuse of power on the part of men who, not long before, had so
often authorised and stimulated their subordinates to indulge in all
the excesses of liberty.   At the same time five soldiers signed and
presented to Fairfax a petition to complain of the obstacles thus
placed in the way of their right of petition.   " Be pleased to
consider," they wrote, " that we are English soldiers, engaged for
the freedom of England, and not outlandish mercenaries, to butcher
the people for pay, to serve the pernicious ends of ambition and
will in any person under Heaven."[3]

Fairfax immediately referred this petition to the council of war,
which condemned the five soldiers to ride with their faces towards
their horses' tails in front of their respective regiments, to have their
swords broken over their heads, and to be cashiered.   This sentence
was carried into execution at once, on the very day that the High
Court of Justice condemned Lord Capell to death.   A few days
after, Lilburne published a new pamphlet, entitled " The Hunting
of the Foxes from Newmarket and Triploe Heath to Whitehall by
Five small Beagles, or the Grandie-Deceivers Unmasked;" a
narrative at once burlesque and tragical of the petition and punishment of the five soldiers; and a burning invective against the
commander who had inflicted such chastisement upon them.

---

[1] Whitelocke's Memorials, p. 383.
[2] On the 22nd of February, 1649. See Guizot's Etudes Biographiques,
pp. 172, 173.
[3] Old Parliamentary History, vol. ix. p. 49; Commons' Journals, vol.
vi. p. 151; Whitelocke, pp. 383—385; The Hunting of the Foxes from Newmarket and Triploe Heath to Whitehall by Five small Beagles, p. 17;
Godwin's History of the Commonwealth, vol. iii. pp. 45—59; Guizot's Etudes
Biographiques sur la Révolution d'Angleterre, pp. 149—173.

"Was there ever," says Lilburne in his introduction, "a generation of men so apostate, so false, and so perjured as these? Did ever men pretend an higher degree of holiness, religion, and zeal to God and their country than these? They preach, they fast, they pray, they have nothing more frequent than the sentences of sacred Scripture, the name of God and of Christ, in their mouths. You shall scarce speak to Cromwell about anything but he will lay his hand on his breast, elevate his eyes, and call God to record; he will weep, howl, and repent, even while he doth smite you under the first rib. * * It is evident to the whole world that the now present interest of the officers is directly contrary to the interest of the soldiers : if you will uphold the interest of the one, the other must down; and as well may you let them bore holes through your ears, and be their slaves for ever, for your better distinction from freemen For what are you now? Your mouths are stopped, you may be abused and enslaved, but you may not complain, you may not petition for redress. They are your lords, and you are their conquered vassals. There must be no standing against the officers; if they say the crow is white, so must the soldier; he must not lisp a syllable against their treacheries and abuses, their false musters, and cheating the soldiery of their pay; that soldier that is so presumptuous as to dare to article against an officer must be cashiered."[1]

And at the same time that he thus denounced the officers to the soldiers, Lilburne addressed to the Parliament the second part of his "England's New Chains Discovered;" another invective, equally furious and severe, in which he denounced to the civil power the leaders of the army, who were labouring, and had ever laboured, to possess themselves of the mastery. "If your honourable House," he said, "should fail in performing that supreme trust which is really and essentially resident in your integrity, yet we shall not doubt but that what we have here presented and published will open the eyes and raise the hearts of so conscionable a number of the soldiery and people in all places, and make them so sensible of the bondage and danger threatened, as that these men, this faction of officers, shall never be able to go through with their wicked intentions."[2]

The Parliament and the General Council of officers were equally irritated by these publications, and combined, against their

---

[1] Hunting of the Foxes, pp. 12, 13.
[2] Lilburne, England's New Chains Discovered, part ii. p. 16; Old Parliamentary History, vol. xix. p. 51; Whitelocke, pp. 389, 390; Godwin's History of the Commonwealth, vol. iii. p. 60; Heath's Chronicle, p. 430.

new enemies, the weapons both of revolutionary violence and of
constituted authority.   Petitions arrived from several counties,
expressing censure of the nascent opposition, and promising devoted
adherence to the Parliament.   Various congregations of sectaries,
Anabaptists and others, sent to declare that it was against their wish
that Lilburne's pamphlet, "England's New Chains Discovered,"
had been read in some of their meetings, and to express their entire
disapprobation of it.   Several regiments, at the suggestion of their
officers, formally protested against the rising rebellion.   The
General Council of the army addressed to the House, on the 28th
of March, 1649, a "humble petition," in which, after demanding
the redress of certain administrative abuses which were injurious
to the soldiers, they bore witness to the good understanding which
subsisted between the Parliament and the army; and the House
attached so much importance to this proceeding, that it returned
official thanks to the petitioners.   "This day," said the Speaker to
them, in the name of the House, "will be a day of much discontent
to all the common enemies of you and us; but to all good men
that have engaged to carry on the good of the kingdom with us, it
will be a great rejoicing and satisfaction, by this your modest and
discreet petition.   And, as in yourselves, it shows your moderation,
so all those whose mouths are open to malice and detraction, will
see that both the army and Parliament are unanimous in promoting
the public good.   The things contained in your petition they
consider as matter of great concernment, and intend to take them
into immediate consideration; and as you have showed yourselves
forward and faithful in former services, they have commanded me
to return you the heartiest thanks I can for these your discreet and
serious representations."   And to sustain, by the energy of its own
resolutions, these public manifestations on the part of its adherents,
the House voted that Lilburne's pamphlet contained "much false,
scandalous, and reproachful matter, highly seditious, and destructive
to the present Government;" that its authors and distributors were
guilty of high treason, and should be proceeded against as traitors;
and that the Council of State should be enjoined to carry these
resolutions into effect.   The Council of State, on its part, directed
Milton to prepare an answer to Lilburne's book; and on the following day, Lilburne himself, and his three principal associates,
William Walwyn, Thomas Prince, and Richard Overton, were
arrested and imprisoned in the Tower.[1]

---

[1] Commons' Journals, vol. vi. pp. 153, 168, 174, 177; Whitelocke's
Memorials, p. 393; Godwin's History of the Commonwealth, vol. iii. pp. 60, 343.

Evidently, the majority of the republican party, both in the army and throughout the country generally, with greater good sense than consistency, disavowed factious opponents, and wished to support its leaders and the Parliament. But extreme factions are never conscious of their weakness, for their feverish excitement makes them believe themselves strong, and hope is always found associated with the courage which leads men to brave martyrdom. From his confinement in the Tower, Lilburne published, under the title of " A Picture of the Council of State," a full narrative of his own arrest and that of his companions, with details of their examination, defence, and imprisonment; a remarkable exhibition of dignified pride and puerile bravado, of outspoken honesty and absurd vanity. Apostrophising Cromwell and Ireton, he says—" Let them do their worst, I for my part bid defiance to them, assuredly knowing they can do no more to me than the devil did to Job. They have an army at command, but if every hair on the head of each officer or soldier were a legion of men, I would fear them no more than so many straws, for the Lord Jehovah is my rock and defence, under the assured shelter of whose wings I am safe and secure, and therefore will I sing and be merry. * * * Courteous reader and dear countryman, excuse, I beseech thee, my boasting and glorying, for I am necessitated to it, my adversaries' base and lying calumniations putting me upon it, and Paul and Samuel did it before me. And so I am thine, if thou art for the just freedoms and liberties of the land of thy nativity, JOHN LILBURNE, that never yet changed his principles from better to worse, nor could ever be threatened out of them, nor courted from them, that never feared the rich or mighty, nor ever despised the poor or needy, but always hath continued, and hopes by God's goodness to continue, *semper idem*."[1]

Lilburne did not limit his opposition to pamphlets, or to invectives against a few eminent men; he had in his mind certain moral and political ideas, very imperfectly systematised, but very popular among the lower classes, and which he ardently hoped to render triumphant. Already, on the 26th of February preceding, he had committed them to writing, and presented them, in the form of an address, to the House; as he was eager to oppose his own plan of government to that presented by the republican leaders, and to bring his Commonwealth into competition with theirs. The House had received his address as the propositions of an enemy are generally received, and had not honoured it with any answer.

[1] Lilburne's Picture of the Council of State, pp. 22, 23.

Wounded at once in his self-love and his political faith, Lilburne published, while in prison, and in concert with his companions in captivity, a new "Agreement of the People of England," which contained a summary of their views with regard to social organisation, and would, as they fondly hoped, bring into contempt that other "Agreement," which, three months before, the Council of Officers had submitted to Parliament. Composed of thirty articles, Lilburne's Constitution was not so different as he imagined from that for which he aspired to substitute it : it was unlike it, however, in several particulars, some of its arrangements being more just and liberal, and others more futile and impracticable. On the one hand, Lilburne gave far greater extent to the rights and liberties of individuals, and especially to liberty of conscience ; on the other, he paid far less attention to the means of government, and instituted, against abuses of authority, many of those pretended guarantees which disorganise both society and government : for instance, he deprived the members of the existing legislative assembly of the right of being elected to sit in the succeeding Parliament. The republic of the General Council of officers could not have existed for any length of time,—that of Lilburne could not even have begun to exist.[1]

At the very moment when he brought it forward, it received, from an originally obscure incident, a name which was fatal to its success. A band of thirty men appeared in Surrey, and announced that they would shortly number four thousand. Everard and Winstanley, the former of whom had once been a soldier, were their leaders. They began to dig the ground, and deposit in it seeds and roots, calling to them the people of the neighbourhood, promising food and clothing to all who should join them, and threatening to pull down the palings of the adjacent parks. At the request of the county magistrates, Fairfax sent two troops of horse to arrest them. The leaders appeared before him with their hats on their heads, and on being asked why they did not remove them in the general's presence, replied, " Because he is only our fellow-creature." Everard defended their conduct, and asserted their rights. "We are," he said, "of the race of the Jews ; all the liberties of the people were lost by the coming in of William the Conqueror, and ever since the people of God have lived under tyranny and oppression worse than that of our forefathers under the Egyptians. But now the time of deliverance is at hand, and

---

[1] Commons' Journals, vol. vi. p. 151 ; Whitelocke, p. 384 ; Lilburne's Agreement of the Free People of England.

God will bring his people out of this slavery, and restore them to their freedom in enjoying the. fruits and benefits of the earth. There has lately appeared to me a vision, which bade me, 'Arise and dig and plough the earth, and receive the fruits thereof, to distribute to the poor and needy, and to feed the hungry, and clothe the naked.' We intend not to meddle with any man's property, nor to break down any pales or enclosures, but only to meddle with what is common and untilled, and to make it fruitful for the use of man. But the time will suddenly be when all men shall willingly come in and give up their lands and estates, and submit to this community. We will not defend ourselves by arms, but will submit unto authority, and wait till the promised opportunity be offered, which we conceive is at hand."[1]

These men called themselves the Diggers, but the public named them the Levellers; and the name was immediately applied to all the small groups, either in the army or in the country, who, influenced by political or religious ideas of a variously anarchical nature, desired another republic than that which was attempting to govern England, and gave it their most strenuous opposition. In vain did Lilburne and his friends protest against this name; in vain did they add to their scheme of constitution an article formally declaring that "no estates should be levelled, nor all things held in common."[2] The cognomen had a natural origin; scattered but striking facts and speeches served from time to time to confirm its applicability; it continued to be used as the designation of the whole party; and the republicans in possession of power, both in Parliament and in the army, had the good fortune that their revolutionary enemies were called the Levellers.

The struggle daily bordered more closely upon war; the slightest incident, whether serious or frivolous, might have kindled it. By the external relations which he maintained, and by the letters which he wrote, Lilburne, even while in prison, continued to foment an increasingly dangerous agitation, both in the city and in the army. On the 11th of April, 1649,[3] the Parliament resolved to bring him and his three companions to trial; a committee of councillors of state and chief judges, presided over by Bradshaw, was appointed to consult as to the form of procedure most suitable under the circumstances; and six barristers were retained to plead against the

---

[1] Whitelocke, pp. 396, 397; Godwin's History of the Commonwealth, vol. iii. p. 82; Cromwell's Letters and Speeches, vol. ii. pp. 29, 30.

[2] Whitelocke, pp. 399, 400.

[3] Commons' Journals, vol. vi. p. 183.

prisoners at the trial. Such formidable preparations excited the most passionate emotions among the partisans of Lilburne; the House was inundated with petitions on his behalf, including one signed by ten thousand citizens of London and its vicinity, and another presented by thousands of women, who thronged the approaches to Westminster Hall from day to day. To the first of these petitions the House replied with severity that the four prisoners would be tried according to the laws, and that it expected all persons in England to acquiesce in the judgment of Parliament. To the second petition no answer was returned. The women persisted. "There was a design," they said, "to fetch Lilburne and his fellow-prisoners out of the Tower at midnight to Whitehall, and there murder them. The House, by declaring the abettors of Lilburne's book traitors, have laid a snare for people, as hardly any discourse can be touching the affairs of the present time, but falls within the compass of that book: so that all liberty of discourse is thereby utterly taken away, than which there can be no greater slavery." In answer, the House bade the women, "Go home and wash their dishes;" to which some replied, "They had neither dishes nor meat left."[1]

In the midst of this excitement, eight regiments, four of infantry and four of cavalry, were appointed by lot to proceed to Ireland, where the civil war had recommenced. The soldiers, who felt little inclination for such an expedition, murmured violently; it was a difficult and an unpleasing service, in a despised and detested country: and they were to be sent thither without having had justice done them, before either their arrears had been paid or their rights recognised, before the government of the country had been firmly established, or the liberties of England definitely secured. A printed paper was immediately circulated through the barracks and in the streets, calling on the soldiers to claim their rights, and, in the mean while, not to stir. A squadron of Colonel Whalley's regiment of cavalry, which had not been appointed by lot for service in Ireland, received orders to leave London: the men demanded previous satisfaction of their claims, seized upon their standard, and formally refused to obey orders. Fairfax and Cromwell hastened to the spot, quelled the mutiny, sent off the regiment on its march, and selected fifteen of the mutineers to be tried by court-martial. Five of them were condemned to death. Lilburne

[1] Commons' Journals, vol. vi. pp. 178, 189, 196; Whitelocke, pp. 393, 396—398; Clement Walker's History of Independency, part ii. p. 106; Godwin's History of the Commonwealth, vol. iii. p. 103.

immediately wrote to the Lord General, to protest against the "exercise of martial law, against any whomsoever, in time of peace," and to remind him that the violation of this principle "was one of the chiefest articles for which the Earl of Strafford lost his head." The republican general, however, did not hesitate. "You must make an end of this party," said Cromwell, in the Council of State, at the time of Lilburne's arrest, "or it will make an end of you, and you will be held the most foolish and ridiculous persons in the world, to have been overcome by so contemptible a sort of enemies." Cromwell understood both how to flatter and how to strike: without a moment's delay, four of the five condemned mutineers were pardoned, and the fifth, Robert Lockyer, was immediately shot in St. Paul's Churchyard. He was a brave young soldier, a pious sectary, an enthusiastic republican, greatly beloved by his comrades: his death produced upon them, and their friends among the people, a profound impression of grief and anger; his corpse was watched, wept, and prayed over; and two days after, a procession as solemn as it was popular, conveyed it to the new churchyard in Westminster. A hundred horsemen, five or six abreast, went before the corpse; "the coffin was then brought, with six trumpets sounding a soldier's knell; then the trooper's horse came, clothed all over in mourning, and led by a footman. The corpse was adorned with bundles of rosemary, one half stained in blood; and the sword of the deceased along with them. Some thousands followed in rank and file; all had sea-green and black ribbon tied on their hats, and to their breasts; and the women brought up the rear." At the churchyard, a vast multitude of the better class of citizens, who had not thought fit to march through the city, awaited the arrival of the procession. It was the general opinion that such a funeral was a great affront to the leaders of the Parliament and army.[1]

Six days after this, news reached London that insurrections had broken out at Banbury and Salisbury, in the regiments of Colonels Reynolds, Scroop, and Ireton; the soldiers had driven away their officers, with the exception of a few who had sided with them: and one of these, Captain Thompson, had published, under the title of "England's Standard Advanced," a manifesto demanding the abolition of the Council of State and of the High Court of Justice, the election of a new Parliament, the adoption of Lilburne's plan of

---

[1] Whitelocke's Memorials, pp. 397—399; Clement Walker's History of Independency, part ii. pp. 161—164; Cromwelliana, pp. 55, 56; Carlyle's Letters and Speeches of Cromwell, vol. ii. pp. 31, 32.

government, and the immediate liberation of Lilburne and his
fellow-prisoners; and declaring that "if a hair of their heads shall
perish, they will, God enabling them, avenge it seventy times seven
fold upon the tyrants." Simultaneously with this news, information
was received that, at Oxford and Gloucester, in the regiments of
Colonels Harrison, Ingoldsby, and Horton, the excitement was
extreme; and that most of the soldiers in those corps were already
in correspondence with the insurgents, and were quite disposed to
march and join them.[1]

It redounds greatly to the credit of the republican leaders, both
Parliamentary and military, that, at this critical moment, they exaggerated neither the evil nor the danger, but met it with prompt
and firm, though moderate measures. They proceeded without fear
or irritation, with faith in their right and in their power, acting as
a government against rebels, and not as a faction against rivals.
The Parliament voted that every attempt to overthrow, by action
or writing, the established government of the Commonwealth, the
authority of the House of Commons, or of the Council of State, or
to excite any sedition in the army, should be considered an act
of high treason; it enjoined its committee to terminate without
delay the law against abuses of the liberty of the press; it took
measures for strengthening the internal police of the city of
London; and it ordained that Lilburne and his companions in the
Tower should be separated from one another, and that all visits, all
communications from without, should be forbidden them. This
done, it remained calm, and left the generals to act as they
thought best.[2]

Fairfax and Cromwell, on their part, were anxious first of all to
make sure of the troops which they had with them, for the mutiny
had spread in every direction; they accordingly reviewed, in Hyde
Park, the two regiments which they commanded in person, and
which bore their names. Cromwell spoke a good deal, sometimes
to the troops generally, and sometimes to individual soldiers. What
could they do better, he said, than adhere faithfully to the Parliament? It had punished delinquents; it had got a good navy afloat,
which would effectually protect commerce; it had guaranteed the
exact payment of all that remained due to the army; it had passed
resolutions for bringing its own session to a speedy termination, and
for the assembling of future Parliaments; and as to martial law,

[1] Clement Walker's History of Independency, part ii. pp. 168—173;
Godwin's History of the Commonwealth, vol. iii. p. 71.
[2] Commons' Journals, vol. vi. pp. 205, 207—209; Whitelocke's Memorials,
p. 401; Old Parliamentary History, vol. xix. p. 122.

whoever could not stand it was not fit to be a soldier, and his best
plan would be to lay down his arms ; he should have his ticket and
get his arrears, just as those would who remained faithful to their
standard. One trooper only made some objections, in a very unbecoming tone. Cromwell had him arrested ; but immediately after,
at the request of his comrades, who answered for his future good
behaviour, he pardoned him, and allowed him to resume his place in
the ranks. Some of the men wore the sea-green badges of the
Levellers, but they tore them from their hats. Both regiments
manifested the utmost ardour ; and when the review was over, the
two generals, full of confidence, set their troops at once in movement.[1]

Five days after, having marched nearly fifty miles in one single
day, they came up, at Burford in Oxfordshire, with the insurgents,
who were already somewhat dispirited by a check which they had
received at Banbury, where Captain Thompson had begun the insurrection. Surprised and defeated by the vigorous attack of his
colonel, Thompson's troop had been dispersed, and he himself had
found safety in flight ; a messenger, sent to the insurgents by
Fairfax, had moreover lulled them into false security, and they
imagined that negotiations would be opened with them. Cromwell
entered Burford suddenly, in the middle of the night, with two
'thousand men, whilst Reynolds posted himself with a strong party
at the other extremity of the town, to cut off the retreat of the
rebels. They defended themselves for a few moments, " firing
some shots out of windows ; " but soon losing all hope, destitute of
leaders, and scantily supplied with ammunition, about four hundred
of them surrendered, and the others succeeded in making their
escape. Fairfax immediately assembled a court-martial, which
decided that the mutineers should be decimated. On the following
day, in Burford churchyard, Cornet Thompson, brother to the chief
leader of the insurrection, was brought out and shot first. All
those who were to suffer the same punishment were on the leads of
the church, witnessing the execution of their comrades, and
awaiting their own turn. After Cornet Thompson came a corporal,
and then a third, who all died with indomitable firmness, expressing
sorrow for nothing they had done, and themselves giving the signal
to fire. Cornet Dean was the fourth to be shot, a brave old soldier,
whom the General knew well ; he expressed penitence ; Fairfax
pardoned him, and no others were shot. Cromwell went into the
church, called down the rest of the condemned mutineers, rebuked

[1] Cromwelliana, p. 56 ; Cromwell's Letters and Speeches, vol. ii. pp. 32, 33.

and admonished them, and reproached them for having so wickedly imperilled the good cause,—the cause of God and of the country. "They wept," says a newspaper of the period; "they retired to Devizes for a time, were then restored to their regiments, and marched cheerfully for Ireland."[1]

Some bands were still roving about in Oxfordshire and Northamptonshire: Captain Thompson rallied them, and kept them together for a few days; but being vigorously attacked by Colonel Butler, he was soon left alone, and fled to a wood. Butler's soldiers pursued him thither; Thompson issued from his retreat, fell upon his assailants, killed or wounded three of them, was wounded himself, fell back again into the wood, and again desperately charged his pursuers, declaring he would never yield alive: whereupon "a corporal, with seven bullets in his carbine," shot him dead.[2] With him ended the first and only serious insurrection of the Levellers.

At this success, the Parliament manifested an excess of joy which, for the first time, revealed its fears. The Speaker received orders to address the formal thanks of the House to Fairfax, Cromwell, and all their officers. Cromwell alone was present when the vote was passed, and to him the Speaker addressed himself. Three members were appointed to pay the same compliment to Fairfax. A day was named for a solemn general thanksgiving: two celebrated preachers among the Independents, John Owen and Thomas Goodwin, were requested to prepare sermons for the occasion; and when the day arrived, after having attended the religious services, the whole House went into the city, to a public dinner of congratulation, to which the Lord Mayor and Common Council had invited them. All the officers then in London, above the rank of lieutenant, were present at this dinner. When the members arrived at Grocers' Hall, the Lord Mayor presented to the Speaker, who immediately returned it to him, the sword which was borne before him—an honour which had never been paid to any but the King; and at the banquet the Speaker occupied the royal seat. Just as the guests were about to sit down, the Earl of Pembroke, then simply a member of the House of Commons, but who, in reward for his baseness, and out of respect for his former dignity, had been placed next to the Lord General, called to Whitelocke to take that seat as senior Commissioner of the Great Seal. Whitelocke declined the honour. "What!" said the Earl,

[1] Cromwelliana, pp. 56, 57; Cromwell's Letters and Speeches, vol. ii. pp. 33—35; Whitelocke, p. 402; Heath's Brief Chronicle, pp. 431, 432.
[2] Whitelocke's Memorials, p. 403.

in a loud voice, so as to be heard by all the guests, " do you think that I will sit down before you ? I have given place heretofore to Bishop Williams, to my Lord Coventry, and my Lord Littleton ; and you have the same place that they had ; and as much honour belongs to the place under a commonwealth as under a king; and you are a gentleman as well born and bred as any of them therefore I will not sit down before you." Whitelocke yielded, with humble but satisfied vanity; and Lord Pembroke received the praises, and with them the contempt, of all the assembly.[1]

At the conclusion of the banquet, the Lord Mayor, on the part of the city, presented to Fairfax a basin and ewer of beaten gold, worth one thousand pounds, and to Cromwell plate worth five hundred pounds; and the House, delighted at this flattering reception in a place where they had recently found it so difficult to obtain the proclamation of the Commonwealth, returned official thanks to the Lord Mayor, and appointed a special committee " to consider of some mark of favour and respect " whereby the Parliament might express its satisfaction with the city. Five weeks after, the House passed an act for settling the new park of Richmond on the mayor and commonalty, and citizens of London, and their successors for ever ;[2] thus offering the spoils of the King for the pleasures of the city.

The leaders, however, fell into no illusion with regard to the dangers which still threatened them ; they were too close observers of the people and the army to believe that the hopes they had just crushed were really extinct ; they had been firm and calm during the struggle ; they were prudent and moderate after the victory. They made it their endeavour to satisfy the legitimate or popular demands of the malcontents, or at least to awaken hopes that those demands would eventually be complied with. Measures were taken to secure the regular payment of the troops, to save the people from any abuse of military billets, to assist wounded soldiers and their families, to procure some relief for prisoners for debt, and to supply the poor of London with work.[3] Committees were appointed to report on the best means for improving the debased coinage, and for rendering the civil procedure of the law courts

---

[1] Whitelocke, p. 400 ; Cromwelliana, p. 59 ; Letter of M. de Croullé to Cardinal Mazarin (June 21, 1649), in the Archives des Affaires Etrangères de France.

[2] Whitelocke, pp. 400, 411 ; Leicester's Journal, p. 73 ; Commons' Journals, vol. vi. pp. 227, 263.

[3] Commons' Journals, vol. vi. pp. 155, 202, 208.

more expeditious and less onerous.[1] A general amnesty was also
proposed;[2] and the question of the term and system to be adopted
for the election of a new Parliament was frequently brought forward.[3]
Laws were passed, on the one hand, for abolishing the constraints
anciently imposed on the faith and worship of various denominations of Christians, and on the other hand, for repressing licentiousness of manners: for the opposition demanded at once more liberty
and greater severity.[4] Nor were they content with general measures
and legislative promises; they were anxious to show kindly dispositions towards the men who were most deeply compromised: several
leading men in the Parliament and army had conferences with the
principal Levellers, with a view to endeavour to come to some agreement with them as to the reforms to be accomplished, and the
means to be adopted for carrying on the government.[5] This spirit
of conciliation extended as far even as to Lilburne himself: by
placing him and his companions in solitary confinement, they had
been deprived of the liberty of conversation generally allowed to
prisoners; this was now restored to them.[6] One of the confidants
of the dominant party, and even of Cromwell himself, the Reverend
Hugh Peters, went apparently of his own accord, and from a pure
feeling of affectionate interest, to visit Lilburne in the Tower, to
endeavour to mollify him by suggesting to him prospects of
accommodation and liberty. The prosecution which had been commenced against him was postponed; his eldest son fell ill, paternal
anxiety triumphed over political stubbornness, and Lilburne wrote
to Henry Martyn, who had continued to regard him with friendly
feelings, to request permission to leave the Tower and visit his wife
and children. Permission was granted him, and this indulgence
was afterwards almost habitually extended both to himself and to
his companions.[7] The republican Parliament really felt a strong
desire to make a sincere peace with the democratic and fanatical
opposition which it had vanquished, and to induce them to return
into the ranks of the party which, with all its forces united, was
scarcely strong enough to maintain itself and govern the country,
even by violence.

But there is nothing more indomitable than a narrow, subtle,

[1] Commons' Journals, vol. vi. pp. 154, 211, 224, 240, 244.
[2] Ibid. p. 195; Whitelocke, p. 398.
[3] Ibid. pp. 199, 207, 210.
[4] Ibid. pp. 245, 295, 474, 359, 410.
[5] Whitelocke's Memorials, p. 424.
[6] Commons' Journals, vol. vi. pp. 208, 210.
[7] Ibid. pp. 264, 292.

and vain mind, joined to a brave and honest heart. Lilburne would perhaps, though detesting them, have treated with enemies whom he believed as sincere in their convictions as himself; but he despised his conquerors as ambitious, interested, and abandoned hypocrites. Even their favours were, in his eyes, only concessions of their weakness, or artifices of their perfidy. He treated Hugh Peters, when he paid him a visit in the Tower, with coarse bluntness, and repelled his insinuations as assaults or snares. Peters reproached him with having, by his attacks, caused the misfortunes of the late rebellion, and laid bare the wounds of the Commonwealth. "If the sun shining upon the dunghill," answered Lilburne, "make it stink, whether is the fault in the sun or the dunghill?"[1] And in the space of three months, four new pamphlets bore witness to his indefatigable hostility. One of these pamphlets, addressed "to his honoured friend, Cornelius Holland, Councillor of State," was a public challenge to political discussion. "Let your House," wrote Lilburne, "choose two men, I will choose two more, and they shall have power finally to decide the business betwixt us; and I will be content they shall appoint Cromwell, Ireton, Bradshaw, and all the orators or pleaders they had against the King and the beheaded lords, or as many of them as they please, to plead against me, and I will have none but myself, singly, to plead my own cause against them all, provided the debate may be public, and that I may have free liberty to speak for myself; and if I cannot maintain mine own innocency and integrity, I will lose and forfeit all I have, yea, and my life to boot: but if you return me not an effectual answer to my present proposition within the next five days, I shall hold myself at liberty to do the best I can for my own preservation, by anatomising what I know, either privately or publicly, of you or the rest of your associates."[2] And in two pamphlets, in fact, one directed by name against Cromwell and Ireton,[3] and the other containing a seditious provocation, addressed by ten city apprentices to the soldiers of the army in general, and of Fairfax's regiment in particular,[4] Lilburne took ample advantage of the right which he had thus reserved to himself.

These provocations were not altogether ineffectual. A new

[1] A Discourse betwixt Lieut.-Colonel John Lilburne, close prisoner in the Tower of London, and Mr. Hugh Peters, upon May 25, 1649, p. 3.

[2] John Lilburne to his honoured friend, Mr. Cornelius Holland, p. 5.

[3] An Impeachment of High Treason against Oliver Cromwell and Henry Ireton, by John Lilburne. London, August 10, 1649.

[4] An Outcry of the Young Men and Apprentices of London, August 22, 1649.

sedition broke out at Oxford, in Colonel Ingoldsby's regiment: the soldiers arrested and imprisoned their officers, including their colonel himself, who had been sent down in all haste by the Parliament to repress the mutiny. They chose a council of agitators from their own ranks, fortified themselves in the buildings of New College, and from that stronghold renewed all the demands of the Levellers. They expected, they said, a reinforcement of six thousand men from Northamptonshire, and as many more from the western counties, and from Kent; and indeed, in many places, and among several regiments, their example had its effect. Cornet Dean, whom Fairfax had recently pardoned in Burford churchyard, re-appeared at the head of a band. But the ill success of the first insurrection, and the clement firmness of the generals, had left a profound impression, both on the army and the people: the movement succeeded neither in gaining ground nor in prolonging its existence. The officers who had been imprisoned at Oxford quietly resumed their authority, first over the very sentinels who were guarding them, and next over the soldiers who were scattered through the streets. Ere long the entire regiment made submission to its colonel, and ten days after it had first broken out, the rebellion was entirely quelled.[1]

But a new and most important fact then became known for the first time. When Hugh Peters paid Lilburne a visit in the Tower: " Tell your masters from me," said the prisoner to him, " that if it were possible for me now to choose, I had rather choose to live seven years under old King Charles's government, (notwithstanding their beheading him as a tyrant for it,) than live one year under the present government that now rule; nay, let me tell you, if they go on with that tyranny they are in, they will make Prince Charles have friends enough, not only to cry him up, but also really to fight for him, and to bring him into his father's throne."[2] Two months after, in his " Outcry of the Apprentices to the Soldiers," Lilburne reminded the army that " the apprentices ran in to their assistance, to uphold and maintain the fundamental constitution of this Commonwealth, viz., the interest and right of the people in their Parliaments, not engaging in the least against the person of the King, as King, or with any thoughts or pretence of destroying, but regulating kingship."[3] These sentiments and this language had borne their fruit: the Levellers had entered into communication

---

[1] Commons' Journals, vol. vi. p. 293; Whitelocke's Memorials, pp. 424, 429.

[2] A Discourse between John Lilburne and Hugh Peters, p. 8.

[3] The Outcry of the Young Men of London, p. 4.

with the Cavaliers; and at the very moment when the Oxford mutiny broke out, a letter was intercepted from a Cavalier prisoner in the Tower to Lord Cottington, one of the intimate advisers of Charles II., in France, which ran thus:—

" All our hopes depend on his Majesty's seeming compliance with Lilburne and the Levelling party, whose discontents increase daily. As touching the state of affairs here, his Majesty's friends have no possibility of embodying, unless the Levellers lead the way, which will be, I hope, suddenly put in execution. To that purpose, I desire some assistance may be given me, for without supplies of money, little can be expected, those I converse withal being either extremely needy or covetous."[1]

The Parliament could not fail to turn such facts to its advantage ; and it used them as its principal argument in a long declaration, which it published against the Levellers, to justify the more rigorous measures which it proposed to adopt against them, and to strengthen the allegiance of its own partisans.[2] Accordingly, combining action with words, it ordained that Lilburne's trial should at once be proceeded with ; and appointed an extraordinary commission of forty members to preside over the sentence, though the right of pronouncing upon the facts charged against the prisoner was left to the jury.[3]

The relatives and friends of Lilburne—his wife, who loved him tenderly, and shared his courage ; and his brother, Colonel Robert Lilburne, an officer greatly respected by both the generals and the army—made every effort to save him from this trial. He even manifested some desire to avoid it himself, and offered to emigrate to the West Indies ; but he published at the same time a pamphlet, to explain the motives of his departure, and keenly to debate the conditions on which he would consent to leave his native land.[4] No answer was returned to his proposition. Yielding to the entreaties of his wife, he then consented to request a delay. But to this application also he received no reply; the republican government had resolved to make a last effort against this insupportable enemy, and thought they were now sure to rid themselves of him.

The trial began at Guildhall, on the 24th of October, 1649. Lilburne displayed all the resources of his mind, and all the vigorous energy of his character, in making head against the learned and subtle magistrates who were his judges,—some of them

[1] Old Parliamentary History, vol. xix. p. 193.
[2] Ibid. pp. 177—200.
[3] Commons' Journals, vol. vi. p. 293.
[4] This pamphlet is entitled " The Innocent Man's Second Proffer."

servile adherents of the government, and anxious to trammel his
defence; the others honest and upright men, desirous to protect
the prisoner in his just rights, but piqued and irritated at every
instant by his abrupt sallies, and by the bitterness of his sarcasms
or the violence of his invectives against the power whose representatives they were. The trial had lasted two days, and was
approaching its termination, when Lilburne, turning suddenly
towards the jury, thus addressed them :—

"Gentlemen of the Jury,—You are my sole judges, the keepers
of my life, at whose hands the Lord will require my blood. And
therefore I desire you to know your power, and consider your duty,
both to God, to me, to your own selves, and to your country;
and the gracious assisting spirit and presence of the Lord God
Omnipotent, the Governor of heaven and earth, and all things
therein contained, go along with you, give counsel, and direct you
to do that which is just, and for His glory!"

"Amen! amen!" cried all the spectators with one voice. The
judges looked at each other with some uneasiness, and requested
Major-General Skippon to send for three more companies of foot-
soldiers. The Attorney-General Prideaux, and the Lord Chief
Justice Keble, who presided in the court, renewed their endeavours
to convince the jury that both justice and necessity required the
condemnation of the prisoner. After they had deliberated three
quarters of an hour, the clerk of the court addressed the jury :—

"Gentlemen of the jury, are you agreed of your verdict?"

"Yes."

"Look upon the prisoner; is he guilty of the treasons charged
upon him, or any of them, or not guilty?"

"Not guilty of all of them."

"Nor of all the treasons, or any of them that are laid to his
charge?"

"Not of all, nor of any one of them."

At these words Guildhall resounded "with such a loud and
unanimous shout as is believed was never heard before." It lasted
for half an hour, during which the judges remained motionless on
their seats, exposed to this wild outburst of popular satisfaction.
The prisoner stood calmly at the bar, and it was observed that he
appeared rather less haughty and animated than before. When the
tumult had in some degree subsided, the clerk resumed :—

"Gentlemen of the jury, hearken to your verdict; the Court
has heard it. You say that John Lilburne is not guilty of all the
treasons laid unto his charge, nor of any one of them; and so you
say all?"

" Yes, we do so."[1]

Lilburne was taken back to the Tower, followed by the acclamations of the multitude ; and during the whole of the night bonfires were lighted in the streets. The government made an attempt to detain him still in prison ; but in about a fortnight the discontent of the people, and the efforts of some prudent or friendly members of the House of Commons,—among others, of Ludlow and Henry Martyn,—obtained his liberation.

The Parliament was greatly irritated by this defeat, which was far more offensive to its self-love than dangerous to its power ; for though Lilburne escaped from its hands, it retained its victory over the Levellers, who thenceforward gave up all attempts to rouse the country and army to rebellion, and remained satisfied with conspiring in secret. But this very victory was a futile one ; the republican government derived no increase of strength from its triumph ; its enemies, the King, the Cavaliers, and the anarchists, all fell beneath its blows, and yet it found itself compelled to continue, and even to aggravate, the severity of its proceedings towards them. To the ancient statutes regarding treason, it added new clauses of a more menacing character, for they provided that words should be considered equivalent to overt acts, and punished capitally.[2] Though the office of licenser of the press was abolished, a law was passed enacting the most tyrannical prohibitions and inquisitions in reference to obnoxious publications ; not only did it impose very heavy penalties on the authors, printers, vendors, and distributors of seditious writings, but even the purchasers were bound, within twenty-four hours, to surrender their purchase to the nearest magistrate. It forbade all printing, except in the four cities of London, Oxford, Cambridge, and York. The publication of journals or collections of news, and the trade in books, both at home and abroad, were placed entirely under the control of the government. All hawkers and public singers were suppressed, and whenever any one was found exercising either of these callings, he was seized, and taken to a house of correction to be whipped as a common rogue ; and a fine was inflicted on every magistrate who neglected to fulfil this provision of the law.[3] The publication of the proceedings and debates before the High Courts of justice was stringently prohibited. In contravention of the laws and traditions

---

[1] State Trials, vol. iv. cols. 1270—1470.
[2] This bill was proposed on the 1st, and adopted on the 14th of May, 1649. Commons' Journals, vol. vi. pp. 199, 200.
[3] This bill was proposed on the 9th of August, and adopted on the 20th of September, 1649. Commons' Journals, vol. vi. pp. 276, 298.

of the country, the House of Commons, in several instances, constituted itself a court of justice, and condemned offenders, whom it could not hope to reach in any other way, to severe penalties, to exile, to heavy fines, and even to the pillory.[1] It enacted that no Cavaliers, Catholics, military adventurers, or other suspected persons, should be allowed to reside in London.   When it found itself unable to bring any legal action against enemies of whom it stood in dread, it detained them arbitrarily in prison. At the moment when Lilburne, acquitted by the jury, took his departure from the Tower, a Presbyterian royalist, named Clement Walker, who had been expelled from Parliament in 1648 with the rest of his party, published his " Anarchia Anglicana," a passionate and partial history, but full of important facts and curious anecdotes relative to the republican party and its leaders.   Walker took Lilburne's place in the Tower, and remained there untried until his death, which took place in 1651.[2]   During that year, the Council of State transferred to different towns five of the most distinguished among the old Presbyterian leaders,—Sir William Waller, Sir William Lewis, Sir John Clotworthy, Major-General Browne, and Commissary-General Copley; and this order reveals the fact, that they had been confined in Windsor Castle ever since the establishment of the Commonwealth.[3]

All these severities did not succeed in inspiring the country, or even the republicans themselves, with faith in the strength and security of the Commonwealth.   They were in full possession of power; they had deprived of all political activity both the high aristocracy and the radical democracy of their time,—both the Royalists and the Levellers.   Their internal anxieties already tormented them far more than all their enemies could have done.   Conquerors and masters, they beheld arising in their midst a conqueror and a master with whom they knew not how to dispense, and against whom they were incapable of defending themselves.   The new-born Commonwealth already felt that Cromwell dominated over it ; at every crisis of peril or alarm it had recourse to him, and when the crisis was passed, it grew terrified at the credit and renown which he had acquired by saving it ; and Cromwell, on his side, whilst lavish in his demonstrations of the most humble devotedness to the Commonwealth, gave continual expression to the aspirations of his ambition and his pride.   Henry Martyn, who lived on terms of great

---

[1] Commons' Journals, vol. vi. pp. 354—356, 591 ; vol. vii. pp. 71—73, 75, 78, 79; Whitelocke, p. 340.

[2] Godwin's History of the Commonwealth, vol. iii. p. 347.

[3] Ibid. p. 250; Order Book of Council, March 11, 1651.

familiarity with him, ventured one day, in the House, obstinately to thwart him in some of his wishes in regard to the army. Cromwell drew his dagger abruptly, and clapping it on the seat by him, expressed great anger against " Harry and his levelling crew." On another occasion, in a more gay and friendly mood, he called Martyn " Sir Harry;" upon which the republican arose, and bowing profoundly, said, " I humbly thank your Majesty ! I always thought when you were king that I should be knighted."[1] The first year of the Commonwealth had not reached its term, and yet already pamphlets were seized at Coventry, entitled, " The Character of King Cromwell;"[2] and on the 14th of June, 1651, M. de Croullé wrote to Cardinal Mazarin : " According to the belief of many persons, Cromwell is carrying his ideas beyond what would be warranted by the most reckless ambition."[3] The republican leaders met with no resistance in the government; but they stood alone, forced continually to extend the limits of their power, in the midst of irreconcilable enemies, whilst Cromwell grew in greatness beside them, to work their ruin by acting as their servant.

A desolating scourge, civil war, occurred to defer the outburst of these elements of discord, and to restore for a time to the Commonwealth that feverish unity and energy which were the sole conditions of its existence.

[1] Forster's Statesmen of the Commonwealth, vol. iii. p. 328; Mercurius Pragmaticus, Feb. 27 to March 5; Cromwelliana, p. 53.
[2] Whitelocke's Memorials, p. 434.
[3] Archives des Affaires Etrangères de France,

BOOK II.

STATE OF PARTIES IN SCOTLAND AND IRELAND—CHARLES II. IS PROCLAIMED
KING — SCOTTISH COMMISSIONERS AT THE HAGUE — WAR IN IRELAND —
CROMWELL ASSUMES THE COMMAND—HIS CRUELTY AND SUCCESSES—MON-
TROSE'S EXPEDITION IN SCOTLAND—HIS DEFEAT, ARREST, CONDEMNATION,
AND EXECUTION—CHARLES II. LANDS IN SCOTLAND—CROMWELL RETURNS
FROM IRELAND, AND TAKES THE COMMAND OF THE WAR IN SCOTLAND—
HIS DANGEROUS POSITION — BATTLE OF DUNBAR — CHARLES II. ENTERS
ENGLAND—CROMWELL FOLLOWS HIM—BATTLE OF WORCESTER—FLIGHT AND
ADVENTURES OF CHARLES II.—HE RETURNS TO FRANCE—CROMWELL RE·
TURNS TO LONDON—TRIUMPHANT SUCCESS OF THE COMMONWEALTH.

Of the three kingdoms which had owned the sway of Charles I.,
England was the only one which contained a republican party sufficiently strong to obtain a temporary victory, and sufficiently bold to
attempt to govern its conquest. From very different causes, Scotland and Ireland both remained thoroughly royalist, but with dispositions and under conditions which rendered them incapable of
efficiently supporting the King, with whom they neither could nor
would dispense. In neither of these two kingdoms the royalists,
properly so called, were dominant: in Scotland the Presbyterians
were the masters, and in Ireland the Catholics ;—masters un-
equally tyrannical on account of the diversity of their positions, but
equally malignant and blind, equally led by their religious passions
to overstep their political designs, and unable either to estimate the
rights and power of their adversaries, or to measure their own
pretensions by their own real strength. Both were divided: in
Scotland, the violent Presbyterians predominated both in the Parliament and in the Church ; but they had to contend with an
opposition consisting of the moderate Presbyterians, who, in 1648,
had made war against the English Parliament on behalf of Charles I.,
and who still reckoned numerous adherents, both among the aris
tocracy and in the army. In Ireland, a large portion of the
Catholic aristocracy, from loyalty or from prudence, frankly supported,

in concert with the majority of the Irish Protestants, the cause of the Protestant king ; but they were trammelled, at every step, by the passions, suspicions, and exactions, as natural as they were ill-advised, of the Catholic population who marched beneath their banners. And in both kingdoms, around the dominant party thus internally disunited, other parties were in agitation, attached to contrary principles, inferior in numbers and influence, but active, brave, and persevering. In Scotland, on the one hand, were the pure royalists, who were so either from adherence to the Anglican faith, or from devotion to the principle of monarchy; and on the other, the independent sectaries, who were in communication with the English republicans and their Parliament. In Ireland, on the one hand, were the intractable Catholics, who were hostile to every Protestant government, whether monarchical or republican, and who opposed them both by turns, as their own temporary interest suggested ; on the other, a small number of Protestant and republican English who had settled in Ireland, and a rather large number of timid Irish Catholics, who ranged themselves under the banner of the Parliament, because they believed in its strength, and for the sole purpose of delivering themselves from the perils of a conflict which could not possibly result in any victory to their own most cherished cause.

The rivalries of their leaders aggravated the dissensions of these parties. In Scotland, at the head of the fanatical Presbyterians, stood the Marquis of Argyle, a prudent, persevering, and crafty man, fond of power and fearful of danger, a royalist more from tradition than from taste, more faithful to his dependents than to his masters, chiefly anxious to maintain his influence and secure his personal safety, and skilful in gaining for himself, in the party to which he was opposed, allies against his rivals. The execution of the Duke of Hamilton in London, had deprived the moderate Presbyterians of their old leader, who was ill replaced by his brother, Lord Lanark, who inherited his title and not his credit, and by Lord Lauderdale, a servile courtier with an independent mind, passionately malignant although profoundly indifferent, and thoroughly corrupt, notwithstanding his fanaticism. Montrose seemed born to charm and to command the pure royalists, as he was by far the most brilliant, the most alluring, the boldest, the most devoted, and the most presumptuous of them all. And from the ranks of the Edinburgh bar sprang up, for the small party of Scottish republican sectaries, a leader whom the English Parliament might have envied them ;— Archibald Johnstone, Lord Warristoun, ardent, inventive, prompt, indefatigable, learned, and eloquent, with all the subtlety of a knave,

and all the sincerity of a martyr. Ireland numbered among her
leaders fewer men of eminence, whose names have survived the age
in which they lived. More respected than he was feared or followed,
the Marquis of Ormonde, Viceroy of Ireland for Charles II., as he
had been for Charles I., presided over the efforts and discords of the
royalist party in that country, with inexhaustible though often
ineffective devotedness; and among the independent Irish who
attached themselves exclusively to neither Parliament nor King,
Owen Roe O'Neil is the only one who, by his successful audacity
and his continual defections, has obtained any name in history.
But a host of secondary leaders, important then though unknown
now, were at work either among the people, or near the Viceroy
ardently pursuing, sometimes against their enemies, and sometimes
against their rivals, their own advancement, or the deliverance
of their faith and fatherland.

A fter the death of Charles I., the royalist feeling triumphed, at
the outset, over these diversities and discords. At Edinburgh, on
the 5th of February, and in Ireland, wherever Ormonde was the
master, Charles II. was proclaimed king. The Parliament of Scotland had a new grievance against the English Parliament : the Commissioners who had been sent by it to London, first to advise, and
then to protest, against the judgment of Charles I., had been
brutally arrested at the moment when they were preparing to return
to their country,[1] and conducted under escort to the Scottish frontier,
in order to prevent any publication or communication with the
people on their parts.[2] The conscience and the self-respect of the
Scots were alike offended. Their Parliament decided that Commissioners should immediately be sent to the new King to invite
him to return among them. Ormonde urged him at the same time
to come to Ireland, where he would find three-fourths of the nation
devoted to his cause ; and the most formidable of the Irish chieftains, Owen Roe O'Neil himself, who had refused to treat with
Ormonde, conveyed to Charles, by a private messenger, the strongest
assurances of his fidelity.[3]

All these envoys arrived almost simultaneously at the Hague,
where Charles was residing, under the protection of the Stadtholder,
the Prince of Orange, his brother-in-law, and treated with considerate

[1] Commons' Journals, vol. vi. p. 452 ; Whitelocke, pp. 384, 385, 388.
[2] Parliamentary History, vol. xix. pp. 16—36, 40—48 ; Commons' Journals,
vol. vi. pp. 131—135, 145.
[3] Whitelocke, pp. 381—383, 389, 392; Laing's History of Scotland, vol. iii.
p. 436; Clarendon's History of the Rebellion, vol. vi. pp. 269—272, 282, 283,
304—306; Carte's Ormonde Letters, vol. i. pp. 213, 291.

though reserved respect by the States-General of Holland. He was there surrounded by his wisest counsellors, those men whose advice the King his father, with the experience of misfortune, had expressly recommended him to follow—Lord Cottington, Sir John Colepepper, and particularly Sir Edward Hyde, the last passionately attached to monarchy and the Anglican Church, but a serious and able man, who remained faithful in exile, as on his native soil, to the religion, the laws, and the manners of his country They had strongly urged Charles neither to establish himself in France, where they regarded the policy of Mazarin with great suspicion, nor to join his mother, the Queen-dowager, who resided partly at St. Germains, and partly at Paris, still little loved by the true English whom she loved little. and surrounded by Catholic priests and those frivolous and reckless courtiers, who, under the late King, had exercised, sometimes on the King's conduct, and always on the royal cause, so fatal an influence.

The perplexity of Charles was great: the Commissioners of the Parliament and Kirk of Scotland offered him very rigorous conditions: they required that he should separate from all his old friends, and especially from Montrose (who was detested by all the Presbyterians), that he should proceed almost alone to Scotland, that he should place himself entirely in the hands of the dominant party, that he should sign their Covenant of 1638, and, in short, that he should become, whether sincerely or hypocritically, a Presbyterian with them and like them.   Although opposed to the fanatical Presbyterians, and while deploring their exactions, the moderate men, Lord Hamilton and Lord Lauderdale, advised Charles to resign himself to these conditions; and they insisted as strongly as any that he should absolutely give up Montrose, refusing to have any communication with him themselves, and insolently leaving the King's cabinet when he entered it. Montrose, in his turn, exhorted Charles to repel all these pretensions, which would reduce him to servitude under the pretext of restoring him to his throne, and to rely, for his restoration to his kingdom, only on the sword ; offering to be the first to draw it, and to lead the van, in order to open the way for him.   Charles found the advice of Montrose the most to his taste, though he did not altogether believe in its soundness ; but the Prince of Orange, backed by the letters of the Queen-mother, and by the general opinion of Holland, strongly urged him not to adopt it, but on the contrary to accept the propositions of the Scottish Commissioners—being unable to conceive that he should persist in refusing a kingdom which thus sought his acceptance, for the sake of supporting the Anglican Church and the bishops, who had already cost the King his father his crown and his life.[1]

It was suggested to Charles, who as yet had neither said nor done anything since the death of his father, that, on proceeding to Scotland, he should address a declaration to the English people, to explain to them his views and feelings, to revive the courage of his adherents, and to prevent any false interpretations to which his conduct might give rise. Hyde, who, in the council, had strongly opposed this step, was appointed to draw up the manifesto ; but when he submitted the draft to his colleagues, notwithstanding the extreme pains he had taken to weigh every word of it, so many discordant objections were raised against it, and the impossibility of giving verbal satisfaction to the royalists of England without alienating those of Scotland and Ireland became so evident that, by common consent, it was resolved to persevere in that silence which had at first been maintained by instinct.[2]

Difficulties soon wearied Charles : the prospect of the unpleasantnesses and compromising falsehoods which awaited him in Scotland was regarded by him with repugnance ; he started objections to the Scottish Commissioners, and gave them an evasive answer, which was equivalent, for the moment, to a refusal. At the same time he gave Montrose a secret commission, with the title of Lieutenant-Governor and Commander-in-chief of all the royal forces in Scotland, authorising him to levy men and money in Europe, wheresoever he could obtain them, and to attempt a royalist expedition in his own country, at all risks. Then, announcing his resolution to proceed to Ireland, where nothing was required of him but his presence, Charles actually embarked and sent off, in two small ships, a portion of his suite and baggage : but alleging the propriety, before leaving the Continent, of going to France to pay a farewell visit to the Queen his mother, he indefinitely postponed his own departure.[3]

In reality, and although, as far as the number and loyalty of his partisans were concerned, his chief hope was in Ireland, he was by no means eager to repair thither, and thus to show himself to the Protestants of England and Scotland, surrounded by a Catholic people and army as his primary supporters. But precisely for

[1] Carte's Ormonde Letters, vol. i. p. 238; Clarendon's History of the Rebellion, vol. vi. p. 306.

[2] Clarendon's History of the Rebellion, vol. vi. pp. 318—323.

[3] Carte's Ormonde Letters, vol. i. pp. 263, 345; Clarendon's History of the Rebellion, vol. vi. pp. 285, 306—309; Wishart's Memoirs of Montrose, pp. 338—360.

these reasons, Ireland, immediately after the death of the King, became the object of serious attention and vigorous action on the part of the republican Parliament. In that country most of all, it expected to witness the outbreak of a royalist war, and there also it preferred to meet it. War against Ireland had always excited passionate enthusiasm in England, in almost all parties. This hostility of race, religion, and politics had been used against Charles I. with unfailing success; and from it the republicans hoped to derive the same advantages against his son. As soon as it became known in London that he had been proclaimed king in Ireland, and that Ormonde rallied almost the whole nation beneath his standard, it was resolved that he should be attacked there. At the same time that they abolished kingship and suppressed the House of Lords, the Commons voted 120,000*l.* a month for the support of an army of forty-four thousand men, a large portion of whom were to be employed in Ireland; and the Council of State received orders to confer with the General-in-chief and his principal officers "concerning the modelling of the forces that were to go into Ireland."[1]

Five days after, Scott stated to the House, in the united names of the Council of State and the Council of War, that the first measure to be taken for organising the army and modelling the war in Ireland, was the appointment of a general to command the forces in that country. The House referred this appointment to the Council of State. It was thought that Lambert would be nominated, and most of Cromwell's friends had seemed to indicate him as the proper person to be selected. But some, with greater clear-sightedness or quicker comprehension, unexpectedly proposed Cromwell himself, who was not present at the meeting. Being immediately informed of this, he appeared surprised and irresolute, and requested the Council of the army to name two officers of each regiment to join with him in a religious meeting for the purpose of invoking the Divine guidance in so important a matter. The result of this meeting was that he accepted the command, and the House confirmed his appointment. He signified his acceptance with great diffidence, and many expressions of "his own unworthiness, and disability to support so great a charge, and of the entire resignation of himself to their commands, and absolute dependence upon God's providence and blessing, from whom he had received many instances of His favour;" and he desired the House "that no more time

[1] Commons' Journals, vol. vi pp. 157, 159. 163, 170, 172, 182, 186, 188, 208; Whitelocke, pp. 385, 380, 391, 392.

might be lost in the preparations which were to be made for so great a work: for he did confess that kingdom to be reduced to so great straits, that he was willing to engage his own person in this expedition, for the difficulties which appeared in it; and more out of hope, with the hazard of his life, to give some obstruction to the successor which the rebels (for so he called the Marquis of Ormonde and the Irish royalists) were at present exalted with, that so the Commonwealth might still retain some footing in that king-dom, till they might be able to send fresh supplies, than out of any expectation that, with the strength he carried, he should be able, in any signal degree, to prevail over them."[1]

The House complied with his wishes, and in the pains which it took to insure the success of the war, we may recognise at every step the provident solicitude and the practical good sense of the leader whom it had appointed to the command. To console Fairfax for his inactivity, he was invested with the title of Generalissimo of all the Forces of the Parliament, both in England and Ireland. Cromwell was neither vain nor captious, and no one ever made greater concessions to the self-love of his rivals, especially when he was labouring to supplant them. He obtained as his major-general his son-in-law, Ireton, whose capacity, energy, and friendship he had fully tried. The regiments selected for his expedition formed a body of twelve thousand men; they were paid their arrears, were well provided with arms and ammunition, and measures, on which Cromwell strenuously insisted, were taken to secure their regular recruitment. The accounts of the officers were settled, and they received considerable sums in advance of their pay. Other officers, who had abandoned Lord Inchiquin when he declared for the royal cause, returned to the service of the Parliament, and were treated with the same favour. Ample provision was made for the commis-sariat of the army. A number of vessels were placed at the general's disposal, and ordered to cruise off the coast of Ireland. A loan of 150,000l., specially devoted to the necessities of this war, was opened in the City, and Cromwell himself superintended its negotia-tion. The Committee of Sequestrations was directed to press the payment of the sums due from those royalists who had been ad-mitted to compound for their property, and these payments also had Ireland for their destination. Cromwell's prudence extended even beyond his special and warlike mission: a vigilant patron of his friends, he recommended those of them who had business to arrange

---

[1] Whitelocke, pp. 390, 391; Clarendon's History of the Rebellion, vol. vi. pp. 318, 319.

with the Parliament to present their petitions immediately, and he insisted that justice should be done them before his departure. He obtained full justice for himself with regard to the liquidation of his arrears, for the settlement of his pay, which was considerable, and for the various supplementary grants which he needed. Finally, his commission secured to him the civil as well as the military command in Ireland, and its duration was fixed for three years.[1]

Having thus made sure of his material forces, Cromwell's next care was to provide means of moral action. The Commonwealth had few friends in Ireland : it was necessary, therefore, to gain fresh adherents, or at least to thin the ranks of the enemy. Cromwell learned that one of the most influential and able men in Ireland, Lord Broghill—who, after having served by turns the King and the Parliament, had retired to his estates—had just arrived in London with the intention of crossing over to Holland to offer his services to Charles II. He sent one of his officers to say that he would wait on him, as he was anxious to have some conversation with him. Lord Broghill was astonished, and imagined that there must be some mistake, as he had not the honour of knowing the General. But a few minutes after, Cromwell arrived at his house, and, having first expressed the greatest kindness and esteem for him, proceeded to inform him that his designs were perfectly known, and that instead of proceeding to Spa for the benefit of his health, as his passport purported, he was going immediately to Charles Stuart, for purposes hostile to the Government. Broghill denied any such intention. Cromwell upon this assured him that he had good proof of what he said, and that he could show him his own letters to the purpose : "they have already been examined by the Council of State," he added, "who have made an order for your being committed to the Tower ; but I have obtained a delay in executing the order, till I should previously have conferred with you." Lord Broghill admitted everything, thanked Cromwell for his kindness, and requested his advice. "I have obtained permission from the Council," answered Cromwell, "to offer you a command in the Irish war ; you shall have the authority of a general officer, no oaths shall be imposed upon you, and you shall only be required to serve against the Irish Catholics." Broghill manifested some reluctance, and desired some time to consider the proposal. But Cromwell replied that that was impossible, as, the moment he left him with the offer unaccepted, he would instantly find himself

[1] Commons' Journals, vol. vi. pp. 183, 184, 226, 232, 235, 240, 243, 248, 253, 254, 267, 270, 281, 288, 300, 301, 321, 328, 331 ; Whitelocke's Memorials, pp. 399, 401, 404, 409, 410, 412, 415, 421, 423, 426, 430.

a state prisoner.[1]   They parted good friends, and three months
afterwards they were both in Ireland serving the Parliament
together.

About the same time there arrived in London some men well
known for their Catholic fervour—Sir Kenelm Digby, Sir John
Winter, and the Abbé Montague, who had already been frequently
occupied in the affairs of Ireland, and who had always placed the
cause of the Church far above that of the King.   They were led
to hope full liberty for their faith and worship in Ireland, provided
that the Catholics of that country would disavow the temporal
pretensions of the Pope, and raise ten thousand men for the
service of the Commonwealth.   Conferences took place through the
medium of the Spanish ambassador: and to afford some test of
the disposition of the Catholics, a learned priest, named Thomas
White, in a pamphlet entitled, "The Grounds of Obedience and
Government," maintained that the people might be released
from their oath of allegiance by the evil conduct of their governor,
and that, when he was once deposed, the common good might
require them to submit rather than to attempt his restoration.   On
the Continent Charles II. and his counsellors grew alarmed, and
warned Ormonde to be on his guard.   And they had good reason to
do so, for while this civil negotiation was being carried on in secret
in London, Monk, at the suggestion of Cromwell, had concluded a
suspension of hostilities with the great Catholic chief, O'Neil, in
Ireland: which suspension covered the engagement of O'Neil to
lend his assistance underhand to the operations of the army and
generals of the Parliament.   Cromwell had too unprejudiced a mind
to underrate the strength of the Catholics in Ireland; and with
equal unscrupulousness, but greater secrecy than Charles II. had
employed, he prepared to conciliate them, if the Protestant Parliament and public would permit him to do so, or to compromise and
divide them, if he were forbidden to make use of them.[2]

He also attempted to renew some friendly relations with the
Presbyterians themselves, his most recent and most ardent
opponents,—abstaining from all religious hostility to them, and
giving them to understand that, in his opinion, their ecclesiastical
system was the one which the State must eventually adopt and
maintain.   Before his departure for Ireland, he was anxious to

    [1] Carte's Ormonde Letters, vol. i. p. 249; Godwin's History of the Com-
monwealth, vol. iii. pp. 153—155; Cromwell's Letters and Speeches, vol. ii.
p. 95.
    [2] Carte's Ormonde Letters, vol. i. pp. 216—222.

make friends there, and to conciliate, or at least to pacify the enemies whom he left behind him in England.

He still delayed his departure, however. Was he merely desirous to wait until his troops had arrived, and were in readiness in Ireland, before he appeared there himself; or did he meditate some secret design? The Parliament began to feel some anxiety, for it was chiefly to get rid of Cromwell, and to find employment for the army, that it had so vigorously undertaken the Irish war, and made so many sacrifices for its effectual maintenance. The foreign ministers resident in London strongly doubted Cromwell's intention to go at all. "People continue to say," wrote M. de Croullé to Cardinal Mazarin, "that Cromwell will start at the end of this month, at latest. The opinion which I have to the contrary, is so conformable to that of many intelligent persons, that I cannot retract it, and until I am convinced by the news of his journey into that country, I shall persevere in that opinion. It can hardly be possible that Cromwell, who, according to the belief of many, carries his ideas beyond even the suggestions of the most undisciplined ambition, can resolve to abandon this kingdom to the mercy of the plots which may be formed in his absence, and which his presence can prevent from being so much as undertaken."[1]

But, in the beginning of June, Ormonde entered the field, and, notwithstanding the dissensions of his party, and the wretched organisation of his army, his successes were so rapid, that at the end of the month, Londonderry and Dublin were the only towns in Ireland which remained faithful to the Parliament. Cromwell took his resolution. On the 10th of July, a large number of his friends met at Whitehall; three ministers invoked the Divine blessing on his arms; and Cromwell himself, after two of his officers, Goffe and Harrison, had spoken, commented on several texts of Scripture which were appropriate to his undertaking. On the same day, at five o'clock in the evening, he set out for Bristol, "in that state and equipage," says a newspaper of the time, "as the like hath hardly been seen; himself in a coach, with six gallant Flanders mares, whitish-grey; divers coaches accompanying him, and very many great officers of the army; his life-guard consisting of eighty gallant men, the meanest whereof a commander or esquire, in stately habit, with trumpets sounding. Of his life-guard, many are colonels, and, believe me, it's such a guard as is hardly to be paralleled in the world. And now, have at you, my Lord of Ormonde! you will have men of gallantry to encounter, whom to

[1] Letter of the 14th June, 1649; Archives des Affaires Étrangères de France.

overcome will be honour sufficient, and to be beaten by them will be no great blemish to your reputation. If you say, 'Cæsar or nothing!' they say, 'A Republic or nothing!'"[1]

On reaching Bristol, and from motives which it is impossible to ascertain, Cromwell remained there nearly a month, going and coming between the different ports along the coast, superintending the embarkation of his troops, and receiving numerous visitors. The people thronged from the surrounding country to see him. His wife and several members of his family came to pass a few days with him. He seemed still to hesitate, and to quit the soil of England with great doubtfulness and effort.[2]

News, however, arrived from Ireland, which put an end to his lingerings. Before marching upon Dublin, Ormonde had written to the governor, Colonel Michael Jones, who had, until then, been regarded as a moderate Presbyterian, urging him "to leave that pretended Parliament, who had murdered their King, and would introduce anarchy," and promising him great rewards, if he would return to the royal cause. Jones answered, "that he understood not how his lordship came to that power; that the Parliament of England would never have consented to such a peace as his lordship had made with the rebels, without any provision for the Protestant religion; that he knew not how that could be established by an army of Papists; and that he had rather suffer in his trust, than purchase to himself the ignominy of perfidy by any advantage offered to him." Ormonde encamped before Dublin, hoping to reduce the place, as its garrison was weak, and he had adherents among the inhabitants. But, at the end of July, Cromwell's vanguard, assisted by a favourable wind, entered the port of Dublin, in spite of Ormonde's endeavours to prevent it. The garrison, thus strengthened, revictualled, and inspirited, demanded some bold action of its commander; and, on the 2nd of August, Jones made so unexpected, so vigorous, and so successful a sortie against the camp of the besiegers, at the village of Rathmines, that, notwithstanding the desperate efforts of the superior officers and of Ormonde him-self, the whole of the royal army was thrown into disorder, put to rout with considerable loss, and obliged to raise the siege.[3]

Whatever may have been the cause of his delay in quitting England, it did not suit Cromwell's purpose that another should have the honour of subjugating Ireland. On the day following the

---

[1] Cromwelliana, p. 62; Whitelocke, p. 413.
[2] Carlyle, Cromwell's Letters and Speeches, vol. ii. p. 87.
[3] Whitelocke, pp. 391, 419, 420; Commons' Journals, vol. vi. pp. 175, 278·
Clarendon's History of the Rebellion, vol. vi. pp. 310—345.

arrival of this news, he set out; and as soon as he had embarked, while still in the port of Milford Haven, careful to show himself one of the foremost to celebrate the victory of Colonel Jones, he wrote to his friend Richard Mayor, whose daughter had just been married to his eldest son Richard : "The Marquis of Ormonde besieged Dublin with nineteen thousand men or thereabouts; seven thousand Scots and three thousand more were coming to join him in that work. Jones issued out of Dublin with four thousand foot and twelve hundred horse ; hath routed this whole army ; killed about four thousand upon the place ; taken 2,517 prisoners, above three hundred of them officers, some of great quality.[1] This is an astonishing mercy ; so great and seasonable that indeed we are like them that dreamed. What can we say? The Lord fill our souls with thankfulness, that our mouths may be full of His praise,—and our lives too ; and grant we may never forget His goodness to us. These things seem to strengthen our faith and love, against more difficult times. Sir, pray for me, that I may walk worthy of the Lord in all that He hath called me unto ! "

And this outburst of patriotic piety concludes by this trait of paternal solicitude :—" I have committed my son to you ; pray give him advice. I envy him not his contents ; but I fear he should be swallowed up in them. I would have him mind and understand business, read a little history, study the mathematics and cosmography : these are good, with subordination to the things of God. Better than idleness, or mere outward worldly contents. These fit for public services, for which a man is born."[2]

Cromwell always manifested the greatest interest in his children, their temporal affairs as well as their moral tendencies ; and in this as in everything that concerned him, he brought his provident and dominant activity into constant exercise.

He arrived in Dublin two days afterwards, on the 15th of August, and was received with all possible demonstrations of joy. The population crowded out to welcome him, with mingled kindness and curiosity. When nearly in the heart of the city, where the concourse was greatest, he halted, and, rising in his carriage, with his hat in his hand, made a speech to the people. " He did not doubt," he said, " that, as God had brought him thither in safety, he would be able, by Divine Providence, to restore them all to their just liberties and properties : and," he added, " that all persons whose hearts' affections were real for the carrying on of this

---

[1] These round numbers are all greatly exaggerated. See Carte's Ormonde Letters, vol. ii. pp. 403, 407—411.

[2] Cromwell's Letters and Speeches, vol. ii. pp. 41, 45.

great work against the barbarous and bloodthirsty Irish and their confederates and adherents, and for propagating of Christ's Gospel, and establishing of truth and peace, and restoring of this bleeding nation of Ireland to its former happiness and tranquillity, should find favour and protection from the Parliament of England and him, and withal receive such rewards and gratuities as might be answerable to their merits." This speech was received by the people with shouts of "We will live and die with you!"[1] On the following day, a military and puritanic proclamation indicated the character of his government; after reciting "the great mercies of God to the city of Dublin, particularly in the late defeat given to the rebels who encompassed it round about," he expressed his astonishment to learn that, "notwithstanding the goodness of God to them, yet by profane swearing, cursing, and drunkenness, His holy name is daily dishonoured and blasphemed, contrary to the laws of God and the known laws of the land, and to the articles of war;" he enjoined the mayor and magistrates of the city, as well as the officers of the army, "to put in due execution the laws against such offenders;" and he finally declared that he would "punish the neglect and contempt of his proclamation with the severest penalties of the law."[2]

No sooner had his troops rested a few days than he entered the field, but with intentions very different from those he had professed at a distance, whilst his expedition was in preparation. As soon as he was in Ireland, on the theatre of war and in the midst of the combatants, Cromwell became convinced that the prejudices and animosities of the English against the Irish, of the Protestants against the Catholics, of the Republicans against the Royalists, were there fierce and uncontrollable passions, which might be used with powerful efficacy so long as they were allowed free course, but which permitted no politic calculations or wary compromises. He accepted this conclusion without hesitation, as a fact which admitted of no discussion, and determined to take full advantage of it. The instructions and examples which he received from London urged him rather to pursue this course than otherwise. The news from Ireland, and particularly Jones's victory at Dublin, and the confidence which it inspired, dissipated all the schemes of negotiation with the Irish and the Catholics which had recently been in contemplation. The Parliament severely disavowed the suspension of hostilities which Monk had concluded with O'Neil, and the political leaders who had secretly incited Monk to take this step,

[1] Cromwell's Letters and Speeches, vol. ii. p. 48.
[2] Whitelocke's Memorials, p. 423.

felt themselves obliged to be the first to blame his act, in order to succeed afterwards in getting him excused because of his intention. A few days later, the House voted that Sir Kenelm Digby and Sir John Winter.—those ardent Catholics whom it had allowed, and almost invited, to come to London, that it might secure their co-operation in Ireland, at the price of the liberty of their faith and worship,—were dangerous men, whom it was necessary to dismiss without delay; and they were ordered to leave England immediately on pain of death and the confiscation of their property if they ventured to return thither.[1] All tendency to compromise, from motives of either justice or prudence, had disappeared ; and in the councils of England, as in the army in Ireland, religious and political fanaticism alone prevailed.

It was under these sombre auspices that Cromwell marched from Dublin, on the 31st of August, at the head of about ten thousand men, to lay siege to Drogheda, the most important town in the province of Leinster. Ormonde, on retiring from the siege of Dublin, had thrown into this town a garrison of three thousand men, nearly all English, commanded by Sir Arthur Ashton, an old wooden-legged officer, of tried courage and fidelity, in the hope that it would long arrest the progress of the enemy. After employing six days in preparing for the siege, Cromwell summoned the governor to surrender, and on his refusal, on the 10th of September, the storm commenced. The first attack, although vigorous, failed, with great loss to the assailants; Colonel Castle and several other officers were killed in the breach. Cromwell headed the second attack himself, and, notwithstanding the energetic resistance of the besieged, the intrenchments were carried in succession, as well as the towers and churches of the town, to which the most obstinate had retreated. "In the heat of action," wrote Cromwell to the President of the Council of State and to the Speaker of the House of Commons, "I forbade our men to spare any that were in arms in the town ; and, I think, that night they put to the sword about two thousand men, among whom were the governor, Sir Arthur Ashton, and divers considerable officers. The next day the two towers were summoned, in one of which was about six or seven score ; but they refused to yield themselves : and we, knowing that hunger must compel them, set only good guards to secure them from running away until their stomachs were come down. From one of the said towers, notwithstanding their condition, they killed and wounded some of our men. When they

---

[1] Commons' Journals, vol. vi. pp. 277, 289; Whitelocke, pp. 419, 422, 423.

submitted, their officers were knocked on the head, and every tenth man of the soldiers killed, and the rest shipped for the Barbadoes. I believe all their friars were knocked on the head promiscuously. I am persuaded that this is a righteous judgment of God upon these barbarous wretches, who have imbrued their hands in so much innocent blood; and that it will tend to prevent the effusion of blood for the future—which are the satisfactory grounds to such actions, which otherwise cannot but work remorse and regret.

"P.S.—The following officers and soldiers were slain at the storming of Tredah:—The governor, one colonel, two lieutenant-colonels, one major, eight captains, eight lieutenants, and eight cornets,—all of horse; three colonels, with their lieutenants and majors, forty-four captains, and all their lieutenants, ensigns, &c.; 220 reformadoes and troopers; 2,500 foot soldiers, besides staff officers, surgeons, &c., and many inhabitants."[1]

According to other reports, by royalist and even parliamentary writers, not only did the carnage last two days, but officers who were discovered after the lapse of five or six days, during which they had been concealed by the humanity of some of the soldiers, were put to death in cold blood; and at the moment of the massacre, women and children met with the same fate as armed men. "It was," says a contemporary panegyrist of Cromwell, "a sacrifice of three thousand Irish to the ghosts of ten thousand English, whom they had massacred some years before."[2]

The sacrifice did not produce the effect which Cromwell had anticipated would justify it; it did not suffice to prevent the further effusion of blood; another such example had to be made. Wexford, a month afterwards, defended itself with the same obstinacy as Drogheda, and witnessed a similar massacre. Other places, it is true, from intimidation or treachery, surrendered: Cork, Ross, Youghal, and Kilkenny, submitted without resistance; but other places again, Callan, Gowran, and Clonmel, made a bold defence; and some, Waterford for instance, resisted so vigorously that Cromwell was obliged to raise the siege. And, even where success seemed won most easily, it was sullied by acts of wanton cruelty: at Gowran the soldiers obtained their lives on surrendering the place, but on the condition of giving up their officers, who were all put to death. The Bishop of Ross was hanged in his episcopal robes, under the walls of a fortress defended by his troops.

---

[1] Carlyle, Cromwell's Letters and Speeches, vol. ii. pp. 56—68; Old Parliamentary History, vol. xix. pp. 201—210; Whitelocke, pp. 424—427.

[2] Old Parliamentary History, vol. xix. p. 210; Clarendon's History of the Rebellion, vol. vi. p. 396; Ludlow's Memoirs, p. 129.

Clonmel made an heroic resistance, and when at length it surrendered, Cromwell found not a single man belonging to the garrison in it; whilst he was signing the articles of capitulation with the inhabitants, they had left the town by night with their arms and baggage, to recommence the war elsewhere.[1]

It is the ordinary artifice of bad passions to impute the cruel satisfaction with which they glut themselves, either to some great idea whose accomplishment they are earnestly pursuing, or to the absolute necessity of success. History would be dishonoured by admitting these lying excuses: it is her duty to refer evil to its source, and to render to the vices of mankind that which is their due.

Human fanaticism also lies, or allows itself to be deluded by pride, when it pretends to be the executor of the high decrees of Divine justice: it is not the office of man to pronounce upon nations the sentences of God.

Cromwell was not bloodthirsty; but he was determined to succeed rapidly and at any cost, from the necessities of his fortune, far more than for the advancement of his cause: and he denied no outlet to the passions of those who served him. He was an ambitious and selfish, though really great, man, who had narrow-minded and hard-hearted fanatics for his instruments.

His great and true means of success did not consist in his massacres, but in his genius, and in the exalted idea which the people had already conceived of him. Sometimes by instinct, sometimes from reflection, he conducted himself in Ireland towards both his friends and his enemies with an ability as pliant as it was profound; for he excelled in the art of treating with men, and of persuading, or seducing, or appeasing those even who naturally regarded him with the greatest distrust and aversion. At the same time that he gave up to murder and pillage the towns which fell into his hands, he maintained in other respects the severest discipline in his army, not suffering it to do the inhabitants any wrong, and taking care that it paid for all it consumed. That very man who boasted that at Drogheda " all the friars were knocked on the head promiscuously," and who always pompously excepted the Catholics from his promises of Christian toleration, that very man maintained, by means of Irish monks, a most active police among his enemies, who kept him always well informed of their designs and movements,

---

[1] Carlyle, Cromwell's Letters and Speeches, vol. ii. pp. 50—166; Commons' Journals, vol. vi. pp. 314, 323; Whitelocke, pp. 433, 434, 456; Godwin's History of the Commonwealth, vol. iii. pp. 151—161.

and were sometimes influential enough to procure their failure by promoting dissensions among them.   He laboured incessantly to detach all men of importance from the royal cause, and he even carried his attempts of this sort, unsuccessfully of course, as far as the Marquis of Ormonde himself, for whom he openly professed the highest esteem, and frequently asked,—" What Lord Ormonde had to do with Charles Stuart, and what obligations he had ever re-ceived from him ?"   Towards the Parliament his behaviour was very independent, but without vanity or bluster; his language, on the contrary, was deferential even to humility.   After the capture of Ross, he wrote to the Speaker of the House of Commons :—" Having given you this account, I shall not trouble you with particular desires.   Those I shall humbly present to the Council of State. Only, in the general, give me leave humbly to offer what in my judgment I conceive to be for your service, with a full submission to you.   We desire recruits may be speeded to us.   The forces desired will not raise your charge, if your assignments already for the forces here do come to our hands in time.   Wherefore I humbly beg that the moneys desired may be seasonably sent over; and those other necessaries, clothes, shoes, and stockings, formerly desired ; that so poor creatures may be encouraged ; and through the same blessed presence that has gone along with us, I hope, before it be long, to see Ireland no burden to England, but a profitable part of its Commonwealth."[1]

It was not long before he discovered and put into practice the most effectual means for succeeding in this object.   When he per-ceived that, notwithstanding some partial successes, he would never be able to disorganise the royalist party in Ireland, by depriving it of its leaders, he turned his attention towards the soldiers ; they were numerous and brave, but for the most part utterly destitute and de-spondent.   He published throughout the country that they were free to go and serve abroad ; and that he authorised all the officers, or any other persons who chose to engage in the undertaking, to levy as many men as they could find, and to convey them out of Ireland for the service of the Continental powers.   He communi cated this permission to the Ministers of France and Spain in London.   Numbers of royalist officers, both English and Irish, without employment or resources, saw a future thus opened to them, and offered their services to the foreign agents, for levying regi-ments and transporting them into France or Spain.   Don Alonzo

[1] Carlyle, Cromwell's Letters and Speeches, vol. ii. pp. 99, 100 ; Claren-don's History of the Rebellion, vol. vi. pp. 427, 428 ; Whitelocke, p. 426; Godwin's History of the Commonwealth, vol. iii. p. 151.

de Cardeñas, the Spanish ambassador in London, and Cardinal Mazarin, eagerly availed themselves of this offer; in a few months, nearly twenty five thousand Irish were enrolled for Spain, and twenty thousand for France, and that Catholic territory on which Ormonde found it very difficult to keep together a body of eight or ten thousand men for the King's service, furnished more than forty thousand soldiers, hostile to the Parliament, for the service of France and Spain.[1]

So many successes, both military and political, gained so rapidly, and so skilfully extolled by his zealous friends, soon caused the Parliament almost as much alarm as they had won it security. Cromwell in London was, at every moment, a subject of embarrassment; but Cromwell, so powerful and glorious in Ireland, seemed more dangerous and threatening still. Moreover, a report was current that Charles Stuart, in consequence of fresh negotiations with the Scots, was on the point of proceeding to Scotland. Cromwell would probably be needed in that direction. On the 8th of January, 1650, it was determined that he should be recalled, and the Council of State was ordered to inform him of this resolution. He was then in winter quarters, scarcely recovered from a rather severe illness. He suddenly re-entered the field, and vigorously recommenced his marches and sieges in various parts of Ireland. On the 25th of February, letters were read from him, in the House of Commons, announcing new successes. It was voted first, that a letter of thanks should be sent to him, and next that, on his return to London, he should "have the use of the lodgings called the Cockpit (a portion of the palace of Whitehall), of the Spring Garden and St. James's House, and the command of St. James's Park." Cromwell's wife and family, with considerable reluctance, made preparations for removing to their new abode; as for Cromwell himself, he continued to remain and conquer in Ireland. At length, on the 2nd of April, he thus wrote to the Parliament:—

"I have received divers private intimations of your pleasure to have me come in person to wait upon you in England; as also copies of votes of the Parliament to that purpose. But considering the way they came to me was but by private intimations, and the votes did refer to a letter to be signed by the Speaker, I thought it would have been too much forwardness in me to have left my charge here, until the said letter came; it being not fit for me to prophesy whether the letter would be an absolute command, or

[1] Clarendon's History of the Rebellion, vol. vi. pp. 429—431; Cromwell's Letters and Speeches, vol. ii. p. 103.

having limitations with a liberty left by the Parliament to me, to consider in what way to yield my obedience. Your letter came to my hand upon Friday the 22nd of March, the same day that I came before the city of Kilkenny. And I understood by Dr. Cartwright, who delivered it to me, that reason of cross winds, and the want of shipping in the West of England where he was, hindered him from coming with it sooner; it bearing date the 8th of January, and not coming to my hands until the 22nd of March.

"The letter supposed your army in winter quarters, and the time of the year not suitable for present action; making this as the reason of your command. And your forces have been in action ever since the 29th of January; and your letter, which was to be the rule of my obedience, coming to my hands after our having been so long in action,—with respect had to the reasons you were pleased to use therein, I knew not what to do. And having received a letter signed by yourself of the 26th of February, which mentions not a word of the continuance of your pleasure concerning my coming over, I did humbly conceive it much consisting with my duty, humbly to beg a positive signification what your will is; professing (as before the Lord) that I am most ready to obey your commands herein with all sincerity; rejoicing only to be about that work which I am called to by those whom God hath set over me, which I acknowledge you to be; and fearing only in obeying you, to disobey you. I most humbly and earnestly beseech you to judge for me, whether your letter doth not naturally allow me the liberty of begging a more clear expression of your command and pleasure: which, when vouchsafed unto me, will find most ready and cheerful obedience."[1]

He had gained as much time as he wished, and while he was delaying, the course of events was such as to render his return to London a new source of power and greatness to him.

When Charles II., after having left the Hague to pay a visit to the Queen, his mother, at St. Germains, received certain information that Cromwell had assumed the government of Ireland, he hesitated more and more to proceed thither, as he was unwilling to risk his future and his life upon so dangerous a ground, and against so formidable an adversary. He spent three months at St. Germains; a monotonous residence which the Court of France took little pains to render agreeable to him, and the ennui of which the imperious ill-temper of his mother did not tend to dissipate. At the news of Ormonde's defeat before Dublin, the young prince's first

---

[1] Cromwell's Letters and Speeches, vol. ii. pp. 157, 158.

impulse was to set out at once for Ireland, and take his personal share in the struggle : to those who told him that it would be imprudent for him to go thither to share in defeat, he replied : " Then must I go there to die, for it is disgraceful for me to live anywhere else." " This speech appeared to proceed from a noble heart," says Madame de Motteville, who lived on almost as intimate terms with Queen Henrietta Maria as with Anne of Austria ; " the greatest men of antiquity never spoke better ; but young people pass easily from this rigid virtue into laxity ; they afterwards endure with indifference those very evils which at first appeared to them the most insupportable in life, and the pleasures which they meet with in life are the cause of this. So it happened in the case of this prince."[1] His own courtiers were not long in estimating the character of their sovereign. " Foreign princes," wrote one of them to the Marquis of Ormonde, " begin to look upon him as a person so lazy and careless in his own business, that they think it not safe, by contributing anything to his assistance, to irritate so potent enemies as they fear his rebellious subjects are like to prove."[2] Charles soon experienced the effects of this feeling ; Cardinal Mazarin gave him clearly to understand that his prolonged residence at St. Germains was becoming a source of embarrassment to the Court of France, which had no wish to quarrel with the Commonwealth of England ; Queen Henrietta Maria herself, who stood in great need of Mazarin's favour, urged her son to take the Cardinal's hint, without requiring a more precise explanation of his wishes ; and about the middle of September, 1649, Charles set out through Normandy for the island of Jersey, the only part of his dominions of which he still retained possession.[3]

No sooner had he arrived there than he received intelligence of the disaster of Drogheda, and almost at the same moment the Parliament of Scotland sent to request him to resume the negotiations which had been opened at the Hague for his return to his kingdom. Since the failure of that first attempt, the general feeling of the Scottish people in favour of the King had not ceased to manifest itself ; several insurrections of the pure royalists had occurred in various parts of the kingdom ; and although the Presbyterian Parliament had promptly repressed them, its leaders, Argyle amongst others, were convinced that they could not refrain from making another serious effort to induce Charles to return, or at

---

[1] Mémoires de Madame de Motteville, vol. iii. pp. 329, 333 ; in Petitot's Collection.
[2] Carte's Ormonde Letters, vol. i. p. 319.
[3] Clarendon's History of the Rebellion, vol. vi. pp. 351—354.

least attempting a striking demonstration of their willingness to receive him. The propositions which their envoy, Lord Winram of Liberton, brought to Jersey, were in substance the same, and to the full as harsh, as those which Charles had recently rejected at the Hague; but his position was now less advantageous; his enemies were triumphant in England and Ireland; from Paris and the Hague, his mother and brother-in-law urged him more strongly than ever to accept the propositions of the Scots, one writing to him that the Court of France, and the other that the people of Holland, were decidedly of opinion that he should do so. Charles wished to consult Ormonde; Ormonde replied that there was no possible ground for hope unless they could succeed in bringing about a war between England and Scotland, and thus operating a diversion which would enable the Irish royalists to take breath and attempt fresh efforts. Nearly all the most trusted counsellors of Charles, who were with him at the time, held the same opinion. he yielded to their unanimous advice, and, either because Jersey seemed an inconvenient place for negotiating, or in order to gain more time, he appointed the Scottish Commissioners to meet him at Breda, a town in the private domain of his brother-in-law, the Prince of Orange, where he felt himself perfectly free and safe. But as he felt neither satisfaction nor confidence in the negotiation to which he had submitted, he wrote to Montrose, who was then busy raising money and men in Germany: " I entreat you to go on vigorously, and with your wonted courage and care, in the prosecution of those trusts I have committed to you, and not to be startled with any reports you may hear, as if I were otherwise inclined to the Presbyterians than when I left you. I assure you I am upon the same principles I was, and depend as much as ever upon your undertaking and endeavours for my service."[1]

Montrose did not require to be stimulated to activity; passionately proud and devoted to his King, he had confidence in his cause, in himself, and in his destiny. A popular prediction had affirmed that he would restore the King to his throne; and he had been supplied by Charles with all the powers necessary to enable him to act. He travelled through the Netherlands, Germany, Denmark and Sweden, seeking the means of accomplishing his mission wherever he went, daily witnessing the failure of some of those on which he had relied, and daily returning to his work with the same conviction and the same ardour. That part of Europe,

<hr>

[1] Laing's History of Scotland, vol. iii. pp. 441, 581; Clarendon's History of the Rebellion, vol. vi. pp. 399—401; Whitelocke, pp. 429, 430; Carte's Ormonde Letters, vol. i. pp. 338, 350.

and especially Sweden, had then become the second fatherland of a large number of Scottish officers, who, after having served under Gustavus Adelphus in the Thirty Years' War, had settled there with the fortune or the fame which they had acquired. Montrose lived among them as a pleasant companion both in war and revel, attracting some by the brilliancy of his expectations, alluring others by his open-handed liberality; they had all promised him their personal support or influence for his great enterprise, and some had even furnished him with funds. The King of Denmark and several of the petty princes of Germany had given him similar assurances.[1] When he believed himself ready to enter upon action, he published from Copenhagen, a declaration in which he announced and justified his undertaking, and invited all faithful subjects of the King to join with him in Scotland for its accomplishment; he then appointed Hamburgh as the place of rendezvous for his recruits, and took up his own residence there, with greater pomp than his resources warranted, for the purpose of awaiting, organising, and despatching his forces.[2]

Recruits arrived slowly and in small numbers; the Court of Denmark was zealous but poor; Queen Christina of Sweden, who had at first appeared favourable, was suddenly seized with admiration for the English Commonwealth and for Cromwell. Montrose collected with great difficulty at Hamburgh and Gothenburgh, a body of twelve hundred men, poorly armed and equipped; a first division, which he sent off in September, 1649, perished at sea; the second, under the command of the Earl of Kinnoull, arrived safely at Kirkwall, the capital of Pomona, the principal of the Orkney islands, and fixed themselves there until the arrival of their general. Montrose on his side was awaiting fresh recruits, and the promised insurrections of the royalists in the Scottish Highlands. But the first attempt at insurrection, beginning too prematurely, had been too easily repressed;[3] no general rising took place; the friends of Montrose wrote to him that his presence was indispensable, and would certainly be efficacious. He set out, at length, and reached the Orkneys in the early part of March, 1650, with five hundred men, and a few Scottish nobles who were devoted to his person and fortune.

A short time before his arrival, and in answer to his declaration, the Kirk and Parliament of Scotland had published two other decla-

---

[1] Wishart's Memoirs of Montrose, Appendix xix. pp. 454—458.
[2] Clarendon's History of the Rebellion, vol. vi. pp. 408—410; Whitelocke, pp. 426, 430, 434—436; Wishart's Memoirs of Montrose, pp. 361—369.
[3] Browne's History of the Highlands, vol. ii. pp. 26—28.

rations against him, remarkable for their violence even in that age of unbridled passion. "It may seem strange," they said, "that we should think it worth the while to answer the slanders and groundless reproaches of that viperous brood of Satan, James Grahame, whom the Estates of Parliament have long since declared traitor, the church hath delivered into the hands of the devil, and the nation doth generally detest and abhor; yet, because our silence may be subject to misconstruction, and some of the weaker sort may be inveigled by the bold assertions and railing accusations of this impudent braggart, presenting himself to the view of the world, clothed with his Majesty's authority as Lieutenant-Governor and Captain-General of this Kingdom, we shall shortly answer what is said against us, take off the mask which he hath put on, and expose him to public view in his own apparel."[1] All the old grievances of the dominant party, and the variations of conduct imputed to Montrose at the beginning of the civil war, and the acts of cruelty of which he had been accused during his campaign on behalf of Charles I., in 1645, were ably set forth in these two documents, which were read and commented upon from every Presbyterian pulpit; and at the moment when he set foot again in Scotland, the rage and terror of the people combined, against Montrose, with the hatred and alarm of his rivals.

On disembarking at the northern extremity of Scotland, he displayed somewhat pompously three banners, two in the name of the King, on one of which was painted the severed head of Charles I., with this motto, "Judge and revenge my cause, O Lord!"—on the third, which was his own standard, was a naked arm, holding a blood-stained sword, on a black ground, with this motto, "*Nil medium.*" He then advanced slowly through the counties of Caithness and Sutherland, expecting to be joined by recruits from the country itself. These recruits, however, did not appear; on the contrary, he learned that many chieftains, on whose support he had reckoned, had ranged themselves on the side of the Parliament; and he was visibly surprised and disappointed at the little sensation produced by his name and progress. The government at Edinburgh, whilst a larger body of troops were collecting under the command of David Lesley, sent forward some squadrons of cavalry under Lieutenant-Colonel Strahan, an impetuous sectary and valiant officer; five hundred infantry, collected by the Earl of Sutherland, joined Strahan's force, and they were lying together at Tain, on the eastern coast of Ross-shire, when they were informed that Mon-

---

[1] Wishart's Memoirs of Montrose, pp. 464, 465.

trose was encamped at a short distance, and carelessly guarded, as he did not know that the enemy was already so near him. It was Saturday, the 10th of April, and Strahan hesitated to march forward, as he was unwilling to run the risk of being obliged to fight on Sunday; but a movement made by Montrose brought the two troops still more closely together. Strahan then took his resolution, and advanced to within a league of Montrose's camp at Corbiesdale, which was still unaware of his proximity, and in considerable disorder. Strahan's squadrons charged it suddenly and in succession, as if they had been the vanguard of an army. Montrose tried to fall back upon a neighbouring wood : the soldiers whom he had brought with him from Germany fought valiantly, but the recruits that he had raised in the Orkneys dispersed. With his accustomed bravery, he endeavoured, but in vain, to rally them ; his horse was killed under him, and he would have been taken on the field of battle, if his friend, Lord Frendraught, had not generously re-mounted him. The battle soon turned into a rout and massacre ; ten officers, and more than three hundred soldiers, were slain ; more than four hundred prisoners were taken, and a hundred Irish, who were found among them, were instantly shot. Montrose fled at full speed, and as soon as he was out of sight, he forsook his horse, threw away his George and his Order of the Garter, changed clothes with a peasant, and betook himself across the fields in search of an asylum. He wandered for many days among the Highlands of Ross and Sutherlandshire, sometimes received with enthusiasm, sometimes repulsed with horror, frequently exhausted with fatigue and hunger, and vainly endeavouring to reach the coast. At length, on the 3rd of May, either from mischance or treachery, he was discovered and arrested in a cottage on the estate of Neil Macleod, Laird of Assynt ; from whence he was taken to the castles of Skild and Brane, until orders arrived for his immediate transfer to Edinburgh.[1]

He was now in the worst possible position ; he had against him both the government and the people, the implacable hatred of his rivals, and the brutal fury of the multitude. They thronged on his route to load him with insults, but could not succeed in humbling him for a moment. He endured with the same firmness of soul the outrages of his enemies and the farewell meeting with his children, with whom he was allowed a brief interview at the house of his father-in-law, the Earl of Southesk. But marks of sympathy were

<hr/>

[1] Wishart's Memoirs of Montrose, pp. 372—377 ; Balfour's Annals of Scotland, vol. iii. p. 432, vol. iv. p. 9; Laing's History of Scotland. vol. iii. pp. 443—444; Browne's History of the Highlands, vol. ii. pp. 30—36.

not altogether denied him. At the castle of Grange, where he lodged with his escort a short time before reaching Dundee, the Lady of Grange made an almost successful attempt to procure his escape during the night ; and at Dundee itself, which in 1645 had suffered severely from his arms, the inhabitants, far from triumph-ing over him in his misfortune, treated him with the greatest respect, and, by their remonstrances, obtained permission from his guards to supply him with clothes suitable to his rank, instead of the tattered garments in which he had been captured, and which he had until then been insultingly obliged to wear.[1]

On the 17th of May he arrived at Leith, near Edinburgh. The Parliament met on the same day, and voted that "James Grahame should be brought on a cart, bareheaded, and bound to the cart by a rope,—the hangman, in his livery, covered, riding on the horse that draws the cart,—from the Watergate to the Tolbooth of Edinburgh, and from thence to the Parliament House ; and there, in the place of delinquents, on his knees should receive his sentence, viz., to be hanged on a gibbet at the Cross of Edinburgh, with his book and declaration tied by a rope about his neck, and there to hang for the space of three hours until he were dead ; and thereafter to be cut down by the hangman ; his head, hands, and legs to be cut off, and distributed as follows : his head to be affixed on an iron pole on the west pinnacle of the new prison of Edinburgh : one hand to be set on the gate of Perth, the other on the gate of Stirling ; one leg and foot on the gate of Aberdeen, the other on the gate of Glasgow. If he was at his death penitent, and released from excommunication, then the trunk of his body should be interred in the Greyfriars ; otherwise it should be interred in the Borrowmuir, by the hangman's men, under the gallows."[2] The manners of that age were still rude enough for the hatred of his enemies to take pleasure in such a spectacle, which was then calculated to inspire beholders with greater dread than disgust.

On the following day, at four o'clock in the afternoon, Montrose was conducted, on an old brokendown horse, from Leith to the Watergate of Edinburgh, where he was met by the magistrates of the city in their robes, escorted by the town-guard and hang-man. A copy of his sentence was delivered to him ; he read it, and returned it, saying with the greatest calmness and com-posure, "That he was ready to submit to it ; only he was sorry that through him the King's majesty, whose person he represented,

[1] Wishart's Memoirs of Montrose, pp. 379—382.
[2] Balfour's Annals of Scotland, vol. vi. pp. 12, 13.

should be so much dishonoured." The procession then moved forward; Montrose did not remove his hat, and the hangman knocked it off; thirty-four of his officers, his companions in captivity, walked, tied two and two together, before the cart. Along the whole route an immense crowd had collected for the purpose of assailing Montrose with abuse, and even with dirt and stones; but the tranquil firmness of his demeanour, the gravity of his looks, and the undaunted courage which he displayed, produced so powerful an impression upon the people that outrage ceased, silence reigned around the mournful cavalcade, or was broken at intervals only by expressions of compassion, and prayers on behalf of the illustrious prisoner. As the procession passed in front of the house of the Earl of Moray, the cart stopped for a moment; all looked up in surprise; the Marquis of Argyle was at the window, with his family and several friends; he had desired to feast his eyes upon the humiliation of that enemy before whom, five years previously, he had been forced to fly.[1] Although the distance was little more than a mile, three hours were spent in going from the gate of the city to the Tolbooth. On dismounting from the cart, Montrose gave the hangman some money, as a reward, he said, "for driving his triumphal chariot so well." The Parliament was in session; five commissioners were sent to the prison " to ask James Grahame if he had anything to say before he repaired to the House to receive his sentence." On their return to the Parliament, they reported that Montrose had refused to give any answer until he knew upon what terms they stood with the King, and whether they had come to any agreement with him. Seven commissioners were immediately sent to interrogate him, and to inform him that an agreement had been concluded with the King, who was on the point of returning to Scotland. Somewhat moved, doubtless, by this intelligence, Montrose declined giving any further answer, saying that he had made a long journey, and that after the wearisome and tedious ceremony and compliment they had paid him that day," he desired some repose.[2]

Two days after, when he was brought to the bar of the Parliament, he allowed himself the pleasure of following his natural

[1] This fact is placed beyond doubt by a letter from the French agent Graymond to Cardinal Mazarin, dated 31st May, 1650. " Plusieurs prirent garde, et en ont bien discouru après, qu'on fit halte vis-à-vis la maison du Comte de Moray, où estoit entre autres M. le Marquis d'Argyle, que considéroit son ennemi par une fenestre entr'ouverte." Archives des Affaires Etrangères de France.
[2] Wishart's Memoirs of Montrose, pp. 383—386; Balfour's Annals of Scotland, vol. iv. p. 14.

tastes, and appeared before his enemies in splendid attire. He
wore a rich dress of black silk embroidered with silver, and over it
a scarlet cloak, trimmed with silver lace, and lined with crimson
taffety ; and a beaver hat, with a broad silver band. On being
placed on the raised platform appointed for criminals, he glanced
proudly around him ; his face was pale and careworn, but expressive
of invincible courage and dignified resolution. The Chancellor,
Lord Loudon, addressed him in a long and bitter speech, and concluded by saying, " that for the many horrible murders, treasons, and
impieties he had committed, God had now brought him to suffer
condign punishment." When the Chancellor had terminated his
harangue, Montrose obtained, with some difficulty, permission to say
a few words in his own defence ; he spoke with reserved hauteur,
and considerable address, as if he had anticipated some result from
his speech. " He considered the Parliament," he said, " as sitting
by the King's authority ; and therefore he had appeared with
reverence, and bareheaded, which otherwise he would not willingly
have done." He defended himself from the charges of cruelty
which had been brought against him during the late war, saying,
" that it was not in the power of the greatest generals to prevent
disorders altogether in their army, but he had endeavoured what he
could to suppress them, and to punish them as soon as they were
known ; he had never spilt any blood--no, not of his most inveterate
enemies—but on the field of battle ; and even in the greatest heat
of action, he had preserved the lives of many thousands. As to
his late invasion, he had undertaken it at the command of his
Majesty ; and he might justly affirm that no subject ever acted
upon more honourable grounds, nor by a more lawful power and
authority than he had done. Wherefore," he said in conclusion,
" he desired them to lay aside all prejudices, private animosity, and
desire of revenge, and consider him, in relation to the justice of
his cause, as a man and a Christian ; as an obedient subject, in
relation to the commands of his royal master, which he had faithfully executed ; as their fellow-subject, and one to whom they lay
under great obligations, for having preserved the lives and fortunes
of many of them, at a time when he had the power and authority,
and wanted only the cruel inclination, to have destroyed both. He
entreated them not to be too rash in their judgment against him,
but to judge him according to the laws of God, the laws of nature
and nations, and particularly by the laws of the land ; which, if they
refused, he appealed to the just Judge of the world, who must at
last judge them all, and always gives righteous judgment." The
Chancellor replied to him with anger and invectives. Montrose

attempted to speak a second time, but he was stopped, and ordered to kneel down and receive his sentence : which he did.[1] His execution was fixed for the following day.

During the evening, the Presbyterian ministers and magistrates of Edinburgh besieged Montrose with their visits, in the hope of extorting from him some expression which would imply a recognition of the rightfulness of their Church and government. But their persevering endeavours only served to increase his enthusiasm. He told them " that he was much beholden to the Parliament for the great honour they had decreed him ; for he was prouder to have his head fixed upon the top of the prison, in the view of the present and succeeding ages, than if they had ordered a golden statue to be erected to him in the market-place, or that his picture should be hung in the King's bedchamber. He thanked them for taking so effectual a method to preserve the memory of his loyalty and regard for his beloved sovereign, even to the latest posterity, by transmitting such lasting monuments of them to the four principal cities of the kingdom, and wished heartily that he had flesh enough to have sent a piece to every city in Christendom, as a testimony of his unshaken love and fidelity to his King and country." He spent the night in prayer, and in composing verses, in which he gave noble expression to the same sentiments. Early in the morning, the noise of drums and trumpets resounded through the town, he asked the captain of the guard what it meant, and was told that it was to call the soldiers and citizens to arms, because it was feared that some of the people might attempt to rescue him. " What! " said Montrose, " do I, who was such a terror to these good men, when alive, continue still so formidable to them now, when I am to die ? But let them look to themselves, for even after I am dead, I will be continually present to their wicked consciences, and become more formidable to them than while I was alive." He then began to dress with great pains. Whilst he was at his toilette, Sir Archibald Johnstone, a member of Parliament, and one of his bitterest enemies, derisively expressed his surprise that a man in such a position should bestow so much care on the frivolous adornment of his person. Montrose answered with a smile, " that while his head was his own, he would dress and adorn it; but to-morrow, when it becomes yours, you may treat it as you please."

He dressed himself with great magnificence, and threw over his shoulders a handsome cloak of scarlet velvet, trimmed with

---

[1] Wishart's Memoirs of Montrose, pp. 387—392 ; Balfour's Annals of Scotland, vol. iv. p. 16.

gold lace, which his friends had sent him. As he walked from his prison to the place of execution, his grand air, and the proud and calm expression of his countenance, produced a more powerful effect than ever upon the spectators. He assisted the executioner to hang round his neck, in conformity with his sentence, the history of his wars, and his late declaration, and said "he reckoned himself more honoured thereby, than when it had pleased his Majesty to create him a knight of the most noble Order of the Garter." He was not allowed to stand forward and address the people, but he addressed a few words to those who stood near him, expressive of his persistence in the sentiments which had guided his life hitherto, and of the utmost piety and tranquillity of soul. He requested permission to die with his hat on, it was refused; to retain his cloak,—this also was denied him; upon which he desired the magistrates "to inflict what further degree of ignominy and disgrace they could possibly invent, for that he was ready to submit with the greatest cheerfulness to the highest indignities for the sake of that cause for which he suffered." His last words were, "May God have mercy upon this afflicted kingdom!"[1] It is said that the hangman himself wept, after having obeyed the fatal signal; that a murmur of indignant sorrow burst from the crowd; and that Argyle, on learning the particulars of his great rival's death, became agitated and melancholy, as if seized with regret, or struck by a presentiment of his own future fate.

The Commissioners of the Parliament had not deceived Montrose when they told him that they had treated with the King, and that he was about to return amongst them. At the very moment that Montrose began in Scotland his brief and fatal campaign, Charles received the Scottish Commissioners at Breda, and resumed with them the discussion of their harsh propositions. Great difference of opinion existed among his advisers upon this subject. His most sensible and honest counsellors exhorted him not to submit to such thraldom, and supported their opinions by the authority of Hyde, in whom Charles had the utmost confidence, and whom he had just despatched on an embassy to Madrid. "If the King puts himself into the hands of the Scots," Hyde had written to Mr. Secretary Nicholas, "they cannot justly be accused of deceiving him, for, on my conscience, they will not use him worse than they promise, if he does all they require him to do in this last address. I wish, with all my heart, they who advise the

---

[1] Wishart's Memoirs of Montrose, pp. 392—405; Balfour's Annals of Scotland, pp. 19—22; Laing's History of Scotland, vol. iii. pp. 414—417, 582.

King to comply and join with them, would deal as clearly, and say that the King should now take the Covenant, and enjoin it to others, and all observe it; but to say he should put himself into their hands, and hope to be excused taking it, and be able to defend others from submitting to it, or that he and we should take it and break it afterwards, is such folly and atheism, that we should be ashamed to avow or think it. Oh, Mr. Secretary! if I were now at Breda, I would fly to the Indies, rather than be involved in such councils."[1]

So long as there was any uncertainty as to the issue of Montrose's expedition, Charles hesitated. His good sense and dignity both led him to think with Hyde; but when he learned at Breda that Montrose was defeated, a fugitive, and, ere long, a prisoner, his frivolous and reckless counsellors carried their point. They had on their side the Queen-mother, the Prince of Orange, and that unwillingness to wait patiently, which is ever the result of exile. The friends of Hyde took no part in the deliberations of the Council, and Charles consented to everything. He promised to swear fidelity to the Scottish Covenant, to disavow and annul every treaty of peace which had been concluded with the Irish, never to permit the free exercise of the Catholic religion in Ireland, or in any part of his dominions, to acknowledge the authority of the various Parliaments held in Scotland since the commencement of the war, and finally, to govern, in civil affairs, according to the advice of the Parliament, and in religious matters, according to that of the Church. And in order to give to his promise the sanction of an enormous falsehood, he wrote to the Parliament, that, as he had forbidden Montrose to engage in his expedition, he could not regret the defeat of a man who had dared to act in disobedience to his authority.[2]

It is said that Charles hoped by this means to save the life of Montrose, and that, when he was informed of his execution, he was on the point of breaking off all further negotiation. It is said also, that at Edinburgh, when Montrose's expedition began, the violent party wished to recall the Commissioners of the Parliament from Breda, and to cease all negotiation with Charles; and that the immediate execution of Montrose was the bribe given by the moderate men to the fanatics, in order to induce them to concur in

---

[1] Clarendon's State Papers, vol. iii. p. 14; Carte's Ormonde Letters, vol. i. p. 373; Clarendon's History of the Rebellion, vol. vi. pp. 401—408.

[2] Clarendon's State Papers, vol. iii. pp 13—19; Balfour's Annals of Scotland, vol. iv. pp. 24, 25; Lingard's History of England, vol. xi. p. 51; Thurloe's State Papers, vol. i. p. 117.

the King's return.   No positive trace has remained of these mutual concessions : parties, like individual consciences, have their shameful secrets, which they employ all their arts to conceal.   However this may be, no change was made in the existing state of things on either side ; the Scottish Commissioners declared that they were satisfied with the King's promises ; Charles acquiesced in Montrose's execution, as he had yielded to his own humiliation ; and on the 2nd of June, 1650, he embarked at Ter-Veere for Scotland, on board a flotilla which the Prince of Orange had placed at his disposal.[1]

He arrived three weeks afterwards on the coast of Scotland ; but, before he was allowed to set foot on shore, he was required to sign the Covenant.   The Scottish nobles who had advised him to consent to everything, Hamilton and Lauderdale among others, left him and retired to their estates ; they were of the number of those whom, ever since the 22nd of March, 1649, the Presbyterian Parliament had formally excluded from all participation in public affairs ; and their presence with the King was not only compromising to him, but fraught with danger to themselves.   Two days after his disembarkation, nearly all the English who had accompanied Charles were expressly sent out of the kingdom ; the Duke of Buckingham, Lord Wilmot, and a few others of his household, the most frivolous and hypocritical of his courtiers, were alone authorised to remain with him.   The Parliament had minutely arranged beforehand the route which he was to take to his palace of Falkland, near Edinburgh ; and he was conducted thither with great marks of respect, but under the strictest guard and surveillance.[2]

At about the same time, Cromwell, yielding obedience at length to the wishes of the Parliament, returned from Ireland to England ; on his disembarkation at Bristol, he was greeted with honours and acclamations by the whole town, who came out *en masse* to welcome him.   As soon as it became known that he was near London, Fairfax and most of the officers of the army and members of Parliament went out to meet him at Hounslow Heath ; at Hyde Park he found the Lord Mayor and train-bands waiting for him ; and from thence to St. James's Palace, where he was to lodge, it was, say the newspapers of the time, one vast tumult of salutation, congratulation, artillery-volleying, and human shouting. " What a crowd come out to see your Lordship's triumph !" said

---

[1] Laing's History of Scotland, vol. iii. p. 440; Clarendon's State Papers, vol. iii. p. 22.

[2] Godwin's History of the Commonwealth, vol. iii. p. 226; Clarendon's History of the Rebellion, vol. vi. pp. 436, 437.

one of the bystanders to Cromwell; to which he replied, with his rough and frank good sense, "Yes; but if it were to see me hanged, how many would there be!"[1]

As soon as Montrose's expedition in the Highlands, and the arrangements concluded at Breda between Charles II. and the Scottish Commissioners, had become known in London, the Parliament had given the Council of State full powers to repel any invasion, and had voted a considerable increase of the army. Immediately on Cromwell's return from Ireland, Fairfax and he were appointed, the one Lord General of the Forces, the other Lieutenant-General, to command what was vaguely called the "Northern Expedition." They both signified their acceptance of these appointments; but a few days after, the Council of State having decided that, instead of waiting until the Scots invaded England, the English army should take the initiative, and carry the war into Scotland, Fairfax manifested great reluctance to undertake such a command. His wife, a zealous Presbyterian, and the Presbyterian ministers by whom she was surrounded, had, it is said, suggested these scruples; but perhaps, also, Fairfax was beginning to perceive that Cromwell and the republicans had used, and wished still to use, him as a cloak to cover, and an instrument to accomplish, designs utterly at variance with his feelings and wishes. In any case, his resistance was, in the eyes of the public, a cause of serious embarrassment, which could not be treated lightly, and to overcome which every effort should be made. Five commissioners—Cromwell, Lambert, Harrison, St. John, and Whitelocke—were appointed by the Council of State to wait upon Fairfax, to confer with him on the subject, and endeavour to remove his difficulties.

"My Lord General," said Cromwell, "we are commanded by the Council of State to endeavour to give your Excellency satisfaction on any doubts of yours which may arise concerning the command in Scotland, and the grounds of the resolution of the Council for the journey into Scotland."

FAIRFAX.—"I am very glad of the opportunity of conferring with this committee, where I find so many of my particular friends, as well as of the Commonwealth, about this great business; for I do acknowledge myself not fully satisfied as to the justice of our invasion of our Scottish brethren."

LAMBERT.—"Will your Excellency be pleased to favour us with the particular causes of your dissatisfaction?"

FAIRFAX.—"I shall very freely do it, and I think I need not

Cromwell's Letters and Speeches, vol. ii. pp. 103, 104; Whitelocke, p. 457.

make to you or to any that know me any protestation of the continuance of my duty and affection to the Parliament, and my readiness to serve them in anything wherein my conscience will give
me leave."

HARRISON.—"There cannot be more desired nor expected from
your Excellency."

FAIRFAX.—"Give me leave, then, my Lords, with all freeness
to say to you that I think it doubtful whether we have a just cause
to make an invasion upon Scotland. With them we are joined in
the National League and Covenant; and now, for us, contrary
thereunto, and without sufficient cause given us by them, to enter
into their country with an army, and to make war upon them, is
that which I cannot see the justice of, nor how we shall be able to
justify the lawfulness of it before God or man."

CROMWELL.—"I confess, my Lord, that if they have given us
no cause to invade them, it will not be justifiable for us to do it.
But, my Lord, they have invaded us, as your lordship knows they
have done. since the National Covenant, and contrary to it, in that
action of Duke Hamilton, which was by order and authority from
the Parliament of that kingdom, and so the act of the whole nation
by their representatives. And they now give us too much cause of
suspicion that they intend another invasion upon us, joining with
their King, with whom they have made a full agreement, without
the assent or privity of this Commonwealth; and are very busy at
this present in raising forces and money to carry on their design.
I humbly submit it to your Excellency's judgment, whether these
things are not a sufficient ground and cause for us to endeavour to
provide for the safety of our own country, and to prevent the
miseries which an invasion of the Scots would bring upon us? That
there will be a war between us, I fear, is unavoidable. Your Excellency will soon determine whether it be better to have this war
in the bowels of another country or of our own."

FAIRFAX.—"It is probable there will be war between us; but
whether we should begin this war and be on the offensive part, or
only stand upon our own defence, is that which I scruple. And
although they invaded us under Duke Hamilton, who pretended the
authority of the Parliament then sitting for it, yet their succeeding
Parliament disowned that engagement, and punished some of the
promoters of it. If we were assured of their coming with their
army into England, I confess it were prudence for us to prevent
them, and we are ready to advance into Scotland before they can
march into England; but what warrant have we to fall upon them
unless we can be assured of their purpose to fall upon us?"

HARRISON.—" I think, under favour, there cannot be greater assurance or human probability of the intentions of any State than we have of theirs to invade our country."

FAIRFAX.—" Human probabilities are not sufficient grounds to make war upon a neighbour nation, to whom we are engaged in a solemn league and covenant."

ST. JOHN.—" But, my Lord, that league and covenant was first broken by themselves, and so dissolved as to cease, and the disowning of Duke Hamilton's action by their latter Parliament, cannot acquit the injury done to us before."

CROMWELL.—" I suppose your Excellency will be convinced of this clear truth, that we are no longer obliged by the league and covenant which themselves did first break."

FAIRFAX.—" I am to answer only for my own conscience; and what that yields unto as just and lawful, I shall follow: and what seems to me, or what I doubt to be, otherwise, I must not do. Every one must stand or fall by his own conscience: those who are satisfied of the justice of this war may cheerfully proceed in it; those who scruple at it, as I confess I do, cannot undertake any service in it. I acknowledge that which hath been said to carry much weight and reason with it, and none can have more power upon me than this Committee, nor none be more ready to serve the Parliament than myself in anything wherein my conscience shall be satisfied; in this it is not, and therefore, that I may be no hinderance to the Parliament's designs, I shall willingly lay down my commission, that it may be in their hands to choose some worthier person than myself, who may upon clear satisfaction of his conscience undertake this business, wherein I desire to be excused."

CROMWELL.—" I am very sorry your lordship should have thoughts of laying down your commission, by which God hath blessed you in the performance of so many eminent services for the Parliament. I pray, my Lord, consider all your faithful servants, us who are officers, who have served under you, and desire to serve under no other general. It would be a great discouragement to all of us, and a great discouragement to the affairs of the Parliament, for our noble general to entertain any thoughts of laying down his commission. I hope your lordship will never give so great an advantage to the public enemy, nor so much dishearten your friends as to think of doing so."

FAIRFAX.—" What would you have me do? As far as my conscience will give way, I am willing to join with you still in the service of the Parliament; but where the conscience is not satisfied, none of you, I am sure, will engage in any service ; and that is my condition in this, and therefore I must desire to be excused."[1]

The Commissioners immediately reported this answer to the Council of State. "The Lieutenant-General," says Ludlow, "acted his part so to the life that I really thought him in earnest; which obliged me to step to him as he was withdrawing with the rest of the Committee out of the council-chamber, and to desire him that he would not, in compliment and humility, obstruct the service of the nation by his refusal; but the consequence made it sufficiently evident that he had no such intention."[2] Two days afterwards, Whitelocke and Lord Pembroke presented their report to the House, both on the main question of the invasion of Scotland, and on the conference between the Council of State and Fairfax. The House voted unanimously that it was both just and necessary that the English army should enter Scotland, and that it should be set in movement without delay. A declaration justifying this resolution was read and adopted. The House was informed that Mr. Rushworth, Secretary to the Lord-General, was at the door. He was at once admitted, and informed the House that the Lord-General had commanded him to present, from him, to the Parliament, the last commission he had received from the Parliament for the Scottish war, and likewise his first commission as Lord-General, if the Parliament pleased to desire it. A resolution was immediately passed, withdrawing all military command from Fairfax. This was the rupture of the Commonwealth with the only Presbyterian leader who had served it. Cromwell was at once appointed Captain-General and Commander-in-Chief of all the forces of England. Three days after, he left London to rejoin his army ; and three weeks after, he crossed the Tweed and entered Scotland at the head of about fifteen thousand men. On setting foot on Scottish soil, he harangued his troops. "As a Christian and a soldier, I exhort you to be doubly and trebly diligent, to be wary and worthy, for sure enough we have work before us ! But have we not had God's blessing hitherto? Let us go on faithfully, and hope for the like still."[3]

If he had been aware of the proceedings in the councils of Scotland, and of the relation in which the Scots stood to the King

---

[1] Whitelocke's Memorials, pp. 460—462; Old Parliamentary History, vol. xix. pp. 266—275.

[2] Ludlow's Memoirs, p. 135.

[3] Commons' Journals, vol. vi. pp. 431, 432; Godwin's History of the Commonwealth, vol. iii. pp. 215, 221, 222; Cromwell's Letters and Speeches, vol. ii. p. 180.

whom they had recalled, Cromwell would undoubtedly have felt full confidence in his success. Neither demonstrations of public respect, nor the pomp of royalty, were wanting to complete the illusion of Charles's position; he had been voted an allowance of 9,000*l.* a month for the maintenance of his household; and he had been surrounded with a numerous retinue. In the absence of the Parliament, which then stood adjourned, the members of the intermediate committee, or Committee of Estates as it was called, with the Marquis of Argyle at their head, paid the King the most assiduous homage. Argyle was a consummate courtier, careful to observe every point of etiquette, and to seize every opportunity of pleasing the King in small matters. At the same time, great preparations were being made for the impending war; the Parliament had taken measures for providing Scotland with an army of thirty thousand men; an experienced general, David Lesley, was to command it; and fortifications were in process of construction around the capital. But this show of zeal for monarchy ill concealed the forced nullity of the King, and the incoherence of the ideas and actions of the party who were desirous at once to support him and to make him a nonentity. Charles was not present at the councils at which public affairs were discussed, and whenever he attempted to converse seriously with Argyle on the subject, that wily courtier respectfully eluded any such conversation. The theologians, on the other hand, attacked the young Prince whom the politicians took such pains to nullify; observances, remonstrances, and sermons occupied the leisure which was forced upon him; and notwithstanding all his efforts to appear a hypocrite, he always passed, and deservedly, for a libertine. Although Presbyterians above all things, the Scots were sincere royalists; and Charles, who was but little inclined to indulge in illusions, knew perfectly well that, out of Scotland, he had neither kingdom nor army; but, on both sides, the distrust and dissatisfaction were profound, and although they were mutually necessary to one another, they differed too widely to come either to a thorough understanding or a lasting union.[1]

When it became known that Cromwell had passed the border, it was thought impossible to avoid showing the King to the army. He accordingly went to the camp, and the troops received him with demonstrations of joy which soon aroused the suspicions of both ardent theologians and jealous politicians. Charles was gay, witty, and affable; his presence in the camp gave a great impulse to free

---

[1] Clarendon's History of the Rebellion, vol. vi. pp. 436—441; Whitelocke, p. 462; Laing's History of Scotland, vol. iii. p. 450.

conversation, occasioned many expressions of devotedness to his person, and probably led to some symptoms of insubordination and dislike of his keepers. The fanatics eagerly availed themselves of this opportunity; they loudly inveighed against the composition of the army, which contained, they said, a large number of malignants, old Hamiltonians, and episcopalian or libertine royalists. A purification was ordered; eighty officers were cashiered, and according to some authorities, several thousand soldiers were also disbanded. The King was not permitted to remain any longer in the camp. He was conducted with all haste to Leith, further north than he had yet been. But even these precautions were insufficient to calm the fears or satisfy the passions of the fanatics; they resolved to intimidate and compromise Charles more thoroughly still. They required him to sign an expiatory declaration, in which he should formally acknowledge and condemn the evil deeds of his father, the idolatry of his mother, and his own sin in consenting to a treaty with the Irish rebels; and should renew, against Popery and heresy, and in favour of free Parliament and the Presbyterian government of the church, all the protestations and promises which had already been obtained from him.[1]

Charles's first impulse was to refuse, saying that he would never again be able to look his mother in the face after signing such a document. He then requested time to take the advice of the council. The fanatics refused to wait; the Committee of Estates and that of the Kirk declared "that they espoused no malignant quarrel or party, nor acknowledged the King or his interest, otherwise but in subordination to God; but they would vindicate themselves from the aspersion that they owned and supported his Majesty in all the proceedings of the late King."[2] Most of the officers of the army assured the Committee of Estates of their adherence to this declaration. Some of them even, including Colonel Strahan, the conqueror of Montrose, had secret communications with the English army and Cromwell on this subject; at which the royalists were justly alarmed. The Presbyterian ministers thundered from their pulpits that the King was the very root of malignancy, and that he had sworn to observe the Covenant without any intention of keeping his oath. Political reservations cannot withstand the contact of sincere passions. Charles was intimidated, yielded, and signed the expiatory declaration. Overjoyed at their triumph, the

---

[1] Godwin's History of the Commonwealth, vol. iii. p. 226; Clarendon's History of the Rebellion, vol. vi. pp. 453, 454; ·Brodie's History of the British Empire, vol. iv. p. 280.

[2] Laing's History of Scotland, vol. iii. p. 455.

fanatics, and the people and army with them, celebrated a solemn fast in honour of this expiation; and more than one preacher assured his audience that "now the anger of heaven had been appeased, they would gain an easy victory over a blaspheming general and a sectarian army."[1]

A few months after this humiliation, Charles gave an audience to Dr. King, Dean of Tuam, who was about to return to the Marquis of Ormonde, in Ireland. "Mr. King," he said, "I have received a very good character of you, and do therefore give you assurance that however I am forced by the necessity of my affairs to appear otherwise, yet I am a true child of the Church of England, and shall remain firm unto my first principles. Mr. King, I am a true Cavalier. I understand you are willing to go into Ireland. My Lord of Ormonde is a person that I depend upon more than any one living. I much fear that I have been forced to do some things which may prejudice him. You have heard how a declaration was extorted from me, and how I should have been dealt withal, if I had not signed it. Yet what concerns Ireland is no ways binding, for I can do nothing in the affairs of that kingdom, without the advice of my Council there, nor hath that kingdom any dependence upon this, so that what I have done is nothing; yet I fear it may prejudice my Lord of Ormonde, and my friends with him, so that if you would satisfy him in this, you would do a very acceptable service unto me; and tell him that I account it not only an error, but a misfortune that I came not into Ireland when he invited me thither."[2]

Cromwell was not ignorant of these dissensions in the Scottish government; but he soon found himself, with his army, in so difficult a position, that he was more occupied with escaping from his own dangers, than in taking advantage of the weakness of his enemies. As fast as he advanced into the Scottish territory, between the border and Edinburgh, the population retired before him with their cattle, furniture, and provisions, leaving in their villages only a few old women, who refused even to brew and bake for the English troops. This was in consequence of the orders of Lesley, and the sermons of the Presbyterian ministers, who were never weary of denouncing the republican sectaries, declaring that they would massacre all the inhabitants between the ages of sixteen and

---

[1] Laing's History of Scotland, vol. iii. pp. 454—457; Whitelocke, pp. 468, 469; Cromwell's Letters and Speeches, vol. ii. p. 191; Lingard's History of England, vol. xi. pp. 59, 60; Brodie's History of the British Empire, vol. iv. pp. 281—284; Burnet's History of His Own Time, vol. i. p. 99.

[2] Carte's Ormonde Letters, vol. i. pp. 391—393.

G

sixty—that they would cut off the right hand of all between six and sixteen years old—that they would burn the breasts of the women with hot irons—and destroy everything they found in their way. In vain had Cromwell published and distributed along his route, two proclamations addressed, one "To the People of Scotland," and the other, "To all that are Saints and Partakers of the Faith of God's Elect in Scotland;" and intended, the first to dissipate the terrors of the people, and the second to satisfy their pious passions. In vain did he maintain the strictest discipline in his army, and sent back to Edinburgh, in his own carriage,—in order to disprove the reputation for stern cruelty which was attributed to him—some Scottish officers, who had been taken prisoners in a skirmish: the feeling of terror and antipathy continued and increased. Cromwell was able to victual his troops only by keeping near the sea-coast, and obtaining supplies of provisions from England. Although it was the month of August, the weather was bad; it rained continually, and illness broke out in the English army. The Scottish general kept his men within their intrenchments, between Edinburgh and Leith, and was evidently determined to rest satisfied with covering the capital, and to avoid any general action, leaving the English to waste their strength in the solitude of the country, and the dearth of their camp. Cromwell more than once attempted to draw Lesley out of his lines, and to give him battle; he even risked his own person so openly in these skirmishes, that a Scottish soldier recognised him, and fired at him; upon which Cromwell shouted to him, "that if he had been one of his soldiers, he would have cashiered him for firing at such a distance." All these attempts, however, led to no result. Lesley remained steadily within his lines. "They hope," wrote Cromwell to Bradshaw, from Musselburgh, "we shall famish for want of provisions, which is very likely to be, if we be not timely and fully supplied."[1]

His position soon became so critical, that Cromwell resolved to escape from it at any risk. It was decided in a council of war, that the army should fall back upon Dunbar, there to await supplies and reinforcements, and should retreat from thence, along the coast, towards the English border, if reinforcements were not sent. On the following day, five hundred invalids were embarked at Musselburgh, and the retreat began. Lesley issued immediately from his camp, and closely followed the English army, harass-

[1] Cromwell's Letters and Speeches, vol. ii. pp. 179—184; Whitelocke, p. 469; Old Parliamentary History, vol. xix. pp. 298—312; Brodie's History of the British Empire, vol. iv. pp. 278, 284—287; Godwin's History of the Commonwealth, vol. iii. p. 228.

ing and attacking it at every step, without ever consenting to a general action. One of these attacks, during the night, was so vigorous, that "our rear-brigade of horse," writes Cromwell, "had like to have engaged with their whole army, had not the Lord, by his providence, put a cloud over the moon, thereby giving us opportunity to draw off those horse to the rest of our army." The English reached Dunbar in great distress, and on his arrival, Cromwell learned that Lesley had just occupied, with a considerable detachment, the pass of Cockburnspath, between that town and the English border; a narrow defile, "where," says Cromwell himself, "ten men to hinder are better than forty to make their way." As incapable of illusion as of discouragement, Cromwell wrote at once to Sir Arthur Haslerig, governor of Newcastle: "We are upon an engagement very difficult. The enemy hath blocked up our way at the pass at Copperspath, through which we cannot get without almost a miracle. He lieth so upon the hills, that we know not how to come that way without great difficulty; and our lying here clearly consumeth our men, who fall sick beyond imagination. I perceive your forces are not in a capacity for present release, wherefore, whatever becomes of us, it will be well for you to get what forces you can together, and the south to help what they can. The business nearly concerneth all good people. If your forces had been in a readiness to have fallen upon the back of Copperspath, it might have occasioned supplies to have come to us. But the only wise God knows what is best. All shall work for good. Our spirits are comfortable, praised be the Lord,—though our present condition be as it is. And indeed we have much hope in the Lord, of whose mercy we have had large experience. Indeed, do you get together what forces you can against them. Set to friends in the South to help with more. Let H. Vane know what I write. I would not make it public, lest danger should accrue thereby. You know what use to make hereof."[1]

Great agitation, but of a very different character—the agitation of joy and pride—pervaded the Scottish camp. They saw retreating before them, "that Antichrist, that arrogant man, Cromwell, over whose head the curse of God hung for murdering the King and breaking the Covenant, who termed his guns his twelve apostles, and put his whole confidence in them." They held both his army and himself hemmed in between their mountains, their ocean, and their battalions. Lesley convoked his council; his own position was not exempt from difficulties; he could find neither water nor forage on

---

[1] Cromwell's Letters and Speeches, vol. ii. pp. 198—201, 212, 213.

the hills which were occupied by his troops; and it would be exceedingly dangerous to prolong his stay there. He persisted, however, in his opinion: they must, he said, continue to avoid any action, and to drive the English army, day by day, towards the border; what victory could be greater than to compel it to return home sick and humiliated, vanquished without a battle? Nearly all his officers were of the same opinion. But Lesley's council was not a simple council of war: delegates from the Committee of Estates and of the Kirk accompanied him; many ministers, and those most zealous fanatics, lived and preached in his camp; they taxed him with sloth, and urged him not to allow the escape of those enemies whom God had delivered into their hands. "They had disposed of us, and of their business," writes Cromwell, "in sufficient revenge and wrath towards our persons; and had swallowed up the poor interest of England, believing that their army and their King would have marched to London without any interruption." Although unconvinced, Lesley made but little resistance; he, also, had doubtless his illusions and temptations of pride. In a skirmish with an outpost, an English soldier, " a very stout man, though he had but a wooden arm," who had made himself conspicuous by his desperate resistance, was taken prisoner, and brought before Lesley, who asked him, " If the enemy intended to fight?" " What do you think we come here for?" answered the soldier; " we come for nothing else." " Soldier," said Lesley, " how will you fight, when you have shipped half of your men and all your great guns?" The man replied, " Sir, if you please to draw down your men, you shall find both men and great guns too." Lesley, more moved by the soldier's firmness than by his suggestion, sent him away free, and determined to seek the battle which he had until then so carefully avoided. " By seven o'clock to-morrow," he said to his officers, " we will have the English army, dead or alive."[1]

On the same day, in the morning, Cromwell, perplexed in spite of his firmness, had invited his most faithful friends to meet him, to pray together, and invoke the aid of God in their peril. " We lay very near the enemy," he writes, " being sensible of our disadvantage; having some weakness of flesh, but yet consolation and support from the Lord himself to our poor weak faith, wherein I believe not a few amongst us stand: That, because of their number, because of their advantages, because of their confidence, because of

Brodie's History of the British Empire, vol. iv. pp. 286—292; Lingard's History of England, vol. xi. pp. 61, 62; Cromwell's Letters and Speeches, vol. ii. pp. 202, 203; Carte's Ormonde Letters, vol. i. pp. 381—384.

our weakness, because of our strait, we were in the mount. and in the mount the Lord would be seen; and that He would find out a way of deliverance and salvation for us: and, indeed, we had our consolations and our hopes."[1] When this devotional service was ended, at about four o'clock in the afternoon, Cromwell mounted his horse, and rode with Lambert, his major-general, about the neighbourhood of Dunbar, in the park of Brocksmouth House, the residence of the Earl of Roxburgh. While looking towards the enemy from this point, he discerned through his glass an extraordinary movement in their camp; a portion, first of their cavalry and then of their artillery, marched from their left wing to their right, and descended the hills towards the sea, as if they intended more effectually to cut off all retreat for the English army, and to give it battle as soon as it began to move. "They are coming down," cried Cromwell; "the Lord hath delivered them into our hands!" He called Lambert's attention to this movement, and asked if it was not his opinion that they would now be able to attack the Scots with advantage. Lambert quite agreed with him, and Monk, coming up, likewise assented. A council of war was immediately convoked; Cromwell proposed that at daybreak the army should begin its march, and attack the Scots, who appeared determined to give battle, and to dispute their passage at every point. Monk energetically supported this proposition, and offered to lead the van, at the head of his brigade of foot.[2] The resolution was unanimously adopted, and the English spent the night in noiseless preparations for the combat.

The night was wild and wet, and just before daybreak, a thick fog arose, which caused the attack to begin a little later than Cromwell had intended. At the outset the English had the worst of it: their advanced guard of cavalry were vigorously received and repulsed by the Scottish artillery and lancers; the first regiment of English infantry restored the action, but did not decide it; and the fight continued hotly for some time, amid cries of "The Lord of Hosts!" from the English, and "The Covenant!" from the Scots. At about seven o'clock, Cromwell's own regiment of foot charged suddenly, and broke the Scottish lines. At this moment the fog dispersed, the sun shone brightly over hill and ocean. "Now, let God arise," exclaimed Cromwell, "and his enemies shall be scattered!" His words gave fresh courage to his men, and were repeated by all who stood near him. "He was a strong man," says

---

[1] Cromwell's Letters and Speeches, vol. ii. pp. 213, 214.
[2] Burnet's History of his Own Time, vol. i. p. 100; Carte's Ormonde Letters, vol. i. p. 382; Laing's History of Scotland, vol. iii. p. 459.

one of his contemporaries ; " in the dark perils of war, in the high places of the field, hope shone in him like a pillar of fire, when it had gone out in all the others." Enthusiasm is as contagious as discouragement; the English charged with redoubled vigour; the Scottish cavalry gave way ; a body of infantry, which made a bold resistance, was broken through and scattered by the English squadrons; the cry arose, " They run! they run!" Disorder spread rapidly throughout the Scottish army, which took to flight in every direction. " After the first repulse," writes Cromwell, " they were made by the Lord of Hosts as stubble to our swords." At nine o'clock the battle was over ; three thousand Scots had been slain ; more than ten thousand prisoners, with all their artillery and baggage, and two hundred standards, were in the hands of the English. " I believe I may speak it without partiality," wrote Cromwell on the following day to the Parliament, " both your chief commanders and others in their several places, and soldiers also, acted with as much courage as ever hath been seen in any action since this war. I know they look not to be named, and therefore I forbear particulars."[1]

Two days afterwards, on the 5th of September, Cromwell resumed the offensive ; and within four days he was master of Leith, of the whole country around Edinburgh, and of Edinburgh itself, with the exception of the castle, which was occupied by a strong garrison. Charles II. and the whole Scottish government retired northwards, to Perth ; Lesley, with the wreck of his army, westwards, to Stirling. The republican Parliament had attained its object : Scotland was invaded, and had fully enough to do to defend her own territory.

Amidst the general alarm, Charles rejoiced, in his heart, at the defeat of the fanatics, whose yoke he endured so impatiently. To them, to their malevolent exclusions and blind requirements, public opinion was beginning to ascribe these unexpected reverses. In vain did the six ministers who formed the Committee of the Kirk endeavour, in a sombre manifesto, to throw all the responsibility on the obstinate wickedness of their adversaries ; maintaining that God would have given Lesley the victory, if the army and court had been thoroughly purged of all malignants. There is, even under the sway of the most ardent fanaticism, a degree of absurdity which, in presence of imperious and melancholy events,

1 Carlyle's Letters and Speeches, vol. ii. pp. 206—216 ; Carte's Ormonde Letters, vol. i. pp. 380—384; Ludlow's Memoirs, p. 141 ; Whitelocke, pp. 470, 471 ; Brodie's History of the British Empire, vol. iv. pp. 292—294; Forster's Statesmen of the Commonwealth, vol. iv. pp. 286—290.

does not easily obtain credence. Charles deemed the moment favourable for escaping from his masters: by means of some of his officers, and particularly of Dr. Frazier, his physician, a determined enemy of Argyle, who had recently procured his banishment from court, he entered into secret negotiations with the royalist chiefs of the Scottish Highlands, among others with the Lords Huntly, Middleton, Ogilvy, and Dudhope, who promised to rise in arms as soon as he appeared among them. But at the very moment when his escape was finally arranged, the secret was communicated to Argyle, and the Committee of Estates immediately ordered all the Cavaliers, who still remained with the King, to leave the court within twenty-four hours, and the kingdom within twenty days. Three only were excepted from this order, and one of these was the Duke of Buckingham, who was suspected of having revealed the secret. Charles demanded that nine others of his friends should be excepted; his demand was refused. He did not press it; but, a week after, he left Perth at about one o'clock in the afternoon, in hunting costume, attended only by five servants; and as soon as he was out of sight, he set spurs to his horse, joined Lord Dudhope and Lord Buchan, who were waiting for him, and arrived at night-fall, escorted by a few Highlanders, at the house of the Laird of Clova, distant about fifty miles from Perth. He was sleeping quietly on a mattress, when, at break of day, entered Colonel Montgomery and three other officers sent from Perth by the Committee of Estates, who had discovered almost simultaneously the flight of the King and the place of his retreat. Charles parleyed with them; he had escaped, he told them, only because he had been informed that the Committee of Estates intended to give him up to the English, and to hang all his servants. Montgomery averred that this was a calumny. The chiefs who had escorted the King in his escape urged him to remain with them, assuring him that, some few miles further, he would find a numerous body of Highlanders ready to obey his orders. But the promise seemed vague, and Charles, like his father, had no great taste for hazardous adventures. Whilst he was hesitating, two squadrons of Scottish cavalry arrived to support Montgomery's representations. Seeing the house surrounded with troops, Charles yielded, and was immediately taken back to Perth.[1]

This ridiculous *Start*, as it was called, was not, however, lost to Charles. Argyle and the Committee of Estates became alarmed,

[1] Laing's History of Scotland, vol. iii. p. 464; Baillie's Letters, vol. ii. p. 356; Clarendon's History of the Rebellion, vol. vi. pp. 484—486; Lingard's History of England, vol. xi. pp. 64, 65.

both at the antipathy with which they inspired him, and at the facilities which he could find for escaping from them. In the Presbyterian church also, there were not wanting ministers more sensible than their fanatical colleagues, who said that they were not treating the King well, that they were unjust and harsh towards the moderate royalists, and that they should strive to rally all parties together, instead of perpetuating and exacerbating old dissensions. These opinions had their influence in the Parliament which met at Perth ; it manifested as much zeal for the King's cause, and greater toleration of royalists of all shades ; it voted all that was necessary for the re-organisation of the army ; and two resolutions, though violently opposed by the fanatics, were adopted—the one declaring that the expressions of repentance of the partisans of the late Duke of Hamilton should be accepted ; and the other that, this done, they should be permitted to serve the King and defend the kingdom. A large number of moderate Presbyterians, and even of Cavaliers, hastened to profit by this permission : Hamilton and Lauderdale returned to court.   Charles presided over the council, and gave his attention, without obstacle, to the affairs of the Parliament and army. Finally it was announced that, ere long, according to ancient usage, he would be solemnly crowned at Scone, and the preparations for this ceremony began.   Argyle was not altogether free from anxiety at this movement, which brought his adversaries once more into contact with the King, and irritated his firm friends, the fanatics ; but he felt the necessity of yielding, and Charles graciously took pains to quiet his distrust and calm his displeasure.   He even went so far as to lead him to suppose that he might probably marry his daughter ; and Captain Titus, a Presbyterian who was on good terms with Argyle, was sent into France to the Queen-mother, as if to obtain her consent.[1]

Cromwell, freed from the great care which had momentarily absorbed his whole attention, attentively observed these political resolutions of his adversaries, and anticipated much advantage from them.   He was equally well able to address masses and individuals, to appeal to religious convictions, and to treat with material in-terests.   The declaration which, on his arrival in Scotland, he had addressed " To all that are Saints and Partakers of the Faith of God's Elect in Scotland," had met with a vehement answer from the Scottish Kirk.   Cromwell immediately seized upon this oppor-tunity for entering into correspondence and controversy with them,

[1] Clarendon's History of the Rebellion, vol. vi. pp. 487, 488 ; Laing's History of Scotland, vol. iii. pp. 464, 465 ; Burnet's History of his Own Time, vol. i. p. 105.

discussing both their arguments and their acts, referring them to various passages of Holy Scripture in support of his own views, and inviting them to appeal to the general judgment of believers on the question at issue between them and himself. "You conceal from your own people," he says, "the papers we have sent you, as they might thereby see and understand the bowels of our affection to them, especially to such among them as fear the Lord." As soon as he was master of Edinburgh, he sent a letter to the governor of the Castle, in which most of the Presbyterian ministers had taken refuge, to inform them, "that they have free liberty granted them, if they please to take the pains, to preach in their several churches; and that he had given special commands both to officers and soldiers that they should not in the least be molested." They refused to avail themselves of this permission, saying that they found nothing in his letter "whereupon to build any security for their persons while in the town, and for their return to the castle." He upbraided them for their pusillanimity in his reply, saying, "that if their Master's service (as they call it) were chiefly in their eye, imagination of suffering would not have caused such a return" to his proposal; and boldly affirming that "no man had been troubled in England or Ireland for preaching the Gospel, though none had liberty under pretence thereof, to overtop or debase the civil power."[1] He cared little about the strict accuracy of his assertions, provided that they produced, at the time when he spoke, and upon the public whom he addressed, the impression which he required.

A few months later, during a visit to Glasgow, he frequently attended at Presbyterian sermons, taking care to protect the liberty of the preachers, even when they attacked him, and always manifesting the greatest eagerness to enter into discussion with them. "He one day sent to them," says one of his officers, "to give us a friendly Christian meeting, to discourse of those things which they rail against us for: that so, if possible, all misunderstandings between us might be taken away. Which accordingly they gave us, on Wednesday last. There was no bitterness nor passion vented on either side; all was with moderation and tenderness. My Lord General and Major-General Lambert, for the most part, maintained the discourse; and on their part, Mr. James Guthrie and Mr. Patrick Gillespie. We know not what satisfaction they have received. Sure I am, there was no such weight in their arguments

[1] Carlyle's Letters and Speeches, vol. ii. pp. 231—233; Old Parliamentary History, vol. xix. pp. 320—323; Thurloe's State Papers, vol. i. pp. 158—162.

as might in the least discourage us from what we have under-taken."[1]

Cromwell took as much care to conciliate individuals as to exercise a directing and favourable influence upon popular opinion. He found, among his prisoners, Mr. Alexander Jaffray, Provost of Aberdeen, and Mr. Carstairs, a Presbyterian minister of Glasgow, both intelligent and influential men ; he conversed familiarly with them, and treated them so well that he succeeded in obtaining a strong hold upon their minds; upon which he made haste to exchange them for some English prisoners who were detained in Dumbarton Castle, and they became useful agents to him in the country.   He never let slip any opportunity of showing politeness and confidence to the men who he knew were more favourable to the Common-wealth than to Charles Stuart; he was particularly attentive, for instance, to Sir Archibald Johnstone, who thenceforward became his secret friend, and ultimately his vigorous ally.   Even under the most insignificant circumstances, from natural character or from calculation, he was careful to please those who were indifferent or hostile to him.   Riding one day on a reconnoitring expedition in Lanarkshire, with some officers, he was in want of a guide, and could find none, "save one valetudinary gentleman," son of Sir Walter Stewart of Allertoun, a royalist and covenanter, another of whose sons had served as a captain in the Scottish army at the battle of Dunbar.   When he had completed his survey, Cromwell called in at the house ; Sir Walter had absconded; and his wife, " who was as much for the King and royal family as her husband,'' was alone to entertain the republican General.   Cromwell entered into conversation with her, spoke with interest of her husband, her relatives, and her children ; and said that change of climate would be beneficial to her invalid son, and that Montpellier, in the south of France, would be the place for him.   Another of her sons, a lad of ten years, went up to Cromwell, and began to handle the hilt of his sword : Cromwell patted him on the head, and said, " You are my little captain."   On rising from table, he returned thanks to God for his repast in his usual manner, and prayed for a blessing upon the family.   He then set off to rejoin the army, leaving the lady of the house full of admiration for his amiability and piety , " she was sure," she said, " that Cromwell was one who feared God, and had the true interest of religion at heart."[2]

Thus fomented by the able policy of Cromwell, division broke

---

[1] Cromwell's Letters and Speeches, vol. ii. p. 310.
[2] Ibid. vol. ii. pp. 311, 312.

out among the Scots. In proportion as the Presbyterian leaders became more moderate, and manifested greater deference to the King, and tolerance of his friends, the fanatics became more violent, and separated more widely from him. They were especially incensed at certain resolutions of the Parliament, which, in consideration of a few expressions of repentance, had allowed the old royalists to resume their positions both in the court and the army. They addressed a violent remonstrance, on this subject, to the Committee of Estates, in which they openly attacked the King, regretted that he had ever been recalled; demanded that he should be excluded, for a time at least, from all participation in the government, and that his ministers, Argyle and Loudon among others, should be dismissed; and protested against all idea of an invasion of England, and even against the continuation of the war, as essentially unlawful, if it were to be carried on in the interest, and by the exertion of the libertine or hypocritical royalists. After the defeat at Dunbar, five counties of the south-west of Scotland, in which these opinions were predominant—Renfrew, Ayr, Galloway, Wigton, and Dumfries —had formed themselves into a separate association, and had demanded permission to levy troops on their own account, declaring that they would continue to resist the English sectaries, but that they would no longer serve under Lesley. The Parliament at Perth had weakly consented to this; three or four thousand men had been levied in the remonstrant counties, and were under the command of Colonels Kerr and Strahan, the two most impetuous officers in the army, and both of them, or at least Strahan, in close correspondence with Cromwell. The fanatics, therefore, had both troops and leaders in that district. The Scottish government began to feel alarmed; the remonstrance was voted calumnious, treacherous, and dangerous: and Colonel Montgomery was sent, with two regiments of cavalry, to take the command of all the King's forces in the west. But the discussion had been long, and the execution was far from rapid; before it was possible to re-establish the authority of the government in the confederated counties, Cromwell sent Lambert thither with a body of troops, and eventually proceeded thither himself. Either by force of arms, or by the connivance of its leaders, the little army of fanatics was defeated and dispersed: and of its two commanders, one, Colonel Kerr, was wounded and taken prisoner without much resistance, and the other, Colonel Strahan, openly went over to Cromwell with several officers. "There is at this time," wrote Cromwell after this expedition, "a very great distraction, and mighty workings of God upon the hearts of divers, both ministers and people, much of it tending to the justification of our cause. And although some are as bitter and as bad as ever, making it their business to shuffle hypocritically with their consciences and the Covenant, to make it seem lawful to join with malignants, which now they do—as well they might long before, having taken in the head malignant of them : yet truly others are startled at it; and some have been constrained by the work of God upon their consciences to make sad and solemn accusation of themselves: charging themselves as guilty of the blood shed in this war, by having a hand in the treaty at Breda, and by bringing the King in amongst them. This lately did a lord of the session, and withdrew from the Committee of Estates. And lately Mr. James Livingston, a man as highly esteemed as any for piety and learning, who was a commissioner for the Kirk at the said treaty, charged himself with the guilt of the blood of the war, before their assembly; and withdrew from them, and is retired to his own house."[1]

Charles was as much rejoiced as Cromwell at this disorganisation of the Presbyterian party, for at the same time, and by a natural coincidence, the royalist party became reconstituted: the moderate men daily allied themselves more closely with it, in order to escape from the yoke of the sectaries, who lost ground in the opinion of the quieter part of the population, by their acts of violence and by their reverses of fortune; while the royalist nobles regained their former influence. The coronation took place in the cathedral church of Scone, on the 1st of January, 1651, with all the old regal solemnities; and notwithstanding the Presbyterian harshness of the sermon delivered on the occasion by Robert Douglas, the moderator of the general assembly of the Kirk—notwithstanding the unintelligent stringency of the oaths required from Charles—a feeling of serious and devoted loyalty animated the whole proceeding; the spectators, both lay and clerical, nobles and people, however ill-assorted their ideas in regard to government may have been, all sincerely desired a monarchical régime for their country, and Charles Stuart for their King.[2] Out of respect for his right they exposed themselves, by crowning him, to a very unequal conflict: happy would it have been if they could have reckoned, on his part, upon a just return of sincerity and affection!

Almost at the very moment that Charles was crowned at Scone, the republican Parliament of England sent into Scotland a celebrated engraver, named Symons, to take the portrait of Cromwell,

[1] Cromwell's Letters and Speeches, vol. ii. pp. 263—265; Baillie's Letters, vol. ii. pp. 348—369; Burnet's History of his Own Time, vol. i. pp. 103—105; Laing's History of Scotland, vol. iii. pp. 401—406.
[2] Somers' Tracts, vol. vi. pp. 117—143.

for the purpose of transferring it to a medal to be struck in commemoration of the battle of Dunbar. " It was not a little wonder to me," wrote Cromwell, " to see that you should send Mr. Symons so great a journey, about a business importing so little, as far as it relates to me; whereas, if my poor opinion may not be rejected by you, I have to offer to that which I think the most noble end, to wit, the commemoration of that great mercy at Dunbar, and the gratuity to the army; which might be better expressed upon the medal, by engraving on the one side the Parliament, which I hear was intended, and will do singularly well; and on the other side an Army, with the inscription over the head of it, *The Lord of Hosts!* which was our word that day. Wherefore, if I may beg it as a favour from you, I most earnestly beseech you, if I may do it without offence, that it may be so. And if you think not fit to have it as I offer, you may alter it as you see cause; only I do think I may truly say it will be very thankfully acknowledged by me, if you will spare the having my effigies in it."[1] The medal was struck without regard to this desire, and as it had been originally projected. No great man ever carried the hypocrisy of modesty so far as Cromwell, or so easily subordinated his vanity to his ambition.

Two incidents now occurred to give a new and unexpected direction to the progress of affairs and of the war. Cromwell fell seriously ill. Royalist plots broke out in England.

Ever since Charles II. had been in Scotland, the English royalists had been agitating in every direction to go to his assistance. He had sent blank commissions with his signature to many of them, giving them authority to raise men, to confer appointments, to make promises, in short, to act for him and in his name. Among the Cavaliers who resided in England, many were indiscreet, either from temerity or vanity; those who were living in safety on the Continent, in Holland, or at Paris with the Queen-mother, frequently compromised their friends at home by their correspondence or conversation; great jealousy and distrust existed among the different groups of these exiles, who were incessantly disputing for influence in their banishment, or quarrelling about their future hopes. Sometimes they refused to communicate or co-operate with one another; and sometimes they betrayed each other, from animosity or levity. The republican Council of State had organised, against them and among their own ranks, a very active police. One of its members, Scott, was specially intrusted with its manage-

---

[1] Cromwell's Letters and Speeches, vol. ii. pp. 290, 291; Harris's Life of Cromwell, p. 519.

ment, and wanted neither ability nor funds for the proper discharge of his duty. During the years 1650 and 1651, four royalist plots were set on foot, either by old Cavaliers, or by Presbyterians who were all the more zealous, because their conversion was both recent and sincere : but all failed, and in the space of thirteen months, twenty-seven royalists, military and civil, lay and ecclesiastic, known and obscure, were brought to the scaffold, some by sentence of court-martial, but most after trial by those High Courts of Justice which were erected, not for the purpose of judging in accordance with the laws, but in order to defend the Commonwealth against the opinions of the people, and the enterprise of its enemies. All these reverses, however, did not discourage the English royalists ; they were devoted, harassed, and unoccupied ; their King was in Scotland ; his friends there were fighting for him ; and thence they obtained, with regard to his danger, his strength, and his designs, vague notions which kindled both their animosities and their hopes. They could not make up their minds to remain quiet, when their cause was being so vigorously debated at their very gates ; and, in their turn, they sent into Scotland reports of their attempts at insurrection, their illusions, and their promises.[1]

Whilst the royalist spirit was thus reviving in Scotland and fermenting in England, Cromwell, on his return from a long winter's march at the head of his troops, through a heavy storm of hail, snow, and rain, was seized at Edinburgh with a violent attack of fever. This illness became serious ; the Parliament and Council of State grew alarmed, and sent an express messenger to Cromwell with the strongest assurances of their concern and solicitude : to which he thus replied in a letter to Bradshaw : " I do with all humble thankfulness acknowledge your high favour and tender respect of me, in sending an express to inquire after one so unworthy as myself. Indeed, my lord, your service needs not me : I am a poor creature ; and have been a dry bone ; and am still an unprofitable servant to my Master and you. I thought I should have died of this fit of sickness ; but the Lord seemeth to dispose otherwise. But truly, my lord, I desire not to live, unless I may obtain mercy from the Lord to approve my heart and life to Him in more faithfulness and thankfulness, and to those I serve in more profitableness and diligence."[2] He soon got better, and resumed his ordinary mode of life. " The Lord General is now well re-

[1] Milton's State Papers, pp. 33, 34, 37 ; Commons' Journals, vol. vi. pp. 501, 506 ; Whitelocke, pp. 484, 486 ; Curte's Ormonde Letters, vol. i. p. 414 ; Clarendon's History of the Rebellion, vol. xi. p. 490.
[2] Cromwell's Letters and Speeches, vol. ii. p. 302.

covered," was the news sent from Edinburgh to London ; " he was in his dining-room to-day with his officers, and was very cheerful and pleasant ; so that there is not any fear, by the blessing of God, but that he will be enabled to take the field when the provisions arrive."[1] And so, in fact, he did ; but his disease soon broke out again, and three successive relapses bore witness to its obstinacy. The Parliament sent two celebrated physicians, Dr. Bates and Dr. Wright, to Edinburgh without delay, and Fairfax gave them his own carriage for the journey. And finally, the House voted that " in regard of the Lord General's relapse, and present indisposedness, and the nature and sharpness of the air where he is, he be desired, in relation to his health, to remove himself into some part of England, until by the blessing of God upon means used, he be restored into a condition of health and strength to return to the army ; he disposing thereof, in the mean time, and the management of affairs there, into such hands as he shall think fit."[2]

When these votes reached Scotland, an important event had just occurred, which led to the expectation that fresh resolutions would be adopted by the royalist party. The moderate men, with Hamilton and Lauderdale at their head, had decidedly gained the ascendency in the Scottish Parliament. Argyle and his friends made vain efforts to oppose them ; and Charles, while treating the rigid Presbyterians with courtesy and consideration, successfully employed all his address and influence to secure and enhance the triumph of their adversaries ; the army was re-organised in accordance with his wishes ; in spite of violent debates, and the formal protest of the Chancellor, Lord Loudon, a number of old royalists, and those of the most obnoxious class, were appointed colonels. Finally, the Parliament invited the King to take the command in person,[3] and Charles actually became the leader of his troops, as well as the head of his council, at the very moment when the English Parliament advised Cromwell, for the sake of his health, to leave Scotland, where he seemed on the point of death.

A month had scarcely elapsed, and, either from the vigour of his constitution or the energy of his will, Cromwell was convalescent, and had actively recommenced the campaign ; manœuvring round about the Scottish army, which was again shut up within its in-

---

[1] Cromwelliana, p. 101.

[2] Commons' Journals, vol. vi. p. 579 ; Cromwell's Letters and Speeches vol. ii. p. 314 ; Whitelocke's Memorials, p. 494.

[3] Laing's History of Scotland, vol. iii. p. 467 ; Browne's History of the Highlands, vol. ii. p. 69 ; Godwin's History of the Commonwealth, vol. iii. pp. 246, 247.

trenchments at Stirling ; reducing to submission the adjacent counties ; gaining possession, by storm or treachery, of most of the fortresses which still held out against him ; defeating, either in person, or by his lieutenants, the detached bodies of troops which attempted to hamper his movements ; and finally laying siege to Perth—thus threatening to deprive Charles, who lay encamped at Stirling with his army, of the seat of his government.

Charles then abruptly took the resolution which he had long been meditating : he announced to his council his intention of breaking up the camp, and carrying the war into England, where his partisans only awaited his presence to rise in insurrection against the Parliament. Many of the Scottish leaders, assuredly, though staunch royalists, were far from approving, in their hearts, of such a design ; they had little inclination to compromise themselves so far with their formidable neighbours ; sometimes even they had suggested to Charles that he would do well to content himself with the crown of Scotland, and to leave England to struggle, as long as it pleased, beneath the yoke of the Commonwealth, and of its revolutionary factions. The recollection of the invasion attempted in 1647, by the late Duke of Hamilton, and of its ill success, was still present to their minds. Nevertheless, most of them silently assented to the plan, being either intimidated by the will of the King, or carried away by the irresistible influence which is always exercised over men's minds by a bold resolution in critical circumstances. Argyle, almost alone, used every effort to dissuade the King from this step ; out of jealousy for the loss of his power, perhaps, for it marked the triumph of his rivals, the Hamilton faction ; but also from prudence and political sagacity. He estimated more correctly than the little court of Charles, the state of the public mind in England, the ardour of the young republican party, and the slight chances in favour of a royalist insurrection. Why run such risks, and leave Scotland destitute both of its army and its King, after it had shown so much devotion to his cause ? Why plunge, with his little Scottish army, into the midst of his enemies, when he might, by remaining in Scotland on the defensive, waste and destroy the English army, and Cromwell himself, by the severities of a second winter ? Charles gave no heed to his advice. Argyle insisted, declaring that, for his part, he would never share in such an undertaking, and requested permission to retire to his estates. Some persons advised Charles to have him immediately arrested ; it was dangerous, they said, to leave so powerful a malcontent behind him in Scotland. Charles refused, however, either out of consideration for his recent intimacy with Argyle, or from fear of the consequences of an open rupture. Argyle set out at once for his seat at Inverary. The King publicly announced, by proclamation, his intention to begin his march for England on the following day, accompanied by those of his subjects who were willing to prove their loyalty to him by sharing his fortune; and on the following day, in fact, the 31st of July, 1651, he was on his road to Carlisle, at the head of an army of eleven, or according to some authorities, fourteen thousand men, with David Lesley for his lieutenant-general.[1]

Cromwell was encamped before Perth, of which he had just gained possession, when he learned this news. It is doubtful whether he was either surprised or grieved to hear it; he was strongly impressed with the difficulties and dangers, both to his army and himself, of the prolongation of the inconclusive war which he had been carrying on for a year in Scotland; and he thought himself far more certain to obtain prompt and decisive success in England. As early as the month of January preceding, he had intimated to the Parliament that the Scots might probably attempt an invasion; and his recent manœuvres, by placing him in the rear of the Scottish army, so clearly opened the way to England to the King, that they almost seemed to invite him to take it. He did not conceal from himself the impression of terror, anger, and distrust which would be produced in London by such a movement; all the more because, a week before, when he was marching on Perth, he had written, " The enemy's great expectation now is to supply themselves in the West with recruits of men, and what victual they can get; for they may expect none out of the North, when once our army shall interpose between them and Perth, to prevent their prevalency in the West, and making incursions into the borders of England."[2] With dignified and sagacious firmness, he immediately encountered the reproaches and suspicions which he anticipated, and wrote to the Parliament, on the 4th of August, " While lying before Perth, we had some intelligence of the enemy's marching southward, though with some contradictions, as if it had not been so. But doubting it might be true, we marched with all possible expedition back again, and have passed our foot and many of our horse over the Frith this day, resolving to make what speed we can up to the enemy, who, in his desperation and fear, and out of inevitable necessity, is run to try what he can do this way. I

[1] Clarendon's History of the Rebellion, vol. vi. p. 491; Whitelocke, p. 501; Laing's History of Scotland, vol. iii. p. 469; Godwin's History of the Commonwealth, vol. iii. pp. 253, 260.
[2] Cromwell's Letters and Speeches, vol. ii. p. 320.

H

do apprehend, that if he goes for England, being some few days' march before us, it will trouble some men's thoughts, and may occasion some inconveniences, which I hope we are as deeply sensible of, and have been, and I trust shall be as diligent to prevent, as any. And, indeed, this is our comfort, that in simplicity of heart as towards God, we have done to the best of our judgments; knowing that if some issue were not put to this business, it would occasion another winter's war, to the ruin of your soldiery, for whom the Scots are too hard in respect of enduring the winter difficulties of this country; and to the endless expense of the treasure of England in prosecuting this war. It may be supposed we might have kept the enemy from this, by interposing between him and England: which truly I believe we might; but how to remove him out of this place, without doing what we have done, unless we had had a commanding army on both sides of the river of Forth, is not clear to us!

"We pray therefore that (seeing there is a possibility for the enemy to put you to some trouble) you would, with the same courage, grounded upon a confidence in God, wherein you have been supported to the great things God hath used you in hitherto, —improve, the best you can, such forces as you have in readiness, or as may on the sudden be gathered together, to give the enemy some check, until we shall be able to reach up to him; which we trust in the Lord we shall do our utmost endeavour in. And indeed we have this comfortable experience from the Lord, that this enemy is heart-smitten by God; and whenever the Lord shall bring us up to them, we believe the Lord will make the desperateness of this counsel of theirs to appear, and the folly of it also. When England was much more unsteady than now; and when a much more considerable army of theirs, unfoiled, invaded you; and we had but a weak force to make resistance at Preston, upon deliberate advice we chose rather to put ourselves between their army and Scotland; and how God succeeded that, is not well to be forgotten! This present movement is not out of choice on our part, but by some kind of necessity; and, it is to be hoped, will have the like issue. Together with a hopeful end of your work, in which it's good to wait upon the Lord, upon the earnest of former experiences, and hope of His presence, which only is the life of your cause."[1]

Cromwell had not deceived himself; the disturbance was great

---

[1] Cromwell's Letters and Speeches, vol. ii. pp. 327—329; Godwin's History of the Commonwealth, vol. iii. p. 253; Old Parliamentary History vol. xix. pp. 455, 498.

in London: fear concealed itself beneath the mask of anger; in
the Parliament as in the city, and even in the interior of the
Council of State, Cromwell was declaimed against and loaded with
blame, and it was even suggested that he had treated with Charles
Stuart to betray the Commonwealth. " Some," says Mrs. Hutchinson, "could not hide very pale and unmanly fears; and Bradshaw
himself, stout-hearted as he was, privately could not conceal his
fear."[1] But among the leaders at least, the alarm was of short
duration; Vane, Scott, Robinson, and Henry Martyn were men of
active and obstinate courage, passionately devoted to their cause,
and moreover compromised to that point at which courage, without
ceasing to be a virtue, becomes a necessity. They immediately took
measures for making a bold stand against the invaders, and reviving
public confidence. The army, to which they had recently added three
thousand horse and a thousand dragoons, received a fresh augmenta-
tion of four thousand infantry. The militia were called out throughout the country. Three regiments of volunteers were formed in
London and its neighbourhood, for the special purpose of serving
as a guard to the Parliament. Several earnest and influential men,
among others Colonel Hutchinson and John Claypole, Cromwell's
son-in-law, raised similar troops by their own exertions; and the
Parliament voted the necessary sums for defraying all these
expenses. On entering England, Charles had published a proclamation of general amnesty, from which three men only, Cromwell,
Bradshaw, and Coke, the three principal actors in the trial of the
King his father, were excepted. The Parliament replied to this by
ordering it to be burned, in London, by the common hangman, in
presence of the militia regiments; and by declaring Charles Stuart,
and his abettors, agents, and accomplices, rebels and traitors to the
Commonwealth of England. They also voted the punishment of
death against all who should, in any way, maintain any correspondence with him; imprisoned or banished all the old royalists;
and in fine established so rigorous and minute a system of police
that, among other provisions, all masters of families, in certain
parts of the country, were enjoined to keep their children and
servants within their houses, except at certain hours of the day,
and if they remained absent from home for more than twelve hours,
to notify their absence to the committee of the militia of the place,
under penalty of being held responsible for their actions.[2]
Meanwhile Charles advanced with his army, through the north-

---

[1] Memoirs of Colonel Hutchinson, p. 356.
[2] Commons' Journals, vol. vi. pp. 557, 614, 619—622; vol. vii. pp. 3, 6, 7, 9.

western counties of England, without meeting with any opposition. On learning his departure, Cromwell had immediately detached Lambert and Harrison, with most of his light troops, to follow him, and either separately or together to harass his flanks and rear, so as to straiten his quarters and impede his progress in every way, without risking a general action, in which they could not fail to be worsted, and which Cromwell wished to reserve for himself. " His Majesty," wrote Lord Lauderdale to his wife, from Penrith, " is thus far advanced into England with a very good army ; I dare say, near double the number of those that the King of Sweden entered Germany with, if they be not more. As soon as we came into England, his Majesty was by an Englishman, whom he made King-at-Arms for that day, proclaimed King of England, at the head of the army, with great acclamation, and shooting off all the cannon. Yesterday he was proclaimed here in Penrith, and will be in all the market-towns where we march. Never was an army so regular as we have been since we came into England ; I dare say we have not taken the worth of a sixpence ; and whatever our enemies print or write, trust me this is the best Scots army that ever I saw, and I hope shall prove best. All those that were unwilling to hazard all in this cause with their King, have on specious pretence left us. This is a natural purge, and will do us much good. Nothing of action yet, except the driving of some small parties, with which I will not trouble you. One thing I cannot forget : this morning, my Lord Howard of Escrick's son came in to us from the enemy, with his whole troop ; his Majesty received him graciously, and immediately knighted him. He is the first, but I am confident a few days will show us more that will return to their duty."[1]

Lord Lauderdale was deceived in his expectation. Few Englishmen joined Charles on his march : he was invading England at the head of an army of Scotsmen and Presbyterians, foreigners and sectaries. The national pride was wounded, the adherents of the episcopal church were discontented and disquieted, and these feelings lent fresh influence to the fear inspired by the Parliament and its severities. Charles met with no more support than resistance : in most of the towns through which he passed, he was received with acclamations ; but the population did not rise in his favour, and the royalist leaders themselves arrived only in small numbers, and with but few followers. On his departure from Scotland, Charles had sent information of his movement to one of his most devoted and

_____

[1] Carey's Memorials of the Civil War in England, vol. ii. pp. 307—309 ; Cromwell's Letters and Speeches, vol. ii. p. 327 ; Whitelocke's Memorials, p. 501.

bravest adherents, the Earl of Derby, who, since the termination of the civil war, had been living in retirement in the Island of Man, with Charlotte de la Tremouille, his wife, quite as royalist and heroic as himself. Derby hastened to rejoin the King with a small troop of chosen friends and servants, and Charles directed him to go through Lancashire for the purpose of rousing and collecting his partisans in that county. But whilst the earl was engaged in the performance of this mission, he was surprised and defeated at Wigan by Colonel Robert Lilburne, whom Cromwell, with his habitual prudence, had sent thither, to put down any royalist movements which might be attempted. Derby was taken prisoner, but contrived to escape, and made his way, a fugitive, and almost alone, to join the King once more at Worcester. Another of Charles's lieutenants, of a different religious and political creed, General Massey, an excellent officer, who had been a Presbyterian and Parliamentarian in the early part of his career, also received orders to rally the royalists in Lancashire and Cheshire, where he was supposed to have considerable influence; and he had met with tolerable success in his work, when the Scottish ministers, who attended the march of the royal army, perceived that he recruited among Episcopalians and Catholics, as well as among Presbyterians. Without saying anything to the King, they sent a declaration after him, which they required him to publish, to the effect that no one was to be admitted into the army who did not first subscribe the Covenant. Charles no sooner heard of this declaration, than he wrote to Massey to suppress it; but his letter was intercepted, and published by the Parliament, and only served to give another proof of the King's duplicity, and the internal dissensions of his party. Whilst the royalists manifested this timidity, the republicans displayed the utmost firmness: the commandant of the little town of Biggar, on being summoned to surrender, replied, that "he would keep it for the Parliament, from whom he held it." Charles had intended to make Shrewsbury the centre of his operations in the west, and he hoped that its governor, Colonel Mackworth, a lawyer who had turned soldier, would open its gates to him; but Mackworth refused to do so, and immediately received from the Parliament a chain of gold, in thanks for his fidelity. On arriving at Warrington, on the Mersey, the royal army perceived on its left a considerable body of troops. It was Lambert and Harrison, who had combined to prevent their passing the river, by destroying the bridge; but they did not succeed in this; the royal army passed over, and some squadrons of Cavaliers vigorously charged Lambert's vanguard with shouts of " Oh, you rogues, we will be with you before your Cromwell comes!" Lambert refused to give battle, and retreated in some disorder. Charles thought it inexpedient to pursue him—he was anxious to get forward. But at the very moment that the enemy were retiring before him, Charles observed his lieutenant-general, David Lesley, looking sad and melancholy, and keeping aloof from his officers. The King "rode up to him, and asked him with great alacrity how he could be sad, when he was at the head of so brave an army, which looked so well that day? to which David Lesley answered him in his ear, that he was melancholic indeed, for he well knew that army, how well soever it looked, would not fight."[1]

On the 22nd of August, Charles arrived at Worcester, where he had promised his tired troops good quarters, and ample repose. For a moment he was tempted to start again immediately, and to march upon London without halting; but he was one of those men who have mind enough to conceive great designs, but too weak a will to execute them. Worcester was an important and well-situated town; the Council of State had made it a place of banishment for a number of gentlemen of the neighbourhood, who thus found themselves collected there on the King's arrival, and who received him with transports of delight. The mayor and all the local authorities manifested equal devotedness to his cause; and measures were immediately taken for the provisioning of his army. Charles resolved to establish his head-quarters in the town, and on the 23rd of August, 1651, exactly nine years, day for day, since the King his father had planted the royal standard at Nottingham, to begin the civil war, Charles set up his standard at Worcester, and summoned, by solemn proclamation, all his male subjects between the ages of sixteen and sixty, to join him at the general muster of his forces on the 26th of August, in the meadows between the city and the river Severn, which flows near it. Thirty or forty gentlemen only, with about two hundred followers, appeared at the rendezvous. The royal army was then found to consist of about twelve thousand men, of whom ten thousand were Scots, and scarcely two thousand English.[2]

A very strong movement, on the contrary, had taken place in

[1] Clarendon's History of the Rebellion, vol. vi. pp. 494—498; Whitelocke, pp. 266, 501—503; Godwin's History of the Commonwealth, vol. iii. pp. 260—267; Lingard's History of England, vol. xi. pp. 76—78; Boscobel Tracts, pp. 27—29.

[2] Whitelocke, pp. 503, 504; Clarendon's History of the Rebellion, vol. vi. pp. 506, 507; Boscobel Tracts, pp. 173, 180; Cromwell's Letters and Speeches, vol. ii. p. 330; Lingard's History of England, vol. xi. p. 77.

the republican party, and even throughout the country generally, against those insolent neighbours who had come to impose a king upon England by force of arms, and those tyrannical Presbyterians who proposed to establish their creed upon the oppression of Christian consciences. All diversity of political ideas and desires disappeared almost entirely before this national feeling. The militia of a great many large towns—London, Bristol, York, Gloucester, Coventry, Hereford—rose with ardour to defend their homes, or even to join the army which was defending their country. Regiments of volunteers were formed in several counties for the same purpose. Fairfax, who had refused to invade Scotland, placed himself at the head of his neighbours in Yorkshire, and offered his services to Cromwell, to repulse the men who had dared to invade England. The Parliament, by the measures it adopted, and the rewards it distributed, and Cromwell, by the commands he issued, and the examples he made along his whole route, from the north-east to the south-west of England, unremittingly fostered this move-ment, and when, after a march of twenty-one days, Cromwell, who had left Scotland with ten thousand men, arrived before Worcester, on the 28th of August, he had under his command an army of thirty-four thousand men, of whom twenty-four thousand were infantry, and ten thousand cavalry.[1]

The royal army was much less numerous, less animated, and less ably commanded. It was not even accurately known who was to com-mand it. At the time when it entered England, the ambitious, pre-sumptuous, and restless Duke of Buckingham had told the King that it would be unwise to leave it under the command of a Scottish general, and had proposed himself as Lesley's successor. At Worces-ter, when the moment for decisive action drew near, he renewed his demand with such importunity that the King grew angry, and told him he could hardly believe he was in earnest, or that he could really consider himself fit for such a charge. The Duke asked wherein his unfitness lay. "You are too young," replied Charles. "But, sire," urged Buckingham, "Harry the Fourth of France commanded an army and won a battle when he was younger than I am;" and he persisted so strongly in his request, that at last the King was compelled to tell him he would have no generalissimo but himself; "upon which the duke was so dis-contented that he came no more to the Council, scarce spoke to the King, and would not converse with anybody; nor did he recover

[1] Whitelocke, pp. 497, 502, 504; Commons' Journals, vol. vii. pp. 6, 8; Godwin's History of the Commonwealth, vol. iii. pp. 263, 268, 407, 408; Brodie's History of the British Empire, vol. iv. p. 307; Boscobel Tracts, p. 180.

this ill-humour whilst the army stayed at Worcester."[1] Misunder-standing prevailed among the other generals also. Lesley, who was dispirited and unpopular, detested Middleton, who was confident and beloved by the soldiers; Massey had been grievously wounded in an attempt to prevent the enemy from passing the Severn and taking up a position on both banks of the river, and was confined to his bed, incapable of active service. Charles was constantly employed in reconciling or pacifying his lieutenants, but he was himself frivolous and careless; he had but little authority, little faith in his own success; and traitors were not wanting within the walls of Worcester to inform Cromwell of the bad internal condition of the royal army—its dissensions, hesitations, movements, and projects.[2]

Cromwell did not hesitate a moment: without waiting for the slow results of a siege, he resolved to attack Worcester at once on both sides of the Severn, at both extremities of the town, and to carry it at all risks. He encamped on the left bank of the river, and on the very day of his arrival, in spite of the obstinate resistance of the royalists, he passed a body of troops to the right bank, under Lambert's orders; and five days after, during the evening of the 2nd of September and the morning of the 3rd, numerous reinforcements, commanded by Fleetwood, executed the same movement, with orders to attack the western suburb of Worcester, whilst Cromwell himself, at the eastern extremity, directed the principal attack against the city itself. Charles, whose information was very imperfect, did not expect any serious affair on that day, and was quietly resting his troops; but at about one o'clock in the afternoon, while on the tower of the cathedral with his staff, he noticed several of Cromwell's regiments crossing the river by a bridge of boats, and marching against the Scottish troops, who had been posted, under Major-General Montgomery, to defend the western approaches to the city. Almost at the same moment he heard, on the eastern side, the volleys of the republican artillery, which was beginning to batter the approaches to the place. Charles descended hastily from the tower, mounted his horse, and rode to the western suburb to support Montgomery. Cromwell was already there in person, warmly pushing the attack: before acting himself on the left bank, he had desired to make sure that the orders which he had given were well executed on the right. The Scots made a bold resistance. Charles thought that the bulk of the parliamentary army were

[1] Clarendon's History of the Rebellion, vol. vi. pp. 507—509.
[2] Boscobel Tracts, pp. 30, 125, 180, 220; Whitelocke, p. 505; Cromwell's Letters and Speeches, vol. ii. p. 335.

engaged on this side, and returning immediately into the town, he put himself at the head of his best infantry and his squadrons of English cavalry, left the city by the eastern gate, and marched upon Cromwell's camp, hoping to find it weakly guarded, and to be able to destroy it. But Cromwell also had passed rapidly over to the left bank of the river, and re-appeared at the head of the troops which he had left there. The battle, thus engaged at both extremities of Worcester, lasted for four or five hours,—" as stiff a contest as I have ever seen," wrote Cromwell; but begun and maintained by the royalists in the midst of great confusion. The troops led by Charles himself charged the republicans so vigorously that they gave way at first, abandoning a part of their artillery; three thousand Scottish cavalry, commanded by Lesley, were under arms behind the King, who sent them orders to follow up his movement, and charge in their turn. "Oh, for one hour of Montrose!" shouted the English Cavaliers; but Lesley remained motionless. Cromwell meanwhile rallied his troops, and resumed the offensive; the royal infantry, failing in ammunition, fell back; the Duke of Hamilton and Sir John Douglas were mortally wounded. Cromwell, everywhere present and full of confidence, carried the attack in person to the intrenchments of Fort Royal, which covered the city on that side, and summoned the commandant, who occupied it with fifteen hundred men, to surrender; a volley of artillery was his reply; but the fort was soon stormed, and the garrison put to the sword. Both royalists and republicans fought hand to hand up to the gates of the city: there the disorder was extreme,—an ammunition waggon had been overthrown, and blocked the passage; Charles was obliged to dismount from his horse, and enter Worcester on foot; the republicans dashed through the breach after him. Meanwhile the conflict in the west had the same issue: Montgomery's Scots, after having exhausted their ammunition, fell back upon the town, pursued by Fleetwood's troops, who entered with them. The combat was renewed in the streets in the form of partial encounters, and intermingled with acts of pillage and heroism, devotedness and flight. Charles remounted on horseback, and endeavoured to rally his men, but in vain. "Then shoot me dead!" he cried. "rather than let me live to see the sad consequences of this day." But ere long it became his most imperative duty not to fall into the hands of the enemy. About fifty royalists, led by Lord Cleveland, Colonel Wogan, Sir James Hamilton, and Major Careless, formed themselves into a compact body, and with ardent courage charged the republican troops in every direction, in order to cover the retreat of the King, who at length left Worcester by St. Martin's gate, and took the northern road. Before he had ridden far he came up with some of Lesley's cavalry, who were flying without having fought; for a moment he felt disposed to try once more to induce them to turn and renew the action. "But no," he said to himself, "men who deserted me when they were in good order, would never stand to me now they are beaten." So he left Lesley and his Scotsmen to effect their retreat as they best might, and concentrated his attention on providing for his own safety. The idea occurred to him of going to seek an asylum in London—the best place, perhaps, both for concealment and for taking advantage of any opportunity that might present itself for renewing the war. But he mentioned this plan only to Lord Wilmot, his most intimate confidant; and, followed by about sixty devoted Cavaliers, he pursued his way towards the north, protected for the moment by the night, and anxiously consulting with his companions as to their means of safety for the morrow.[1]

At about the same time, at ten o'clock in the evening, Cromwell, who had hardly made his entry into Worcester, which was still a prey to confusion and pillage, sent a short announcement of his victory to the Parliament, and a fuller account on the following day. "The battle," he wrote, was fought with various success for some hours, but still hopeful on our part; and in the end became an absolute victory,—and so full a one as proved a total defeat and ruin of the enemy's army. We took all their baggage and artillery. What the slain are, I can give you no account, because we have not taken an exact view; but they are very many: and must needs be so; because the dispute was long and very near at hand, and often at push of pike. There are about six or seven thousand prisoners taken here; and many officers and noblemen of very great quality: Duke Hamilton, the Earl of Rothes, and divers other noblemen,— I hear, the Earl of Lauderdale; many officers of great quality; and some that will be fit subjects for your justice. . . . . The dimensions of this mercy are above my thoughts. It is, for aught I know, a crowning mercy. Surely, if it be not, such a one we shall have, if this provoke those that are concerned in it to thankfulness, and the Parliament to do the will of Him who hath done

[1] Boscobel Tracts, pp. 30—38, 123—130, 134; Clarendon's History of the Rebellion, vol. vi. pp. 510—514; Clarendon's State Papers, vol. iii. p. 30; Whitelocke, p. 507; Cromwell's Letters and Speeches, vol. ii. p. 337; Bates, Elenchus Motuum Nuperorum, part ii. pp. 219—225; Godwin's History of the Commonwealth, vol. iii. pp. 271—274; Lingard's History of England, vol. xi. pp. 77, 78; Cromwelliana, p. 115; Old Parliamentary History, vol. xx. pp. 59—68.

His will for it, and for the nation ;—whose good pleasure it is to establish the nation and the change of the government, by making the people so willing to the defence thereof, and so signally blessing the endeavours of your servants in this late great work."[1]

When this letter was read, the Parliament called in Major Cobbett, who had brought it, and wished to hear from him a circumstantial narrative of the battle.   Cobbett at the same time produced the Collar and Garter of the King, which had been found at Worcester, in the house which he had occupied.   Two members of the House, Mr. Scott and Major Salwey, on their return from the camp to which they had been sent on a special mission, also satisfied, by numerous details, the curiosity of their colleagues.   Every day brought the names of new and important prisoners ; the Earls of Derby, Cleveland, Lauderdale, Shrewsbury and Kelly, Generals Massey, Middleton and Lesley, indeed, nearly all the royalist leaders fell, during their flight, into the hands of the republican authorities.   It was truly, as Cromwell had said, a crowning victory.   The Parliament was anxious to show its grateful joy by all means in its power.   It ordered a solemn thanksgiving service throughout the three kingdoms, and gave a great banquet in White-hall.   Four members, Whitelocke, St. John, Lisle and Pickering, were appointed to wait on Cromwell, to express to him, in terms officially voted by the House, the sense which Parliament entertained of his glorious services.   The palace of Hampton Court was assigned to him for a residence, with an estate in land of the yearly value of 4,000l.   His principal officers, and even the obscure messengers who had brought the news, received splendid rewards.   But while favours were thus lavished on the victors, severities were not forgotten towards the vanquished.   Nine of the principal prisoners were chosen to be tried by court-martial for high treason ; one of them, the Duke of Hamilton, died of his wounds before judgment could be pronounced upon him ; three, the Earl of Derby, Sir Timothy Fetherstonhaugh, and Captain Benbow, were tried at Chester, and condemned to death.   They met their fate with the courage of martyrs.   " For the cause in which I had a great while waded," said the Earl of Derby on the scaffold, " I must needs say, my engagement or continuance in it hath laid no scruple upon my conscience.   It was on principles of law, and on principles of religion, that I embraced it ; my judgment is satisfied, and my conscience rectified ; for which I bless God.   I will not presume to decide controversies.   I pray God to prosper that side that hath

[1] Cromwell's Letters and Speeches, vol. ii. pp. 339—341.

right with it; and that you may enjoy peace and plenty, when I shall enjoy peace and plenty, beyond all you possess here."[1]

Either because such speeches from the vanquished seemed to the Parliament more dangerous than their punishment was useful, or because the completeness of its triumph inclined it to moderation, these painful spectacles were not multiplied. The other prisoners of mark remained confined in the Tower. The common soldiers were treated with severity, but their fate was kept as secret as possible; thousands of them were sold or given away to merchants or planters, and sent to work either in the colonies, or in the mines of Africa. Finally, it was decreed, and solemnly proclaimed all over the country, that a reward of one thousand pounds should be given to any person who should "bring in to the Parliament Charles Stuart, son of the late tyrant."[2]

Whilst the Parliament was passing this decree in London, its soldiers were traversing the western counties in all directions in search of the king, and finding traces of him everywhere, but himself nowhere. Five days after the battle, a detachment of infantry arrived suddenly at the old monastery of Whiteladies, the seat of a Catholic gentleman named Giffard, and required him, on pain of death, to tell them what had become of the king, who, they said, had recently been concealed in his house. Mr. Giffard resolutely denied having seen the fugitive, and begged, if he must die, that they would first give him leave to say a few prayers. "If you can tell us no news of the king," said one of the soldiers, "you shall say no prayers." He persisted in his silence, and the soldiers, after having carefully searched the whole house, rode off without doing him any further injury. Whiteladies, however, had been the first asylum of Charles; he had arrived there at daybreak on the 4th of September, scarcely twelve hours after having escaped from Worcester. He had immediately cut off his hair, stained his hands and face, and assumed the coarse and threadbare garments of a peasant; and five brothers Penderell, all of them labourers, woodmen or domestics in the service of Mr. Giffard, had undertaken to secure his safety. "This is the king," said Mr. Giffard to William Penderell; "thou must have a care of him, and preserve him as thou didst me." They accordingly took Charles to

---

[1] Commons' Journals, vol. vii. pp. 12—16; Old Parliamentary History, vol. xx. p. 72; State Trials, vol. v. pp. 294—323; Boscobel Tracts, pp. 187, 193, 198; Clarendon's History of the Rebellion, vol. vi. pp. 515—518; Whitelocke, p. 508.

[2] Godwin's History of the Commonwealth, vol. iii. pp. 273—276; Commons' Journals, vol. vii. p. 14.

Boscobel House, and concealed him in the adjoining woods. It was raining heavily: Richard Penderell procured a blanket, and spread it for the king under one of the largest trees; while his sister, Mrs. Yates, brought a supply of bread, milk, eggs, and butter. "Good woman," said Charles to her, "can you be faithful to a distressed Cavalier?" "Yes, Sir," she replied, "and I will die sooner than betray you." Some soldiers passed on the outskirts of the wood, but did not enter it, because the storm was more violent over the wood than in the open fields. On the next day, the king concealed himself among the leafy branches of a large oak, and from this cover he could see the soldiers scouring the country in search of him. One night he left his hiding-place, to endeavour to cross the Severn, and take refuge in Wales; but as he was passing a mill with Richard Penderell, his guide, the miller called out, "Who goes there?" "Neighbours going home," answered Penderell. "If you be neighbours, stand," cried the miller, "or I will knock you down." They fled as fast as they could, and were pursued for some time by several men who came out of the mill with the miller. In another of their attempts to escape, while fording a small river, the King, who was a good swimmer, helped his guide across, as he was unable to swim. He wandered for seven days in this manner through the country, changing his place of refuge almost daily, sometimes hidden beneath the hay in a barn, sometimes concealed in one of those obscure hiding-places which served as a retreat to the proscribed Catholic priests; hearing or seeing, at every moment, the republican soldiers who had been sent in search of him. In concert with his faithful guards, and with Lord Wilmot, who had rejoined him, he resolved to make for the sea-coast, near Bristol, in the hope of being able to find a vessel to take him over to France. He now changed his disguise, assumed a servant's livery instead of his peasant's garb, and set off on horseback, under the name of William Jackson, carrying behind him his mistress, Miss Jane Lane, sister of Colonel Lane, of Bentley, his last place of refuge in Staffordshire. "Will," said the colonel to him at starting, "thou must give my sister thy hand to help her to mount:" but the King, unused to such offices, gave her the wrong hand. "What a goodly horseman my daughter has got to ride before her," said old Mrs. Lane, the colonel's mother, who was watching their departure, though unacquainted with the secret. They set off, but they had scarcely ridden two hours, when the King's horse cast a shoe, and they halted at a little village to get another shoe. "As I was holding the horse's foot," says the King in his narrative of his escape, "I asked the smith what news. He told me that there was no news that he knew of, since the good news of the beating of those rogues, the Scots. I asked him whether there were none of the English taken that had joined with the Scots. He answered that some of them were taken, but he did not hear that that rogue, Charles Stuart, had been taken yet. I told him that, if that rogue were taken, he deserved to be hanged more than all the rest, for bringing in the Scots. Upon which he said that I spoke like an honest man; and so we parted."[1]

On the 13th of September he reached Abbotsleigh, near Bristol, the residence of Mr. Norton, a cousin of Colonel Lane. He there learned, to his great sorrow, that there was not in the port of Bristol any vessel on board which he could embark; and he was obliged to remain in the house four days. Under pretence of indisposition, he was indulged with a separate chamber, and by Miss Lane's request, particular care was taken of him. He was really much harassed and fatigued, though but little inclined to endure patiently either hunger or ennui. On the morning after his arrival, he rose early, and went to the buttery-hatch to get his breakfast, where he found Pope, the butler, and two or three other servants, "and," he says, "we all fell to eating bread and butter, to which Pope gave us very good ale and sack. As I was sitting there, there was one that looked like a country fellow, sat just by me, who gave so particular an account of the battle of Worcester to the res' of the company, that I concluded he must be one of Cromwell's soldiers. But I asking him how he came to give so good an account of that battle? he told me he was in the King's regiment; and on questioning him further, I perceived that he had been in my regiment of guards. I asked him what kind of a man I was? To which he answered by describing exactly both my clothes and my horse; and then looking upon me, he told me that the king was at least three fingers taller than I. Upon which I made what haste I could out of the buttery, for fear he should indeed know me; being more afraid when I knew he was one of our own soldiers, than when I took him for one of the enemy's."[2]

Charles had no sooner returned to his room, than one of his companions came to him in great agitation, and said "What shall we do? I am afraid Pope the butler knows you, for he says very positively to me that it is you, but I have denied it." Charles had already learned that, in positions of danger, bold confidence is often no less a source of safety than a necessity; he sent for the

[1] Boscobel Tracts, pp. 40—46, 131, 136—146, 190, 192, 218, 223—226, 239—241.

[2] Boscobel Tracts, pp. 54, 108—110, 146—150, 243.

butler, told him all, and received from him, during his stay at Mr. Norton's house, the most intelligent and most devoted care.

But attentions, even when shown most discreetly, sometimes prove most compromising: at the end of four days Charles had to seek a new asylum: and on the 14th of September, he left Abbotsleigh for Trent House, in the same county, the residence of Colonel Wyndham, a staunch royalist. In 1636, six years before the outbreak of the war between Charles I. and his Parliament, Sir Thomas Wyndham, the Colonel's father, when on the point of death, had said to his five sons—"My sons, we have hitherto seen serene and quiet times, but now prepare yourselves for cloudy and troublesome. I command you to honour and obey our gracious sovereign, and in all times to adhere to the crown; and though the crown should hang upon a bush, I charge you forsake it not." The injunctions of the dying man were obeyed; three of his sons and one of his grandsons fell on the battle-field, fighting for Charles I.; and Colonel Wyndham, who had also served with honour in the royal army, was, in 1651, a prisoner on parole in his own house. He received the king with the utmost devotedness, and set to work immediately to obtain some means of embarkation for him in one of the neighbouring ports. He thought he had succeeded in doing so at Southampton; but the vessel which he had fixed upon was required by the agents of the Parliament, to transport a body of troops to Jersey. A sea-captain of Lyme, named Limbry, undertook, not without considerable hesitation, to convey to St. Malo some royalist gentlemen who had been engaged in Worcester fight; every arrangement was made as to the price, the day, the hour, and the place of embarkation: on the 23rd of September, the vessel was to set sail from Charmouth, a little port near Lyme, and during the night, the long-boat was to fetch the fugitive royalists, from an appointed place on the beach.

Guided by Colonel Wyndham, Charles proceeded to the spot agreed upon, where he was met by Lord Wilmot; they waited there all night, but the boat did not make its appearance. Limbry, at the moment when he was about to send his things on board, had been detained by the anger and despair of his wife. On that very day, at the fair of Lyme, proclamation had been made of the act of Parliament which offered a reward of a thousand pounds for the king's arrest, and at the same time menaced with the severest punishment all who should give him refuge. Limbry's wife, without suspecting that the king himself was concerned in the matter, declared to her husband that she would not suffer him to take on board his vessel any royalist, or to expose her children and

herself to utter ruin for the sake of any lord, however high his rank;
and with the help of her two daughters, she locked her husband in
his room, threatening that, if he persisted in his design, she would
denounce it immediately to Captain Macy, who commanded a
company of the Parliament's troops at Lyme. Limbry yielded
to the fears and violence of his wife. The king's position was
now becoming dangerous; the presence of so many strangers at
Charmouth had been remarked; Lord Wilmot's horse required shoe-
ing; the smith to whom it was taken said "that he was sure his three
shoes had been set in three several counties, and one of them in
Worcestershire." Suspicions were aroused; the puritan minister
of the place, a zealous republican, went to the hostess of the inn
where Charles had been staying, and said to her, "Why how now,
Margaret, you are a maid of honour now." "What mean you by
that, Mr. Parson?" said she. "Why Charles Stuart lay last night
at your house," he answered, "and kissed you at his departure;
so that now you can't but be a maid of honour." The hostess grew
angry, and told him he was a scurvy-conditioned man to go about
to bring her and her house into trouble; "but," she added, "if I
thought it was the King, as you say it was, I would think the better
of my lips all the days of my life; and so, Mr. Parson, get you out
of my house, or else I'll get those shall kick you out." Charles
left Charmouth in all haste, but on arriving at Bridport, a neighbouring town, he found the streets filled with soldiers; it was the
regiment which the Parliament was about to send to take possession of Jersey. "What is to be done?" asked Colonel Wyndham, in great alarm; Charles, with his accustomed presence of
mind, and still acting the part of a domestic, dismounted, took the
bridles of the horses, and passing boldly among the troopers, with
many a coarse jest and rough word, he went straight to the best inn
of the place, and remained there until his party had quietly dined.
In the mean while, at Charmouth and its neighbourhood, the report
that Charles Stuart had been there had assumed consistency;
Captain Macy mounted his horse with some of his men, rode at full
speed to Bridport, and, after making full inquiries there, set off
immediately in pursuit of the fugitives; but at a short distance from
the town, Charles and his companions had left the high road, and
continued their journey across country. Macy lost all trace of
them; and from village to village, they returned to Colonel
Wyndham's house in Somersetshire, divided between feelings of
increased perplexity, and the delight of finding rest after danger.

Charles remained for eleven days at Trent House, still seeking,
but in vain, the means of transport to France. It then became

necessary for him once more to change his residence. Colonel Wyndham was informed that his house was becoming more and more suspected; and ere long, troops arrived in the neighbourhood. On the 6th of October, the King left Trent House to take refuge at Hele House, the residence of Mr. Hyde, in Wiltshire; where he would be nearer the small seaports of Sussex, at one of which his friends hoped to be able to procure him a vessel. They at last succeeded in obtaining one, and on the morning of the 13th of October, Charles left his last hiding-place, escorted by a few faithful friends, who had brought their dogs, as if for a coursing expedition on the downs. They slept at Hambledon, in Hampshire, at the house of a brother-in-law of Colonel Gunter, one of the King's guides: and the master of the house, on his return home, was astonished to find his table surrounded by unknown guests, whose gaity exceeded the bounds of "decent hilarity." The King's cropped hair, and the reproof which he administered to the honest squire for a casual oath, redoubled his surprise; he bent towards his brother-in-law, and asked if that fellow were not "some round-headed rogue's son." The colonel assured him that his suspicions were unfounded, upon which he sat down at table with his guests, and gaily drank the King's health " in a good glass of beer, calling him brother roundhead." On the following day, the 14th of October, they proceeded to Brighthelmstone, where they were to meet the master of the promised vessel, and the merchant who had engaged it for them. They all supped together at the village inn; during the meal, the captain, Anthony Tettersall, scarcely once took his eyes off the King; and after supper he took the merchant aside, and told him "that he had not dealt fairly with him; for though he had given him a very good price for carrying over that gentleman, yet he had not been clear with him;—for," said he, " he is the King, and I very well know him to be so." The merchant assured him that he was mistaken, but he answered: " No I am not; for he took my ship, together with other fishing vessels at Brighthelmstone, in the year 1648, when he commanded his father's fleet; but be not troubled at it, for I think I do God and my country good service in preserving the King, and by the grace of God, I will venture my life and all for him, and set him safely on shore, if I can, in France." At about the same time, at another part of the room, the innkeeper came up to the King, who was standing by the fire, with his hand resting on the back of a chair, and kissed his hand suddenly. " God bless you wheresoever you go!" he said; "I do not doubt, before I die, to be a lord, and my wife a lady." Charles laughed, and went into another

I

room, putting full trust in his host; and at five o'clock on the morning of the 15th of October, the King and Lord Wilmot were on board a little vessel of sixty tons, which only waited for the tide to leave Shoreham harbour.   As soon as they were at sea, Captain Tettersall came into the cabin where the King was lying, fell on his knees, kissed his hand, and protesting his entire devotedness, suggested that, in order to prevent all difficulty, he should himself persuade the crew, who imagined that they had embarked for the English port of Poole, to sail towards the coast of France, by representing himself to them as a merchant in debt, who was afraid of being arrested in England, and wished to recover some money that was owing to him at Rouen.   Charles willingly acceded to this proposition, and contrived to ingratiate himself so thoroughly with the sailors, that they joined him in requesting the captain to turn aside from his course in favour of his passengers.   The weather was fine and the wind favourable, and at one o'clock in the afternoon of the 16th of October, the ship's boat landed the King and Lord Wilmot in the little port of Fécamp.   They proceeded on the following day to Rouen, clothed so wretchedly and looking so disreputable, that when they presented themselves at an inn, the host hesitated to give them admittance, taking them "to be thieves, or persons that had been doing some very ill thing."   Charles sent for an English merchant who resided at Rouen, to supply his immediate necessities; and wrote at once to the Queen his mother, who was in the utmost anguish as to his fate.   The most contradictory reports had been spread regarding him : some stated that he had been captured by Cromwell's soldiers, others that he had succeeded in making his escape to Holland.   As soon as it became known that he was at Rouen, the English refugees flocked to meet him; he left that city on the 29th of October, and on the 30th, he met his brother, the Duke of York, at Magny, and afterwards at Monceaux, near Paris, the Queen his mother, the Duke of Orleans his uncle, with a large number of French and English gentlemen who had come out on horseback to welcome him.   He proceeded that same evening to the Louvre, saved from all peril, but conquered and without hope.[1]

He had wandered about England for forty-two days, and had been concealed successively in eight different hiding-places; forty-five persons of all ranks in life, whose names have reached us, and doubtless many others of whom we have no information, had known

[1] Boscobel Tracts, pp. 67—73, 119—122, 156—163, 251—259; Clarendon's State Papers, vol. iii. pp. 30, 31; Bates, Elenchus Motuum Nuperorum, pp. 226—266.

who he was and where he was. Not one of them betrayed, even by
an indiscretion, the secret of his presence or of his movements.
Sincere devotedness can inspire the most simple-minded with
sagacity, and the weakest with virtue.

Whilst Charles was thus experiencing at once the severest
trials of his destiny and the fidelity of his friends, Cromwell had
returned in triumph to London, preceded by the prisoners whom
he had taken, and surrounded by the officers who had shared in his
victory. The four commissioners who had been delegated by
the Parliament went, on the 11th of September, beyond Aylesbury
to meet him. "We come," they said to him, " in the name of
the Parliament, to congratulate your Lordship on your good recovery of health, after your dangerous sickness. Your unwearied
labours and pains, in the late expedition into Scotland, for the
service of this Commonwealth ; your diligence in prosecution of
the enemy, when he fled into England ; the great hardships
and hazards you have exposed yourself unto, and particularly
in the late fight at Worcester ; your prudent and faithful managing
and conducting throughout this great and important affair, which
the Lord from heaven hath so signally blessed, and crowned
with so complete and glorious an issue :—of all these things
the Parliament have thought fit, by us, to certify to your Lordship their good acceptance, and great satisfaction therein ; and
for the same, to return to you in the name of the Parliament
and Commonwealth of England, their most hearty thanks ; as
also, to the rest of your officers and soldiers, for their great and
gallant services. And since, by the great blessing of God upon
your Lordship's and the army's endeavours, the enemy is so totally
defeated, and the state of affairs, as well in England as in Scotland, such as may very well dispense with your Lordship's continuance in the field, the Parliament do desire your Lordship, for the
better settlement of your health, to take such rest and repose as
you shall find most requisite and conducing thereunto ; and for
that purpose, to make your residence at or near London ; whereby
also, the Parliament may have the assistance of your presence, in
the great and important consultation for the further settlement of
this Commonwealth, which they are now upon." On his entry
into London, Cromwell was met by the Speaker and a large number
of members of the House of Commons, by the President of the
Council of State, the Lord Mayor and aldermen of the city, and
many thousands of notable citizens, who accompanied him to Whitehall, amid salutes of artillery and popular acclamations ; and when,
four days afterwards, he made his appearance again in the House,

the Speaker reiterated to him the solemn thanks of the Parliament and country.[1]

Cromwell received all these honours with pious modesty, saying but little of himself, and ascribing, first to God and then to his soldiers, the whole merit of his success. Through his humility, however, glimpses of an irrepressible internal exultation occasionally manifested themselves : his affability towards the commissioners whom the Parliament had sent to meet him wore an air of magnificence and grandeur : he presented to each of them a fine horse and some of the prisoners of rank whom he brought with him, and who would certainly redeem their liberty at a high price. To White-locke he gave two of them, and he liberated them without ransom. Cromwell proceeded slowly towards London, receiving the homage of the population on his route, and sometimes even halting to share in the hawking expeditions of the gentlemen whom he met. At Aylesbury, it was remarked that he remained long in private conversation with the Chief Justice St. John, one of the Parliament's commissioners, and also one of Cromwell's most intimate confidants. His air, his language, and his manners, seemed to undergo a natural transformation ; and Hugh Peters, a clear-sighted sectarian preacher, who had long been used to understand and serve him, said, as he noticed his altered appearance : " This man will be king of England yet."[2]

His good fortune extended to his lieutenants ; on leaving first Ireland, and then Scotland, he had delegated the command in the former country to Ireton, and in the latter to Monk—the one a republican, the other a royalist at heart, but both of them sensible, capable, rough-mannered men, well fitted to carry on a work of war, and of government by the sword when the victory was won. Both of them obtained complete success. Monk met with desperate resistance at several places, and especially at the siege of Dundee : Ireton continued the system of cruel severity which Cromwell had put in practice, and died of the plague, it is said, after the siege and capture of Limerick. But, at the end of the year 1651, both Ireland and Scotland were in entire subjection ; Ormonde had returned to the Continent ; the Scottish Highlanders, unable to undertake any serious enterprise, had great difficulty in maintaining some remnant of independence in their rude mountain fastnesses. At the same time, the fleet and troops of the Parliament had re-

[1] Commons' Journals, vol. vii. pp. 13, 14, 18; Whitelocke's Memorials, p. 509.

[2] Whitelocke, p. 500; Ludlow's Memoirs, p. 189; Cromwell's Letters and Speeches, vol. ii. p. 343.

gained possession of the islands of Guernsey, Jersey, Scilly, and
Man, the last refuges of the royal dominion : the chief colonial de-
pendencies, New England, Virginia, and Barbadoes, had either
hastened or been compelled to accept the new government of the
home country ;[1] and a few months after that battle which had consummated the defeat of royalty in England, the republican Parliament was master of all the English territories, in both hemispheres.

[1] Commons' Journals, vol. vii. pp. 31, 35, 62, 90, 124, 172; Whitelocke,
pp. 523, 527; Clarendon's History of the Rebellion, vol. vi. pp. 515—554.

BOOK III.

IMPRESSION PRODUCED ON THE CONTINENT BY THE TRIAL AND EXECUTION OF CHARLES I.—ASSASSINATION OF DORISLAUS AT THE HAGUE, AND OF ASCHAM AT MADRID—ATTITUDE OF THE CONTINENTAL STATES TOWARDS THE COMMONWEALTH OF ENGLAND—DEVELOPMENT AND SUCCESSES OF THE ENGLISH NAVY—FOREIGN POLICY OF THE REPUBLICAN PARLIAMENT—RIVALRY BETWEEN FRANCE AND SPAIN IN THEIR RELATIONS WITH ENGLAND—RECOGNITION OF THE COMMONWEALTH BY SPAIN—RELATIONS BETWEEN ENGLAND AND THE UNITED PROVINCES—ENGLISH AMBASSADORS AT THE HAGUE—DUTCH AMBASSADORS IN LONDON—THEIR WANT OF SUCCESS—NEGOTIATIONS OF MAZARIN IN LONDON—LOUIS XIV. RECOGNISES THE ENGLISH COMMONWEALTH—WAR BETWEEN ENGLAND AND THE UNITED PROVINCES—SUCCESSES OF BLAKE—EFFECTS OF THE WAR IN ENGLAND.

THOUGH victorious over its enemies at home, the Commonwealth was, as yet, neither at peace nor at war with the States of the Continent.

The trial and execution of Charles I. had produced the deepest emotion throughout Europe. It was the second time, within a period of sixty years, that royalty had fallen, in England, beneath the axe of the executioner. It was the first time that the sovereignty of the people and a republican form of government had been proclaimed and established in a great Christian country. The surprise, anxious curiosity, pity, and indignation which these occurrences awakened were universal. Protestant countries felt the necessity of clearing the Reformation from the reproach of having instigated or contributed to so great a crime. In Germany, in Denmark, in Sweden, and most of all in Holland, the ministers of religion hastened loudly to express their reprobation; the pulpits resounded with maledictions against the anarchical and sacrilegious sectaries; and the clergy of the Hague waited in a body upon Charles II., and solemnly expressed to him their grief and horror, in a Latin oration. The feelings of the people corresponded with these manifestations on the part of the Church; the details of the trial and death of Charles I. were collected and published with pious respect; a woman at the Hague fell into travail and died with terror at hearing the news. The representatives or partisans of the regicides were treated with aversion and insult in the streets: from popular instinct, or Christian conscientiousness, or political wisdom, Protestant and republican Holland shrank from any manifestation of indulgence for so unprecedented an act, considering it as full of social danger as of moral iniquity.[1]

In Catholic countries—Spain, Portugal, Italy, and Southern Germany—the impression was equally strong, but of a different nature. Both clergy and people regarded the fate of Charles I. as the natural consequence of heresy, and as an exhibition of the justice of God, who punishes peoples and kings by one another, when they separate from His Church. The crime excited deep aversion, but it was accompanied by less surprise than in Protestant Europe, and perhaps also by less sympathy and sorrow.

In France the impressions were of a more mingled character. At the very moment when pure monarchy was on the point of predominating in that country, the spirit of reform and of political liberty had attempted a sincere and earnest, but superficial and vain, effort to arrest its progress. The English Parliament found many admirers among the partisans of the Fronde; its maxims were welcomed, and its acts observed, with eager curiosity; and more than one pamphlet pointed out the House of Commons and the city of London as models for the Parliament and bourgeoisie of Paris. But the trial of Charles I., the violent mutilation of the House of Commons, the abolition of the House of Lords, and the tyrannical establishment of the Commonwealth, gave the royalist opinion in France, with regard to the affairs of England, an ascendency in harmony with the course of French affairs, and which the prolonged disorders of the Fronde, and the relations of its leaders with the English republicans, strengthened rather than diminished. The revolution of England, far from alluring, excited only mingled reprobation and alarm: it was attacked in a multitude of pamphlets; Joan of Arc was represented as exhorting the French to take arms to avenge the cause of royalty upon the English parricides; and the monarchical opinion with regard to England soon prevailed among the French people, always eager spectators of public events.

Two tragical incidents which occurred at this time, give a striking proof of the state of public opinion in Europe.

---

[1] Clarendon's History of the Rebellion, vol. vi. pp. 267, 268; Wicquefort's Histoire des Provinces Unies, vol. iv. p. 155; Whitelocke, pp. 386—390.

On the 3rd of May, 1649, Dr. Isaac Dorislaus, a native of Holland, who had long been settled in England, and had been appointed one of the counsel to conduct the prosecution of the King, arrived at the Hague, having been sent by the Parliament in the capacity of an assistant to Walter Strickland, the Commonwealth's resident ambassador to the United Provinces. He was quietly supping in the evening, with several other persons, at the Swan Inn, when six men in masks arrived at the house; two of them remained outside to guard the door; the others entered, put out the lights in the hall, and presenting themselves suddenly in the dining-room, told those who were at table not to stir, for there was no harm intended to any but the agent that came from the rebels in England, who had recently murdered their King. " They then dragged Dorislaus from the table, and put him to death; and quietly sheathing their swords, they left the room, rejoined their companions in the street, and quitted the Hague, before any one had either time or inclination to arrest them."[1]

About a year afterwards, in the early part of May, 1650, Anthony Ascham, an author of small reputation, who had taken part in the overthrow of the monarchy and the trial of the King, disembarked at Cadiz, on a mission from the Parliament to the King of Spain. Before he left London, his thoughts had dwelt much on the fate of Dorislaus, and he had expressed his anxiety on the subject to M. de Croullé, the French Chargé-d'affaires.[2] On his arrival at Cadiz, the governor, the Duke of Medina Celi, placed him under the care of Colonel Don Diego de Moreda, and two other officers, who were ordered to escort him to Madrid, and not to leave him until he was safely established in that city. They arrived there on the 5th of June, and either from negligence or ill-will, the Spanish officers, after having taken Ascham to a little inn, left him there alone, and went in search of a lodging for themselves elsewhere. On the following day, at noon, Ascham was at table with his secretary, Rivas, a renegade Franciscan monk; a man entered; Ascham advanced to meet him, taking him for a friend; but on catching sight of three other strangers who entered at the same time, he started quickly back to seize his pistols, which lay on a table near him; when the first comer, calling him a traitor,

[1] Wicquefort's Histoire des Provinces Unies, vol. iv. p. 157; Leclerc's Histoire des Provinces Unies, vol. ii. p. 271; Clarendon's History of the Rebellion, vol. vi. pp. 297, 298; Whitelocke, pp. 368, 401; Commons' Journals, vol. vi. p. 206.

[2] Letters from M. de Croullé to Cardinal Mazarin, June 30, 1650; in the Archives des Affaires Etrangères de France.

caught him by the hair, and struck him dead with his stiletto. His secretary, Rivas, attempting to escape and shouting for help, was also killed on the spot; one English domestic alone escaped, and spread the alarm. The four murderers left the room, returned to their companions who were awaiting them at the street-door, and proceeded without hinderance to seek sanctuary, one in the house of the Venetian ambassador, and the other five in a church adjoining the hospital of St. Andrew.[1]

At Madrid and at the Hague, the public excitement, and the anxiety of the two governments, Dutch and Spanish, were very great. The republican Parliament resented, as was anticipated, these bloody outrages; it manifested its sympathy for the two victims by public honours; Vane presented a solemn report on the assassination of Dorislaus; his body was brought to London, and buried in Westminster Abbey; and the whole Parliament attended the funeral. Similar respect, though in a less degree, was paid to Ascham. Pensions and employments were bestowed on both their families. Urgent and even threatening demands were made at the same time, and frequently renewed, at the Hague and at Madrid. to obtain justice upon the assassins. Both governments promised redress, and attempted to give it. The murderers were well known: those of Dorislaus were dependents of Montrose; those of Ascham were English Cavaliers who had taken refuge at Madrid, and one of them was a servant in the house of Lord Cottington and Sir Edward Hyde, who then resided at Madrid, as the ambassadors of Charles II. But at the Hague no one was arrested. At Madrid, although the civil authorities removed the murderers from their asylum, the Church asserted its privileges, and the prolonged conflict between the two jurisdictions ended in the impunity of the assassins; one only, who was found to be a Protestant, was delivered over to the secular arm and hanged. Both in Holland and Spain public feeling protected them; they had, it was said, only punished by murder men guilty of more heinous murder; and far from showing any repentance for their action, they gloried in it: those who had killed Ascham told the magistrates of Madrid that they would have killed him in presence of the King of Spain, if they had not found a more convenient opportunity. And the secret indulgence of the governments connived with the popular feeling; they pursued the crime from complaisance or fear, but without any serious desire to punish the criminals. A few weeks

[1] Thurloe's State Papers, vol. i. pp. 148—153, 202—204; Clarendon's History of the Rebellion, vol. vi. pp. 441—444; Old Parliamentary History, vol. xix. p. 285; Commons' Journals, vol. vi. pp. 407, 428.

after the assassination of Ascham, in a conversation with Lord Cottington and Hyde, the prime minister of Spain, Don Luis de Haro, did not hesitate to say: " I envy those gentlemen for having done so noble an action, how penal soever it may prove to them, to revenge the blood of their king. If the king my master had such resolute subjects, he would never have lost his realm of Portugal, for want of one brave man to take away the life of the usurper."[1]

But far more in the seventeenth century than in our own times, politicians cared little to act in accordance with their real feelings and their private speeches; and whilst the public on the Continent gave free vent to their ill-will towards the republican judges of Charles I., the governments, either from calculation or fear, manifested either indifference or reserve. The Dutch ambassadors who had been sent to London to attempt to save the King, demanded, after his death, that their negotiations with the Parliament should not be published; and though one of them, Adrian Pauw, left England immediately, the other, Albert Joachim, continued to reside there. Anne of Austria and Cardinal Mazarin thought it fitting that the young King of France should make some effort to save the life of the king his uncle; and Louis XIV., accordingly, wrote two solemn letters to Cromwell and Fairfax; but before M. de Varennes, who was appointed to deliver them, had left Paris, Charles I. was executed. M. de Bellièvre, then ambassador of France in London, made no attempt on his behalf; he did not even ask permission to see him. Some surprise was manifested at this at Paris, in the king's council; but Bellièvre was warmly defended and approved. " I see the necessity which I have for your protection," he wrote to M. Servien, " and the kindness with which you have extended it to me. I thought that it was better to be blamed for not having taken a step which any one might have seen could produce no advantage to the King of England, than to be guilty of the harm which that step might have done to the affairs of the king my master. For, as you know very well, they are so suspicious here with regard to everything that proceeds from France, that that which would pass unnoticed from others is declared criminal when it comes from us; and as, of foreign powers, they fear us alone, they pay such attention to our actions and our words that the least expression of the resentment which we must feel for

[1] Commons' Journals, vol. vi. pp. 209, 211, 313; Old Parliamentary History, vol. xix. pp. 286, 287; Leclerc's Histoire des Provinces Unies, vol. ii. p. 272; Wicquefort's Histoire des Provinces Unies, vol. iv. p. 158; Clarendon's History of the Rebellion, vol. vi. pp. 444—450; Papers from the Archives of Simancas.

that which they have done, might be enough to lead them to make alliance with Spain; and the knowledge of this fact, combined with the general instructions which I have always received not to irritate these fellows (ces gens-ci), made me resolve to act as I have done. I cannot repent of having been too circumspect, as I now find myself supported by your approval."[1]

After the King's death, Bellièvre persisted in his circumspection. "If there were a Court here," he wrote, "I should need no other rule as to the time for putting on mourning, and the manner of wearing it; but as there is none, I think it right to wait the orders it may please you to send me."[2] He was ordered to go into mourning and leave the country; for Mazarin was as little inclined to recognise the English Commonwealth as to irritate it. Bellièvre quitted London, but not till after a delay of three months, and leaving behind him his secretary, Croulle, who was directed to watch over the interests of France, though not in any official character. The last relations of the ambassador with the Parliament were somewhat difficult; he attempted, but in vain, to obtain his passports without taking leave; and he was obliged to wait upon the Speaker, who reported his visit to the House. "Here," wrote Bellièvre, "no affair is unimportant, and no despatch prompt, especially where France is concerned: and at this time, when those who govern are so jealous of their newly-acquired authority, and so unaware of how much they may obtain or preserve in regard to strangers, that everything gives them umbrage; and they forget that which is due, out of fear of doing too much. . . . Moreover, so uncertain are they in their resolutions that they are capable of passing in a moment from a compliment to an insult, or from an offensive action to an excess of civility."[3]

The Court of Madrid treated the new Commonwealth with even greater consideration than that of Paris, for it left its ambassador, Don Alonzo de Cardenas, in London, without at first renewing his credentials, but confidentially authorising him to continue his relations with the republican Parliament. This was a less difficult position for Don Alonzo than for any other person, as he had for a long while displayed great coolness, and even malevolence, towards Charles I., and had assiduously cultivated the favour of the revolutionary leaders; so that between them and him an interchange of

---

[1] Wicquefort's Histoire des Provinces Unies, vol. iv. p. 162: MSS. de Brienne, in the Bibliothèque Impériale, Paris; Archives des Affaires Étrangères de France.

[2] M. de Bellièvre to M. Servien; Archives des Affaires Étrangères de France.

[3] The same to the same.

friendly feelings and good offices had been established, from which Spanish policy hoped to gain great advantage.[1]

The Emperor and Princes of Germany, the King of Denmark, and the Queen of Sweden, were less reserved in their manifestation of the feelings with which they were inspired by the republican Parliament and its acts; but, alone among the sovereigns of Europe, the Czar of Russia, Alexis Michaelowitz, the father of Peter the Great, broke off all connection with the revolutionary Commonwealth and expelled the English merchants from his dominions.[2]

But all was not done by the powers of the Continent when they had assumed an uncertain and expectant attitude towards the republican Parliament; they had also to regulate their conduct towards the exiled King, and here their perplexities and the inconsistent weaknesses of their policy were still greater. Charles II. resided among the sovereigns of Europe, sometimes with the Prince of Orange, his brother-in-law, and sometimes at the Court of the King of France, his cousin-german; the Queen of Spain, Elizabeth of France, was his aunt. He was everywhere able to invoke, and he did in fact invoke, the ties of consanguinity, as well as the common interest and honour of kings. He sent Lord Cottington and Hyde to Madrid, Sir John Colepepper to Moscow, Lord Wilmot to Ratisbon, and Mr. Crofts to Poland. Sovereigns and their ministers found themselves incessantly in presence of his rights, his hopes, his demands, his complaints, and his agents. Nothing is more offensive to power than the sight of misfortunes which it will not succour, but which it is bound to respect; it has, however, many ways of ridding itself, at small cost, of such burdens. William of Orange alone was a warm and active friend to Charles Stuart; he was an ambitious and imperious young prince, inclined to violent enterprises and to absolute power, but of a noble and sincere heart; to restore the fortunes of his brother-in-law, he wasted his strength in efforts and sacrifices which were too limited to be effectual, and to which his unexpected death soon put an end. Excited by the Stadtholder and by the popular feeling of Holland, the States-General of the United Provinces bestowed on Charles great marks of interest and respect: on the news of the death of the King his father, they waited on him in a body to express their condolence,

[1] Letter of Cardeñas to King Philip IV., February 18, 1649; Deliberations of the Council of State at Madrid on the Letters of Cardeñas, March 13, 1649; in the Archives of Simancas. Clarendon's History of the Rebellion, vol. vi. p. 328.

[2] Wicquefort's Histoire des Provinces Unies, vol. iv. p. 156; Clarendon's History of the Rebellion, vol. vi. pp. 248—250; Whitelocke, p. 466.

and the Grand Pensionary, Van Ghent, in his harangue called him Sire, and your Majesty; but those words were pronounced with some embarrassment, and in a low voice, as though he were unwilling to compromise himself too deeply with the rising Commonwealth by recognising the new King in too pointed a manner. The Court of France considered that it was quite enough to give an asylum and a pension to the widow and children of Charles I.; it abstained from any other expression of feeling, and Charles Stuart received from it, on his father's death, neither letter nor message—indeed no mark whatever of sympathy or support. The King of Spain, who had not to answer for the presence of the Stuarts in his dominions, thought it his duty to write a letter of friendly condolence to Charles II., in which he gave him the title of King; but he long delayed sending it. When Charles, on leaving the Hague for Paris, passed through the Spanish Netherlands, he was received with great honours at Antwerp and Brussels; a splendid carriage and six fine horses were presented to him; he was even supplied with a loan of money; the Archduke Leopold and the Spanish ambassador in Holland, Anthony Lebrun, gave him encouragement in their private conversations: but at the same time they took the most minute precautions to deprive these demonstrations of all political value, and to represent them as mere acts of politeness. The Court of Madrid absolutely forbade any act or speech on their part which might be regarded in London as a positive declaration in favour of the King; they were even ordered to antedate certain letters which seemed to present this character.[1] The crowned heads of Europe were willing to treat Charles II. with respect and to do him service, provided that no meaning could be attached to their conduct which might be incompatible with the maintenance of strict neutrality between him and the republican Parliament.

To this political coolness were added acts of cynical indifference in private life. The furniture and pictures of Charles I., who loved the arts, and had patronised them with taste, were sold in London. Cardenas and Croullé gave full information of this to Don Luis de

---

[1] Clarendon's History of the Rebellion, vol. vi. pp. 310—313, 323—333, 470, 569; Leclerc's Histoire des Provinces Unies, vol. ii. p. 270; Letter from the Archduke Leopold, Governor of the Netherlands, to King Philip IV., March 4, 1649; Letter of Condolence from King Philip IV. to his Majesty King Charles of England, April 5, 1649: a first draft had been prepared in the month of March preceding; Letters from the Conde de Penaranda and the Archduke Leopold to King Philip IV., July 4—8, 1649; Deliberations of the Council of State at Madrid on the Title to be given to Charles II., August 2, 1649: in the Archives of Simancas.

Haro and Cardinal Mazarin, who, either for their sovereigns or for themselves, eagerly purchased, often at low prices, these spoils of the royal martyr. "If the pictures are sold at the prices marked in the list which you have sent me, I think them very dear," wrote Mazarin to Croullé; "that, however, will not prevent me from sending some intelligent person to buy several for me." Queen Christina of Sweden, and the Archduke Leopold, governor of the Spanish Netherlands, also purchased several; and when, in 1651, in the middle of winter, the King of Spain requested Lord Cottington and Hyde to leave his dominions, one of the secret causes of that resolution was the expected arrival of eighteen mules from Corunna, laden with pictures and curosities belonging to Charles I., which had been purchased in London for Philip IV., and which he thought he could not decently display in his palace, so long as the ambassadors of Charles II. were at Madrid.[1]

Both great and small, at home and in exile, the English royalists were offended and indignant at this eager readiness to profit by their disasters, while rendering them so little help. "The neighbour princes," says Clarendon, "joined in this manner to assist Cromwell with very great sums of money, whereby he was enabled to prosecute and finish his wicked victory; whilst they enriched and adorned themselves with the ruins and spoils of the surviving heir, without applying any part thereof to his relief, in the greatest necessities which ever king was subject to." And Graymond, the agent of Cardinal Mazarin in Scotland, wrote to him: "The servants of the King of Great Britain here utter imprecations against the kings and sovereigns of the earth, and principally against His Majesty (Louis XIV.), if he does not assist their King, after whose ruin they desire that of all others; and they do not scruple to say they will contribute with all their power to their destruction, which will be, they say, very easy to effect, when once the people have, in imitation of England's example, breathed the sweetness of popular government. They already point to Cromwell as the author of this great design, and the reformer of the universe . . . . and they say that he will begin with us, and that we well deserve it, because we do not endeavour the restoration of the King of England, though we are under the greatest obligations to do so."[2]

[1] Clarendon's History of the Rebellion, vol. vi. pp. 249, 458—460; Letters from Croullé to Mazarin, February 11 and May 23, 1650; and from Mazarin to Croullé, June 17, 1650: in the Archives des Affaires Etrangères de France.

[2] Clarendon's History of the Rebellion, vol. vi. p. 249; Letters from Graymond to Mazarin, October 23, 1649: in the Archives des Affaires Etrangères de France.

Such anger was very natural on the part of earnest and devoted adherents of a persecuted cause. But they ill understood the political state of Europe, and did not appreciate the general causes which rendered the kings of the Continent so cold and inert in presence of events which seemed to affect them so nearly.

The progress of affairs in England was watched with the closest attention by the European powers, but it did not inspire them with any serious alarm. Though they regarded the English revolutionaries with the utmost antipathy, they did not feel themselves really menaced by them, and their own position did not furnish any necessity for engaging in a direct and open struggle against them. At precisely the same period when royalty was tottering to its fall in England, it was gaining strength on the Continent; in all the great States of Europe, feudal and municipal liberties, the independent aristocracy, and the turbulent democracy of the Middle Ages, were disappearing, or giving way before it; the necessity for order in society, and for unity in the supreme power, everywhere predominated: the general tendency of ideas, as well as of events, was towards monarchy. The Commonwealth appeared a singular fact, purely local in its character, and the contagious influence of which was not greatly to be dreaded on the Continent, even in those States which were still agitated by civil dissensions.

The name of Commonwealth, or Republic, moreover, was not then necessarily a cause of distrust and alarm: although that form of government had, until then, prevailed only in secondary States, it had maintained its place in Europe, without disturbing European order by its presence; the great European monarchies had lived on good and peaceable terms with the Republics of Italy, Switzerland, Germany, and the Netherlands. Europe had not yet contracted the habit of considering the republican form of government as the precursor and promoter of revolutions and anarchy.

The English revolution furthermore presented itself as much in a religious as in a political character. The great wars of religion were now at an end; the Treaty of Westphalia had just laid the foundation of a new European order; the Catholic States and the Protestant States had mutually come to an understanding, and among the latter, the most recent and most opposed, the United Provinces, had at length conquered their position and tranquillity. The prevalence of peace between the various Christian communions, if not in the interior of every State, at least in the external relations of countries with one another, had been definitely established; and although religious prejudices and animosities were far from being extinct, neither government nor people were willing to renew a conflict by which all had cruelly suffered, and in which neither party could any longer hope to crush its rival. It is by exhaustion and necessity that God imposes justice and good sense upon nations.

Religious peace restored liberty to politics; religious passions and creeds no longer regulated the designs and alliances of States; the spirit of ambition or of resistance to ambition, of preponderance or independence, of aggrandisement or equilibrium, became the principal motive of the conduct of governments in their international relations; they sought to obtain thereby means of attack or defence in their temporal hopes or fears, and weapons to serve them in their rivalries. The English revolution profited by this new and purely lay character of continental politics. Of the two great powers, France and Spain, which then contested for the ascendency in Europe, neither wished to quarrel with the young Commonwealth; they both did their best either to draw it into their camp, or keep it from joining the enemy; and two systems of alliance, more or less complete, and more or less openly avowed between France, England, and the United Provinces on the one side, and between Spain, England, and the United Provinces on the other, were the constant thought of Mazarin and Don Luis de Haro at Paris and Madrid, and the object of the unceasing labours of their agents in London.[1]

The republican Parliament had a just, though confused and incomplete consciousness of its position: it understood that it was detested, but in no respect menaced, by the great European monarchies, and it conducted itself towards them with caution and dignity, but without uneasiness or angry feeling. It showed no anxiety to be recognised by them, neither did it hasten to accredit representatives of the Commonwealth to their courts. Not that it felt no impatience on this subject; it frequently sounded the foreign agents who still remained in England, Bellièvre, Croullé, Cardenas, and Joachim; sometimes in order to learn from them what sort of a reception would be given at their respective courts to the ministers whom the Commonwealth might send, and sometimes to intimate to them that they could not themselves continue to reside in London unless they received from their govern-

[1] Letters of Anthony Lebrun, Spanish Ambassador in Holland, to Don Alonzo de Cardeñas, November 29, 1649; of Cardeñas to Philip IV., January 23 and February 15, 1652; and of the Archduke Leopold to Philip IV., February 6, 1652: in the Archives of Simancas. Letters of Croullé to Mazarin, January 10, 1650; and of Servien to Croullé, January 28, 1650: in the Archives des Affaires Etrangères de France.

ments fresh credentials accrediting them to the Parliament.[1] This strong desire to be formally recognised was exhibited from time to time by indirect means. " It has been printed here," wrote Croullé to Mazarin. " that the State-councillors of France had treated with the English merchants on the subject of the business they transact, and had thereby recognised the Parliament as representing the Commonwealth. I hope they will rest contented with this imaginary recognition."[2] The Parliament was not thus easily satisfied ; it continued, on the contrary, to prove itself at once exacting and impatient in this respect; determined to wait for the recognition of the Commonwealth so long as it was not complete and satisfactory ; and deliberating, on various occasions, and with jealous susceptibility, upon the formalities to be observed in the relations of the Commonwealth with foreign governments.[3] But its attitude was calm and dignified at the same time : it publicly declared its intention to maintain all the existing treaties between England and other States ;[4] it recommended the Council of State to employ consuls in all foreign countries, in order that friendly commercial relations might not be broken off ;[5] it retained in France an officious agent, named Angier, who actively watched over English interests ;[6] and it remained in frequent and courteous communication with some of the foreign ministers in London, particularly the Spanish envoy Cardenas and the Dutch ambassador Joachim, who had not yet received fresh letters of credence, but who were known to be well disposed towards the Commonwealth. In spite of numerous marks of inexperience, and some tendency to arrogance, the conduct of the republican leaders, in regard to foreign policy, was characterised by dignified reserve and intelligent prudence, and by a desire to remain at peace abroad, so as not to aggravate the difficulties and burdens of their government at home.

On one point only they engaged, unreservedly and at all risks,

---

[1] Letters from Croullé to Mazarin, November 15 and December 6, 1649, and November 7, 1650; and from Servien to Croullé, November 6, 1649 : in the Archives des Affaires Etrangères de France. Letters from Cardenas to Philip IV., June 20 and August 13, 1649; and Deliberations in the Council of State at Madrid on the Recognition of the Commonwealth of England, October 9, 1649, and May 7, 1650 : in the Archives of Simancas.

[2] Archives des Affaires Etrangères de France.

[3] Commons' Journals, vol. vi. pp. 416, 517, 618; vol. vii. p. 64.

[4] Thurloe's State Papers, vol. i. p. 133.

[5] Commons' Journals, vol. vi. p. 333.

[6] Ibid. pp. 132, 491.

K

in a bold and even violent course of action. In the month of June,
1648, a considerable portion of the fleet, eleven vessels, had revolted from the Parliament, and sailed over to Holland to place
themselves under the orders of the Prince of Wales, for the service
of the imprisoned King. In the month of October following, Prince
Rupert was appointed admiral of this royal fleet: though until then
unused to the sea, he was a man of dashing bravery, fond of adventure, fearless of a life of hardship and uncertainty, familiar and
liberal towards his inferiors ; he soon became as popular with the
sailors as with the soldiers, and he continued on sea, against the
Commonwealth, the same determined, wandering, and predatory
warfare which he had waged on land against the Parliament.
Charles II. was then living in a state of deep distress ; he was in
want of money to help his partisans, to pay his servants, to send
messages to the Queen his mother, and even to undertake a journey
himself. His brother-in-law, the Prince of Orange, could not, notwithstanding his generous friendship, supply all his wants ; some
few of the princes of the Continent, the Duke of Lorraine, the
Queen of Sweden, the King of Poland, and the Czar of Russia, made
him occasional loans or presents; his faithful friends in England sent
him a part of what was left them after confiscations and sequestrations ; but these supplies were speedily exhausted : Charles had no
permanent or certain income.   He sought and found, in the fleet
commanded by Prince Rupert, precarious though sometimes abundant
resources ; it sailed up and down the Channel, in the North Sea,
and all round England, making numerous and rich prizes from the
mercantile fleet of the Commonwealth, and often at haphazard from
that of any country : it was a fleet of corsairs under a royal flag,
sent out to provide for the expenses of a proscribed king. Many
private shipowners, English, Scotch, French, and Dutch, requested
permission to share in this life of adventure and profit, by equipping
ships at their own cost ; leave was readily granted or sold to them ;
orders were issued by Charles II. for the regulation of this service
and the division of the booty ; a fifteenth part of the value of all
the prizes taken was allotted to the King, and a tenth to the
admiral ; the remainder was divided into three parts, one for the
owners of the vessel, one for the purveyors of provisions and
stores, and the third for the crew, among whom it was distributed
in proportion to the rank and position of every man, from the
admiral down to the common sailor. All commercial and personal
security disappeared from the British waters ; they became an
arena of incessant depredations, — of a privateering warfare, in
which the vessels even of the King of France, and of the States-

General of Holland, disguising their flags, did not fail frequently to engage.[1]

Against this ruinous and insulting danger, the republican Parliament immediately took the most vigorous measures. No sooner had it acceded to power than it re-organised and augmented, by all available means, the fleet which remained at its disposal: on the 2nd of February, 1649, thirty merchant vessels were engaged for the service of the State, and equipped for war; the naval forces voted in March, 1650, for the campaign of the following summer, amounted to sixty-five ships and 8150 men; and during the winter of 1650–1651, thirty-nine vessels, manned by 4190 sailors, and carrying 954 guns, were specially set apart for the protection of the English coasts. The impressment of sailors was rigorously carried on. Large provision was made for all the expenses of the naval forces, for the payment and promotion of the officers, and for the wages, maintenance, and rewarding of the sailors. Vane was president of the committee of the navy, and introduced his spirit of intelligent and zealous activity into all the departments of the service. Blake, Dean, Popham, Ayscue, Penn and Baddeley were placed in command of various squadrons, and sent to cruise in the Channel or the North Sea, off the coasts of Ireland, France, Holland, Portugal, and Spain, and even in the Mediterranean, the Levant, and the West Indies. Most of them were officers of the land army, without nautical experience, but of tried boldness and capacity, devoted to the Commonwealth, eager for success and glory for their country and themselves, caring little what it might cost either themselves or their country, and firmly resolved to maintain everywhere and at any price the honour and safety of the English name and flag.[2]

To these well-provided and ably commanded material forces, the Parliament added legislative measures no less efficacious for the protection of the national commerce. It regulated the laws relating to maritime prizes in the way most calculated to excite the ardour and to recompense the efforts of its seamen.[3] It called home all those who were serving in foreign fleets; and to such English merchants as had suffered heavy losses at sea by visits from foreign

[1] Clarendon's History of the Rebellion, vol. vi. pp. 23, 31, 110, 148—152; Granville Penn's Memorials of the Life of Sir William Penn, vol. i. pp. 260, 266; Hepworth Dixon's Life of Admiral Blake, pp. 114—118; Warburton's Memoirs of Prince Rupert and the Cavaliers, vol. iii. pp. 250, 266, 286—297; Whitelocke, pp. 308, 349, 447.

[2] Commons' Journals, vol. vi. pp. 129, 134, 148, 149, 156, 375, 407; Memorials of Sir William Penn, vol. i. pp. 291—297, 302—304.

[3] Commons' Journals, vol. vi. pp 202, 204.

vessels, it secured the means of obtaining redress for their injuries.[1]
A declaration of Louis XIV. had recently prohibited the introduction
into France of all woollen stuffs or silks manufactured in England ;
the Parliament directed the Council of State to prepare a report
upon the different treaties which had hitherto regulated the commercial relations of the two countries, and on the ground that the
recent prohibition was illegitimate, it forbade in its turn the introduction into England of wines, woollen stuffs, and silks from
France.[2]   " And to those who told them that this exclusion would
not be effectual, and that they could not do without our wines,"
wrote Croullé to Mazarin, " they answered jocosely that men soon
got accustomed to anything, and that, as they had without inconvenience dispensed with a king, contrary to the general belief, so they
could also easily dispense with our French wines."[3]

Success attended these vigorous measures, ordered by an imperious government, and executed by bold and able agents.   The
republican fleet sailed into every sea, sometimes convoying the
English merchant ships, sometimes making rich prizes of foreign
traders, chasing the flag of Charles II. everywhere to the death, and
inspiring wherever it went that mingled fear and respect which is
always felt for a power which acts with rapidity and energy.   Prince
Rupert, towards the end of the winter of 1649, was cruising off the
eastern and southern coast of Ireland, with a view to second the
operations of the royal army in that island, and to seize the merchant
vessels which were always numerous in those waters.   Blake sailed
thither in pursuit of him, and blockaded him in the port of
Kinsale.   Rupert managed to escape with his fleet; but he lost
three of his ships, and repaired with the rest to the coast of Portugal, to resume his random life of freebooting and adventure.   Blake
followed him thither by order of the Parliament, taking with
him Charles Vane, a brother of Sir Harry Vane, who had been
commissioned to lay before the King of Portugal the complaints and
demands of the Commonwealth.   Both fleets anchored opposite
each other at the mouth of the Tagus, and both began negotiations
with the Court of Lisbon,—Rupert that it should continue to
support him, and Blake that it should cease to do so.   Rupert
found great favour both at the Court and among the people of Portugal : on his arrival, King John IV. had sent several of his officers
to meet him, and conduct him in state to the palace ; and whenever
he came on shore, the populace of Lisbon thronged around him

[1] Commons' Journals, vol. vi. pp. 379, 397.
[2] Ibid. pp. 284, 285.
[3] Archives des Affaires Etrangères de France.

with noisy acclamations. Blake, on the contrary, was an object of deep antipathy both to the Court and people, who were ardently royalist and Catholic in their opinions: whenever his sailors left their ships, they were insulted and sometimes maltreated, either by Prince Rupert's men, or by the Portuguese themselves. Paying but little attention to these manifestations of ill-will, Blake demanded of King John to rid his dominions of pirates who had robbed the Commonwealth of England of a portion of its fleet by debauching its sailors; and stated that he had orders to pursue and destroy them as enemies of all regular commerce between civilised nations; but if the King of Portugal would not himself undertake to drive the pirates from his ports, he desired that at least he would not take it ill that the English admiral should enter the harbour with his squadron, and execute the commission which he had received from his government. The indignation which this demand produced at Lisbon was immense; the Queen and the Prince Royal sustained the somewhat tottering courage of the King, who was advised by some of his ministers to yield. A nobleman of high rank was sent to Blake with complimentary messages and presents, but with orders to repulse his pretensions and to refuse him admittance into the harbour. Blake tried to force an entrance, but without success: his ships were fired on by the forts at the mouth of the river, and he was obliged to desist. He then began to make reprisals upon the commerce of Portugal; no ships, either royal or mercantile, were allowed either to enter or leave the port of Lisbon; Blake seized first five, and then nine, and he afterwards destroyed a rich fleet of twenty-three vessels from Brazil, declaring that he would not cease hostilities until the royalist pirates were either delivered up or ordered away. The Court of Lisbon alternated between anger and fear; it ordered the arrest and imprisonment of the English merchants resident in that capital; and Charles Vane, finding it impossible to obtain the restoration of their liberty and property, re-embarked on board the fleet, and returned to England. But at the same time, the King of Portugal urged Prince Rupert to withdraw, unless he considered himself strong enough to attack Blake's fleet and deliver the kingdom of his presence. Rupert one day appeared disposed to give battle; but Blake had received a reinforcement of eight vessels under Admiral Popham, and he manifested such eagerness to begin the attack himself, that Rupert retired beneath the protection of the forts, and at last contrived to escape, with great difficulty, from the port of Lisbon, to seek fortune and safety in the Mediterranean. Blake pursued him along the Spanish coast as he had done along that of Portugal;

and the same hesitations between favour and disfavour, the same
alternations of anger and fear which had agitated the Court
of Lisbon when in presence of these two rival fleets, disturbed,
though more remotely, the Court of Madrid.   As soon as
Prince Rupert appeared off Malaga, the two ambassadors of
Charles II. in Spain, Cottington and Hyde, informed the Spanish
government of his arrival, and claimed a favourable reception for
the cousin and fleet of their King.   Don Luis de Haro readily
promised it, as much from disquietude at the presence of so
formidable a foreign force, as from favour to a royal fleet.   But it
was learned soon after at Madrid that the republican fleet was
also off the coast of Spain, pursuing that of King Charles, and
demanding, as at Lisbon, admittance into the Spanish ports,
in order to attack and destroy it.   Equally violent and imperious
claims were asserted by both parties simultaneously: Rupert, after
having sunk several English merchant vessels before Malaga,
demanded of the governor to arrest on shore, and deliver into
his hands the master of one of those ships, who had taken
an active part against King Charles, that " he might boil him in
pitch."   This the governor refused to do.   Blake, on his side,
learning that Prince Rupert had landed, urged the Spanish
authorities to deliver him up to him, as a leader of pirates, and an
enemy of all nations.   The Court of Madrid took refuge against
these impetuous demands, in delay and inactivity.   The war
between the two fleets continued for some months longer on
the Spanish coast: at length, Blake destroyed the greater part of
the royal fleet in an engagement off Malaga; and Rupert, left with
two vessels only, wandered for some time in the Mediterranean, and
then, passing through the Straits, sailed to the Atlantic and along
the Western coast of Africa, in search of opportunities for making
new prizes without having to fight the fleet of the Commonwealth.
The republican navy remained predominant in the seas of south-
western Europe; Penn and Lawson were sent out in pursuit of
Rupert, of whose whereabouts nothing was known; and Blake was
recalled to England, to resume, in concert with Dean and Popham,
the command of the fleet in the Channel and the North Sea.   There
the republican navy was in presence of more formidable rivals; but
there also it had already given abundant proof of its vigour
and daring.   French commerce especially had paid dear for the
prizes which its privateers had made at first upon the English.   In
the month of September, 1651, the Parliament declared that, as it
could not obtain justice from the King of France, it had determined
to do itself justice; six French ships, arrested by captains of

vessels in the service of the State, were definitively confiscated, and no satisfaction was given to the remonstrances which arrived from Paris on the subject.[1] At sea the Parliament felt its strength, and had made it felt; its flag floated proudly on the breeze, feared by its enemies and respected by its rivals.

But its success and skill, in matters of foreign policy, extended only thus far: though, in its maritime affairs, it displayed great ability and energy, in its diplomatic relations and undertakings it was equally deficient in sagacity and good sense, in moderation and resoluteness.

It was in presence of two powers, at ardent rivalry with each other, but placed in very different positions and animated by very different tendencies. Spain, yet glorying in her recent greatness, of which Europe still stood in dread, was rapidly declining; the empire of Germany belonged to her no longer; notwithstanding protracted and sanguinary efforts, she had lost the United Provinces; her dominion in Italy was limited: a conspiracy had in one day robbed her of Portugal: afar off, and in the New World only, her possessions continued immense: she was, to use the pithy phrase of Sully, "one of those States which have strong arms and legs, but a weak and debilitated heart."[2] Amid the splendour of its court, and the pomposity of its language, the Spanish government felt itself really weak, and sought to conceal its weakness by immobility. Philip IV. and Don Luis de Haro, both of them sensible and moderate men—the one from idleness, and the other from prudence—and tired of conflicts which resulted only in defeat, aspired solely to the security of peace, and devoted their utmost care to avoiding all questions and circumstances which would have imposed upon them efforts of which they did not feel themselves capable. Divided and enervated, the House of Austria retained perhaps less ambition than power, and, except in cases of absolute necessity, pompous inertness was the policy of the successors of Charles V.

France and the House of Bourbon, on the contrary, were advancing together with bold and rapid progress. a potent spirit of activity and ambition animated both the councils of the crown and

---

[1] Memorials of Prince Rupert, vol. iii. pp. 288—388; Clarendon's History of the Rebellion, vol. vi. pp. 270,390—395; vol. vii. pp. 65. 66; Thurloe's State Papers, vol. i. pp. 134, 137, 138, 140—142, 154—158; Whitelocke, pp. 410, 423, 446, 449, 458, 463, 470, 471, 475, 476, 484—486, 515, 520; Dixon's Life of Blake, pp. 122—165.

[2] Sully to Président Jeannin, in the Négociations du Président Jeannin, p. 261.

the various classes, more especially the superior classes, of citizens; a taste for great designs and striking enterprises everywhere pre- vailed, without any fear of the labours and responsibilities which they entail.   Thus, notwithstanding civil dissensions and fruitless endeavours for political liberty, the State grew stronger and more extended ; the national unity and the royal authority received simultaneous development.   As persevering as he was supple, and by turns a conqueror and a fugitive, but always a favourite and first minister, whether in exile or at Paris, Mazarin pursued the work of Henry IV. and of Richelieu, through alternate successes and reverses, in war and at court.   The government and the country displayed at once the characteristics of youth and age, were guided by powerful traditions in the midst of an entirely new movement, and yet were full of strength and thirsting for greatness.

Between these two powers, England might either have chosen an ally at her will, or have firmly maintained the balance · notwith- standing their repugnance to the regicide Commonwealth, they were so passionate in their jealousy and fear of one another that they subordinated all other feelings to the desire of mutually depriving each other of so important a supporter.   The republican Parliament adopted neither of these courses : imperfectly appreciating the real strength and future prospects of the two powers, and swayed by old habits of routine, it remained wavering, but not impartial, between Spain and France—affecting neutrality without knowing either how to abandon it opportunely, or to maintain it unimpeachably.

Spain had some slight claims to preference : it was not from Madrid that Queen Henrietta Maria, the constant object of the anti- pathy and hostility of the Parliamentarians, had come ; it was not at Madrid that she still found an asylum and the means of support. At the time of the King's trial, Don Alonzo de Cardenas, on being urged by the royalists to make some demonstration in his favour, had formally refused to do so, saying that he had no instructions from his Court on the subject.[1]   After the proclamation of the Commonwealth, he had remained in London on very good terms with the republican leaders, and he had solicited from his Court the renewal of his letters of credence, giving it to understand that he would turn them to good account, both for the political interests of Spain, and for the religious interests of the English Catholics.[2]

[1] Letter from Cardeñas to King Philip IV., February 15, 1649; in the Archives of Simancas.

[2] The same to the same, February 18, 1649.

Philip IV. and Don Luis de Haro were less hasty than Cardenas; they would have preferred to declare neither for nor against Charles II. or the Commonwealth, to take secret advantage of the favourable tendencies of the one, to give some underhand expressions of sympathy with the other, and to wait events in complete inaction. Such was the constant drift of the opinions of the Spanish Council of State, when consulted by its King, sometimes upon the despatches of Cardenas, and sometimes on those of Charles II. and his ambassadors. For more than a year, this policy of indifference and inertness was pursued at Madrid: no fresh instructions, no new powers were sent to Cardenas; an attempt was made to prevent Cottington and Hyde from coming to Madrid, and as that failed, no heed was taken of their presence.[1] When they learned that Anthony Ascham was about to arrive in Spain, on a mission from the Parliament, they expressed their indignant surprise "that his Catholic Majesty should be the first Christian Prince that would receive an ambassador from the odious and execrable murderers of a Christian King, his brother and ally; which no other prince had yet done, out of the detestation of that horrible parricide."[2] The Council of State deliberated upon their remonstrance; and again, some months after, upon their request that Prince Rupert and his fleet might be well received in all the ports of Spain.[3] A direct answer either to their demands or complaints was sedulously avoided: both in regard to the republican Commonwealth and the proscribed King, the chief desire of the Court of Madrid was to say nothing, and to remain in inactivity.

But their relative positions gradually altered: the Parliament became more exacting; Cardenas wrote to his King that they refused to treat with him, and that he would be obliged to leave England, unless he received fresh letters of credence, in which the Commonwealth was expressly recognised.[4] The assassination of Ascham, and the perseverance of the Parliament in its endeavours to obtain justice upon his murderers, plunged the Court of Madrid into great embarrassment. Charles II., on his side, treated Spain with ill humour; he went to Paris, under the pretext of visiting the Queen his mother, but in reality, it was said, for the purpose of

[1] Deliberations of the Council of State at Madrid, March 13—29, May 4, June 6, and August 2, 1649; in the Archives of Simancas.
[2] Clarendon's History of the Rebellion, vol vi. p. 412; Note from Lord Cottington and Hyde to Philip IV., May 10, 1650; in the Archives of Simancas.
[3] Deliberations of the Council of State at Madrid, May 10 and October 22, 1650; in the Archives of Simancas.
[4] Cardenas to King Philip IV., June 20, 1649.

receiving the advice and directions of Mazarin : and he bestowed
the name of *brother* on the King of Portugal, who in Spain was
always termed a *tyrant* and *usurper*.[1]   The republican Parliament,
on the other hand, was rough in its treatment of the House of
Braganza, and had almost made war on it, because of the support
it had given to Prince Rupert and his fleet.   After hesitating
twenty-one months, the Court of Madrid at length came to a decision ; it dismissed from Spain the two ambassadors of Charles II.,
and sent fresh letters of credence to Cardenas, accrediting him
to the Parliament of the Commonwealth.   At the same time Juan
de Guimaraes arrived in London, sent by the King of Portugal to
put an end to the misunderstanding between the two countries.
The Parliament made Guimaraes wait fifteen days before giving
him permission to come to London ; and even then it was carried
by a majority of one vote only, and it was decided that he should
be received without public ceremony by a committee of eleven
members.[2]   But only two days after Cardenas had announced the
arrival of his new letters of credence, he was received by the entire
Parliament in solemn audience.[3]   Three Commissioners, one of
whom was the Earl of Salisbury, went to fetch him from his house
in a carriage belonging to the State ; thirty or forty other carriages
accompanied him, filled with Spanish and English gentlemen ; two
regiments of cavalry were drawn up before Whitehall as he
passed ; and he was escorted by a regiment of infantry.   On his
entrance into the hall in which the Parliament was assembled,
he took his seat in an arm-chair which had been prepared for
him, delivered to the Speaker his letters of credence, which were
written in the Latin language, and pronounced a long speech
in Spanish, in which he congratulated himself on being the first
who came, in the name of the greatest prince of Christendom,
to recognise that House as the supreme power in the nation,
and narrated with much detail the steps taken by the King his
master to secure the punishment of the murderers of Ascham, and
to make Prince Rupert withdraw from the ports of Spain.   Republican pride took pleasure in receiving with such pomp this
striking homage from a monarch ; a few austere Puritans alone
were dissatisfied by it.   " I fear," wrote Bradshaw to one of Cromwell's officers, " our impatient haste to ingratiate with neighbouring

---

[1] Antoine Lebrun to Cardenas, from the Hague, November 29, 1649;
and Cardenas to King Philip IV., December 14, 1649 ; in the Archives of
Simancas.
[2] Commons' Journals, vol. vi. pp. 504, 510, 511, 516, 519, 522, 529, 530.
[3] Ibid, vol. vi. pp. 513, 515.

nations hath done us neither honour nor profit. God grant we may depend upon Him, and seek aright for His owning of us, and that we may be independent enough as to all others! But in these things I have many dissenting brethren, and I write to one much abler to judge, and therefore abstain."[1]

At the same time that the Parliament was bestowing upon, and receiving from, the Spanish ambassador these striking marks of mutual good-will, the house of the French Chargé-d'affaires, Croullé, was broken into by a band of soldiers, and he was himself arrested, taken before the Council of State, and ordered to leave England within ten days. "Although Messieurs les Espagnols have waited till the last moment," he wrote immediately to Cardinal Mazarin, "they have not failed to be well received; and as it cannot have been without conditions that they have resolved to take this step, the principal of which conditions would be to be on bad terms with France, they thought fit to precede that ceremony by an action which would prove their desire to disoblige that country. Yesterday when, in accordance with the permission I have received from Court to keep a priest in my service, he was saying mass before an audience of several Frenchmen and a very few English, a company of soldiers came into my house, secured the doors, and, having entered, began to beat and maltreat all whom they met, and I was of the number. A French gentleman and I, by opposing ourselves to the violence which they were about to do to the altar, gave sufficient time to the officiating priest to divest himself of his robes and to mix with the crowd, whence I found means to take him, and to shut him up in my cabinet, so that he was not seen. The soldiers having made themselves absolute masters of everything, I went with an English nobleman and two French gentlemen to lay my complaint before the President of the Council, who, without deigning to hear me, had me arrested and confined in the guard-house and in a wretched inn until nightfall. At about six o'clock I was summoned before the Council of State, where, having given a simple and truthful narrative of the affair, it was resolved to order me to leave the country; which having been communicated to me by the President, I told him that I was here by the command of the King my master, whom I would inform of what he had stated to me, and that as soon as I had received his Majesty's orders, I would obey them without delay. To which the President having replied, that what I had then said evinced more contempt of the Council than anything I had said before, that no kings had authority to give

<hr />

[1] Milton's State Papers, p. 40.

orders in that country, and that, if I did not obey, they would proceed against me in the usual course; I answered that when I had spoken of his Majesty's commands, I had understood them as referring only to myself, who, wherever I was, received no other, and that they had in their hands the power and the force to do what they pleased, but not to make me do anything contrary to my duty; upon which I withdrew. This morning a messenger from the Council of State has brought me their orders, with a passport for me to leave the country within ten days, with which I must comply. I shall, however, wait the commands which it shall please your Eminence to send me."[1]

Mazarin felt the utmost displeasure at this incident; he had long been disturbed by the intrigues of Cardenas in London, and by the preference given to Spain by the English Government. On the 6th of August, 1649, he had written to Croullé, by M. Servien:— "I beg you not to lose any opportunity for filling the Parliament with the greatest distrust of the Spaniards, which I doubt not you will do vigorously and adroitly upon all occasions;" and a few months later he wrote:—"It would be well for the Parliament of England to furnish us secretly with some assistance in men or money, to enable us to defend ourselves against the great preparations which the Spaniards are making to attack us on all sides in the coming campaign. . . . At least you must always make it your object to prevent them from giving any help to the enemy, on the false representations which Cardenas will make to them."[2] The information which Croullé transmitted to Mazarin had never been calculated to allay his anxieties: at one time he sent him an account of the marks of favour which the Parliament was bestowing on Cardenas; at another, the announcement, well or ill founded, that a hundred thousand pounds sterling had been sent from London to Madrid, to help Spain in the war against France. MM. de Bouillon and Turenne, who were then the leaders of the Fronde, had, it was said, written to Cromwell to request his support, and the republican Council of State contemplated sending part of the fleet which was cruising off Lisbon to assist the insurgent Frondeurs at Bordeaux.[3] A report was spread that Cromwell, after having subjugated Ireland, would make a journey into France: by a

[1] Letter from Croullé to Mazarin; Archives des Affaires Etrangères de France.

[2] Letters from Servien to Croullé; Archives des Affaires Etrangères de France.

[3] Letters from Croullé to Mazarin, January 10, May 16, July 4, and September 12, 1650; in the Archives des Affaires Etrangères de France.

singular misapprehension, Mazarin at first saw in this only a friendly
intention, and Servien immediately wrote to Croullé :—" If, at the
close of his expedition in Ireland, Mr. Cromwell comes into France,
being, as he is, a person of merit, he will be well received here ; for
assuredly every one will go to meet him at the place where he dis-
embarks."[1] But Croullé's letters quickly disabused the Cardinal :—
" I know of no persuasion strong enough," he wrote, " to remove
from the minds of all that, as soon as Cromwell has done in
Ireland, he will pass into France with his army. . . . . All
that is said about his design proceeds from those who desire it
from different motives of interest ; and from this cause he is made
to say a quantity of things which I have always neglected to write,
as being destitute of certainty and likelihood ; as, among other
things, that, looking at his hair, which is already white, he said
that, if he were ten years younger, there is not a king in Europe
whom he would not make to tremble, and that, as he had a better
motive than the late King of Sweden, he believed himself still
capable of doing more for the good of nations than the other ever
did for his own ambition."[2]

Whether true or false, these rumours and sayings gave Mazarin
great anxiety ; the declared hostility of England would have seriously
aggravated the difficulties of his precarious position at home, and
the embarrassments of his foreign policy, which he obstinately
pursued, in spite of all personal inconveniences. By his side,
Colbert,. as yet a mere councillor of State, and intendant of the
Cardinal's household, but already passionately devoted to the maintenance of the national prosperity, unremittingly denounced the
sufferings and losses which were inflicted upon French commerce
by the prohibitive measures of the republican Parliament, and the
underhand and irregular warfare waged between the navies of the
two States. Mazarin absolutely needed powerful allies in Europe ;
Colbert required security for French commerce, both on land and
sea. For a moment, Mazarin indulged the hope of being able to
conclude an effectual alliance with the United Provinces against
Spain and England : the Count d'Estrades, who had long been
ambassador in Holland, was, in 1650, governor of Dunkirk ; and on
the 2nd of September, the Prince of Orange wrote to him—" The
confidence which I have in your friendship, and in that which you
entertained for my late father, leads me to hope that you will not

[1] Letter from Servien to Croullé ; in the Archives des Affaires Etrangères
de France.
[2] Letters from Croullé to Mazarin ; Archives des Affaires Etrangères de
France.

refuse me the request which I make to you to come and visit me at
the Hague as soon as possible, as I have very important affairs to
communicate to you." This communication was a project of a
treaty by which Louis XIV. and the Prince of Orange were to bind
themselves "to make war in common against Spain, and at the
same time to break with Cromwell, by endeavouring, by all sorts of
means, to restore the King of England to his kingdom." D'Estrades
sent for instructions to Mazarin, who immediately replied : " The
Queen has commanded me to give you orders to proceed without
delay into Holland, to the Prince of Orange ; and in order that you
may be in a position to treat with him, if you find him disposed to
break with Spain, I send you the King's authority to conclude the
treaty ; and it would be the greatest service you could possibly
render his Majesty. For my own part, I shall be very grateful to
you if you induce that Prince to break with Spain ; which would
frustrate all the measures of my enemies, and dissipate the cabals
and factions which are appearing at Court and in the Parliament
against me. I beg you to neglect no effort to secure the success of
this affair, which is most important."[1]

The affair did not succeed : the Prince of Orange died on the
6th of November, 1650 ; and towards the end of the same year,
Mazarin found himself standing alone, in presence of Spain, which
still continued hostile, of the British Commonwealth, which had
been officially recognised by Spain, of the United Provinces,
which had been detached from the cause of monarchy by the
death of their Stadtholder ; and without any relations, even
officious, with England, from whence his agent had been expelled.

From character as much as from policy, it was impossible for
him to remain in this position ; as impatient as he was crafty, and
making small account of mortifications, he was one of those men
who rush into action in order to escape from embarrassment, and
who expose themselves to a fresh repulse rather than make no
attempt to repair those which they have suffered. The French
merchants insisted strongly upon the renewal of pacific relations
with England; they attempted themselves to enter into direct
correspondence with the republican Parliament and Council.
Salomon, Vicomte de Virelade, wrote in their name from Paris, to
the British Council of State, to request a safe conduct to come to
London and negotiate on their behalf: " No one here," replied
Walter Frost, the Secretary of the Council of State, " could treat

[1] Lettres, Mémoires et Négociations de M. le Comte d'Estrades, vol. i.
pp. 99—103.

with you concerning these affairs, excepting only the sovereign power, or those whom it might depute; and that power will receive no address from any but the sovereign power of France, which alone can give the necessary authority for treating of such affairs. I cannot therefore obtain for you a passport to come hither in the capacity which you indicate. . . . But if the State of France will, by you, make overtures of a public address to this Commonwealth regarding these affairs, in the manner usual between sovereign States, I have no doubt that this State will be glad to receive any honest and just propositions which will tend to terminate differences, and restore freedom of trade for the common advantage."[1]

Colbert now came to the assistance of the merchants: he drew up a statement in which, after laying down the principle that " for the restoration of trade two things were necessary—safety and liberty," he proceeded to enumerate the facts which deprived all trade between France and England of these two conditions of existence, and indicated, without hesitation, the means by which they might be recovered. " The point on which the English most strongly insist," he said, at the close of his report, " is the recognition of their Commonwealth, in which the Spaniards have preceded us. A closer union is consequently to be feared as the result of the negotiations of the Spanish ambassador in England. It is for our lords, the ministers, to prescribe the form of this recognition, how far it should extend; in which France will be excusable before God and men, if she be compelled to proceed to a recognition of that Commonwealth, in order to prevent the leagues and evil designs of the Spaniards, who are guilty of all kinds of injustice, and submit to all imaginable meannesses, in order to injure us."[2]

If he alone had had to decide, Mazarin would probably have acted with promptitude and thoroughness; but he had also to consult Anne of Austria, her council, and her confidants. He presented to her a report, in which the question of the recognition of the Commonwealth of England was carefully discussed. " It seems at first sight," he says, " that if we are guided by the laws of honour or justice, we ought not to recognise this Commonwealth; as the King could do nothing more prejudicial to his reputation than to consent to a recognition by which he would abandon the interest of the legitimate king, his near relative, neighbour, and ally; and

[1] Documents Inédits sur l'Histoire Diplomatique de France, Revue Nouvelle, vol. v. pp. 413—416.
[2] Ibid., vol. v. pp. 409—413.

nothing more unjust than to recognise usurpers who have imbrued their hands in the blood of their sovereign. . . . But as the laws of honour or justice should never lead us to do anything contrary to the dictates of prudence, it must be considered that all the demonstrations which we might now make in favour of the King of England, would not lead to his restoration ; that a longer refusal to recognise the Commonwealth will serve in no way to augment or confirm the rights of the King ; . . . . . that whatever the necessities of the time and of our affairs may compel us to do in favour of the Commonwealth, will not prevent us from afterwards being able to take advantage of any favourable conjunctures that may present themselves, when we shall be in a better condition to attempt some great enterprise ; . . . . . that, moreover, there is reason to fear that, if the Spaniards once become more intimately allied with the English, as they are ardently labouring to be, they will prevent them from consenting to any accommodation with us, and will persuade them, if not to make open war upon us, at least to give them powerful assistance against us. There accordingly remains no room for doubt that we should without delay enter into negotiations with the Commonwealth of England, and give it the title which it desires. One condition is, nevertheless, absolutely necessary ; and without it, it would be useless to pledge ourselves to grant this recognition ; and that is, to be assured beforehand that we shall derive from it some utility, capable of counter-balancing the prejudice which may accrue by it to our reputation : . . . . . it would be doubly prejudicial to condescend to an act of meanness, if, after we had done it, the English should continue in a state of indifference and coolness towards us ; and if our advances only served to make them more haughty and un-yielding, in the conditions of the treaty which must be made with them for the accommodation of the differences which exist between us."[1]

To escape from this danger, and not " expose themselves to public disgrace with no profit," it was resolved first of all to send to London a secret agent, M. de Gentillot, a man of talent, well acquainted with England, and who had already been employed more than once on similar missions. " His Majesty," it was stated in his instructions, " has thought fit that the Sieur de Gentillot, as he is going into England, should labour adroitly and quietly, by means of the friends and connections which he has in that country,

[1] Documents Inédits sur l'Histoire Diplomatique de France, in the Revue Nouvelle, vol. v. pp. 416, 419 ; MSS. de Brienne, in the Bibliothèque Impériale, Paris.

to obtain accurate information whether there is a real disposition to put an end, by a fair accommodation, to the difference which exists between the two nations, and to re-establish a good correspondence between them. He must be assured above all things that the Parliament of England has not made any private treaty with the Spaniards against France, and that it is not so far pledged to them that it will be unable to enter into all the accommodations and confederations which may be judged useful for the two kingdoms. The English will not fail to demand whether the King will openly recognise their Commonwealth by letters and other public demonstrations; in answer to which the Sieur de Gentillot will represent that there will be no difficulty upon that head, and that it is a point which the Parliament may consider as conceded in accordance with its desire; but that it is important for us to be assured that, after the recognition has taken place, we shall not relapse into any rupture or bad understanding, and that hostilities shall entirely cease. This assurance can be no other than the agreement, at the same time, upon a plan of accommodation of the differences which exist between the two nations." Here followed an enumeration of these differences, and of the precise conditions of the treaty which was to terminate them; and the instructions ended thus: "The Sieur de Gentillot may even intimate that, if the Commonwealth of England desires any closer engagement with France, especially against Spain, we are entirely disposed towards such an alliance. . . . In case the said Sieur de Gentillot should find such a disposition on the part of the English, on his giving information thereof, the ambassador who will be sent into England, will be instructed, and will have full powers, to treat of such an alliance."[1]

In taking this step, Mazarin had forgotten to give due consideration to two things—the weakness of his own position, and the pride of the English republicans. At the moment when M. de Gentillot arrived in London, the Frondeurs were victorious in Paris: the Cardinal, obliged to fly, had found an asylum, with great difficulty, first at Havre, and then at Sedan; and the British Parliament, on its side, wishing to be recognised by France as it had recently been by Spain, openly and without further delay, refused to listen to, and even to admit into London, any secret and officious agent. "I regret above all things in the world," wrote M. de Gentillot to M. Servien, "that I did not rightly understand matters be-

[1] Documents Inédits sur l'Histoire Diplomatique de France; Revue Nouvelle, vol. v. pp. 419—422.

L

fore I undertook this journey: these people have too much
cause for complaint; they wish to be addressed in due form,
and to be treated with in the same way as other powers. I have
done everything that was possible to be done ; but all has been of
no avail.   It was thought that you had sent me hither only to act
as a spy upon their affairs.   Either from that or some other reason,
or to show us that they cannot admit any kind of negotiation which
evades a recognition of their power, it is certain that very abruptly
they sent for me on Friday, as a private individual, to come to
them : six deputies of the Council of State examined me a little,
went away to make their report, and shortly afterwards sent a
secretary to give me an act which ordains that I must leave London
within three days : in obedience to which, I leave this to-day, which
is my third day ; and I shall cross over to Calais to await an answer
to this despatch."[1] No further orders were given to M. de Gentillot ;
he returned to Paris, and the rest of the year 1651 passed away,
without any fresh attempt at an accommodation being made between
the Court of France and the republican Parliament.

This was thought of very little consequence in London, for the
Commonwealth and its leaders were in one of those periods of good
fortune and hope which deceive governments, and especially new
governments, as to their real strength, and give manifestation to all
the dreams of their pride.   At the same time that its recognition
by Spain introduced the young Commonwealth into the society of
European States, the death of William, Prince of Orange, laid
open to the influence of England the United Provinces, the very
one of those States to which it was bound by the most natural links
of position and interest.   Both of them Protestant and republican,
the one hardly victorious, and the other still engaged in the struggle
for the defence of its faith and liberties, the two nations had the
same cause to maintain, in the name of analogous ideas, and frequently against the same enemies.   Everything invited them to a
close alliance.   A serious obstacle opposed this at the outset : two
great parties—the patrician burghers of the towns on the one side,
and on the other, the House of Nassau, supported by the remains
of the feudal nobility, and by the masses—disputed for the government of the United Provinces : both were powerful and worthy of
respect, for both had gloriously fought and suffered for the independence of their country.   When the victory was won, they
immediately began a secret as well as an open conflict; the one

[1] Documents Inédits sur l'Histoire Diplomatique de France ; MSS. de
Brienne, in the Bibliothèque Impériale, Paris.

party aspiring to found an aristocratic and federal republic, the other tending to transform, under the name of a Stadtholderate, the confederation of the United Provinces into a sole and hereditary sovereignty; a deplorable disunion, in which both parties, obeying noble impulses, and sustaining legitimate interests, aggravated beyond measure, by their passions, the importance of their disagreements, and were, in turn, equally regardless of what their strength could effect, and of what their country desired. As long as the Prince of Orange lived, he secured the preponderance, in the councils of the United Provinces, of a policy hostile to the British Commonwealth, not, however, without great efforts, or with complete success. He would have desired to engage the confederation in the cause of Charles II., even at the cost of war : this was evidently more than was consistent with the welfare or the public feeling of the country. The province of Holland, in which commercial interests and the patrician burghers predominated, energetically supported a peaceful and neutral policy; it maintained friendly relations, on its own account, with the English Parliament, taking care to keep on good terms with its merchants, and to show it particular respect on all occasions ; it even sent and maintained for some time in London, a special agent, Gerard Schaep, whom the Parliament received and treated with great distinction.[1] A rupture between the two States was thus prevented, but this was the limit of the influence of the province of Holland and its magistrates ; they could not prevent the Prince of Orange, seconded by the jealousies of the other provinces, and by the popular feeling of the country, from securing the preponderance of a royalist policy in the general conduct of affairs. Not only did the States-General bestow on Charles II. all such marks of interest, and all such indirect support, as would not absolutely pledge them to his service, but they admitted him to confer with them, to explain to them his position and views, to ask their advice ; and at the same time, they refused to grant any audience to the Resident of the English Commonwealth, Walter Strickland, who had remained at the Hague after the murder of his colleague, Dorislaus, and neither his repeated demands, nor the formal protest of the States of the province of Holland, could overcome their refusal.[2] Strickland returned to London, and in giving an account of his mission to Parliament, with the bitterness of a disappointed diplomatist, made it aware of the deep-rooted enmity with which it

---

[1] Commons' Journals, vol. vi. pp. 414, 421, 422, 425.
[2] Leclerc's Histoire des Provinces Unies, vol. ii. p. 272 ; Commons' Journals, vol. vi. pp. 295, 315 ; Thurloe's State Papers, vol. i. pp. 113—115, Clarendon's History of the Rebellion, vol. vi. p. 470.

was regarded by the Prince of Orange, and the States-General, over which he had complete control.[1]

On the death of the Prince of Orange, a complete change took place in this state of things. Notwithstanding that great marks of respect and affection were shown towards his family, neither his dignities nor his power were transmitted to the child to whom his widow, the Princess Mary Stuart, gave birth a few days after his death, and who afterwards became William III., King of England. The magistrates of the principal towns, the families of De Witt, Bicker, De Waal, Ruyl, Voorhout, and others, resumed the functions of which the Prince had violently deprived them; the municipal aristocracy and the province of Holland, in which its chief strength resided, regained their ascendency in the central government; an extraordinary assembly of the States-General restored to vigour the republican traditions of the confederation; everything announced that a pacific and even friendly policy towards the Commonwealth of England would be substituted for the royalist and hostile policy of the Prince of Orange. Never could a more favourable opportunity have presented itself for the conclusion, between the two Protestant republics, of that intimate alliance which their position seemed to indicate to them.[2]

The Parliament hastened to seize it, and determined that ambassadors extraordinary should be sent to the Hague to settle all differences, and treat of an alliance, between the two States. In order to give this embassy greater authority, it was intrusted to the Chief-Justice, Oliver St. John, one of the ablest leaders of the Parliament during the civil war, and of the Commonwealth since its victory, and moreover, an intimate friend and councillor of Cromwell. St. John refused at first, on the ground of ill-health. He was a selfish, arrogant, and timid revolutionist, satisfied with his judicial position and his indirect influence in the government, and unwilling to compromise either his self-respect or his safety in a mission which would certainly be difficult, and might perhaps be dangerous. The House would not accept his refusal, appointed Walter Strickland as his colleague, gave them their instructions, and despatched them on their mission, which was surrounded with unusual splendour. Forty gentlemen, and a retinue of about two hundred servants, accompanied them. St. John took Thurloe with him as his secretary. On their arrival in Holland,

<hr>

[1] Commons' Journals, vol. vi. p. 452.

[2] Wicquefort's Histoire des Provinces Unies, vol. iv. pp. 200—220; Leclerc's Histoire des Provinces Unies. vol. ii. pp. 288—303; Wagenaar's Vaderlandsche Historie, vol. xii. p. 118, et seq.

first at Rotterdam, and then at the Hague, they were received with no less attention and solemnity. A deputation from the States-General came to meet them, attended by twenty-seven carriages; they expressed great regret that they could not lodge them in the house devoted by the State to the reception of foreign ambassadors, as it was already occupied by the French ambassador, M. de Bellièvre; they were therefore established in a private house, and most of their suite were lodged in the neighbourhood, going and coming through the streets incessantly, but always in parties of three or four, and carrying their swords in their hands or under their arms, as though they thought themselves in a hostile country, and surrounded by the murderers of Dorislaus. The English royalists were indeed very numerous at the Hague, in the train of the Princess of Orange and of the Duke of York, and very much inclined to insult the ambassadors of the Commonwealth. The Dutch population itself was also ill-disposed towards them, and followed them about with offensive curiosity, ridiculing their attitudes, and saying that they were doubtless afraid.[1]

The feelings of the men who were then at the head of the government of Holland were of a very different character. From position as well as from prudence, for their own sakes no less than for the sake of their country, they sincerely desired to be on good terms, and even to form a true alliance, with the Commonwealth of England. Three days after their arrival at the Hague, St. John and Strickland were received by the States-General in solemn audience, with the most distinguished marks of friendly consideration, and seven commissioners were appointed to confer with them. They were instructed to declare to the ambassadors " that the United Provinces offered their friendship to the Commonwealth of England, and that they were inclined not only to renew and maintain inviolably the affection and friendly relations which had at all times existed between the English nation and themselves, but also to make a treaty of common interest with the Commonwealth." The first words of the two ambassadors made it evident that such offers would not suffice them. " We propose," they said, " that the amity and good correspondence which hath anciently been between the English nation and the United Provinces, be not only renewed and preserved inviolably, but that a more strict and intimate alliance and union be entered into by them, whereby there may be a more

[1] Commons' Journals, vol. vi. pp. 525, 527, 528, 541, 513 ; Whitelocke, pp. 487, 488, 490 ; Clarendon's History of the Rebellion, vol. vi. pp. 594—596 ; Wicquefort's Histoire des Provinces Unies, vol. iv. p. 287 ; Leclerc's Histoire des Provinces Unies, vol. iii. pp. 307, 308.

intrinsical and mutual interest of each in other, than has hitherto
been, for the good of both."[1]

What was this "more strict and intimate alliance" to be?
What was the meaning of the "more intrinsical and mutual interest?" For six weeks, St. John and Strickland refused to give
any more definite explanation of their meaning: it was, they said,
for the States-General to explain, with precision and detail, their
views in this negotiation; as for themselves, they did not consider
the first offer which had been made to them at all satisfactory;
and as the Parliament had appointed a fixed and limited term
for the duration of their embassy, they insisted that a clear and
peremptory answer should be promptly given to their general
proposition.[2]

A design of vast and chimerical ambition, one of those designs
which men hesitate to acknowledge even while they are labouring
to accomplish them, was entertained in the secret souls of St. John
and the Parliamentary leaders who had sent him on his mission.
At once presumptuous and restless, they were under the influence
of that exuberance of rash activity, that necessity of gaining strength
by extension, which characterises new powers when intoxicated by
their first successes. The reports spread about Cromwell's plans
for an expedition into France had no other origin; sensible, even in
the midst of the utmost revolutionary ferment, Cromwell probably
never entertained such an idea; but in the army, in the Parliament, everywhere throughout republican England, ideas of this
kind formed the theme of passionate discussion among men of bold
and unquiet minds, who imagined everything would be possible
to their country and themselves, after what they had already
done. The United Provinces were not like France; there was no
necessity to conquer them by war; half the work was done already;
all moral and material ties, religion, institutions, politics, commerce,
connected and assimilated the United Provinces with England.
Why should not the assimilation be carried as far as union? Why
should two republics so similar and so near to one another remain
separated? "*Faciamus eas in unam gentem*—let us make of them
one nation," was the idea of the republican leaders in England.
Strickland, during his first mission to the Hague, had already
expressed it in a letter to Walter Frost, the Secretary of the
Council of State; it inspired the embassy of St John, and swayed
the entire negotiation.[3]

[1] Wicquefort's Histoire des Provinces Unies, Preuves, vol. ii. pp. 379—391.
[2] Ibid. vol. ii. pp. 392—394.
[3] Thurloe's State Papers, vol. i. p. 130; Clarendon's History of the

It was a dream as full of imprudence as of pride. The union into a single State, and under the same government, of the two great Protestant republics would assuredly have met with desperate resistance in Europe, and might perhaps have rekindled the wars of religion. The population of Holland would have indignantly rejected any such proposal; it was the loss of their national existence, and their absorption into the more powerful State of England, which was already exceedingly unpopular in the United Provinces, as their former protector, their present rival, and probably their future enemy. Satires, songs, and other small compositions in prose and verse, expressive of deep hatred and violent threats against the English, were already in circulation among the people : even the heads of the Dutch government, the men most decidedly in favour of a good understanding with England, were too high-minded not to place the independence of their country far above all other considerations, and their good-will in the negotiation diminished as soon as they caught a glimpse of the ambitious design of the foreign envoys. Deploring, some years later, the Orangist intrigues and popular passions which had led to the rupture between the two countries, John de Witt said, with patriotic bitterness : " To this must be added the insupportable humour of the English nation, its continual jealousy of our prosperity, and the mortal hatred of Cromwell to the young Prince of Orange, the son of the sister of that banished king, who was the person he most feared in the world."[1]

Various incidents, some of them natural and almost unavoidable, others the result of deliberate design, occurred still further to augment the difficulties of the negotiation. The populace of the Hague frequently exhibited the coarsest ill-feeling towards the ambassadors ; in the streets and suburbs of the town, their servants were insulted and maltreated by the servants of the Princess of Orange, or by the Cavaliers in the train of the Duke of York, who was then residing with his sister. The Prince and Princess themselves often passed and repassed, slowly and with a brilliant cavalcade, in front of the residence of the ambassadors, as if to brave them ; puerile pleasures, in which party hatreds and humours indulge in order to obtain consolation or recreation in the time of their impotence. One day Prince Edward, a younger brother of

---

Rebellion, vol. vi. p. 594; Godwin's History of the Commonwealth, vol. iii. p. 372; Leclerc's Histoire des Provinces Unies, vol. ii. p. 309.

[1] Leeven en Dood der Gebroeders Cornelis en Johan de Witt, rp. 23, 27, 35; Histoire de Corneille et Jean de Witt, vol. i. p. 64.

Prince Rupert, seeing the ambassadors pass in their carriage, shouted after them: "O you rogues! you dogs!" On another occasion, St. John, while walking in the park at the Hague, met the Duke of York, on foot like himself, and they did not recognise one another until they were almost face to face. As the ambassador of the Commonwealth would not give way, the Prince snatched his hat off his head, and threw it in his face, saying: "Learn, parricide, to respect the brother of your King." "I scorn," answered St. John, "to acknowledge either you or him of whom you speak, but as a race of vagabonds." They both laid their hands on their swords, but the gentlemen who were with them surrounded them, and prevented an encounter. A Colonel Apsley boasted, it is said, that he would go and strangle St. John in his house. The ambassadors complained of these affronts to the States-General. The magistrates instituted prosecutions, took measures of police, and placed guards all round their residence. Official satisfactions were not wanting; but the animosities of the royalists and of the populace continued to exist, and constantly found some new form and fresh opportunity for manifesting themselves."[1]

The ambassadors sent a report to London of the almost equally perilous and difficult position in which they were placed: they even sent Thurloe to give a detailed explanation of the state of affairs in Holland, and to inquire whether they should continue to negotiate or return home.[2] The Parliament, which clung strongly to its plan, authorised them to prolong their stay; but at the same time, to give the States-General a proof of their dissatisfaction and power, it ordered the arrest at sea of nine merchant vessels belonging to Amsterdam, and bound for Portugal; and sent to the Hague for explanation of the attitude of Admiral Tromp, who was cruising with his squadron off the Scilly Islands, as though he intended to take possession of them. The States-General explained the instructions which had been given to Tromp, and complained of the seizure of the nine ships.[3] Neither country was willing to take the initiative in the rupture; but the

---

[1] Commons' Journals, vol. vi. pp. 560, 568; Whitelocke, pp. 491, 493, 494; Clarendon's History of the Rebellion, vol. vi. pp. 594—596; Old Parliamentary History, vol. xix. p. 473; Carte's Ormonde Letters, vol. i. p. 447, vol. ii. p. 2; Raguenet's Histoire de Oliver Cromwell, p. 261; Leclerc's Histoire des Provinces Unies, vol. ii. pp. 308—310; Wicquefort's Histoire des Provinces Unies, vol. iv. p. 289; Thurloe's State Papers, vol. i. p. 170.

[2] Commons' Journals, vol. vi. p. 568.

[3] Thurloe's State Papers, vol. i. p. 177; Whitelocke, pp. 491, 492; Wicquefort's Histoire des Provinces Unies, Preuves, vol. ii. pp. 397—402; Leclerc's Histoire des Provinces Unies, vol. iii. p. 311.

temper of both parties daily became more unfriendly, and was displayed even in the actions and words of courtesy which were intended to conceal it.

After more than two months had been spent in useless conference—months wasted by the English ambassadors in not stating what they were endeavouring to effect, and by the Dutch in not giving an answer to what was asked of them thus indirectly, although they understood it quite well,—St. John and Strickland at length decided to announce with precision some of their pretensions, in seven articles.[1] These alone would have resulted in the complete connection of the policy and fate of the United Provinces with the policy and fate of England in all matters of peace, war, and alliance; and they moreover bound the States-General to abdicate, in certain cases, on their own territory, the rights and free exercise of sovereignty. And to indicate that their mission was far from being limited to even these extreme terms, the two ambassadors hastened to add that, if their first demands were acceded to, " the Parliament had given them power to propound and bring to effect on their part, matters of greater and higher concernment to the good of both commonwealths."[2]

Evidently, with such after-thoughts, nothing was possible; no further explanation was necessary to produce a complete mutual understanding : from politeness, the negotiation was continued a few days longer; but on the 29th of June, 1651, St. John and Strickland announced that the Parliament had recalled them, and requested an audience to take leave, which was granted to them on the following day. In presence of the States-General, the official language of St. John was moderate and courteous, but on separating from the Dutch commissioners, with whom he had been negotiating for three months, he said to them : " I perceive that their High Mightinesses are waiting the issue of affairs in Scotland, that they may regulate their carriage to our government accordingly, and that for that reason they have slighted the generous overtures with which we were charged. It is true that some members of our Parliament dissuaded this embassy, and advised that we should first finish our war in Scotland, and then expect your representatives on our shores. But I thought more honourably of you. I was wrong : and I now confess that these cautious advisers understood you better. Take my word for it, however, our Scottish campaign will soon be terminated as our warmest friends would wish, and you will

[1] Thurloe's State Papers, vol. i. p. 182; Wicquefort's Histoire des Provinces Unies, Preuves, vol. ii. pp. 410—414.
[2] Ibid. p. 188 ; ibid. pp. 415—418.

then repent your having so lightly treated the proposals we have made."[1] Two days afterwards, the English ambassadors left Holland, refusing, in obedience to the express commands of the Parliament, the rich presents which were offered them by the States-General: and on the 7th of July, Whitelocke announced to the House that they had returned to London, and were ready to give a report of their mission.[2]

Two decisive measures promptly followed the presentation of this report. On the 5th of August, Whitelocke proposed to Parliament the famous bill known as the Act of Navigation, which provided that no foreign ships should be allowed to bring 'nto England any commodities which were not the proper produce or manufacture of the countries to which they respectively belonged. This was the hardest blow which could possibly be struck at Holland, whose prosperity mainly depended upon its carrying trade. Before the end of the year, the bill was definitively adopted, and put into operation.[3] At the same time, letters of marque were granted to many English merchants, to enable them, it was said, to indemnify themselves for the losses which had been inflicted on them by the Dutch navy. The United Provinces had refused to allow themselves to be conquered by negotiation : war was now proposed against them.

The victory of Worcester carried to a climax the proud confidence of the republican Parliament ; and the States of the Continent, by their attitude and conduct after that great defeat of the royalist party, served only to justify and increase it. From all parts there came to London declarations of recognition of the Commonwealth, overtures of official relations, and almost even diplomatic congratulations and compliments. Tuscany, Venice, Genoa, the Hanseatic Towns, the Swiss Cantons, and the petty Princes of Germany, sent and received agents.[4] From Sweden, Denmark, and Portugal, extraordinary ambassadors brought letters from their sovereigns to the Parliament, were presented to it in solemn audience, and commenced eager negotiations with it, either to put an end to existing differences, or to enter into immediate alliance.[5] Wonder-

---

[1] Histoire de Corneille et Jean de Witt, vol. i. p. 63 ; Wicquefort's Histoire des Provinces Unies, Preuves, vol. ii. p. 428; Heath's Brief Chronicle, pp. 524—527; Thurloe's State Papers, vol. i. pp. 189—192.

[2] Commons' Journals, vol. vi. pp. 593, 595 ; Whitelocke, p. 496; Leclerc's Histoire des Provinces Unies, vol. ii. p. 313.

[3] Commons' Journals, vol. vi. p. 617, vol. vii. p. 27 ; Leclerc's Histoire des Provinces Unies, vol. ii. pp. 313, 314.

[4] Commons' Journals, vol. vii. pp. 19, 28, 96, 142, 256.

[5] Ibid. vol. viii. pp. 77, 103, 104, 130, 135, 136, 137, 230, 234, 243, 177,

struck by the success of the Commonwealth, all Europe took measures to live on good terms with it, whether it believed or not in its future stability.

Mazarin could not remain passive amid this movement, for no one was readier than he to bend before power, either to attract and use it for his advantage, or to conceal from it his real views. He renewed his attempts to resume friendly relations with the English Commonwealth; M. de Gentillot made a fresh journey to London, where Mazarin maintained numerous secret agents, both French and English, partly for the purpose of collecting information, and partly to form connections which he hoped some day to turn to his profit. His anxiety became still more intense when he learned that Sir Harry Vane had been to Paris, and had an interview with Cardinal de Retz. "On my return home at about eleven o'clock in the evening," says De Retz, "I found a certain Fielding, an Englishman, whom I had known formerly at Rome, who told me that Vane, a great Parliamentarian and intimate confidant of Cromwell, had just arrived in Paris, and had orders to see me. I found myself somewhat embarrassed by this; however, I thought I ought not to refuse this interview, at a conjuncture when we were not at war with England, and when the Cardinal himself was making both base and continual advances to the Protector. Vane gave me a short letter from him, which was only a letter of credence. The substance of his discourse was that the sentiments which I had expressed in defence of public liberty, combined with my reputation, had inspired Cromwell with a desire to make friendship with me. This was adorned by all the courtesies, all the offers, and all the temptations that you can imagine. Vane appeared to me a man of surprising capacity. I answered with all possible respect: but assuredly I neither said nor did anything that was not worthy both of a true Catholic and of a good Frenchman."[1] Mazarin judged otherwise, and from his place of exile at Bruhl he wrote thus to the Queen: "The Coadjutor has always spoken with veneration of Cromwell, as of a man sent by God into England, saying that he would raise up similar men in other kingdoms; and once, in jovial company when Ménage was present, hearing some one extol the courage of M. de Beaufort, he said in express terms: 'If M. de Beaufort is Fairfax, I am Cromwell.'"[2]

178, 182, 185, 186, 187, 190, 191, 194, 203, 223, 229, 149, 159, 165, 215, 252, 261, 269, 270, 273, 276, 277.

[1] Mémoires du Cardinal de Retz, p. 211.

[2] Lettres du Cardinal Mazarin à la Reine Anne d'Autriche, publiées par M. Ravenel, pp. 5, 6.

Mazarin excelled in the art of ruining his enemies by exaggerating the meaning of their actions or words, and by immediately appropriating to his own use, with the utmost effrontery, their tactics and weapons. Whilst he thus represented to the Queen as a crime in the Coadjutor the sentiments which he entertained with regard to Cromwell, he was himself labouring to enter into intimate relations with Cromwell: too sagacious not to perceive that in him were centred all the power and ability then existing in England, it was to the future master of the Commonwealth, and no longer to the republican Parliament, that his advances were addressed. Cromwell willingly received them; he also was busily engaged in securing to himself powerful friends in every direction. "He adroitly leaves to others the conduct and care of everything unpopular," wrote Croullé to M. Servien, as early even as 1650, "and reserves to himself such things as give satisfaction; or at least he spreads a report to this effect, in order that, if they succeed, they may be attributed to him, and if not, that it may be thought that it was in his will to do them, but that their realisation was prevented by others."[1]   On the 5th of February, 1652, the Comte d'Estrades, who was still governor of Dunkirk, wrote to Mazarin, who had then returned into France, and had just rejoined the Queen at Poitiers: "The Protector Cromwell has sent to me Mr. Fitz-James, his colonel of guards, to propose to me to treat about Dunkirk, that he would give me two millions for it, and that he would engage to furnish fifty vessels and fifteen thousand foot-soldiers, to declare against Spain, and against the enemies of the King and of your Eminence, with whom he would wish to make a close friendship. I replied to Mr. Fitz-James that, if the troubles and civil war which existed in France did not oblige me to send to the Queen and your Eminence, I would have had him thrown into the sea for having supposed me capable of betraying my King, but that the present state of affairs obliged me to detain him with me until I had received an answer from the Court." Mazarin replied to D'Estrades: "My opinion was that we should accept Cromwell's proposition; but M. de Châteauneuf opposed it, and carried the Queen with him, so that she would not consent to it. . . . I leave it for the Sieur de Las to express to you the sentiments which I feel towards you: your interests are as dear to me as my own." D'Estrades understood his wishes, and did not lose a moment; five days afterwards he wrote to Mazarin: "As soon as I had received from M. de Las the letter which acquainted me with the intentions of your Eminence touching

---

[1] June 20, 1650: Archives des Affaires Étrangères de France.

the proposition of England, I communicated the same to my friend
in London, and begged him to give me an answer on the point contained in my letter, as speedily as possible. He arrived in this
town this morning, and told me, on the part of Mr. Cromwell, that
what the Commonwealth demands is that the King should recognise
them, and send an ambassador as soon as possible, and that he
should pay their subjects that which has been taken from them at
sea. . . . He told me afterwards that Mr. Cromwell had charged
him to tell me that, if your Eminence could not remain in France,
and your enemies should oblige you to leave your country, he assured me that you would be well received in England if you should
wish to retire thither, and treated by the Commonwealth with all
kinds of honour; that they would give you a good house to live in,
entire safety for your person, and the free exercise of your religion;
and that whenever you wished to go to Rome, you should be furnished with vessels to convey yourself and all your train whither-
soever you might wish."[1]

Mazarin now thought himself near the accomplishment of his
wishes: powers were immediately sent to the Comte d'Estrades
"to treat of a new alliance with the Commonwealth of England.
. . . In judging," Louis XIV. was made to say, "that the
Sieur Cromwell might send some one to us to be better informed
of our good intentions, you will have to acquaint him with them,
and to open yourself in all confidence, not only respecting any
treaty with the Commonwealth, but also with the said Sieur Cromwell personally, for the common welfare of the two kingdoms as
well as for his private interests; as I give you, by these presents,
power to act, negotiate, treat, and promise in my name all that
you may judge fitting with regard to the said Cromwell, and I will
ratify and execute all that you shall have promised in my name."[2]
D'Estrades, however, did not leave Dunkirk: it was not until a
month after the date of his powers, that he received precise instructions, and a letter from Mazarin with comments upon them.
The Cardinal wished to sell dearly the recognition of the Commonwealth, and to grant it only in exchange for an immediate
treaty which should not merely put an end to all differences
between the two States, but should secure to France the alliance, or
at least the secret support, of England against Spain. In this hope,

---

[1] Lettres, Mémoires et Négociations du Comte d'Estrades, vol. i. pp. 103
—107; Letter from the Comte d'Estrades to Cardinal Mazarin, in the Archives
des Affaires Etrangères de France.
[2] Letter from Louis XIV. to the Comte d'Estrades; MSS. de Brienne, in
the Bibliothèque Impériale, Paris.

he even authorised D'Estrades to resume the question of the cession
of Dunkirk to the English.[1] Being doubtless informed by his
friends in London that he would have but little chance of success,
D'Estrades never went on this mission.   In his stead, almost
identical instructions were given to M. de Gentillot, who furthermore had orders to deliver to Cromwell a letter from Louis XIV.
himself, to the following effect : " Mr. Cromwell, as I am sending
expressly to London the Sieur de Gentillot, a gentleman of my
chamber, with letters of credence to the Parliament of the Commonwealth of England and to the Council of State, in order to
acquaint them with my good intentions; and as it is advantageous
to both States to live in good neighbourhood, peace, and amity, I
have charged him with this letter for you, to assure you of my good
will and entire disposition to do whatever may conduce to the
security and liberty of the trade, well-being, and mutual advantage
of the two nations; and feeling assured that you will contribute
willingly to so good a result, I leave it to the said Sieur de Gentillot
to tell you more, begging you to give him credence as a person in
whom I place entire confidence."[2] Whether it was never carried
out, or whether it failed obscurely, the mission of Gentillot produced no more result than that of D'Estrades.   Both parties were
feeling their way, without advancing.   Meanwhile, Mazarin became
more and more anxious and hurried.   Some months previously, at
the very moment when he had commenced these negotiations, the
Prince de Condé and the Frondeurs of Bordeaux had also sent to
London two agents, MM. Barrière and De Cugnac, with instructions
to solicit the support of the Commonwealth, and to offer in return
free trade with Guienne, certain favours towards the French Protestants, and even the cession of the island of Oleron.   These
agents had, in the first instance, no public character ; they addressed themselves to all the men of importance, and particularly to
Cromwell, stating their demands and offers to all whom they thought

---

[1] MSS. de Brienne, in the Bibliothèque Impériale, Paris.
[2] The text of this letter is as follows :—" Monsieur Cromwell, envoyant
exprès à Londres le Sieur de Gentillot, gentilhomme de ma chambre, avec
lettres de créance au Parlement de la République d'Angleterre, et au Conseil
d'Etat, pour leur faire entendre mes bonnes intentions, et comme il est avan-
tageux à l'un et à l'autre Etat de vivre en bon voisinance, paix et amitié, je l'ai
chargé de cette lettre pour vous, pour vous assurer de ma bonne volonté et
disposition entière à faire ce qui servira à la sureté et liberté du commerce,
bien et utilité réciproque des deux nations ; et m'assurant que vous contri-
buerez volontiers à un si bon effet, je me remets au dit Sieur de Gentillot de
vous en dire davantage, vous priant de lui donner créance comme en une
personne en qui je prends une confiance entière." MSS. de Brienne, in the
Bibliothèque Impériale, Paris.

able to help them. But on the 31st of March, 1652, the Speaker informed the Parliament that he had received a letter signed "Louis de Bourbon," and addressed "Au Parlement de la République d'Angleterre," accrediting M. de Barrière. This letter was read and referred to the Council of State, who received Barrière and heard his propositions. Whitelocke presented a report on the subject to the Parliament. The mission now appeared to assume a definite character; the Spanish ambassador warmly supported it; the Comte de Daugnon, governor of Brouage, and an ally of the Prince de Condé, also sent agents and promises to London. Finally the city of Bordeaux itself, in its own name, despatched two special deputies, MM. de Blarut and de Trancons, "to demand of the Commonwealth of England, as of a just and powerful State, assistance in men, money, and ships to support the city and commons of Bordeaux, now united with our lords the Princes; and not only to shelter them from the oppression and cruel vengeance which is in store for them, but also to effect their restoration to their ancient privileges, and to enable them to breathe a freer air than they have hitherto done. And as the said lords of the Parliament of the Commonwealth of England," continued their instructions, "will probably demand of them reciprocal advantages, they will let them first explain their pretensions, and afterwards, if necessary, they may grant them a port in the river of Bordeaux, where their vessels may find retirement and safety, such as Castillon, Royan, Talmont or Paulhac, or that of Arcachon if they wish, which they may fortify at their own expense. We may even permit them to besiege and capture Blaye, in which our troops will help them as much as possible. They may also make a descent upon La Rochelle and capture it, if they please."[1]

The alarm was great, both at Court and in the Council. Whilst, in the southern provinces, civil war thus invited a foreign army into France, foreign war still continued in those of the north: the Spaniards were vigorously pushing the siege of Gravelines; Dunkirk was expected shortly to fall, and the news arrived suddenly that seven vessels, which had left Calais for the purpose of conveying thither provisions and reinforcements, had been arrested and captured at sea by the English squadron, under the command of Admiral Blake. In vain did all the French authorities make the most urgent remonstrances; in vain did the Duke de Vendôme, Grand Admiral of France, write to Blake, to the republican Council

<hr/>

[1] Commons' Journals, vol. vii. pp. 112, 117, 129, 133; Documents Inédits sur l'Histoire Diplomatique de France, in the Revue Nouvelle, vol. v. pp 381—393; Thurloe's State Papers, vol. i. pp. 216, 224, 226, 250.

of State, and even to the Parliament;[1] they replied that the letters
of marque issued by the French government had caused, and still
continued to cause, the greatest injury to English commerce, for
which they had resolved to obtain or take reparation, and they
refused to release the ships which had been seized.[2] Evidently,
the Parliament was resolved not to purchase the recognition of the
Commonwealth at the price which Mazarin wished to make it pay;
it was determined to maintain its wavering neutrality between
France and Spain, and inclining always rather towards Spain, it
willingly seized upon all opportunities for making France feel its
power to do her harm. Don Alonzo de Cardenas had carefully
fostered this tendency in London : the proceedings and messengers
of Mazarin had caused him the utmost anxiety, and he had sent
minute information of all that had' passed to his Court, urging it to
make to the Parliament, on its side, the advances and concessions
necessary to prevent any alliance between England and France.
Sometimes he laboured to induce Spain to enter into an intimate
alliance with the two Protestant republics of London and the Hague,
against France and Portugal; sometimes he urged his Court to
second the English in an enterprise against Calais, on condition that
they should aid the Spaniards in the siege of Gravelines, Dunkirk,
and Mardyke. Finally, he undertook to conclude between Spain
and the Commonwealth of England, a formal treaty of friendship,
which should securely bind both States; and on the 20th of
September, 1652, he sent to Madrid a draft in twenty-four articles,
which he had already submitted, on the 12th, to the republican
Council of State, who had manifested a strong disposition to
accept it.[3]

Urged by these dangers, Mazarin at length determined to
recognise the Commonwealth, without deriving any immediate
advantage from the step. On the 2nd of December, 1652, M. de
Bordeaux, Councillor of State and Intendant of Picardy, received
directions to convey a letter from the King to the Parliament, and
to re-establish official relations between the two States. This
resolution was adopted and executed without either boldness or
gracefulness, with an air at once haughty and embarrassed. The

    [1] MSS. de Brienne, in the Bibliothèque Impériale, Paris.
    [2] Commons' Journals, vol. vii. pp. 175, 195, 224; Dixon's Life of Blake,
pp. 208—210.
    [3] Letters from Cardeñas to Philip IV., January 23, February 5, 15, 25,
July 19, September 12, 20, 1652; Deliberations of the Council of State at
Madrid on the Despatches of Cardeñas, August 14, 1652: in the Archives of
Simancas.

instructions of M. de Bordeaux formally stated that he was not an ambassador, and he was ordered to declare as much on his arrival ; they seemed to make the commercial interests of the two countries, and the restitution of the seven vessels captured on their way to Dunkirk, the almost entire object of his mission ; they recommended him, it is true, " to say nothing which might lead to a rupture, or offend the English, so as not to give them any pretext for declaring themselves enemies of the crown, as it appears to His Majesty that it is better for a time that they should rove the seas and practise the piracy with which they reproach others, than that they should do anything worse, namely, join their forces with the Spaniards, and take the rebels under their protection ; " but at the same time, Bordeaux was enjoined, "if he could obtain no satisfaction regarding the special business with which he was charged, to return to France without waiting for further orders," whilst, if he found the Parliament favourably disposed and ready to appoint commissioners to examine the old treaties with him, he was to wait, "and send at once to His Majesty, to receive his commands, together with the necessary powers and instructions." In reality, the step was decisive, and carried with it the full recognition of the Commonwealth ; but either from natural hesitation, or from complaisance to the scruples of the Queen and Court, Mazarin had attempted to give it the appearance of an experimental mission of a limited and conditional character, and one which could be receded from at any time without discredit.[1]

Republican pride quickly detected and frustrated this petty artifice. When the Speaker announced to the Parliament that he had received a letter from the King of France, its superscription was first of all examined: it was addressed, " A nos très chers et grands amis les Gens du Parlement de la République d'Angleterre." The master of the ceremonies was directed to state to M. de Bordeaux, that this was not the style in which foreign princes wrote to the Parliament, and that a letter thus addressed could not be received. Two days afterwards, Bordeaux sent back the letter with this new address : " Au Parlement de la République d'Angleterre ;" it was immediately admitted, and the 21st of December following was fixed for the reception of M. de Bordeaux, but he was informed that " as he was not an ambassador, he would have audience neither of the Parliament, nor of the Council of State, but of a Committee." When admitted before this committee, " The King of France, my

---

[1] Archives des Affaires Etrangères de France; MSS. de Brienne, in the Bibliothèque Impériale, Paris.

master," he said, "having judged it fitting, for the good of his service, to send me to the Parliament of the Commonwealth of England, has commanded me to greet it on his part, and to assure it of
his friendship, from the confidence which he has of finding in it a
mutual correspondence to his good intentions. The union which
should exist between neighbouring states is not regulated by the
form of their government; wherefore, though it has pleased God, in
His providence, to change that which was formerly established in
this country, there does not cease to be a necessity for trade and
friendship between France and England. This kingdom may have
changed its aspect, and from a monarchy have become a Commonwealth, but the position of places does not change; people always
continue neighbours, and remain interested in one another, for
trading purposes; and the treaties which exist between nations are
not so much binding upon princes as upon peoples, as they have
for their principal object their common advantage." Having thus
formally recognised the Commonwealth, Bordeaux proceeded at
once to the special object of his mission, and after a few phrases
against the intrigues of Spain, and upon the power of France, he
ended by demanding the restitution of the seven vessels, and by
giving the Parliament full assurance that "His Majesty, who
regards justice as the principal support of his sceptre, and the solid
foundation of legitimate empires, will not fail to have compensation
given to all those of this State who may have just claims against his
subjects; and that, having obtained the satisfaction which is his
due, he will embrace all means likely to maintain a perfect correspondence between the two States."[1]

On learning that this step had been taken by the King of France
towards the republican Parliament, the Queen of England, Henrietta Maria, wrote to her second son, the Duke of York:—"My
son, this letter is to inform you that, as they have sent from here to
England to recognise those infamous traitors, notwithstanding all
the reasons which we could give against the measure, the King,
your brother, has resolved to leave this place, and has already communicated his intention to the Queen. He has not yet taken any
resolution with regard to you. Wherefore you must still act as if
you were ignorant of this embassy, and in case any one should
mention it to you, you must say that you cannot believe it. . . .
I confess to you, since my great misfortune, I have never felt anything equal to this. May God take us under His holy protection,

---

[1] Commons' Journals, vol. vii. pp. 228, 230, 233; Archives des Affaires
Etrangères de France; MSS. de Brienne, in the Bibliothèque Impériale.

and give us the patience which we shall need to support this blow!"[1]
Charles II., however, did not leave Paris—he was not asked to do
so; and the pension of six thousand livres a month which he
received from Louis XIV. was continued ; but his position became
more and more isolated and melancholy, and his most faithful
advisers urged him thenceforth to seek an asylum elsewhere.

The Commonwealth seemed equally triumphant both at home
and abroad—in European diplomacy as well as in the civil war ;
but the fatal effects of its imprudent and arrogant policy towards
the United Provinces had begun to manifest themselves, and far
overbalanced the advantages which accrued to it from its recognition
by Louis XIV., and its imperfect neutrality between France and
Spain.

When the Dutch leaders had rejected the propositions of the
English ambassadors, and refused to connect the fate of their
country with that of a Commonwealth so dangerous and tottering, they had done a deed of equal patriotism and courage, and had
discharged their duty towards the dignity as well as the safety of
the State which they governed.   But they were sincerely desirous
of peace, and even of an alliance, with England ; the victory of the
Parliament at Worcester and its Act of Navigation, by showing
them that war was at once most probable and most perilous, determined them to attempt a last effort to avoid it.   As soon as they
learned the flight of Charles II. after his defeat, a decree was proposed in the States-General, enacting that no foreign prince should
be allowed to enter their territory without their formal consent ; and
shortly afterwards they sent three ambassadors to London, with
orders to resume the negotiations which St. John and Strickland, on
leaving the Hague, had so abruptly broken off.   At their first
audience, the principal of the three ambassadors, Jacobus Catz, formerly Grand Pensionary of the United Provinces, endeavoured, in
a long speech, which was too flattering to be adroit. to conciliate the
friendly feeling of the Parliament.   Their reception had been attended with great pomp ; the master of the ceremonies had been
ordered to fetch them from Gravesend, in barges decorated with
official ensigns ; three members of Parliament had met them at
Greenwich, and conducted them on the following day to Westminster.   On their entrance into the hall, the Speaker and all the
members rose, and took off their hats : the English republicans
were anxious to treat the republic of the United Provinces with dis-

---

[1] MSS. de Brienne, in the Bibliothèque Impériale, Paris; Clarendon's
History of the Rebellion, vol. vi. p. 605; vol. vii. p. 49.

tinction, and to diffuse among both nations the conviction that they
regarded it with sincere sympathy : but at the same time, swayed
by mingled feelings of pride and rancour, they received and discussed its propositions with the haughty obstinacy of a power confident in its own strength, and burning to avenge a misapprehension
which it regarded as an insult.   In both countries the popular feeling was in accordance with this disposition of the English government : in Holland, either from an Orangist spirit, or from national
rivalry, the people expected a war, and manifested a greater inclination to desire than to fear it ; the fishermen of the Meuse related,
with patriotic confidence, their visions of great navies, which had
appeared in the air, just above their coasts, engaging in mighty conflicts, from which they prognosticated the victory of the Dutch flag.
In London the populace were still more animated : they daily received news of hostile proceedings at sea, between English and
Dutch ships, sometimes relating to the affronts and losses which
English commerce had experienced, and sometimes to the bold reparation which it had taken for itself at the expense of its rivals ;
and more than once, on hearing such news, whether true or false,
the mob thronged round the house which the Dutch ambassadors
occupied at Chelsea, and showed so strong a tendency to insult
them, that Parliament was obliged to assign them a guard for their
protection.[1]

  Among the negotiators themselves the difficulties daily grew
more insurmountable ; unexpected questions arose ; old or new pretensions were put forward on both sides.   The Dutch, having become a powerful nation, were also anxious to establish their entire
independence at sea, and to free themselves from the admissions of
inferiority which England had been, or assumed to be, entitled to
impose upon them.   The English accused their kings of the House
of Stuart of having abandoned, or allowed to fall into desuetude,
those external tokens of their empire over the sea which in former
days, and especially during the glorious reign of Elizabeth, their
sailors had possessed, or laid claim to.   The salute of their flag, the
right of visiting, and the right of fishery, became the subjects of animated debates · the more they were prolonged, the haughtier became
the demands and tone of the English ; they even began to speak
without evasion of their sovereignty over the seas which surrounded
their island : the Dutch ambassadors, from loyalty as much as from
prudence, declared that their government was equipping a large

<hr />

[1] Commons' Journals, vol. vii. pp. 45, 53, 54, 56, 58, 64; Whitelocke, pp.
512, 518, 521. 533 ; Leclerc's Histoire des Provinces Unies, vol. ii. p. 314 ;
Wicquefort's Histoire des Provinces Unies, vol. iv. pp. 307—310.

fleet to protect their trade in those waters. The English commissioners almost contested their right to do this, saying that they would themselves maintain the police of the sea for the common advantage of all. Whilst quarrels about principles were thus growing in bitterness, actual hostilities spontaneously commenced between the two nations: their ships never met without exchanging some mark of enmity; it was soon learned that an embargo had been laid in the ports of Holland upon all English ships; and that a Dutch merchant fleet, returning from the Mediterranean, had refused to lower its flag to the English squadron, upon which Commander Young had attacked it, to compel it to do so. Explanations were demanded and given on both sides; the embargo in Holland was raised; but the ill-feeling which it had excited in England continued. The Dutch negotiators did their best to extenuate grievances, and to resolve questions pacifically; but they were not all three animated by this desire to an equal extent: their dissensions were remarked, and they were called ironically, "The disunited ambassadors of the United Provinces." They insisted in vain upon the abolition, or at least the temporary suspension, of the Act of Navigation; the Parliament was inflexible on this point; and, both from external incidents and from the turn taken by the negotiations themselves, the maintenance of peace daily became more doubtful and more difficult.[1]

In the midst of these diplomatic agitations, it suddenly became known that, on the 12th of May, in the Downs, not far from Dover roadstead, the Dutch fleet, under the command of Tromp, and the English fleet, under Blake, had met and fought. Informed that Tromp was cruising in that part of the Channel, and suspecting that some hostile design was in contemplation on his part, Blake had immediately sailed thither, and on his arrival, he had, by firing three signal-guns in succession, summoned the Dutch admiral to lower his flag in presence of the English squadron. Tromp kept on his course without taking any notice of his summons. Soon after he fell in with a ketch coming from Holland, which evidently brought him important orders, for he suddenly veered round and made towards Blake, who lay to, and repeated his summons. According to the account given by the English admiral, Tromp's only answer was to send a broadside into the James, Blake's flagship, which caused it considerable damage. "Well," said Blake

[1] Commons' Journals, vol. vii. pp. 103, 135, 139; Whitelocke, pp. 512, 517, 522, 529, 530; Dixon's Life of Blake, pp. 189—191; Wicquefort's Histoire des Provinces Unies, vol. iv. pp. 310—318; Leclerc's Histoire des Provinces Unies, vol. ii. pp. 314—316; Heath's Brief Chronicle, p. 585.

"it is not very civil in Van Tromp to take my flag-ship for a
brothel, and break my windows;" and in his turn, he opened a
vigorous cannonade upon the *Brederode*, Tromp's own vessel. The
action thus unexpectedly begun, lasted more than four hours ;
Tromp had forty-two ships, and Blake only twenty-three. The
English admiral had more than fifty men of his own crew killed or
wounded : the Dutch lost one of their ships. When night fell,
Tromp made sail towards the coast of Holland ; and on the following day at dawn, Blake, who had remained on the scene of action,
could discover no trace of his enemy.[1]

Two sensations of a very different character, in London anger,
and at the Hague anxiety, were excited by this news. " Tromp
came to brave us on our own seas," said the English ; " he wished
to surprise our fleet, that he might attack and destroy it by
treachery." " Tromp was driven towards the English coast by
stress of weather," answered the Dutch ; " he was returning, and
about to salute the English fleet, when he was violently summoned
and attacked ; he merely stood on the defensive, and withdrew as
soon as he could do so honourably ; with his superior force, he
could easily have destroyed the English fleet, if such had been his
design." These explanations, and especially the last, were received
with ironical derision, as falsehoods almost equivalent to fresh
insults. The populace manifested their furious ill-feeling towards
the ambassadors more strongly than ever. A fourth ambassador
extraordinary arrived suddenly from the Hague,—Adrian de Pauw,
Pensionary of the Province of Holland, already well known and
esteemed in England, attached to a pacific policy, and of a prudent
and conciliating character : he brought, on the part of his government, the strongest denials of any hostile or offensive intention
towards England ; he declared that Tromp had neither received any
instructions, nor entertained any purpose, to attack the English
fleet, and that what had happened had only been the result of unfortunate misconceptions and accidents ; he demanded that an
inquiry should be instituted into the facts, and into the conduct of
the two admirals, offering the dismissal of Tromp from his command, if the charges imputed to him were substantiated ; and, in
the mean while, he insisted that the negotiations should be pursued
and brought to a conclusion. Pauw was received with great consideration ; but, in their suspicions as in their desires, the Parlia-

---

[1] Whitelocke, pp. 523, 524; Dixon's Life of Blake, pp. 191—195; Memorials of Sir William Penn, vol. i. pp. 419—423; Leclerc's Histoire des Provinces Unies, vol. ii. pp. 315—317; Wicquefort's Histoire des Provinces
Unies, vol. iv. pp. 318—320.

ment and the Council of State proved inflexible ; and after several
conferences, feeling somewhat embarrassed by the urgency of the
Dutch negotiators, they suddenly set up, as a preliminary condition,
the claim that the United Provinces should indemnify them for the
expenses which the prospect of a war had already forced them to
incur ; which being granted, they would pursue the negotiations.
It would be impossible, I think, carefully to examine these facts
and documents without coming to the conclusion that, in spite of
the intrigues of the Orangist party, the rulers of the United Provinces were sincerely desirous of peace, whereas, either from passion
or premeditation, the English republicans, both Parliament and
people, obstinately clung to every cause of war, in the hope of
establishing their supremacy at sea, and even of carrying out, by
force of arms, those ambitious designs upon the United Provinces,
which negotiation had failed to crown with success. Perceiving
the inutility of further efforts, Pauw and his colleagues at length
requested an audience to take leave ; on the following day they
were received with great marks of official respect by the Parliament,
to which, before their departure, they delivered a series of documents
in which their propositions and conduct were, in their point of view,
faithfully stated and fully justified. Five days afterwards, on the
7th of July, 1652, the Parliament published its declaration of war,
with an exposition of its motives; and fifteen days afterwards, the
manifesto of the States-General also appeared, accepting, with spirit,
though with regret, the defiance which had been offered them.[1]

Although with forces, in reality, very unequal, the two nations
entered upon the conflict with the same ardour, and almost with
the same confidence. The navy of the United Provinces was, at
that time, superior to that of England, both in reputation and
ability ; it had been formed, for nearly a century, by commercial
enterprise with distant lands, by the conquest and administration
of remote possessions in America and the Indies, and in difficult
and dangerous fisheries ; its sailors were numerous and practised ;
its admirals had begun to introduce, into the command of great
fleets, the art of executing scientific and connected manœuvres,
which was almost unknown at that period, according to their own
historians, to the best English seamen. The latter, on their side,
possessed vessels generally of a larger size, manned by more
numerous crews, and furnished with heavier guns ; they were,

[1] Commons' Journals, vol. vii. pp. 140—142, 147, 149, 150, 152; White-
locke, pp. 537, 538; Dixon's Life of Blake, pp. 195—197; Wicquefort's
Histoire des Provinces Unies, vol. iv. pp. 322—324, Leclerc's Histoire des
Provinces Unies, vol. ii. pp. 318—320.

moreover, thoroughly under the influence of the most energetic human passions, patriotism, pride, ambition, and jealousy: and they had, to back them, a country far more populous and wealthy than the United Provinces, and placed, not under the feeble and mutable direction of a confederation of States, but under the sole authority of a revolutionary assembly, proud of its triumphs at home, and accustomed to lavish men and money for the successful accomplishment of its designs. A month after his encounter with Tromp off Dover, Blake had under his command a fleet of 105 ships of war, carrying 3961 guns, and manned, in addition to their crews, by two regiments of infantry. The Dutch had not been less vigilant in their preparations; they had hired, on account of the State, all the merchant ships of large tonnage which they could obtain ; sixty men-of-war, of immense size, were in process of construction ; a multitude of expert foreign sailors were lured into their service by the promise of high wages; and when Tromp put to sea, he had under his command a fleet of 120 ships, which, in the opinion of every Dutch patriot, would be able to sweep the English navy from the face of the ocean.[1]

On the 21st of June, before even the Dutch ambassadors had left London, or war had been officially declared, Blake set sail from Dover with sixty vessels, leaving one of his lieutenants, Sir George Ayscue, to defend the Channel, whilst he himself sailed northwards, either to protect the numerous English merchantmen which were returning from the Baltic, or to destroy the Dutch fishing-boats, which thronged in vast numbers to the coasts of Scotland and the neighbouring islands for the herring fishery. This fishery had become an important feature in Dutch trade ; a host of small vessels, called busses, were engaged in it, each manned by a family of fishermen, for even the women and children took part in the adventure. It was an unfailing means of subsistence to the poorer classes, and to the State the source of an extensive trade, and a nursery of hardy seamen. More than six hundred barques of all sizes, protected by twelve Dutch men-of-war, were collected in the seas of the north of Scotland when Blake arrived there. Falling suddenly upon them with infinitely superior forces, Blake, notwithstanding their courageous resistance, sank three of the men-of-war, captured the other nine, and seized the six hundred herring-busses ; after taking a tenth of the produce of their fishery as a tribute, from a feeling of generous humanity, he sent

---

[1] Dixon's Life of Blake, pp. 197—202; Memorials of Sir William Penn, vol. i. pp. 395—432.

them home with the remainder, ordering them never again to fish in those waters without having first obtained permission of the Council of State. Meanwhile Tromp, informed by the Dutch ambassadors, on their return, of the English admiral's plan of campaign, came out of the Texel as soon as he knew that Blake was on his way to the north, and made all sail towards the British Channel, with seventy-nine men-of-war and ten fire-ships, in the hope that he would be able to destroy Ayscue's very inferior fleet, and afterwards to effect a landing, or to commit great ravages, along the coast of England. The alarm was great in London and the adjacent counties; the militia of Kent rose in arms to repel the menacing invader; batteries were hastily erected on several points along the coast; courier after courier was sent to Blake to inform him of what was going on in the Channel, and to urge his return. Nature lent the Parliament the aid which Blake could not have had time to afford. In the very midst of the Channel, Tromp's fleet was delayed by a dead calm which rendered all movement impossible, and when the wind returned, it blew from the land, and with such violence, that, notwithstanding the skill and perseverance of the Dutch sailors, they found it impossible to get near enough to the English coast to attack Ayscue, who lay in safety under the cliffs. Immediately renouncing a project which he saw he could not accomplish, Tromp set out with his whole fleet for the North, where he would be sure to fall in with Blake, separated from Ayscue, and distant from any place which might have supplied him with reinforcements; and he promised himself that he would inflict, on the English admiral himself, the defeat which his lieutenant had just escaped. On the 5th of August, the English and Dutch fleets fell in with one another between the Orkneys and the Shetland Isles; the English were considerably weakened, for, on receipt of the news from London, Blake had despatched eight of his best frigates southwards, to reinforce Ayscue; he did not attempt, however, to avoid a battle, and he was making every preparation on board his flag-ship, the *Resolution*, to attack Tromp, when he perceived in the sky, signs of an approaching tempest; feeling certain, that on that day, any engagement would be impossible, he signalled his captains to shelter their ships as they best could in the little archipelago of the Shetland Isles, and so to await the morrow. The storm burst ere long, and lasted all night with unusual violence even for those seas; the wind, rain, thunder, and darkness rendered any concerted manœuvre, and almost all communication, impossible between the ships; the Dutch fleet was dispersed and cruelly damaged; many vessels were wrecked either at sea or on the coast; others fled for refuge to Norway ; the fire-ships were dashed in pieces ; and when morning broke, instead of the noble squadron which he had brought with him, Tromp, as he stood on the deck of the *Brederode*, could only see a few vessels drifting at hap-hazard, dismasted, with their sails in tatters, and still struggling with great difficulty against a sea which was covered with wrecks. He could succeed in collecting only forty-two of his ships, with which he returned in despair to Scheveling in Holland, where he was received with surprise, sorrow, and unjust indignation by his countrymen. Blake, whose fleet had suffered much less severely, pursued the Dutch to their retreat, and as he was unable to come up with them, and bring them to an engagement, he ravaged and insulted their western coasts from Wadden to Zealand, and then ran across to Yarmouth with the ships he had captured, and nine hundred prisoners.[1]

Tromp was proud and sensitive ; wounded and disgusted by the clamours which assailed him because a calm and a tempest had by turns prevented him from engaging the enemy, he resigned his command. He was moreover inclined towards the Orangist party, and the republican aristocracy, who were then predominant, made no efforts to retain his services ; they thought they could give him a successor worthy to fill his place. Not long before, they had appointed to the command of part of their naval forces Michael Ruyter, a man of obscure origin but great popular reputation, beloved by the sailors, a stranger to all political parties, and always ready to serve his country with equal modesty and heroism. No sooner had he embarked on board his ship the *Neptune*, than Ruyter entered the Channel with thirty vessels, fell in with an English fleet off Plymouth under the command of Ayscue, consisting of forty vessels larger and better equipped than his own, attacked it suddenly, and compelled it to retire into Plymouth harbour, leaving the Dutch masters of the open sea. Ruyter himself was humbly astonished at this success : " It is only," he wrote, " when it pleases God to inspire courage that victories are gained : this is a work of Providence for which men could not possibly account." The Parliament, dissatisfied with Ayscue, who was moreover suspected of royalism, deprived him of his command, but not discourteously, and gave him a pension of three hundred pounds, and a landed estate of the same annual value in Ireland . his squadron was placed under the command of Blake. The

[1] Dixon's Life of Blake, pp. 202—207 ; Memorials of Sir William Penn, vol. i. pp. 432—435 ; Whitelocke, pp. 538, 542 ; Heath's Chronicle, pp. 597—599 : Leclerc's Histoire des Provinces Unies, vol. ii. pp. 320, 321 ; Wicquefort's Histoire des Provinces Unies, vol. iv. pp. 331—333.

States-General, on their side, being resolved to carry on the war with energy, had, immediately after Tromp's retirement, fitted out a new squadron; and one of the boldest of the leaders of the aristocratic party, Cornelius de Witt, had been appointed its admiral. He was brave to excess, and thoroughly experienced in nautical matters, but stern, passionate, obstinate and short-sighted, and no favourite with the sailors, who feared his severity, without having confidence in his good fortune. This choice was regarded as political rather than military, and gave great dissatisfaction to the friends of Tromp, who were numerous in the fleet. Before putting to sea, at the very moment when he embarked, Cornelius de Witt was compelled to inflict severe punishment on some mutineers. Ruyter was ordered to join him, and serve under him. Their forces, which effected a junction on the 2nd of October, 1652, between Dunkirk and Newport, amounted to sixty-four sail. Blake had for some time been cruising in the neighbourhood, with a fleet of sixty-eight ships, in search of the enemy, and in the hope of an engagement. Being informed on the 8th of October, that the Dutch fleet was in sight to the north-east of Dover, he pushed rapidly in front of his squadron, signalled all his ships to rally, and gave the order to the crew of his own vessel: " As soon as some more of our fleet comes up, bear in among them !" In a council of war held the previous evening on board the Dutch admiral, Ruyter had given his opinion that a battle should be avoided rather than invited; he had found that several ships in the squadron were in a bad state, and scantily provided with ammunition: perhaps also he had not entire confidence in the good-will of all the crews, and even of all the officers. Cornelius de Witt absolutely insisted upon fighting; and although, during the previous night, a storm had separated from him several of his ships, which were slow in rejoining him, he accepted Blake's attack with an ardour which five hours of unsuccessful conflict did not abate for an instant. Two of the Dutch vessels foundered at the first onset; two others were boarded and taken; and several captains executed the admiral's orders without the zeal and alacrity which are essential to victory. Just before the action began, De Witt wished to remove his flag to the *Brederode*, Tromp's old flag-ship; but the unwillingness of the crew to receive him was so evident that he gave up the idea, and remained on board his own vessel, a huge and unwieldy Indiaman. Ruyter, with his vanguard division, performed prodigies of skilful and devoted valour; De Witt, by his indomitable courage, gained the admiration even of his enemies. But their efforts were vain; the advantage everywhere remained with the English; and when night fell upon the two

fleets, very different feelings swayed the combatants : on board the
English ships reigned the activity of satisfaction and hope, both
officers and sailors laboured cheerfully to repair their damages, to
collect their ammunition, and to prepare for the renewal of the
battle on the morrow ; in the Dutch fleet, on the contrary, extreme
discontent and anxiety prevailed.   De Witt once more assembled
his council of war ; he wished to recommence the fight at daybreak ;
but he was informed that twenty of his captains, without waiting
any orders, or giving any intimation of their purpose, had separated,
under cover of the darkness, from the main body of the fleet, and
sailed no one knew whither.   Ruyter and all the other captains
declared that a second action was impossible : De Witt was obliged
to yield, and to consent to return to Holland to refit his squadron
in its ports, and to receive fresh instructions from the States-
General.   Blake followed the Dutch in their retreat, without
hanging too closely on their rear, and cruised for some days along
their coast, proud of his victory, and jealously determined to make
it unquestionable.[1]

Misfortune and impending danger teach nations justice : the
eyes of all Holland turned once more towards Tromp ; he had not
done all that had been expected of him, but he had not been
defeated ; he had yielded to calm and tempest, not to the English.
It was he who, for twenty years, had commanded the fleets of Holland
against those of Spain, and conquered the independence of his
country at sea.   He was known to be an implacable enemy of the
English navy, by one of whose cruisers he had been taken prisoner
in his youth, and detained more than two years on board his captor.
The voice of the people urged the States-General to restore him to
his command.   The King of Denmark, alarmed at the maritime
preponderance of England, employed his influence at the Hague
to the same purpose.   Tromp was recalled ; all the naval forces of
the State were placed once more under his command ; Cornelius
De Witt, Ruyter, Evertz, and Floritz, the most renowned sea-
captains of Holland, were appointed his vice-admirals.   De Witt
declined, on the ground of ill-health ; he was really ill of fatigue,
chagrin, and anger ; Ruyter accepted without hesitation.   An ally
more brilliant than powerful, Charles II., offered the States-General
to serve, as a simple volunteer, on board their squadron ; he was

[1] Dixon's Life of Blake, pp. 208—215 ; Memorials of Sir William Penn,
vol. i. p. 435 ; Commons' Journals, vol. vii. p. 166 ; Whitelocke, pp. 542, 543 ;
Leclerc's Histoire des Provinces Unies, vol. ii. pp. 321—324 ; Wicquefort's
Histoire des Provinces Unies, vol. iv. pp. 333—336 ; Gerard Brandt's Life of
Ruyter, pp. 18—23.

sure, he said, that many captains in the English fleet were only waiting for an opportunity to come over to him, and would do so as soon as they knew he was near at hand. By the advice of John De Witt, then Pensionary of the Province of Holland, the States-General declined this offer; they had already refused to link their destiny with that of the regicide Commonwealth; and they were equally unwilling to connect their cause with that of the proscribed King. With a staff thus composed, Tromp set to work with earnest energy to refit the fleet with all possible speed; all the ports and arsenals of the United Provinces put forth their utmost resources. The Parliament and Blake believed they would not need to make any fresh efforts for some months: a naval campaign in winter then appeared, even to the bravest seamen, almost an impossibility: several divisions of the English fleet had been sent to their special stations, in the Baltic, the north of Scotland, and the western entrance to the Channel. Blake, modest even in success, and always impressed with a deep sense of his responsibility, had requested the Parliament to associate with him, in the naval command, two experienced generals who would aid him in bearing its weight. Monk and Dean had been appointed to this service; but both were still occupied in completing the subjection of Scotland; and while waiting their arrival, Blake was cruising with his squadron from port to port between Essex and Hampshire, when a report reached him that a large Dutch fleet had put to sea under the command of Tromp, and a few days afterwards, from the outlook of his vessel the *Triumph*, he perceived their ships in full sail between Dover and Calais. Tromp's fleet consisted of seventy-three sail, and Blake had only thirty-seven. He convoked a council of war without delay, to give his captains his instructions rather than to consult them, for he was determined to fight; he inspired them with his own confident ardour, and the battle took place on the following day, with equal impetuosity on both sides. It was a series of individual combats, the brunt of which was chiefly borne by Ruyter, Evertz, and Tromp for the Dutch, and by Blake for the English. Blake was for some time surrounded by a number of the enemy's ships, who boarded him thrice, and were thrice repulsed; but for the obstinate fidelity of two of his own vessels, the *Sapphire* and the *Vanguard*, which stood by him with unwavering steadiness and devotion, the English admiral must have fallen before the overwhelming numbers of his foes. Thick fog and darkness at length separated the two squadrons; but Blake's fleet was *hors de combat;* two of his ships, the *Garland* and the *Bonadventure*, after a desperate resistance, had fallen into the hands of the Dutch; several others, with their sails in shreds, their masts shattered, and their crews disabled, could no longer keep the sea; and Blake accordingly retired into the Thames to repair damages, recall the other divisions of his scattered fleet, and await their arrival in a safe anchorage. Tromp meanwhile sailed up and down the Channel as a conqueror, with a broom at his mast-head, thus braving the English navy in those very seas in which she claimed unrivalled sovereignty: and the States-General, prouder even than their admiral, officially informed the European powers of their victory, and prohibited all correspondence or communication with the British Isles, fancying themselves strong enough to place them in a state of naval blockade.[1]

Blake unreservedly declared his reverse, with firm and sorrowful disinterestedness. "I am bound," he wrote to the Council of State, "to let your honours know that there was much baseness of spirit, not among the merchantmen only, but in many of the State's ships. And therefore I make it my earnest request that your honours would be pleased to send down some gentlemen to take an impartial and strict examination of the deportment of several commanders, that you may know who are to be confided in, and who are not. It will then be time to take into consideration the grounds of some other errors and defects, especially the discouragement and want of seamen. . . . . And I hope it will not be unseasonable for me, in behalf of myself, to desire your honours that you would think of giving me, your unworthy servant, a discharge from this employment as far too great for me ; so that I may spend the remainder of my days in private retirement, and in prayers to the Lord for blessings on you and on this nation." The Council of State did everything that Blake proposed, except granting his petition to be allowed to retire ; three of its members were sent on board the fleet, and subjected the conduct of the officers to a strict examination; several were dismissed, and some even arrested ; the admiral's own brother, Benjamin Blake, being found guilty of some neglect of duty, was cashiered and sent on shore. At the same time, all the disposable ships in the neighbouring ports were required to form the fleet; a resolution was carried to raise the effective marine force to thirty thousand men ; the stores necessary for equipping and repairing the ships were provided without delay ; Monk and Dean were ordered to hold themselves

---

[1] Dixon's Life of Blake, pp. 216—225; Memoirs of Sir William Penn, vol. i. pp. 556—560; Whitelocke, p. 551 ; Clarendon's History of the Rebellion, vol. vi. pp. 601—606; Leclerc's Histoire des Provinces Unies, vol. ii. p. 324; Wicquefort's Histoire des Provinces Unies, vol. iv. p. 336; Brandt's Life of Ruyter, p. 24; Heath's Chronicle, p. 611.

ready to embark, and take their share in the responsibility and dangers of the ensuing campaign. And as to Blake himself, the Council of State wrote to him, " to acquaint him with what they had done for the giving him an addition of strength, and to let him know that they do leave to him, upon the place, to do what he may for his own defence and the service of the Commonwealth."[1]

Two months after his reverse off the Naze, Blake sailed from the mouth of the Thames with sixty men-of-war ; the two most experienced seamen of his country, Penn and Lawson, commanded his van and rear guard ; and he was accompanied by two of the most valiant generals of the land army, Monk and Dean, with twelve hundred veteran soldiers. Twenty other ships from Portsmouth joined him in the Straits. It was the most numerous, the best equipped, and the most ably commanded fleet the Commonwealth had ever put to sea. Blake sailed westward down the Channel, full of impatience and hope that he would soon meet the enemy ; he knew that Tromp would, at that period, be probably on his return from the western coast of France, whither he had gone to meet a large fleet of traders which had been ordered to rendezvous at the Isle of Rhé, and which he was to convoy to Holland. On the 18th of February, at daybreak, between Cape La Hogue and Portland Bill, the Dutch fleet came in sight; and Blake himself, from his flag-ship, the *Triumph*, was one of the first to perceive its advance. Seventy-five men-of-war, and two hundred and fifty merchantmen, sailing under their escort, covered the sea far and wide. Blake at that moment was fortunately within call of his two vice-admirals, Penn and Lawson, though not of his whole fleet ; Monk, among others, was some miles astern with a division. Tromp perceived the temporary superiority of his forces, and giving orders to his convoy to keep to windward, he resolved to begin the engagement at once. At that very moment Blake bore down upon him, and the *Triumph* sent a broadside into the *Brederode*. Tromp received the fire without returning it at first ; but as soon as the two vessels were within musket-shot of each other, he poured his first tremendous broadside into the English flag-ship, then, suddenly tacking round, gave her a second, and quickly reloading his batteries, and passing under his enemy's stern, he discharged into her a third broadside, which took terrible effect on the crew and tackling of the *Triumph*. On seeing the flag-ship surrounded with fire and wreck, Vice-Admiral Penn dashed gallantly in, and attacked

---

[1] Memorials of Sir William Penn, vol. i. pp. 456—466; Dixon's Life of Blake, pp. 225—228; Whitelocke's Memorials, p. 551; Commons' Journals, vol. vii. p. 222.

Tromp in his turn. The entire English squadron arrived successively, and a furious battle was engaged on all sides. It lasted all day long, with alternations of success and defeat which hourly redoubled the ardour of the combatants, making each in turn hope that the victory would remain on his side. Tromp, Ruyter, De Wildt, Kruik, and Severs, among the Dutch captains, and Blake, Penn, Lawson, and Barker, among the English, performed prodigies of valour and skill; Ruyter, surrounded by the English just as he had boarded and taken one of their ships, narrowly escaped being made prisoner. None of the English vessels suffered so severely as that of the admiral himself; his flag-captain, Andrew Ball, and his secretary, Sparrow, were killed by his side; more than half his crew fell before the fire of the Dutch; Blake himself was at last wounded in the thigh, and the same bullet, after hitting him, tore away part of General Dean's buff-coat. At the approach of evening, however, Blake, believing himself in possession of the advantage, ordered some of his ships to sail towards the Dutch convoy and prevent it from escaping. Tromp perceived this manœuvre, and immediately fell back with the main body of his fleet, to cover his convoy. Night fell and put an end to the action. The next day at dawn, Tromp, dispersing his squadron so as to guard his whole convoy, crowded sail and stood up the Channel. Blake followed him with his whole force, came up with him about noon, and the battle was renewed with the utmost fury. Ruyter, on all occasions the boldest and most resolute of the Dutch, was again very near falling into the hands of the English; he owed his safety entirely to the vigilance of Tromp, who, seeing him in imminent peril, sent a ship to support and extricate him from his position. But the efforts of the Dutch admiral were various and divided; whilst fighting, he was incessantly obliged to protect his convoy, and got gradually near the coast of Holland, in order to place it in safety. The second day of the battle was less advantageous to him than the first; four or five of his ships were taken or destroyed. Either from party animosity or from weakness, some of his captains sent, in the evening, to inform him that they had no more powder, and could no longer take part in the fight; he ordered them to withdraw during the night, fearing they might on the morrow be guilty of some treasonous act, or some contagious example of cowardice. On the following day Blake perceived that the Dutch fleet was reduced in number, and with fresh ardour he immediately renewed both the attack upon Tromp and the pursuit of the convoy. Neither the ability nor the energy of the Dutch admiral slackened for a moment; he maintained the fight, rallying with great difficulty his disordered convoy, and gradually retiring along the French coast in order to reach that of his own country. He succeeded in this design on the fourth day after his encounter with Blake, by dint of persevering and intelligent courage, but after having lost, according to the statements of the Dutch, nine ships of war and twenty-four merchantmen, and, according to the English reports, seventeen ships of the first class and more than forty of the second. The States-General, in this emergency, proved themselves worthy of being so faithfully served, for they acted with justice: not only did they express their gratitude to Tromp, Ruyter, Evertz, and Floritz, but, in order to give them an unmistakable proof of their approbation, they made them rich presents, to which the particular States of the province of Holland added gifts of their own. The Parliament, on its side, gave way, somewhat noisily perhaps, to transports of joy; not only did it address official thanks to the commanders of the squadron, and take measures, first by opening a subscription, and afterwards, in the name of the State, to provide for the families of the men who had fallen in the action: but it appointed the celebration of a solemn service of thanksgiving throughout the dominions of the Commonwealth. Wherever the Dutch prisoners landed, they were escorted to London by troops of horse, and in all the towns through which they passed, the bells rang merry peals in celebration of a victory, which had been preceded by such intense anxiety, and which had cost such desperate efforts.[1]

It was at once real and futile; it was an additional vicissitude in a struggle already full of vicissitudes, but not one of those triumphs which definitively settle questions, and decide the fate of nations. Victorious not long before, the United Provinces were now defeated, but not despondent; it soon became known that a new fleet was in preparation in their ports: whoever was the victor, the war only became more ruinous and desperate after every battle.

The Catholic powers of the Continent, France and Spain especially, watched with secret satisfaction this ardent conflict between the two Protestant republics; which, in spite of all their expressions of courtesy, they regarded, in reality, with distrust and ill-will. The English Parliament had found it impossible either to remain

<hr/>

[1] Whitelocke, p. 551; Dixon's Life of Blake, pp. 230—244; Old Parliamentary History, vol. xx. pp. 116—121; Memorials of Sir William Penn, vol. i. pp. 472—485; Wicquefort's Histoire des Provinces Unies, vol. iv. pp. 336—339; Leclerc's Histoire des Provinces Unies, vol. ii. pp. 128—333; Brandt's Life of Ruyter, pp. 28—32.

really neutral between the Courts of Paris and Madrid, or to secure, by a decided choice, an alliance with either of them ; in its indecision, it had always inclined towards Spain, whose inert and feeble policy could lend it no effectual assistance, and had constantly manifested a kind of hostile coolness towards France, whose ambitious activity and increasing strength might have rendered her a most useful ally. Both Courts remained motionless, seeking rather to aggravate than to terminate the war. The Protestant Courts of the North, on their side—Sweden and Denmark, among others—were divided between the two rival republics : the King of Denmark, Frederick III., after having first made the most marked advances in London, took the side of the United Provinces, with which he was connected by commercial interests and prior treaties ; Queen Christina of Sweden showed some favour rather towards the British Commonwealth, but did not declare herself on its side, or lend it any assistance.[1] The ambitious and short-sighted arrogance of the republican Parliament had thrown all the foreign relations of England into disorder, and forced it to adopt a policy which set it at variance with its natural friends, without anywhere providing it with other allies.

At home this policy imposed enormous burdens on the nation, and necessitated an increase of tyranny on the part of the new government. It was requisite to maintain the army constantly on a war-footing, to defend the Commonwealth against the disaffection of the country ; and incessantly to augment the fleet, to defend the country against foreign foes. In December, 1652, the Parliament voted 120,000l. per month for this double defence during the coming year,—80,000l. for the army, and 40,000l. for the fleet ; and new acts of a special character were passed on several occasions, during the course of 1653, to supply the deficiencies of this inadequate budget. And as the public taxes, although very heavy, were not enough to meet such necessities, recourse was constantly had, either to further sales of crown or church lands, or to fresh confiscations either of the revenues, or of the entire property, of delinquent royalists. In November, 1652, the Parliament voted that the parks and palaces of Windsor and Hampton Court, Hyde Park, Greenwich Park, and Somerset House, should be sold, and that the proceeds should be devoted to the expenses of the navy ; bills were also proposed for the sale of the royal forests, and even of several cathedrals, which it was doubtless intended to

[1] Leclerc's Histoire des Provinces Unies, vol. ii. pp. 326, 327; Wicquefort's Histoire des Provinces Unies, vol. iv. pp. 352—361 ; Commons' Journals, vol. vii. pp. 103, 104, 119, 133, 135, 137, 149, 182, 190, 191, 194, 203, 234.

demolish. Many of these measures were either not carried into effect, or were afterwards revoked; but the confiscations and fines inflicted on the royalists were always rigorously levied. In 1651, at the time when the negotiations with the United Provinces were broken off, seventy wealthy Cavaliers were condemned to the confiscation of all their property, both real and personal : during the following year, amid the exigencies of the war, twenty-nine others suffered the same fate; and six hundred and ninety-two others were allowed to ransom their sequestrated possessions only by paying one-third of the value to the Commonwealth within four months.[1] Civil tyranny thus undertook to supply the necessities which an unwise foreign policy had created.

A united and unopposed government would have found it exceedingly difficult to endure such a burden for any length of time. The republican Parliament, with all its feverish enthusiasm, was weak and tottering; for it was rent by violent internal dissensions, and Cromwell, at once powerful and at leisure, made it his sole business to turn its faults to his own advantage, and to undermine the ground beneath its feet.

[1] Commons' Journals, vol. vi. p. 604; vol. vii. pp. 160, 211, 212, 216, 222, 224; Old Parliamentary History, vol. xx. pp. 103—113; Scobell's Collection of Acts, pp. 156, 210.

BOOK IV.

CONFLICT BETWEEN CROMWELL AND THE PARLIAMENT—ATTEMPTS TO OBTAIN A
REDUCTION OF THE ARMY—PROPOSITION OF A GENERAL AMNESTY AND A
NEW ELECTORAL LAW—PROJECTS OF CIVIL AND RELIGIOUS REFORM—CON-
VERSATION BETWEEN CROMWELL AND THE PRINCIPAL LEADERS OF THE
PARLIAMENT AND ARMY—PETITION OF THE ARMY IN FAVOUR OF REFORM,
AND FOR THE DISSOLUTION OF THE PARLIAMENT—CHARGES OF CORRUPTION
AGAINST THE PARLIAMENT—IT ATTEMPTS TO PERPETUATE ITS EXISTENCE
BY SANCTIONING NEW ELECTIONS—URGENCY OF THE CRISIS—CROMWELL
DISSOLVES THE PARLIAMENT.

On the 9th of September, 1651, three days after the Parliament
had appointed four of its members to wait upon Cromwell, and offer
him their most thankful congratulations upon the victory of Worcester, it voted that the charges of the Commonwealth should be
lessened without delay, and directed the Council of State and the
Committee of the Army to furnish it with a return of all the forces
then on foot, that it might consider how the army might be most
conveniently reduced, and the expenses of the State diminished.
On the following day it was resolved, that four thousand cavalry and
four thousand infantry should be disbanded. Six days afterwards,
Cromwell, on resuming his seat in the House, received the solemn
thanks of the Speaker, a gift of lands of the yearly value of four
thousand pounds, and the palace of Hampton Court as a residence ;
but at the same time the House referred it to the Council of State
to consider what forces were necessary to be kept up for the safety
of the country; and in consequence, on the 2nd of October, it
determined that five regiments of foot and three regiments of horse
should be dismissed, that a large number of garrisons should be
reduced, and that the army should be left at an establishment of
about twenty-five thousand men, whereby a saving of thirty-five
thousand pounds per month would be effected.[1]

These measures were evidently dictated by a regard for the

---

[1] Commons' Journals, vol. vii. pp. 15, 18, 19, 23.

public interest : the country groaned beneath the weight of taxation, and it was to be expected that victory would remove at least a part of the burdens imposed by war. But apart from these considerations, the attitude of the Parliament disclosed the prevalence of other feelings and other motives : in its anxiety to disband the troops, its chief object was to weaken a dangerous rival. Such an attempt must be perilous, however necessary and legitimate ; revolutionary governments are never welcome to break the sword which has saved their life ; the service is so great that they can never adequately reward or forget it, and their prudential measures to check ill-satisfied ambition are regarded as evidences of ingratitude and fear. Those powers only, which are based upon right, and sanctioned by time, can recompense and disarm great conquerors without fear of making them their masters.

Cromwell made no resistance, no objection even ; the measure was too natural, and too indisputably necessary to admit of opposition. He was, moreover, greatly pleased at the dismissal of the militia regiments, whose independent habits, and patriotic rather than military spirit, were by no means agreeable to him. But too clear-sighted to mistake the intentions of the Parliament, he hastened, in his turn, to take precautions, and prepare to be avenged upon it. At his instigation, and with his support, two propositions, both popular in the country, although with different parties, were immediately revived, and carried with all expedition through the House : these were a general amnesty, and an electoral law to regulate the period of the dissolution of the Parliament, and the nomination of its successors. Neither of these propositions was a new one ; for more than two years they had figured among the number of those questions which the Parliament announced its intention to determine, and which it made some show of taking into consideration. On the 25th of April, 1649, it had decided, upon the report of Ireton, that an Act of amnesty should be prepared,—the basis of such an Act had been indicated by the House. The bill was produced, read a first and second time on the 5th of July, and referred to a committee, which was to meet on the following day ; after which, nothing more was heard of it. At about the same period, on the 15th of May, 1649, a committee had been appointed to prepare a law for the election of future Parliaments. On the 9th of January, 1650, Vane made a long report on this subject, in which the principles of the new electoral system were set forth : the House resolved that it would meet once a-week to discuss the measure ; and during the years 1650 and 1651, forty-eight sittings were actually held, or at least convoked, for this

purpose. But neither the amnesty nor the electoral law made any
real progress ; the Parliament's only serious occupation was to
maintain itself in power, and defend itself against its enemies. As
soon as, by Cromwell's influence, the two measures were again
brought forward, their supporters allowed the House no rest. The
Act of amnesty was revived on the 17th of September, 1651, and
reported on the 27th of November, and, after being vigorously
debated during sixteen sittings, it was at length adopted on the
24th of February, 1652, with certain modifications and restrictions.
The country took so lively an interest in it, that, on ordering its
publication, the House directed the Council of State to take care
that it was not abusively and incorrectly reprinted, so that no
mischief or inconvenience might arise thereby.   The discussion of
the electoral law was carried on with even greater heat and expedition : it occupied the committee appointed to draft it, and the
House itself, from the 17th of September, 1651, to the 18th of
November following ; special meetings, frequent divisions, and very
small majorities attested both the keenness of the debate, and the
importance of the question ; forty-nine votes against forty-seven,
decided that the moment had come for fixing a term to the duration
of the existing Parliament ; and in all the divisions, we find Cromwell at the head of the most ardent supporters of the dissolution.
They at length gained their point, but the realisation of their triumph
was deferred to a long date: on the 18th of November, 1651, the Parliament voted that it would not continue its sittings beyond the 3rd
of November, 1654.[1]   Thanks to Cromwell's victories, the civil war
between the Parliament and the King had ceased, and yet it was
attempted to assign a duration of three years to the duel which was
about to commence between Cromwell and the Parliament.

From good sense, rather than from moderation or patience of
character, Cromwell could wait ; under all circumstances, he
judiciously estimated how much was possible, and attempted
nothing more, although his desires and intrigues had a much wider
range.   He had succeeded in obtaining the fixation of a term to
the existence of the Parliament ; he did not attempt to abridge that
term to suit his pleasure ; but indirect means presented themselves
to him for harassing, and more speedily exhausting, the power with
which he had to contend ; and he set them in operation, sometimes
with passionate earnestness, and sometimes with profound astute-
ness, according as occasion suggested or allowed.

[1] Commons' Journals, vol. vi. pp. 195, 250, 210, 344; vol. vii. pp. 19, 44,
96, 36, 37; Ludlow's Memoirs, p. 189.

At that period the spirit of innovation in England was not confined to questions of government and political order alone; it extended to civil order also, and demanded, in the laws and judicial procedure, reforms in which the daily interests of the entire population were concerned. On these subjects, numerous ideas were in fermentation, which, though still obscure, vague, and incoherent, were always powerful, because of the rude necessities to which they corresponded, and the unbounded prospects which they opened to view. It was proposed to abolish burdensome taxes, to render the administration of justice less tedious and costly, to simplify the laws relating to property, to lessen the weight of the public debts, to remove the restraints which pressed upon the condition of persons and the ordinary relations of life, and to supply the necessaries of existence at a cheaper rate, and with less difficulty. Among the higher and more enlightened classes, whether from selfishness, or from a love of order and a just understanding of the conditions of the social state, these ideas obtained but little credit; the lawyers, especially, obstinately rejected them, and rallied numerous and respectable interests to resist them. But among the inferior classes, the Levellers, the Mystics, the honest dreamers, or the men of perverse and ill-regulated mind, indeed, all that section of the people, in whom just feelings and bad passions, practical instincts and chimerical absurdities are so closely associated, welcomed with enthusiasm the hope of such reforms, and loudly demanded their immediate accomplishment.

In religious matters, also, desires at once ardent and confused, acute sufferings and grave disorders, excited and maintained a continual agitation. The Anglican Church had fallen; there were no more bishops, no more chapters, no longer an exclusive and official ecclesiastical establishment. But the English nation retained an earnestly religious character; it required an assured form of worship, regular practices of devotion, and an assiduous preaching of the Gospel. The sects satisfied these wants of the soul as far as their own particular adherents were concerned; but the sects formed only a small minority; beyond the sectaries, the proscribed Catholics, and the infidels (who were more numerous at that period than is commonly believed), was the mass of the people, sorrowful and indignant sometimes at being unable to find ministers of their faith, and sometimes at being deprived of those in whom they had confidence, and compelled, by destitution, if not by force, to listen to others in whom they placed no reliance, and whom they regarded with no respect. The Presbyterians had come forward, and towards the close of 1649, the Parliament had given them permission to organise their ecclesiastical establishment, under the title of a National Church;[1] but they met with only very incomplete success, for they were thought to be as exclusive and tyrannical as the Anglican Church had been, and the other dissenting sects rejected them as utterly as the Anglicans themselves. The result of all this, in regard to religion, was a state now of abandonment and death, and now of persecution and anarchy, giving rise to endless clamours, recriminations, disputes, and complaints, which were invariably addressed to the Parliament, as the source of all evils as well as of all remedies, and which it was at a loss for means how either to stifle or to satisfy.

With regard to all these questions of organisation, both civil and religious, Cromwell had no fixed principles, and no unalterable determination : no mind could have been less systematic than his, or less governed by general and preconceived ideas ; but he had an unerring instinct of popular feelings and wishes; and without much caring to inquire how far they were legitimate or capable of satisfaction, he boldly became their patron, in order to make them his allies. He had long ago perceived with what favour any ideas of reform in civil suits would be welcomed, and he had lent them his support. In 1650, writing to the Parliament after the victory of Dunbar, he said : " Relieve the oppressed, hear the groans of poor prisoners in England. Be pleased to reform the abuses of all professions ; and if there be any one that makes many poor to make a few rich, *that* suits not a Commonwealth."[2] When, after the termination of the civil war, he took up his residence in London, with nothing to do but attend to what was passing among the people, or in the Parliament, he became the centre of all projects of this nature, and the hope of their promoters and partisans. On the 27th of October, 1651, certain prisoners confined in the prisons of London addressed him to the effect—" That the law was the badge of the Norman bondage, and that prisons were sanctuaries to rich prisoners, but tortures to the poorer sort, who were not able to fee lawyers and gaolers. They, therefore, pray the General, into whose hands the sword is put, to free them from oppression and slavery, and to restore the nation's fundamental laws and liberties, and to gain a new Representative; and that the poor may have justice, and arrests and imprisonments may be taken away." Six weeks after, numerous petitions arrived from the country, addressed to the General and his officers, and demanding of them " the abolition of

---

[1] Neal's History of the Puritans, vol. iii. pp. 248—250; Grant's Summary of the History of the English Church, vol. ii. p. 413.

[2] Cromwell's Letters and Speeches, vol. ii. p. 217.

tithes, of the excise, and of the managing and unlawful using of the laws of the land, through the number, pride, subtlety, and covetousness of lawyers, attorneys, and clerks, whereby the poor countrymen find the cure worse than the malady." The movement of the people, in this respect, towards the army and its leaders was so universal, that, in several places, officers received authority from the General to sit as judges, and decide suits, " wherewith the people were much satisfied for the quick despatch they received with full hearing."[1]

When religion and the Church were concerned, Cromwell was somewhat more embarrassed ; for, in reference to these matters, he had, not inflexible resolutions, but engagements and allies which he had no wish to abandon. The enthusiastic sectaries of the army, the soldiers of the fifth monarchy (which was to be the reign of Jesus Christ), had constituted his strength, first against the King, and afterwards against the Presbyterian party in the Parliament. He knew all that was to be apprehended or expected from them ; from their military fidelity and their mystical fanaticism, they were, in critical moments, his most necessary and surest instruments ; and he carefully kept up his intimacy with them. But he required, in the religious order of things, a more elevated and extensive influence : this he sought and obtained from two sources, —the regular preaching of the Gospel, and liberty of conscience : he became the avowed protector of these two interests ; by the first he conciliated the Presbyterians, who alone, after the ruin of the Anglican Church, could supply the country with any considerable number of learned, pious, and honoured ministers ; whilst in the name of liberty of conscience he became the man most necessary to all under persecution, even to the Episcopalians and Catholics, who were denied the free exercise of their faith, but who promised themselves that they would obtain from him tacit toleration and secret support. Among all ranks of society, and within the pale of every Christian community, he thus maintained relations and inspired hopes, which furnished him sometimes with grievances, and sometimes with weapons, against the Parliament.

He did not, however, confine himself to this indirect opposition, or rest satisfied with the slow progress which it enabled him to achieve ; he was as full of passionate energy as of cautious artifice, and as eager to strike a decisive blow, when it became possible, as he was persistent in secretly pursuing his object, when it was necessary to wait for opportunities of success. He was anxious to know with some degree of certainty what were the views of those men

[1] Whitelocke's Memorials, pp. 512, 517, 519.

whose co-operation was necessary to him, and how far he might reckon upon their friendly support. On the 10th of December, 1651, he "desired a meeting with divers members of Parliament, and some chief officers of the army," at the house of the Speaker, Lenthall; on the one side were Fleetwood, Desborough, Harrison, and Whalley, his old companions in war and victory; on the other, Whitelocke, Widdrington, St. John, and Lenthall, the civil leaders of the revolution. The conversation is thus reported by Whitelocke.

CROMWELL.—"Now that the old King is dead, and his son defeated, I hold it necessary to come to a settlement of the nation. And in order thereunto, I have requested this meeting that we together may consider and advise, What is fit to be done, and to be presented to the Parliament."

SPEAKER LENTHALL.—"My Lord, this company were very ready to attend your Excellence, and the business you are pleased to propound to us is very necessary to be considered. God hath given marvellous success to our forces under your command; and if we do not improve these mercies to some settlement, such as may be to God's honour, and the good of this Commonwealth, we shall be very much blameworthy."

HARRISON.—"I think that which my Lord General hath propounded, is, To advise as to a settlement both of our civil and spiritual liberties; and so, that the mercies which the Lord hath given in to us may not be cast away. How this may be done is the great question."

WHITELOCKE.—"It is a great question indeed, and not suddenly to be resolved! Yet it were a pity that a meeting of so many able and worthy persons as I see here, should be fruitless. I should humbly offer, in the first place, Whether it be not requisite to be understood in what way this settlement is desired? Whether of an absolute republic, or with any mixture of monarchy?"

CROMWELL.—"My Lord Commissioner Whitelocke hath put us upon the right point; and indeed, it is my meaning that we should consider, Whether a republic, or a mixed monarchical government will be best to be settled? And, if anything monarchical, then, In whom that power shall be placed?"

SIR THOMAS WIDDRINGTON.—"I think a mixed monarchical government will be most suitable to the laws and people of this nation. And if any monarchical, I suppose we shall hold it most just to place that power in one of the sons of the late King."

FLEETWOOD.—"I think that the question, Whether an absolute republic, or a mixed monarchy, be best to be settled in this nation, will not be very easy to be determined."

LORD CHIEF JUSTICE ST. JOHN.—"It will be found, that the government of this nation, without something of monarchical power, will be very difficult to be so settled as not to shake the foundation of our laws, and the liberties of the people."

SPEAKER LENTHALL.—"It will breed a strange confusion to settle a government of this nation without something of monarchy."

DESBOROUGH.—"I beseech you, my Lord, why may not this, as well as other nations, be governed in the way of a republic?"

WHITELOCKE.—"The laws of England are so interwoven with the power and practice of monarchy, that to settle a government without something of monarchy in it, would make so great an alteration in the proceedings of our law, that you will scarce have time to rectify it, nor can we well foresee the inconveniences which will arise thereby."

COLONEL WHALLEY.—"I do not well understand matters of law; but it seems to me the best way, Not to have anything of monarchical power in the settlement of our government. And if we should resolve upon any, whom have we to pitch upon? The King's eldest son hath been in arms against us, and his second son likewise is our enemy."

SIR THOMAS WIDDRINGTON.—"But the late King's third son, the Duke of Gloucester, is still among us, and too young to have been in arms against us, or infected with the principles of our enemies."

WHITELOCKE.—"There may be a day given for the King's eldest son, or for the Duke of York his brother, to come into the Parliament. And upon such terms as shall be thought fit and agreeable both to our civil and spiritual liberties, a settlement may be made with them."

CROMWELL.—"That will be a business of more than ordinary difficulty! But really I think if it may be done with safety and preservation of our rights, both as Englishmen and as Christians, that a settlement with somewhat of monarchical power in it would be very effectual."[1]

The conversation continued for some time in this strain, but no other result was arrived at than to make the leading men in the Parliament and army aware of the designs of Cromwell, and to acquaint him with their feelings and wishes. He also perceived that he might find a dangerous opponent in the young Duke of Gloucester, who was at that time in England, and in the hands of the Parliament. A few months after, the Prince's tutor, Mr.

---

[1] Whitelocke's Memorials, pp. 516, 517.

Lovel, received secret encouragement to request that the Duke of Gloucester might be liberated from prison, and sent into Holland to the Princess of Orange, his sister. He had no difficulty in obtaining this permission, together with a sum of five hundred pounds for the expenses of the voyage, on condition that the Prince should embark at the Isle of Wight, the place of his confinement, and should not touch at any point on the English coast on his way to Holland.[1] Thus a royal competitor was removed, under a show of generosity and kindness.

The republican leaders of the Parliament were not ignorant of the views and intrigues, which Cromwell took so little pains to conceal, and they used their utmost efforts to thwart him. For a considerable period they had attempted to give some satisfaction, or at least to excite hopes that satisfaction would be given, to the desires for reform which were rife all over the country. A committee had been appointed to inquire into the changes necessary to be introduced into the civil law, and the Parliament had more than once urged this committee, which went languidly to work, to proceed with greater energy and assiduity.[2] But these recommendations, which probably were not of a very forcible character, had produced but little effect, and only one important result had emanated from the deliberations of the Committee. It had proposed, and Parliament had adopted, an Act ordaining that in future all the laws, and all proceedings before all Courts of Justice, should be conducted in English, and not in French or Latin ; and to secure the execution of this really popular measure, the Parliament had carefully gone into the minutest details.[3] Some abuses had also been reformed in the practice of the Court of Chancery, and the expense of lawsuits considerably diminished.[4] But either from professional obstinacy, or from a just dread of the consequences of innovation, the lawyers, who predominated in the committee, had strenuously opposed nearly all the plans of the reformers, and it had relapsed into its former languor when the struggle between Cromwell and the Parliament occurred to revive its activity. As soon as it found that Cromwell was seeking this kind of popularity, the Parliament ordained, " That the Committee for regulating the law be revived, and sit to-morrow in the afternoon, and so *de die in diem:* with power to confer with what persons they shall think fit,

---

[1] Clarendon's History of the Rebellion, vol. vii. pp. 87, 88; Heath's Brief Chronicle, p. 614.

[2] Commons' Journals, vol. vi. pp. 280, 328, 485.

[3] Ibid. vol. vi. pp. 487, 488, 490, 493, 500.

[4] Ibid. vol. vi. pp. 509, 525.

and to send for persons, papers, witnesses, and what else may conduce to the business; and to report to the House from time to
time, as often as they shall think fit."[1] But this was only a promise,
that had been renewed several times already, and had always proved
unproductive; it was felt necessary to do something more novel,
and better calculated to inspire the partisans of reform with fresh
confidence. It was determined that a commission should be appointed of persons not members of the House, "to take into
consideration what inconveniences there are in the law, and how
the mischiefs that grow from the delays, the chargeableness, and
the irregularities in law proceedings, may be prevented, and the
speediest way to reform the same;" and that they should report
their opinions and suggestions to a Parliamentary Committee.[2]
Twenty-one persons, nearly all of them eminent for rank or learning,
were selected to form this commission, and the celebrated juris-
consult, Matthew Hale, was the first on the list.[3] The most
important questions of civil legislation were fully discussed: the
registration of marriages, births, and deaths, the transfer of property
and its registration, the abolition of fines upon bills, declarations,
and original writs, the speedy recovery of rents, and other matters
of equal importance; on all these subjects, the commission drafted
schemes of reform for the consideration of the House, several of
which were actually submitted to it by Whitelocke, who, according
to his estimation of the chances of success, became by turns the
opponent or the reporter of innovations.[4] A general work, "containing the system of the law," was also prepared by this Commission
and laid before the House, which heard it read, and ordered that
three hundred copies of it should be printed, "to be delivered to
members of the Parliament only."[5]

In religious matters also, the Parliament would have been glad
to obtain some popularity, and gain for itself, as Cromwell had
done, clients and friends among all denominations. In the year
1650, it had abolished the laws passed during the reign of Queen
Elizabeth to enforce uniformity of faith and worship;[6] but at the
same time, it had continued and even aggravated the persecution
of the Catholics and Episcopalians, and promulgated new laws
against immorality of conduct, "obscene, licentious, and impious

[1] Commons' Journals, vol. vii. p. 26.
[2] Ibid. vol. vii. p. 58; Whitelocke, p. 519.
[3] Ibid. vol. vii. pp. 71, 74.
[4] Ibid. vol. vii. pp. 107, 110.
[5] Ibid. vol. vii. pp. 249, 250.
[6] Ibid. vol. vi. p. 474.

practices," and " atheistical, blasphemous, and execrable opinions ;"[1] attempting by this means to give satisfaction at once to religious animosities, to liberty of conscience, and to austerity of character. Such a task cannot possibly be performed by the power whose duty it is to put all the laws into daily application, and which, even in the eyes of the people whose passions it has adopted, must bear the punishment of their inconsistencies and iniquities. Cromwell, carefully keeping himself aloof from the Government, was able to protect by turns, and with greater or less reserve, sectaries of all sorts, Episcopalians, Catholics, and even freethinkers of the worst kind ; whilst the Parliament, whose duty it was to govern, found itself taxed sometimes with harshness for repressing them, and sometimes with laxity for tolerating them, and gained only enemies where Cromwell recruited partisans.

High-minded and high-spirited men, and Vane especially, were unable patiently to endure this position, and earnestly strove to rise above it. Some great event or some important act could alone achieve their deliverance; they stood in need of some splendid success, which should not be gained for them by Cromwell. This was probably one of the causes which, either from reflection or instinct, instigated them to their project for a close alliance between England and Holland, and to the war which the failure of this attempt occasioned between the two States. Just about this period, another prospect, not wanting in grandeur, presented itself before them. Scotland was subjugated. Monk was governing it with soldier-like sternness, but sensibly and justly. Argyle alone retained, in his domains, some remnant of independence; but it was fraught with no danger to the conquerors. Why should they not incorporate Scotland with England? Great Britain would then form only a single State, as it already formed a single island; and the Commonwealth would have the glory of accomplishing that which England's greatest kings had attempted in vain to effect. On the 9th of September, 1651, scarcely six days after the battle of Worcester, this design was mooted in the Parliament, and before the year was at an end, it was transformed into an express declaration of the entire union of the two countries. Eight commissioners, with Vane and St. John at their head, set out for Scotland, with detailed instructions for its execution. They arrived at Edinburgh on the 20th of January, 1652, and took up their residence at Dalkeith, whither they summoned delegates from all the counties and boroughs of Scotland, in order to obtain their consent to the

---

[1] Commons' Journals, vol. vi. pp. 410, 423, 430, 453.

union. The undertaking was attended with great difficulty; and
had it not been for the authority of Monk and his garrisons, all
Vane's eloquent persuasiveness would probably have failed of
success. The Scottish people were indignant at the idea of losing
their nationality; the Presbyterian clergy protested against any
infraction of the independence of their church, and abjured any
admission of the spiritual power of the Parliament. The vassals
of Argyle refused to obey the orders of the English commissioners.
The Provost of Edinburgh attempted in vain to induce the ministers
of the town to preach in favour of the union; he only obtained
this answer,—"that they knew better what to preach than the
Provost could instruct them."[1] The counties and boroughs which
refused to send delegates, or whose delegates refused to accede to
the union, were deprived of their franchises; and yet, even according
to the computation most favourable to the English, twenty counties
and thirty-five boroughs only, out of ninety, gave their consent.
But victorious force does not need even so much as this to proclaim
that its right is recognised. Argyle, on receiving a promise that
his domains should be protected, and that he should be paid whatever was due to him, consented at length to come to terms. Vane
returned to London, on behalf of the commissioners, to report to
Parliament their success. It was agreed that twenty-one Scottish
delegates should proceed thither soon afterwards, to discuss the
definitive terms of the union; and, on the 13th of April, 1652. on
the report of Whitelocke, in the name of the Council of State, a
bill was brought forward to decree the abolition of royalty in
Scotland, and the union of the two countries under the sole authority
of the Parliament, into whose body a certain number of Scottish
representatives were to be admitted.

A few weeks afterwards, either because this imperfect success
had inspired the Parliament with greater confidence, or because the
necessity of providing for the expenses of the naval war with
Holland appeared to it a favourable opportunity, the question of the
reduction of the army was revived. The House resolved, "that
it be referred to the Council of State (upon conference with the
Lord General and such other persons whom they shall think fit).
to take into consideration both the garrisons and forces in England
and Scotland; and how some considerable retrenchment may be

[1] Cromwell's Letters and Speeches, vol. ii. pp. 315—317; Burnet's History
of his Own Time, vol. i. pp. 112—115; Guizot's Life of Monk, pp. 39—42;
Commons' Journals, vol. vii. pp. 14, 21, 30, 31, 53, 85, 96, 110, 118, 129;
Whitelocke, pp. 519, 521—523, 528, 529; Balfour's Annals of Scotland, vol. iv.
p. 350; Ludlow's Memoirs, p. 172.

made of the charge, with safety to the Commonwealth ; and report the same to the House on to-morrow se'ennight." This resolution had no sooner been passed than the Speaker received a letter from Cromwell, which was read to the House; it has not been inserted in the journals, but it evidently referred to the desire for a reduction of the army which the House had expressed ; for, twelve days after, the expenses of the army in England and Scotland were voted without any reduction.[1]

The Parliament anticipated, and indeed appeared to obtain, better success with regard to the army in Ireland. Although several parts of that island were still in a state of insurrection, or at least of insubordination, the war there was virtually at an end ; all the places of any importance had surrendered, and the enemies of the Commonwealth were nowhere able to make any stand against its soldiers. Another operation, more cruel even than war, had begun, namely, the expropriation and transplantation, either completely or partially, of all the Catholic population of Ireland, for the purpose of paying, in the first place, the adventurers in the loan contracted in 1642, with the Irish confiscations as security ; and secondly, the arrears due to the disbanded soldiers. Such a prospect could not fail to render the reduction of this part of the army more easy of accomplishment. As soon as this terrible remodelling of landed property and the population was effected, the Parliament proposed to incorporate Ireland, as well as Scotland, with England, by granting it also a small amount of influence in the general assembly in which the government of the Commonwealth was vested; and it hoped to exercise a decisive preponderance in a country where it was thus able to dispose everything at its pleasure.[2]

But Cromwell, ever careful to allow no opportunity to escape which might be made conducive to his fortune, had been furnished, by a frivolous incident, with the means of extending his influence to Ireland, and he had hastened to avail himself of them. After the death of Ireton, who, under the title of Lord Deputy, had commanded in Ireland as the lieutenant of Cromwell (who still retained the rank of Governor-General of that kingdom), Lambert, who was then serving in Scotland, was appointed to succeed him, under the same name and with the same powers. Vain and fond of display, he left Scotland in all haste to take possession of his new honours, and made his entry into London, with a large and magnificent train ; having, it is said, spent five thousand pounds on

---

[1] Commons' Journals, vol. vii. pp. 136, 138, 139, 142.

[2] Ibid. vol. vii. pp. 79, 123, 161, 220; Ludlow's Memoirs ; Leland's History of Ireland, vol. iii. pp. 887—897.

his equipage. A few days after, Lady Lambert, his wife, who was as vain as himself. met Ireton's widow, Cromwell's daughter Bridget, in St. James's Park, and pompously took precedence of her. Notwithstanding her piety and sorrow, Lady Ireton felt this insult keenly. Fleetwood, Cromwell's lieutenant-general in the command of all the forces of the Commonwealth, happened by chance to be present at this scene; he was himself a widower, and he offered Lady Ireton first his sympathy and condolence, and ultimately his hand. She accepted without hesitation; the wife of the Lieutenant-General of the Commonwealth would, of course, take precedence on all occasions of the wife of the Lord Deputy of Ireland. This marriage met with Cromwell's entire approval; Fleetwood belonged to a wealthy and important family, and could not fail to prove a useful son-in-law. An opportunity soon presented itself for turning this new connection to profit; Cromwell's commission as Governor-General of Ireland was nearly expired; a proposition was made in the House for its renewal, but Cromwell himself declined this favour, saying that he had enough honours and authorities already. The office of Lord-Lieutenant or Governor-General was therefore suppressed. A Lord-Deputy without a Governor-General was held to be a solecism; and another title, with various compensations, was offered to Lambert; but he would not accept what he considered a diminution of his glories, and resigned his office. It was then decided that the Commander-in-chief of the forces of the Commonwealth should appoint some officer to the command in Ireland, and Cromwell named Fleetwood. But careful to heal the wound that he had inflicted, he attempted, and successfully, to persuade Lambert that the ill-will of the Parliament alone had deprived him of the title of Lord Deputy, which he, Cromwell, would have been delighted that he should retain; and with a thorough comprehension of the meanness which may lie hid under a show of vanity, he expressed to Lambert his regret that his brief dignity should have involved him in such enormous expenses, and requested permission to make up his loss from his own purse; to which Lambert consented, thus placing himself, in his misadventure, under obligation to Cromwell, who, by this means, made his son-in-law the commander in Ireland, and converted the man whom some had attempted to set up as his rival in the army, into a deadly enemy of the Parliament.[1]

He excelled in thus vigorously pushing his advantages. The

[1] Ludlow's Memoirs, p. 177; Hutchinson's Memoirs, pp. 360, 361; Whitelocke, pp. 528, 533, 536.

House, notwithstanding the check which it had just received, persisted in its design of reducing the army. Cromwell resolved openly to engage in the conflict between the army and the Parliament, in the name of all the grievances, real or imaginary, and all the desires, practicable or chimerical, which were rife in the country, and to which the House was continually promising, though it never gave, satisfaction. On the 12th of August, 1652, the House ordered the Council of State, with all convenient speed, to report to it what had been done touching the retrenchment of the forces, particularly in the three garrisons of Exeter, Gloucester, and Bristol. On the same day, a general council of officers met at Whitehall; and on the day following, six of the leaders, Commissary-General Whalley, Colonels Hacker, Barkstead, Okey, and Goffe, and Lieutenant-Colonel Worsley, presented themselves at the door of the House with a petition in which all these grievances and desires, in reference to both civil and religious matters, were summed up in twelve articles, in respectful but peremptory terms, and insisting, at the close, on the enactment of "such qualifications for future and successive Parliaments, as should tend to the election only of such as were pious, and faithful to the interest of the Commonwealth."[1]

The House felt some surprise at this proceeding; such petitions had formerly been used against the Crown; but, since the establishment of the Commonwealth, the army had ceased thus to interfere in the government. Cromwell himself had contributed to lull the fears of the House, for without any scruple about contradicting or belying himself, at the very moment when he was thus secretly instigating the officers to urge the Parliament to dissolve, he had appeared desirous of diverting them from this step, and had given his word to the House that if it should order the army to break their swords and throw them into the sea, they would obey without hesitation.[2] The petition was received with great respect, and referred to a special committee, which was ordered to inquire how many of its particulars were already under consideration, how far they had been proceeded in, and what method might be adopted for their more speedy expedition. The Speaker, on behalf of the House, thanked the officers for their constant affection to the Parliament, and for the vigilant care for the public interest expressed in their petition. But, when these official demonstrations were over, the principal members of the House unreservedly

[1] Commons' Journals, vol. vii. pp. 163, 164; Whitelocke, p. 541; Cromwell's Letters and Speeches, vol. ii. p. 372.
[2] Ludlow's Memoirs, p. 191.

expressed their dissatisfaction at a proceeding, and at language, "so improper if not arrogant, for the officers of the army to use to the Parliament their masters." "You had better stop this way of petitioning by the officers of the army with their swords in their hands," said Whitelocke to Cromwell, "lest in time it may come too home to yourself."[1] But Cromwell made light of his anxiety; no one cared less for the embarrassments which success might one day entail upon him.

About six weeks after this, meeting Whitelocke walking one evening in St. James's Park, Cromwell saluted him "with more than ordinary courtesy," and desired him to walk aside with him that they might have some private discourse together. The following conversation then ensued.

CROMWELL.—"My Lord Whitelocke, I know your faithfulness and engagement in the same good cause with myself, and the rest of our friends; and I know your ability in judgment, and your particular friendship and affection for me; and therefore I desire to advise with you in the main and most important affairs relating to our present condition."

WHITELOCKE.—"Your Excellency hath known me long, and I think will say that you never knew any unfaithfulness or breach of trust by me: and for my particular affection to your person, your favours to me, and your public services, have deserved more than I can manifest. Only there is, with your favour, a mistake in this one thing, touching my weak judgment, which is incapable of doing any considerable service to yourself or this Commonwealth; yet to the utmost of my power, I shall be ready to serve you, and that with all diligence and faithfulness."

CROMWELL.—"I have cause to be, and am, without the least scruple of your faithfulness, and I know your kindness to me, your old friend, and your abilities to serve the Commonwealth; and there are enough besides me that can testify it. I believe our engagements for this Commonwealth have been and are as deep as most men's; and there never was more need of advice and solid hearty counsel, than the present state of our affairs doth require."

WHITELOCKE.—"I suppose no man will mention his particular engagement in this cause, at the same time when your Excellency's engagement is remembered; yet to my capacity, and in my station, few men have engaged farther than I have done; and that, besides the goodness of your own nature and personal knowledge of me, will keep you from any jealousy of my faithfulness."

[1] Commons' Journals, vol. vii. p. 104; Whitelocke, p. 541

CROMWELL.—" I wish there were no more ground of suspicion of others than of you. I can trust you with my life and the most secret matters relating to our business, and to that end I have now desired a little private discourse with you. Really, my Lord, there is very great cause for us to consider the dangerous condition we are all in, and how to make good our station, to improve the mercies and successes which God hath given us, and not to be fooled out of them again, nor to be broken in pieces by our particular jarrings and animosities one against another, but to unite our councils, and hands and hearts, to make good what we have so dearly bought, with so much hazard, blood, and treasure ; and that, the Lord having given us an entire conquest over our enemies, we should not now hazard all again by our private janglings, and bring those mischiefs upon ourselves which our enemies could never do."

WHITELOCKE.—" My Lord, I look upon our present danger as greater than ever it was in the field ; and, as your Excellency truly observes, our proneness is to destroy ourselves, when our enemies could not do it. It is no strange thing for a gallant army, as yours is, after full conquest of their enemies, to grow into factious and ambitious designs ; and it is a wonder to me that they are not in high mutinies, their spirits being active, and few thinking their services to be duly rewarded, and the emulation of the officers breaking out daily more and more, in this time of their vacancy from their employment ; besides, the private soldiers, it may be feared, will in this time of their idleness, grow into disorder ; and it is your excellent conduct which, under God, hath kept them so long in discipline, and free from mutinies."

CROMWELL.—" I have used, and shall use, the utmost of my poor endeavours to keep them all in order and obedience."

WHITELOCKE.—" Your Excellency hath done it hitherto even to admiration."

CROMWELL.—" Truly God hath blessed me in it exceedingly, and I hope will do so still. Your Lordship hath observed most truly the inclinations of the officers of the army to particular factions, and to murmurings that they are not rewarded according to their deserts, that others who have adventured least, have gained most, and they have neither profit, nor preferment, nor place in government, which others hold, who have undergone no hardships nor hazards for the Commonwealth. And herein they have too much of truth ; yet their insolency is very great, and their influence upon the private soldiers works them to the like discontents and murmurings. Then, as for the members of Parliament, the army begins to have a strange distaste against them, and I wish there were not too much cause for it. And really their pride and ambition, and self-seeking, engrossing all places of honour and profit to themselves; and their daily breaking forth into new and violent parties and factions; their delays of business, and design to perpetuate themselves, and to continue the power in their own hands; their meddling in private matters between party and party, contrary to the institution of Parliaments, and their injustice and partiality in those matters; and the scandalous lives of some of the chief of them;—these things, my Lord, do give too much ground for people to open their mouths against them, and to dislike them. Nor can they be kept within the bounds of justice, and law or reason; they themselves being the supreme power of the nation, liable to no account to any, nor to be controlled or regulated by any other power; there being none superior, or co-ordinate with them. So that, unless there be some authority and power so full and so high as to restrain and keep things in better order, and that may be a check to these exorbitances, it will be impossible in human reason to prevent our ruin."

WHITELOCKE.—" I confess the danger we are in by these extravagances and inordinate powers is more than I doubt is generally apprehended; yet, as to that part of it which concerns the soldiery, your Excellency's power and commission is sufficient already to restrain and keep them in their due obedience; and, blessed be God! you have done it hitherto, and I doubt not but by your wisdom you will be able still to do it. As to the members of Parliament, I confess the greatest difficulty lies there, your commission being from them, and they being acknowledged the supreme power of the nation, subject to no control, nor allowing any appeal from them. Yet I am sure your Excellency will not look upon them as generally depraved; too many of them are much to blame in those things you have mentioned, and many unfit things have passed among them; but I hope well of the major part of them, when great matters come to a decision."

CROMWELL.—" My Lord, there is little hope of a good settlement to be made by them,—really there is not: but a great deal of fear, that they will destroy again what the Lord hath done graciously for them and us. We all forget God, and God will forget us, and give us up to confusion; and these men will help it on, if they be suffered to proceed in their ways. Some course must be thought on to curb and restrain them, or we shall be ruined by them."

WHITELOCKE.—" We ourselves have acknowledged them the supreme power, and taken our commissions and authority in the highest concernments from them; and how to restrain and curb them after this, it will be hard to find out a way for it."

CROMWELL. — "What if a man should take upon him to be King?"

WHITELOCKE. — "I think that remedy would be worse than the disease."

CROMWELL. — "Why do you think so?"

WHITELOCKE. — "As to your own person, the title of King would be of no advantage, because you have the full kingly power in you already, concerning the militia, as you are General. As to the nomination of civil officers, those whom you think fittest are seldom refused; and, although you have no negative vote in the passing of laws, yet what you dislike will not easily be carried; and the taxes are already settled, and in your power to dispose the money raised. And as to foreign affairs, though the ceremonial application be made to the Parliament, yet the expectation of good or bad success in it is from your Excellency, and particular solicitations of foreign ministers are made to you only. So that I apprehend indeed less envy, and danger, and pomp, but not less power and real opportunities of doing good, in your being General, than would be if you had assumed the title of King."

CROMWELL. — "I have heard some of your profession observe, that he who is actually King, whether by election or by descent, yet being once King, all acts done by him as King are lawful and justifiable, as by any King who hath the crown by inheritance from his forefathers; and that, by an Act of Parliament in Henry the Seventh's time, it is safer for those who act under a King (be his title what it will) than for those who act under any other power. And surely the power of a King is so great and high, and so universally understood and reverenced by the people of this nation, that the title of it might not only indemnify in a great measure those that act under it, but likewise be of great use and advantage in such times as these, to curb the insolences and extravagances of those whom the present powers cannot control, or at least are the persons themselves who are thus insolent."

WHITELOCKE. — "I agree in the general with what you are pleased to observe as to this title of King; but whether for your Excellency to take this title upon you, as things now are, will be for the good and advantage of yourself and friends, or of the Commonwealth, I do very much doubt, notwithstanding that Act of Parliament of 11 Henry VII., which will be little regarded or observed to us by our enemies, if they should come to get the upper hand of us."

CROMWELL.—" What do you apprehend would be the danger of taking this title?"

WHITELOCKE.—" The danger, I think, would be this. One of the main points of controversy betwixt us and our adversaries, is whether the government of this nation shall be established in monarchy, or in a free State or Commonwealth; and most of our friends have engaged with us upon the hopes of having the government settled in a free State, and to effect that, have undergone all their hazards and difficulties—they being persuaded (though I think much mistaken) that, under the government of a Commonwealth, they shall enjoy more liberty and right, both as to their spiritual and civil concernments, than they shall under monarchy; the pressures and dislike whereof are so fresh in their memories and sufferings. Now, if your Excellency shall take upon you the title of King, this state of our cause will be thereby wholly determined, and monarchy established in your person; and the question will be no more whether our government shall be by a monarch or by a free State, but whether Cromwell or Stuart shall be our king and monarch. And that question, wherein before so great parties of the nation were engaged, and which was universal, will by this means become in effect a private controversy only. Before it was national, what kind of government we should have; now it will become particular, who shall be our governor, whether of the family of the Stuarts, or of the family of the Cromwells. Thus, the state of our controversy being totally changed, all those who were for a Commonwealth (and they are a very great and considerable party), having their hopes therein frustrated, will desert you; your hands will be weakened, your interest straitened, and your cause in apparent danger to be ruined."

CROMWELL.—" I confess you speak reason in this; but what other things can you propound that may obviate the present dangers and difficulties, wherein we are all engaged?"

WHITELOCKE.—" It will be the greatest difficulty to find out such an expedient. I have had many things in my private thoughts upon this business, some of which perhaps are not fit or safe for me to communicate."

CROMWELL.—" I pray, my Lord, what are they? You may trust me with them. There shall no prejudice come to you by any private discourse betwixt us. I shall never betray my friend. You may be as free with me as with your own heart, and shall never suffer by it."

WHITELOCKE.—" I make no scruple to put my life and fortune in your Excellency's hand; and so I shall, if I impart these fancies to you, which are weak, and perhaps may prove offensive to your Excellency; therefore, my best way will be to smother them."

CROMWELL.—"Nay, I prithee, my Lord Whitelocke, let me know them. Be they what they will, they cannot be offensive to me; but I shall take it kindly from you. Therefore I pray do not conceal those thoughts of yours from your faithful friend."

WHITELOCKE.—"Your Excellency honours me with a title far above me; and since you are pleased to command it, I shall discover to you my thoughts herein, and humbly desire you not to take in ill part what I shall say to you."

CROMWELL.—"Indeed I shall not; but I shall take it, as I said, very kindly from you."

WHITELOCKE.—"Give me leave, then, first to consider your Excellency's condition. You are, environed with secret enemies. Upon your subduing of the public enemy, the officers of your army account themselves all victors, and to have had an equal share in the conquest with you. The success which God hath given us, hath not a little elated their minds, and many of them are busy and of turbulent spirits, and are not without their designs how they may dismount your Excellency, and some of themselves get up into the saddle. They want not counsel and encouragement herein, it may be, from some members of the Parliament, who may be jealous of your power and greatness, lest you should grow too high for them, and in time overmaster them; and they will plot to bring you down first, or to clip your wings."

CROMWELL.—"I thank you that you so fully consider my condition. It is a testimony of your love to me and care of me; and you have rightly considered it; and I may say without vanity that in my condition yours is involved and all our friends; and those that plot my ruin will hardly bear your continuance in any condition worthy of you. Besides this, the cause itself may possibly receive some disadvantage by the strugglings and contentions among ourselves. But what, sir, are your thoughts for prevention of those mischiefs that hang over our heads?"

WHITELOCKE.—"Pardon me, sir, in the next place, a little to consider the condition of the King of Scots. This prince being now, by your valour, and the success which God hath given to the Parliament, and to the army under your command, reduced to a very low condition; both he and all about him cannot but be very inclinable to hearken to any terms, whereby their lost hopes may be revived of his being restored to the crown, and they to their fortunes and native country. By a private treaty with him, you may secure yourself and your friends, and their fortunes; you may make yourself and your posterity as great and permanent, to all human probability, as ever any subject was, and provide for your friends. You may put such limits to monarchical power, as will secure our spiritual and civil liberties ; and you may secure the cause in which we are all engaged (and this may be effectually done) by having the power of the militia continued in yourself, and whom you shall agree upon after you. I propound therefore for your Excellency to send to the King of Scots, and to have a private treaty with him for this purpose. And I beseech you to pardon what I have said upon this occasion ; it is out of my affection and service to your Excellency, and to all honest men ; and I humbly pray you not to have any jealousy thereupon of my approved faithfulness to your Excellency and to this Commonwealth."

CROMWELL.—" I have not, I assure you, the least distrust of your faithfulness and friendship to me, and to the cause of this Commonwealth ; and I think you have much reason for what you propound. But it is a matter of so high importance and difficulty, that it deserves more of consideration and debate than is at present allowed us. We shall therefore take a further time to discourse of it."[1]

Cromwell could at his pleasure postpone a conversation with Whitelocke, when it took a turn which was not agreeable to him, but he could not adjourn the impending conflict between the Parliament and himself, which was made manifest, and hastened onwards, by such confidential communications ; it was war, and one of those wars which do not admit of a pacific settlement. Notwithstanding the hypocrisy displayed in the personal relations and language of the antagonists, the conflict was thenceforward avowed and active. Irritated and paralysed at once by the intrigues of its enemy, the Parliament introduced into its management of public affairs the consciousness of its own danger,—and the precautions requisite for its own defence. Never had it manifested so much anxiety to give satisfaction to the wishes of the country ; law reform, the alleviation of the condition of the poor, the measures necessary for securing the preaching of the Gospel, and the maintenance of its ministers in every part of the empire,—indeed all questions of a popular character, whether civil or religious, were the subjects of repeated discussion and deliberation ; and those great political acts which were calculated to throw lustre on the ruling power, such as the union of England and Scotland, the settlement of the affairs of Ireland, and the necessities of the war with the United Provinces,

---

[1] Whitelocke's Memorials, pp. 548—551.

were incessantly under debate. The Government strove hard to obtain a little dignity or favour from every available source. But most of these attempts resulted in nothing ; debates were indefinitely prolonged and resumed, conferences and reports of committees were multiplied to no effect, resolutions which seemed decisive were revoked or called in question. The Parliament was evidently under the sway of a continuous perplexity, which urged it to redouble its efforts, at the same time that it doomed them to unproductiveness.

Cromwell, on his side, was not exempt from anxiety and hesitation ; he had frequent conversations, sometimes with the officers only, sometimes with the officers and members of Parliament together, and sometimes even with Presbyterian or other ministers, whom he consulted as it were upon a case of conscience, in order to bring them over to his views: but he sometimes met with opposition as frank and decided as his own words were indiscreet and passionate. At one of these conferences, Dr. Edmund Calamy, a preacher of great eminence in the city, boldly opposed the system of a sole ruler as unlawful and impracticable. Cromwell answered readily upon the first head of unlawful, and appealed to the safety of the nation being the supreme law. " But," said he, " pray, Mr. Calamy, why impracticable ? " Calamy replied, " Oh! 'tis against the voice of the nation ; there will be nine in ten against you." " Very well," said Cromwell ; " but what if I should disarm the nine, and put a sword in the tenth man's hand, would not that do the business ? "[1] This bold language on the part of a conqueror whose prowess had so often been tried, proved sufficiently seductive to most of the bystanders, but filled others with alarm. The enthusiastically mystical sectaries, with Harrison at their head, were entirely devoted to Cromwell ; the Parliament was, in their eyes, only a profane power which held the place of the government of Christ, the only legitimate King ; and they anticipated, from the piety of Cromwell, the advent of the reign of the saints, and from his valour the overthrow of Antichrist as personified in the Pope and the Turks. Men of unbiassed mind, the secular politicians, clearly understood that the struggle between their General and the Parliament could not be long continued, and that the moment of its termination was at hand. Numerous letters arrived from the army in Scotland, to assure the English army of their sympathy and support. In the army of Ireland the feeling was less unanimous ; Ludlow, who had served there for many years with great distinction,

[1] Forster's Statesmen of the Commonwealth, vol. v. p. 52 ; Life of Oliver Cromwell (London, 1743), p. 225 ; Neal's History of the Puritans, vol. iv. p. 374.

possessed considerable influence, which he employed wholly to keep up the republican spirit. Three officers, Colonel Venables, Quartermaster-general Downing, and Major Streater, went to London to oppose the designs which they saw were in contemplation. Cromwell either gained over or silenced Downing and Venables; but Streater remained firm, and even went so far as to say in a conference, "That the General intended to set up himself, and that it was a betraying of their most glorious cause, for which so much blood had been spilt." Harrison denied this accusation, saying, "That he was assured the General did not seek himself in it, but did it to make way for the rule of Jesus, that He might have the sceptre." "Well," replied Streater, "Christ must come before Christmas, or else he will come too late."[1]

The danger was not so pressing as Streater imagined. Cromwell had the sense to perceive the obstacles which stood in his way, and to take time to surmount them. In the midst of the conflict in which he was so hotly engaged, and doubtless with a view to moderate it by lulling suspicions, he suddenly withdrew his opposition to the plan for a fresh reduction of the army, which had been thrown out by his influence, five months previously; and on the 1st of January, 1653, by agreement between the Parliament and the General, this reduction was positively ordered,—about three thousand infantry, and a thousand cavalry were disbanded, several garrisons were reduced, and a saving of 10,000*l.* a-month was effected in the charges of the Commonwealth.[2]

Cromwell could afford to make the House this sacrifice; it had already received from him, and more especially from itself and from time, the fatal blows beneath which it was finally to succumb. For more than twelve years, in its entire or mutilated state, this Parliament had held the reins of power, and was responsible, in the eyes of England, for events, as well as for its own acts, for what it had failed to foresee, as well as for what it had decreed, for what it had not prevented, as well as for what it had done. And not only for twelve years had the Parliament governed, but it had absorbed into itself all powers; it alone treated and decided on a multitude of questions which, before its time, would have devolved upon the Crown or its agents, the magistrates and the local authorities : confiscations, sequestrations, sales of royal and ecclesiastical domains, the disputes which arose upon these questions, appointments to public offices, the conduct of war by land and sea—the whole

[1] Forster's Statesmen of the Commonwealth, vol. v. p. 44; Life of Oliver Cromwell, p. 228; Whitelocke, p. 553.

[2] Commons' Journals, vol. vii. p. 241.

revolutionary administration and government—were in the hands of the Parliament, which was thus charged with an infinite number of private as well as public interests.   The journals of the House give evidence, on every page, of this monstrous centralisation of affairs of every kind, daily debated and decided either by the House itself, or by its committees ; and this was carried to such an extent, that, from time to time, the House was obliged to determine that for one or two weeks, it would set aside all private affairs, and attend only to the public business of the country.[1] A deplorable state of confusion, truly, in which the Parliament lost not only its time, but its virtue.   Neither the good sense nor the honesty of the majority of mankind could stand against this prolonged enjoyment of power in the midst of chaos : abuses, vexations, malversations, and unlawful transactions sprang up and multiplied, as the natural fruit of such a state of things ; and the Parliament, absolute master of the fortune and fate of a host of citizens, as well as of the fate and fortune of the State, soon became notorious as a den of iniquity and corruption.

Politically, this accusation was unjust.   The political leaders of the republican Parliament, Vane, Sidney, Ludlow, Hutchinson, and Harrington, were men of spotless integrity, passionately devoted to their cause, but pledged to no other interest than the triumph of their cause and passion.   The cause itself, though incompatible with common sense, and regarded with antipathy by the country, was a noble and a moral one ; the principles which presided over it were a firm faith in truth, an affectionate esteem for humanity, respect for its rights, and a desire for its free and glorious development.   But among the secondary, though active ranks of the party, in the minds of a large number of members, both of the Parliament and of the local committees connected with it, and under the influence either of political disappointments, or personal temptations, a spirit of greedy selfishness, license, and indifference, a tendency to despise or doubt the virtues of justice and probity, had made frightful progress, and given rise to disorders which had entailed upon the party and the Parliament, universal disrespect and dislike.

Several disgraceful scandals occurred to justify and exasperate this public feeling.   Lilburne, ever rabid to maintain his rights, and satisfy his animosities, had, on behalf of one of his uncles, claimed the proprietorship of certain mines in the county of Durham, held unlawfully (as he said) by Sir Arthur Haslerig, who was as

---

[1] Commons' Journals, vols. vi. and vii. *passim;* Whitelocke, p. 551.

stirring and popular in the Parliament, as Lilburne in the city. The demand was twice rejected by the committee appointed to inquire into the case. Lilburne accordingly published against his judges a pamphlet,[1] in which he termed them "four of the most unjustest and unworthiest men that ever the Parliament made judges, fit for nothing but to be spewed out of all humane society by all ingenuous rational men, and deserving to have their skins flayed over their ears, stuffed full of straw, and hung up in some public place." He also addressed to the Parliament itself, a petition no less insulting to Haslerig. The Parliament ordered that it should be examined by a committee of fifty members; and after a long investigation, Lilburne was condemned to pay a fine of 3,000*l.* to the State, 2,000*l.* as damages to Haslerig, and 500*l.* a-piece to the four members of the committee which had decided upon his claim, and to be banished from England for life.[2] Whether Lilburne's claim was a just one or not, and whatever may have been the violence of his complaint, such a sentence pronounced, not by judges, but by political enemies, revolted the public by its excessive rigour. The popular feeling became still stronger when this severity was compared with an even more glaring act of indulgence. Lord Howard of Escrick, a member of the House, had been expelled from his seat in Parliament, imprisoned in the Tower, and condemned to pay a fine of 10,000*l.*, for a notorious act of corruption;[3] but his fine was afterwards remitted, and he was set at liberty.[4] In reference to some business about naval prizes, a merchant, named Jacob Stainer, was brought to the bar of the House, and examined with regard to certain letters, in which, alluding either to the Parliament, or to the Council of State, he had written to his correspondent at Antwerp: "We have made a great many friends amongst the great ones, to speak for us in the business, when it comes before them." He gave a rather confused explanation, and was set at liberty on bail a fortnight afterwards.[5] Mr. Blagrave, a member of Parliament, was formally accused, by a person who gave his name, and offered to prove his charge, of having received money for certain appointments: the matter was referred to a special committee, and there remained.[6] The disgraceful avidity of private

---

[1] This pamphlet is entitled: "A just Reproof to Haberdasher's Hall," and was published in August, 1651.
[2] Commons' Journals, vol. vii. pp. 71, 72, 74.
[3] Ibid. vol. vi. p. 591.
[4] Ibid. vol. vi. p. 318; vol. vii. p. 274.
[5] Ibid. vol. vii. pp. 223, 229.
[6] Ibid. vol. vii. p. 257.

interests, and sometimes even the dishonesty of certain members, were thus screened, if not by the complicity, at least by the timorous complaisance of the entire Parliament.

These excessive severities and favours were equally odious on the part of an assembly worn out by its prolonged existence as much as by its numerous mistakes, mutilated by its own hands, still full of discord notwithstanding the smallness of its numbers, which even the defeat of its enemies at home had not strengthened, and which abroad was daily involving the country more deeply in a ruinous war against the only Protestant and republican nation among its neighbours. The public weariness and disgust were manifested on every side; a multitude of pamphlets, which daily became more insolent in their tone, were in circulation; contempt was mingled with hatred; ironical refutations were published of the declarations " of the imaginary Parliament of the unknown Commonwealth of England ;"[1] and it was loudly called upon to make way for an assembly of better men. The House, in great irritation, ordered the Council of State " to suppress the weekly pamphlets, or any other books, that go out to the dishonour of the Parliament and prejudice of the Commonwealth," and gave it powers " to imprison the offenders, and to inflict such other punishment on them as they shall think fit.[2] But neither the anger of the House, nor the powers of the Council of State, were any longer sufficient to repress the hostility of a public who felt they had Cromwell for their ally. The Parliament struggled in vain to live; it was wanting at once in moral force and in material strength ; united at length in a common antipathy, neither the people nor the army would any longer tolerate its existence.

Under the pressure of this position, the republican leaders were preparing with much debate the bill of dissolution, which had so long been demanded of them, when an event occurred which suddenly modified their intentions. The great victory which, about the middle of February, 1653, Blake gained over Tromp in the Channel, appeared to them a favourable circumstance; it threw lustre upon their government ; and soon after overtures of peace arrived from Holland. In the private conclaves of his party, Vane strongly urged them to renounce all dangerous slowness of action. One of his friends, Roger Williams, who was then staying at his house, wrote to a correspondent in New England :—" Here is great thoughts and preparations for a new Parliament. Some of our

[1] Commons' Journals, vol. vii. p. 195.
[2] Ibid. vol. vii. pp. 236, 241.

friends are apt to think a new Parliament will favour us and our cause more than this has done."[1] It was determined that the existing Parliament should dissolve on the 3rd of November in that same year,—that is, a year sooner than had previously been intended; and the House began seriously to discuss the provisions of the Act which was to regulate the election of its successors.[2]

This Act has been lost; it does not exist on the registers of the House, and has been found nowhere else; its essential provisions are, however, known. It established a system almost identical with that which, on the 20th of January, 1649, the general council of officers of the army had submitted to the Parliament: an assembly of four hundred members, to be elected in the counties by all the possessors of an annual income of two hundred pounds in real or personal property, and in the boroughs by all the inhabitants who paid a certain rent, the amount of which was not yet fixed. The schedule of the boroughs to be invested with electoral rights was minutely debated, and it suppressed many ancient privileges. But the electors were called upon only to make up the number of the existing Parliament, and not to renew it entirely; the members then sitting, to the number of about one hundred and fifty, remained *de jure* members of the new Parliament, for the counties or boroughs which they had until then represented. More than this: they alone formed the committee invested with the right of pronouncing upon the validity of the new elections, and the qualifications of the persons elected,—so that, far from running any risk of being excluded from the future Parliament, they continued to be its permanent and predominant nucleus.[3]

This assuredly was not the kind of dissolution which the country and the army expected: the falsehood was gross and palpable. Cromwell, however, grew anxious, and resolved in himself not to suffer such an Act to pass into a law. He was well aware of the powerful influence of legality, and the weaknesses of factions; and he knew how many people there are who, when the crisis approaches, are ready to be satisfied with a little. His intimate confidants, the preachers who were devoted to his person, went about in all directions repeating, even from the pulpit, that the Parliament decidedly was determined not to dissolve, and that in one way or

[1] Forster's Statesmen of the Commonwealth, vol. iii. p. 149.

[2] Commons' Journals, vol. vii. pp. 241, 261, 263, 265, 268, 270, 273, 277.

[3] Cromwell's Letters and Speeches, vol. ii. pp. 379, 380; Godwin's History of the Commonwealth, vol. iii. p. 448; Forster's Statesmen of the Commonwealth, vol. iii. pp. 157—162; Commons' Journals, vol. vii. pp. 273, 752.

another, it would be necessary to force it to do so. Cromwell him-self appeared to be more than ever undecided and perplexed. "I am pushed on," he said one day to Quarter-master-general Vernon, " by two parties to do that, the consideration of the issue whereof makes my hair to stand on end. One of these is headed by Major-General Lambert, who, in revenge of the injury the Parliament did him in not permitting him to go into Ireland with a character and conditions suitable to his merit, will be contented with nothing less than their dissolution. Of the other Major-General Harrison is the chief, who is an honest man and aims at good things, yet, from the impatience of his spirit, will not wait the Lord's leisure, but hurries me on to that which he and all honest men will have cause to re-pent."[1] He sought out all the men of any importance, whether as soldiers or civilians, sometimes assembling them in conference at his house, sometimes sounding them in private conversations, and varying his confidential communications or his falsehoods, according as he wished to divert the suspicions of those whom he addressed, or hoped to gain them over to his design.

On the 19th of April, 1653, a more than usually numerous meeting was held at Whitehall ; all the leading officers, the most eminent lawyers, Whitelocke, Widdrington, and St. John, and some twenty other members of the House, among whom were Sir Arthur Haslerig and Sir Gilbert Pickering, had been summoned or had come thither, either to concert together on what was to be done, or to explain their views. It had become known that the Parlia-mentary leaders, Vane especially, wished to press the adoption of the proposed bill. Cromwell urged the meeting to seek out some means of putting an end to the existing Parliament, and of pro-viding for the government of the Commonwealth until a new Par-liament should be called. He proposed that, as soon as ever the Parliament was dissolved, forty persons, selected from among the members of the House and of the Council of State, should be pro-visionally invested with the administration of public affairs. He had often declared that, "if they should trust the people in an election of a new Parliament according to the old constitution, it would be a tempting of God ; and that his confidence was that God did intend to save and deliver this nation by few, as he had done in former times ; and that five or six men, and some few more, setting themselves to the work, might do more in one day than the Parliament had done or would do in a hundred, as far as he could perceive ; and that such unbiassed men were like to be the

---

[1] Ludlow's Memoirs, p. 190; Whitelocke, p. 553.

only instruments of the people's happiness." The discussion was animated and long ; the bill which the Parliament then had under consideration was attacked as delusive, and destined, not to dissolve, but to perpetuate the Parliament, and as dangerous to the Commonwealth, for it opened the doors of the House to the Presbyterians, its mortal enemies. Widdrington and Whitelocke expressed themselves strongly against any plan for dissolving the Parliament against its own will, and instituting a provisional government in its stead ; in their opinion, such a proceeding was warrantable neither in conscience, nor in wisdom. ' "The work you go about is accursed," cried Haslerig, " it is impossible to devolve this trust." St. John maintained, on the other hand, that, in one way or another, the existing state of things must be brought to an end, and that the power of the Parliament could not be prolonged. Nearly all the officers were of this opinion. Cromwell reproved those who used violent language, and the conference broke up about midnight, without adopting any resolution. It was agreed, however, that they should meet again on the next day, and that the members of the House should take care that no abrupt decision was arrived at upon the bill in question, in order that they might still have time to consult together on the course they intended to pursue.[1]

The next day, the conference was less numerously attended : irritated or alarmed, several of those who had been present on the previous evening did not return, and others went to the House to watch its proceedings, and report to Cromwell. Whitelocke returned to the General's house, and renewed his objections to a dissolution of the Parliament, and the formation of a provisional government; foreseeing that he would be appointed a member of it, and, as he would not dare to refuse to serve, that he would be thereby compromised. While the discussion between them on this point was in progress, Cromwell was informed that the Parliament was sitting, and that Vane, Martyn, and Sidney were pressing the immediate adoption of what they called the dissolution bill. The members of the House who were with Cromwell at Whitehall went off immediately to Westminster; but Cromwell himself remained with his officers, determined still to wait, and not to act unless forced to do so by extreme necessity. Presently Colonel Ingoldsby arrived, exclaiming, " If you mean to do anything decisive, you have no time to lose." The House was on the point of coming to a

[1] Whitelocke, p. 554; Heath's Flagellum, p. 130; Cromwell's Letters and Speeches, vol. ii. p. 380.

P

vote; Vane had insisted with such warmth and earnestness on passing the bill, that Harrison had deemed it necessary " most sweetly and humbly" to conjure his colleagues to pause before they took so important a step. Cromwell left Whitehall in haste, followed by Lambert and five or six officers; and commanded a detachment of soldiers to march round to the House of Commons. On his arrival at Westminster, he stationed guards at the doors and in the lobby of the House, and led round another body to a position just outside the room in which the members were seated. He then entered alone, without noise, "clad in plain black clothes, with grey worsted stockings," as was his custom when he was not in uniform. Vane was speaking, and passion- ately descanting on the urgency of the bill. Cromwell sat down in his usual place, where he was instantly joined by St. John, to whom he said, "that he was come to do that which grieved him to the very soul, and that he had earnestly with tears prayed to God against. Nay, that he had rather be torn in pieces than do it; but there was a necessity laid upon him therein, in order to the glory of God, and the good of the nation." St. John answered, "that he knew not what he meant; but did pray that what it was which must be done, might have a happy issue for the general good;" and so saying, he returned to his seat. Vane was still speaking, and Cromwell listened to him with great attention. He was arguing the necessity of proceeding at once to the last stage of the bill, and with that view, adjured the House to dispense with the usual formalities which should precede its adoption. Cromwell, at this, beckoned to Harrison. "Now is the time," he said; " I must do it!" "Sir," replied Harrison, anxiously, "the work is very great and dangerous." "You say well," answered Cromwell, and sat still for another quarter of an hour. Vane ceased speaking; the Speaker rose to put the question, when Cromwell stood up, took off his hat, and began to speak. At first, he expressed himself in terms of commendation of the Parliament and its members, praising their zeal and care for the public good; but gradually his tone changed, his accents and gestures became more violent; he re- proached the members of the House with their delays, their covetousness, their self-interest, their disregard for justice. "You have no heart to do anything for the public good," he exclaimed; "your intention was to perpetuate yourselves in power. But your time is come! The Lord has done with you! He has chosen other instruments for the carrying on His work, that are more worthy. It is the Lord hath taken me by the hand, and set me on to do this thing." Vane, Wentworth, and Martyn rose to reply to him, but he would not suffer them to speak. "You think, perhaps," he said, "that this is not parliamentary language; I know it; but expect no other language from me." Wentworth at length made himself heard; he declared that this "was indeed the first time that he had ever heard such unbecoming language given to the Parliament; and that it was the more horrid, in that it came from their servant, and their servant whom they had so highly trusted and obliged, and whom, by their unprecedented bounty, they had made what he was." Cromwell thrust his hat upon his head, sprang from his seat into the centre of the floor of the House, and shouted out, "Come, come, we have had enough of this; I'll put an end to your prating—Call them in!" he added briefly to Harrison; the door opened, and twenty or thirty musketeers entered, under the command of Lieutenant-Colonel Worsley.

"You are no Parliament," cried Cromwell; "I say, you are no Parliament! Begone! Give way to honester men." He walked up and down the floor of the House, stamping his foot, and giving his orders. "Fetch him down," he said to Harrison, pointing to the Speaker, who still remained in his chair. Harrison told him to come down, but Lenthall refused. "Take him down," repeated Cromwell; Harrison laid his hand on the Speaker's gown, and he came down immediately. Algernon Sidney was sitting near the Speaker. "Put him out," said Cromwell to Harrison. Sidney did not move. "Put him out," reiterated Cromwell. Harrison and Worsley laid their hands on Sidney's shoulders, upon which he rose and walked out. "This is not honest," exclaimed Vane, "it is against morality and common honesty!" "Sir Harry Vane! Sir Harry Vane!" replied Cromwell; "you might have prevented this extraordinary course; but you are a juggler, and have not so much as common honesty. The Lord deliver me from Sir Harry Vane!" And, amidst the general confusion, as the members passed out before him, he flung nicknames in the face of each. "Some of you are drunkards!" he said, pointing to Mr. Challoner; "some of you are adulterers!" and he looked at Sir Peter Went-worth: "some of you are corrupt unjust persons!" and he glanced at Whitelocke and others; then, turning to Henry Martyn, he said, "Is a whoremaster fit to sit and govern?" He went up to the table on which the mace lay, which was carried before the Speaker, and called to the soldiers, "What shall we do with this bauble? here, take it away." He frequently repeated; "It is you that have forced me to this, for I have sought the Lord night and day, that he would rather slay me than put me upon the doing of this work." Alderman Allen told him, "That it was not yet gone so far, but all things might be restored again; and that, if the soldiers were commanded out of the House, and the mace returned, the public affairs might go on in their course." Cromwell rejected this advice, and called Allen to account for some hundred thousand pounds which, as Treasurer of the army, he had embezzled. Allen replied, "That it was well known that it had not been his fault that his account was not made up long since; that he had often tendered it to the House, and that he asked no favour from any man in that matter." Cromwell ordered him to be arrested, and he was led off by the soldiers. The room was now empty; he seized all the papers, took the Dissolution-Bill from the Clerk, and put it under his cloak; after which he left the House, ordered the doors to be shut, and returned to Whitehall.[1]

At Whitehall, he found several of his officers, who had remained there to wait the event. He related to them what he had done at the House. "When I went there," he said, "I did not think to have done this. But, perceiving the Spirit of God so strong upon me, I would not consult flesh and blood." A few hours later, in the afternoon, he was informed that the Council of State had just assembled in its ordinary place of meeting, in Whitehall itself, under the presidency of Bradshaw. He went to them immediately, followed only by Harrison and Lambert. "Gentlemen," he said, "if you are met here as private persons, you shall not be disturbed, but if as a Council of State, this is no place for you; and since you can't but know what was done at the House this morning, so take notice that the Parliament is dissolved." "Sir," answered Bradshaw, "we have heard what you did at the House in the morning, and before many hours all England will hear it. But, Sir, you are mistaken to think that the Parliament is dissolved; for no power under heaven can dissolve them but themselves. Therefore take you notice of that." All then rose and left the room. On the following day, the 21st of April, this announcement appeared in

---

[1] Whitelocke, p. 554; Leicester's Journal, pp. 139—141; Ludlow's Memoirs, pp. 193, 194; Old Parliamentary History, vol. xx. p. 128; Heath's Chronicle, p. 628; Bates, Elenchus Motuum Nuperorum, part ii. p. 284; Echard's History of England, vol. ii. p. 744; Peck's Memoirs of Oliver Cromwell, pp. 34—36; Clarendon's History of the Rebellion, vol. vii. pp. 1—7; Burton's Parliamentary Diary, vol. iii. pp. 98, 209.

In giving an account of the expulsion of the Long Parliament to M. Servien, in a letter dated May 3, 1653, M. de Bordeaux gives some details which I have not thought it right to insert, as I find them mentioned by no contemporary English writer. They, moreover, appear to me very improbable, as they are at variance both with the general character of the event, and with all other accounts of it.

the *Mercurius Politicus*, which had become Cromwell's journal: "The Lord-General delivered yesterday in Parliament divers reasons wherefore a present period should be put to the sitting of this Parliament, and it was accordingly done, the Speaker and the members all departing. The grounds of which proceedings will, it is probable, be shortly made public." And, on the same day, a crowd collected at the door of the House to read a large placard which had probably been placed there during the night by some Cavalier who was overjoyed at finding his cause avenged on the republicans by a regicide; it bore this inscription:

"This House to be let, unfurnished."[1]

[1] Ludlow's Memoirs, p. 194; Mercurius Politicus, No. 50, p. 238; Forsters Statesmen of the Commonwealth, vol. v. pp. 56—59.

BOOK V.

PUBLIC INDIFFERENCE TO THE EXPULSION OF THE LONG PARLIAMENT—CROM-
WELL'S MANIFESTO TO JUSTIFY HIS CONDUCT—HE ASSUMES POSSESSION OF
THE GOVERNMENT—CONVOCATION OF THE BAREBONE PARLIAMENT—CROM-
WELL'S OPENING SPEECH—CHARACTER AND ACTS OF THE BAREBONE PAR-
LIAMENT—PREVALENCE OF THE MYSTICAL REVOLUTIONARY SPIRIT AMONG
ITS MEMBERS—ITS INEFFICIENCY AND RESIGNATION—CROMWELL IS PRO-
CLAIMED PROTECTOR—PLOTS OF THE REPUBLICANS AND CAVALIERS—LIL-
BURNE, GERARD, AND VOWELL—GOVERNMENT OF CROMWELL ; HIS COURT ;
HIS REFORMS—SCOTLAND AND IRELAND ARE INCORPORATED WITH ENGLAND
—FOREIGN POLICY OF CROMWELL—PEACE WITH HOLLAND—WHITELOCKE'S
EMBASSY TO SWEDEN—CROMWELL'S TREATIES WITH SWEDEN, DENMARK,
AND PORTUGAL—CROMWELL'S RELATIONS WITH SPAIN AND FRANCE—ELECTION
OF A NEW PARLIAMENT—CROMWELL'S OPENING SPEECH—HOSTILITY OF THE
PARLIAMENT—CROMWELL'S SECOND SPEECH, AND SECESSION OF A NUMBER
OF MEMBERS—RENEWAL OF HOSTILITIES BY THE PARLIAMENT—CROMWELL'S
THIRD SPEECH—DISSOLUTION OF THE PARLIAMENT.

THE expulsion of the Long Parliament awakened no feeling but
indifferent and derisive curiosity, both in London and throughout
the country. Not an arm, not a voice was raised in its defence.
" We do not even hear a dog bark at their going," said Cromwell,
in his coarse delight at his triumph. To this hatred and contempt
for the vanquished, was added that movement of popular admiration
which daring and victorious force always inspires : Cromwell had
alone decided, and personally accomplished, this great act. A host
of congratulatory addresses were sent to him, dictated, some by that
servile enthusiasm which hastens to hail the conqueror, but most
by the mystical exultation of the sectaries, who hoped that the
fall of the Parliament would introduce the reign of the Lord.
Other addresses, of a far more important character, arrived,—from
the army in Scotland, which approved unrestrictedly of all that had
been done ; from the army in Ireland, which merely signified its
submission, and recommended the maintenance of discipline, without giving any pledge of political adherence ; and finally, from the
fleet, which the Parliament had treated with such care and predi-

lection, but which was controlled, in Blake's absence, by the influence of Monk, who had long been disposed to connect his own fortunes with Cromwell's greatness, and whose co-operation Cromwell had secured, before attempting his *coup d'état*. Either from accident or design, Blake had been sent, a fortnight previously, on a cruise to the north of Scotland; while moored before Aberdeen, he received the news of the fall of the Parliament; he immediately assembled his captains on board his own vessel. Some of them, sincere republicans like himself, urged him to declare against Cromwell. " No," he said, " it is not for us to mind affairs of state, but to keep foreigners from fooling us;" and from that day forward, abandoning politics, his only aim was to conquer for his country, whoever might be its master.[1]

In the City of London, some of the aldermen ventured a petition " to his Excellency the Lord General," begging him " that the late dissolved Parliament might be suffered again to sit, in order to a new Representative, and that they might regularly dissolve themselves." But a counter-petition immediately arrived from the City, accusing the aldermen who had signed the first, of not having forgotten monarchy, assuring Cromwell of support, and humbly desiring " that he would not look backward, but proceed vigorously in effecting what the Lord and his people, and this poor languishing nation, expect from him, and he has often published."[2]

Both from desire and instinct, it was Cromwell's plan to proceed boldly; but, on the very day after his easy victory, and although no open resistance was offered, obstacles appeared. Great acts of the Divine justice are always combined with great severities, and are frequently executed by instruments which neither inspire confidence, nor command respect. When it fell, the Long Parliament had deserved its fate; it had sometimes misunderstood, and sometimes violated its own principles; it had assumed as rights the evil necessities created by its faults; it had proved itself equally incapable of governing and being governed. Nevertheless, it numbered among its members many men of rare talent and virtue, who, even after their fall, were still held in just estimation; and many honest men who, notwithstanding their obstinate adherence to false views, had been sincerely anxious to promote the welfare of their country, and consequently met with respect and sympathy, on their retirement

---

[1] Cromwell's Letters and Speeches, vol. ii. p. 383; Old Parliamentary History, vol. xx. pp. 143—147; Milton's State Papers, pp. 90—97; Cromwelliana, pp. 119—124; Ludlow's Memoirs, p. 195; Gumble's Life of Monk, p. 71; Dixon's Life of Blake, pp. 241—249.

[2] Cromwelliana, p. 124; Whitelocke, p. 557.

into private life. They no longer had any power to exercise or
defend ; men were therefore more disposed to listen to them ; they
made no attempt to overthrow their conqueror, but they spoke more
freely of him, of his past actions, of his future designs.—Whom
had not Cromwell deceived ? To whom had he not stated the
exact opposite of what he had said elsewhere ? Was he not himself
obnoxious to all the charges which he had brought against the
Parliament ? Who could now believe in his disinterestedness, or rely
on his promises ? Was it to bow before the sword of a general that
England had broken the sceptre of a king ? Questions like these,
occurring to every mind, awakened old animosities, and aroused
unfortunate suspicions; and M. de Bordeaux was well informed
when, a fortnight after the successful accomplishment of the *coup
d'état*, he wrote to the Count de Brienne : " The little satisfaction
which the public manifest at being governed by the officers of war,
and at finding themselves deprived of their ancient privileges, by
the suppression of the Parliament, added to the diversity of opinions
and religions of which the army is composed, gives the general considerable anxiety, it is said, and causes him to fear that his enterprise
will not be so durable or successful as he expected."[1]

Cromwell, however, had not lost a moment in attempting to
gain public approval of his conduct. Two days after the expulsion
of the Parliament, a Declaration appeared, in the name of the
Lord General and his Council of Officers, explaining their motives,
and setting forth the misdeeds of the Parliament, the dangers of
the Commonwealth, and the vain efforts of the army to prevent a
rupture. A few days after this, a second Declaration, emanating
from the same authorities, made a fresh effort to the same end.
But these documents, cold and embarrassed in style, produced little
effect. It was necessary to get out of this precarious position, and
to obtain, for a power which was as yet without form and name, some
real or apparent sanction on the part of the country. Cromwell
sent for Mr. John Carew and Major Salway, two staunch republicans
with whom he had remained on good terms. He complained to
them " of the great weight of affairs that by this undertaking was
fallen upon him, affirming that the thought of the consequences
thereof made him tremble ; and he therefore desired them to free
him from the temptations that might be laid before him, and,
to that end, to go immediately to the Chief-Justice St. John,
Mr Selden, and some others, and endeavour to persuade them to
draw up some instrument that might put the power out of his

---

[1] Archives des Affaires Etrangères de France.

hands." "Sir," answered Major Salway, "the way to free you from this temptation is for you not to look upon yourself as being under it, but to rest persuaded that the power of the nation is in the good people of England, as formerly it was."[1]

Cromwell accordingly assembled at Whitehall the principal men, both officers and civilians, who were near at hand; and at this meeting, at which Carew and Salway were present, it was resolved to summon, from all parts of the Commonwealth, a certain number of "known persons, men fearing God, and of approved integrity," to whom the supreme power should be intrusted. But, as time would be required for their selection and arrival, a Council of State was, in the interim, appointed to conduct the government. Opinions differed as to the number of members of whom it should be composed. Lambert and the more worldly men wished that it should consist of ten persons only, that affairs might be carried on more rapidly; Harrison proposed seventy, the number of the Jewish Sanhedrim; Colonel Okey and other saints insisted on thirteen, as symbolical of Christ and his twelve apostles. Their opinion prevailed, and on the 29th of April, a State Council of thirteen members, nine military men and four civilians, was installed at Whitehall, under the presidency of Cromwell, who announced it to the public, on the next day, by a declaration in his own name, and signed by himself alone: a circumstance which was remarked even then, as indicative of his future designs.[2]

It is said that, notwithstanding the public affronts which he had so recently received at Westminster, Sir Harry Vane, who had retired to his country-seat in Lincolnshire, received an invitation to form part of this new Council of State; and replied that "he believed the reign of the Saints would now begin, but, for his part, he was willing to defer his share in it until he came to Heaven."[3]

Meanwhile, inquiry was made in every direction for those unknown depositaries to whom the sovereignty was to be transferred. Pious and faithful men were wanted, who should not have put themselves forward as candidates, who should not have issued, maimed and mutilated, from the conflicts of popular election, and who

[1] Old Parliamentary History, vol. xx. p. 137; Cromwell's Letters and Speeches, vol. ii. p. 385; Godwin's History of the Commonwealth, vol. ii. p. 520; Ludlow's Memoirs, p. 195; Forster's Statesmen of the Commonwealth, vol. v. p. 133.
[2] Old Parliamentary History, vol. xx. p. 151; Cromwell's Letters and Speeches, vol. ii. p. 386; Cromwelliana, p. 122; Thurloe's State Papers, vol. i. pp. 240—395; Whitelocke, p. 555; Godwin's History of the Commonwealth, vol. iii. pp. 514—520; Forster's Statesmen of the Commonwealth, vol. v. p. 128.
[3] Thurloe's State Papers, vol. i. p. 265.

should owe their appointment solely to the holiness of their life, duly attested, by the common consent of true Christians, to the power whose duty it was to select them.   Those preachers who had influence in the counties assembled their congregations, to consult with them before making such difficult choice.   Cromwell and his officers held frequent meetings, either to invoke the Divine guidance and blessing, or to examine the names and particulars transmitted to them.   The malcontents of every sort, Royalists and Parliamentarians, did their best to cast derision and insult on these proceedings of the new masters of England.   Cromwell, they said, pretended that he was in direct communication with the Holy Spirit, and invested his own wishes with the authority of orders dictated by God himself.   But mockery is an unavailing weapon against enthusiasm and discipline ; neither the sectaries, nor the soldiers of Cromwell were moved by it, and he pursued his work, without caring for such attacks, and ready to laugh at them himself when opportunity offered.   "The reports spread about the Lord General are not true," wrote M. de Bordeaux to M. de Brienne ; "he does really affect great piety, but not any special communication with the Holy Spirit, and he is not so weak as to allow himself to be caught by flattery.   I know that the Portuguese ambassador having complimented him on this change, he made a jest of it."[1]   After a month spent in inquiries and consultations, Cromwell and his Council made a final selection of a hundred and thirty-nine persons— a hundred and twenty-two for England, six for Wales, five for Scotland, and six for Ireland.   All these names had been carefully discussed ; many, that of Fairfax for instance, though at first suggested, were rejected on further consideration ; and several, which had been incorrectly written, were rectified, on the list, by the hand of Cromwell himself.   Some disaffected soldiers, who thought they had as much right to interfere in this operation as their officers, protested, by petition, against certain of those chosen. Cromwell took no notice of their petition, and on the 6th of June, 1653, when he had carefully determined on his list, he addressed, in his own name alone, letters of summons to the hundred and thirty-nine persons whom it specified.   The summons was in these terms :—

"Forasmuch as, upon the dissolution of the late Parliament, it became necessary that the peace, safety, and good government of this Commonwealth should be provided for : and in order thereunto, divers persons fearing God, and of approved fidelity and honesty,

---

[1] Archives des Affaires Etrangères de France.

are, by myself, with the advice of my council of officers, nominated ; to whom the great charge and trust of so weighty affairs is to be committed : and having good assurance of your love to, and courage for, God and the interest of His cause, and that of the good people of this Commonwealth :—I, Oliver Cromwell, Captain-General and Commander-in-Chief of all the armies and forces raised and to be raised within this Commonwealth, do hereby summon and require you, being one of the persons nominated, personally to be and appear at the Council Chamber, commonly known or called by the name of the Council Chamber at Whitehall, within the City of Westminster, upon the Fourth day of July next ensuing the date hereof ; then and there to take upon you the said trust, unto which you are hereby called, and appointed to serve as a Member for the County of ——. And hereof you are not to fail."[1]

This satisfaction being once given to the constitutional scruples of those who surrounded him, until the meeting of this strange Parliament, Cromwell, by means sometimes of the Council of State, and sometimes of the General Council of Officers, took into his hands the entire government. Orders were issued for the continuation of the taxes voted by the expelled Parliament, for the maintenance of the army and fleet. Four judges, respecting whom suspicions were entertained, were dismissed, and two others appointed to try cases in Wales. "The General has sent the Master of the Ceremonies to all the foreign ambassadors," wrote M. de Bordeaux to M. de Brienne, "to assure them that this change will in no degree alter the good understanding and friendship which may exist between their masters and this State, and that, in a few days, we shall know with whom we have to treat."[2] The Council of State, indeed, soon after appointed five of its members to resume the negotiations which had been commenced with the ministers of France and Portugal. Envoys arrived from the States-General of Holland, and from the Grand Duke of Tuscany ; they were received without delay.[3] Neither the diplomatic relations nor the internal affairs of the country suffered any interruption. " Our great change from a hundred and fifty or two hundred governors to ten, has been effected without noise or sorrow," wrote a London merchant, named Morrell,

---

[1] Cromwell's Letters and Speeches, vol. ii. pp. 386, 387 ; Old Parliamentary History, voi. xx. p. 151; Thurloe's State Papers, vol. i. pp. 256, 274, 289, 306 ; Commons' Journals, vol. vii. p. 282 ; Whitelocke, p. 557 ; Heath's Chronicle, p. 639; Godwin's History of the Commonwealth, vol. iii. pp. 521—524.

[2] Archives des Affaires Etrangères de France.

[3] Thurloe's State Papers, vol. i. p. 239 ; Godwin's History of the Commonwealth, vol. iii. pp. 525—528.

to Cardinal Mazarin, with whom he maintained a regular correspondence ; "seeing that the others in four years have done nothing
for the good of the people, either by land or sea, we hope better
things of ten than of two hundred—greater secrecy, more promptitude, less speechifying, more work, without wasting four years in
harangues."[1]

At the same time that he thus took possession of the administration of public affairs, Cromwell was not inattentive to the
security of private interests—his own as well as those of others.
Disturbances, with which political passions were not unconnected,
broke out in Cambridgeshire, in reference to a great draining of the
fens which had been undertaken by a company of which he was
one of the principal promoters ; he wrote at once to the agent of
the company—" I hear some unruly persons have lately committed
great outrages in Cambridgeshire, about Swaffham and Botsham, in
throwing down the works making by the adventurers, and menacing
those they employ thereabout.   Wherefore I desire you to send one
of my troops, with a captain, who may by all means persuade the
people to quiet, by letting them know they must not riotously do
anything, for that must not be suffered ; but that if there be any
wrong done by the adventurers, upon complaint, such course shall
be taken as appertains to justice, and right will be done."[2]   He
further induced the Council of State to take the necessary measures
for securing the reparation of any damages, if the troops were not
sufficient to prevent them.

A few days afterwards he experienced one of those accidents of
fortune, which give strength and grandeur to newly established
authorities, as they appear to be special marks of the Divine favour.
After having been suspended for a time by the victory gained by
Blake over the Dutch in the month of February preceding, the
naval war had recommenced, and was sustained, on the part of the
English, by the squadrons equipped, and the admirals appointed,
by the Parliament.   Tromp held the sea for the United Provinces ;
he was despondent and hopeless, for his fleet, though numerous,
was composed for the most part of battered and ill-manned ships ;
but his courage and skill were undiminished, and he had Ruyter,
De Witt, and Floritz for his lieutenants.   He had just returned
from escorting a large convoy of merchantmen, when he learned
that the English fleet was divided, that Blake had sailed northwards, and that Monk and Dean, with about a hundred sail, were

    [1] Archives des Affaires Etrangères de France.
    [2] Cromwell's Letters and Speeches, vol. ii. p. 385 ; Cromwelliana, p. 128.

cruising to the north of the Straits of Dover, between Ramsgate and Nieuport. He immediately sailed to encounter them, and on the 2nd of June, the action, in which both fleets were equally desirous to engage, began with great vigour, especially on the part of the English. At the first broadside, Dean, who that very morning, beset by gloomy presentiments, had spent a longer time than usual in prayer in his cabin, was struck dead by a cannon shot as he stood by the side of Monk on board their flag-ship, the *Resolution*. Monk threw his cloak over the mangled corpse of his colleague, and continued the fight with renewed ardour. Night at length separated the two fleets, which had suffered almost equally in the conflict. The action began again, on the following day, somewhat late, for Tromp had spent the whole morning in unsuccessful attempts to recover the weather-gage. He was unaware that, either from instinct or from information which had reached him announcing a battle, Blake was at that very moment making all sail towards the south, in order to take part in the action. Suddenly the booming of his artillery was heard behind the Dutch fleet, and in a few moments, a young officer who bore his name, Captain Robert Blake, breaking through the Dutch line, was the first to rejoin the English squadron, amid the joyous cheers of the sailors, whose courage revived at this announcement of the speedy arrival of the Sea King, as they called Blake. Tromp's energy and obstinacy increased with the danger; animated by his reproaches and example, the crew of his vessel, the *Brederode*, boarded Vice-Admiral Penn's flag-ship, the *James;* the English vigorously repulsed their assailants, entered the *Brederode* pell-mell with them, and had already gained possession of the quarter-deck, when Tromp, determined not to be taken alive, threw a lighted match into the powder-magazine, and blew up the deck of the *Brederode* with all those who occupied it. The report immediately spread through the Dutch fleet that their admiral was dead; the whole fleet was thrown into disorder; and several captains took to flight. Tromp, who had escaped by miracle, left the disabled *Brederode* for a fast-sailing frigate, in which he flew through the line of Dutch ships, encouraging the brave to renew the fight, and firing on the timid as they fled. But all his efforts were vain; he was obliged to retreat in his turn, and make sail towards the ports of Holland, hotly pursued by the English. On the following day, the 4th of June, Monk and Blake wrote to announce their victory to Cromwell, and to report the capture of eleven Dutch vessels and 1350 prisoners. Tromp, Ruyter, and De Witt, on their side, hastened to communicate their defeat and its causes to the States-General; declaring that they would go to sea no more unless their fleet were better armed, more abundantly provided with stores, and reinforced by a number of larger ships. " Why should I keep silence any longer?" said Cornelius de Witt, in the Assembly of the States. "I am here before my sovereigns; I am free to speak; and I must say that the English are at present masters both of us and of the seas."[1]

The thanksgiving ordered by the Council of State for this victory had scarcely ceased to resound throughout England, when the assembly of Cromwell's election met, on the 4th of July, in the Council Chamber at Whitehall, in obedience to the order he had issued. Two only of those summoned did not attend. They were seated on chairs arranged around the room, when Cromwell entered, accompanied by a large number of officers. All rose and uncovered at his appearance. Cromwell also took off his hat, and, placing himself with his back to a window opposite the middle of the room, with his hand resting on a chair, he thus addressed them: " Gentlemen, I suppose the summons that hath been instrumental to bring you hither gives you well to understand the occasion of your being here. Howbeit I have something further to impart to you, which is an instrument drawn up by the consent and advice of the principal officers of the army; which is a little (as we conceive) more significant than the letter of summons. We have that here to tender you; and somewhat likewise to say farther to you for our own exoneration, which we hope may be somewhat farther for your satisfaction. And withal, seeing you sit here somewhat uneasily by reason of the scantiness of the room, and heat of the weather, I shall contract myself with respect thereunto." And feeling rather warm himself, he took off his cloak and gave it to an officer, who held it until the assembly broke up, just as he would have done for the king on a similar occasion.[2]

Cromwell did not keep his word, for he spoke for more than two hours. He had not written his speech, and his ideas, however fixed they may have been at the outset, crowded upon his mind with such abundance and rapidity that he seemed rather to abandon himself to their current, than to attempt to arrange, extend, or limit them at

[1] Old Parliamentary History, vol. xx. p. 148; Cromwelliana, pp. 124, 125; Whitelocke, p. 557; Dixon's Life of Blake, pp. 249—253; Memorials of Sir William Penn, vol. i. pp. 491—499; Leclerc's Histoire des Provinces Unies, vol. ii. p. 333; Wicquefort's Histoire des Provinces Unies, vol. iv. p. 379; Brandt's Life of Ruyter, pp. 33—37; Thurloe's State Papers, vol. i. pp. 269, 270.
[2] Old Parliamentary History, vol. xx. p. 152; Cromwell's Letters and Speeches, vol. ii. pp. 390, 391; Leicester's Journal, p. 147.

his will. He was an entire stranger to oratorical art, to harmony of composition, and to elegance of language; he jumbled together, in chaotic confusion, narrative, reflection and argument, pious quotations, commentaries, interpellations, allusions, reminiscences, and speculations on the future; but a deeply political, practical, and precise intention animated all his words, pierced through their confusion, pervaded all their windings; and he impelled his auditors with resistless force towards the object which he wished to attain, by exciting in their minds, at every step, the impression which it was his object to produce. He began by reminding them of the great events they had witnessed from the opening of the Long Parliament to the battle of Worcester: civil war, the trial of the king, the defeat of his son, the subjugation of the three kingdoms—"those strange windings and turnings of Providence, those very great appearances of God, in crossing and thwarting the purposes of men, that he might raise up a poor and contemptible company of men, neither versed in military affairs, nor having much natural propensity to them, into wonderful success." He was anxious to fill the new assembly with a feeling of the power and right of the army, as the instrument and representative of the will of God, who had given it the victory over all its enemies. Thence he passed to a review of his recent conflict with the Parliament, and after having sanctified the army in the name of success, he justified it in the name of necessity. The Parliament had been willing neither to effect the reforms which the people demanded, nor to dissolve really, and restore to the people their free right of suffrage; the lawyers had spent three months in disputing on the meaning of the word *incumbrances*, without coming to an agreement; the conferences which had been obtained, with great difficulty, between the leaders of the Parliament and the officers of the army, had invariably ended in this answer—"the perpetuation of the Parliament can alone save the nation." And not only had they maintained themselves in possession of their seats, by the act which they had prepared for the regulation of new elections, but they had admitted into Parliament many Presbyterians, deserters and enemies of the good cause. "If we had been fought out of our liberties and rights," he said, "necessity would have taught us patience; but to deliver them up would render us the basest persons in the world, and worthy to be accounted haters of God and of his people." The Parliament had, therefore, been dissolved; "and," he continued, "the necessity which led us to do that, hath brought us to the present issue, of exercising an extraordinary way and course to draw you together here. Truly God hath called you to this work, by, I think, as

wonderful providences as ever passed upon the sons of men in so
short a time.   And truly, I think, taking the argument of necessity,
for the Government must not fall ; taking also the appearance of
the hand of God in this thing,—I think you would have been loth
it should have been resigned into the hands of wicked men and
enemies.   I am sure God would not have it so.   It has come,
therefore, to you by the way of necessity ; by the way of the wise
Providence of God, through weak hands."   He then, according to
his custom, made a parade of humility at the very moment that he
was proving his authority and power.   "Truly," he said, "it's
better to pray for you than to counsel you ; and yet, if he that
means to be a servant to you, who hath now called you to the
exercise of the supreme authority, discharge what he conceives to
be a duty to you, we hope you will take it in good part;" and he
proceeded to enlarge upon the conditions of good government,
advising them to do justice to all, "to be as just towards an unbeliever as towards a believer," to show sympathy for the saints,
and to be very compassionate to the infirmities of the saints.
"Therefore, I beseech you," he continued, "though I think I need
not, have a care of the whole flock !   Love the sheep, love the
lambs ; love all, tender all, cherish and countenance all, in all
things that are good.   And if the poorest Christian, the most mistaken Christian, shall desire to live peaceably and quietly under
you,—I say, if any shall desire but to lead a life of godliness and
honesty, let him be protected.   I confess I have said sometimes,
foolishly it may be, I had rather miscarry to a believer than an
unbeliever.   This may seem a paradox : but let's take heed of
doing that which is evil to either !   I think I need not advise,
much less press you, to endeavour the promoting of the Gospel ; to
encourage the ministry ; such a ministry and ministers as be faithful in the land.   Indeed I have but one word more to say to you,
though in that, perhaps, I shall show my weakness ; it's by way of
encouragement to go on in this work.   Perhaps you are not known
by face to one another ; indeed, I am confident you are strangers,
coming from all parts of the nation as you do.   I dare appeal to all
your consciences ; neither directly nor indirectly did you seek for
your coming hither.   You have been passive in coming hither—
being called.   Therefore own your call !   I think it may be truly
said that there never was a supreme authority consisting of such a
body, above one hundred and forty, I believe ; never such a body
that came into the supreme authority before, under such a notion
as this, in such a way of owning God, and being owned by him ;—
if it were a time to compare your standing with that of those that

have been called by the suffrages of the people! Who can tell how soon God may fit the people for such a thing? None can desire it more than I! But this is some digression. I say, own your call, for it is of God!"[1]

How admirable are these instincts on the part of a profound genius, anxious to derive from God that pretended supreme power which he had himself established, and the inherent infirmity of which he already perceived!

The assembly listened to Cromwell with favour and respect. It was not, as some have stated, composed entirely of men of obscure origin and low condition; it included many names illustrious by birth or achievements, and a considerable number of country gentlemen and citizens, of importance in their respective towns and counties, landed proprietors, merchants, tradesmen, or artisans. Most of its members were unquestionably men of orderly life, neither spendthrifts nor in debt, not seekers after employments or adventures, but devotedly attached to their country and their religion, and deficient neither in courage nor in independence. But their habits, their ideas, and even their virtues were narrow and petty, like the social position of most of them. They had more private honesty than political intelligence and spirit; and, notwithstanding the uprightness of their intentions, the probity of their character, and the earnestness of their piety, they were incapable of feeling, and even of comprehending, the high mission to which the will of Cromwell had called them.

They began, however, by appropriating to themselves the name, the forms, and all the external signs of their new rank. They transferred their sittings to Westminster, to the room in which the House of Commons had formerly met. There they received and solemnly read an instrument, signed by the Lord General and his officers, which devolved upon them the supreme authority, and imposed on them an obligation not to retain it after the 3rd of November, 1654, but three months before that time, to make choice of other persons to succeed them, who were not to sit longer than a year, and were then to determine the future government of the country. They resolved, after a long debate, and by a majority of sixty-five votes against forty-six, that they would assume the name of the Parliament. They elected as their Speaker Mr. Francis Rouse, who had been a member of the Long Parliament; ordered

[1] Cromwell's Letters and Speeches, vol. ii. pp. 390—420; Old Parliamentary History, vol. xx. pp. 153—175; Milton's State Papers, pp. 106—114; Despatch from Don Alonzo de Cardeñas to King Philip IV., July 17, 1653, in the Archives of Simancas.

that the mace, which Cromwell had removed, should be replaced on their table; appointed a Council of State of thirty-one members, with instructions similar to those given to the preceding Council; and, in short, resumed all the prerogatives and re-established all the usages of the expelled Parliament.[1]

Cromwell and his officers had made them a Parliament; to show their gratitude, they voted, in their turn, that the Lord General, Major-Generals Lambert, Harrison, and Desborough, and Colonel Tomlinson should be invited to sit with them as members of the House.[2]

On the day on which they installed themselves at Westminster, they devoted nearly their whole sitting to pious exercises; not, as the previous Parliament had done, by attending sermons preached by specially appointed ministers, but by themselves engaging in spontaneous prayers, without the assistance of any professional ecclesiastic. Eight or ten members often spoke in succession, invoking the Divine blessing on their labours, or commenting on passages of Scripture; " and some affirmed," says one of them, " they never enjoyed so much of the spirit and presence of Christ in any of the meetings and exercises of religion in all their lives as they did that day." They therefore persisted in this practice, and instead of appointing a chaplain every day, as soon as a few members had arrived, one of them engaged in prayer, and others followed him, until a sufficient number had assembled to open the sitting and begin business. On the day after their installation, they voted that a special day should be devoted to the solemn invocation of the Divine blessing upon their future acts; and having discharged this duty, with a view to induce the nation to join its prayers to their own, for the same purpose, they published a Declaration, which is expressive at once of proud hopes, of mystical enthusiasm, and of feelings of the deepest humility. " We declare ourselves," they said, " to be the Parliament of the Commonwealth of England. . . . When we look upon ourselves, we are much afraid, and tremble at the mighty work and heavy weight before us, which we justly acknowledge far above, and quite beyond, our strength to wield or poise; so that we oft cry out and say with Jehoshaphat, *O Lord, we know not what to do, but our eye is towards thee!* . . . We hope that God, in His great and free goodness, will not forsake His people; and that we may be fitted and used as instru-

---

[1] Commons' Journals, vol. vii. pp. 281—285; Godwin's History of the Commonwealth, vol. iii. p. 531; Forster's Statesmen of the Commonwealth, vol. v. p. 163.

[2] Commons' Journals, vol. vii. p. 281.

ments in His hand, that all oppressing yokes may be broken, and all burdens removed, and the loins also of the poor and needy may be filled with blessing; that all nations may turn their swords and spears into ploughshares and pruning-hooks, that the wolf may feed with the lamb, and the earth be full of the knowledge of God, as waters cover the sea. This is all we say, If this undertaking be from God, let Him prosper and bless it, and let every one take heed of fighting against God; but if not, let it fall, though we fall before it."[1]

Thus strengthened and confident, they set to work finally to effect those reforms which had been so long and so earnestly desired. Twelve committees were appointed for this purpose: two were intrusted with the settlement of the affairs of Scotland and Ireland, and their incorporation with England; a third had instructions to prepare various measures of law reform; and to a fourth was submitted the question of tithes, which was regarded with the liveliest interest, not only by the clergy and sectaries, but also by political men generally. The naval and military establishments, the public revenue, the public debts and frauds upon the State, petitions, commerce, and corporations, the condition of the poor, the state of the prisons, the promotion of education, and the advancement of learning, occupied the attention of eight other committees. The bills thus prepared were to be immediately submitted to the Parliament for discussion, and voted upon without delay.[2]

The ardour and assiduity of these committees, and of the Parliament itself, in their respective labours, were great. The Parliament voted that it would meet at eight o'clock in the morning of every day in the week, excepting Sunday. Neither the Committees nor the Council of State were to meet while the Parliament was sitting, for the presence of all their members was required in the House itself, and they had to attend to their special missions before and after the general sittings of the House. In a short time, they presented numerous reports to Parliament; the question of tithes, reforms in civil and criminal law, the administration of the finances, the condition and payment of the army, the settlement of debts and the division of lands in Ireland, pauperism, prisons, and petitions formed, one after another, the subjects of long and animated debates.[3] A sincere zeal animated the assembly; questions and

[1] Commons' Journals, vol. vii. pp. 281—283; Old Parliamentary History, vol. xx. pp. 181—189; Forster's Statesmen of the Commonwealth, vol. v. pp. 166—171; Leicester's Journal, p. 148.

[2] Commons' Journals, vol. vii. pp. 285, 286, 287, 288, 323, 326.

[3] Ibid. vol. vii. pp. 338, 285, 286, 288, 290, 292, 293, 297, 298, 299, 300, 301, 302, 303, 304, 308, 310, 315, 316, 324, 326, 327, 330, 331, 334, 341, 354.

considerations of private interest had but little influence in their deliberations; like bold and honest men, their only thought was how they might best serve and reform the State.

But two contingencies which popular reformers never foresee, obstacles and speculative theories, soon arose. In order to accomplish great reforms in a great society, without destroying its peace, the legislator must possess extraordinary wisdom and a high position: reforms, when they originate with the lower classes, are inseparable from revolutions. The Parliament of Cromwell's election was neither sufficiently enlightened, nor sufficiently influential to reform English society, without endangering its tranquillity; and as, at the same time, it was neither so insane, nor so perverse, nor so strong, as blindly to destroy instead of reforming, it soon became powerless, in spite of its honesty and courage, and ridiculous, because it combined earnestness with impotence.

It found, however, one part of its task in a very advanced state: the two committees which the Long Parliament had appointed in 1651, one consisting of members of the House and the other of private individuals, for the purpose of preparing a scheme of law-reform, had left a large body of materials, in which most of the questions mooted were solved, and the solutions even given at length. Twenty-one bills,—seventeen on various points of judicial organisation and civil legislation, and four on points of criminal law and police regulations, as to religion and morals, were ready prepared to receive the force of laws by the vote of the House. The new Parliament ordered that they should be reprinted and distributed among its members. After long debates, however, four measures of reform were alone carried; one to place under the control of the civil magistrates, the celebration and registration of marriages, and the registration of births and deaths; the other three, for the relief of creditors and poor prisoners for debt, for the abolition of certain fines, and for the redress of certain delays in procedure. The collection of taxes, the concentration of all the revenues of the State in one public treasury, and the administration of the army and navy, also formed the subject of regulations which put an end to grave abuses. The question of the distribution of confiscated lands in Ireland, first among the subscribers to the various public loans, and then among the disbanded officers and soldiers, was finally settled. The salaries of the persons employed in several departments of the public service were reduced; and serious and persevering efforts were made to meet all the expenses, and discharge all the liabilities of the State. In these administrative matters, important, though but secondary, the Parliament was guided by a spirit of order, probity, and economy, highly honourable to itself, and useful to the State, though frequently narrow and harsh in its application.[1]

But, when it came to treat of really great political questions, when it was in presence of the obstacles and enemies which those questions raised up against it, then the insufficiency of its information, its chimerical ideas, its anarchical tendencies, its internal dissensions, and the weakness of its position, became fully apparent. A large number of its members ardently longed to accomplish four innovations ; — in ecclesiastical matters, they desired the abolition of tithes, and of lay patronage in presentations to benefices ; in civil affairs, they demanded the suppression of the Court of Chancery, and the substitution of a single code for the vast collections of statutes, customs, and precedents which formed the law of the country. Not only were these innovations naturally opposed by those classes whose interests would be seriously affected by their adoption, by the clergy, the lay impropriators, the magistrates, the lawyers, and all the professions dependent on these ; but they interfered, more or less directly, with those rights of property and hereditary succession which could not be infringed upon, even in the slightest degree, without shaking the whole framework of society. Accordingly, whenever these vital questions were mooted, a deep schism arose in the Parliament : the men who were swayed by class or professional interest, or by a conservative spirit, vehemently opposed the suggested innovations ; and those who, in their desires for reform, had still retained their good sense, demanded that, before the institutions and rights in question were abolished, the House should inquire into the best means of supplying the place of the institutions, and indemnifying the possessors of the rights for their loss. But the reformers, wilfully or blindly obedient to the revolutionary spirit, required that, in the first instance, the innovations which they demanded should be resolved upon, and the principle which they involved be absolutely admitted, and that the House should then inquire what was to be done to fill up the vacancies, and repair the losses which they had occasioned. They did not know what powerful and intimate ties connected the institutions which they attacked with the very foundations of English society, nor how much time and care would be necessary to reform an abuse without injury to the sacred right, or the necessary power, on which it rested. They gained a temporary victory, however, on three questions : the abolition of tithes, of lay patronage, and of the

<hr />

[1] Somers' Tracts, vol. vi. pp. 177—245 ; Commons' Journals, vol. vii. pp. 283, 292, 293, 297, 298, 299, 300, 301, 302, 303, 304, 308, 310, 315, 316, 323, 324, 326, 327, 329, 330, 356—360.

Court of Chancery, and the compilation of a single code, were adopted in principle; but the interests thus injured were strong and skilful; they formed a powerful coalition, and opposed to the practical execution of these general resolutions, such hinderances and delays as rendered them entirely nugatory. Irritated at this resistance, the revolutionary spirit became increasingly manifest; strange propositions multiplied,—some of them puerile, as this, "that all who have applied for offices shall be incapable of public employment;" others menacing, not only to the higher classes, but to all who had a settled occupation, from the demagogic and destructive mysticism which they exhibited. Although strongly opposed in their progress through Parliament, these propositions were always sooner or later adopted; for the zealous and mystical sectaries, with Major-General Harrison at their head, daily obtained a greater preponderance in the House. From their friends out of doors they received impetuous encouragement and support: all questions, whether political or religious, which at any time occupied the attention of Parliament, were discussed at the same time by meetings of private citizens, unlimited as to numbers, unrestricted as to ideas and language. Two Anabaptist preachers, Christopher Feake and Vavasor Powell, may be particularly mentioned: these eloquent enthusiasts held meetings every Monday at Blackfriars, which were crowded by multitudes of hearers, mutually encouraging one another to a spirit of opposition and revolution. At these meetings, foreign politics were treated of, as well as home affairs, with equal violence and even greater ignorance; war with the United Provinces was a favourite theme of the two preachers. "God," they maintained, "had given Holland into the hands of the English: it was to be the landing-place of the saints, whence they shall proceed to pluck the whore of Babylon from her chair, and to establish the kingdom of Christ on the Continent." "Last Monday, in the afternoon," wrote Beverning, the Dutch ambassador in London, to his friend, John de Witt, "I went to the meeting at Blackfriars. The scope and intention of it is to preach down governments, and to stir up the people against the United Netherlands. Being then in the assembly of the saints, I heard one prayer and two sermons; but, good God! what cruel and abominable, and most horrid trumpets of fire, murder, and flame! I thought upon the answer which our Saviour gave to James and John,—'Ye know not what manner of spirit ye are of.'"[1]

[1] Commons' Journals, vol. vii. pp. 283, 284, 285, 286, 290, 304, 352, 335, 336, 321, 325, 333, 334, 346, 340; Cromwell's Letters and Speeches, vol. ii. pp. 429, 430; Thurloe's State Papers, vol. i. pp. 442, 591, 641; Godwin's

Cromwell was an attentive observer of these disorders and conflicts. It was in the name and with the support of the reforming sectaries that he had expelled the Long Parliament, and assumed possession of the supreme power; and he had very recently combined with them in demanding what they now sought to obtain. But he had quickly perceived that such innovators, though useful instruments of destruction, were destructive to the very power they had established: and that the classes among whom conservative interests prevailed, were the natural and permanent allies of authority. Besides, he was influenced by no principles or scruples powerful enough to prevent him, when occasion required, from changing his conduct and seeking out other friends. To govern was his sole aim; whoever stood in the way of his attainment of the reins of government, or of his continuance at the head of the State, was his adversary; he had no friends but his agents. The landed proprietors, the clergy, and the lawyers, had need of him, and were ready to support him if he would defend them: he made an alliance with them, thus completely changing his position, and becoming an aristocrat and conservative instead of a democrat and revolutionist. But he was an able and prudent man, and he knew the art of breaking with old allies only so far as suited his purpose, and of humouring them even when he intended to break with them. He sent for the principal leaders of the sectaries, the Anabaptist preacher, Feake, among others; upbraided them with the blind violence of their opposition which, both at home and abroad, tended only to the advantage of their common enemies, and declared that they would be responsible for all the consequences that might ensue. "My lord," said Feake, "I wish that what you have said, and what I answer, may be recorded in heaven; it is your tampering with the king, and your assuming an exorbitant power, which have made these disorders." "When I heard you begin with a record in heaven," answered Cromwell, "I did not expect that you would have told such a lie upon earth; but, rest assured, that whensoever we shall be harder pressed by the enemy than we have yet been, it will be necessary to begin first with you." And he dismissed them without further rebuke.[1] But his resolution was taken; and, in his soul, the fate of a Parliament in which such persons had so much influence, was irrevocably determined.

On Monday, the 12th of December, 1653, a number of members

History of the Commonwealth, vol. iii. pp. 570—576, vol. iv. pp. 58—60; Forster's Statesmen of the Commonwealth, vol. v. p. 215.

[1] Thurloe's State Papers, vol. i. p. 621; Ludlow's Memoirs, p. 199.

devoted to Cromwell, were observed to enter the House of Commons at an unusually early hour. Francis Rouse, the Speaker, arrived shortly after them, and as soon as ever it was possible, a House was formed. The members of the reform party, astonished at an enthusiasm for which there was no apparent motive, and suspecting some secret design, sent messengers in all directions to entreat the immediate attendance of their friends. But no sooner had prayers been said, than Colonel Sydenham rose to address the House. "He must take leave," he said, "to unburthen himself of some things that had long lain upon his heart. He had to speak, not of matters relating to the well-being of the Commonwealth, but that were inseparable from its very existence." He then made a most violent attack upon the measures of the Parliament, and particularly of a majority of its members. "They aimed," he went on to say, "at no less than destroying the clergy, the law, and the property of the subject. Their purpose was to take away the law of the land, and the birthrights of Englishmen, for which all had so long been contending with their blood, and to substitute in their room a code, modelled on the law of Moses, and which was adapted only for the nation of the Jews. In the heat of a preposterous fervour, they had even laid the axe to the root of the Christian ministry, alleging that it was Babylonish, and that it was Antichrist. They were the enemies of all intellectual cultivation, and all learning. They had also brought forward motions which, in no equivocal manner, indicated a deep-laid design for the total dissolution of the army. In these circumstances," continued Sydenham, "he could no longer satisfy himself to sit in that House; and he moved that the continuance of this Parliament, as now constituted, would not be for the good of the Commonwealth; and that, therefore, it was requisite that the House, in a body, should repair to the Lord-General, to deliver back into his hands the powers which they had received from him." Colonel Sydenham's motion was at once seconded by Sir Charles Wolseley, a gentleman of Oxfordshire, and one of Cromwell's confidants.[1]

Notwithstanding their surprise and indignation, the reformers defended themselves; one of them rose immediately, to protest against the motion. He treated most of Colonel Sydenham's assertions as calumnies, enumerated the various measures conducive to

[1] Commons' Journals, vol. vii. p. 363; Somers' Tracts, vol. vi. pp. 266—284; Ludlow's Memoirs, pp. 199, 200; Old Parliamentary History, vol. xx. pp. 239—244; Whitelocke, p. 570; Cromwelliana, p. 130; Harris's Life of Cromwell, p. 331; Godwin's History of the Commonwealth, vol. iii. pp. 523—592; Forster's Statesmen of the Commonwealth, vol. v. pp. 216—222.

the public advantage that had been passed, or were still in progress, extolled in the highest terms the disinterestedness of the Parliament, and its zeal for the public good, and earnestly protested against the adoption of a measure fraught with such incalculable calamities as the voluntary resignation of that Parliament would prove. Other members spoke to the same effect; some said that they had to propose means of reconciliation which would satisfy all parties. The debate promised to be of considerable duration. Many of the reformers, who had been sent for, were now arriving, and the issue seemed exceedingly doubtful. Rouse, the Speaker, suddenly left the chair, and broke up the sitting. The sergeant took up the mace and carried it before him, as he left the hall. About forty members followed him, and they proceeded together towards Whitehall. Thirty or thirty-five members remained in the House, in great indignation and embarrassment, for they were not sufficiently numerous to make a House; but twenty-seven of them, Harrison among the number, resolved to keep their seats, and proposed to pass the time in prayer. But two officers, Colonel Goffe and Major White, suddenly entered the House, and desired them to withdraw; they answered that they would not do so, unless compelled by force. White called in a file of musketeers; the House was cleared, and sentinels were placed at the doors, in charge of the keys.[1]

The Cavaliers, in their ironical narratives of the occurrence, assert that, on entering the House, White said to Harrison : " What do you here?" " We are seeking the Lord," replied Harrison. " Then," returned White, " you may go elsewhere, for, to my certain knowledge, he has not been here these twelve years." [2]

Meanwhile, the Speaker, and the members who had accompanied him, had arrived at Whitehall. They first of all went into a private room, and hurriedly wrote a brief resignation of their power into Cromwell's hands. This they signed, and then demanded an interview with the Lord General. He expressed extreme surprise at their proceeding, declaring that he was not prepared for such an offer, nor able to load himself with so heavy and serious a burden. But Lambert, Sydenham, and the other members present, insisted; their resolution was taken ;—he must accept the restoration of power which he had himself conferred. He yielded at last. The act of abdication was left open for three or four days, for the signatures of those members who had not come to Whitehall; and it soon exhibited eighty names—a majority of the whole assembly.

[1] Forster's Statesmen of the Commonwealth, vol. ii. pp. 219, 220.
[2] Ibid.

Cromwell had slain the Long Parliament with his own hand ; he did not vouchsafe so much honour to the Parliament which he had himself created ; a ridiculous act of suicide, and the ridiculous nick-name which it derived from one of its most obscure members, Mr. Praisegod Barebone,[1] a leather-seller in the city of London, are the only recollections which this assembly has left in history. And yet, it was deficient neither in honesty nor in patriotism ; but it was ab-solutely wanting in dignity when it allowed its existence to rest on a falsehood, and in good sense when it attempted to reform the whole framework of English society : such a task was infinitely above its strength and capacity. The Barebone Parliament had been intended by Cromwell as an expedient ; it disappeared as soon as it attempted to become an independent power.

Four days after the fall of the Barebone Parliament, on the 16th of December, 1653, at one o'clock in the afternoon, a pompous caval-cade proceeded from Whitehall to Westminster, between a double line of soldiery. The Lords Commissioners of the Great Seal, the Judges, the Council of State, the Lord Mayor and Aldermen of the City of London, in their scarlet robes and state carriages, headed the procession. After them came Cromwell, in a simple suit of black velvet, with long boots, and a broad gold band round his hat. His guards and a large number of gentlemen, bareheaded, walked before his carriage, which was surrounded by the principal officers of the army, sword in hand, and hat on head. On arriving at Westminster Hall, the procession entered the Court of Chancery, at one end of which a chair of state had been placed. Cromwell stood in front of the chair, and as soon as the assembly was seated, Major-General Lambert announced the voluntary dissolution of the late Parliament, and in the name of the army of the three nations, and of the exigencies of the time, prayed the Lord General to accept the office of Protector of the Commonwealth of England, Scotland, and Ireland.

After a moment's modest hesitation, Cromwell expressed his readiness to undertake the charge. One of the clerks of the council, Mr. Jessop, then read the act or instrument in which the consti-tution of the Protectoral Government was embodied in forty-two

---

[1] Mr. Godwin (History of the Commonwealth, vol. iii. p. 524) and Mr. Forster (Statesmen of the Commonwealth, vol. v. p. 144) have taken con-siderable pains to establish that this person's real name was *Barbone*, and not *Barebone*, and thus to remove the ridicule attaching to the latter name ; but, by their own admission, the writ of summons addressed to this member spells his name as *Barebone* ; I have therefore retained this spelling, which seems to be at once officially and historically correct.

articles. Cromwell thereupon read and signed the oath, "to take upon him the protection and government of these nations, in the manner expressed in the form of government hereunto annexed." Lambert, falling on his knees, offered to the Lord Protector a civic sword in the scabbard, and Cromwell, on receiving it, laid aside his own, to denote thereby that he intended to govern no longer by military law alone. The Commissioners of the Great Seal, the Judges, and the officers, pressed him to take his seat in the chair of state provided for him. He did so, and put on his hat, while the rest remained uncovered. The Lord Mayor, in his turn, offered his sword to the Protector, who delivered it back again to him immediately, exhorting him to use it well. The ceremony was now consummated; the procession returned to Whitehall, greeted rather by general curiosity than by popular acclamations. Cromwell's chaplain, Mr. Lockier, delivered a solemn exhortation in the Banqueting Hall; and between four and five o'clock a triple discharge of artillery announced that the Lord Protector had taken up his residence in his palace of Whitehall. He was proclaimed without delay, under this title, in every quarter of London, and in all the counties and cities of England. The original intention had been, it is said, to confer upon him at once the title of king, and the instrument of government had been at first prepared in conformity with that idea; but either from natural prudence, or from consideration for the open opposition of some of his most intimate confidants, Cromwell himself discountenanced so abrupt a return to the monarchical system, and, in order still to retain the name of Commonwealth, would accept no other title but that of Protector.[1]

The Parliament might abdicate, but the Sectaries, Anabaptists, Millenarians, and others, did not feel disposed to do so. Two days after the installation of the Protector, a more numerous audience than usual assembled at Blackfriars, around the pulpit of their favourite preacher, Mr. Feake, whose denunciations of Cromwell were violent in the extreme. "Go and tell your Protector," he said, "that he has deceived the Lord's people, that he is a perjured villain. But he will not reign long; he will end worse than the last Protector did, that crooked tyrant, Richard. Tell him I said it." Feake was summoned before the Council, and placed in custody. Major-General Harrison, the most eminent man of the Anabaptist party, was asked whether he would acknowledge the new Protectoral Government; he frankly answered, "No." His com-

---

[1] Old Parliamentary History, vol. xx. pp. 216--265; Cromwelliana, pp. 130, 131; Thurloe's State Papers, vol. i. pp. 632, 611, 641, 669; Whitelocke, pp. 571—577; Forster's Statesmen of the Commonwealth, vol. v. pp. 223—228.

mission was accordingly taken from him, and he received orders to retire home to Staffordshire, and keep quiet.[1]

Cromwell was not mistaken when he foresaw that from this source would proceed, if not his most serious danger, at all events his most troublesome embarrassments. Already, six months previously, he had found himself once more in presence of that indomitable Leveller, who, in the early days of the Commonwealth, had waged against him so vigorous and unceasing a warfare. On the 3rd of May, 1653, as soon as he heard of the expulsion of the Long Parliament, Lilburne wrote to Cromwell, in respectful but uncringing language, to request permission to return to England. As he had been banished by the Long Parliament, he hoped that Cromwell, though formerly his enemy, would grant him reparation for the injustice done him by that assembly. Having received no answer to his letter, he returned to England without permission, and published, on his arrival in London, a pamphlet, entitled: "The Banished Man's Suit for Protection to General Cromwell." He was immediately arrested and imprisoned in Newgate. But he infinitely preferred imprisonment to exile, for while in Newgate, his own intrepid skill and the devoted attachment of his partisans enabled him daily to speak, write, and act, and to employ others to speak, write, and act for him. Cromwell, the Council of State, the law courts, and the Barebone Parliament, were incessantly assailed by petitions from himself and his friends. Six of his adherents, in the name of "the young men and apprentices of the cities of London and Westminster, borough of Southwark, and the parts adjacent," appeared one day at the bar of the House to present a petition couched in violent and almost threatening language. The Speaker asked their names; one of them answered, "Our names are subscribed to the petition." And being again asked "If he knew of the making of this petition, he said, "He was commanded by the rest of his friends and fellow-apprentices not to answer any questions, but to demand an answer to their petition." The Parliament declared the petition to be seditious and scandalous, sent the petitioners to Bridewell, and ordered that Lilburne should be closely confined in Newgate. But it was impossible either to silence him or to make his friends forget him. Tired at last of this ceaseless and troublesome contest, Cromwell himself determined that he should be brought to trial. "Freeborn John," wrote one of his confidants, "has been sent to the Old Bailey, and

---

[1] Thurloe's State Papers, vol. i. p. 641; Cromwell's Letters and Speeches, vol. iii. pp. 4, 5.

I think he will soon be hanged." To secure his condemnation, all those precautions were taken which the subtle or shameless dexterity of the servants of a powerful tyranny could possibly devise. The trial was to be hurried through with the utmost rapidity. It took place at the time when the most celebrated advocates, who might otherwise have lent Lilburne their assistance, had left London to go on circuit. The prisoner was refused a copy of his indictment, and was not allowed publicly to read the Act of the Long Parliament by which he had been banished, and on which his indictment rested. In order to give the jurors an unfavourable impression of his case, his accusers published the reports of the agents who had denounced his connection with the royalists in Holland, and particularly with the Duke of Buckingham. Lilburne strove with exhaustless energy against all these premeditated obstacles. He succeeded in obtaining, before their departure from town, the written opinions of two eminent lawyers, one of whom was the learned Presbyterian, Maynard. He compelled the Court to give him a copy of his indictment, and to promise that the Act ordaining his banishment should be publicly read. He opposed obstinacy by obstinacy, argument by argument. The Attorney-General, Prideaux, who had very irregularly taken his seat among the judges, was very bitter against him. Lilburne immediately called on him to come down from his seat, with that contemptuous and insulting impetuosity which can disconcert and weaken even the most arrogant and overbearing power. And when the Court proved inflexible, when Lilburne's efforts failed to obtain what he demanded, he exclaimed with passionate and forceful despair. " My lord, rob me not of my birthright, the benefit of the law, which again and again I demand as my right and inheritance. And, my lord, if you will be so audacious and unjust, in the face of this great auditory of people, to deny me, and rob me of all the rules of justice and right, and will forcibly stop my mouth and not suffer me freely to speak for my life, according to law, I will cry out and appeal to the people that hear me this day, how that this Court by violence rob me of my birthright by law, and will not suffer me to speak for my life."

The audience were powerfully affected; Lilburne's relatives and friends, his aged father, a number of brave soldiers, who had formerly been his companions in arms, and a host of apprentices and artisans surrounded him, most of them armed, and all equally irritated and anxious. They distributed in the court and in the streets a multitude of tickets bearing these words :—

"And what! shall then honest John Lilburne die ?
Threescore thousand will know the reason why."

"On Saturday last," wrote Beverning to John de Witt, "there were at his trial six thousand men at least, who, it is thought, would never have suffered his condemnation to have passed without the loss of some of their lives."[1] The judges, in spite of their anger, could not conceal their alarm. They were, however, strongly guarded: Cromwell had sent for four regiments; detachments of soldiers scoured the streets from time to time: two companies were stationed round the court-house, and reinforcements were in readiness, if required. The trial, with all its varied incidents, lasted from the 13th of July to the 20th of August, 1653; at the last moment, Lilburne thus addressed the jury:—"The act whereupon I am indicted is a lie and a falsehood; an act that hath no reason in it, no law for it; it was done as Pharaoh did, resolved upon the question that all the male children should be murdered. Since the king's head was cut off, they could not make an act of Parliament. By the same law by which they voted me to death, they might vote any of you honest jurymen. And I charge you to consider, whether, if I die on the Monday, the Parliament on Tuesday may not pass such a sentence against every one of you twelve, and upon your wives and children, and all your relations; and then upon the rest of this city, and then upon the whole county of Middlesex, and then upon Hertfordshire; and so by degrees there be no people to inhabit England but themselves."

Impossible suppositions and exaggerated language pass uncriticised by a crowd, when under the influence of strong emotion; popular sympathy, and respect for the ancient laws of the land prevailed against the earnest efforts of all the civil and military leaders of the revolution. Lilburne was a second time acquitted by the jury. Three days after, by order of the Barebone Parliament, the Council of State sent for the jurors, and ordered them, with threats, to explain their reasons for pronouncing such an acquittal. Seven of them flatly refused to give any answer, saying they were answerable for their verdict only to God and their own consciences. Four gave some reasons for their vote, but justified what they had done, and stood by their colleagues. Against this firmness on the part of obscure citizens, neither Cromwell nor his Parliament ventured any further intimidation; and they were allowed to return quietly home. But Lilburne, though acquitted, was not set at liberty; the Parliament, after having received official reports of the trial and subsequent examination of the jury, directed the Lieutenant of the Tower still to detain the prisoner in custody, "notwithstanding any *Habeas*

[1] Thurloe's State Papers, vol. i. pp. 367, 441.

Corpus granted, or to be granted, by the Court of Upper Bench, or any other Court."[1]

Lilburne, who had fancied himself victorious, sank beneath this rigour. Imprisoned, first in the Tower, and afterwards in the island of Jersey, he consented at length to live peaceably in order to live at liberty; and he died obscurely, four years afterwards, at Eltham in Kent, leaving to his country an unyielding example of legal resistance, and of a vain appeal to the laws. Convinced, by this trial, that the jury would expose his power to defeat, in those very conjunctures in which he would have most need of success, Cromwell resolved to rid himself of its interposition, as he had already got rid of the Long Parliament, but with less noise. He intimated his wishes to the Little Parliament by means of his confidants, and three weeks before its dissolution, that Parliament granted him the restoration of that exceptional and altogether political jurisdiction which had sentenced first the King, then Lord Capell, and afterwards the various royalist conspirators with whom the Commonwealth had had to deal. On the 21st of November, 1653, a High Court of Justice was instituted, composed of thirty-four members, among whom Bradshaw was again conspicuous: for, though he was too sincere a republican to serve Cromwell in his councils, he was too passionate a revolutionary to refuse to judge the enemies of the revolution. And that nothing might be wanting that could add to the safety of the Protector, the Barebone Parliament also ordained that the statute regarding acts of treason should be revised and adapted to the character and requirements of the new government.[2]

These precautions were not superfluous, for, as Whitelocke had predicted to Cromwell, as soon as monarchical power, under the name of a Protectorate, was restored in the person of a single man, all attacks were immediately directed against him: Cavaliers and Levellers, Episcopalians and Anabaptists, all renewed their conspiracies, sometimes separately, sometimes in concert with one another. Cromwell treated these different kinds of enemies in very different ways. Towards the mystical and republican sectaries, he continued to act with moderation and almost with kindness; even when he punished them, he contented himself with depriving them

[1] Commons' Journals, vol. vii. pp. 295, 294, 297, 298, 306, 309, 358; State Trials, vol. v. cols. 407—452; Guizot's Études Biographiques sur la Révolution d'Angleterre, pp. 187—192; Thurloe's State Papers, vol. i. pp. 367, 368, 369, 429, 435, 412, 449, 451, 453.

[2] Commons' Journals, vol. vii. pp. 297, 306, 353, 354; Guizot's Etudes Biographiques, p. 192.

of their commissions, or imprisoning them for a short time, and
was always ready to restore them to their employments or to liberty,
when they manifested the least sign of repentance, or as soon as the
danger had passed.   Immediately after the proclamation of the
Protectorate, he became aware that Colonels Okey, Overton, Alured,
and Pride were engaged in intrigues hostile to his authority; he
merely separated them from their regiments, recalling them indi-
vidually from Scotland and Ireland, and detained them in London.
When he had to deal with influential but unofficial men belonging
to this party, with famous preachers or popular dreamers, he would
request them to come and see him, and " would enter with them
into the terms of their old equality, shutting the door, and making
them sit down covered by him, to let them see how little he valued
those distances that, for form sake, he was bound to keep up with
others."   At these interviews, he opened his heart to his visitors as
to old and true friends.   " He would rather," he told them, " have
taken a shepherd's staff than the protectorship, since nothing was
more contrary to his genius than a show of greatness; but he saw
it was necessary at that time to keep the nation from falling into
extreme disorder, and from becoming open to the common enemy ;
and, therefore, he only stepped in between the living and the dead
(as he phrased it), in that interval, till God should direct them on
what bottom they ought to settle ; and he assured them that then
he would surrender the heavy load lying upon him, with a joy equal
to the sorrow with which he was affected while under that show of
dignity."[1]   He would then pray with them, powerfully impressing
their hearts, and becoming himself often moved even to tears.   The
most suspicious were disarmed, the most irritated were grateful to
him for his confidence, and although he did not succeed in stifling
all hostile feeling in the party, he at least prevented it from spread-
ing more widely or finding dangerous expression ; and he either
held most of these pious enthusiasts bound to his service, or left
them embarrassed and incapable of action in spite of their ill-
humour.

Towards royalist conspirators, his behaviour was very different ;
against them were directed all his demonstrations of severity, and
when necessary, his acts of rigour, either in order to defend himself
effectually against their plots, or to rally around him the timorous
or distrustful republicans.   Opportunities of this kind were not
wanting ; conspiracies, both serious and frivolous, real or imagi-

[1] Thurloe's State Papers, vol. ii. pp. 285—294, 313, 414 ; Burnet's History
of His Own Time, vol. i. p. 125.

nary, are the most usual weapon and pastime of vanquished or unemployed factions. At the time of Lilburne's arrest, several Cavaliers were also arrested; during his exile in Holland, he had entered into intimate relations with them, and had boasted that, if 10,000l. were placed at his command, he would, within six months, ruin both Cromwell and the Parliament, by means of his pamphlets and friends. It was even stated that, when he returned to England, the Duke of Buckingham had accompanied him as far as Calais. A month after the establishment of the Protectorate, a committee of eleven royalists were surprised in a tavern in the city, plotting a general insurrection of their party and the assassination of Cromwell. He contented himself with sending them to the Tower, and publishing an account of their conspiracy. But ere long was mysteriously circulated a proclamation published, it was said, at Paris, on the 23rd of April, 1654, which ran as follows:—
"Charles the Second, by the grace of God, King of England, Scotland, France, and Ireland, Defender of the Faith, to all our good and loving subjects, peace and prosperity. Whereas a certain mechanic fellow, by name Oliver Cromwell,—after he had most inhumanly and barbarously butchered our dear father, of sacred memory, his just and lawful sovereign,—hath most tyrannically and traitorously usurped the supreme power over our said kingdoms, to the enslaving and ruining the persons and estates of the good people, our free subjects therein: These are, therefore, in our name, to give free leave and liberty to any man whomsoever, within any of our three kingdoms, by pistol, sword, or poison, or by any other way or means whatsoever, to destroy the life of the said Oliver Cromwell; wherein they will do an act acceptable to God and good men, by cutting so detestable a villain from the face of the earth. And whosoever, whether soldier or other, shall be instrumental in so signal a piece of service, both to God, to his king, and to his country, we do, by these presents, and on the word and faith of a Christian king, promise to give him, and his heirs for ever, five hundred pounds per annum free land, or the full sum in money, and also the honour of knighthood to him and his heirs; and if he shall be a soldier of the army, we do also promise to give him a colonel's place, and such honourable employment wherein he may be capable of attaining to further preferment answerable to his merit."

Nothing can be less probable than that this proclamation really emanated from Charles II., or that, as has been asserted, it was the work of Hyde; it presents indisputable proofs of a subaltern origin, and statesmen, even if they commanded an assassination, would

R

be careful not to proclaim it. But it was circulated and welcomed, under the seal of secrecy, throughout the royalist party; and men were not wanting, even among the higher ranks of the king's adherents, to whom such an assassination would not have been at all repugnant. Cromwell, though naturally neither pusillanimous nor easily annoyed, regarded this proclamation as a very serious matter. "Assassinations," he said, "were such detestable things, that he would never begin them; but if any of the king's party should endeavour to assassinate him, and fail in it, he would make an assassinating war of it, and destroy the whole family; and he asserted he had instruments to execute it, whensoever he should give order for it."[1]

On the night of the 20th of May, 1654, five royalists, among whom were Colonel John Gerard, a young gentleman of good family, and Peter Vowell, a schoolmaster at Islington, were arrested in their beds, by order of Cromwell, on the charge of having conspired to assassinate the Protector. The plot was to have been carried into execution on the previous evening, as Cromwell rode from Whitehall to Hampton Court, and he had escaped only in consequence of information received a few hours previously, by crossing the Thames at Putney, and thus avoiding the ambuscade. Charles II. was to have been proclaimed immediately in the city, and Prince Rupert had promised to land without delay on the coast of Sussex, with the Duke of York and ten thousand men, English, Irish, and French. More than forty persons, many of them men of importance, were also arrested on the two following days, on the ground of being implicated in the conspiracy But Cromwell sent only three of them, Gerard, Vowell, and Somerset Fox, before the High Court of Justice which had been erected to try them.[2]

Somerset Fox pleaded guilty and admitted the fact, whereby he obtained his pardon. Gerard and Vowell denied having entertained any project of assassination. Vowell demanded to be tried by his peers, twelve jurymen, in conformity with the terms of Magna Charta, and with the sixth article of the constitution of the Protectorate. "We are your peers," replied Lord Lisle, the President of the Court, "not your superiors, but your equals. We are present, near twice twelve, as you see; and we are to proceed by

[1] Thurloe's State Papers, vol. i. pp. 306, 441, 442, 453, vol. ii. pp. 95, 105, 114, 151, 248; Clarendon's State Papers, vol. iii. pp. 75, 79, 98; Godwin's History of the Commonwealth, vol. iv. pp. 60, 74; Forster's Statesmen of the Commonwealth, vol. v. pp. 184, 191, 241; Burnet's History of His Own Time, vol. i. p. 121.

[2] Scobell's Collection of Acts and Ordinances, part ii. p. 311.

the power of the ordinance appointing us." Glynn, one of the Judges, affirmed that this ordinance undoubtedly had the force of law ; for, in the old law of treason, the word *King* signified merely the supreme governor of the State, and as it had been so construed in the case of the Queen, it equally extended to a Lord Protector. The trial was, however, conducted with moderation, although the police were the principal witnesses ; and one of the chief conspirators, Major Henshaw, was not brought forward to give evidence, probably because he had discovered the plot to the Council. Notwithstanding the denials of the prisoners, the evidence against them, even at the present day, seems incontrovertible. Henshaw and Gerard had evidently been to Paris, where they had communicated their plan to Prince Rupert, who had given them the greatest encouragement, and introduced them to Charles II.; and, on their return to London, they had made every preparation for the execution of their design. Had they informed the King of the extremities to which they intended to proceed, and received his approbation? Hyde, at this very period, and in his most private correspondence, absolutely denies that they had done so. "I do assure you, upon my credit," he wrote to his friend, Secretary Nicholas, on the 12th of June, 1654, "I do not know, and upon my confidence the king does not, of any such design. Many light foolish persons propose wild things to the king, which he civilly discountenances, and they and their friends brag what they hear or could do ; and no doubt, in some such noble rage, that hath now fallen out which they talk so much of at London, and by which many honest men are in prison : of which whole matter the king knows no more than you do." After his condemnation, and even on the scaffold, Gerard persisted in his protestations of innocence. But whatever may have been the amount of his participation in the plan for the assassination of the Protector, and whether Charles was aware of it or not, the fact itself was incontestable, and probably even more serious than Cromwell allowed it to appear ; for there is reason to believe that M. de Baas,—at that time an envoy extraordinary of Mazarin to London, and temporarily connected with the embassy of M. de Bordeaux,—was not unacquainted either with the conspirators or with their design. Cromwell was so convinced of this that he summoned M. de Baas before his council, and sharply interrogated him on the subject. But he had too much good sense to magnify the affair beyond what was required by a due regard for his own safety, or by laying too much stress on this incident, to interrupt, for any length of time, his friendly relations with Mazarin and the Court of France, which manifested the greatest anxiety to remain on good terms with him. He merely

sent M. de Baas back to France, openly stating to Louis XIV. and
Mazarin, his reasons for so doing, and showing in this the same
moderation which had induced him to bring to trial only three of
the conspirators. He had escaped the danger, made known to
England and Europe the active vigilance of his police, and proved
to the royalists that he would not spare them. He attempted
nothing further. He possessed that difficult secret of the art of
governing which consists in a just appreciation of what will be
sufficient in any given circumstance, and in resting satisfied
with it.[1]

He was careful also not to affect a servile adherence to his own
policy; but he borrowed from his enemies anything which he
thought useful or likely to serve his purpose. He had dismissed
the Barebone Parliament in order to preserve the fabric of society in
England from anarchical and chimerical reformers; and the establishment of the Protectorate, which vested "the supreme legislative
authority of the Commonwealth of England, Scotland, and Ireland,
in one person, and the people in Parliament assembled,"[2] had been
the first step in the monarchical reaction which had now commenced.
This reaction was warmly promoted by Cromwell. The act of
government conferred upon him alone, or assisted by a Council of
State dependent upon him, nearly all the attributes of royalty.[3]
He hastened to make use of this power. Immediately after his
installation, he issued new patents under his own hand to the judges
and great officers of state.[4] All public acts, whether administrative
or judicial, were passed in his name. He formally appointed his
Council of State, and subjected it, in its deliberations, to most of
the rules which had been laid down for the guidance of the Parliament.[5] On the 8th of February, 1654, he was entertained at a
pompous banquet by the City of London, at the termination of
which he conferred the honour of knighthood on the Lord Mayor,
and presented him with his own sword, just as a king would have

---

[1] State Trials, vol. v. cols. 517—540; Thurloe's State Papers, vol. ii.
pp. 309, 321, 330—334, 338, 350—357, 382—384, 412, 437, 510—514, 523;
Clarendon's History of the Rebellion, vol. vii. pp. 28—30; Clarendon's State
Papers, vol. iii. p. 247; Harleian Miscellany, vol. x. pp. 210—251; Heath's
Chronicle, pp. 663, 667; Godwin's History of the Commonwealth, vol. iv.
pp. 75—79; Forster's Statesmen of the Commonwealth, vol. v. pp. 243—245.

[2] Old Parliamentary History, vol. xx. p. 248.

[3] Ibid. vol. xx. pp. 249—262.

[4] Ibid. vol. xx. p. 274; Godwin's History of the Commonwealth, vol. iv.
p. 23.

[5] Godwin's History of the Commonwealth, vol. iv. pp. 29—32; Forster's
Statesmen of the Commonwealth, vol. v. pp. 229, 230.

done at his accession to the throne.[1] He left the Cockpit, where he had until then resided, and took up his abode in the royal apartments of Whitehall, which were magnificently fitted up and furnished for his reception.[2] His residence assumed the state and splendour of a court ; and the quarterly expenditure of his household amounted, in 1655, to thirty-five thousand pounds.[3] In his communications with foreign ambassadors, he introduced the rules and etiquette of the great continental monarchies ; the three ambassadors of Holland, Beverning, Nieuport, and Jongestall, who had come to London to treat of peace, thus describe, in a letter to the States-General, the audience which he granted them on the 4th of March, 1654 : " We were fetched in his Highness's coach, accompanied with the Lords Strickland and Jones, with the Master of the Ceremonies, and brought into the great banqueting-room at Whitehall, where his Highness had never given audience before. He stood upon a pedestal, raised with three steps high from the floor, being attended by the Lords President Laurence, Viscount Lisle, Skippon, Mackworth, Pickering, Montague, and Mr. Secretary Thurloe, together with the Lord Claypole, his Master of the Horse. After three reverences made at entrance, in the middle, and before the steps, which his Highness answered every time with reciprocal reverences, we came up to the steps, and delivered to him, with a compliment of induction, our letters of credence. He did receive them without opening them ; the reason whereof we suppose to be our delivering of the copies and translations thereof in the morning to Mr. Thurloe ; so that we presently began our discourse with a compliment of thanks for his good inclination shown in the treaty of our common peace, of congratulation in this new dignity, of presentation in all reciprocal and neighbourly offices on the behalf of your High and Mighty Lordships, and wishing all safety and prosperity to his person and government. To which he answered with many serious and significant expressions of reciprocal inclination to your High and Mighty Lordships, and to the business of peace ; for which we once 'more' returned him thanks, and presented unto his Highness twenty of our gentlemen, who went in before us, being followed by twenty more, to have the honour to kiss his hand ; but instead thereof, his Highness advanced near the steps, and bowed to all the gentlemen one by one, and put out his hand to them at a distance, by way of congratulation. Whereupon we were conducted back

[1] Old Parliamentary History, vol. xx. p. 27 ; Cromwelliana, p. 134.
[2] Cromwelliana, pp. 132, 139 ; Cromwell's Letters and Speeches, vol. iii. p. 10.
[3] Forster's Statesmen of the Commonwealth, vol. v. p. 248.

again after the same manner."[1] The audience could hardly have been conducted otherwise if Cromwell had been king.[2]

It was not surprising, therefore, that reports were everywhere current that he was about to assume that title, nay, that he had already assumed it, and that he had been crowned in secret. Even the composition of his royal household was announced; Lambert was to be Commander-in-chief and a duke, St. John Lord Treasurer, Sir Anthony Ashley Cooper Lord Chancellor, and Lord Say Lord High Chamberlain. The House of Peers was to be restored; all the peers were about to repair immediately to London, and submit to the new government. Plays, players, and public festivals were soon to make their appearance again, and all was to go on once more merrily and brilliantly, as in the old times. It was even stated that the Prince of Condé had proposed to the Protector a matrimonial alliance between their two families.[3]

Such rumours, we may be sure, were not unpleasing to Cromwell; but he had no intention of allowing himself to be led astray by their seductive influence; he had reached that happy period of combined ardour and prudence when the genius and fortune of great men, still in the full vigour of youth, manifest themselves without inebriety or excess. At the same time that he once more erected, under a modest name, the throne on which he wished to take his seat, he felt it necessary to give to the men of the popular party, to which he had until now belonged, such satisfactory reasons as might determine them to follow him in so complete a change of policy; and as he had just quarrelled with the ultra-reformers, it devolved upon him to effect those reforms which were really demanded by public opinion and sanctioned by good sense. He accomplished with rapidity and moderation, many of those measures which the Long Parliament and the Barebone Parliament had so wordily and uselessly discussed. The administration of the finances, the repair and conservation of the public highways, the condition of prisoners for debt, and the internal economy of prisons, the police of the city of London, and the regulation of public amusements, such as horse-races and cock-fights, all formed the subject of legislative acts, framed with a view to promote good order and general civilisation. Duels were prohibited, and precautions marked by no excess of rigour were taken for their prevention. An elaborate ordinance, prepared with the utmost care, limited the jurisdiction and modified

[1] Thurloe's State Papers, vol. ii. p. 154; Cromwelliana, p. 136.
[2] Letters from Bordeaux to Brienne, January 1—5, 1654.
[3] Thurloe's State Papers, vol. i. p. 645; vol. ii. pp. 2—8; Forster's Statesmen of the Commonwealth, vol. v. p. 231.

the procedure of the Court of Chancery. Cromwell intrusted its preparation to those very lawyers, who, in the Barebone Parliament, had strenuously opposed the abolition of that Court. "I am resolved," he told them, " to give the learned of the robe the honour of reforming their own profession, and I hope that God will give them hearts to do it."[1] A central committee, composed of thirty-eight persons—nine laymen, and twenty-nine clergymen—was appointed to examine all preachers who aspired to hold a church living, and no one could be inducted without having received their approval. In every county, moreover, a special committee was nominated to make inquiry into the character and conduct of all ministers of the Gospel and schoolmasters within their county, and to eject such as should appear "scandalous, ignorant, or insufficient." Preaching and Christian instruction, as well as the wise administration of parochial matters, were effectually encouraged. Commissioners, nearly all of them men of learning and influence, were directed to visit the universities of Oxford and Cambridge, and the great classical schools of Eton and Winchester, in order to reform abuses and to introduce necessary improvements. In less than nine months, from the 24th of December, 1653, to the 2nd of September, 1654, eighty-two ordinances, bearing upon almost every part of the social organisation of the country, bore witness to the intelligent activity, and to the character, at once conservative and reformatory, of the Government.[2]

At the same time, Cromwell completed another work, which the Long Parliament and the Barebone Parliament had both undertaken and left unfinished. Under favour of the discussions which had arisen between the great powers of the Commonwealth, the Scottish royalists had once more conceived hopes and taken up arms; while Ireland, and even the republican army in Ireland, was not at all in a satisfactory condition. When the news of the establishment of the Protectorate arrived in Dublin, in January, 1654, the new system of government was adopted by the Council of Government, although presided over by Cromwell's son-in-law, General Fleetwood, by a majority of only one vote; and one of its principal members, Ludlow, instantly resigned all civil functions, but retained his military command, of which no one could tell what use he intended to make. In Scotland, the insurrection, though chiefly confined to the Highlands, descended occasionally to ravage the plains; and towards the beginning of February, 1654, Middleton had been sent

---

[1] Whitelocke's Journal of the Swedish Embassy, vol. ii. p. 133.
[2] Scobell's Collection of Acts and Ordinances, part. ii. pp. 275—368; Cromwell's Letters and Speeches, vol. iii. pp. 8—10.

from France, by Charles II., to attempt to give, in the king's name, that unity and consistency of action in which it had until then been deficient. No sooner had he been proclaimed Protector, than Cromwell took decisive measures to crush these dangers in their infancy; he despatched to Ireland his second son, Henry, an intelligent, circumspect, and resolute young man, and to Scotland, Monk, whom that country had already once recognised as her conqueror. Both succeeded in their mission; Henry Cromwell, at Dublin, encouraged the friends of the Protector, won the uncertain, intimidated the factious, embarrassed even Ludlow himself by his firm but courteous conversation, and returned to London after an absence of three weeks, leaving his brother-in-law, Fleetwood, in peaceful possession of power. Monk, with his usual prompt and intrepid boldness, carried the war into the very heart of the Highlands, established his quarters there, pursued the insurgents into their most inaccessible retreats, defeated Middleton and compelled him to re-embark for the Continent, and, after a campaign of four months, returned to Edinburgh at the end of August, 1654, and began once more, without passion or noise, to govern the country which he had twice subjugated. Cromwell had reckoned beforehand on his success, for, on the 12th of April, 1654, at the very period when he ordered Monk to march against the Scottish insurgents, he had, by a sovereign ordinance, incorporated Scotland with England, abolished all monarchical or feudal jurisdiction in the ancient realm of the Stuarts, and determined the place which its representatives, as well as those of Ireland, should occupy in the common Parliament of the new State.[1] Thus was the internal unity of the British Commonwealth accomplished and organised, under the authority of its Protector.

The foreign affairs of the country, at the moment when Cromwell took possession of the supreme power, were, though not in danger, in a state of painful and barren confusion. The war with Holland still continued, and at the same time, negotiations had been opened for the restoration of peace; ambassadors were constantly passing between the Hague and London, endeavouring to obtain an accommodation, while the fleets were cruising in search of one

---

[1] Thurloe's State Papers, vol. ii. pp. 149, 162, 193; Ludlow's Memoirs, pp. 207, 208; Guizot's Etudes Biographiques sur la Révolution d'Angleterre, pp. 66—68; Guizot's Monk, pp. 48—52; Whitelocke's Memorials, pp. 581—583. 587—589, 592, 597—599; Scobell's Acts and Ordinances, part ii. pp. 288—298; Cromwelliana, pp. 134, 136, 138; Burnet's History of His Own Time, vol. i. pp. 107, 108; Laing's History of Scotland, vol. iii. pp. 482—485; Godwin's History of the Commonwealth, vol. iv. pp. 62—69.

another, in order to come to an engagement. On the 29th of July, 1653, Monk, who acted as commander-in-chief during the absence of Blake, whom ill-health had compelled to go on shore for repose, issued orders to his captains that " no English ship should surrender to the enemy, and that they should accept no surrender of the vessels against which they fought.   Their business, he said, was not to take ships, but to sink and destroy to the utmost extent of their power."[1] The event of the battle, fought with this redoubled animosity, was still uncertain when, on the 31st of July, Tromp, who had dashed into the very midst of the English fleet, was struck to death with a ball. " It is all over with me, but keep up your courage," were his last and only words. Neither his lieutenants, Ruyter, Cornelius de Witt, Floritz, and Evertz, nor the States-General, his masters, lost their courage, but their hopes declined as they found the resources of their country exhausted, and as the designs of their enemy became apparent in the conflict.[2]   By a singular coincidence, on the very day on which Monk and Tromp encountered each other, not far from the mouth of the Meuse, Beverning wrote from London to John de Witt : " Your lordship hath seen by my foregoing letters that I always made but little account of our agreeing with this nation. . . .   The veil is now at length taken off by the last answer of the Council, where they durst propound that the two commonwealths should coalesce and become united, and that the whole thus united should be subject to one supreme government, composed of persons belonging to each nation. . . . Whereupon we delivered in a further memorandum, with a desire, by reason of the opportunity, to take our leaves of the Council ; but after two days waiting, we are not yet despatched. . . .   I doubt not but that the exorbitant proceedings, and extravagant propositions of these men, will open the eyes of all the princes of Europe, and cause them to look to their ambitious and execrable designs."[3] Three of the Dutch ambassadors, Nieuport, Van de Perre, and Jongestall, did in fact return to the Hague, but Beverning remained in London. Neither side was desirous to break off all negotiations ; Cromwell used all his efforts to prevent such an extremity. Beverning had several conferences with him, which led him to hope there was some possibility of an accommodation. " Last Saturday," he wrote, on the 22nd of August, 1653, " I had a discourse with His Excellency Cromwell for above two hours, being without anybody present with us. His Excellency spoke his

[1] Gumble's Life of Monk, pp. 59—64.
[2] Leclerc's Histoire des Provinces Unies, vol. ii. p. 334.
[3] Thurloe's State Papers, vol. i p 382.

own language so distinctly that I could understand him. I answered him in Latin. I urged much upon some particulars which His Excellency did confess to be of very great consideration, and took them into his thoughts to reflect upon;"[1] and three weeks later, on the 19th of September, he wrote, "I find now at present somewhat more moderation; and I hope they will be contented with a good and strict alliance."[2] But the Barebone Parliament was still in existence; the arrogant pretensions of the fanatics revelled in unrestrained liberty; authority was scattered, and unreason let loose; no one dared to decide and conclude any matter of public import. War and negotiations continued simultaneously between London and the Hague, without leading to any result.

The same uncertainty and feebleness were manifested in the relations of the Commonwealth with the other States of Europe. Cromwell obtained the appointment of Whitelocke as ambassador to the Queen of Sweden, whose good will he hoped might be converted into a strong and lasting alliance. Whitelocke hesitated about accepting this distant mission, which seemed to him a mark of distrust rather than a token of favour. His wife besought him with tears to refuse, on the ground of their happiness, and of their twelve children, conjuring him to remember the fate of Dorislaus and Ascham. Cromwell, however, insisted. "This business," he said, "is of exceeding great importance to the Commonwealth; and there is no prince or State in Christendom with whom there is any probability for us to have a friendship, but only the Queen of Sweden. . . . If you should decline this mission the Protestant interest would suffer by it. . . Your going may be the most likely means to settle our business with the Dutch and Danes, and all matters of trade. . . . I will engage to take particular care of your affairs myself; and you shall neither want supplies, nor anything that is fit for you. I shall hold myself particularly obliged to you if you will undertake it; and I will stick to you as close as your skin to your flesh."[3] Whitelocke consented; but when his consent had once been given, he did not meet, either in the Parliament or in the Council of State, with the good treatment which he had been led to expect. Doubts were raised as to his piety; he was not allowed all that he considered necessary for the accomplishment of his embassy; he demanded a salary of fifteen hundred pounds a month, but only a thousand was granted; he

---

[1] Thurloe's State Papers, vol. i. pp. 417, 418.

[2] Ibid. vol. i. p. 463.

[3] Whitelocke's Journal of the Swedish Embassy, vol. i. pp. 1, 9, 13, 16—22, 31—36, 41, 46, 99.

requested a retinue of a hundred persons, and the number was reduced to seventy. Delayed by these difficulties and disappointments, he did not set out until three months after his nomination.

Affairs, even when decided, were transacted with similar slowness and reluctance. Sometimes even the simplest matters were left undone altogether. The ambassador of Portugal, the Count de Sa, had been in London for more than eighteen months; in order to put an end to the differences between the two States, he had consented to all the conditions and indemnities demanded by the Parliament,—"conditions of such a character," wrote Bordeaux to M. Servien, "that it would be always very easy to terminate affairs at that rate."[1] And yet the treaty with Portugal was not concluded. The project of alliance which Don Alonzo de Cardenas, in the name of the King of Spain, had submitted to the Long Parliament, on the 12th of September, 1652, also remained in suspense, as though it had been forgotten and void of meaning. The minister of France, notwithstanding the obstinate refusal given to his demand for the restitution of the vessels which Blake had captured off Calais, seemed to have made greater progress with his negotiation: some desire had been intimated to him that an ambassador should be sent into France; the Commissioners appointed to treat with him had given him to understand that "if His Majesty had any intention to form an alliance with their State, the interests of the merchants should not stand in the way of it," and had said to him in a contemptuous manner, "What! shall we waste our time upon merchants?" "This, however," he adds, "is not the turning-point of the affair."[2] The Long Parliament felt that it was in imminent danger, and sought friends on every side: at the period of its expulsion, Bordeaux believed that he was on the point of concluding a treaty with it. He resumed his labours, with renewed hopes, on the accession of the new authorities to power. Mazarin, ever lavish of flattering advances, wrote to Cromwell to propose a reciprocation of useful friendship. Cromwell replied to him with a rare excess of affected humility. "It's surprise to me that your Eminency should take notice of a person so inconsiderable as myself, living, as it were, separate from the world. This honour has made, as it ought, a very deep impression upon me, and does oblige me to serve your Eminency upon all occasions, so as I shall be happy to find out; so I trust that very honourable person, Monsieur Burdoe (Bordeaux),

[1] Bordeaux to M. Servien, Jan. 27, 1653, in the Archives des Affaires Etrangères de France.

[2] Bordeaux to Brienne, April 10, 1653; in the Archives des Affaires Etrangères de France.

will therein be helpful to your Eminency's thrice humble servant, Oliver Cromwell."[1]   But these demonstrations of good-will led to no result : France, her king, and her cardinal, were regarded by the republicans and anabaptists of the Barebone Parliament with a distrustful antipathy which Cromwell was as yet unwilling to brave. " You have possibly not yet been informed of all the rebuffs which your envoy has received in London," wrote M. de Gentillot to M. de Brienne ; " his Eminence has stated publicly that General Cromwell caused him to be treated with all kinds of civility, and that everything was in a good train.   A different opinion prevails here ; and it is thought that he has treated your envoy very roughly, never having been willing to grant him any private audience, nor receive any particular compliment.   I say this in order to lead you to persuade yourself of the bad feeling of this government, that you may take your own precautions against them."[2]   Bordeaux ere long received the same impression, and transmitted it to Paris : " The General," he wrote to M. de Brienne, " does not appear to me very warm towards France : the first answer which he gave me when I told him that the king was strongly inclined to an accom- modation between the two nations, was, that a just war was better than an unjust peace—*justum bellum præstabat iniquâ pace.*"[3]   Two months later, this coolness and reserve had greatly increased. " For some time," wrote Bordeaux, " Mr. Cromwell has informed me, by means of the Master of the Ceremonies, that he wished me no longer to address myself to him about matters of business, although I have hitherto done so only twice ; and as he has even avoided me on several occasions, I have been unable to converse with him, and I have been obliged, by means of third persons, to insinuate the reasons which should oblige England to seek the friend- ship of France, since his Majesty is acting with sincerity, and is willing to concede all that propriety will permit, in order to assure them of it."[4]   In presence of a fanatical and narrow-minded Parlia- ment, and in the midst of the tottering Commonwealth, torn by the conflicts of opposing parties and popular prejudices, no decided and consistent policy could be adopted ; and no one, not even Cromwell, felt himself strong enough boldly to undertake the

[1] Cromwell to Mazarin, June 9, 1653; in the Archives des Affaires Etrangères de France.
[2] Gentillot to Brienne, July 30, 1653; in the Archives des Affaires Etrangères de France.
[3] Bordeaux to Brienne, August 7, 1653; in the Archives des Affaires Etrangères de France.
[4] Bordeaux to Brienne, October 23, 1653; in the Archives des Affaires Etrangères de France.

responsibility of any great act, or the prosecution of any great enterprise.

Affairs changed their aspect when Cromwell became Protector. In regard to foreign policy, his government was guided by two fixed ideas—peace with the United Provinces, and an alliance of the Protestant States: these were, in his eyes, the two vital conditions of the safety and power of his country in Europe, as well as of his own safety and power in his own country and in Europe. He applied himself without delay to the realisation of these projects.

Peace with the United Provinces was, to him, a matter of some difficulty. He had openly approved and supported the ambitious plan for the incorporation of the two republics; and not only did the dreamy fanatics refuse to abandon this project, but many of the leaders of the army, and those remarkable for good sense, Monk among others, had imbibed during the war such a strong feeling of hatred and contempt for the Dutch, that they could not endure the thought of any concession to those rivals whom they had already conquered, and whom they hoped ere long to crush. From Protestant sympathy, for the interest of commerce, and from weariness of taxation, the English nation desired peace; but the revolutionary and military party were in general opposed to it; they accused Cromwell of desiring it only on his own account, and for the sole purpose of consolidating his power. He was not unaware of this opposition, and he took care not to irritate it either by his language or by the terms of the negotiation, but he neither hesitated nor swerved in the slightest degree from his design. Though he showed himself haughty and exacting in his dealings with the envoys of the States-General, he was in private communication with Beverning and Nieuport, who belonged to the province of Holland, and who, like himself, were decidedly in favour of peace. He abandoned the idea of the incorporation of the two States, and certain other stipulations which would have been too offensive or too burdensome to the Dutch; he admitted their allies, and among others, the King of Denmark, to participate in the advantages of the treaty; and on these terms, he secured to England not only a close alliance with the United Provinces, but most indisputable pledges of her maritime preponderance and commercial prosperity. On one point alone, on a revolutionary interest which narrowly affected his own personal safety, he was inexorable: after having imposed on the United Provinces an obligation never to receive into their territories any enemy of the Commonwealth, and thus deprived the Stuarts of that asylum, he demanded that they should further promise never to make the young Prince of

Orange, or his descendants, either Stadtholder, or commander of their forces by land or sea, or governor of any of their fortified towns. He was anxious to remove from all participation in power, both at the Hague and in London, all princes sprung from the House of Stuart, and attached to its cause. Such a stipulation evidently was destructive of the sovereignty and dignity of the Confederation; the partisans of the House of Orange, who were numerous and popular, indignantly protested against it. The States-General refused to allow this clause, and the treaty was on the point of being broken off. For direct and public negotiation, Cromwell now substituted secret intrigue; he told Beverning and Nieuport that he would be satisfied with a private engagement to this effect on the part of the province of Holland, which he considered sufficiently powerful alone to decide such a question. This was a strong temptation to the interest and passions of the Pensionary of Holland, John de Witt, and his friends, who governed that province: Cromwell merely demanded of them to exclude for ever from the government of their country the prince and party whom they had recently overthrown. Were the efforts which they made to repulse this pretension perfectly sincere and real? All the documents relating to the negotiation, both public and confidential, seem to attest that they were. However this may be, Cromwell's demand became known; most of the United Provinces, and some even of the towns of Holland, protested against acceding to it; but Cromwell peremptorily insisted, offering no alternative but the adoption of his terms or the continuation of the war. After great agitation, the States of Holland, by fourteen votes against five, determined to give the pledge which Cromwell required; but they sent orders to their envoys in London to make a fresh effort, before affixing their signatures to the treaty, to induce him to omit, or at least to modify, this clause in the accommodation. The public treaty had been signed on the 5th of April, 1654, but the negotiations were continued for two months after; Cromwell refused to hear of any modification, and it was not until the 5th of June that, the secret article having at length been ratified, the treaty of peace was solemnly proclaimed, amid the loudest and most enthusiastic demonstrations of popular satisfaction. The King of Denmark, the Swiss Protestant cantons, the Hanseatic towns, and several of the petty Protestant princes of the north of Germany were included in the treaty.[1]

[1] Guizot's Monk, p. 46; Forster's Statesmen of the Commonwealth, vol. v. p. 251; Thurloe's State Papers, vol. i. pp. 517, 519, 520, 530, 566, 570, 607, 612, 614, 621, 624, 643, vol. ii. pp. 16, 20, 28—30, 35, 37, 46—106, 211, 227, 245, 251, 257; Leclerc's Histoire des Provinces Unies, vol. ii. pp. 391, 410,

In the mean time, Whitelocke was in Sweden, negotiating the second of those treaties which were to place England at the head of Protestant Europe. Serious obstacles, of an unforeseen character, threatened to prevent the success of his mission. Neither Queen Christina nor her subjects shared in the religious passions which inspired the policy of which he was the organ. Though firm and sincere Protestants, the Swedes were cold both in creed and practice. Whitelocke, who was far from being a strict Puritan, was astonished at the laxity of their morals, at their want of earnestness in worship, and at their almost entire neglect of religious rest on the Sabbath day. At their very first conversation (which took place on the 20th of December, 1653), the Queen spoke to him slightingly of the Puritan enthusiasm of his country. "I pray," she asked him, "what religion do you profess in England? The world reports a great number of different religions in England, some Lutherans, some Calvinists, some called Independents, some Anabaptists, and some yet higher, and different from all the rest, whose names we know not."[1] When they began to speak of political alliances, the Queen expressed herself in favour of the union of Sweden and England with Spain. "Probably some," said Whitelocke, "may object the difference in religion." "That will be no hinderance to the force of the union," answered the Queen: "the Dutch and Danes being Protestants, unite with the French, though Papists. You English are hypocrites and dissemblers." Whitelocke expostulated. "I do not mean either your General or yourself," added the Queen, "but I think that in England there are many who make profession of more holiness than is in them, hoping for advantage by it."[2] Cromwell's ambassador often had to encounter very hostile prejudices and feelings, on the part of the Swedish populace; the mob came at night to assail his servants with insults for having killed their king, and derisively termed the Parliament "a company of tailors and cobblers." Whitelocke more than once had to take precautions against public insult, and plots were even formed for his assassination.[3] When he entered into conference with old Chancellor Oxenstiern—"the wisest statesman of the Continent," as Cromwell called him—he had to deal with serious

---

432—450; Dumont's Corps Diplomatique Universel, vol. vi. part ii. treaty 17; Godwin's History of the Commonwealth, vol. iv. pp. 45—52; Bordeaux to Brienne, August 11—14, September 22, 1653, and Bordeaux to Servien, December 6, 1653, in the Archives des Affaires Etrangères de France.

[1] Whitelocke's Journal, vol. i. pp. 275, 276.

[2] December 30, 1653; Whitelocke's Journal, vol. i. pp. 275, 297.

[3] Ibid. vol. i. pp. 205, 215, 451, 504.

objections, many of which he found it difficult to refute. "I desire to know," said Oxenstiern, "what stability and settlement there is in your Commonwealth and government, and how it came to pass that the late Parliament, which they called by the late king's authority, was dissolved, and another constituted, which, some report, may probably be as soon dissolved as the other was ; and then how shall our treaty have a good and fixed foundation ? Do you hold kingly government to be unlawful, that you have abolished it ?" Whitelocke defended and explained, to the best of his ability, occurrences which he did not himself approve; but he succeeded poorly in convincing the Chancellor, who was reserved and cautious from disposition as well as from prudence, and who protracted the negotiation with a view to watch the course of events between England and the United Provinces, and to learn whether they would make war or peace. Whitelocke's anxiety increased when he discovered that Oxenstiern had, in his inmost soul, "a little envy towards the Protector, because he had done greater things than the Chancellor had done, and had advanced himself to that estate which the Chancellor had proposed to himself to have done when the Queen was young, but could not arrive at it."[1] He communicated to the Queen the objections which Oxenstiern had raised, and the fears with which he had inspired him ; she expressed her entire approval of his answers, and told him " that in case her Chancellor and he could not agree, it must come to her at last, and he should find her to be guided by honour and reason." But at the very moment when Christina gave Whitelocke this assurance, she drew her chair close to him, and said : " I shall surprise you with something which I intend to communicate to you, but it must be under secrecy." " Madam," returned Whitelocke, " we that have been versed in the affairs of England, do not use to be surprised with the discourse of a young lady ; whatsoever your Majesty shall think fit to impart to me, and command to be under secrecy, shall be faithfully obeyed by me." " I have great confidence of your honour and judgment," replied the Queen, " and therefore, though you are a stranger, I shall acquaint you with a business of the greatest consequence to me in the world, and which I have not communicated to any creature. Sir, it is this: I have it in my thoughts and resolution to quit the crown of Sweden, and to retire into private life, as much more suitable to my contentment than the great cares and troubles attending upon the government of my kingdom. What think you of this resolution ?"[2]

[1] January 12, 1654 ; Whitelocke's Journal, vol. i. pp. 319—323, 375.
[2] January 21, 1654; Whitelocke's Journal, vol. i. pp. 360, 361.

Nothing could have been more unwelcome to Whitelocke than this communication, for it was upon Queen Christina herself that all his hopes rested. Cromwell had told him that it would be so when he left England, and since his arrival in Sweden, everything had tended to confirm the Protector's opinion. His mission would be a ridiculous failure if he had come merely to receive the confidence, and witness the abdication, of the princess who could alone grant him success. He made earnest but useless efforts to divert her from her purpose, and withdrew in great perturbation of mind from the interview which had gained him the honour of hearing so great a secret.

Whitelocke did not reckon sufficiently on the influence which the wonderful genius and fortune of a great man could not fail to exercise over the imagination of a woman, who was herself remarkable for intellect and eccentricity, and who made it her delight and boast to act according to the dictates of her fancy, rather than in obedience to the rules of reason, and of her high position. At the very first private audience which she granted him, she said to him : " Your General is one of the gallantest men in the world ; never were such things done as by the English in your late war. Your General hath done the greatest things of any man in the world ; the Prince of Condé is next to him, but short of him. I have as great a respect and honour for your General, as for any man alive, and I pray, let him know as much from me."[1] A few days after this, she made particular inquiries of Whitelocke respecting Cromwell's family, his wife and children. "Much of your General's history," she said, " hath some parallel with that of my ancestor, Gustavus I., who, from a private gentleman of a noble family, was advanced to the title of Marshal of Sweden, because he had risen up and rescued his country from the bondage and oppression which the King of Denmark had put upon them ; and, for his reward, he was at last elected King of Sweden. I believe that your General will be King of England, in conclusion." " Pardon me, madam," said Whitelocke, " that cannot be, because England is resolved into a Commonwealth ; and my General hath already sufficient power and greatness, as general of all our forces both by sea and land, which may content him." " Resolve what you will," answered Christina, " I believe he resolves to be king."[2] She received the news of the establishment of the Protectorate before Whitelocke ; and as soon as she saw him, she inquired : " Have you yet received your letters?" " Not yet, madam," said the ambassador, " but I have reason to believe the

[1] Whitelocke's Journal, vol. i. p. 251.
[2] Ibid. vol. i. pp. 295, 296.

news. and to expect your Majesty's inclinations thereupon." "Pardieu." replied the Queen, "I bear the same respect, and more, to
your General and to you than I did before; and I had rather have
to do with one than with many."[1] Christina's imagination had
been strongly impressed, not by Cromwell alone, but by the entire
English revolution; she took delight in judging it, and speaking of
it, with the independence of a philosopher; she frequently expressed
to Whitelocke great admiration for Milton, extolling the force of his
reasoning, as well as the beauty of his language. One day, at a
ball, she invited Whitelocke to dance with her; he begged earnestly
to be excused, as he was rather lame. "I am fearful, madam," he
said, "that I shall dishonour your Majesty, as well as shame myself,
by dancing with you." "I will try whether you can dance," said
the Queen. "I assure your Majesty," urged Whitelocke, "I cannot
in any measure be worthy to have you by the hand." "I esteem
you worthy," said Christina, "and therefore make choice of you to
dance with me." "I shall not so much undervalue your Majesty's
judgment," answered Whitelocke, "as not to obey you herein, and
I wish I could remember as much of this as when I was a young
man." When they had done dancing, and as he was leading the Queen
back to her seat, "Pardieu," she said, "these Hollanders are lying
fellows." "I wonder," said Whitelocke, "how the Hollanders should
come into your mind upon such an occasion as this!" "I will tell
you," said the Queen; "the Hollanders reported to me a great
while since that all the noblesse of England were of the king's
party, and none but mechanics of the Parliament party, and not a
gentleman among them; now I thought to try you, and to shame
you if you could not dance: but I see that you are a gentleman,
and have been bred a gentleman; and that makes me say the
Hollanders are lying fellows."[2]

The personal feelings of the Queen overcame the hesitation of
her Chancellor: after having skilfully imposed upon Whitelocke
certain concessions which she thought would be useful or complimentary to her people, she indulged her self-love, by exhibiting her
power, before she descended from the throne, in an act which would
tend to the advantage of the great man whom she admired. On
the 28th of April, 1654, Whitelocke and Oxenstiern signed between
England and Sweden, a treaty of friendship and alliance, in which
the essential articles of Cromwell's propositions were embodied. A
month after, on the 5th of May, Christina solemnly abdicated her
throne, in presence of the assembled Diet at Upsal; and, on the

[1] Whitelocke's Journal, vol. i. p. 321.
[2] Ibid. vol. ii. p. 155.

following day, Whitelocke embarked at Stockholm on his return to England, where he arrived on the 30th of June, having achieved a success of the utmost importance to Cromwell's policy, and bearing messages which could not fail to flatter his pride.[1]

A special treaty with the King of Denmark,[2] which secured to English commerce, in regard to passage through the Sound, advantages which until then the Dutch had alone enjoyed, and the establishment of a permanent embassy in the Swiss Cantons for the maintenance of constant influence in that quarter,[3] completed the work of Cromwell's Protestant policy. In that respect, his object was attained; he had entered into intimate relations with all the Protestant States of Europe, by skilfully combining interests with creeds, and securing the weak as his clients and the powerful as his allies.

It was said in France that he meditated still vaster and more difficult designs, for the promotion of Protestantism. "The Protector purposes," wrote one of his emissaries to Cardinal Mazarin, "to assemble a council of all the Protestant communions, in order to unite them in one body by the common confession of one faith." Some particular facts indicate that this idea had really entered his mind. He was one of those powerful and fertile geniuses in whom great designs and great temptations are constantly originating; but he unhesitatingly applied the test of his strong good sense to his most alluring dreams, and never attempted to realise those which did not resist the trial.

Towards the Catholic powers he assumed an attitude of complete and fearless liberty, unmarked by prejudice or ill-will, but equally void of courtship or flattery, showing himself disposed to maintain peace, but always leaving open the prospect of war, and watching over the interests of his country and of his own family with stern and uncompromising haughtiness. He put an end, at length, to the negotiation which had been so long pending with the King of Portugal, and signed, with the Count de Sa, a treaty by which England obtained important advantages for her trade. Cromwell was not sorry, moreover, to impress the court of Spain with his power, by living on good terms with a sovereign who had but

---

[1] Whitelocke's Journal. vol. i. pp. 262, 265, 299, 301, 311—314, 319—323, 381—384, 395, 418, 423, 429—431, 461, 486—489, 492, 493—499, 519, 524; vol. ii. pp. 9, 23, 26, 57—60, 61, 64, 109—113, 386, 401, 412.

[2] This treaty was not finally signed until the 14th of September, 1654; see Dumont's Corps Diplomatique Universel, vol. v. part ii. pp. 80, 92.

[3] See Vaughan's Protectorate of Oliver Cromwell, illustrated in a series of letters between Dr. John Pell, Resident Ambassador with the Swiss Cantons, and Sir Samuel Morland, &c.

recently liberated himself from her dominion, and who was treated by her as an usurper. But, at the same moment, a tragical incident afforded him an opportunity of giving striking satisfaction, at the expense of Portugal, to the republican pride of England, and to the instinctive aversion of the people for foreigners. A brother of the Portuguese ambassador, Don Pantaleon de Sa, had brutally engaged in a street-quarrel, near the New Exchange, in the very heart of the City ; and, having returned to the spot, on the following day, with about fifty officers and servants, attached to the embassy, all armed to the teeth, they caused a great tumult, in which one bystander was killed, and several others severely wounded. The outrage was public, the murder flagrant, and the popular exasperation ardent in the extreme ; the rank of the principal offender only aggravated the offence. Cromwell resolved that justice should be done. Neither the earnest entreaties of the ambassador, nor his vehement assertion of diplomatic privileges, could shake the resolution of the Protector. Don Pantaleon de Sa was arrested, tried, condemned, and beheaded, on the 10th of July, at the Tower of London, in presence of a vast multitude, whose fierce pride revelled in such a spectacle. On that very day, a few hours before the execution of his brother, the Count de Sa had signed the treaty which he had come to negotiate, and had left London to escape from witnessing a punishment which he had been unable to avert.[1]

In presence of such successes, and of such acts, convincing proofs of formidable power and indomitable energy, the two great rival Catholic powers, France and Spain, paid their court to Cromwell with jealous anxiety, aiming to secure his friendship, and, if possible, to deprive each other of it. As soon as he was proclaimed Protector, Don Alonzo de Cardenas, in a private interview, offered him the support of Spain for the establishment of his power, promising that the king, his master, would undertake to repulse the pretensions of Charles Stuart, and would not lay down his arms until the Court of France had also been compelled to acknowledge the government of Cromwell. In return for this assistance, Cardenas demanded that the Protector should ally himself with Spain against France, and should supply the Court of Madrid with an army and a fleet, the expenses of which should be borne in common, so long as the war lasted.[2] Some months after, Cardenas

---

[1] State Trials, vol. v. cols. 461—518; Thurloe's State Papers, vol. i. pp. 610, 616, vol. ii. pp. 222, 427—429, 447, 473, 517 ; Whitelocke's Memorials, pp. 569, 595 ; Clarendon's History of the Rebellion, vol. vii. pp. 30—33.

[2] Thurloe's State Papers, vol. i. pp. 705, 759—763.

further offered to Cromwell a considerable sum of money, as much, even, as six hundred thousand crowns a-year, "without having, either in London or in Flanders," wrote Mazarin to Bordeaux, "the first sou wherewith to pay him, if he took them at their word; they would promise him with the same readiness a million or two, to gain him to their side, since it will certainly not cost them more to keep and perform one promise than the other."[1]

The offers of Mazarin were more positive, and he better understood how to back them by the indirect artifices of vigilant diplomacy. On the 21st of February, 1654, on sending M. de Baas to London, he induced Louis XIV. to write to the Protector a letter full of flattering and almost friendly expressions. Bordeaux was raised to the rank of an ambassador, and received orders to maintain his rank with fitting splendour.[2] Inquiry was made as to the terms in which Cromwell and his Council desired that his credentials should be couched: they would have wished Louis XIV. to address the Protector as *Mon frère*, but monarchical complaisance was not yet ready to go quite so far; the title of *Mon cousin* was accordingly suggested, but Cromwell rejected it, declaring that he desired no other than that of *Monsieur le Protecteur*.[3] If the treaty of alliance were concluded, Mazarin offered him, first 1,200,000, then 1,500,000, and finally 1,800,000 livres a-year, and the restoration of Dunkirk to the English, as soon as the combined French and English troops should have gained possession of it.[4] The residence of the proscribed princes in France was a continual subject of distrust and protest on the part of Cromwell. Charles II. had indeed gone to live at Cologne,[5] but the Queen, his mother, and his two brothers, the Dukes of York and Gloucester, still resided either at St. Germains, or at Paris; the Duke of York even served in the French army. Mazarin intimated that it would be easy "to send that prince, in some civil manner, to join his brother, and to assign to the Queen-mother some town in the kingdom, as an appanage,

[1] Mazarin to Bordeaux, April 18, 1654, in the Archives des Affaires Etrangères de France.
[2] In February, 1654; Bordeaux to Brienne, March 2 and April 7, 1654; Baas to Mazarin, April 7, 10, 1654, in the Archives des Affaires Etrangères de France.
[3] Bordeaux to Brienne, March and April, 1654, in the Archives des Affaires Etrangères de France.
[4] Mazarin to Baas, March 27, 1654; Mémoire pour servir d'instructions au Sieur de Bordeaux, July 16, 1654, in the Archives des Affaires Etrangères de France.
[5] At the beginning of June, 1654; Clarendon's History of the Rebellion, vol. vii. p. 113.

to which she could retire with the Duke of Gloucester, who, at a more advanced age, when his designs were capable of giving umbrage, should also be sent to rejoin the king, his brother." And to these political advances, Mazarin added all kinds of personal attentions. " Let me know," he wrote to M. de Baas, " whether the ambassador and yourself, on consulting together, think it would be well for me to send some Barbary horses to M. le Protecteur, and tell me whether it would be too great a familiarity to send him a present of wine ; and, in short, advise me what other things would be most agreeable to him." [1]

The Cardinal was all the more anxious to please the Protector, because the Court of Spain was not his only rival in seeking his favour. On learning the establishment of the Protectorate, the Prince of Condé had hastened to write to Cromwell—" I rejoice infinitely," he said, " that justice has been done to the merit and virtue of your Highness. Therein alone could England expect to find safety and repose ; and I hold the people of the three kingdoms to have reached the climax of their happiness, in finding their property and lives now intrusted to the guidance of so great a man. For my own part, I beseech your Highness to believe that I shall deem myself very happy if I can serve you on any occasion." [2] The prince's agents, Barrière and Cuguac, as well as the deputies from the town of Bordeaux, were still in London, striving to obtain, for the Fronde, the support of the Protector, as they had formerly sought that of the Parliament. [3]

Cromwell received all these advances with the same appearance of good will : not that he looked at them all with the same favourable eye, or that he hesitated careless or uncertain which to choose among allies so diverse. Unlike the Long Parliament, he inclined far more towards France than towards Spain ; with superior sagacity, he perceived that Spain would thenceforward be an apathetic and decadent power, and, in spite of all her friendly demonstrations more hostile than any other European State to Protestant England, for she was devoted, more exclusively than any other, to the maxims and influences of the Church of Rome.

And at the same time that there was but little to be expected from Spain, her vast possessions in the New World offered a rich

---

[1] Mazarin to Baas, April 8, 1654, in the Archives des Affaires Etrangères de France.

[2] Condé to Cromwell, December, 1653 ; in the Manuscrits de Brienne, Bibliotheque Impériale, Paris.

[3] Thurloe's State Papers, vol. i. p. 760, vol. ii. pp. 259, 685 ; Bordeaux to Brienne, March 27, 1654, in the Archives des Affaires Etrangères de France.

and easy prey to the maritime ambition of England. From France, on the other hand, Cromwell had much to fear, for she held the Stuarts in her grasp; and also much useful assistance to hope for, as she was ruled by a free and active government, capable of thinking boldly and executing vigorously. But most of Cromwell's companions, Lambert among others, had not equally just notions as to the state of facts, and the interests of their country abroad; slavishly obedient to the routine of popular ideas and passions, they held France in especial abhorrence, and longed to be at war with her, for the honour, they said, as well as for the safety of their Commonwealth. Cromwell, always full of consideration for the opinions of the men of whom he had to make use, attempted to set them right on this particular; sometimes in private interviews, and sometimes in meetings at the house of his son Henry, his intimate confidants laboured to make Lambert, and the other officers who thought with him, understand the danger of a definitive rupture with France, and the advantages which her alliance would afford. The Spanish ambassador sometimes had an inkling of these public intimations of Cromwell's private sentiments, "and he would then indulge," says Bordeaux, "in great imprecations against this Government, expressing his earnest wish that the King, his master, and the King of France would free themselves by a mutual accommodation, from all the cringings and fawnings which jealousy obliged them both to manifest towards the Protector, in order to gain him over to their interests." But Cromwell, who was in no anxiety to take any decided course, easily dispelled the ill humour of Cardenas and of Bordeaux, by giving them each in turn reason to hope for his preference. He replied to their proposals by declaring his own. From Spain, besides the sum of fifty thousand crowns per month, which Cardenas had offered him, he demanded the right of free navigation in the West Indies, and an assurance that English merchants might freely practise their religion in Spain, without being exposed to prosecution by the Inquisition, and with liberty to use the English Bible, and other religious books relating to their particular form of belief. From France, he wished to obtain first four millions, and then, at least, two millions of livres, per annum; the custody of some great maritime town, Brest for instance, until Dunkirk should be taken; the expulsion of the Stuarts, and of a certain number of royalists, whose names he stated; and, finally, liberty of conscience, and security of person and property, for the French Protestants. Cardenas and Bordeaux protested, each in his turn, against pretensions so exorbitant. "To demand immunity from the Inquisition, and free navigation in the

West Indies," said Cardenas, " is to demand the two eyes of my master;—nothing can be done, in this respect, except in conformity with ancient usage." " Demands so excessive," replied Bordeaux, " can be considered only as a pretext which M. le Protecteur wishes to employ in order to liberate himself from the promise he has given to come to an accommodation with France." Both negotiations, however, continued with various oscillations,—sometimes Cromwell lessened his pretensions, sometimes more extensive concessions were offered him : matters were carried so far, especially on the side of France, as the careful preparation and minute discussion of drafts of a treaty, but nothing was concluded with either power ; Cromwell held them both in suspense, and became more and more the object of their jealous assiduities.[1]

Thus caressed and sought after by all foreign powers, and victorious at home over all parties—seeing that civil order had been strengthened and peace restored by his authority—he believed himself in a position to face without danger the trial imposed on him by the seventh article of the Protectoral Constitution, and he issued writs for the election of a new Parliament, to meet on the 3rd of September, 1654, the anniversary of his victories at Dunbar and Worcester.

It was the first time, for fourteen years, that England had been called upon to elect a Parliament, and the electoral system itself was altogether new : the Constitutional Act had borrowed it almost entirely from the plan which Vane was on the point of getting voted by the Long Parliament, on the very day of its expulsion by Cromwell. There were to be four hundred and sixty members,— four hundred for England and Wales (of whom two hundred and fifty-one were to represent counties, and a hundred and forty-nine, cities and boroughs), thirty for Scotland, and thirty for Ireland ; all persons possessing real or personal property to the value of 200l. were entitled to vote ; no one was eligible for election unless he were a man of acknowledged integrity, fearing God, of unblemished morals, and twenty-one years of age ; all persons who had taken part against the Parliament since the 1st of January, 1641, and all Catholics were deprived of the right of voting and of being voted for : this, briefly, was the system. Three parties strongly contested the elections : the adherents of the Protector, the Republicans, and

[1] Thurloe's State Papers, vol. i. pp. 705, 760, 761; Correspondence of Bordeaux with Brienne and Servien, July and August, 1654, in the Archives des Affaires Etrangères de France; Correspondence of Cardeñas and the Archduke Leopold with Philip IV., and Deliberations of the Spanish Council of State in March, April, and August, 1654, in the Archives of Simancas.

the Presbyterians who had made war against the king, but who re-gretted the abolition of kingship. All the important members of Cromwell's Government, with the exception of Lord Lisle, were elected; among the republican leaders, Vane, Ludlow, Sidney, and Hutchinson either did not become candidates, or were rejected; but Bradshaw, Scott, Haslerig, and others, equally staunch, though less known, were chosen in preference to the Protector's candidates. The Presbyterians were numerous; they came, not as determined opponents, but as independent and not very friendly neutrals. The same condition was imposed on all, both by the twelfth article of the Instrument of Government, and by the form of the writ ordain-ing their election: "That the persons elected shall not have power to alter the Government as it is hereby settled in one single person and a Parliament."[1]

At their first meeting, on the suggestion of Lambert, who, when the sermon was over, proposed that the members present should wait on the Protector in the Painted Chamber, where he was ex-pecting them, some symptoms of ill-humour were manifested; several members cried out, "Sit still!" It was a Sunday, and no business could be done on that day. Cromwell had no intention of neglecting his religious duties; he merely gave a gracious reception to the Parliament, and begged the members to assemble on the fol-lowing day in the same place, when he would make to them certain communications which he judged necessary for the welfare of the Commonwealth.[2]

"Gentlemen," he said to them on the next day, "you are met here on the greatest occasion that, I believe, England ever saw; having upon your shoulders the interests of three great nations; and truly, I believe I may say it without any hyperbole, you have upon your shoulders the interests of all the Christian people in the world. . . . . . The end of your meeting, I judge to be, healing and settling." He abstained from reference to past transactions, which, he said, "instead of healing, might set the wound fresh a-bleeding;" but he paused to describe the state of the country at the time when the Protectoral Government had com-menced. "What was our condition?" he asked. "What was the face that was upon our affairs as to the interests of the nation? as

[1] Old Parliamentary History, vol. xx. pp. 250—255, 291—294; Cromwell's Letters and Speeches, vol. iii. pp. 21, 22; Godwin's History of the Common-wealth, vol. iv. pp. 106—112; Forster's Statesmen of the Commonwealth, vol. iii. pp. 158—162; vol. iv. pp. 262—264.

[2] Commons' Journals, vol. vii. p. 365; Goddard's Diary in the Introduction to Burton's Diary, vol. i. p. 18.

to the ranks and orders of men, whereby England has been known
for hundreds of years? A nobleman, a gentleman, a yeoman,—the
distinction of these, that is a good interest of the nation, and a
great one. The natural magistracy of the nation, was it not almost
trampled under foot, under despite and contempt, by men of levelling principles? Did not that levelling principle tend to the
reducing of all to an equality—not only for the orders of men and
ranks of men, but for property and interest also? What was the
purport of it but to make the tenant as liberal a fortune as the land-
lord?—which, I think, if obtained, would not have lasted long.
The men of that principle, after they had served their own turns,
would then have cried up property and interest fast enough. And
that the thing did extend far, is manifest; because it was a pleasing
voice to all poor men, and truly not unwelcome to all bad men.
   . . .   In spiritual things, the case was still more sad and
deplorable." He then went on to describe the unrestrained propa-
gation of all the wild theories which, under the garb of religion,
tended only to produce licentiousness, blasphemy, and madness.
'The grace of God," he said, " was turned into wantonness; and
Christ and the Spirit of God made a cloak for all villany and spu-
rious apprehensions. . .   . And men can tell the magistrate
that 'he hath nothing to do with men holding such notions; these
are matters of conscience and opinion; he is to look to the outward
man, not to the inward.' . . . To what are such considerations
and pretensions leading us? Liberty of conscience, and liberty of
the subject—two as glorious things to be contended for, as any that
God hath given us; yet both these abused for the patronising of
villanies!   . . These things were in the midst of us; and
nothing in the hearts and minds of men but, 'Overturn, overturn,
overturn!' . . . To add to our misery, whilst we were in
this condition, we were deeply engaged in war with the Portuguese; and not only this, but we had a war with Holland; and, at
the same time also, we were in a war with France. Besides the
sufferings caused by these wars, in respect to the trade of the nation,
it's most evident that the purse of the nation could not have been
able much longer to bear it; . . . and either things must have
been left to sink into the miseries these premises would suppose, or
else a remedy must be supplied. A remedy hath been applied:
that hath been this Government; a thing I shall say little unto.
The thing is open and visible, to be seen and read by all men; and,
therefore, let it speak for itself. . . . But truly I may,—I
hope, humbly before God, and modestly before you,—say somewhat
on the behalf of the Government. Not that I would discourse of

the particular heads of it, but acquaint you a little with the effects it has had, and what the state of our affairs is. . . .

"The Government hath had some things in desire, and hath done some things actually. It hath desired to reform the laws, and for that end bills have been prepared, which in due time, I make no question, will be tendered to you. . . . The Chancery hath been reformed, I hope to the satisfaction of all good men. . . . The Government hath further endeavoured to put a stop to that heady way of every man making himself a minister and preacher. It hath endeavoured to settle a method for the approving and sanctioning of men of piety and ability to discharge that work. . . . The Government hath also taken care, we hope, for the expulsion of all those who may be judged any way unfit for this work; who are scandalous, and the common scorn and contempt of that function. One thing more this Government hath done, it hath been instrumental to call a free Parliament, which, blessed be God, we see here this day. I say, a free Parliament! . . . I perhaps forgot, but indeed it was a caution upon my mind, and I desire now it may be so understood, that if any good hath been done, it was the Lord, not we His poor instruments.

" I did instance the wars, which did exhaust your treasure, and put you into such a condition that you must have sunk therein, if it had continued but a few months longer. Now you have peace with Swedeland; peace with the Danes; peace with the Dutch; a peace unto which I shall say but little, seeing it is so well known in the benefit and consequences thereof. . . . Nothing so much gratified our enemies as to see us at odds with that Commonwealth; and so I persuade myself nothing is of more terror or trouble to them than to see us thus reconciled. Truly, as a peace with the Protestant States hath much security in it, so it hath as much of honour and of assurance to the Protestant interest abroad. I wish it may be written upon our hearts to be zealous for that interest. . . . You have a peace likewise with the crown of Portugal, which, your merchants make us believe, is of good concernment to their trades; . . . and moreover, by this treaty, our people which trade thither have liberty of conscience—liberty to worship in chapels of their own. Indeed peace is desirable with all men, as far as it may be had with conscience and honour. We are upon a treaty with France. . . . And I dare say that there is not a nation in Europe but is very willing to ask a good understanding with us. . . .

" Truly I thought it my duty to let you know, that though God hath dealt thus bountifully with you, yet these are but entrances

and doors of hope, whereby, through the blessing of God, you may
enter into rest and peace. But you are not yet entered.   .   .   .
I have not spoken these things as one who assumes to himself
dominion over you, but as one who doth resolve to be a fellow-servant
with you to the interest of these great affairs, and of the people of
these nations. I shall trouble you no longer, but desire you to
repair to your House, and to exercise your own liberty in the choice
of a Speaker, that so you may lose no time in carrying on your work."[1]

It would seem that words like these, marked by so much good
sense, should have produced a strong impression upon men who
were pledged, like Cromwell himself, to oppose the ancient
monarchy, and who were interested in strengthening the government of the revolution; but when parties have reached a certain
degree of separation and excitement, they will neither understand
nor listen to one another; each follows its own special ideas, and
advances towards its own particular object, without paying the
slightest attention to any unwelcome truths that it may hear, and
disregarding them even more contemptuously when they are uttered
by suspicious lips. After the Protector's speech, the republicans,
on their return to their place of meeting, renewed all the maxims
and pretensions of the Long Parliament, which he had so recently
expelled. They could remain satisfied neither with exercising
the very extensive powers secured to them by the Instrument of
Government, nor with restoring to vigour the legal and necessary
privileges of the House,—such, for instance, as entire liberty of
discussion and speech: three days after their installation, they
decided, after an animated debate, by a hundred and forty-one votes
against a hundred and thirty-six, that, on the following day, they
would form themselves into a committee of the whole House to
deliberate upon the question, "whether the House shall approve of
the system of government by a single person and a Parliament."[2]

This was far more than the assertion of a rival ambition : it was
a systematic determination to admit the legitimacy of no government
and of no power which did not emanate from the Parliament,
as the creature from its creator; it was the proclamation of the
primordial, individual, and absolute sovereignty, in principle, of
the people, and in fact, of the Parliament, as representing the
people.

Cromwell was not a philosopher, he did not act in obedience to
systematic and premeditated views; but he was guided in his

---

[1] Cromwell's Letters and Speeches, vol. iii. pp. 23—45; Old Parliamentary
History, vol. xx. pp. 318—333.

[2] Commons' Journals, vol. vii. pp. 365—367.

government by the superior instinct and practical good sense of a man destined by the hand of God to govern. He had watched the operation of this arrogant design to create the entire government by the sole will of the people, or of the Parliament; he had himself audaciously promoted the work of destruction which had preceded the new creation ; and, amidst the ruins which his hands had made, he had perceived the vanity of his rash hopes ; he had learned that no government is, or can be, the work of man's will alone ; he had recognised, as essential to its production, the hand of God, the action of time, and a variety of other causes apart from human deliberation. Entering, so to speak, into council with these superior powers, he regarded himself as their representative and minister, by the right of his genius, and of his manifold successes. He resolved not to suffer interference with what they had done, and he had done, to establish, in the stead of fallen monarchy, the new government over which he presided.

The Parliament had spent four days in discussing the question whether it should give this government its approbation. On the morning of the 12th of September, 1654, the members were proceeding to the House, as usual, to continue this debate; and on their way they were constantly met by reports that the Parliament was dissolved, and that the Council of State and Council of War, sitting together as one body, had decided upon its dissolution. On their arrival at Westminster, they found the doors of the Parliament House shut, and guarded by soldiers; some of them attempted to go up the stairs: "There is no passage that way," said the guard; "the House is locked up, and we have orders to give no admittance to any person. If you are a Member, go into the Painted Chamber, where the Protector will presently be."[1] Westminster Hall, the Court of Requests, and the Painted Chamber, were full of Members walking up and down, anxiously questioning one another, and awaiting the Protector's arrival. At about ten o'clock, Cromwell appeared, attended by his officers and life-guards, and took his stand on the raised dais where he had stood a week before to open the Parliament. "Gentlemen," he said to them, " it is not long since I met you in this place, upon an occasion which gave me much more content and comfort than this doth. . . . I did then acquaint you what was the first rise of this government, which hath called you hither, and by the authority of which you have come hither. Among other things which I then told you, I said you were a free Parliament; and truly, so you are,—whilst you own

<hr/>
[1] Burton's Diary, vol. i. p. xxxiii.

the government and authority which called you hither. But certainly that word, free Parliament, implied a reciprocity, or it implied nothing at all : and I think your actions and carriage ought to be suitable. But I see it will be necessary for me now a little to magnify my office. . . . I called not myself to this place . . . I was by birth a gentleman, living neither in any considerable height, nor yet in obscurity. I have been called to several employments in the nation—to serve in Parliament and elsewhere ; and I did endeavour to discharge the duty of an honest man in those services. . . . Having had some occasions to see, together with my brethren and countrymen, a happy period put to our sharp wars and contests with the then common enemy, I hoped, in a private capacity, to have reaped the fruit and benefit of our hard labours and hazards. . . . I hoped to have had leave to retire to a private life. I begged to be dismissed of my charge ; I begged it again and again ;—and God be judge between me and all men if I lie in this matter. That I lie not, in matter of fact, is known to very many ; but whether I tell a lie in my heart, as labouring to represent to you what was not upon my heart, I say, the Lord be judge." He then proceeded to narrate, in this tone, all his past career—his struggle with the Long Parliament, the overtures he had received from that body, and the necessity he had been under to dissolve it. " Because of my manner of life," he continued, "which had led me up and down the nation, thereby giving me to see and know the temper and spirits of all men, and of the best of men ; I knew that the nation loathed their sitting. . . . . Under their arbitrary power, poor men were driven, like flocks of sheep, by forty in a morning, to the confiscation of goods and estates, without any man being able to give a reason why two of them had deserved to forfeit a shilling. . . . And so far as I could discern, when they were dissolved, there was not so much as the barking of a dog, or any general and visible repining at it !" He then referred to the convocation of the Barebone Parliament. " I have appealed to God before you already," he said : "though it be a tender thing to make appeals to God, yet I trust in such exigencies as these it will not offend His majesty. And I say to you again, in the presence of that God who hath blessed, and been with me in all my adversities and successes, that my greatest end was to lay down the power which was in my hands. The authority I had was boundless,—for by Act of Parliament, I was General of all the forces in the three nations ; in which unlimited condition I did not desire to live a day,—wherefore, we called that meeting. What the event and issue of that meeting was, we may sadly remember. It hath much teaching in it, and I hope will make us all wiser for the future. . . . The result was that they came and brought to me a parchment, signed by very much the major part of them, expressing their re-delivery and resignation of the power and authority that had been committed them, back again into my hands. And I can say it, in the presence of divers persons here who know whether I lie in that, that I did not know one tittle of that resignation, till they all came and brought it, and delivered it into my hands. . . . My power was again, by this resignation, become as boundless and unlimited as before. All government was dissolved: all civil administration was at an end. I was arbitrary in power; having the armies in the three nations under my command; and truly not very ill-beloved by them, nor very ill-beloved by the people—by the good people. The gentlemen that undertook to frame this government did consult divers days together, how to frame somewhat that might give us settlement; and that I was not privy to their councils they know. When they had finished their model in some measure, they told me that except I would undertake the government, they thought things would hardly come to a composure or settlement, but blood and confusion would break in upon us. I refused it again and again; not complimentingly,—as they know, and as God knows! . . . They urged on me, 'That I did not hereby receive anything which put me into a higher capacity than before; but that it limited me—that it bound my hands to act nothing without the consent of a Council, until the Parliament met, and then limited me by the Parliament. After many arguments, and at the entreaty and request of divers persons of honour and quality, I did accept of the place and title of Protector. . . . I shall submit to your judgment, that I brought not myself into this condition. . . . This was not done in a corner: it was open and public. . . . I have a cloud of witnesses. I have witnesses within, without, above! . . . I had the approbation of the officers of the army, in the three nations. And with their express consent, there went along an implied consent also of a body of persons who had had somewhat to do in the world; who had been instrumental, under God, to fight down the enemies of God and of His people—I mean, the soldiery. And truly, the soldiery were a very considerable part of these nations, especially when all government was thus dissolved, and nothing to keep things in order but the sword. And yet they,—which many histories will not parallel—even they were desirous that things ought to come to a consistency, and arbitrariness be taken away, and the government be put into the hands of a person limited and bounded, as in the

Act of Settlement, whom they distrusted the least, and loved not the worst. . . . I would not forget the approbation I found in the great city of London,—and from many cities, and boroughs, and counties :—express approbations in name of the noblemen, gentlemen, yeomen, and inhabitants, giving very great thanks to me for undertaking this heavy burden at such a time. . . . Nor is this all. The judges did declare, that they could not administer justice to the satisfaction of their consciences, until they had received commissions from me. . . And I have yet more witnesses. . . . All the sheriffs in England are my witnesses; and all that have come in upon a process issued out by sheriffs are my witnesses. All the people in England are my witnesses; and many in Ireland and Scotland. And I shall now make you my last witnesses—and shall ask you, whether you came not hither by my writs, directed to the several sheriffs? To which writs the people gave obedience; having also had the Act of Government communicated to them, which was required to be distinctly read unto the people at the place of election, to avoid surprises, or mis-leadings of them through their ignorance. There also they signed the indenture, with proviso, ' That the persons so chosen should not have power to alter the government as now settled in one single person and a Parliament.'

" This being the case, though I told you in my last speech that you were a free Parliament, yet I thought it was understood withal that I was the Protector, and the authority that called you; that I was in possession of the government by a good right from God and men. . . . May not this character, this stamp, bear equal force with any hereditary interest that could furnish or hath furnished, in the common law or elsewhere, matter of dispute and trial of learning? I do not know why I may not balance this Providence, in the sight of God, with any hereditary interest. . . . And for you to disown or not to own it; for you to act with Parliamentary authority, especially in the disowning of it, contrary to the very fundamental things, yea, against the very root itself of this establishment; to sit, and not own the authority by which you sit—is that which I believe astonisheth more men than myself, and doth as dangerously disappoint and discompose the nation as anything that could have been invented by the greatest enemy to our peace and welfare, or that could well have happened. It is true, as there are some things in the establishment which are fundamental, so there are others which are not, but only circum-stantial. But some things are fundamentals! In every govern-ment there must be somewhat fundamental, somewhat like a Magna

Charta, which should be standing, unalterable. The government by a single person and a Parliament is a fundamental. . . . That Parliament should not make themselves perpetual is a fundamental. . . . And, again, is not liberty of conscience in religion a fundamental? Liberty of conscience is a natural right; and he that would have it ought, to give it. . . . But I told you some things were circumstantials—as, for example, this is: that we should have 200,000l. to defray civil offices; or that we should have twenty thousand foot-soldiers and ten thousand horse, though, if the spirits of men were composed, five thousand horse and ten thousand foot might serve. These things are circumstantials, and, therefore, matters of consideration between you and me. . . . But I can sooner be willing to be rolled into my grave, and buried with infamy, than I can give my consent unto the wilful throwing away of this government, in the fundamentals of it!

"I would it had not been needful for me to call you hither to expostulate these things with you, and in such a manner as this. But necessity hath no law. Feigned necessities, imaginary necessities, are the greatest cozenage that men can put upon the Providence of God; but it is as contrary to God's free grace, as carnal, and as stupid, to think there are no manifest and real necessities, because necessities may be abused or feigned. I had a thought within myself, that it would not have been dishonest nor dishonourable, nor against true liberty, not even the liberty of Parliaments, if,—when a Parliament was so chosen as you have been, in pursuance of this Instrument of Government, and in conformity to it, and with such an approbation and consent to it,—some owning of your call and of the authority which brought you hither, had been required before your entrance into the House. This was declined, and hath not been done, because I am persuaded scarce any man could doubt you came with contrary minds. And I have reason to believe the people that sent you least of all doubted thereof. And therefore I must deal plainly with you. What I forebore upon a just confidence at first, you necessitate me unto now! Seeing the authority which called you is so little valued, and so much slighted,—till some assurance be given and made known that the fundamental interest shall be settled and approved, according to the proviso in the writ of return, and such a consent testified as will make it appear that the same is accepted,—I have caused a stop to be put to your entrance into the Parliament House.

"I am sorry, I am sorry, and I could be sorry to the death, that there is cause for this. But there is cause. . . . There is therefore somewhat to be offered to you: a promise of reforming as

T

to circumstantials, and agreeing in the substance and fundamentals,
that is to say, in the form of government now settled. The making
of your minds known in that, by giving your assent and subscription
to it, is the means that will let you in, to act those things as a Parliament which are for the good of the people. . . . The place
where you may come thus and sign, as many as God shall make free
thereunto, is in the lobby without the Parliament door."[1]

So much boldness in displaying his power, and in making in-
discriminate use of force and right, truth and falsehood, in the assertion of his authority, struck all minds with stupor. Indignant, but
powerless, the republican leaders, Bradshaw, Scott, and Haslerig,
refused to give any pledge, and returned home again ; and to the
honour of the party, about a hundred and fifty members followed
their example. But the majority of members either approved or
submitted ; on the very first day, a hundred and forty signed the
required engagement ; before the end of the month, more than
three hundred had subscribed it, and the Parliament resumed its
labours. Cromwell manifested no ill feeling towards the recusant
members : " I had rather they would stay without," he said ; " one
malcontent that is within the House may do more harm than ten
that are without."[2] Those who remained, however, considered that
some explanation and some reservation were due to the principles of
legal order, and to their own honour : on the 14th of September, at
the suggestion of Whitelocke, the Parliament declared that the
pledge to make no change in the government did not apply to the
whole forty-two articles of the Protectoral Constitution, but only to
the first article which established the government of the Commonwealth by a single person and successive Parliaments. Four days
after, on the 18th of September, in order to give an air of independence to their servility, the House converted the whole of
Cromwell's recent conduct into a measure of their own, and resolved :
" That all persons returned, or who shall be returned, to serve in
this Parliament, shall before they be admitted to sit in the House,
subscribe the recognition of the Government—to be true and faithful to the Lord Protector, and not to propose, or give consent, to
alter the government, as it is settled in one person and a Parliament."[3] A disreputable artifice of a mutilated assembly, which

---

[1] Burton's Diary, vol. i. pp. xxxii.—xxxvi.; Cromwell's Letters and
Speeches, vol. iii. pp. 50—76 ; Old Parliamentary History, vol. xx. pp. 348—
371 ; Commons' Journals, vol. vii. p. 367 ; Ludlow's Memoirs, pp. 211, 212.

[2] Thurloe's State Papers, vol. ii. p. 715.

[3] Commons' Journals, vol. vii. p. 368 ; Old Parliamentary History, vol. xx.
pp. 370, 371 ; Whitelocke's Memorials, p. 605.

falsely ascribed to itself an act of violence, in order to cover its humiliation by the lie !

A singular accident was well nigh causing the abrupt overthrow of the precarious edifice, so laboriously supported by the strong arm of one man.   On the 29th of September, Cromwell had taken it into his head to dine in the open air, in Hyde Park, with Thurloe and some of his household ; his carriage was harnessed with six Friesland horses which the Duke of Oldenburgh had sent him not long before ; and he resolved to try, with his own hand, the mettle of these animals, " not doubting," says Ludlow, " but they would prove as tame as the three nations which were ridden by him." Thurloe could not resist the desire to ride in a carriage driven by the Protector, and so got inside.   Cromwell " drove pretty handsomely for some time, but, at last, provoking the horses too much with the whip, they grew unruly ; " the postilion was thrown ; Cromwell fell from the coach-box upon the pole, and from the pole to the ground ; his foot caught in the harness, and he was dragged along for a moment, but he quickly extricated himself, and the carriage passed on without touching him.   During his fall, a pistol went off in his pocket, revealing, in the accidental danger which he had incurred, his secret precautions against the constant dangers by which he was surrounded.   He was immediately taken up—as well as Thurloe, who had dislocated his ankle by jumping out of the carriage —and conveyed to Whitehall, where he was let blood, and remained confined to his room for nearly three weeks, during which time he received few visitors, and gave but little attention to business.   The Government newspapers made no allusion to the accident ; those of the opposition merely mentioned the danger to which the Protector had been exposed, without specifying its cause ; the court poets celebrated his miraculous deliverance ; so long as he remained confined to his room, his enemies said that he was very ill, and his friends that he was in health ; but, in reality, the accident was more dangerous in possibility than in fact, and the terms in which the various foreign ministers speak of it in their letters to their Courts, show that the public was neither long nor seriously alarmed at it.[1]

Cromwell's real or apparent inactivity lasted much longer than his indisposition ; for more than three months, he remained almost utterly unmoved and silent, as if his only intention were to watch and wait.   Meanwhile Parliament was discussing the constitution of the Protectorate.

[1] Thurloe's State Papers, vol. ii. pp. 652, 653, 656 ; Ludlow's Memoirs, p. 215 ; Bates's Elenchus Motuum Nuperorum, part ii. p. 350 ; Godwin's History of the Commonwealth, vol. iv. p. 133.

The leaders of the republican opposition, and the majority of their party, were no longer in the House; but their presumptuous and obstinate rashness remained after their withdrawal. Convoked for the purpose of establishing a government, the sole anxiety of the House was to discuss a constitution; for more than three months they were employed in dissecting and amending the forty-two articles, which they increased to sixty, with that democratic mistrust and theological subtlety which are equally tiresome and dangerous to the ruling power. Should the Protector have a share in the legislature, or should he be strictly limited to the executive? Should his veto on the resolutions of the Parliament be always merely suspensive, and if so, for what period of time; or sometimes peremptory, and if so, in what cases? In whom should the right of declaring war and making peace be vested? Under what limitations should the Protector be intrusted with the disposal and command of the army and militia? Who should appoint the Council of State? What should be the extent of the powers of the Protector, in the matter of making laws and imposing taxes, during the absence of the Parliament, and in cases of urgency? These questions, though already settled in the Instrument of Government establishing the Protectorate, were resumed and discussed as though that Instrument had never existed, or were only an unauthoritative text for debate; and their discussion occupied all the sittings of the House, and often two sittings daily, from the 20th of September, 1654, to the 20th of January, 1655. There was a fixed determination to take no note of what had been done already, and to institute the Protectoral government afresh, in virtue of the exclusive sovereignty of the people and Parliament. And the debates, though animated, were hypocritical, for the opposing parties were all secretly influenced by views which they did not openly avow; the partisans of the Protector wished to give still further development to the monarchical reaction which had begun under that name; the republicans who had submitted to Cromwell, struggled to maintain, in the institutions of the country, means of return for the expiring republic; and the Presbyterians endeavoured once more to introduce those principles of parliamentary monarchy, in furtherance of which they had begun the revolution. Some Cavaliers who had gained admission into the House by dissembling their opinions and origin, laboured, under the mask of great zeal for liberty or the Commonwealth, to foment dissensions which they hoped would terminate in the common ruin of their various enemies. In presence of these incoherent elements, ever ready to coalesce against him, though for contrary purposes, Cromwell and his adherents vainly attempted

. to exercise an amount of influence in the House which might make it an instrument of strength and stability to his government: but it only served to hamper or to menace his power, and he frequently suffered repulses from it, as offensive as they were unexpected.[1]

Upon the question which affected him most closely, he had bitter experience of the small amount of influence which he possessed. In the general committee by which the constitution had been just discussed, the question arose whether the Protectorate should be elective or hereditary; but as an hereditary succession had seemed to meet with but little favour, the proposition had been indefinitely postponed. It was brought forward again on the 16th of October, 1654, upon occasion of the examination of the thirty-second article of the constitution, and the discussion lasted three days. "There was little appearance," wrote Bordeaux to the Count de Brienne, "that the resolution would be favourable; nevertheless, the Protector, either being persuaded to the contrary, or influenced by some other consideration not known to all the world, has again ventilated this question. At first his party appeared to be the strongest; even General Lambert made an harangue to persuade the Parliament that it was necessary to make the office of Protector hereditary; but when the votes were taken, all his relatives and friends were in favour of making it elective, so that, out of the two hundred and sixty members of whom this body is composed, two hundred were of the same opinion; which has surprised not only the public, but also the family of the Protector, who, on the previous day, thought themselves sure of retaining . that dignity in their house."[2]

Not satisfied with thus opposing or trammelling the Protector in his political views, the House waged an almost continual warfare with him on religious matters also, though in this respect their hostility was less direct and open. In order to secure liberty of conscience, within the limits allowed by the spirit of his age, Cromwell had obtained the insertion of the following article in the Instrument of Government: "That such as profess faith in God by Jesus Christ (though differing in judgment from the doctrine, worship, or discipline publicly held forth) shall not be restrained from, but shall . be protected in, the profession of their faith and exercise of their

---

[1] Commons' Journals, vol. vii. pp. 368—413; Burton's Diary, vol. i. pp. xl. cxxxiii., vol. iii. pp. 550, 551; Bates's Elenchus Motuum Nuperorum, part ii. p. 392.

[2] Bordeaux to Brienne, October 29, 1654, in the Archives des Affaires Etrangères de France; Thurloe's State Papers, vol. ii. p. 681; Burton's Diary, vol. i. p. li.; Godwin's History of the Commonwealth, vol. iv. pp. 134—136.

religion; so as they abuse not this liberty to the civil injury of others, and to the actual disturbance of the public peace on their parts: Provided this liberty be not extended to Popery or Prelacy nor to such as, under the profession of Christ, hold forth and practise licentiousness."[1]   These restrictions, though already severe, were not enough for the Presbyterians, who were numerous and powerful in the House; and they determined to augment them in every possible way.   A committee of fourteen members, assisted by an equal number of divines, among whom Presbyterian influences prevailed, was appointed to prepare the creed which was to be subscribed by all ministers holding public benefices.   The same commissioners were further directed to define, by the essential characteristics implied therein, the words—" Such as profess faith in God by Jesus Christ," in order to confine, within the limits of that definition, the liberty promised to dissenting Christians.   Another committee was appointed to prepare a list of all heresies that should be considered damnable.   And suiting their practice to their maxims, Parliament ordered the prosecution and imprisonment of several heretics,—one John Biddle among others, a sincere and humble, but obstinate freethinker, who had published various works subversive of Christian doctrine.   Parliament commanded that the books should be burned by the common hangman, and that a bill should be prepared for the punishment of their author.[2]

At the same time that, upon questions of constitutional organisation, the House proved itself thus indefatigable and untractable, it neglected from carelessness or premeditation, all other questions, and all other business.   Several bills were brought forward in reference to the Court of Chancery,[3] the Court of Wards,[4] the equalisation of taxation, the celebration of marriages,[5] the treatment of idiots and lunatics,[6] the abolition of purveyance,[7] the relief of prisoners for debt,[8] indeed, almost all the subjects in which the public was at all deeply interested ; but not one of these propositions was finally discussed and adopted.   At the same time the measures of reform which, in the absence of the Parliament, the Protector

[1] Old Parliamentary History, vol. xx. p. 261.
[2] Commons' Journals, vol. vii. pp. 373, 399, 400, 416; Baxter's Life, vol. i. part ii. pp. 197—205; Neal's History of the Puritans, vol. iv. pp. 122, 123; Godwin's History of the Commonwealth, vol. iv. pp. 144—149; Whitelocke, p. 609.
[3] Commons' Journals, November 15 and 25, 1654.
[4] Ibid. October 31, 1654.
[5] Ibid. September 26, 1654.
[6] Ibid. January 15, 1655.
[7] Ibid. November 21, 1654.
[8] Ibid. October 25, 1654.

had promulgated on his own authority,—especially those which related to proceedings before the Court of Chancery, and the expulsion of ignorant or inefficient ministers and schoolmasters, were suspended and referred to committees which were directed to subject them to complete revision.[1] This was at once a postponement of reform, and an insult to the Protector. Another committee had been appointed to inquire what reductions could be effected in the army and fleet, and to confer with Cromwell on the subject:[2] the conferences, however, were infrequent or dilatory, and although certain reductions were determined upon,[3] particularly in the fleet, it does not appear that they were ever carried out. When the question of supplies arose, the delays, which were then far more serious, became far more voluntary and premeditated : two months elapsed without the Parliament appearing to think that any supplies were necessary; and when at last it did take the subject into consideration, the resolutions which it adopted were merely provisional and altogether ineffectual.[4] An ordinance issued by the Protector had fixed the sum to be devoted to the payment of the army and fleet, first at 120,000*l.*, and then at 90,000*l.* per month ; the Parliament, without appearing to suspect or care about the insufficiency of the sum, reduced it to 60,000*l.*;[5] and even after this reduction, the bill was indefinitely delayed, and was never presented to the Protector for his sanction. Sometimes the House, from intimidation or a spontaneous feeling of anxiety, suddenly rescinded its hostile or dilatory votes, and adopted resolutions in conformity with the wishes of the Government ; but it soon relapsed into its former course, having only added proofs of its hesitation and weakness to those which already existed of its ill-will. Evidently, its only serious occupation was its secret struggle with the Protector, and it laboured unceasingly to make his government insupportable or impossible to him, without possessing courage or power to take it from him by force.[6]

For a long time, Cromwell endured this hostility with patience, as he hoped it would involve the Parliament in greater discredit than it would entail danger upon himself ; finally, however, it began to annoy and alarm him : such constant criticisms, though

[1] Ibid. October 5, 10, 13, and 23, 1654.
[2] Commons' Journals, September 26, 1654.
[3] Ibid. October 5, 1654.
[4] Ibid. November 7 and 21, 1654.
[5] Ibid. November 28, 29, and December 4 and 20, 1654.
[6] Commons' Journals, vol. vii. pp. 370, 373, 375, 376, 377, 378, 379, 382, 385, 387, 390, 392, 394, 405, 413 ; Godwin's History of the Commonwealth, vol. iv. pp. 140—145, 148—151

indirect, and timidly uttered, tarnished and undermined his power; by the delay and insufficiency of the supplies granted, the House tended to the indefinite prolongation of the session. Cromwell, in his turn, grew angry, and hinted a dissolution. His more moderate advisers, Whitelocke among others, who had, apparently, acquired considerable influence in the House, endeavoured to dissuade him from this course; sudden dissolutions, they said, had always proved fatal to the power which effected them; and besides, what reason was there for such rash haste? The legal term of the session was at hand; for as, by the eighth article of the constitution, the House was to sit for five months only, its tenure of office would legally expire on the 3rd of February; and he might then, with far less noise and inconvenience, pronounce its dissolution if he pleased. But these arguments had little effect upon Cromwell; the House, while devolving upon him all the responsibility of the government, prevented him from governing; he was embarrassed and irritated; he longed to answer these stealthy and indirect attacks by a bold and decisive act; and courtiers were not wanting around him to stimulate his passion, and urge him to execute his design.[1]

Whilst he was thus deliberating, the House itself supplied him with the pretext and the opportunity for which he waited. It had at length brought its debates on the constitution to a close; and on the 10th of January, 1655, the partisans of Cromwell demanded that before they finally passed the bill,—which was entitled "An Act declaring and settling the Government of the Commonwealth of England, Scotland, and Ireland, and the dominions thereunto belonging,"—they should have a conference with the Protector on the subject; but the proposition was rejected by one hundred and seven votes against ninety-five. Six days afterwards, on the 16th of January, the House further resolved, by eighty-six votes against fifty-five, that this bill should become law without the Protector's consent. No sooner had they adopted this resolution, than they became conscious that they had gone too far, and they retracted it on the following day, by voting "that the bill be engrossed, in order to its presentment to the Lord Protector, for his consideration and consent;" but at the same time, they decided that unless the Protector and Parliament should agree to the whole and every part of the bill, it should be void and of no effect; thus depriving Cromwell of all liberty to amend or alter its provisions.[2]

[1] Old Parliamentary History, vol. xx. p. 250; Whitelocke, p. 610.
[2] Commons' Journals, vol. vii. pp. 411, 418, 419.

Cromwell took his resolution at once. An expedient was suggested to him by which he would be able, in appearance at least, to
act with legality. It was customary, in paying the troops, to reckon
by lunar months of twenty-eight days. By applying this method to
the duration of the Parliament, the five months of session, to which
it was entitled by the Instrument of Government, would expire on
the 22nd of January, 1655. On the morning of that day, the Protector, with his usual retinue, proceeded to Westminster, and summoned the House to attend him in the Painted Chamber. They
came, in much surprise and apprehension, expecting some rough
remonstrance, but not at all anticipating an immediate dissolution.
" Gentlemen," said Cromwell, " when I first met you in this room,
it was to my apprehension the hopefullest day that ever mine eyes
saw, as to the considerations of this world : and I came with very
great joy and contentment, and comfort. . . . I met you a
second time here, and I confess, at that meeting, I had much abate-
ment of my hopes, though not a total frustration. . . . I did
think, as I have formerly found in that way that I have been
engaged in as a soldier, that some affronts put upon us, some
disasters at the first, had made way for very great and happy successes ; and I did not at all despond but the stop put upon you, in
like manner, would have made way for a blessing from God. . . .
But we, and these nations, are, for the present, under some disappointment! . . . Sure I am you will all bear me witness
that, from your entering into the House upon the recognition, to
this day, you have had no manner of interruption or hinderance of
mine, in proceeding to what blessed issue the heart of a good man
could propose to himself. You have me very much locked up as to
what you have transacted among yourselves, from that time to this.
But as I may not take notice what you have been doing, so I think
I have a very great liberty to tell you that I do not know what you
have been doing. I do not know whether you have been alive or
dead. I have not once heard from you all this time ; and that you
all know.—If I have had any melancholy thoughts, and have sat
down by them, why might it not have been very lawful for me to
think that I was a person judged unconcerned in all these businesses ? I can assure you I have not so reckoned myself. Nor
did I reckon myself unconcerned in you. . . . I have been
careful of your safety, and the safety of those that you represented,
to whom I reckon myself a servant. I have been caring for you,
for your quiet sitting, for your privileges, that they might not be
interrupted. I have been consulting if possibly I might in anything promote the real good of this Parliament. And I did think it

to be my business rather to see the utmost issue, and what God would produce by you, than unseasonably to intermeddle with you.　.　.　.

"I will tell you somewhat, which, if it be not news to you, I wish you had taken very serious consideration of.　If it be news, I wish I had acquainted you with it sooner.　And yet, if any man will ask me why I did not, the reason is, because I did make it my business to give you no interruption.　There be some trees that will not grow under the shadow of other trees; there be some that choose to thrive under the shadow of other trees.　I will tell you what hath thriven,—I will not say what you have cherished,—under your shadow; that were too hard.　Instead of peace and settlement,—instead of mercy and truth being brought together, and righteousness and peace kissing each other, by your reconciling the honest people of these nations, and settling the woeful distempers that are amongst us,—weeds and nettles, briers and thorns, have thriven under your shadow.　Dissettlement and division, discontent and dissatisfaction, together with real dangers to the whole State, have been more multiplied within these five months of your sitting, than in some years before.　Foundations have also been laid for the future renewing of the troubles of these nations, by all the enemies of them abroad and at home.　Let not these words seem too sharp, for they are true as any mathematical demonstrations are, or can be. · . . .　During your sittings and proceedings, the Cavalier party have been designing and preparing to put this nation in blood again. . . . 　They have been making great preparations of arms. .　. 　Banks of money have been framing, for these and other such like uses.　Letters have been issued with privy seals, to as great persons as most are in the nation, for the advance of money.　Commissions for regiments of horse and foot, and command of castles, have been likewise given from Charles Stuart, since your sitting.　And what the general insolences of that party have been, honest people know and can very well testify.—Nor is this all.　Men have appeared of another sort than those before mentioned to you; 'a company of men like briers and thorns;' and worse, if worse can be.[1]　These also have been, and yet are, endeavouring to put us into blood and into confusion; more desperate and dangerous confusion than England ever yet saw. . .　If a commonwealth must fall, it is some satisfaction that it perish by men, and not by the hands of persons differing little from beasts. if it must needs suffer, it should rather suffer from rich men than from poor men, who, as Solomon says, 'when they

---

[1] The Anabaptist Levellers.

oppress, leave nothing behind them, but are as a sweeping rain.'
Now such as these also are grown up under your shadow. . . .
They have taken encouragement from your delays; . . . they confess they built their hopes upon the assurance they had of the
Parliament's not agreeing to a settlement. . . . Yet you might
have had an opportunity to have settled peace and quietness
amongst all professing godliness, and have rendered them and
these nations both secure, happy, and well satisfied. There was a
government already in the possession of the people; a government
which hath now been exercised near fifteen months, . . .
wherein I dare assert there is a just liberty to the people of God, and
the just rights of the people in these nations are provided for. . . .
For myself, I desire not to keep my place in this government an
hour longer than I may preserve England in its just rights, and
may protect the people of God in such a just liberty of their
consciences as I have already mentioned. And therefore, if this
Parliament have judged things to be otherwise than as I have
stated them, it had been huge friendliness for you to have convinced me in what particulars my error lay. Of which I never yet
had a word from you. But if, instead thereof, your time has been
spent in setting up somewhat else upon another bottom than this
stands upon, it looks as if the laying grounds for a quarrel had
rather been designed, than to give the people settlement. If it be
thus, it's well your labours have not arrived to any maturity
at all!   . .

    "But wherein have you had cause to quarrel? What demonstra-
tions have you held forth to settle me to your opinion? I would
you had made me so happy as to have let me know your grounds.
. . . Was there none amongst you to move such a thing? . .
If it be not folly in me to listen to town-talk, such things have
been proposed, and rejected, with stiffness and severity, once and
again. . . . I would not have been averse to alteration, of the
good of which I might have been convinced. . . . But
I must tell you this: That as I undertook this government, in the
simplicity of my heart and as before God, to do the part of an
honest man, and to be true to the Commonwealth,—so I can say
that no particular interest, either of myself, estate, honour, or
family, are, or have been, prevalent with me to this undertaking.
For if you had, upon the old Instrument of Government, offered
me this one, this one thing,—I speak as thus advised, and before
God, as having been to this day of this opinion; and this hath been
my constant judgment, well known to many who hear me speak;—
if, I say, this one thing had been inserted, that the government

should have been placed in my family hereditarily, I would have rejected it! And I could have done no other according to my present conscience and light: . . . though I cannot tell what God will do with me, nor with you, nor with the nation, for throwing away precious opportunities committed to us. . . .

"I know that I am like to meet with difficulties; and that this nation will not, as it is fit it should not, be deluded with pretexts of necessity in that great business of raising money. . . . If I had not a hope fixed in me that this cause and this business was of God, I would many years ago have run from it. If it be of God, He will bear it up. If it be of man, it will tumble, as everything that hath been of man since the world began, hath done. And what are all our histories, and other traditions of actions in former times, but God manifesting Himself, that He hath shaken and tumbled down, and trampled upon, everything that He had not planted? And, as this is, so let the All-wise God deal with it. If this be of human structure and invention, and if it be an old plotting and contriving to bring things to this issue, and that they are not the births of Providence, then they will tumble. But if the Lord take pleasure in England, and if He will do us good, He is very able to bear us up! Let the difficulties be whatsoever they will, we shall in His strength be able to encounter them. And I bless God, I have been inured to difficulties; and I never found God failing when I trusted in Him. I can laugh and sing, in my heart, when I speak of these things to you, and elsewhere. And though some may think it is an hard thing to raise money without Parliamentary authority upon this nation; yet I have another argument to the good people of this nation, if they would be safe, namely: whether they prefer the having of their will, though it be their destruction, rather than comply with things of necessity? That will excuse me. But I should wrong my native country to suppose this.

"I have troubled you with a long speech: and I believe it may not have the same resentment with all that it hath with some. But because that is unknown to me, I shall leave it to God—and conclude with this: that I think it my duty to tell you that it is not for the profit of these nations, nor for common and public good, for you to continue here any longer, and therefore I do declare unto you, that I do dissolve this Parliament."[1]

---

[1] Cromwell's Letters and Speeches, vol. iii. pp. 89—119; Old Parliamentary History, vol. xx. pp. 403—431; Whitelocke, pp. 610—618; Ludlow's Memoirs, p. 216; Godwin's History of the Commonwealth, vol. iv. pp. 153—157.

BOOK VI.

GOVERNMENT OF CROMWELL WITHOUT A PARLIAMENT—ROYALIST AND REPUB-
LICAN CONSPIRACIES—DIFFERENT ATTITUDE OF CROMWELL TOWARDS THE
TWO PARTIES—INSURRECTIONS IN THE WEST AND NORTH OF ENGLAND—
ATTEMPTS AT LEGAL RESISTANCE—APPOINTMENTS OF MAJOR-GENERALS—
TAXATION OF THE ROYALISTS—CROMWELL'S RELIGIOUS TOLERATION—HIS
CONDUCT TOWARDS THE JEWS, TOWARDS THE UNIVERSITIES, AND TOWARDS
LITERARY MEN—GOVERNMENT OF MONK IN SCOTLAND, AND OF HENRY
CROMWELL IN IRELAND—CROMWELL'S CONVERSATIONS WITH LUDLOW.

· CROMWELL'S indignation was not feigned; he returned to Whitehall,
dissatisfied but confident; he was conscious of his strength, had
implicit faith in his good fortune, and heartily despised the adversaries who attempted to prevent him from governing. Were they
capable of taking the government themselves? Whom had they to
substitute in his stead? He alone could preserve them from the
return of Charles Stuart, by maintaining order and peace throughout the country. Besides, theoretically, he did not aspire to absolute power; he did not set it up as a legal and durable system;
he was well acquainted with the conditions of government in
England,—a monarch, a Parliament, and the law. But he, personally, required a Parliament that would admit his past conduct
and present authority as indisputable facts; and that would act as
his accomplice, not as his rival. He had once hoped that the Parliament which he had just dissolved would understand this position,
and satisfy both the requirements of the new Prince, and the
ancient traditions of the country. This had proved an utter miscalculation; and he resented it with that irritated pride which per-
vades great hearts that have been deceived in their expectations,
and are determined not to endure a reverse.

To this miscalculation was added danger. Cromwell spoke the
truth when he reproached the Parliament with having revived the

hopes and conspiracies of the Royalists and Levellers by their
opposition to the Protectorate. The royalist party was in motion
throughout England, Scotland, and Ireland : in the counties, the
gentlemen frequently visited one another or met together, to kindle
their loyalty by an exchange of their plans, and of the news they
had received : between them and the little court of Charles II. at
Cologne, correspondence was constantly kept up, and messengers
were continually passing. The central committee, which alone in
England had instructions and secret powers from the proscribed
king, were opposed to any armed outbreak ; nothing was ripe,
nothing was ready yet, they said ; it would be better to wait until
the internal dissensions of the army and the unfavourable feelings
of the country had received further development ; by too much pre-
cipitancy, they might lose their opportunity. The high-spirited
Cavaliers, the men of action, complained, on the other hand, of the
lukewarmness of the committees, which allowed every opportunity
to escape, and gave Cromwell time to discover every plot. Beyond
the limits of their own party, circumstances, in the opinion of the
boldest, seemed favourable to their cause : a feeling of republican
dissatisfaction, more violent than general, was fermenting in the
army. Among the troops stationed near his residence or within his
reach, Cromwell was easily able to dispel or crush these symptoms
of opposition ; but at a distance, the ill-will was more undisguised,
and men were not wanting to head the malcontents. Ludlow was
still in Ireland, and though not at all an enterprising man, he was
a blunt, rough soldier, openly opposed to the Protector, and had
formally refused to promise not to engage in any movement against
him. Cromwell had sent back to his command in Scotland, Colonel
Overton, a brave and pious officer, rash with mystic gentleness, who
possessed the confidence of the saints in the lower ranks of the
army, and believed it his duty, if they required it, to make himself
the faithful instrument of the Lord, in the midst of so many worldly
backslidings. Colonels Okey, Alured, Cobbett, and Mason shared
the sentiments of Overton, but like him, they were full of hesitation
and uneasiness when the moment drew near for acting against their
general, who was Protector still of the name of the Commonwealth.
But they were swayed and hurried on by some old comrades, such
as Major Wildman and Colonel Sexby, men who had risen altogether from the ranks, who were passionate enemies of Cromwell,
uncompromising inheritors of Lilburne's hostility and fanaticism,
and who lived in intimate and permanent conspiracy with the adherents of Charles Stuart : either because, from hatred to the Protector, they were resigned to accept the old King, or because they

hoped easily to set him aside and establish the republic, when they had overthrown the Protector.[1]

Left sole master of the field, and free from all restraint in the government, amid such a host of enemies, Cromwell placed himself at once in readiness for the struggle, and extended the range of his power to its utmost limit. He issued an ordinance for the levying of the various taxes, including the sixty thousand pounds a month which the Parliament had assigned for the payment of the army and fleet, though it had come to no final vote on the subject. As soon as the rumour of a royalist conspiracy began to spread, the Protector summoned the Lord Mayor and all the municipal authorities of the city of London to attend him, communicated to them the information which he had obtained, and enjoined them to maintain order with the strictest severity, giving them power to raise a body of troops, of which Major-General Skippon was to have the command. He revived the laws which enacted judicial prosecutions and banishment against all Jesuits, Catholic priests, and Popish recusants. He published a proclamation commanding all known royalists to leave London, Westminster, and the suburbs, within six days; horse-races and all popular meetings were prohibited for six months. The measures taken against suspected republicans were of a different character; for some time, they had been under the surveillance of a vigilant police: but no steps had been publicly taken against them; some had been warned, some directed to change their residence, some deprived of their employments, and some quietly arrested. Orders had been sent to Fleetwood, in Ireland, that "whereas Major-General Ludlow has declared himself dissatisfied with the present government, Lieutenant-General Fleetwood is hereby required to take care that his charge in the army be managed some other way, and to send him prisoner to England, if necessary." Thurloe, and Cromwell himself, maintained a constant correspondence with Monk, in Scotland, regarding the disaffected officers in the army under his command, and Monk faithfully devoted his silent but effectual vigilance to the service of the Protector. He was informed that Overton, who commanded at Aberdeen, was the centre of a network of combined royalist and republican intrigues, the object of which, it was said, was to surprise Dalkeith, where Monk resided, to seize his person, and to march immediately towards the north of England, where an insur-

---

[1] Clarendon's History of the Rebellion, vol. vii. pp. 33—35, 41—44, 129—134; Clarendon's State Papers, vol. iii. p. 265; Ludlow's Memoirs, pp. 217—221; Cromwelliana, p. 149; Thurloe's State Papers, vol. iii. pp. 47, 55, 185, 217, Whitelocke, pp. 606, 618.

rection was to break out under the direction of Bradshaw and Haslerig. The conspirators expected they would be able to dispose of about two thousand cavalry and several regiments of infantry. They were in communication also with the fleet, and particularly with Vice-Admiral Lawson. It was even affirmed that Fairfax, then quietly residing at his seat at Nun Appleton, was favourable to their plan, and would bestir himself in Yorkshire on their behalf, when they arrived in that county. Cromwell, in London, and Monk, at Dalkeith, followed the development of this conspiracy step by step, for the plot was betrayed on every hand. Monk sent orders to Overton to come to him; Overton hesitated to obey; Monk at once superseded him in his command, assigned him Leith as a residence, and shortly afterwards (on the 10th of January, 1655), had him arrested, and sent him to London, where he was confined in the Tower. Among his papers, proofs were found of his dealings with the Cavaliers, and some lines against the Protector, written in his own hand :—

> " A Protector! what's that? 'Tis a stately thing,
> That confesseth itself but the ape of a king .
> A counterfeit piece, that woodenly shows
> A golden effigy, with a copper nose . . .
> In fine, he is one, we may Protector call,
> From whom the King of Kings protect us all !" [1]

Overton had been confined in the Tower for about three weeks, when Major Wildman, the most violent of the republican conspirators, was sent thither also. He had been arrested on the 10th of February, while dictating a " Declaration of the free and well-affected people of England, now in arms against the tyrant Oliver Cromwell." In this manifesto he recapitulated the hopes of liberty, in whose name Cromwell had formerly roused England to revolt, the falsehoods by which he had deceived her, the oppression with which he had afflicted her; and he conjured all honest men, all his old comrades in the army, to join in the insurrection which aimed at delivering their country from so shameful a yoke. In his obscure house in the little town of Exton, Wildman believed himself in perfect safety; the door of his room was open, and he had not yet finished dictating, when a body of soldiers, sent by Cromwell's order, entered suddenly and seized him, his papers, and his arms, which Colonel Butler sent at once to the Protector. Several other

[1] Old Parliamentary History, vol. xx. pp. 431, 432 ; Thurloe's State Papers, vol. iii. pp. 46, 47, 55, 67, 75, 76, 1.0, 185, 217, 280; Whitelocke, pp. 618, 625; Cromwelliana, pp. 149—152; Ludlow's Memoirs, p. 221.

leaders of the Anabaptists and Levellers—Harrison, Carew, and Lord Grey of Groby—before they had engaged in any hostile undertaking, were arrested, dispersed, and confined in various prisons, but no prosecution was instituted against them.[1] When he had to deal with men of his old party, Cromwell's aim was to forestall and stifle their plans; to render them powerless, not to make them public victims.

Towards the royalists, he acted very differently. At the same time that, to promote the security of civil interest, and to maintain the conservative character of his government, he endeavoured to obtain the adherence of the great landowners,—quiet men who were fatigued with the contest,—he allowed the ardent, hot-headed members of the party to involve and compromise themselves as much as they pleased,—watching their intrigues without checking them, exaggerating rather than diminishing their importance, and punishing them severely as soon as he caught them in action. When the Parliament was dissolved, they were in a state of great hopefulness and effervescence; they reckoned confidently on the support of their republican allies in the army, on the irritation likely to be produced by the violent measures of the Protector, on a promised rising in the Highlands of Scotland, and on the weakness and irresolution of Fleetwood's government in Ireland. A great insurrection was planned; it was to break out simultaneously in the western and northern counties, where the principal strength of the party lay. The leaders sent message after message to Cologne, beseeching the King to give them authority to act, and to hold himself in readiness at no great distance, for they would soon be in a position to execute their design. They had already fixed on the 14th of February as the day on which the insurrection was to break out; the King would easily land in Kent, which would rise to a man on his behalf, and where Dover Castle would be in their hands; and they would at last revenge their cruel defeat at Worcester.[2]

Charles had little faith in these assurances, and little inclination to trust himself again to so much uncertainty and risk; his wisest counsellors, Hyde and Ormonde in particular, shared his doubts; but how could he persistently refuse to risk somewhat with those who were ready to risk all for his sake? Among the refugees by

[1] Thurloe's State Papers, vol. iii. p. 147; Whitelocke, pp. 618—620; Godwin's History of the Commonwealth, vol. iv. pp. 159—165; Cromwelliana, p. 151; Clarendon's History of the Rebellion, vol. vii. pp. 42, 43.
[2] Clarendon's History of the Rebellion, vol. vii. pp. 129—134; Ludlow's Memoirs, p. 218; Cromwelliana, p. 149; Clarendon's State Papers, vol. iii. pp. 265—269.

whom he was surrounded, the greater number, from imprudence or ennui, urged him to accede to such pressing solicitations : his most intimate favourite, Lord Wilmot, whom he had recently created Earl of Rochester, begged leave to go to England to form an idea of the preparations, resources, and chances of their friends on the spot. Wilmot was a clever and pleasant companion, and no one could know as yet that, after having shown such impatience to make the attempt, he would not be firm when the moment for action arrived. From concession rather than from conviction, Charles gave him leave to go to London, to approve in his name of the projected insurrection, and to promise his presence as soon as it was required ; and secretly leaving Cologne, Charles himself proceeded to Middleburg, in the island of Walcheren, on the coast of Zealand, there to wait, in the house of a trusty host, until Wilmot should invite him to cross the sea.[1]

But secrecy is difficult to Kings, even when dethroned, and no man was more skilful than Cromwell in setting spies upon his enemies. A Cavalier named Manning, who resided with the Court at Cologne, and was on intimate terms with Rochester, kept the Protector informed of all that was going on about the King : Rochester himself was indiscreet and boastful, and, as he travelled through the Netherlands on his way to embark at Dunkirk, he made no secret of the object of his journey to England. The States of the province of Holland, learning the intentions of Charles, and fearing that he might make their territory his point of departure, wrote to his sister, the Princess of Orange, that, on account of their recent treaty with the Commonwealth of England, they would be unable to allow anything of the kind. Revelations and information reached Cromwell from every side ; and before the royalist insurrection had broken out, he was acquainted with its plan, its means of success, the hopes of its promoters, and even the hiding-places of its leaders.[2]

Whether from accident or design, he took no effectual means to prevent it. As soon as it began to be rumoured abroad, he ordered the arrest of a large number of royalists, but not of those who were actually preparing for the speedy execution of the plot. Rochester

---

[1] Clarendon's History of the Rebellion, vol. vii. pp. 135—137 ; Clarendon's State Papers, vol. iii. pp. 265—269; Heath's Chronicle, pp. 677, 678; Thurloe's State Papers, vol. iii. pp. 182, 207.

[2] Clarendon's History of the Rebellion, vol. vii. pp. 134, 140; Heath's Chronicle, pp. 678, 680; Clarendon's State Papers, vol. iii. p. 266 ; Thurloe's State Papers, vol. iii. pp. 190, 195, 224, 301, 330, 390, 457, 501 ; Bates's Elenchus Motuum Nuperorum, vol. ii. p. 326.

spent several days in London, concerting measures with the Cavaliers who had come thither to meet him, discussing their plans, sending messengers into the counties, and transmitting to the King, at his asylum at Middleburg, such hopeful assurances that he only awaited a last signal in order to embark. The measures which Cromwell was taking could not fail to redouble the confidence of the royalists, for he appeared anxious, and had sent to Ireland for reinforcements of troops, but he had found them so disaffected that, before they left Dublin, the Council of War had been obliged to break one company and to hang a soldier, in order to intimidate those who refused to embark.[1]

On the 11th of March, 1655, at five o'clock in the morning, a troop of Cavaliers suddenly entered the town of Salisbury, where the county assizes were at that time being held, under the presidency of Chief Justice Rolle. They were about two hundred in number, mostly gentlemen of Wiltshire, under the command of Sir Joseph Wagstaff, a brave and dashing officer, who had formerly been a Major-General of infantry in the royal army, and had recently arrived from London to place himself at the head of the insurgents in the West. They posted themselves in the market-place, and immediately brought thither the Chief Justice, his colleague Justice Nicholas, and the High Sheriff of the county, who had been seized in their beds. Wagstaff ordered the sheriff to proclaim King Charles the Second; but he boldly refused. Wagstaff proposed that the sheriff and the two judges should be hanged on the spot: "We must use them," he said, "how we ourselves should be used, if we were under their hands." But his companions, and especially Colonel John Penruddock, a gentleman of large estate in the neighbourhood, strenuously opposed any such proceeding, as they were determined to commit neither violence nor disorder at a time when they came to restore the violated laws of the country. The judges were set at liberty, and requested to remember to whom they were indebted for their lives. The sheriff was detained as a hostage, and the King proclaimed without his assistance. The insurgents threw open the doors of the prison, and took all the horses in the town, but, in every other particular, they respected the tranquillity and property of the inhabitants. No resistance was offered to them, but scarcely any one joined them; most persons thought them too weak to declare in their favour.

[1] Clarendon's History of the Rebellion, vol. vii. pp. 137, 138; Heath's Chronicle, p. 678; Bates's Elenchus, pp. 322—325; Cromwelliana, p. 150; Thurloe's State Papers, vol. iii. pp. 161, 162, 164, 172, 179, 190, 273; Ludlow's Memoirs, pp. 217, 218.

They expected that reinforcements from the neighbouring counties would have met them at Salisbury; but finding that they gained no additions to their numbers, they left the place on the same day, in the hope of meeting with better success elsewhere. At Blandford, in Dorsetshire, the town-crier, when brought to the market-place, seemed not unwilling to proclaim the King; but when Penruddock, who was dictating the proclamation, required him to pronounce the words, " Charles II., King of England," the man became terrified, and declared that he would not utter those words even if he should be burnt alive for refusing. In the opinion of the people, the royal cause was a lost cause, which entailed destruction on all who embraced it. The insurgents made no progress; from republican fanaticism, fear, ignorance, or love of order, the populace stood aloof from them. Three or four hundred Cavaliers from Hampshire, who had begun their march to rendezvous at Salisbury, paused when they heard that Wagstaff had left that city, and dispersed instead of going to join him elsewhere. Colonel Butler, who was quartered in that district, sent out four companies of infantry with orders to pursue the insurgents, and attack them if a favourable opportunity should present itself. Major-General Desborough arrived from London with troops. Discouragement hourly thinned the already scanty ranks of the Cavaliers. On the 14th of March, at South Molton, in Devonshire, they were met and instantly attacked by Captain Hutton Crooke. They defended themselves valiantly, but in vain; Penruddock and about fifty of his companions were taken; Sir Joseph Wagstaff and a few others succeeded in reaching the sea-coast, and embarking for France. The insurgents, after having wandered about for four days like a band of fugitives, were all captured or dispersed; and the insurrection in the western counties was crushed in a single engagement.[1]

In the northern counties, the rebellion was even more short-lived and futile; there Rochester had resolved to act in person; and, on his arrival, several influential gentlemen, Sir Henry Slingsby, Sir Richard Maleverer, and others, took up arms, and brought their friends to join him. But he found them less numerous and less well-provided than, he said, he had been led to expect: he vented his ill-humour in complaints, questions, and objections, which, though

[1] Clarendon's History of the Rebellion, vol. vii. pp. 139—145; Thurloe's State Papers, vol. iii. pp. 246—248, 259, 262, 263; Cromwelliana, p. 152; Ludlow's Memoirs, pp. 218, 219; Heath's Chronicle, pp. 678—680; Bates's Elenchus Motuum, part ii. pp. 322—325.

reasonable, came too late, and which certainly ought to have prevented him from entering upon an enterprise in which he now refused to proceed. After some few unsatisfactory meetings, and
before he was aware of the sad issue of the movements in the west,
Rochester set out once more for London, leaving the Cavaliers of
the north in equal humiliation and irritation at having compromised
themselves in reliance upon his mission and name. He was arrested
at Aylesbury by a suspicious justice of the peace, but he succeeded
in escaping and in making his way to London, where he remained
concealed for a few days, and sent news to the King that the whole
enterprise had failed. Charles, in no way surprised at this intelligence, left Middleburg and returned quietly to Cologne, where
Rochester speedily rejoined him; and the little exiled Court con-
soled itself by imputing the ill-success of the undertaking to the
spy Manning, whose treachery was discovered, and whom Charles,
with the permission of Duke Philip William of Neuburg, ordered
to be shot in the dominions of that prince.[1]

Almost at the same moment, the blood of Penruddock and his
companions, the most distinguished among the western insurgents,
flowed on the scaffold at Exeter and Salisbury.[2] Cromwell, in the
first instance, ordered the prisoners to be brought to London, and
interrogated them himself, in order that he might be able to form
a correct impression of the character of the insurrection, and thus
be better qualified to exaggerate its importance. He then sent
them back to the west, that they might be tried and executed on
the scene of their rebellion. He was not afraid, in this instance,
to trust their sentence to a jury: the movement had not met with
popular favour, and Cromwell was quite sure of the sheriffs who
would have to nominate the jurymen. Penruddock and his friends
died without any manifestation of weakness, but without enthusiasm,
like courageous, but disheartened men, who would have been glad
to have saved their lives, but who valued their honour far more than
life, and were able to meet death with dignity and firmness. Cromwell did not multiply trials and executions; he ordered the arrest
of a large number of royalists, detained the most important of them
for some time in prison, and shipped the remainder for the West
Indies, where they were sold as slaves. Seventy were purchased
by the planters of Barbadoes. The Long Parliament, after the

[1] Clarendon's History of the Rebellion, vol. vii. pp. 145—160; Thurloe's
State Papers, vol. iv. pp. 462–468; Slingsby's Diary, pp. xi.—xiii.; Bates's
Elenchus Motuum, part ii. p. 323; Whitelocke, p. 633.

[2] The trial lasted from the 19th to the 23rd of April, and the execution
took place on the 16th of May, 1665.

battle of Worcester, had established a precedent for this barbarous conduct.[1]

The victory was as complete as it had been easy. Cromwell magnified it, as well as the danger, to the utmost possible extent; for he needed some such excuse to justify his recent dissolution of the Parliament, to which he had ascribed this recurrence of civil discord; and to screen the rigorous measures which he saw it would be necessary for him to adopt in future. It is one of the vices of absolute power that, in order to maintain itself in existence, it is obliged to foster and aggravate in society the dread of those evils which it has undertaken to remedy. Of all great despots, Cromwell is, perhaps, the one who made least use of this falsehood, for his despotism was of short duration, and had its origin in natural and real causes; and he himself attempted, more than once, to transform it into a constitutional government. But even he occasionally made a deceptive use of seditions and conspiracies; and in 1655, particularly, he derived, from their feeble and fleeting appear ance, far more strength for his sway than was warranted by the danger to which they had exposed him.

Though delivered for a time from plots, he encountered another kind of obstacle, certainly more inconvenient, if not more formidable; he had to overcome attempts at legal resistance. A merchant in the city, named Cony, who had long been on intimate terms with Cromwell, refused the payment of certain custom duties, which, he said, had been illegally levied: as they had been imposed in virtue of an ordinance of the Protector which had not received the sanction of Parliament. This was on the 4th of November, 1654; on the 6th, Cony was summoned before the Commissioners of Customs; and on the 16th he was condemned to pay a fine of five hundred pounds. On his refusing to pay either the fine or the duties, Cromwell sent for him, "reminded him of the old kindness and friendship that had been between them, and said that, of all men, he did not expect this opposition from him, in a matter that was so necessary for the good of the Commonwealth." Cony, in his turn, reminded the Protector of their old principles, and recalled to his memory his own expression in the Long Parliament—"that the subject who submits to an illegal impost is more the enemy of his country than the tyrant who imposes it." Cromwell grew angry, and said, "I have a will as stubborn as yours

---

[1] State Trials, vol. v. cols. 767—790; Whitelocke, p. 621; Cromwelliana, pp. 149—153; Clarendon's History of the Rebellion, vol. vii. p. 144; Bates's Elenchus Motuum, part ii. p. 458; Burton's Diary, vol. iv. pp. 256, 258, 259, 262, 271, 272.

is, and we will try which of the two will be master:" and Cony was
sent to prison on the 12th of December. He claimed his writ of
habeas corpus from the Court of Upper Bench ; and retained three
of the most eminent lawyers at the bar—Maynard, Twisden, and
Wadham Windham—to plead his cause. They did so, and Maynard in particular is said to have argued the case with such vigour
that Cromwell took the alarm; the argument tended to nothing less
than the absolute denial of the legality of his authority, and if Cony
had been acquitted, every Englishman might, in virtue of the same
principles, refuse to pay any taxes at all. On the day after the
pleading,[1] Maynard and his two colleagues were sent to the Tower,
on the charge of having held language destructive to the existing
government. This was an extreme measure, but it proved
insufficient ; Cony did not give up his point ; he appeared before
the Court unsupported by Counsel, and defended himself so ably
that Chief Justice Rolle, feeling embarrassed at his position, and
not knowing how to cover the dishonour of the sentence which he
was expected to pronounce, deferred judgment and adjourned the
case until the next term, leaving Cromwell in anxious suspense, and
Cony in prison.[2]

This was not the first mark of scrupulosity and independence
which Rolle had exhibited in his conduct towards the Protector.
When called upon, a month previously, to preside at the Exeter
assizes, where Penruddock and the other western insurgents were to
be tried, he had refused on the ground that, after the treatment he
had received from the prisoners at Salisbury, any sentence he might
pronounce would be subject to suspicion. Such delicacy was not
to Cromwell's taste ; Rolle was removed from the Court of
Upper Bench on the 7th of June, 1655, and Glynn, who had
given proof of greater complaisance, was appointed in his stead. It
was still more urgent to bring Cony's case to a conclusion, for his
example was becoming contagious ; and Sir Peter Wentworth, in
his county, had already refused to pay the taxes, and had brought
actions against the collectors. In this case, no dismissal was
possible. By other means, which have remained secret, Cony was
prevailed upon to take no further proceedings ; and the three counsel
were discharged from the Tower on their submission. Cromwell
sent for the judges, and blamed them for having allowed the bar

---

[1] On the 17th of May, 1655.
[2] Ludlow's Memoirs, p. 223; Heath's Chronicle, p. 691; Life of Oliver
Cromwell (London, 1743), pp. 317—319; Clarendon's History of the
Rebellion, vol. vii. pp. 294—296; Godwin's History of the Commonwealth,
vol. iv. pp. 175—181.

such license. They submitted that the law and Magna Charta
permitted it. "Your Magna Charta," said Cromwell, with a
vulgar oath, "shall not control my actions, which I know are for
the safety of the Commonwealth. Who made you judges? Have
you any authority to sit there but what I gave you? If my
authority were at an end, you know well enough what would become
of yourselves, and therefore I advise you to be more tender of that
which alone can preserve you, and not suffer the lawyers to prate
what it does not become you to hear."[1] Sir Peter Wentworth,
when summoned before the Council, at first defended what he had
done, saying that, "by the law of England, no money ought to be
levied upon the people without their consent in Parliament."
Cromwell asked him abruptly : "Will you withdraw your action, or
not?" "If you will command it," said Wentworth, "I must
submit." Cromwell immediately gave the order, and the action was
abandoned.[2] Legal resistance thus seemed, like conspiracy, to
have been conquered without any great effort.

But it had taken too deep root in the traditions and manners of
the nation, to be so easily extirpated. It is one of the chief glories of
the magistrature, in stormy times, to furnish liberty and order with
their last and boldest defenders. When, after the condemnation of
the western insurgents, it became necessary to proceed to the trial
of those in the north, two of the chief justices, Thorpe and Newdi-
gate, refused to do so, and were accordingly superseded. The most
illustrious of them all, Sir Matthew Hale, had already set an
example of resistance on several occasions : he had declined to
attend the assizes at which Penruddock was tried, on the ground
that his private affairs required his attention ; "and if he had been
urged," says Burnet, "he would not have been afraid of speaking
more clearly." On another occasion, learning that a jury had been
selected in obedience to special orders from Cromwell, Hale rejected
that list, and required the sheriff to prepare another. When he
next saw him, Cromwell was very angry, and told him : "You are
not fit to be a judge." "That is very true," said Hale, quietly.
Yet Cromwell did not dismiss him. He had with great difficulty
persuaded Hale to sit as a judge in the Court of Upper Bench,
under his government, and he thought the services of such a man
did him honour. Scrupulous magistrates, however, were not the
only persons who refused to serve the Protector with unquestioning
obedience ; some even of his habitual counsellors, from *esprit de*

---

[1] Clarendon's History of the Rebellion, vol. vii. p. 296.
[2] Ludlow's Memoirs, p. 224.

corps, or from prudence, occasionally ventured to oppose him. In April, 1655, he attempted to put in force the ordinance which he had issued, in August, 1654, for the reform of the Court of Chancery, and the execution of which had been suspended by the late Parliament. Two of the Commissioners of the great seal, Whitelocke and Widdrington, refused to concur in this proceeding, justifying their resistance by reasons which implicitly denied the right of the Protector thus to change the laws by his sole authority. Cromwell at first was patient, and allowed his two opponents time to reflect on their refusal; but when he found that they persisted, he dismissed them from their office, and placed the great seal in other hands. But he did not believe in the resistance offered by either Whitelocke or Widdrington, and was unwilling altogether to lose their services: a few days afterwards he appointed them both Commissioners of the Treasury, with a salary equal to that which they had received as Commissioners of the Great Seal; an act of disdainful conciliation which Whitelocke, in his Memorials, attributes to " the Protector being good-natured, and sensible of his harsh proceedings against me and Widdrington, for keeping to that liberty of conscience which himself held to be every one's right."[1]

If Cromwell had only had to overcome such insurrections as that headed by Rochester, and such resistance as that offered by Whitelocke, his task would have been an easy one; but, in the midst of his success, he had to face two of the greatest difficulties that can beset any Government—an inadequate public revenue, and an army on which he could not firmly rely. Notwithstanding the assurance of his language in dissolving the last Parliament, he did not venture, on his own authority alone, to impose altogether new taxes on the country generally; it was enough to perpetuate, by that authority, those which already existed. And although the army, as a whole, was submissive and faithful to him, he was not ignorant that the Anabaptists, Fifth-monarchy men, and malcontent republicans were numerous and active in its ranks. He stood in absolute need of more money and other soldiers; what he already possessed did not satisfy the necessities of his power.

To supply this deficiency, he had recourse to an act of revolutionary tyranny and iniquity; and the difficulty of his position was such that his genius could discover no better expedient. Under the pretext of maintaining the public peace and repress-

---

[1] Whitelocke, pp. 621—627; Biographia Britannica, vol. iv. p. 2477; Ludlow's Memoirs, p. 219; Thurloe's State Papers, vol. iii. pp. 359, 360, 385; Godwin's History of the Commonwealth, vol. iv. pp. 179—183; Noble's Memoirs of the Protectoral House of Cromwell, vol. i. p. 434.

ing royalist plots, he resolved to establish in every county a local militia, composed of men whom he determined to select himself, and to pay well. In order to pay them, he proposed to levy a tax of a tenth part of their revenue on the royalists alone ; and he anticipated that the proceeds of this tax would amount to a much greater sum than the militia would be likely to cost. For the effectual organisation of this militia and collection of this tax, he proposed to divide England and Wales into twelve districts, the government of which was to be intrusted to twelve of his most reliable and devoted officers, who, under the name of Major-Generals, were to exercise all political and administrative powers, and, to a certain point, all judicial authority, in their respective districts, and from whose decisions there was to be no appeal, but to the Protector himself and his Council. Thus revolutionary tyranny and military despotism were combined for the purpose of treating royalist England as a vanquished and subject nation.

Always governed by prudence, even in his deeds of violence, Cromwell instituted this measure by a partial and almost unperceived experiment. On the 28th of May, 1655, a short time after the insurrection in the west, he appointed his brother-in-law Desborough major-general of the militia levied, and to be levied, in the six counties in the south-west of England. Two months later, on the 2nd of August, Desborough took the direct command of the twelve squadrons of newly-enrolled militia in those counties; and on the following day, the question of the establishment of a general militia was discussed in the Council. It was finally settled the following week by the division of the whole country first into ten, then into twelve districts, the command of the new troops in which was intrusted to the following twelve major-generals : Fleetwood (who had just returned from his government of Ireland), Desborough, Lambert, Whalley, Goffe, Skippon, Berry, Kelsey, Butler, Worsley, Barkstead, and Dawkins.[1]

Whilst the military measure was thus in process of accomplishment, Cromwell had begun to carry out the revolutionary measure. In the course of the month of June, 1655, although the insurrections in the west and north had been suppressed and punished, he ordered the arrest of a large number of the most influential royalists, including the Earls of Newport, Lindsey, Northampton, Rivers, and Peterborough, the Marquis of Hertford, Viscount Falkland, the Lords Willoughby of Parham, St. John, Petre, Coventry, Maynard,

---

[1] Thurloe's State Papers, vol. iii. p. 486, vol. iv. p. 117; Old Parliamentary History, vol. xx. p. 433; Godwin's History of the Commonwealth, vol. iv. pp. 226—230.

Lucas, and more than fifty other Cavaliers of honoured name and character. For this severe treatment, he assigned no particular offence which could have exposed them to justice, but merely a general danger to the Commonwealth from which the Protector was bound, at any cost, to preserve it   At the same time he issued fresh orders that all who had served the late King or his sons should at once leave London; despatched the major-generals to their posts; and on the 31st of October, he officially announced and justified his whole design in a long and careful manifesto.[1]

It was an act of political excommunication against the entire royalist party; treating some as permanent and incorrigible conspirators, and punishing others on account of their incurable hostility and secret connivance with the conspirators.   As they had sincerely accepted neither their own defeat, nor the new government, nor the amnesty which had been granted them; and as they incessantly threatened the state with new dangers, it was just that they should pay the cost of the necessary means for its defence.   They were all deprived of the protection of the common law, and subjected to an annual decimation of their revenue.   Those only whose landed property produced less than 100l. yearly, or whose personal estate was under 1500l. in value, were exempted from the payment of this tax.

The instructions given at the same time to the major-generals enjoined them to make known the Protector's manifesto throughout the country, to obtain the co-operation of trusty commissioners in every county, and to proceed immediately, with their assistance, to a valuation of the incomes of the royalists, and to the collection of the tax.   They were moreover invested with the most extensive authority over persons; they might disarm or arrest them, require bail from them, not only for themselves, but for their children and servants, and compel them to appear from time to time, before an agent appointed for that purpose.   A general register of the persons thus under surveillance in every county was to be kept in London, and none of them were allowed to visit the capital without sending information to the registrar's office of their arrival, their place of abode, and all their movements.   It was a special legislation against a party and class of citizens—not sanguinary in its nature, purely of fiscal and police arrangement, but altogether arbitrary, and

[1] Old Parliamentary History, vol. xx. pp. 431—460; Perfect Proceedings, June 13—21, July 5; Mercurius Politicus, June 14, 21, 28; Perfect Diurnal, July 6; Public Intelligencer, October 8; Godwin's History of the Commonwealth, vol. iv. pp. 223, 224.

accompanied by all the accessory measures which could secure its efficient operation.[1]

Among these measures may be mentioned, in the first place, most vigorous precautions against the license of the press; the number of weekly newspapers published in London had been twelve in 1053, but since the establishment of the Protectorate, it had been reduced to eight, and of those, only two manifested any shade of opposition. An order of Council, dated September 5, 1655, prohibited the future publication of any paper without the special and continued sanction of the Secretary of State; and two weekly sheets, both of which were edited by Marchamont Need-ham,—a writer who had been originally a royalist, but whom Milton had gained over to the service of the Commonwealth and of Cromwell,—alone survived this prohibition.[2]

The execution of this plan, as might have been expected, greatly aggravated its natural and premeditated consequences; from military obedience, party passion, or rival zeal, the major-generals vied with one another in using and abusing the almost un-limited powers with which they were invested; they multiplied domiciliary visits, arrests, and annoyances of every kind, making it their chief object to discover the enemies of the Protector, and to increase the amount produced by the tax; and their vanity was gratified sometimes by the zeal, and sometimes by the fear, which they inspired. " Colonel Birch, who is a prisoner here," wrote Major-General Berry to Secretary Thurloe, on the 24th of No-vember, 1655, " hath applied himself to me as to a little king that could redress every grievance;" and a few weeks later, on the 5th of January, 1656, he wrote: " We have imprisoned here divers lewd fellows, some for having a hand in the plot, others of disso-lute life, as persons dangerous to the peace of the nation; amongst others those Papists who went a hunting when they were sent for by Major Waring; they are desperate persons, and divers of them fit to grind sugar-cane or plant tobacco; and if some of them were sent into the Indies it would do much good." On the 28th of January, Major-General Worsley wrote: " We are fetching in one Sir Charles Egerton, that was a member in the beginning of the Long Parliament, and left it and went to the King's forces; we doubt not of proof to make him a delinquent. We are resolved to find out all such persons as soon as can be." And it was not against the Cavaliers only that this vigilant police were set at work,

[1] Old Parliamentary History, vol. xx. pp. 461—467.
[2] Godwin's History of the Commonwealth, vol. iv. p. 225.

although, according to the manifesto, they alone were the object as they were the cause of the measure ; the major-generals also persecuted, under the same pretext, those republicans and sectaries who were hostile to the Protector. " I find," wrote Worsley to Thurloe, on the 9th of November, 1655, " that Major Wildman hath a great estate in this county, bought and compounded for in his name. I beg a word of that from you by way of direction. If I hear not from you, I intend to sequester all that belongs to him ; " and he did so ; for, on the 24th of December, he wrote to Cromwell himself " We have seized and secured to your Highness's use, a considerable estate belonging to John Wildman, and we hope to find some more." There are few letters, in this voluminous correspondence, in which mention is not made of some persons having been sought out, harassed, arrested, or imprisoned, for no other reason than that their opinions were suspected, or their fortune guessed at, or their declarations as to the value of their property considered incorrect. The most vulgar personal interest sometimes had a great deal to do with the zeal of the major-generals, and some of them exhibited it with coarse bluntness. " I have only one public business of great importance," wrote Major-General Berry to the Protector, on the 1st of December, 1655, " that I make bold to trouble your Highness withal : and that is, that your Highness would please to make good your word to Captain Crooke; but it must be whilst you live, or otherwise we shall fear it will never be done. You know what plotting there is against your person ; and if any of them should take, what will become of our preferments ? " [1]

From the mass of the population, the major-generals did not all meet with the same favourable reception : some of them wrote to complain of the difficulties and repulses which they had encountered in their endeavours to obtain the services of commissioners, willing and able to work with them in establishing and levying the tax ; others had no difficulty in finding commissioners, but they subsequently proved apathetic, inactive, or faint-hearted. Most, however, express their satisfaction at the zeal with which they were received and seconded. " Our commissioners," wrote Major-General Haynes to Thurloe, on the 8th of November, 1655, " seem exceeding real and forward in putting their instructions in execution. I did not expect it would have had so good an acceptance with them." " The business of taxing the Cavalier party," wrote Thurloe to Henry Cromwell, on the 17th of December, " is of wonderful acceptation to all the Parliament party ; all men of all opinions join heartily

---

[1] Thurloe's State Papers, vol. iv. pp. 237, 304, 473, 179, 310, 274.

therein." In several counties the commissioners even went so far as to regret the restriction of the tax to those royalists whose landed revenues exceeded one hundred pounds a year, and they urged the major-generals to advise the Protector to lower this minimum, on the ground that the tax would then become far more productive, and that there were as many royalists with a less as there were with a greater annual income than one hundred pounds. Party jealousies and hatred were much more powerful in the counties than in London; Cromwell's chief power lay among the small tradesmen and the populace; and persons of inferior condition, even when they feel no strong aversion for the higher classes, are always ready to revel in the enjoyment of authority, as of a rare and fleeting pleasure.[1]

The Cavaliers submitted unresistingly; it would even seem that they entertained no idea of resistance, so certain were they that it would be in vain; the most perverse paid no attention to the notices of the commissioners, and allowed themselves to be taxed in silence, saving their honour by refusing to appear, and the rest of their property by passive submission. Even among the great royalist nobles, some few, from pusillanimity, or personal animosity resulting from old political differences, did more than yield the necessary submission. "The Earl of Northumberland," wrote Major-General Goffe to Thurloe, on the 25th of November, 1655, "commends his Highness's declaration much; it seems the Marquis of Hertford broke off a treaty of marriage with him, when it was almost finished, on the score of his having been for the Parliament; which the Earl took very ill." The Earl of Southampton made himself conspicuous by his high-spirited conduct. "He was very stout," wrote Major-General Kelsey to Thurloe, on the 23rd of November, "and would give us no particular of his estate; whereupon we did confine him for disobeying our orders. At last he complied; but afterwards I demanded security, according to my instructions, which he peremptorily refused, whereupon I have secured him; only his mother lying very ill, and himself not well, I let him go to his own house, which is within three miles of this place."[2]

As a financial expedient, the measure succeeded; it was executed promptly and effectually; it met with almost no obstacle, and it supplied the Protector with considerable sums. As a political act it was the ruin of his high glory and of his great future; he

---

Thurloe's State Papers, vol. iv. pp. 171, 321, 140, 179, 215, 216, 224, 225, 227, 235, 308.

[2] Ibid. vol. iv. pp. 229, 234, 162, 208.

had assumed possession of power in the name of the restoration of order and peace, and he had nobly commenced their real restoration ; by the imposition of a tax on the royalists alone, and by the appointment of the major-generals, he tyrannically involved his power in a course of revolutionary violence, and set parties once more at variance, not by civil war, but by measures of oppression. He appealed to necessity, and doubtless believed himself reduced by circumstances to act as he did : if he was right, his was one of those necessities inflicted by the justice of God, which reveal the innate viciousness of a government, and are the inevitable sentence of its condemnation.

From this day forth, he had himself a secret and vexatious consciousness of his position. On bad terms with both royalists and republicans, at once a revolutionist and a conservative, making war and paying court to the higher classes at the same time, he groaned under the weight of these incessant contradictions in his position, maxims, and conduct ; and he sought on every side for just and useful ideas that he might turn to account, and influential interests that he might satisfy, in order to make them points of support, and by their means to supply the absence of fixed ideas and firm friendship. Liberty of conscience was, in this respect, his noblest and best resource. He was very far, as may have been seen already, from admitting it as a general principle, or to its full extent, the Catholics and Episcopalians, who probably constituted the great majority of the population of England at that period, were absolutely excluded from participation in it ; and this exclusion was not merely proclaimed as a maxim of State policy, but it was rigorously put in practice. In June, 1654, a poor Catholic priest, named Southwold, who, thirty-seven years before, had been condemned and exiled for his religion, ventured to return to England, and was arrested in his bed by Major-General Worsley, who sent him to London, where he was tried, condemned, and hanged. "We had a martyrdom here yesterday," wrote M. de Bordeaux, on the 29th of June, to the Count de Charost, governor of Calais ; "a priest was executed, notwithstanding my interposition, and that of other ambassadors, to obtain his pardon : he was accompanied to the scaffold by two hundred carriages, and by a great number of persons on horseback, who all admired his constancy." Cromwell did not seek occasions for such acts of severity : he was always glad when the victims, by a show of submission, enabled him to dispense with punishment ; but when their earnest faith or energetic character led them to refuse such compliance, he unhesitatingly allowed free course to the cruelty of the law. Towards the clergy of the Anglican

Church, he acted with a little more latitude; neither the laws, nor party animosities imposed on him any such sanguinary persecution of them, and he was led by his own inclinations to treat them without harshness, for the political maxims and strong discipline of their church were very much to his taste. Nevertheless, in obedience to revolutionary traditions, in order to please the Presbyterians, and to have benefices to bestow on his partisans, he harassed the Episcopalians, wherever they were found, deprived them of their livings, and forbade all public exercise of their worship. He even went so far as to prohibit, by an ordinance of the 24th of November, 1655, their reception into private families as chaplains or tutors, as had frequently been the case until then. This was to deprive a large number of the unbeneficed clergy of their last refuge against misery, and to deny parents all liberty in even the domestic education of their children. Against so violent a persecution, many urgent protests were made: the learned and illustrious Usher, Archbishop of Armagh and Primate of Ireland, whom Cromwell regarded with much favour, became the representative of his brethren, and with some difficulty obtained from the Protector a promise that this odious interdiction should be repealed. But the promise was not kept: Usher returned to Whitehall, and found Cromwell in the hands of a surgeon, who was dressing a large boil on his breast. The Protector ordered that the Archbishop should be admitted, and begged him to sit down and wait a moment, adding, " if this core (pointing to the boil) were once out, I should be well." " I doubt," said Usher, " the core lies deeper; there is a core at the heart that must be taken out, or else it will not be well." " Ah!" replied Cromwell, with a sigh; "so there is, indeed." But when the Archbishop began to speak to him of the object of his visit, Cromwell interrupted him by saying that he had thought better of it, that he had debated the matter with his Council, and that all were of opinion that it would not be safe for him to grant liberty of conscience to men who had proved themselves the implacable enemies of his person and government. Cromwell was neither so apprehensive nor so hard-hearted as he wished to appear; his declaration against engaging clergymen of the Anglican Church as chaplains and tutors remained almost inoperative; but he had ventured neither to refuse the bait to the fanaticism of his party, nor to revoke it publicly in the name of that liberty of conscience, which he made it his boast to support.[1]

[1] Thurloe's State Papers, vol. ii. p. 406; Whitelocke's Memorials, p. 592; Walker's Sufferings of the Clergy of the Church of England, p. 194; Life of Jeremy Taylor, p. 81; Pell's Life of Dr. Hammond, in Ecclesiastical Bio-

When neither Catholics nor Episcopalians were in question, when the quarrel lay between the various sects which had all taken part in the revolution, Cromwell was more bold in his adherence to his own maxims; he effectually protected the Presbyterians, Independents, Anabaptists, Millenarians, and sectaries of every kind against one another; reminding them that it was not long since they had all been persecuted together; and that they mutually owed one another charity and support. And when he was compelled, in order to put an end to political disorders, or revolting scandals, to repress the excesses of frenzied or licentious mysticism, he still acted with great gentleness towards the leaders of the misguided sectaries, and was always careful to remain on sufficiently intimate terms with them, to induce them to believe that they were his friends, or that they were under obligation to him. Towards the end of the year 1655, the Quakers, and their leader George Fox in particular, had occasioned serious disturbances in several counties. "Fox and two more eminent northern Quakers," wrote Major-General Goffe to Thurloe, on the 10th of January, 1656, "are now in this country, doing much work for the devil, and delude many simple souls; and at the same time, there are base books against the Lord Protector dispersed among the churches. I have some thoughts to lay Fox and his companions by the heels, if I see a good opportunity." George Fox came to London, and made his way into Whitehall. Cromwell received him while dressing; and the valet who was in attendance, one Harvey, "had been a little among Friends," and served to introduce Fox. "I had much discourse with the Protector," Fox relates; "explaining what I and Friends had been led to think concerning Christ and His apostles of old time, and His priests and ministers of new. I exhorted him to keep in the fear of God, whereby he might receive wisdom from God, which would be a useful guidance for any sovereign person. To all which, the Protector carried himself with much moderation; as I spake, he several times said, 'That is very good,' and, 'That is true.' Other persons coming in, persons of quality so called, I was for retiring. He caught me by the hand, and with moist-beaming eyes, said: 'Come again to my house! If thou and I were but an hour of the day together, we should be nearer one to the other. I wish no more harm to thee than to my own soul;'" and he sent Fox away much satisfied, contenting himself with a written promise which the Quaker gave him, to do

graphy, vol. v. pp. 373, 374; Life of Archbishop Usher, p. 75; Biographia Britannica, vol. v. p. 4078.

x

nothing against his government. It is difficult to estimate how much true emotion there may have been in this language: the poet Waller, a sceptic libertine, who was related to Cromwell, and lived on very familiar terms with him, states that he was occasionally present at Whitehall, when the Protector granted audiences to these pious enthusiasts, and that, after he had affectionately taken leave of them, Cromwell would turn to him and say: " Cousin Waller, I must talk to these men after their own way;" and would then resume their previous conversation. However this may be, by this personal affability, and these sympathetic outpourings, Cromwell bound the sectaries to him; and, even while keeping them under strong control, he always retained their confidence and support.[1] He also determined to secure to himself the good will and cordial co-operation of a class of men very unpopular and very much despised,—the Jews, who, though unable to do him harm, might render him essential service. They had been expelled *en masse* from England, in 1290, by King Edward I., and since that period, they had resided in the country in small numbers, connected by no social ties, and with no recognised legal existence. Since his accession to power, however, Cromwell had maintained frequent relations with the Jews both of England and of the Continent. One day, whilst he was conversing with Lord Broghill, he was informed that an unknown visitor was desirous to speak with him; he gave immediate orders for his admission, and an ill-looking and shabbily-dressed man entered, with whom the Protector talked privately for some time. It was a Jew, who had come to inform him that the Spanish government, with which Cromwell was about to commence hostilities, had embarked a considerable sum of money, destined for Flanders, on board a Dutch merchant-vessel, which would soon pass near the English coast. Cromwell took the hint, and the vessel was seized. The Jews had probably already rendered him useful service on more than one occasion, either by acting as spies, or by supplying his pecuniary necessities. It would even appear that his celebrity, destiny, and character had excited their imaginations to such a degree, that some of them, feeling tempted to recognise him as the Messiah they expected, had secretly gone into Huntingdonshire to obtain precise information regarding his family and descent. In October, 1655, a Jew of Portuguese origin, named Menasseh-ben-Israel, who had been long resident in Holland, and was one of the

---

[1] Thurloe's State Papers, vol. iv. p. 408; Cromwell's Letters and Speeches, vol. iii. pp. 149, 150; Waller's Life, prefixed to his Poems.

chief members of the Synagogue at Amsterdam, arrived in England, and published a pamphlet, entitled: "A Humble Address to the Lord Protector in behalf of the Jewish Nation." In this pamphlet, he formally demanded permission for the Jews to establish themselves in England, to have a synagogue and cemetery in London; to enjoy freedom of trade, and the right of settling their lawsuits among themselves, with an appeal to the ordinary tribunals of the country; and the revocation of the ancient laws which ran counter to these privileges. Neither the idea nor the step was altogether novel and unprecedented: struck by the professions of toleration and religious liberty which resounded in England in the midst of all her civil commotions. Menasseh-ben-Israel had already petitioned, first the Long Parliament, and then the Barebone Parliament, for a passport, authorising him to come to London to prosecute his design. But he had not carried his purpose into execution. Another Jew, Manuel Martinez Dormido, had, during the preceding year, presented a petition to Cromwell on the same subject, and Cromwell had referred it to the Council of State, with this endorsement by his secretary: "His Highness is pleased, in an especial manner, to recommend these papers to the speedy consideration of the Council." On the other hand, during the war with Holland, the activity and importance of the Jews had been greatly noticed by the English officers. On the 16th of October, 1654, the three commanders of the fleet had, it is said, urged the Protector to admit that nation into England, for the purpose of diverting their trade thither; and when Menasseh ben-Israel had publicly stated his demand, Major-General Whalley wrote to Thurloe, on the 12th of December, 1655: "It seems to me that there are both political and divine reasons which strongly make for the admission of the Jews into a cohabitation and civil commerce with us; doubtless, to say no more, they will bring in much wealth into this Commonwealth, and where we both pray for their conversion, and believe it shall be, I know not why we should deny the means." It is also stated that the Jews promised to place a considerable sum of money, two or three hundred thousand pounds, in Cromwell's hands, if their demands were granted. It was a great act to be performed, in pursuance of a great idea, and probably in furtherance of a great interest. Cromwell engaged zealously in the matter; he summoned at Whitehall a conference of lawyers, city merchants, and theologians, whom he directed to examine the propositions of Menasseh, under his own presidency. The discussion was long and animated: the conference, which consisted of twenty-seven members, met four times. The lawyers were, in general, favourable to the Jews ; the merchants were doubtful, and somewhat inclined to oppose their pretensions ; the theologians were divided. According to some, the legal admission of the Jews, their social system and form of worship, would be a sin most dangerous and scandalous to Christians ; others, with less severity, seemed disposed to tolerate the Jews, under certain restrictive or humiliating conditions. Cromwell spoke in their favour, and, according to the report of one who was present, with much eloquence ; but he was able to overcome neither the arguments of the theologians, nor the jealousies of the merchants, nor the prejudices of the indifferent; and seeing that the conference was not likely to end as he desired, he put an end to its deliberations. Then, without granting the Jews the public establishment which they had solicited, he authorised a certain number of them to take up their residence in London, where they built a synagogue, purchased the land for a burial-ground, and quietly commenced the formation of a sort of corporation devoted to the Protector, on whose tolerance their safety entirely depended.[1]

At about the same period, Cromwell's lofty and liberal views were displayed with greater success, in a more national undertaking. Since the commencement, and more particularly since the termination, of the civil war, the universities of Oxford and Cambridge had been sometimes indirectly, and sometimes openly attacked. From their devotion to the cause of the King and Church, they suffered, in 1647 and 1649, a first visitation, which proved more dangerous to individuals than to the institutions themselves : their royalist and episcopalian heads and professors were superseded by Presbyterians ; but the internal government of the two establishments was left almost untouched. Under the Commonwealth, however, and more especially after the expulsion of the Long Parliament, when the Independents gained the upper hand, the question assumed a far more serious aspect; the attack was directed against the very nature and existence of the universities. These great schools, in which candidates for the Christian ministry were instructed in ancient and profane literature, simultaneously and in common with other young men destined to various worldly professions—these powerful institutions, which existed of themselves,

[1] Whitelocke, p. 633; Thurloe's State Papers, vol. ii. p. 652 ; vol. iv. pp. 308, 321 ; Bates's Elenchus Motuum, part ii. p. 371; Life of Oliver Cromwell, pp. 320, 321 ; Banks's Critical Review of the Life of Oliver Cromwell, p. 207 ; Neal's History of the Puritans, vol. iv. p. 126; Cromwelliana, p. 154 ; Echard's History of England, vol. ii. p. 779 ; Ellis's Original Letters, Second Series, vol. iv. pp. 3—7 ; Harleian Miscellany, vol. vii. p. 617 ; Burnet's History of His Own Time, vol. i. p. 131.

were self-governed by fixed rules, and formed an independent empire of human knowledge and tradition—greatly scandalised the religious principles and democratic passions of the most ardent sectaries: they could not endure that Christian preachers should be educated and trained by such pagan studies—the perusal of Holy Writ, and the inspiration of divine grace, ought to be sufficient to qualify them for their work. Nor could they tolerate these permanent and independent endowments, by aid of which were formed a race of clergy, in their turn endowed and independent; the ministers of religion, they said, ought to be chosen by the believers themselves, and should be constantly at the disposal of their belief and will Three sectaries, who had long been chaplains in the army, William Dell, William Erbery, and John Webster placed themselves at the head of this crusade against the two universities: it is difficult to ascertain the extent to which the Barebone Parliament, before its abdication, had adopted their views, or what it had done to second them; this much is, however, certain, that nothing less was proposed than the sale of all the property belonging to the universities, and their complete abolition. In popular education, the same conflict was evident as in Church and State; individual mysticism and absolute democracy warring with organised tradition and established aristocracy. It was no longer a contest between two rival churches for benefices and pulpits; it was a war against all the old system of national education—a war waged by its mortal enemies, who thirsted to destroy what they termed "camps of Cain, and synagogues of Satan, stews of Antichrist, and houses of lies."[1]

Cromwell, at the age of seventeen, had spent a year at the university of Cambridge; in 1651, he had been elected Chancellor of the university of Oxford. His mind was great, because it was just, perspicacious, and thoroughly practical: at the same time that he appreciated the social utility of these noble schools of learning, he was charmed by their intellectual beauty. He felt that their destruction would be a source of degradation to his country, and of dishonour to himself; and he therefore took them under his protection. In order to defend them against their enemies, he introduced into them several men, who had once been passionate sectaries themselves, but who had become attached to his fortune and submissive to his influence; among others, two of his chaplains, Thomas Goodwin and John Owen,[2] both of them men of great talent and

---

[1] Godwin's History of the Commonwealth, vol. iv. pp. 86—104; Echard's History of England, vol. ii. p. 705; Clarendon's History of the Rebellion, vol. vii. pp. 15, 16; Huber's English Universities, vol. ii. pp. 12—16.

[2] Goodwin was made President of Magdalen College in the beginning of

ability; and he appointed the latter his Vice-Chancellor at Oxford.
From this introduction of heterogeneous elements, the traditions
and manners of the university received some partial and temporary
modification. Owen made alterations in the costumes and ceremonies at Oxford; instead of conforming to the ancient etiquette
of his office, he often, it is said, wore Spanish boots, large knots of
ribbon at his knees, and a cocked hat. But he energetically defended
the institution itself, in its studies, regulations, and property; and
the universities, with their system of education, and means of action,
were one of those powerful fragments of English society which
Cromwell saved from the attacks of the revolution, which had
raised him to the sovereign power.[1]

Nor did he rest satisfied with saving them from ruin ; he
watched carefully over their prosperity and renown. He presented
the University of Oxford with a collection of valuable manuscripts,
mostly Greek ; and to theological studies, particularly to the publication of the great Polyglot Bible, by Dr. Walton, he granted ready
and effectual encouragement. In order to secure the benefit of a
learned education to the northern counties, which complained of
being too far off to profit by Oxford and Cambridge, he decreed the
foundation of a great college at Durham, to be endowed with the
property of the abolished deanery and chapter. His mind was
neither naturally elegant nor richly cultivated, but his unfettered
genius comprehended the necessities of the human intellect ; and
the great institutions of education and learning were of use to him
as means of patronage and government.[2]

In his conduct towards literary and scientific men themselves,
he was guided by the same feelings,—by no sympathy as a connois-
seur, but by politic benevolence ; honouring their labours, noting
their influence, eager to be praised, or defended, or treated politely
by them, and protecting or conciliating them in his turn, according
as they belonged to his own or the opposite party. Most had
belonged, or still belonged, to the royalist ranks ;—among the poets,
Cowley, Denham, Davenant, Cleveland, Waller, and Butler ; among
philosophers and men of science, Cudworth, Hobbes, Jeremy Taylor,
and Usher, were all either in the service, or favourable to the cause,
of the Church and Crown. Cromwell was under no delusion as to
their principles ; but he was careful not to treat them so harshly as

the year 1650; Owen was made Dean of Christ-Church in March, 1652, and
Vice-Chancellor in the September following.

[1] Wood's Athenæ Oxonienses, vol. iv. cols. 98, 99.
[2] Peck's Memoirs of Oliver Cromwell, pp. 60—72; Harris's Life of Oliver
Cromwell, pp. 420, 421; Cromwelliana, p. 156.

to have them for violent enemies; if he found them involved in any
party intrigue, if even they were arrested, he never failed to order
their release; if he thought it possible, by a little favour or
tolerance, to gain their adherence or respect, he left no means untried for the purpose. Waller resided, as his cousin, at his court;
Cowley and Hobbes were allowed to return from exile; Butler
meditated, in the house of one of Cromwell's officers, his grotesque
satires against the fanatical or hypocritical sectaries; Davenant, on
his liberation from prison, obtained permission from the Puritan
dictator to open a little theatre at Rutland House, for the performance of his comedies. For such amnesty or toleration, these wits
had to give some promises of political neutrality, or some piece of
poetical flattery; but after having imposed on them these acts of
contrition, Cromwell proved neither exacting nor suspicious. When
he had to deal with grave and quiet men, he expressed to them his
esteem, seeking to live on good terms with them, but never exhibiting a despot's fatuity or pretensions. He directed Thurloe to apply
to Cudworth, who was living in learned retirement at Cambridge,
for information regarding persons educated in that university who
aspired to public employments; to Hobbes, whose political doctrines
pleased him, he offered the post of a secretary in his household;
Selden and Meric Casaubon were invited by him to write, one an
answer to the "Eikon Basilikè," and the other, a history of the
recent civil wars. Both of them declined, and Casaubon even refused a purely gratuitous pension; but Cromwell took no offence.
On the death of Archbishop Usher, he was anxious that he should
have a solemn funeral in Westminster Abbey, and purchased his
library, that it might not be sent to the Continent. He did not
always execute all that he had, on the impulse of the moment, promised or planned in matters of this nature. Under the distracting
influence of important affairs the most attentive forget, and the
most powerful want means, always to accomplish the benevolent
designs they may have announced; but if he was not exempt from
these shortcomings of supreme power, Cromwell is perhaps, of all
sovereigns, the one who is least open to the charge.[1]

Towards the literary men of the revolutionary party he had less
need to act with circumspection. Some of them, Thomas May,
Samuel Morland, John Pell, Owen, Goodwin, Nye, and a great
many other dissenting theologians, were either irretrievably pledged

[1] See the Lives of Cowley, Denham, Waller, and Butler, prefixed to their
poetical works; Lives of Cudworth, Davenant, Hobbes, and Usher, in the Biographia Britannica; Harris's Life of Cromwell, pp. 417, 418; Peck's Memoirs
of Cromwell; Godwin's History of the Commonwealth, vol. iv. pp. 240, 241.

to his cause, or actively engaged as members of his government. Others, among whom Milton stands supreme, were ardent republicans, whom the illusions of fancy, the sophisms of interest, or the pressure of circumstances held in allegiance to a despot, in the name of the principles of liberty. Cromwell, profiting by his ascendency, kept them in his service, but without showing affection for them or placing confidence in them. When he became Protector he appointed another Latin secretary to his Council of State, in addition to Milton,[1] and an order of the Council deprived Milton, who had already become blind, of the lodging which he occupied in Whitehall. He continued to receive his salary; he continued to write Latin despatches; he was more than once supplied with funds to afford liberal hospitality at his house and table to such foreign literary men as came to visit England; but he was admitted neither into the State secrets nor into the intimacy of the Protector, to whom, as opportunity offered, he occasionally addressed the warmest eulogies and the most generous advice. He was quite conscious of the small amount of influence which he possessed, but he made no complaint. "You desire," he wrote, on the 18th of December, 1657, to Peter Haimbach, one of his Dutch friends, "that I should recommend you to our envoy who is appointed for Holland; I regret that it is not in my power to do so. I enjoy very little familiarity with the bestowers of favours, and I remain shut up at home, and that very willingly."[2] Other literary men, holding no public offices, Henry Nevill, Cyriac Skinner, one of Milton's disciples, Roger Coke, John Aubrey, and Maximilian Pettie, had grouped themselves around Harrington, with whom they formed a club, called the Rota, which met every evening in a coffee-house near Westminster Hall, and at which they publicly discussed various questions of political organisation, in a spirit not very favourable to Cromwell's government. Some of his soldiers, who were present at these discussions, were more than once tempted to put an end to them by violence, but the great name of Harrington and his moderate language restrained them. Cromwell maintained a strict surveillance over this philosophic coterie, but subjected them to no persecution. Being informed that Harrington was about to publish his republican Utopy, the *Oceana*, he ordered the manuscript to be seized at the printer's and brought to Whitehall. After vain endeavours to obtain its restoration, Harrington, in despair, resolved to apply to the Protector's favourite

---

[1] Philip Meadows was appointed to this post on the 3rd of February, 1654.
[2] Milton's Works, by Todd, vol. i. pp. 152—159; Milton's Works, by Mitford, vol. i. p. xciv., and vol. v. p. 406.

daughter, Lady Claypole, who was known to be a friend to literary men, and always ready to intercede for the unfortunate. While he was waiting for her in an ante-room, some of Lady Claypole's women passed through the room, followed by her daughter, a little girl three years of age. Harrington stopped the child, and entertained her so amusingly that she remained listening to him until her mother entered. "Madam," said the philosopher, setting down the child, whom he had taken in his arms, " 'tis well you are come at this nick of time, or I had certainly stolen this pretty little lady." "Stolen her!" replied the mother, "pray what to do with her?" "Madam," said he, "though her charms assure her a more considerable conquest, yet I must confess it is not love, but revenge, that prompted me to commit this theft." "Lord!" answered the lady again, "what injury have I done you that you should steal my child?" "None at all," replied he, "but that you might be induced to prevail with your father to do me justice, by restoring my child that he has stolen;" and he explained to Lady Claypole the cause of his complaint. She immediately promised to procure his book for him, if it contained nothing prejudicial to her father's government. He assured her it was only a kind of political romance, and so far from any treason against her father, that he hoped to be permitted to dedicate it to him: and he promised to present her ladyship with one of the earliest copies. Lady Claypole kept her word, and obtained the restitution of the manuscript, and Harrington dedicated his work to the Protector. "The gentleman," said Cromwell, after having read it, "would like to trepan me out of my power; but what I got by the sword I will not quit for a little paper shot. I approve the government of a single person as little as any, but I was forced to take upon me the office of a high-constable, to preserve the peace among the several parties in the nation, since I saw that, being left to themselves, they would never agree to any certain form of government, and would only spend their whole power in defeating the designs or destroying the persons of one another."[1]

Few despots have so carefully confined themselves within the limits of practical necessity, and allowed the human mind such a wide range of liberty.

It is in the promotion of material prosperity that absolute power, on emerging from great social disturbances, takes its chief delight, and achieves its completest triumph: Cromwell devoted himself to this task with active solicitude, not only by the general

---

[1] Biographia Britannica, *sub voce* Harrington: Toland's Life of Harrington, prefixed to his edition of the Oceana, p. xix.

maintenance of order, but by the adoption of direct and special measures. In 1655, he appointed a Committee of Trade, to meet under the presidency of his eldest son Richard, composed of the members of the Council of State, the judges, certain lawyers, and the aldermen of the nine principal commercial towns of England, for the purpose of inquiring into the means of assisting the development of the trade and navigation of England, and invested with the necessary powers for carrying their decisions into effect. In 1657, he granted the East India Company a new charter; which led to the subscription of an additional capital of three hundred and seventy thousand pounds, and rescued that important branch of trade from the decay into which it had fallen. The management of the post-office received great extension and valuable improvement in 1654. Commissioners were directed to examine into the abuses which had crept into the administration of numerous charitable institutions, and to procure their redress. Everywhere was visible the activity of a vigilant administration, directed by a man of genius and good sense, and supported by a powerful government.[1]

Whilst Cromwell was thus personally engaged in governing England, he had as his lieutenants, Monk in Scotland, and his son Henry in Ireland; both of them judicious and moderate men, thoroughly understanding his position and policy, and inclined, by their own natural tendencies, to act in conformity with them. With regard to Monk, the Protector was not altogether free from distrust. Scotland was full of royalists; Monk treated them sparingly, and in their turn, they paid him great court, in the hope of gaining him to their side, or compromising him with Cromwell. A letter reached him one day from Cologne. It was from Charles II., who wrote as follows:—

"*Cologne, August* 12, 1656.

"ONE who believes he knows your nature and inclinations very well assures me that, notwithstanding all ill accidents and misfortunes, you retain still your old affection to me, and resolve to express it upon the seasonable opportunity, which is as much as I look for from you. We must all patiently wait for that opportunity, which may be offered sooner than we expect. When it is, let it find you ready; and in the mean time, have a care to keep yourself out of their hands, who know the hurt you can do them in a good conjuncture; and can never but suspect your affection to be, as I am confident it is towards your, &c.   "CHARLES REX."

[1] Old Parliamentary History, vol. xx. pp. 470, 471; Whitelocke, p. 630; Cromwell's Letters and Speeches, vol. iii. p. 169; Pictorial History of England, vol. iii. pp. 547, 548, 552.

Monk sent a copy of this letter to Cromwell, on the 8th of November;[1] but did not say that it had been addressed to himself, and seemed not to know to whom it was to be delivered. Whether Cromwell had discovered the truth or not, he wrote to Monk, some time afterwards—"There be that tell me that there is a certain cunning fellow in Scotland, called George Monk, who is said to lie in wait there to introduce Charles Stuart. I pray use your diligence to apprehend him, and send him up to me."[2] But these mutual precautions did not destroy friendly relations between the two men; without pledging his whole future conduct, Monk could render faithful service to the power which he considered the strongest, and Cromwell knew how to make use of capable men, without trusting entirely to them. In Ireland, the Protector had to deal with more complicated difficulties; nearly the whole population, native and Catholic, was opposed to him; the army still contained many republicans, and Ludlow still resided among them. Cromwell had a double task to perform in that country: on the one hand, he had to dispossess and transplant most of the Irish landholders to the province of Connaught; on the other, he had to satisfy the subscribers to the loan of 1641, and the English officers and soldiers to whom the confiscated estates had been promised. Though it had been decreed before the establishment of the Protectorate, this terrible operation, which brought the passions of victors and vanquished alike into play, had not yet been performed, and Cromwell intrusted its execution to a young man, untried as yet, and who had no other authority but that attaching to his name. He conferred this great and difficult power upon him very gradually: he sent him first of all to Ireland as a mere observer, in February, 1654; and then, in June, 1655, as a major-general of the army, under Lord David Fleetwood. With his usual unflinching adherence to his habits of hypocritical artfulness, he wrote to Fleetwood, on the 22nd of June, 1655: "It is reported that you are to to be sent for, and Harry to be Deputy; which truly never entered into my heart. The Lord knows, my desire was for him and his brother to have lived private lives in the country; and Harry knows this very well, and how difficultly I was persuaded to give him his present commission. The noise of my being crowned is a similar malicious figment." But he added at the end of the letter: "If you have a mind to come over with your dear wife, take the best opportunity for the good of the public and your own

---

[1] Thurloe's State Papers, vol. iv. p. 162.
[2] Guizot's Life of Monk, p. 59.

convenience." Fleetwood did come over to England, and Henry Cromwell remained in Ireland, invested with the sole authority in that country, where, some time after, in November, 1657, he officially assumed the character of Lord Deputy. He fully justified his father's confidence; but his private habits, and the internal arrangements of his household, were far from giving equal satisfaction; the scandal even was so flagrant that his sister Mary, who afterwards became Lady Faulconbridge, thought it her duty to remonstrate with him on the subject. "Dear brother," she wrote, on the 7th December, 1655, "I cannot but give you some item of one that is with you, who, it is much feared by your friends that love you, is some dishonour to you and my dear sister, if you have not a great care. For it is reported here, that she rules much in your family; therefore, dear brother, take it not ill that I give you an item of her,—for truly, if I did not love both you and your honour, I would not give you notice of her." It does not appear that Henry Cromwell paid much attention to his sister's counsels; but his prudent political conduct screened the improprieties of his private life : he lessened the extreme rigour of the measures which he was directed to execute towards the ejected Irish,—he conciliated the Presbyterians, and many even of the royalists,—he removed from the army most of the Anabaptists and republicans who were decidedly hostile to his policy,—and finally, on a vague and imperfect promise of tranquillity, he sent Ludlow to England :—so that Cromwell could say, in speaking of his son, with all the satisfaction of paternal pride, "He is a governor from whom I myself might learn."[1]

On the 12th of December, 1655, Ludlow had only just arrived in London, when the Protector sent for him, and gave him an immediate audience in his bed-chamber, at Whitehall, surrounded by several of his general officers. "You have not dealt fairly with me," said Cromwell to him abruptly, "in making me to believe you had signed an engagement not to act against me, and yet reserving an explanation whereby you made void that engagement; which if it had not been made known to me, I might have relied upon your promise. Wherefore will you not engage not to act against the present Government? If Nero were in power it would be your duty to submit."

[1] Thurloe's State Papers, vols. iii. v. *passim*, for the correspondence between Thurloe and Henry Cromwell; Noble's Memoirs of the Protectoral House of Cromwell, vol. i. p. 197; Cromwell's Letters and Speeches, vol. iii. pp. 137, 138, 169; Leland's History of Ireland, vol. iii. p. 401; Godwin's History of the Commonwealth, vol. iv. pp. 427—463.

LUDLOW.—"I am ready to submit, and I can truly say that I know not of any design against you. But if Providence open a way, and give an opportunity of appearing on behalf of the people, I cannot consent to tie my own hands beforehand, and oblige myself not to lay hold of it."

CROMWELL.—"At all events, it is not reasonable to suffer one that I distrust to come within my house, till he assure me he will do me no mischief."

LUDLOW.—"I am not accustomed to go into any house unless I expect to be welcome ; neither have I come hither but upon a message from you. I desire nothing but a little liberty to breathe in the air, to which I conceive I have an equal right with other men. I have gone as far as I could in that engagement which I gave to Lieutenant-General Fleetwood, and if that be not thought sufficient, I am resolved with God's assistance, to suffer any extremities that may be imposed upon me."

CROMWELL.—"Yes ; we know your resolution well enough, and we have cause to be as stout as you ; but, I pray, who spoke of your suffering?"

LUDLOW.—"If I am not deceived, sir, you mentioned the securing my person."

CROMWELL.—"Yea, and great reason there is why we should do so. I am ashamed to see that engagement which you have given to the Lieutenant-General, which would be more fit for a general who should be taken prisoner, and that hath yet an army of thirty thousand men in the field, than for one in your condition. I have always been ready to do you what good offices I could, and I wish you as well as any of my council. I desire you to make choice of some place to be in, where you may have good air."

LUDLOW.—"I assure you my dissatisfactions are not grounded upon any animosity against your person. If my own father were alive, and in your place, they would, I doubt not, be altogether as great."

CROMWELL.—"Well, well ; you have always carried yourself fairly and openly to me ; but I protest I have never given you just cause to act otherwise."

Here the conversation ended ; Ludlow was conducted into an adjacent room, where he was soon after joined by Fleetwood, who endeavoured to persuade him to engage, as the Protector desired, though but for a week. "Not for an hour," answered Ludlow ; and he returned home, where Cromwell allowed him to remain in peace. Six months afterwards, in August, 1656, Cromwell had issued orders for the convocation of a new Parliament, from which he was

anxious to exclude the influential republicans; and he summoned
Ludlow before his council. "I am not ignorant," he said, "of the
many plots that are on foot to disturb the present power; yet I
would have you to know that what I do proceeds not from a motive
of fear, but from a timely prudence to foresee and prevent danger.
Had I done as I should, I ought to have secured you immediately
upon your coming into England; and therefore I now require you
to give assurance not to act against the Government."

LUDLOW.—"I must beg to be excused in that particular, and to
remind you of the reasons I formerly gave you for my refusal. I
am, however, in your power, and you may use me as you think fit."

CROMWELL.—"Pray, then, what is it that you would have?
May not every man be as good as he will? What can you desire
more than you have?"

LUDLOW.—"It were easy to tell what we would have."

CROMWELL.—"What is that, I pray?"

LUDLOW.—"That which we fought for—that the nation might
be governed by its own consent."

CROMWELL.—"I am as much for a government by consent as
any man; but where shall we find that consent? Among the
prelatical, Presbyterian, independent, anabaptist, or levelling
parties?"

LUDLOW.—"Amongst those of all sorts who have acted with
fidelity and affection to the public."

CROMWELL.—"The people enjoy protection and quiet under my
government; and I am resolved to keep the nation from being
again imbrued in blood."

LUDLOW.—"I am of opinion too much blood has been already
shed, unless there be a better account of it."

CROMWELL.—"You do well to charge us with the guilt of blood;
but we think there has been a good return for what hath been
shed; and we understand what clandestine correspondences are
carrying on at this time between the Spaniard and those of your
party, who make use of your name, and affirm that you will own
them and assist them."

LUDLOW.—"I know not what you mean by my party, and I can
truly say that, if any men have entered into an engagement with
Spain, they have had no advice from me so to do, and that, if they
will use my name, I cannot help it."

CROMWELL.—"I desire not to put any more hardships on you
than on myself. I have always been ready to do you all the good
offices that lay in my power; and I aim at nothing by this pro
ceeding but the public quiet and security."

LUDLOW.—"Truly, sir, I know not why you should be an enemy to me, who have been faithful to you in all your difficulties."

CROMWELL.—"I understand not what you mean by my difficulties. I am sure they were not so properly mine as those of the public; for, in respect to my outward condition, I have not much improved it, as these gentlemen well know." The members of the council, thus appealed to, rose from their seats in token of assent to what he said.

LUDLOW.—"It is from that duty which I owe to the public, whereof you express such a peculiar regard, that I dare not give the security, because I conceive it to be against the liberty of the people and contrary to the known law of England. Here is an Act of Parliament for restraining the Council from imprisoning any of the free-born people of England; and in case they should do so, requiring the Justices of the Upper Bench, upon the application of the aggrieved party, to grant his habeas corpus, and to give him considerable damages. To this act I suppose you gave your free vote, and I assure you that, for my own part, I dare not do anything that may tend to the violation of it."

CROMWELL.—"But did not the army and Council of State commit persons to prison?"

LUDLOW.—"The Council of State did so, but it was by virtue of an authority granted to them by the Parliament; and if the army have sometimes acted in that manner, it has been in time of war, and then only in order to bring the persons secured to a legal trial. Whereas, it is now pretended that we live in a time of peace, and are to be governed by the known laws of the land."

CROMWELL.—"A justice of peace may commit, and shall not I?"

LUDLOW.—"A justice of peace is a legal officer, and authorised by the law to do so, which you could not be, though you were king; because if you do wrong therein, no remedy can be had against you."[1]

The discussion, on both sides, was evidently vain; Cromwell carried it no further, but dismissed Ludlow without ordering his arrest. He was less surprised than he was willing to appear at this resistance and this language. He himself thought, in his inmost heart, that England could be governed neither tranquilly nor long, without the fulfilment of certain conditions of legality, and the co-operation of a Parliament; and experience, more powerful than Ludlow's arguments, confirmed him every day in these convictions.

[1] Ludlow's Memoirs, pp. 233—235, 240—242; Guizot's Etudes Bio graphiques sur la Révolution d'Angleterre, pp. 68—77.

He had succeeded in all his undertakings ; he had overcome all his
enemies, and surmounted all obstacles; and yet obstacles re-
appeared, and enemies rose once more against him ; though universally and invariably victorious, his government had obtained no
stability; neither the defeat of all factions, nor the re-establishment
of order, nor the salutary activity of his home administration, could
suffice to secure him what he sought—the right of present, and the
prospect of future rule.   Great successes abroad, brilliant and
useful alliances, the wide diffusion of the power of England and the
glory of his own name ; would they be more likely to accomplish
this twofold object ?   By gaining more influence and celebrity
throughout the world, would he strengthen his position in his own
country ?   He hoped to do so; and, in his foreign policy, he displayed, with greater confidence than in his home government, his
bold spirit of enterprise, and the absolute power which he had at
his command.

BOOK VII

CROMWELL'S PREPARATIONS FOR WAR AGAINST SPAIN—HIS PROJECTED CAM-
PAIGN IN BOTH HEMISPHERES—BLAKE'S EXPEDITION IN THE MEDITERRA-
NEAN,—BEFORE LEGHORN, TUNIS, TRIPOLI, AND ALGIERS,—AND OFF THE
COAST OF SPAIN—DEPARTURE FROM PORTSMOUTH OF THE FLEET UNDER
PENN AND VENABLES—SECRET OF THEIR DESTINATION—DON LUIS DE HARO,
CONDÉ, AND MAZARIN PUSH THEIR NEGOTIATIONS WITH CROMWELL—PERSE-
CUTION OF THE VAUDOIS IN PIEDMONT—INTERVENTION OF CROMWELL ON
THEIR BEHALF—PENN AND VENABLES ATTACK ST. DOMINGO, UNSUCCESS-
FULLY—CAPTURE OF JAMAICA—RUPTURE BETWEEN CROMWELL AND SPAIN
—TREATY BETWEEN CROMWELL AND FRANCE—THE COURT OF MADRID PRO-
MISES ASSISTANCE TO CHARLES II.—CROMWELL SENDS LOCKHART AS HIS
AMBASSADOR TO PARIS—CROMWELL'S GREATNESS AND IMPORTANCE IN EUROPE
—HE CONVOKES ANOTHER PARLIAMENT.

TOWARDS the end of the summer, and during the course of the
autumn of 1654, whilst the Protector and the Parliament which he
had just called together, were engaged in secret conflict with one
another, two great fleets were being equipped and armed at Portsmouth; one, consisting of twenty-five ships, was under the command of Admiral Blake; the other, comprising thirty-eight vessels,
was to carry the flag of Admiral Sir William Penn, and, in addition
to its crew, was to take on board three thousand soldiers, under the
command of General Venables. The utmost secrecy was maintained as to the destination of these two fleets; the Parliament had
placed them at the disposal of the Protector, without inquiring what
he intended to do with them; and Cromwell merely stated that
their duty would be to establish the maritime predominance of England in all seas. One day, a mob of the wives of the sailors who
were serving on board, pursued him through the streets, inquiring
whither their husbands were to be sent; Cromwell replied with a
smile: "The ambassadors of France and Spain would each of them
willingly give me a million to know that."[1]

[1] Thurloe's State Papers, vol. ii. pp. 542, 571—574, 638, 653, & iii. p. 14;
Whitelocke, p. 621; Dixon's Life of Blake, pp. 266—272; Penn's Memorials

Y

These were preparations for the execution of a plan which he
had determined on in his own mind. In order to maintain himself
in his position, and to mount still higher, he required that England
should be in the enjoyment of prosperity and greatness, and that
he should himself lack neither renown nor money; for neither his
revolutionary measures, nor his major-generals, had provided sufficiently for the expenses of government. Moreover, he was anxious
to employ the national fleet with distinction in distant service ; the
sailors, both officers and men, were in general not very friendly to
him ; they had not, like the land army, been partakers in his victories, and accomplices in his crimes. Some of them were republicans,
but the greater number were royalists. Spain and the New World
alone seemed to furnish the means of giving ample satisfaction to
all these interests of the Protector's policy; there would be expeditions and conquests, booty and trade, enough to occupy ardent
minds, to keep malcontents at a distance, and to satiate even the
most avaricious. And these successes might be obtained at the expense of that country which was pre-eminently Catholic and Papisti-
cal ; of a country which, far from containing within its boundaries,
as was the case in France, a large number of Protestants, who were
tolerated by the law, would not suffer on its territory the slightest
practice of the reformed religion even by strangers, even by English
merchants. Spain, it is true, had been the first of the great continental monarchies to recognise the Commonwealth, and it had
given no legitimate motive, no specious pretext, for such an agres-
sion; but this arose from weakness and timidity on its part, not
from any real feelings of good-will; and Cromwell was as little to be
duped by the actions of others as he was unscrupulous as to his own.
A person named Gage, who had once been a priest, and had lived a
long while in the West Indies, had given him an alluring description of their immense wealth, their great commercial capabilities,
the decay of the Spanish government, and the facility with which
England might obtain complete success, if she would strike a first
vigorous blow. Cromwell resolved to attack Spain in America ; this
was the destination of the squadron and troops commanded by Penn
and Venables ; St. Domingo, Porto Rico, Cuba, and (on the American
continent) Cartagena, were the points specially designated for their
enterprises. " We have no desire to bind you," ran their instructions, " by any precise order, or to any special mode of proceeding ;
we impart to you only those facts and views which have occurred to

of Sir William Penn, vol. ii. pp. 2—27; Letters from Bordeaux to Brienne,
December 21, 1654; in the Archives des Affaires Etrangères de France.

us. Our general design is to obtain an establishment in that part of the West Indies which is possessed by the Spaniards; when you are on the spot, you will deliberate among yourselves, and with persons who are well acquainted with those countries; and you will adopt, both in reference to the enterprises to be attempted, and to the manner of conducting the whole design, such resolutions as shall appear to you most reasonable and efficacious." And whilst Penn, with his squadron, was to sail for Spanish America, Blake was to cruise, with his fleet, all round the coast of Spain, to keep an eye on her ports and ships, to cut off all combination between the mother country and her American settlements, and thus to secure, by a combination of vigorous operations in both hemispheres, the complete success of this great design.[1]

Blake's fleet, which was less numerous, and required less time to equip, was ready three months before Penn's squadron could put to sea. It suited Cromwell's purpose that the co-operation of the two fleets, and the unity of their commission, should at first be concealed. England had to make complaints, to obtain indemnities, and to establish her renown and influence, in the Mediterranean. Blake had time to accomplish this task, before his permanent presence off the coast of Spain became essential to the operations of Penn and Venables in America. He received orders to sail; but, before giving him final instructions, Cromwell, in order to remove all suspicion, wrote the following letter to King Philip IV., on the 5th of August, 1654 :—"As the safety and protection of the trade and navigation of the people of this Commonwealth impose on us the necessity of sending a fleet of ships of war into the Mediterranean, we think it right to inform your Majesty of the same. We do this with no intention to cause any damage to any of our allies and friends, among whom we reckon your Majesty. On the contrary, we enjoin our general, Robert Blake, whom we have appointed to command this fleet, to conduct himself towards them with all possible respect and friendship. We have no doubt that, in return, whenever our fleet may enter your ports and harbours, either to purchase provisions, or for any other purpose, it will be received with all possible good offices. This is what, by this present letter, we demand of your Majesty. We beg you to repose full confidence in our said general, whenever, by letter or otherwise, he may address either your Majesty, or your governors and ministers, in the

[1] Dixon's Life of Blake, p. 273; Memorials of Sir William Penn, vol. ii. pp. 28, 29; Burnet's History of His Own Time, vol. i. p. 137 · Thurloe's State Papers, vol. iii. pp. 11, 16; Clarendon's History of the Rebellion, vol. vii. pp. 172—176.

places where he may find it necessary to touch. May God keep and protect your Majesty!"[1]

Blake put to sea before the end of October, still suffering from the wound he had received in his last engagement with the Dutch, but full of hopefulness and confidence, and inspiring all who served under him with the feelings which animated himself. He was a hero of great simplicity and self-restraint, modest in his boldness, devoted to his faith and profession, influential, though taciturn with his companions, and as much honoured as he was feared by his enemies. The news of his departure created a great sensation at Paris, at Lisbon, at Madrid, and in all the courts of southern Europe; no one knew what he was going to do; but it was believed that he would attempt a great deal, and that, in all he attempted, he would push forward to the end. Almost at the very moment when he left Portsmouth, a French fleet sailed from Toulon, on its way to Naples, containing a body of troops under the command of the Duke of Guise, of whose insane rashness Mazarin was, for the second time, taking advantage, as a pretext for hostility to Spain. On learning that Blake was bound for the Mediterranean, the cardinal was filled with anxiety, and the Count de Brienne wrote, by his order, to M. de Bordeaux :—"I am weighing in my mind the words which I have to write to you, for fear that too lofty an expression may cause an evil of which the consequences might be fearful, or that too low a phrase may cover us with disgrace. . . . It is necessary that you should make it understood that his Majesty, having been informed that Blake has received orders to sail for the straits, to pass them, and to enter the Mediterranean, has resolved to avoid any accident that might render his affairs incapable of an accommodation." Instructions were doubtless given in conformity with this resolution,—for when Blake arrived off Cadiz, one of his tenders was arrested by a Brest squadron on its way to reinforce the Duke of Guise at Toulon; and the French admiral, as soon as he learned that it belonged to the English fleet, sent for the captain into his cabin, told him he was at liberty to continue his voyage, and invited him to drink Admiral Blake's health in a bumper of Burgundy, accompanying the toast with a salute of five guns; after which the French ships, instead of proceeding on their journey, fell back upon Lisbon. The Spanish, Portuguese, Dutch, and even Algerine vessels, which were lying in the roads, received Blake with similar demonstrations of respect. The Count de Molina, governor of Cadiz, invited him to enter the

---

[1] From the Archives of Simancas

port, where he promised him a most friendly reception ; but Blake replied that he was in haste to take advantage of the wind to pass the straits, that he might, without loss of time, execute the Protector's orders in the Mediterranean. He then proceeded rapidly to Naples, to oppose the invasion of the Duke of Guise ; for Cromwell, still wavering between France and Spain, was unwilling to allow either to obtain too great an ascendency, and made it his endeavour to keep them both in check by turns. But when the English fleet arrived off Naples, the Duke of Guise had already failed, and re-embarked for France ; and Blake, free from the care of preventing this frivolous enterprise, was able to pursue the accomplishment of his haughty mission along the whole coast of the Mediterranean.[1]

He presented himself first of all before Leghorn, and sent to the Grand Duke of Tuscany to demand instant redress for the owners of those English merchant vessels which had been captured in 1650 by Prince Rupert, and sold in the ports of Tuscany ; and also permission for the English Protestants to have a church at Florence, and to enjoy the undisturbed exercise of their religion in that city. The alarm spread all along the Italian coast ; some of the prizes had been sold in the Papal States, and the Grand Duke submitted that the pope ought to pay a portion of the indemnity required. Upon this, Blake sent an officer to Rome also, to demand reparation. The terror of the inhabitants was so great that many of them left the city, taking with them or concealing their most valuable property ; and the pope ordered that the wealth deposited in the Cathedral of Loretto should be conveyed into the interior, as he feared a disembarkation and sudden attack on the part of the arrogant English heretics. Blake was no pillager, nor was he regardless of the rules and proceedings of the law of nations ; he peremptorily insisted on the payment of the indemnity, but committed no act of violence. Negotiations began as to the amount of damages to be paid. Blake demanded a hundred and fifty thousand pounds ; the Grand Duke paid him sixty thousand, and the pope added twenty thousand pistoles.[2] As to granting liberty for Protestant worship at Florence, the Grand Duke evaded giving a direct answer, saying that no such privilege had been conceded in any of the Italian States, but that

---

[1] Thurloe's State Papers, vol. ii. p. 731. vol. iii. p. 103 ; Whitelocke, p. 609 ; Dixon's Life of Blake, pp. 272—276 ; Clarendon's State Papers, vol. iii. p. 269 ; Bonille's Histoire des Ducs de Guise, vol. iv. pp. 484—490 ; Papers from the Archives of Simancas, and from the Archives des Affaires Etrangères de France.

[2] The Roman pistole is worth about fourteen shillings.

he would willingly make the concession, if other sovereigns would
do the same.   Blake did not insist further on his demand,—he was
one of those who had religious liberty sincerely at heart, and he
earnestly desired to secure it to Prostestants all over the world ;
but he was sensible and just—he had a due regard for the rights of
sovereigns, and he felt that the condition of the Catholics in
England stood greatly in the way of his claims.[1]

From Leghorn he sailed to the coast of Africa, first to Tunis,
then to Tripoli, and then to Algiers, for the purpose of demanding
indemnity for English merchants, and of obtaining the liberation of
the Christian captives who had fallen into the hands of the pirates.
A report had been spread that, by order of the Grand Signior, the
fleets of all the Mussulman States in the Mediterranean were to
assemble at Tunis, doubtless in order to attack and pillage some
Christian country.   Blake was resolved to defeat any enterprise of
this nature, and to impress the minds of the Barbarescoes with a
due respect for England.   At Tunis only, he had occasion to employ
force.   At the same time that he communicated his demands to the
Dey, he requested permission to take on board a supply of fresh
water.   The Dey brutally refused everything.   " Tell the Dey,"
said Blake, " that God has given the benefit of water to all his
creatures ; and for men to deny it to each other is equally insolent
and wicked."   The Dey's only answer was to show the English
officers his strong fortresses.   " Here," he said, " are our castles of
Goletta and Porto Ferino ; do your worst, and do not think to
brave us with the sight of your great fleet ;" and he was preparing
to repel any attack, when he saw the English fleet stand out to sea
without firing a single gun.   He revelled in the proud enjoyment of
his easy deliverance for a fortnight ; but on the 3rd of April, 1655,
the English fleet appeared again before Tunis ; and at dawn on the
following day, it anchored within half musket-range of the Tunisian
batteries.   Blake had been to Trapani, on the coast of Sicily, to
collect some of his ships, and to complete his supply of ammunition.
After divine service had been solemnly performed on the deck of
every vessel, within sight of the wonder-stricken and respecting
Mussulmans, the action began, and for two hours the Tunisian
forts and the English ships kept up an incessant cannonade.   The
wind was favourable to the English ; they were able to aim their
guns with precision, whilst the Tunisians had to fire almost at
random through clouds of smoke.   The issue was, however, still

[1] Dixon's Life of Blake, pp. 274—278; Thurloe's State Papers, vol. iii-
pp. 1. 41, 103, vol. iv. p. 464; Godwin's History of the Commonwealth, vol. iv.
p. 188 ; Ludlow's Memoirs, p. 215.

uncertain when Blake ordered one of his most trusted officers, John Stoaks, captain of his flag-ship the *St. George*, to lower some of the long-boats of the fleet, and to row alongside nine great Corsair vessels, which lay at anchor in the port, and which constituted the entire naval armament of the Dey; and to set fire to them with lighted brands and torches. The order was boldly executed; notwithstanding the galling fire of the musketeers on shore, the Tunisian fleet was soon in flames; in vain did the Dey's men attempt to arrest the progress of the disaster; the English frigates raked the decks of the burning vessels with terrible broadsides, and destroyed all who had ventured to their relief. The harbour soon became a sea of flame in that direction, and in presence of the dreadful sight, the battle almost ceased. But its issue was no longer doubtful; the Tunisians completely lost courage; the batteries became silent. If he had pleased, Blake might easily have landed and made himself master of the town; but he had attained his object; the Dey had been made to feel the power of England. The fate of Tunis became a warning to the whole coast of Africa; at Tripoli and Algiers, Blake met with no resistance: and with his usual moderation in victory, he arranged, without any arrogant exactions, the demands of his countrymen, and the ransom of the captives.[1]

Even in his conduct towards Mussulmans and barbarians, he did not consider himself at liberty to do as he pleased, and all his acts indicate a prudent respect for the law of nations and his instructions. On the 14th of March, while lying before Tunis, and on the point of attacking it, he wrote to Thurloe: "We are not fully satisfied as touching the power given in that particular instruction authorising us, in case of refusal of right, to seize, surprise, sink, and destroy all ships and vessels belonging to the kingdom of Tunis. I wish that the intent of this and other instructions of this nature might be more clear and explicit, and more plainly significant as to our duty." And on the 18th of April, after his victory, he wrote: "Seeing it hath pleased God so signally to justify us herein, I hope his Highness will not be offended at it, nor any who regard duly the honour of our nation; although I expect to hear of many complaints and clamours of interested men. I confess that, in contemplation thereof, and some seeming ambiguity in my instructions (of which I gave you a hint in my last), I did awhile much hesitate

[1] Dixon's Life of Blake, pp. 280—293; Thurloe's State Papers, vol. iii. pp. 232, 326, 390; Whitelocke, pp. 621—627; Clarendon's History of the Rebellion, vol. vii. pp. 173—178; Bates's Elenchus Motuum, part ii. p. 302.

myself, and was balanced in my thoughts, until the barbarous carriage of those pirates did turn the scale."[1]

Having thus taught the Corsairs a terrible lesson, Blake cruised for some time in the Mediterranean, sailing wherever the power, honour, or fortune of England seemed to require his presence : to Malta, in order to teach respect to the knights, who had more than once detained and captured English merchantmen ; to Venice, in order to receive the congratulations of the Doge and senate, who were delighted that, in the midst of their conflict with the Turks for the possession of Candia, the Mussulmans should receive so effectual a check in the adjacent seas ; to Toulon and Marseilles, in order to intimidate the French privateers, who, in spite of the king's express commands, occasionally sailed from those ports, and committed serious depredations on English trade. Both in law and in fact, the police of the high seas was still, at this period, almost a dead letter, and entirely powerless ; peace between states was not a pledge of unmolested navigation to their respective subjects; and governments did not succeed, or frequently did not attempt, either themselves to repress the maritime disorders of their own subjects, or to protect them against similar disorders or violent attacks on the part of foreign fleets. Blake made large use of his right to watch over the safety of English commerce in the Mediterranean. In order to discourage and punish the depredators, he took prizes of more or less value, in his turn, from the commercial navies of France, Spain, Portugal, Holland, and Hamburgh, which could not fail to lead to unpleasant difficulties with those governments ; but, by his activity and vigour, he animated English merchants with a confidence, and inspired foreign privateers with a dread, which contributed powerfully to promote the prosperity and renown of his country. And, when he thought he had done enough to secure this end, he returned towards the coast of Spain, to await the outbreak of a war between the two States, which was to lead to the expedition against Spanish America, and the conduct of which, in Europe, was to devolve upon himself.[2]

As he lay off Malaga, some of his sailors went on shore, and, happening to meet a procession of the host in the streets, instead of bowing before it with respect, they laughed at it with derision and insult. An indignant priest called on the populace to avenge the honour of their faith ; a violent tumult ensued ; the English

---

[1] Thurloe's State Papers, vol. iii. pp. 232—390.

[2] Dixon's Life of Blake, pp. 289—291; Thurloe's State Papers, vol. iii. pp. 85, 321, 497, 698; Whitelocke, p. 621 ; Bordeaux to Brienne (October 26, 1651), in the Archives des Affaires Etrangères de France.

sailors were beaten and forced to retreat to their ships, where they related their own version of the fray to their admiral. On more than one occasion already, at Lisbon and Venice, and in other Catholic ports, similar scenes had taken place: with the prospect before him of the rupture which he knew was on the point of occurring between England and Spain, he resolved not to pass this by in silence. He sent a trumpeter into the town to demand, not, as was expected, that the violence of the mob should be punished, but that the priest who had excited the tumult should be given up to justice. The governor of Malaga replied that he could not comply with this demand, as in Spain the servants of the Church were not amenable to the civil power. "I will not stay to inquire," replied Blake, "who has the power to send the offender to me; but if he be not on board the *St. George* within three hours, I will burn your city to the ground." No excuse, no delay, was admitted; the priest was sent to the admiral. Blake at once called the sailors before him, and after having heard the story on both sides, he declared that the seamen had behaved with gross rudeness and impropriety towards the Spaniards, and had themselves provoked the attack of which they complained. "Had you sent me an account of what has occurred," he told the priest, "the men should have been severely punished, as I will not suffer them to affront the religion of any people at whose ports we touch; but I feel extreme displeasure at your having taken the law into your own hands; and I would have you and all the world to know that an Englishman is not to be judged and punished except by Englishmen." And he sent the priest on shore again with much civility; having furnished in the midst of the utmost confusion of rights, a rare example of equity and moderation, combined with ardent faith and superior force.[1]

When Cromwell received the letter in which Blake related this incident, he read it out to the Council of State with the utmost approbation, and declared that "by such means, they would make the name of Englishman as great as that of Roman was in Rome's most palmy days."

Cromwell had reason to employ Blake with the fullest confidence, for the republican sailor had sincerely renounced all further interference in the internal dissensions of his country, and resolved to devote himself entirely to the advancement of her glory throughout the world. When Thurloe, in January, 1655, announced to

[1] Burnet's History of His Own Time, vol. i. pp. 147, 148; Dixon's Life of Blake, p. 301—304.

him the dissolution of that Parliament which had aspired to re-constitute, at its pleasure and by its sole authority, the Protectoral government, Blake replied : "I was not much surprised with the intelligence; the slow proceedings and awkward motions of that assembly giving great cause to suspect it would come to some such period ; and I cannot but exceedingly wonder that there should yet remain so strong a spirit of prejudice and animosity in the minds of men, who profess themselves most affectionate patriots, as to postpone the necessary ways and means for preservation of the Commonwealth, especially in such a time of concurrence of the mischievous plots and designs both of old and new enemies, tending all to the destruction of the same. But blessed be God, who hath hitherto delivered, and doth still deliver us; and I trust will continue so to do, although He be very much tempted by us."[1]

About two months after Blake's departure for the Mediterranean, towards the end of December, 1654, the fleet under Penn and Venables, with a strong body of troops on board, left Portsmouth in its turn, and set sail for Spanish America. Although it had been long in preparation, the expedition began under unfavourable auspices : a short time before its departure, a mutiny was on the point of breaking out among the sailors, who complained of the bad quality of their provisions, refused to be enlisted any longer by impressment, and angrily declared that all the world knew whither they were bound, except themselves. The two leaders, Penn and Venables, were not much better disposed than their subordinates; Penn, in his inmost heart, was a royalist, and when he found him-self at the head of a powerful squadron, he sent word to Cologne that, if the King were prepared to act, and would indicate to him a post to which he could conduct his vessels in safety, he was ready to declare in his favour. Venables, a weak and irresolute man, with but little affection for Cromwell, though he had served bravely under him in Ireland, made similar overtures to Charles II. The admiral and general had not communicated their intentions to one another; but they both had but little faith and less liking for Cromwell's future prospects, and were desirous of providing against all contingencies. Charles, who was neither able nor inclined to make any attempt at that time upon England, desired them to pursue, for the advantage of England, the enterprise which they had undertaken, and to wait until a better opportunity should occur for serving him. They set out with no great animation or confi-

[1] Blake to Thurloe, March 14, 1655; Thurloe's State Papers, vol. iii. p. 282.

dence having received orders from the Protector not to open their instructions regarding the object and conduct of the expedition until they reached Barbadoes.[1]

The sailors had reason to believe that the secret had been imperfectly kept. It was in Cromwell's own household, and by one of his most trusted servants, that the indiscretion of divulging it had been committed. He frequently employed, in his transactions with the Continent, and particularly with the Protestants of France, Switzerland, and Germany, an agent named Stoupe, a Grison by birth, and now a minister of the French Church in London; a man of considerable talent and great capacity for intrigue; by turns a theologian, a negotiator, a pamphleteer, and a soldier, with no pretension to appear a person of distinction, but inquisitive and active, fond of secret importance and money, and ready to serve any one who would gratify him by bestowing them. Happening one day to enter the Protector's cabinet, Stoupe found him engaged in the careful examination of a map, on which he was measuring distances. He glanced furtively at it, perceived that it was a chart of the Gulf of Mexico, noticed the engraver's name, and went to him the next day to obtain a copy. The engraver declared that he had no such map. "I have seen it," said Stoupe. "Then," replied the man, "it must have been only in Cromwell's hand, for he only has some of the prints, and has given me strict charge to sell none till I have leave." Stoupe's curiosity was powerfully excited, and soon became indiscreet. Talking one day with some persons about Penn's expedition, he said that, for his part, he believed it was destined for the West Indies. This was reported to Don Alonzo de Cardenas, who sent for Stoupe, asked him what grounds he had for his opinion, and offered him ten thousand pounds if he could discover the secret for him. Stoupe, for once, was not to be tempted, and put the Spanish ambassador on a wrong scent, instead of satisfying his curiosity. But he was in correspondence with the Protestant Frondeurs, who surrounded the Prince de Conti at Brussels, who was then a despondent fugitive, and had been engaged in inglorious warfare under the Spanish flag ever since the defeat of the Fronde had rendered it impossible for him alternately to act the part of a hero and a rebel in his own country. Stoupe sent his correspondents news in return for their good offices, and informed them of his conjecture as to the destina-

[1] Thurloe's State Papers, vol. ii. pp. 512, 571—574, 709; vol. iii. pp. 11, 16; Clarendon's History of the Rebellion, vol. vii. pp. 172, 173; Memorials of Sir William Penn, vol. ii. pp. 14—18; Whitelocke, p. 621; Heath's Chronicle, pp. 674, 682.

tion of Penn's expedition. This was immediately communicated to Condé, who, in his turn, mentioned it to Don John of Austria, who had succeeded the Archduke Leopold in the government of the Netherlands. But Don John attached no importance to a rumour with regard to which he had heard nothing from the Spanish ambassador in London. More attention was, however, paid to it in other quarters. On the 5th of February, 1655, Lord Jermyn wrote from Paris to Charles II., "I cannot forbear allowing myself a great share of hope, out of the several informations that daily come from all parts, that the destination of the fleet is for Hispaniola. Though it be beyond the Line, yet I cannot imagine that the Spaniards can find themselves assaulted in so important a part and remain friends with them that do it." And some months later, on the 5th of May, Mazarin wrote to Bordeaux, "I cannot understand why it should be so difficult on your side of the Channel to discern the purpose of Penn's fleet, seeing that here, where we might be expected to hear much less news than you hear in the place where you are residing, we have learned that, on passing St. Christopher's, he took on board his fleet three hundred Frenchmen and inhabitants of the island, and then continued his course to Cuba."[1]

The court of Madrid was not so careless as its ambassador in London. Alarmed by the indirect information which reached it from all quarters, Don Luis de Haro, by the king's express command, complained to Cardenas, not only of his silence regarding the object of Penn's expedition, but of the incoherence of his statements with respect to the affairs of England, and of the small amount of influence which he possessed with a government which Spain had been the first to recognise and support. Cardenas vigorously defended himself from these censures, attributing the slowness of his proceedings and the unsuccessfulness of his negotiations to the want of positive instructions and the hesitating policy of the court of Spain itself. In reference to Penn's squadron, he added—"The design against the Indies is the only one I have been unable to fathom, because the Protector has kept it carefully concealed from those very persons from whom I could hope to ascertain its object. . . . I have therefore been unable to collect anything but conjectures on this subject, and I have transmitted to your Majesty all that have been made regarding this expedition in all their diversity." He ended by requesting his recall.[2]

[1] Burnet's History of His Own Time, vol. i. p. 137; Clarendon's State Papers, vol. iii. p 264; Letter from Mazarin to Bordeaux, in the Archives des Affaires Etrangères de France.
[2] Cardeñas to King Philip IV. (January 28, 1655); Archives of Simancas.

Instead of recalling him, Philip IV. sent to London a second ambassador, the Marquis de Leyden, a sensible man and valiant officer, who had won himself honours in the wars in the Netherlands by his vigorous defence of Maestricht against the Prince of Orange. He had instructions, acting in concert with Cardenas, to manifest no apprehensions on account of Penn's squadron, but, on the contrary, to renew to the Protector the most formal assurance of the friendly intentions of his sovereign, and to insist on the conclusion of a treaty of intimate alliance between Spain and England, reminding Cromwell of all the causes which should keep him aloof from France, and offering to aid him at once in taking Calais, provided that, on his part, he would help the Prince of Condé to re-enter Bordeaux, and, in concert with the Spaniards, to rekindle the war on the French territory.[1]

Such an advance from the court of Madrid to Cromwell, at the very moment when he was about to commit such an aggression upon Spain, filled Mazarin with anxiety and astonishment. Spain, it appeared, was ready to make any concessions, and undergo any humiliations in order to gain the support of England against France. Orders were sent to M. de Bordeaux to urge the conclusion of the treaty which he had been negotiating for more than two years, and even to announce his departure from England if its ratification were further delayed.[2] He had frequently believed he had reached the end of his negotiation; but sometimes questions which had seemed settled had been resumed, and sometimes new and unexpected difficulties had been raised. It seemed impossible to come to any agreement as to the terms of the secret article, which was to drive the Stuarts and their principal adherents from France. Cromwell, on his side, would give no pledge not to protect the French Protestants, if they should need his support, for the maintenance of their liberties; faithful to the time-honoured pretensions of the kings of England, he demanded that, in the treaty, the King of France should merely assume the title of King of the French; he was determined to treat as an equal with Louis XIV., and to be named before him in the English copy of the treaty, as had been the case in the conventions which he had concluded with the kings of Sweden, Denmark, and Portugal. Whatever desire Mazarin may have had for peace, however strong Colbert may have insisted on the renewal of friendly and secure

[1] Thurloe's State Papers, vol. i. pp. 683, 761, vol. iii. pp. 51, 154; Clarendon's History of the Rebellion, vol. vii. p. 174; Heath's Chronicle, p. 689.

[2] Mazarin to Bordeaux, January 2, 1655; Archives des Affaires Etrangères de France.

commercial relations with England, they long refused compliance with these demands. When Cromwell's fortune seemed tottering, Mazarin drew back, and ceased to be urgent to conclude matters. In October, 1654, when the struggle was at its height between the Protector and his second Parliament, he wrote to M. de Bordeaux:—
"It is advisable to do nothing hastily, and merely to keep things *in statu quo*, until circumstances change, and we are able to see a little more clearly the direction they are likely to take; for it seems to me that prudence does not require that we should make such haste openly to espouse the interests of the Protector, at a conjuncture when, if the opposite party should chance to prevail, all that we had done would only serve to oblige his adversaries to declare against us, and to open their arms to the Spaniards, who would not fail to profit by such a mischance." But when Cromwell was conqueror and sole master at home; when he was seen displaying his power abroad, contracting alliance with all the Protestant states of northern Europe, intimidating both Catholics and Mussulmans in the south, and meditating conquests from Spain; when it became known in Paris that Montecuculi had been to London to attempt to gain the Protector to the interests of the House of Austria, that Whitelocke (at the instigation, it was said, of Queen Christina) had supported his pretensions at Whitehall, and the King of Spain had sent the Marquis of Leyden, in order to give greater weight and dignity to his offers of alliance: in presence of all these facts, Mazarin's hesitation and procrastination disappeared; he sent repeated injunctions to Bordeaux to press the negotiation: the terms of the secret article, relating to the expulsion from France of the Stuarts, and their most intimate friends, were conceded; the use of the old protocol which gave the King of France the title of King of the French, was consented to: and though maintaining the dignity of the crown of France, as to the question of precedence, in the preamble of the treaty, Mazarin added: "We ask for nothing better than to treat on equal terms with England, or even with the Protector himself, provided that he will assume the title of king; and then his Majesty will not hesitate to do him all the honour which the kings of France have been accustomed to do to those of England, and will also send him an ambassador extraordinary to congratulate him, if he desire it:"—an admirably flattering refusal, which, far from offending Cromwell, could not fail to please him! [1]
Cromwell was neither offended nor pleased; he yielded on the

[1] Mazarin to Bordeaux, January 16, 1655; Letters from Bordeaux to Brienne, under various dates; Archives des Affaires Etrangères de France.

question of precedence, but showed no greater haste to bring the treaty to a conclusion. In his heart, he daily inclined more and more towards France;—he knew well that a rupture with Spain would be inevitable, after the blow he was about to strike her, and the patience with which she endured its approach, freed him from alarm as to her anger when the event occurred. The offers of the Marquis of Leyden did not tempt him; on the two points on which England most strongly insisted, free navigation in the West Indies, and religious liberty for the English merchants in Spain, the Court of Spain was inflexible. The words of Condé, and of his agents in London, inspired Cromwell with no confidence. "*Stultus est, et garrulus,*" he said one day to Stoupe, "*et venditur a suis cardinali.*" He was not ignorant that Spain, though she then supported the French malcontents, would never be to them a very helpful patron; she was in great want of money, and had much difficulty in sending to Condé, by the hands of Cardenas, a sum of fifty thousand crowns.[1] He was anxious to have trustworthy information with regard to the feelings of the French Protestants, who, Condé said, were ready to rise in his favour; and Stoupe, by his order, travelled through France as a private individual, visiting the banks of the Loire, Bordeaux, Montauban, Nismes, and Lyons, conversing with the leading Protestants, and informing them of Cromwell's friendly feelings towards them. He found them, for the most part, determined to remain at peace; the edicts were observed,—they were allowed the free exercise of their religion, and left undisturbed in their business transactions; besides, they had a bad opinion of the Prince of Condé: "he is a man," they told Stoupe, "who seeks only his own glory, and is ready to sacrifice to it all his friends, and all the causes that he seems to embrace." Everything concurred to convince Cromwell that he had nothing to expect from Spain and the Frondeurs, and that France, Louis XIV., and Mazarin, possessing, as they did, greater power and ability, were far more formidable neighbours, and would be more useful allies. He granted a solemn audience to the Marquis of Leyden, on the 16th of May, 1655; but the marquis quickly perceived that his embassy would lead to no result, and returned to Flanders. Cromwell ordered that he should be escorted with great pomp to Gravesend; and remained in the same passive attitude towards France, as he did not yet feel it necessary to declare himself, or enter into any more binding engagement. The Court of France still inspired him, and the English public generally, with great distrust: most of the London

---

[1] On the 14th of April, and 15th of July, 1655.

merchants inclined towards Spain, with which country their trade
was considerable. Besides, where would have been the advantage
of deciding, before the issue of the American expedition became
known? Spain would then break the peace herself, and a treaty
with France would be concluded on the ground of necessity.
Bordeaux shrewdly enough divined the causes of the Protector's
tergiversations, and communicated his opinions very faithfully to
his court. "The spirit of conquest, and the pretext of religion,
influence him against Spain," he wrote to M. de Brienne, on the
1st of October, 1654; "his private inclinations, jealousy of our
power, and the interest of the mercantile class, against France.
The discontents which might arise in England, if one of the two
crowns were his declared enemy, keep him in restraint at home;
and confidence that we should not dare to break with him leads
him to despise all the threats and entreaties that I could use to
oblige him to alter his conduct towards us. This is the most
natural sketch I can give of the present disposition of his mind."[1]

An incident, which became European from the sensation which
it everywhere created, though its operation was confined to an obscure
Alpine district, furnished Cromwell with a fresh pretext for still
further postponing any final settlement of the question. In the
retirement of a few valleys of Piedmont dwelt a race of cultivators
and herdsmen, who had been subject for centuries to the house of
Savoy, but who had also for centuries been separate in faith and
worship, from their fellow-subjects and sovereigns. It has been
often discussed, though without leading to any certain solution of
the question, what was the origin of the creed and name of the
Vaudois: the Roman Church treated them as heretics; and in their
turn, they accused the Roman Church of having ceased to be that
primitive apostolic Church of which they regarded themselves as the
faithful representatives. However this may be, they were a poor,
simple, laborious, and pious race of men, passionately attached to
their native mountains, their faith, and their pastors. They had,
on various occasions, obtained from the Dukes of Savoy certain
privileges which secured their religious and local liberties; and,
from the eleventh to the sixteenth century, they had passed through
frequent vicissitudes of toleration and persecution, though they had
been, on the whole, more often unmolested than disturbed in the
practice of their worship, and the enjoyment of their rights. When
the Reformation began, they regarded it but with little attention at

---

[1] Thurloe's State Papers, vol. iii. pp. 570, 613; Dumont's Corps Diplomatique Universel, vol. vi. part ii. p. 106; Burnet's History of His Own Time, vol. i. p. 134.

first; they had no desire for change in their internal government, and the house of Savoy, whose princes were habitually prudent and benevolent towards their subjects, seldom interfered with their tranquillity. They had political reasons for treating them with forbearance : their valleys bordered on the French valleys of Dauphiné, peopled by mountaineers of the same origin, the same faith, and the same manners; their territory was usually passed through by the armies of France, in their expeditions into Italy ; and the Kings of France had frequently taken occasion to show them favour, and sometimes even officially to protect them. On the 28th of September, 1571, less than a year before the massacre of St. Bartholomew, Charles IX. wrote to Duke Emmanuel Philibert, who at that time was treating the Vaudois with great severity:— " I am about to prefer to you a request, not an ordinary one, but as affectionate as any you could have from me ; . . . . for, during the troubles of war, passion does not permit us, any more than illness permits a sick man, to judge what is expedient ; . . . and, as you have treated your subjects extraordinarily in this matter, be pleased now, for my sake, at my prayer and especial recommendation, to receive them into your benign favour, and to restore and re-establish them in their confiscated estates. . . . . This cause is so just in itself, and so full of affection on my part, that I am sure you will willingly grant my request."[1]

When the Reformation had made the conquest of half Europe, and kindled the fires of war and controversy in all minds and in all States, the Vaudois valleys felt the influence of this general agitation ; theological polemics became more frequent among them, and preaching against the Roman Church more violent. The Vaudois pastors, known by the name of *Barbas*, a term of filial deference, were divided into two classes ; the first stationary and attached to the different parishes, the others itinerant missionaries, who travelled through the various countries of Europe, into Italy, France, and Germany, southwards as far as the wilds of Calabria, and eastwards to the mouth of the Danube, for the purpose of teaching and preaching evangelical doctrine. At the close of the sixteenth and commencement of the seventeenth century, they introduced, on their return to their country, the movement which they had met with everywhere else ; in those communes in which there was a mixed population of Catholics and Vaudois, religious dissensions

[1] Léger's Histoire Générale des Eglises Evangéliques et des Vallées du Piémont; Morland's History of the Evangelical Churches of the Valleys of Piedmont; Muston's Israel des Alpes, Histoire Complète des Vaudois du Piémont, vol. ii. p. 109.

z

became embittered; a longing to proclaim their faith and spread
it far and wide around them, sprang up in the hearts of these
mountaineers; they went into the neighbouring valleys, sometimes
as visitors, and sometimes with a view to settlement, discussing and
preaching with obstinate enthusiasm, animated by two powerful
feelings which free and strong governments alone can afford
to tolerate — the spirit of resistance and the spirit of propa-
gandism.

In Catholic Piedmont, for the defence of the opposite cause,
similar ardour was felt; the Roman Church, irritated and alarmed,
commenced an active warfare against the Vaudois.   She had on her
side the legal power and the public passion of the country—the
prince and the people.   The Roman Propaganda undertook the
conversion, and the Court of Turin the subjugation, of the Vaudois;
Catholic priests and doctors traversed their mountains; two voluntary associations, one of men, the other of women, were formed at
Turin to second their efforts.   A lady of high rank, the Marchesa
de Pianezza, beautiful, accomplished, wealthy, and enthusiastic, devoted her time, fortune, and influence to this pious work; her
husband, a stern and valiant officer, undertook to execute the wishes
of his wife, the orders of his sovereign, and the dictates of his creed.
The daughter of Henry IV., Christine of France, who was Regent
of Piedmont, during the minority of her son, Charles Emmanuel II.,
lent them her support.   The Vaudois also possessed, among the
Piedmontese aristocracy, many benevolent patrons, who recommended the government to pursue towards them a moderate policy,
and to respect their ancient liberties.   For some years, and almost
up to the last moment, alternate edicts of toleration and severity,
bore witness to the conflict of the two influences.   But the spirit of
religious tyranny gradually gained ground in the Piedmontese
government; and the Vaudois, by their acts of imprudence or
violence, frequently furnished it with pretexts, and sometimes with
motives, for persecution.   Young men, who were pursued for having
insulted the priests, took refuge in the mountain fastnesses, where
they lived the life of bandits, in revolt against law and order.   In
some of the valleys, at Villar, Bobi, and Angrogna, convents which
had recently been established were burned to the ground; at Fénil
the priest was assassinated.   The mass of the Vaudois population
deplored these crimes, and made sincere efforts to repress and atone
for them, and to comply with the requirements of their sovereign;
but subject as they were to incessant annoyance and insult in their
feelings and rights, they were unwilling either to yield or defend
themselves, and wearied the forced benevolence of their aristocratic

protectors, who were alike powerless to prevent their faults and to restrain their enemies.

On the 25th of January, 1655, the storm which had long been gathering burst at length upon the Vaudois; they were ordered to evacuate within three days—on pain of death and the confiscation of their property—nine of the communes in which they resided They were further enjoined to sell, within twenty days, the lands which they possessed in those communes, and to concentrate themselves and their property in four communes, in which alone their religion was thenceforward to be tolerated; and even in these, for the conversion of the Protestants, mass was to be celebrated every day, and whoever dissuaded a Protestant from becoming a Catholic was to be punished with death. The Vaudois, in consternation, protested against these severities, saying that they were ready to accept any conditions that might be imposed upon them. so long as liberty of conscience was left them; but if it had been determined to deprive them of it, they requested permission to leave the Duke of Savoy's dominions in a body. Their petition was received with some show of attention; negotiations were opened; a day of audience was assigned to their representatives at Turin; but on that very day, the 17th of April, 1655, the Marquis de Pianezza entered the Vaudois valleys with a considerable body of troops, to enforce the evacuation of the nine communes mentioned in the ducal decree. Some attempts at resistance led to a sanguinary conflict, and for eight days the Vaudois were given over to the violence and brutality of a fanatical and licentious soldiery, whose fury knew no bounds against vanquished heretics. The 24th of April, in particular, was, in this obscure spot, one of those days of massacre and outrage, the mere narrative of which, after the lapse of centuries, makes humanity shudder with horror and compassion. I refrain from entering into its hideous details; but it is a source of satisfaction to quote the honest judgment passed on this occurrence, some months afterwards, by a brave French officer who was present. The regiment of Grancey, which had been sent into Italy by Louis XIV., to the assistance of the Duke of Modena, had been stopped on its way, at the request of the Piedmontese authorities, and quartered in their territory, either for the purpose of intimidating the Vaudois, or of lending their oppressors armed assistance in case of need. The Captain du Petit-Bourg, who commanded the regiment, would not take the slightest share in the responsibility; and on the 27th of November following. at Pignerol, in the presence of two officers of the regiment of Sault and Auvergne, he signed this declaration:—

"1, Lord of Petit-Bourg, first captain in command of the regiment of Grancey, having received orders to join the Marquis de Pianezza, and to take orders from him . . . was the witness of numerous acts of great violence and extreme cruelty, practised by the soldiers towards all ages, sexes, and conditions, whom I saw massacred, hanged, burned, and violated, and I also witnessed several terrible conflagrations. . . . When prisoners were brought to the Marquis de Pianezza, I saw the order that all were to be killed, because his Highness would not have any of their religion in all his dominions. . . . Insomuch that I formally deny, and protest before God, that none of the above-mentioned cruelties were committed by my order; on the contrary, seeing that I could afford no remedy thereto, I was constrained to withdraw and to throw up the command of my regiment, in order that I might not assist in such wicked actions."[1]

Cromwell had not waited for the occurrence of this terrible catastrophe before taking an interest in the Vaudois. Careful to keep himself acquainted with the condition of the Protestants in all countries, and to give them all proofs of his good-will, as well as of his power, he had been duly informed of the first measures adopted against them by the Duke of Savoy, and Thurloe had immediately written to John Pell, the English resident in Switzerland, to give him orders secretly to advise the Vaudois to appeal to the Protector, whose aid should not be denied them. When the news of the massacre in the valleys reached England it produced a general outburst of indignation and sympathy. Men listened to and repeated the lamentable story with angry curiosity. Detailed accounts were circulated all over the country, illustrated with little engravings, in which the most hideous scenes of the massacre were roughly depicted. Cromwell became the spokesman and the leader of the popular passion; Milton was immediately set at work; and, on the 25th of May, 1655, the Protector wrote to the Duke of Savoy himself, to Louis XIV., and to Cardinal Mazarin, to the Kings of Sweden and Denmark, to the States-General of the United Provinces, and to the Swiss Cantons, and, finally, to George Ragotzki, Prince of Transylvania, to demand for the Vaudois the justice of their own sovereign, and the protection of all sovereigns who were either Protestant themselves or admitted Protestants within their dominions.[2] Cromwell appointed the learned Samuel Morland, under secretary of the Council of State, his envoy extra-

---

[1] Léger's Histoire Générale des Eglises Vaudoises, part ii. p. 115; Muston's Israel des Alpes, vol. ii. pp. 329–331.
[2] Milton's Prose Works, vol. v. pp. 247–258; Thurloe to John Pell, March 23, 1655, in Vaughan's Protectorate of Cromwell, vol. i. p. 158.

ordinary to convey to Louis XIV. and the Duke of Savoy the
letters which he had addressed to them. At the same time he
directed that a collection should be made throughout England for
the relief of the unfortunate Vaudois, and headed the subscription
with a gift of two thousand pounds from his own purse.

Cromwell's letters contained nothing which could render the
mission of his envoy offensive to the sovereigns to whom they were
addressed, or embarrassing to Morland himself. They were grave,
precise, and urgent. Cromwell proclaimed in them the great principle of liberty of conscience, " which," he said, " is an inviolable
right, over which God alone had any authority ;" and he declared
that " the calamities of the poor people of the Piedmontese valleys
lay as near, or rather nearer to his heart, than if it had concerned
the dearest relative he had in the world." In his letter to the
Duke of Savoy, he insisted on the antiquity of the liberties which
the Vaudois had enjoyed in his dominions, and on the faithful
devotedness which they had always manifested to his family. In
his letter to Louis XIV. he expressed his astonishment at the
report which was current that French troops had taken part in the
massacre of the valleys. He reminded the Protestant States, both
kingdoms and republics, of the necessity of union and common
action on behalf of all the Protestants in Europe, for the maintenance of their own safety no less than in the discharge of their duty
as Christians. But no appearance of menace or bravado, no insolent
provocation, or seditious insinuation, was mingled with his remonstrances. His policy was decided and active, but restrained within
the regular limits of diplomatic communications, and speaking in
moderate, though clear and energetic language.

Morland left London on the 26th of May, 1655, and on the
1st of June he arrived at La Fère, where Louis XIV. and Mazarin
were then residing. He immediately delivered to them the Protector's letters; and three days after, he transmitted to Cromwell
an answer from Louis XIV., in which that prince apologised for the
use which had been made of his troops in Piedmont, announced that
he had already sent to Turin to intercede in favour of the Vaudois,
congratulated himself on having thus anticipated the Protector's
wishes, and ended in these words : " You have well judged in this
affair, not to believe that I had given any order to my troops to do
such an execution as this was ; for there was not any appearance
such a suspicion could possess the spirit of any person well informed,
that I should contribute to the chastisement of any subjects of the
Duke of Savoy, professors of the pretended reformed religion, and
yet in the mean time give so many marks of my good will to those

of mine own subjects who are of the same profession, having also cause to applaud their fidelity and zeal for my service."[1]

At Turin, Morland's mission was of a more stormy character. On delivering to the Duke, on the 21st of June, in solemn audience, the Protector's letter, he accompanied it with a speech, the pathetic and uncomplimentary tone of which offended the Regent Christine, who was present at the interview. "I cannot," she said, "but extremely applaud the singular charity and goodness of his Highness the Lord Protector towards our subjects, whose condition has been represented to him as so exceeding sad and lamentable; but at the same time, I cannot but extremely admire that the malice of men should ever proceed so far as to clothe such fatherlike and tender chastisements of our most rebellious and insolent subjects with so black and ugly a character, in order to render us thereby odious to all neighbouring princes and States. I do not doubt, however, that when his Highness the Lord Protector shall be particularly and clearly informed of all passages, he will be so fully satisfied with the Duke's proceedings, that he will not give the least countenance to these disobedient subjects. For his Highness' sake, however, we will not only freely pardon them for the heinous crimes they have committed, but also accord to them such privileges and graces as cannot but give the Lord Protector a sufficient evidence of the great respect we bear both to his person and mediation." Following the example of the Regent, the Marquis de Saint-Thomas, Chief Secretary of State to the Duke of Savoy, and several of the chief men of his court, both lay and ecclesiastic, hospitably entertained Morland, loading him with politeness, and endeavouring, though with but little success, to convince him of the falsity of the statements which had led to his mission. The French ambassador at Turin. M. Servien, spoke in a more sensible strain: "Duke Emmanuel Philibert," he said, "had made such concessions as were insisted on by the people, in the year 1651; and I do verily believe that his Royal Highness and his mother might easily be pacified towards them, and be inclined to accord to them the same and greater privileges than his royal ancestors had done, were there not some powerful persons in the court, whose zeal for the Catholic religion prompts them to make the worst constructions and representations of all things to their prince. However, I advise you by all means not to add fuel to the fire, but rather to endeavour to satisfy and appease his Highness the Lord Protector,

by a sweet and moderate relation of all these proceedings." These
were the instructions he had received from Mazarin. Morland
sent his report to Cromwell, together with the Duke of Savoy's
answer, full of justifications and reluctant promises; and he left
Turin on the 19th of July, to proceed to Geneva, where he had
orders to await further instructions from the Protector.[1]

In England, the public feeling on the subject still continued the
same. Although the counties had not manifested so much enthusiasm as London, the collection for the relief of the Vaudois
amounted to the sum of 38,241l.; popular indignation against the
Catholics ran very high, and the mob seemed desirous of avenging
upon them the sufferings which the Protestants had to endure in
other countries. The Commissioners appointed to negotiate with
M. de Bordeaux informed him that the Protector would not sign
the treaty until the Court of France had exerted all its influence at
Turin to obtain the restoration of the Vaudois to their liberties.
Cromwell still gave the most earnest and vigilant attention to this
affair, and sometimes with views favourable to the interests of
France : his agent Stoupe, whom Mazarin had also taken into his
service, for a pension of three hundred pounds a year, one day intimated to M. de Bordeaux that the Protector might probably demand
the cession of the Vaudois valleys to the King of France, which
would become a pledge of close friendship between the two States.
But it was in concert more frequently with the Protestant States of
Europe that Cromwell sought to promote the cause of the Vaudois;
he urged the United Provinces and the Swiss Cantons to prepare
for war on their behalf; and he despatched a new envoy, Mr.
George Downing, to Geneva, with instructions to advocate the
adoption of energetic measures, and afterwards to proceed to Turin,
with Morland and the ministers of Switzerland and Holland, in
order to obtain some definite settlement of the business. His confidential friends mentioned Nice and Villafranca, in the Sardinian
States, as points at which English troops might easily disembark.[2]

These rumours, this imminency of war and fresh political com-
plications, greatly disturbed Mazarin, who was always equally ready
to fear and hope. Caring little for general ideas of right and
liberty, he took no interest in the Vaudois, and if no one had inter-

[1] Morland's History of the Evangelical Churches, pp. 567—579.

[2] Ibid. pp. 584—596; Bordeaux to Brienne, May 27, June 3, 10, July 1, 8,
23, August 5, 26, 1655; Mazarin to Bordeaux, July 9, 1655, in the Archives
des Affaires Etrangères de France; Thurloe to John Pell, June 8, 29, July 7,
12, 20, 27, 28, 1655; Vaughan's Protectorate of Cromwell, vol. i. pp. 191, 206,
214, 219, 225, 227, 231; Thurloe's State Papers, vol. iii. p. 690.

fered on their behalf, he would have preferred that they should have been repressed rather than tolerated; but he was a moderate and prudent statesman, and he never lost sight of the difficulties which obstinate violence might occasion. The growing influence of Cromwell on the Continent was regarded by him with suspicion; he dreaded that he might employ it to foment disturbances among the Protestants of France. Above all things, he ardently desired the conclusion of the treaty of peace which had been so long in negotiation in London, and which, in his view, was destined to effect an intimate alliance between France and England, and which alone could enable France to gain a decisive victory in her contest with Spain. "The King," he wrote to M. de Bordeaux, on the 25th of May, 1655, "has commanded me to inform you that, if the Protector is willing, on the same day that we sign the accommodation, to commence another treaty of offensive and defensive alliance, you are ready to proceed with it; that you will even consent to insert, in the first treaty, an article pledging the contracting parties to a more intimate union, in accordance with conditions to be afterwards agreed upon, and which might really be arranged within twenty-four hours."[1] The affair of the Vaudois put an end to all this labour on the part of Mazarin, and delayed the realisation of his hopes: he resolved to bring it at once to a conclusion; peremptory orders were sent to M. Servien, at Turin, to insist on an immediate pacification, and to declare that the King of France would withdraw his support from whichever party refused to consent to it; and on the 18th of August, 1655, a treaty of peace, known by the name of *Patentes de Grâce*, was signed at Pignerol, which put an end to the troubles in the valleys, annulled all prosecutions that had been commenced in reference thereto, and restored to the Vaudois their ancient privileges, namely—liberty of conscience, trade, and transit; under certain conditions, it is true, of considerable severity and harshness, which could not fail to give rise to new disturbances at a subsequent period, and from which Cromwell would probably have saved the Vaudois, if his agents had arrived in time to take part in the final negotiations.[2]

The negotiations were already concluded, and the treaty of Pignerol signed, when Downing, passing through France on his way to Geneva, had an interview, at La Fère, with Mazarin, who

<hr/>

[1] Archives des Affaires Etrangères de France.

[2] Mazarin to Bordeaux, August 19, 1655; in the Archives des Affaires Etrangères de France; Morland to John Pell, August 14, 1655; in Vaughan's Protectorate of Cromwell, vol. i. p. 256; Morland's History of the Evangelical Churches, pp. 613—669; Muston's Israel des Alpes, vol. ii. pp. 386, 395.

overwhelmed him with the politest attentions, placing his servants and carriages at his orders, and even sending him his own supper, with this complimentary message—" As it is too late for Mr. Downing to provide anything, I have sent him what was made ready for myself, and I will seek a supper elsewhere." The Cardinal conversed with Downing for nearly two hours. " Of all things in the world," he said, " I desire a right understanding with his Highness the Lord Protector; I will do anything in my power to evidence it; if a strict alliance be made, nothing will be too hard for us, for I look upon it as necessary to us both. As for Charles Stuart and that family, they shall be of no more consideration than the brotherhood between the Queen of France is at present. As to the Protestants in France, as I have been their friend to keep them from wrong, since I have had the management of affairs here, so if there be anything that his Highness wishes to have done on their behalf, which is consistent with the honour of France, I will do it, though for my part, I have not interposed on behalf of the Catholics in England. The accommodation now in Piedmont is by my master's intercession."[1]

Cromwell was by no means pleased to hear that matter had been thus accommodated—that the envoys of Switzerland had acted in concert with the ambassadors of France, and that the Vaudois no longer needed his assistance. He received the news of the pacification without pleasure, and his councillors more than once intimated to M. de Boreeaux that the Protector was fully aware of the reasons which had caused this eagerness to terminate, without his co-operation, an affair in which he had taken such deep interest.[2] But it was impossible for him to complain. Other intelligence now reached Cromwell, of more serious importance to himself, and which rendered Mazarin's friendship more valuable to him than he had hitherto considered it.

At the beginning of July, 1655, nothing further was known in London regarding Penn's squadron, than that it had arrived at Barbadoes, and sailed thence to the unknown place of its destination. Various rumours had been current about it, both in England and on the Continent: sometimes it was said to have attacked the French colonies, sometimes to have taken St. Domingo or Havanna:

[1] Downing to Thurloe, November 25, 1655; Thurloe's State Papers, vol. iii. p. 734.

[2] Bordeaux to Brienne, September 16, October 7, 1655, in the Archives des Affaires Etrangeres de France; Morland to Pell, August and September, 1655 and Thurloe to Pell and Morland, September 10 and 16, 1655, in Vaughan's Protectorate of Cromwell, vol. i. pp. 258, 264, 265, 268, 272.

the greatest anxiety was felt regarding it, but the utmost uncertainty still prevailed as to its movements. Towards the end of
July, an express messenger, coming by way of Ireland, brought a
letter to the Protector, with whom Stoupe happened to be at the
time. Cromwell read the letter, and immediately dismissed Stoupe,
who went away with the conviction that he had received some bad
news. He learned during the evening that his conjecture was well
founded, and sent immediate information of it to his correspondent
at Brussels; and the Spanish government learned by this means
that the English expedition had disembarked at St. Domingo, and
attempted to gain possession of the island, but that it had completely failed.[1]

When the expedition, towards the end of January, 1655,
arrived at Barbadoes, an unfortunate misunderstanding had already
arisen between the two commanders, the admiral and the general.
Penn was a brave and experienced seaman, but very punctilious
and easily offended; Venables, who had never held a chief command
before, was jealous of his authority, uneasy about his responsibility,
and but little loved by his men, who considered him indolent and
avaricious. The recruits which the army obtained in the West
Indies consisted chiefly of bankrupt colonists, broken Cavaliers,
and foreign adventurers; an undisciplined mob, who were more
intent on pushing their own fortune than on achieving success in
their enterprise, or maintaining the honour of their flag. The
provisions which the fleet was to take on board at Barbadoes had
not arrived on the 31st of March, when she was obliged to set sail.
In obedience to Cromwell's orders, the commanders had waited
until they reached the West Indies before they opened the instructions which informed them of the precise object of their
expedition. On the 14th of April, the squadron, with nearly nine
thousand troops on board, appeared in sight off the south-east
coast of St. Domingo. A council was held on board to arrange the
plan of attack: it appeared that, by landing all their forces at the
same point, near the town of St. Domingo, and falling unexpectedly
upon it, they could hardly fail to gain possession of it; but the
admiral, the general, and Commissary Winslow, who was associated
with them in the conduct of the expedition, could not come to an
agreement on this point. The troops were divided into two bodies:
a small detachment, under Colonel Buller, disembarked near the
town; the main body, under General Venables, landed at a

[1] Thurloe's State Papers, vol. iii. pp. 417, 434, 623, 636, 662; Vaughan's
Protectorate of Cromwell, vol. i. pp. 219, 229; Burnet's History of His Own
Time, vol. i. p. 139.

distance of more than twelve leagues; and it was hoped by this means to distract the attention and divide the force of the Spaniards. But when Venables attempted to rejoin Buller, a three days' march under a burning sun, sometimes over sandy plains, and sometimes through dense jungle, with the accompaniments of thirst, bad food, and excessive fatigue, spread ill-humour, discouragement, and dysentery among the troops. On the 18th of April, having effected a junction and set themselves in movement to attack the place, the two detachments suddenly fell into an ambuscade. The Spaniards, concealed in the ravines and thickets, kept up a deadly fire on the English, who were utterly unable to discover their invisible foes. Several officers were killed, the soldiers murmured, and refused to proceed; the hesitation became general; and, instead of advancing, it was determined to fall back on the nearest point of embarkation, and send to the fleet for provisions and reinforcements. It was not until eight days later, on the 25th of April, after blunderings which disgraced the leaders and disheartened the soldiers, that the army once more began its march to St. Domingo; but on the very next day, in passing through a narrow defile, the vanguard fell into a fresh ambuscade, and was at once thrown into disorder: in vain did a few brave men expose themselves, the cowards fell back on the cavalry, who, in their turn, fell back on the main body, at the head of which was the general's own regiment. The fugitives blocked up the pass in their haste to escape; and but for the energy of brave Major-General Heane, who was killed, with his best officers, in a desperate but glorious attempt to cover this disgraceful retreat, the Spaniards would have destroyed the entire English army. They retreated on this occasion to their most distant landing-place; and there, deliberations and communications were renewed between the army and fleet. Penn made no attempt to conceal his contemptuous censure: Venables, to clear himself from blame, cashiered Adjutant-General Jackson for misconduct, and hanged some of the fugitives: Commissary Winslow fell ill and died. Amid this general disorder, it was unanimously agreed that it would be useless to attempt a third attack on St. Domingo. What was to be done after such a defeat? and how could they consent to do nothing after such great preparations? How could they return to England, and face the Protector, without having at least some victory to allege in their own vindication? The idea occurred to some one of them to seek another conquest in those seas. On the 3rd of May, the fleet, having taken the troops on board once more, sailed from St. Domingo; on the 9th, it appeared before Jamaica, an island far less known and less important than the other, but yet of great extent and fertility. On the following day, a landing was effected, the town was taken, and the Spanish population, who were far from numerous, fled to the mountains. Having thus made a conquest, a portion of the English army was left to garrison the island: twelve ships, under the command of Vice-Admiral Goodson, were stationed along the coast; and towards the end of June, within a few days of each other, Penn and Venables returned to England, where they arrived, the former on the 31st of August, and the latter on the 9th of September, preceded by long apologies for their failure, and very uneasy as to the reception they would meet with from the Protector.[1]

Cromwell sent them both to the Tower for having returned home without orders, and announced his intention to institute a strict examination into their conduct, and, if necessary, to bring them to trial. The failure of their enterprise was a bitter disappointment to him, for he now found himself involved in war with Spain, and had commenced it with a defeat, instead of the brilliant success he had anticipated. He felt it keenly. His enemies took no pains to dissemble their joy: most of his advisers declared at once that they had always disapproved of the expedition; and the examination of Penn and Venables before the Council of State, made it evident that the leaders, whom Cromwell had chosen, were unfit for their post, and that the equipment and supply of the fleet, which he had intrusted to his brother-in-law, Desborough, had not been carefully attended to. Whenever additional details on the subject reached him, Cromwell shut himself up in a room by himself to read them, and could hardly be induced to speak on the matter even to his most trusted friends. His health even seemed to suffer in consequence. "This want of success," wrote Bordeaux to Brienne, on the 21st of October, 1655, "is the principal cause of the Protector's indisposition, if the physician who formerly gave me faithful accounts of his illnesses, is now equally sincere; he assures me that instead of the rumour being true, that he is afflicted by the stone, it is only a bilious colic, which occasionally flies to the brain; and that grief often persecutes him more than either of these, as his mind is not yet accustomed to endure disgrace."[2] But neither this internal agitation, nor his threats of

[1] Thurloe's State Papers, vol. iii. pp. 249—252, 411, 504–508, 509, 545, 646, 689, 755; Memorials of Sir William Penn, vol. ii. pp. 80—132; Harleian Tracts, vol. iii. pp. 510—523; Godwin's History of the Commonwealth, vol. iv. pp. 189—203.

[2] Archives des Affaires Etrangères de France.

severe punishment of the leaders of the expedition, were of long duration; Cromwell was quick in recovering from painful impressions, always ready to look on the bright side of events, and kindly towards his servants. The disastrous narratives that had come from the army and fleet were suppressed; and great stress was laid on the importance of Jamaica, the third of the West Indian isles. Measures were immediately taken for turning its fertility to advantage, and regulating its government. It was even proposed that Lambert should be sent thither as governor; but this proposition was doubtless made rather with a view to enhance the value of the conquest, than with any expectation that he would accept it. Disappointment at the past gave way to cares for the future. Preparations were commenced, in the various ports, for fitting out another expedition to the West Indies; and after a few weeks of detention and examination, Penn and Venables were liberated from the Tower, disgraced, but not prosecuted.[1]

Spain and France, Cardenas and Bordeaux, helped Cromwell to forget his disappointment in the pressure of business. In announcing to his Court the failure of the expedition against St. Domingo, Cardenas denounced the Protector in the harshest terms, characterising his action as one "of infamous malignity and abominable perfidy;" but at the same time, feeling, doubtless, desirous to remain as ambassador in London, he endeavoured to prevent the two nations from coming to open war, and even to renew negotiations of alliance between France and England; "for," he said, "it would be a great advantage to your Majesty that these differences should be accommodated at the outset, and that the Protector should abandon his evil designs."[2] Bordeaux, on his side, hastened to state to the Commissioners, with whom he was negotiating, that "the King, his master, still entertained the same sentiments, and that, if the Protector would make overtures to him, he would meet with every readiness to come to terms."[3] The Court of Madrid acted more worthily than its ambassador: on learning what had occurred at St. Domingo, it conferred the title of marquis and a pension of five thousand ducats on the governor of the island; laid a general embargo on the ships and property of the

[1] On the 25th of October, 1655. Thurloe's State Papers, vol. iv. pp. 1, 6, 21, 22, 28, 38, 177; Memorials of Sir William Penn, vol. ii. pp. 134—142; Don Alonzo de Cardeñas to King Philip IV., December 30, 1655, in the Archives of Simancas.
[2] Cardeñas to King Philip IV., August 12, September 6, and October 4, 1655; in the Archives of Simancas.
[3] Bordeaux to Brienne, September 30, 1655; in the Archives des Affaires Etrangères de France.

English merchants in Spain; threw several of them into prison;
and sent orders to Cardenas to demand an audience to take leave,
and to quit London immediately.[1] Mazarin and Brienne were a
little less hasty than Bordeaux, and seemed inclined to think that,
after the defeat which Cromwell had just experienced, they would
be able to treat with him on better terms.[2] But Cromwell easily
discerned, in spite of these marks of hostility and their indisposition
to make advances, that the Court of Spain feared him, and the
Court of France needed his alliance; he was haughty in his demeanour towards Bordeaux, and rough to Cardenas. " I have just
been informed," wrote Bordeaux to Brienne, on the 30th of
September, 1655, " that the Council considered that they would be
acting meanly if, after the disgrace they have suffered in the Indies,
they were to come to me to propose a peace; and that, now there
no longer remains any obstacle to our treaty, it was for me to propose its signature if my orders continued unchanged."[3] Bordeaux
demanded that the treaty should be signed; and as soon as Cromwell knew that he was fully determined to do so, he sent Cardenas
his passports, with orders to leave England within four days, and
placed a frigate at his disposal for his conveyance home.[4] Cardenas
embarked at Dover on the 24th of October, 1655, and on the same
day the treaty of peace and commerce between France and England
was finally signed. " Our conference," wrote Bordeaux to Brienne,
on the following day, " ended in the expression of mutual wishes
that the treaty might for ever re-establish true friendship between
the two nations. If it have lost its gracefulness by its long postponement, it would seem that the rupture with Spain is likely to
lend it new charms."[5] On the 28th of November following, the
treaty with France and the declaration of war against Spain were
solemnly proclaimed in the streets of London.[6] About six weeks
afterwards Bordeaux took leave of the Protector, as he was about to
spend a few months in Paris;[7] and on the 30th of December, 1655,
Cromwell completed the official connection between the two States.

1 Instructions to Cardeñas, September 1655; in the Archives of Simancas;
Thurloe's State Papers, vol. iv. pp. 19, 21, 24, 45.
2 Brienne to Mazarin, October 7, 1655; in the Archives des Affaires
Etrangères de France.
3 Archives des Affaires Etrangères de France.
4 Cardeñas to King Philip IV., Dover, November 8, 1653; in the Archives
of Simancas.
5 Bordeaux to Brienne, November 4, 1655; in the Archives des Affaires
Etrangères de France.
6 Cromwelliana, p. 154; Thurloe's State Papers, vol. iv. p. 215.
7 Thurloe's State Papers, vol. iv. p. 146.

He appointed his nephew, Sir William Lockhart, to be his ambassador at the Court of Louis XIV. A few months later, in order
to remove every pretext of distrust, by the faithful execution of the
treaty, Barrière, the agent of the Prince of Condé, was requested to
leave England, and he was refused the use of a frigate, which he
had demanded, in order to surround his departure with some éclat.[1]

As soon as it became known that the rupture between Cromwell
and the Court of Madrid was complete, all the enemies of the Protector, both royalists and republicans, in England and on the Continent, set themselves in movement to take advantage of the
chances offered them by this new posture of affairs. Ever since his
return to Cologne, after the failure of the insurrection fomented
and abandoned by his favourite Rochester, Charles II. had resided
there in poverty, idleness, and despondency, incessantly seeking
assistance from all the sovereigns of Europe, and even from the
Pope himself; recklessly pledging his faith and future power in
public to the Protestants, and in secret to the Catholics, as his
necessities dictated, and licentiously devoting himself to his pleasures and his mistresses, from whose arms his honest advisers,
Hyde and Ormonde, had great difficulty in tearing him once a week,
in order to induce him to attend to his affairs. His interest in
them revived in some degree when he began to hope that Spain,
having quarrelled with Cromwell, might at length lend him some
assistance. At the suggestion of some of his partisans he proceeded, without retinue, to Brussels, to confer on this subject with
the Archduke Leopold and the Count de Fuensaldagna, who had
not yet resigned the government of the Spanish Netherlands to
Don John of Austria and the Marquis de Carracena. At the same
time there also arrived in Flanders a man who was, perhaps, Cromwell's most inveterate enemy—Colonel Sexby, a stern, morose, and
indefatigable republican, who, for the last year, had been travelling
incessantly between London and Brussels, Brussels and Madrid,
Madrid and Paris, offering his services wherever he went to get rid
of the Protector, and seeking accomplices for conspiracy, insurrection, war, and assassination in all directions. He had been one of
the first to inform the Spanish government of the English expedition against St. Domingo, and this had gained him a little money
and credit at Madrid. He now came from London, whither he had
gone to continue the preparations of his eternal plot, escaping all
the researches of Cromwell's police, who had seized a portion of his
money, but had been unable to capture his person. Don Alonzo de

---

[1] Thurloe's State Papers, vol. iv. p. 757.

Cardenas, who had been residing at Brussels since the termination of his embassy, and who believed that the republicans were much stronger in England than the royalists, knew Sexby, and was fully cognizant of his intrigues.   Charles II. was urged to see him ; his gravest counsellors, who had by this time rejoined him, were of this opinion also ; and the two exiles had a meeting at Bruges, where they conversed long and anxiously about their affairs.   Agreeing, at least in appearance, as to their object, they differed greatly as to the means to be pursued for attaining it.   Sexby required that the king should keep silence, refrain from putting himself forward, and rest satisfied with giving secret assistance to the conspirators, who would undertake to get up an insurrection in England, to possess themselves of a port, and then, if necessary, to open an entrance into the country to an army of royalists and Spaniards.   Charles and counsellors had but little faith in Sexby's promises, and little inclination to trust the royal fortune to republicans.   But among exiles and conspirators common necessities and animosities remove all objections and screen all falsehoods.   The King and the Leveller fraternised and acted in concert, both at Brussels and Madrid, in order to obtain effectual support from Spain, and in England, in order to arrange a great rebellion.[1]

The Court of Spain accepted these allies, but with hesitation and reluctance ; it had decided upon war against Cromwell, at the last extremity, and with unfeigned regret ; it had no wish to engage irretrievably and desperately in hostilities with the Commonwealth   It was in want of money, even to commence operations.   Its ministers in the Netherlands would not permit Charles II. to fix his residence either at Brussels or Antwerp ; they wished him to return to Cologne, and he had great difficulty in obtaining leave to reside, with a small retinue, at Bruges.   At every step in the negotiation, it was necessary to await orders from Madrid ; and from Madrid the constant order was to avoid precipitation and publicity . they promised to support Charles, but not to avow his cause openly   Like Sexby, the Spaniards requested him to remain in the background, and to commend them to his friends, without committing to them his standard.   Charles, on the contrary. was convinced that, for the achievement of success, as well as for the maintenance of his own dignity, the declared friendship and public

1 Clarendon's History of the Rebellion, vol. vii. pp. 182—186, 237, 278 279 ; Clarendon's State Papers, vol. iii. pp. 159, 170, 180: Thurloe's State Papers, vol. v. pp. 97, 100, 169, 178, 319, 349 ; vol. vi. pp. 829–833 ; vol. vii. p. 325 ; Carte's Ormonde Letters, vol. ii. pp. 85—103 ; Cardeñas to Philip IV., December 28, 1655, in the Archives of Simancas.

demonstration of the Court of Spain were indispensable ; the royalists of England will not move, he said, unless they find themselves strongly supported ; but they would rise all over the country, by land and by sea, if the King of Spain were to proclaim himself the friend and ally of their King. After many protracted conferences, and much lengthy correspondence, and notwithstanding the opposition of the Council of State at Madrid, a treaty of alliance was finally concluded, on the 12th of April, 1656, between the two kings ; Philip IV. promised Charles II. a body of six thousand men, and an annual pension of ten thousand guineas for himself and his younger brother, the Duke of Gloucester, who was living with him, on condition that, on his side, Charles should raise among his subjects four regiments, of which the colonels were immediately appointed ; that he should summon beneath his standard the Irish who had enlisted in the service of France ; and that, with these united forces, he should effect a landing in England, as soon as such an enterprise could be attempted with any chance of success.[1]

Although these mutual promises were executed, on both sides, with great incompleteness and delay, Cromwell and Mazarin were alarmed. It was a serious matter for Cromwell, that one of the great sovereigns of the Continent, who had recently been so indifferent to the cause of Charles II., should have now become his declared and active ally. What would it serve the Protector that he had drained Ireland of royalist soldiers, if they were soon to be assembled again in Flanders, under the banners of the exiled King? With the help of Spain, their embarkation was possible ; and if an invasion were effected from without, an insurrection would assuredly take place within the country. Mazarin, on his side, was desirous to retain the Irish regiments in the service of France, and was greatly displeased to find them ready to disband, and even to march in a body into the Spanish Netherlands, at the call of their King. An expedient occurred to the minds of these two crafty politicians, which might deliver them, in part at least, from their anxieties. The brother of Charles II., the Duke of York, had been serving, for four years, in the French army ; he had earned great distinction by his bravery and military strictness ; and he was regarded with esteem by Turenne, who lost no opportunity of expressing his high opinion of him. In pursuance of the treaty of the 24th of October preceding, that Prince was to be sent

---

[1] Clarendon's History of the Rebellion, vol. vii. pp. 184—186 ; Cardeñas to Philip IV., March 25, July 29, 1656 ; the Archduke Leopold to Philip IV., April 8, 1656 ; Deliberations of the Spanish Council of State, May 7, September 19, and December 16, 1656, in the Archives of Simancas.

out of France; but, on the contrary, why should he not be allowed
to remain there? He strongly desired to remain, and the Queen-
mother desired it still more; he would thus be kept separate from
his brother and from Spain: perhaps, in imitation of his example,
and by means of his influence, the Irish regiments would remain
in the service of Louis XIV. Mazarin sounded Cromwell on this
subject, and he gladly fell in with the idea: it suited them both
thoroughly, both in substance and in appearance. Mazarin, by
treating with kindness one of those proscribed princes whom he had
recently been constrained to abandon, gave pleasure to both his King
and Queen, did a secret service to Cromwell, and kept in his hand
an instrument which might one day be useful. Cromwell proved
his generosity by consenting to the plan, and at the same time
divided the forces of his enemies. But in order to obtain success
in this scheme, it was necessary to create some dispute between the
two brothers, which would prevent them from combining and acting
together: an intrigue managed by the skilful hands of Mazarin,
temporarily produced this result. In consequence of certain pretensions and domestic dispute which arose between the servants of
the two Princes, the Duke of York, who, in obedience to the orders
of Charles II., had gone to join him at Bruges, escaped one day
from Flanders, and passed into Holland, in order to return into
France through Germany. It was believed that the two brothers
had quarrelled irreconcilably; and on the 26th of December, 1656,
Cromwell wrote to Mazarin: "I must return your Eminency
thanks for your judicious management of our weightiest affair; an
affair wherein your Eminency is concerned, though not in equal
degree and measure with myself. I must confess that I did fear
that the Duke had condescended to his brother. But if I am not
mistaken in his character, as I received it from your Eminency,
that fire which is kindled between them will not ask bellows to blow
it and keep it burning. . . . The obligations and many
instances of affection which I have received from your Eminency,
do engage me to make returns suitable and commensurate to your
merits; but although I have this set home upon my spirit, yet I
may not (shall I tell you I cannot?), at this juncture of time, and
as the face of my affairs now stands, answer to your call for toleration. I believe, however, that under my government, your Eminency, in behalf of the Catholics, has less reason for complaint as
to rigour upon men's consciences, than under the Parliament.
Truly, I have plucked many out of the fire—the raging fire of persecution, which did tyrannise over their consciences, and encroached
by an arbitrariness of power upon their estates. And herein it is

my purpose, as soon as I can remove impediments, and some weights that press me down, to make a farther progress, and discharge my promise to your Excellency; but I cannot now give a public declaration of my sense in that point." [1]

Mazarin would have been glad if, in return for his good offices, Cromwell had not compelled him to receive his ambassador Lockhart in Paris. He was at every moment beside him, a troublesome witness of his tergiversations, his double manœuvres, and his coquettings with the enemies of the Protector. As he was less powerful at Court than in the Council, he was afraid that in that gay scene there might be scandal spoken, insults offered, thoughtless or premeditated impertinences committed, perhaps even attacks made, of which the ambassador of the regicide usurper would be the subject and victim. Bordeaux, on his return to London, in April, 1656, had orders to use all his efforts to prevent Lockhart's departure; but it was in vain; and when, after insinuations which no one would understand, he ventured to speak to Thurloe of the inconveniences which might attend such an embassy, "the secretary," he says, "after giving me very patient attention, told me that its sole object was a desire to confirm to his Majesty the sentiments which the Protector had expressed to me here; that propriety would not permit them to alter a resolution which had once been adopted; and that, as joy had been felt on my return here, so Colonel Lockhart would doubtless find a similar feeling in Paris." Mazarin resigned himself to his fate, but not, as he usually did, with courtesy and compliments. Lockhart, who arrived in Paris at the beginning of May, met at first with a cool, and sometimes even disagreeable reception; but he was as adroit as he was high-spirited, and he spoke in the name of a powerful master of whom the Cardinal had need. He quickly surmounted the difficulties of his position, and became the object of Mazarin's caresses, who was too able a statesman not to feel how important it was to secure the good will of a man of such capacity, and so much influence with the Protector. It is part of the consummate art of great politicians to treat matters simply and frankly when they know they are in presence of rivals who will allow themselves to be neither intimidated nor deceived. Mazarin possessed this art, and Cromwell almost always reduced him to this necessity. There was, between these two men, a constant interchange of concessions and resistances,

[1] Thurloe's State Papers, vol. v. pp. 735, 736; Memoirs of James II., vol. i. p. 379; Clarendon's State Papers, vol. iii. p. 318; Bordeaux to Mazarin, April 10, 1656; Mazarin to Bordeaux, April 26, 1656; in the Archives des Affaires Étrangères de France.

services and refusals, in which they ran little risk of quarrelling, for they mutually understood each other, and did not require from one another anything which could not be granted, without doing them greater injury than the grant would have done them service.   The Protector would have been glad for the Cardinal to have furnished him with money for the vigorous execution of his enterprises against Spain in America; but Mazarin, who could see no advantage to France or himself in such a course, formally declined all proposals of this nature; and Cromwell was not offended.   Mazarin, who, in reality, was desirous to arrive at peace with Spain as well as with England, and who was already preparing the way for the Treaty of the Pyrenees, sent M. de Lionne to Madrid, in June, 1656, to open negotiations; and Cromwell, who had just been treating with France as to the basis of their common war against Spain, was somewhat suspicious of this proceeding; but Mazarin clearly explained to Lockhart the motives which had led to this mission, and the circumstances which rendered it almost impossible for peace to ensue from it.   Lockhart saw his meaning, and communicated it to Cromwell; M. de Lionne returned from his embassy without having accomplished any result; and far from having been shaken by this temporary distrust, the union between the Cardinal and the Protector was strengthened and confirmed.   They both judged wisely of their mutual necessities and powers, and maintained, with somewhat suspicious independence, the policy which they had adopted in common.[1]

Cromwell, by that policy, had achieved greatness in Europe, and his greatness was not contested on the Continent as it was in England, for it rested, abroad, on skilful and successful power, unstained by crime or tyranny.   If he had not always scrupulously respected the law of nations, he had at least done nothing to reveal a limitless and unbridled ambition; though raised to power by a revolution, he had not sought to revolutionise even those States with which he was on hostile terms; he had been by turns peaceful and warlike, and more frequently peaceful than warlike; with the exception of the defeat at St. Domingo, and that had led to a useful conquest, he had succeeded in all his undertakings. He was bound by sincere friendship to all the Protestant States, in active alliance with the most powerful of Catholic sovereigns— everywhere present, influential, respected, and feared.   External

[1] Bordeaux to Brienne, May 1—29, 1656; the same to the same, April 10, 1656; Bordeaux to Mazarin, April 10, 1656; Mazarin to Bordeaux, April 26, 1656, in the Archives des Affaires Etrangères de France; Thurloe's State Papers, vol. iv. pp. 739, 759, 771, vol. v. pp. 8, 32, 36, 131, 210, 217, 317, 318, 319, 368; Dumont's Histoire des Traités de Paix, vol. i. p. 606.

testimonies of the respect which his name and powers inspired, reached him from all parts; independently of the foreign ministers who habitually resided at his Court, ambassadors extraordinary were sent from Sweden, Poland, Germany, and Italy, solemnly to present him with the homage or overtures of their masters. Medals, sometimes of quaintly coarse design, were struck in Holland, to celebrate his glory, and humble kings before him. An equestrian portrait of him was displayed in the streets of Paris, accompanied by some disrespectful verses regarding the princes of the Continent.[1] The Grand Duke of Tuscany sent to request his portrait for the picture-gallery of his palace at Florence;[2] and the Venetian ambassador, Giovanni Sagredo, who had come to London from Paris, thus wrote on the 6th of October, 1656, in the peculiar style of his age and country: " I am now in England: the aspect of this country is very different from that of France; here we do not see ladies going to court, but gentlemen courting the chase; not elegant cavaliers, but cavalry and infantry; instead of music and ballets, they have trumpets and drums; they do not speak of love, but of Mars; they have no comedies, but tragedies; no patches on their faces, but muskets on their shoulders; they do not neglect sleep for the sake of amusement, but severe ministers keep their adversaries in incessant wakefulness. In a word, everything here is full of disdain, suspicion, and rough menacing faces. . . King Charles was too good for such bad times. Cromwell has expelled the Parliament; he speaks, and he alone; he has the authority of a king, though he has not the name. His title is that of Protector, but he is destroying the nobility. Such a number of troops secure his power, but they ruin and overburden the country. All pay is for the soldiers. The machine is strong, but I do not think it durable; it works too violently."[3]

Cromwell himself, in the midst of his power and glory, felt that his position was not secure, and longed to change it; for more than eighteen months he had governed alone and arbitrarily; his strong good sense warned him that absolute power soon wears itself out; and that, even though blessed with good fortune, no man can long govern in isolation and without supporters. The war with Spain had already involved him, and threatened to involve him still more deeply, in expenses which he would be unable to meet without fresh taxes. He perceived the necessity of his position; and he believed that, after so many successes, the day had come for establishing a legal and durable order of things: he convoked another Parliament.

[1] Thurloe's State Papers, vol. iii. pp. 502, 540.
[2] Dixon's Life of Blake, p. 294.
[3] Lettere Inedite di Messer Giovanni Sagredo, p. 29 (Venice, 1839).

BOOK VIII.

PROGNOSTICS OF A NEW PARLIAMENT—VANE'S PAMPHLET—THE ELECTIONS—
CROMWELL'S SPEECH AT THE OPENING OF THE SESSION—EXCLUSION OF
NEARLY A HUNDRED MEMBERS—SUCCESS OF THE ENGLISH FLEET OFF
CADIZ—THOROUGH ADHERENCE OF THE PARLIAMENT TO CROMWELL—
PROPOSITIONS AND INTRIGUES TO MAKE CROMWELL KING—THE HUMBLE
PETITION AND ADVICE—FAILURE OF THE ATTEMPT — NEW CONSTITUTION
OF THE PROTECTORATE—CLOSE OF THE SESSION—MANŒUVRES OF CROM-
WELL—DEATH OF BLAKE — SECOND SESSION OF THE PARLIAMENT IN
TWO HOUSES—QUARREL BETWEEN THE TWO HOUSES—CROMWELL DIS-
SOLVES THE PARLIAMENT—AGITATION OF PARTIES—ROYALIST AND REPUB-
LICAN PLOTS—CROMWELL'S ACTIVE ALLIANCE WITH FRANCE—HIS SUCCESSES
ON THE CONTINENT—CAPTURE OF MARDYKE AND DUNKIRK—EMBASSY OF
LORD FAULCONBRIDGE TO PARIS, AND OF THE DUKE DE CREQUI TO LONDON
—CROMWELL CONTEMPLATES THE CONVOCATION OF A NEW PARLIAMENT—
DECLINE OF HIS HEALTH—HIS FAMILY—HIS MOTHER, WIFE, AND CHILDEN—
DEATH OF HIS DAUGHTER, LADY CLAYPOLE—ILLNESS OF CROMWELL—STATE
OF HIS MIND—HIS DEATH—CONCLUSION.

SOME months before adopting this resolution, either from premeditation or instinct, Cromwell had done an act which revealed his
intention to call upon the country to support his power. On the
14th of March, 1656, he published a proclamation ordaining a
general fast and public prayers throughout England, for the purpose
of invoking a blessing from on high on his government, and beseeching " the Lord to discover the Achan, who had so long obstructed
the settlement of these distracted kingdoms."[1] Such ceremonies
were then so frequent that they often passed unnoticed, as simple
manifestations of ordinary and official piety. But the most eminent
of the republican leaders, Sir Harry Vane, did not mistake the
meaning of the present solemnity. Ever since the establishment

---

[1] Forster's Statesmen of the Commonwealth, vol. iii. p. 161; Godwin's
History of the Commonwealth, vol. iv. p. 260.

of the Protectorate, he had lived in retirement at his favourite residence, Belleau, in Lincolnshire; a stranger, in appearance at least, to the intrigues of his party, and to all active opposition. When, however, he saw the Protector addressing himself to the people, and announcing, though remotely, his intention to solicit their aid, he resolved to enter the field once more; and in April or May, 1656, he published a pamphlet entitled, " A Healing Question, propounded and resolved, upon occasion of the late public and seasonable call to humiliation, in order to love and union amongst the honest party; and with a desire to apply balsam to the wound, before it become incurable."

It was a brief, firm, and clear exposition of the essential principles of republican government, as they were understood by Vane and his friends: the complete and absolute sovereignty of the people, as the sole source of all power; a Parliament consisting of one single assembly, as the only representative of the people, and alone in possession of the government; liberty of conscience, a sacred right, laid down as a fundamental maxim, without, however, explicitly including, or formally excluding, the Catholics or Episcopalians; the exclusive reservation of political rights, for an indeterminate time, to the partisans of the good cause, that is, of the revolution; the appointment of a Council of State for life, under the control and by the choice of the Parliament; and, perhaps, if circumstances required, the investiture of a single man with the executive power :—such was the plan of conciliation proposed by Vane to England and to the Protector. To obtain its acceptance by those whose co-operation was evidently indispensable to him, he spoke of the army in flattering terms, saying, " it was in the hands of an honest and wise general, and sober faithful officers ; and he exhorted the soldiers to embody with the rest of the party of honest men, and espouse the same cause, acting in their primitive simplicity, humility, and trust." But beside these hypocritical compliments, were bitter words regarding the danger incurred by public liberties, when their " fair branches are planted on the root of a private and selfish interest; whence sprung the evil of that government which rose in and with the Norman conquest." The whole pamphlet was a singular compound of lofty sentiments and narrow ideas, patriotic sincerity, and blind attachment to unpractical and factious opinions. Vane proposed to establish a government in England, by excluding from it all those great powers, whether ancient or modern, vanquished or victorious, which had ever exercised powerful sway over English society. He outlawed the royalist as well as Charles Stuart himself; and he called upon

Cromwell and his officers either to join the republican clique whom they had formerly expelled, or to abdicate.[1]

There was nothing in this to give Cromwell any new information as to the feelings of his enemies, or to turn him aside from his own firm purpose. The assembling of a Parliament was resolved upon; the writs, issued on the 10th of July, 1656, appointed the elections to take place in August, and fixed the opening of Parliament for the 17th of September following. Great agitation immediately spread throughout England; parties were held in strong restraint, but they were living and ready to start into activity as soon as the slightest movement was allowed them. Vane's pamphlet, though written with no great vigour or brilliancy, was eagerly read. "Sir Harry Vane," wrote Thurloe to Henry Cromwell, on the 16th of June, 1656, "hath lately put forth a new form of government, plainly laying aside thereby that which now is. At the first coming out of it, it was applauded; but now, upon second thoughts, it is rejected as being impracticable, and aiming in truth at the setting up the Long Parliament again. But all men judge that he hath some very good hopes, that he shows so much courage. It doth certainly behove us to have a watchful eye upon that interest." A second pamphlet entitled, "England's Remembrancer, or a word in season to all Englishmen, respecting the ensuing elections," which appeared soon after, greatly increased the excitement of the public and the anxiety of the government. In a few simple and practical pages, the writer advocated the most open and earnest opposition. "It may be," he said, "that some of you tender-hearts, being troubled at what hath been done by the Lord Protector (so-called), are afraid to vote in the choice of your deputies, lest you should seem thereby to approve his power. But if a thief should stop your way to your own house for a time, and afterwards bid you go home, would any of you scruple to go home because the thief had before exercised a power to which he had no right?" And after giving the electors the most energetic advice, he thus concluded :—
"What shall I say more to you, dear Christians and countrymen? —Do not the cries of the widows and the fatherless speak?—Do not your imprisoned friends speak?—Do not your banished neighbours speak?—Do not your infringed rights speak?—Do not your invaded properties speak?—Do not your gasping liberties speak?—Do not all our ruins, at home and abroad, by land and

[1] Vane's Pamphlet, as reprinted entire in the Somers' Tracts, vol. vi. pp. 303—315, and in the Appendix to the third volume of Mr. Forster's Statesmen of the Commonwealth.

sea, speak to you?—Surely they have loud voices; surely they do daily cry in your ears, help! help! or England perishes!"[1]

This second pamphlet was also attributed to Vane, though on unsufficient evidence; but whoever may have been its author, it produced the most astonishing effect. It was distributed in all the towns, hawked through the country districts, and crowds assembled to hear it read. Cromwell felt himself once more in presence of that popular excitement which he had, during his life, so often kindled and checked; and he did not hesitate to engage at once in an ardent conflict with his enemies. When he ordered the elections, he had reckoned on the influence of his Major-generals; they held the whole country under their power; and they had at their command, in every district, obedient soldiers and devoted agents. Pressing instructions were sent to them. The distributors of pamphlets were arrested. The principal republican leaders, Bradshaw, Ludlow, Rich, and Vane himself, were ordered to appear before the Council of State; the summons addressed to Vane was couched in the rudest terms, without the slightest manifestation of politeness or respect; it simply stated, "You are to attend before the Council of State on the 12th of August next." There was evidently a determination to wage a deadly warfare, by all possible means, against the opposition.[2]

Vane, who was not fond of danger, although, from conscientious motives, he never shrank from braving it, believed that he had taken means to screen himself from any such violence. Before publishing his pamphlet, he had sent a copy of it to Fleetwood, in order to show the Protector a mark of deference which, if occasion required, he might afterwards use to his own advantage. Fleetwood returned it to him, after the lapse of a month, without any observation, and probably without having mentioned it to Cromwell, lest he might compromise himself by the proceeding. Vane then published his work; and in a postscript, without naming Fleetwood, he stated that he had taken the precaution of submitting it to a member of the Council. When he received the summons to appear before the Council, feeling almost as surprised at the act itself, as wounded by the offensive form in which it was conveyed, he replied, "It was against the laws and liberties of England that any of the people thereof should be commanded by the king (when

[1] Thurloe's State Papers, vol. v. pp. 123, 149, 176, 268, 317; Carte's Ormonde Letters, vol. ii. p. 109; Burton's Diary, vol. i. p. cxlv.

[2] Thurloe's State Papers, vol. v. pp. 272, 312, 328, 349; Forster's Statesmen of the Commonwealth, vol. iii. p. 171; Godwin's History of the Commonwealth, vol. iv. p. 272.

there was one) to attend him at his pleasure, unless they were
bound thereunto by especial services.   It will, I hope, be permitted
me, without offence, to claim the same privilege and liberty in these
times; yet I have not refused to be at my house in the Strand, and
I am still ready to appear when I shall be sent for." In the mean
while he plunged with characteristic earnestness into the electoral
struggle, and presented himself as a candidate in three different
places.[1]

The earnestness of both sides was extreme; Republicans, Anabaptists, Levellers, Presbyterians, Royalists, and Cavaliers in disguise, all united to oppose the Protector.   "No soldiers! no
courtiers! no salaried men!" was their rallying cry.   Cromwell, on
his side, spread his agents and soldiers all over the country, and set
vigorously to work himself: either personally, or by means of
Thurloe, he maintained a constant correspondence with his Major-
generals, sometimes addressing to them, in his own name, letters
which they publicly read at the electoral meetings, or put into
circulation by means of their adherents.   Both parties, as the
nature of their position and means of action allowed, made unscrupulous use of promises and threats, favours and acts of violence,
in order to insure their success.   "The rabble of the town," wrote
Major-General Kelsey to Thurloe, from Dover, on the 13th of
August, 1656, "are endeavouring to get Mr. Cony chosen, which
will be hard to prevent, if he be not secluded." And Cony probably
was secluded, for Kelsey himself was elected.   The exercise of
arbitrary power was met by outbursts of popular passion ; in several
towns, the elections took place in the midst of tumults which soon
became desperate fights ; at Westminster two men were killed and
a great many wounded ; at Brentford, the Anabaptists, in order that
their candidates might be successful, beat and drove off the magistrates who presided over the election; their adversaries rallied with
shouts of "No Anabaptists!" and the battle became so violent that
the soldiers, resuming their legitimate occupation, had great difficulty in dispersing the combatants.   "Where our honest soldiers
can appear," wrote one of the Protector's agents, on the 22nd of
August, "a reasonable good choice is made ; but the farther off
from London the worse; for even here amongst us, under our noses,
the ill-affected are so bold and ungrateful as at the elections to cry
out . 'No soldiers! no courtiers!'" In order to throw discredit
on the coalition between the Republicans and Cavaliers, and to

---

[1] Thurloe's State Papers, vol. v. p. 323 ; Forster's Statesmen of the Commonwealth, vol. iii. pp. 170, 380.

rekindle revolutionary passions to their disadvantage, Cromwell published the most injurious reports with regard to the exiled Stuarts. "Charles," it was said, "is a sickly, idle, spiritless prince, and his brother, the Duke of York, is a Papist." More than this: one of the mistresses of Charles II., Lucy Waters, the mother of the child who afterwards became the Duke of Monmouth, had come to England, where she had been arrested and imprisoned in the Tower. Cromwell ordered that she should be released, and published her history, together with the text of a warrant for a pension of five thousand livres which Charles had conferred upon her; and the Protector's newspapers thus commented upon the incident: "By this, those that hanker after him may see they are furnished already with an heir apparent, and what a pious, charitable prince they have for their master, and how well he disposeth of the collections and contributions which they make for him here, towards the maintenance of his concubines and royal issue."[1]

The success obtained by the Protector was not commensurate with his efforts; his major-generals and principal adherents were elected. Among the republican leaders, Vane and Bradshaw were defeated; Ludlow and Hutchinson kept aloof from the contest, and the Government secured a majority; but upwards of a hundred declared enemies, and among them some of their most uncompromising opponents, Haslerig, Scott, Bond, and Robinson, had succeeded in getting elected; and when the struggle was over, one of the most sanguine of the Major-generals, Goffe, wrote to Thurloe, on the 29th of August, "Concerning the elections, I hope it may be said that, though they be not so good as we could have wished them, yet they are not so bad as our enemies would have had them."[2]

Some days after this result had been ascertained, on the 21st of August, 1656, Vane appeared before the Council, boldly admitted having written his pamphlet, and gave Cromwell another paper, in which he reiterated his advice and protests. When called upon to pledge himself, under pain of imprisonment, to do nothing to the prejudice of the existing government, he formally refused to do so. "I can do nothing," he said, "which may blemish or bring in question my innocence, or the goodness of the cause for which I suffer. I cannot but observe, however, how exactly you tread in

Thurloe's State Papers, vol. v. pp. 299, 302, 303, 304, 308, 312, 313, 337, 341, 349, 352, 356, 370; Heath's Chronicle, p. 701; Bates's Elenchus Motuum Kuperorum, part ii. p. 375; Cromwelliana, p. 157; Whitelocke, p. 649.
[2] Thurloe's State Papers, vol. v. pp. 311, 365, 299, 313, 296, 349; Old Parliamentary History, vol. xxi. pp. 3—23.

the steps of the late King, whose design being to render the monarchy absolute, thought he could employ no better means to effect it, than by casting into obloquy and disgrace all those who desired to preserve the laws and liberties of the nation. It is with no small grief to be lamented, that the evil and wretched principles by which the late King aimed to work out his design, should now revive and spring up under the hands of men professing godliness." Cromwell allowed fourteen days to elapse before he carried out the threat which had been employed to coerce Vane ; he disliked severities after victory as being more irritating than necessary ; and he left Bradshaw and Ludlow undisturbed, although they had resisted him with equal firmness. On the 9th of September, however, Vane was arrested, and committed to Carisbrook Castle, in the Isle of Wight, the very prison in which Charles I. had been confined by the Long Parliament ; and the governor was ordered not to suffer him to speak to any one, except in the presence of an officer. Colonel Rich and General Harrison, who had also refused to give any pledge, were incarcerated, the former at Windsor, and the latter in Pendennis Castle, in Cornwall; twelve royalists, well known for their active zeal, were sent to the Tower ; and on the 17th of September, after having struck these blows to show that he felt sure of victory, Cromwell opened the Parliament.[1]

He began the session with a speech of more than three hours in length : the longest, as well as the most violent and embarrassed, he had yet delivered. He was under difficulty both as to the topics which he wished to discuss, and those which he wished to pass over in silence. Two motives had made him resolve on assembling a Parliament,—the necessity of having money to carry on the war against Spain, and the hope of making himself king : it was distasteful to him to proclaim his necessity, and he took care not to give the slightest intimation of his hope. He enumerated, with his usual revolutionary bluntness, the dangers which threatened England : " You are at war with Spain. We put you into this hostility upon the ground of necessity ; and the ground of necessity, for justifying men's actions, is above all considerations of instituted law. 　. 　The Spaniard is your enemy, naturally and providentially, by reason of that enmity that is in him against whatsoever is of God. . . . You could not get an honest or honourable peace from him. . . . We desired but such liberty for our traders as that they might keep their Bibles in their pockets, to

<hr />

[1] Thurloe's State Papers, vol. v. pp. 349, 407, 430; Ludlow's Memoirs, p. 211; Godwin's History of the Commonwealth, vol. iv. pp. 275—277 Forster's Statesmen of the Commonwealth, vol. v. pp. 325, 326.

exercise their liberty of religion for themselves, and not be under restraint. But there is no liberty of conscience to be had from the Spaniard. . . . The French, and all the Protestants in Germany, have also agreed that his design was the empire of the whole Christian world, if not more ; and upon that ground, he looks at this nation as his greatest obstacle. . . . If you make any peace with any State that is Popish, and subject to the rule of Rome, you are bound, and they are loose. We have not now to do with any Popish State, except France ; and it is certain they do not think themselves under such a tie to the Pope ; but think themselves at liberty to perform honesties with nations, in agreement with them, and are able to give us an explicit answer to anything reasonably demanded of them. . . .

" Spain is the root of the matter ; that is the party that brings all your enemies before you ;—for Spain hath now espoused that interest which you have all along hitherto been conflicting with,— Charles Stuart's interest . . . with whom he is fully in agreement ; for whom he hath raised seven or eight thousand men, and has them now quartered at Bruges ; to which number, Don John of Austria has promised that, as soon as the campaign is ended, which, it is conceived, will be in about five or six weeks, he shall have four or five thousand added ! . . . And truly Spain hath an interest in your bowels ; for the Papists in England have been accounted, ever since I was born, Spaniolised. They never regarded France ;—Spain was their patron. . . . Can we think that Papists and Cavaliers shake not hands in England ? It is unworthy, un-Christian, and un-English, you say : yes ; but it doth serve to let you see your danger, and the source thereof. . . .

" There is a generation of men in this nation who cry up nothing but righteousness, and justice, and liberty,—and these are diversified into several sects ; and they are known to shake hands with all the scum and dirt of this nation. This levelling party hath some accession lately, which goes under a finer name or notion. I think they will now be called *Commonwealth's men*,— who perhaps have right to it little enough. And it is strange, that men of fortune and great estates, should join with such a people ; but such is the fact. . . . Do not despise these enemies ; they are pretty numerous ; and were to join the Cavaliers at the time when they were risen. . . . It was intended first to assassinate my person, which I would not remember as anything at all considerable, to myself or to you ; for they would have had to cut throats beyond human calculation, before they could have been able to effect their design. But, you know very well, this is no fable

Persons were arraigned for it before the Parliament sat, tried, and, upon proof, condemned. . . . An officer was also engaged, who was upon the guard, to seize me in my bed. And other foolish designs there were—as, to get into a room, to get gunpowder laid in it, and to blow up the room where I lay. . . . The ring leaders in all this are none but your old enemies, the Papists and Cavaliers. . . And they did not only set these things on work, but they sent a fellow, a wretched creature, an apostate from religion and all honesty,—they sent him to Madrid to advise with the King of Spain to land forces to invade this nation. . . . When we knew all these designs, when we found that the Cavaliers would not be quiet,—'there is no peace to the wicked,' saith the Scripture,—we did find out a little poor invention, which I hear has been much regretted; namely, the erecting of your Major-generals, to have a little inspection upon the people thus divided, thus discontented, thus dissatisfied, and upon the workings of the Popish party. . . And truly, I think if ever anything were justifiable, as to necessity, and honest in every respect, this was. And I could as soon venture my life with it as with anything I ever undertook. : . The Major-generals are men of known integrity and fidelity, and men who have freely adventured their blood and lives for the good cause. . . . . And truly England doth yet receive one day more of lengthening out its tranquillity, by that same service of theirs!"[1]

Cromwell had now entered on a difficult course; instead of resting, as he had done at first, upon old revolutionary passions, he was attacking recent and powerful prejudices; the tyranny of the Major-generals had met with general reprobation, and had been censured even by those who had not suffered from its operation. Cromwell himself felt this, and, after having boldly justified the measure, he did not think it wise to dwell upon it at any length. But the next topic of his discourse was not more satisfactory; he had enumerated the evils which beset the country; it now behoved him to suggest remedies for those evils. He could not mention the one at which he was aiming, and which alone he believed would be effectual—the restoration of monarchy, in his person, with its great condition of force, order, and stability. He demanded money for the prosecution of the war, the devoted support of the Parliament for his government, and the reformation of laws and manners. But these were necessities which had been expected, and phrases devoid of deep meaning or virtue. He ended his speech with a paraphrase

---

[1] Cromwell's Letters and Speeches, vol. iii. pp. 193—239.

of the eighty-fifth Psalm, in which King David bursts into thanksgiving and joy, because he trusts that the Almighty God will
pardon his people, bring them back from all their wanderings, and
save them from all their dangers. But there is nothing to indicate
that his peroration produced upon his auditors the impression which
Cromwell hoped it would produce,—piety and the fear of anarchy :
those chords which he had once swept with such powerful effect,
were beginning to lose their influence upon his auditors.

On leaving the Painted Chamber, Cromwell returned to Whitehall, and the members of Parliament proceeded to the hall in which
their meetings were held. At the doors they were met by guards
who, before admitting them, required each of them to produce his
certificate of admission. Most of them did so; but others had no
certificate, and were not allowed to enter. Their surprise and
indignation were great. What was the certificate thus demanded?
By whom, and by what right, was it granted or refused? This
was soon explained; the document was in this form :—" These are
to certify that ———— is returned by indenture one of the
Knights to serve in this present Parliament, for the county of
————, and approved by his Highness's Council. (Signed)
Nathaniel Taylor, Clerk of the Commonwealth in Chancery."
About three hundred members were provided with the certificate ;
a hundred and two had not received it, and were consequently
excluded from the Parliament.[1]

On the following day, the 18th of September, the House met
for the despatch of business. Sir Thomas Widdrington was elected
Speaker, and other preliminary arrangements were in process of
adoption, when the following letter was handed in, signed by sixty-
five persons :—" We whose names are subscribed (with others),
being chosen, and accordingly returned to serve with you in this
Parliament, and in discharge of our trust, offering to go into the
House, were at the lobby door kept back by soldiers ; which, lest
we should be wanting in our duty to you and to our country, we
have thought it expedient to represent unto you, to be communicated to the House, that we may be admitted thereunto."[2]

When this letter had been read, the House ordered that the
Clerk of the Commonwealth in Chancery should be summoned to
the bar on the following day, and should bring with him the indentures of election of all the knights, citizens, and burgesses who
had been returned to serve in that Parliament. When the order

---

[1] Old Parliamentary History, vol. xxi. p. 24; Cromwell's Letters and
Speeches, vol. iii. pp. 240, 241.
[2] Commons' Journals, vol. vii. p. 424.

reached the clerk, he was not in London; but his deputy appeared at the bar of the House, with the indentures of all the elections; the names subscribed to the letter were read, and at each name, the clerk was asked if such a person had been duly elected at the place for which he claimed to sit: in every case the answer was in the affirmative.   The strongest agitation prevailed in the House: members went to and fro, stopping one another, forming into groups, talking and asking questions in the greatest confusion.   The Speaker called to order.   So long as a stranger was in the House, he said, every member should remain quietly and silently in his place.   It was announced that the Clerk of the Commonwealth had returned to London, and was in attendance at the door; he was admitted at once, and required to state how it happened that divers persons who, according to the indentures, appeared to have been well and duly elected, were not allowed to take their seats in the House; he replied that he had received instructions, from his Highness's Council, to deliver certificates of election to those persons only whose return had been approved by the Council; and he produced the order.   The House resolved to demand of the Council for what reasons certain duly elected members had not been approved and admitted to sit.   On the next day, the 22nd of September, Nathaniel Fiennes, one of the Lords Commissioners of the Great Seal, by direction of the Council, made a verbal statement that, in pursuance of the seventeenth article of the Protectoral Constitution, " no persons could be elected to serve in Parliament but such as were of known integrity, fearing God, and of good conversation," and that by the twenty-first article of the same instrument, the Council was authorised and directed " to examine whether the persons elected were agreeable to the above-mentioned qualifications."   The Council, he said, had refused its approval to none of the persons elected who had appeared to it to possess the legal qualifications; and with regard to the persons not approved, his Highness had given orders that they should not be allowed to enter the House.[1]

The admission was boldly made; the articles of the Constitution were formal; the House made some attempt to adjourn any further debate, but the proposal of adjournment was rejected.   Nothing could be done but submit to this mutilation: it was resolved, by a hundred and twenty-five votes against twenty-nine, that the excluded members must apply to the Council, in order to obtain its

[1] Commons' Journals, vol. vii. pp. 425, 426; Old Parliamentary History, vol. xx. pp. 255, 256, vol. xxi. pp. 26—28.

approval; and the House, anxious to proceed to a settlement of the nation, took no further proceedings on the subject.[1]

The excluded members prepared and signed a vehement protest, in which, after a lengthy exposition of their just grievances, they denounced all who should continue to sit in this mutilated Parliament, as "betrayers of the liberties of England, and adherents to the capital enemies of the Commonwealth." Many thousands of copies of this protest, signed by ninety-three persons, were packed in boxes and deposited in various houses in London, whence they were privately taken and circulated throughout the country. Cromwell's police discovered and seized several of these boxes; but the public mind, without growing more generally favourable to the republicans, was becoming tired and indignant at these repeated ✓ acts of tyranny: a strong interest attached to all acts of resistance, by whomsoever attempted; the protest was eagerly sought for, and read with avidity. Some of those who had signed it, however, soon retracted their opposition, for they solicited and obtained from the Protector their admission into that Parliament which they had so lately denounced. But the public impression underwent no alteration, and extended to the House itself; several of the members, regarding whose admission no difficulty had been made, became disgusted and ceased to attend its sittings; and most of those who continued to sit felt, in their inmost hearts, a consciousness of shame from which they hoped some day to find an opportunity of ✓ purging themselves without excessive danger.[2]

At this very moment, and as if to console the insulted nation, fortune sent Cromwell a glorious achievement. On the 2nd of October, 1656, Thurloe announced to the Parliament that the fleet which had been cruising off the coast of Spain, with a view to intercept the Spanish galleons on the way from America, had encountered, fought, and captured several of those richly laden vessels, on their arrival before Cadiz. The honour of this success did not belong to Blake and Montague, the commanders of the fleet: after waiting a long while, they had sailed from the coast of Spain to that of Portugal, leaving before Cadiz one of their officers, Captain Richard Stayner, with seven ships. No sooner had the English admirals taken their departure than the Spanish galleons appeared, four ships of war, and four immense merchantmen; misled by the reports they had received, and believing they would be able to enter the port of Cadiz without difficulty. Stayner

<hr>

[1] Commons' Journals, vol. vii. p. 426.
[2] Old Parliamentary History, vol. xxi. pp. 28—38; Whitelocke, p. 651; Thurloe's State Papers, vol. v. p. 456.

boldly attacked them, within sight of their town, the inhabitants of which, from the roofs of their houses, were able to watch the vicissitudes of the conflict.   After a valiant resistance, the Spaniards yielded : four of the ships were burned, and two captured, with their precious cargo of piastres, ingots, and various wealth.   The Protector and the Parliament combined to extol this victory : the Parliament ordered a solemn thanksgiving service, first for the House itself, and then for the country generally.   A detailed narrative of the affair was drawn up by a committee of the House, and circulated in every direction : the poets, both of the court and people, added their hymns to the official pæans.   Admiral Montague, who arrived soon after, with the prizes, was overwhelmed with favours by Cromwell, and with compliments by the Parliament.   Richard Stayner was knighted   When the treasures of Spain were set on shore at Portsmouth, they were immediately packed in thirty-eight waggons, and conveyed, under a brilliant escort, through the towns and villages of the south-west of England, to the Tower of London, there to be coined into English money.   The imagination of the public and the charlatanry of the government vied with each other in exaggerating the value of the capture ; some said it amounted to three, some to five, and some even to nine, millions of piastres.   "It falls out much less than was expected," wrote Thurloe to Henry Cromwell, on the 4th of November ; "not but that the prize itself fell out to be far richer than we first heard of, there being in the two ships taken near a million of money sterling, which was all plundered to about 350,000l., or 300,000l. sterling. A private captain, they say, hath got to his own share 60,000l., and many private mariners 10,000l. a man ; and this is so universal amongst the seamen, and taken in the heat of the fight, that it is not possible to get it again, any part of it."   It is the privilege of martial glory that even cupidity and falsehood can scarce tarnish its splendour."[1]

Under the influence of this triumph, and in the absence of the old republican opposition, the Parliament passed all the bills, and adopted all the measures that Cromwell could desire.   On the 26th of September an act was passed " for renouncing and disannulling the pretended title of Charles Stuart and his descendants to the crown of England."   On the 9th of October another bill was adopted " for the security of his Highness the Lord Protector's person, and

---

[1] Commons' Journals, vol. vii. pp. 432, 433 ; Thurloe's State Papers, vol. v. pp. 399, 433, 434, 472, 505, 509, 524, 557 ; Clarendon's History of the Rebellion, vol. vii. pp. 212, 213 ; Dixon's Life of Blake, pp. 332—337 ; Cromwelliana, p. 159.

continuance of the nation in peace and safety." On the 1st of
October, it was unanimously voted that "the war against the
Spaniard was undertaken upon just and necessary grounds, and for
the good of the people of this Commonwealth; and the Parliament
will, by God's blessing, assist his Highness therein." The Parliament would willingly have remained satisfied with this promise,
and more than two months elapsed before it seemed to think of
fulfilling it; but the friends of the Protector brought the subject
plainly before the House. "We cannot," said Captain Fiennes,
"kill the king of Spain, nor take Spain or Flanders, by a vote;
there must be monies provided." On the 30th of January, 1657,
a sum of four hundred thousand pounds was voted for the expenses
of the war; and several taxes were remodelled and increased in
order to provide this amount. In all its relations with the
Protector, the Parliament showed him extreme deference; the
forms of official communications between the two powers were
regulated (on the 1st of October, 1656) in a manner most respectful
to him. All the appointments which he had made to high judicial
offices were approved. Nearly all the ordinances which he had
issued, on his own sole authority, were confirmed. The House
published no declaration, and ordained no public ceremony, without
having first requested and obtained his assent. No opportunity was
allowed to escape for bestowing the most substantial marks of favour,
not only on himself, but on his family. On the 27th of December,
1656, the House was discussing an act for regulating the distribution of confiscated lands in Ireland. Whitelocke proposed that a
clause should be added, to settle "the manor-house, town, and lands
of Portumna upon the Lord Henry Cromwell, his heirs and assigns
for ever, in consideration of his many good and faithful services,
and in full satisfaction of all arrears due to him." "A good gift,"
says Thomas Burton, who was present on the occasion; "a manor,
park, house, and four thousand acres:—large things!" No one
opposed the addition of this clause. "I hope," said Sir William
Strickland, "you will readily pass it, for this gentleman has done
you eminent service. It is not a free gift, but for his arrears."
"This is no great matter," said Sir John Reynolds, "not above a
thousand pounds worth. It is as little as can be." "It is less
than his good services and merit," said Mr. Goodwin; "there are
two thousand acres more in Connaught; I desire they may be added;
all is too little." The two thousand acres were added, making six
thousand acres in all: and there were only two noes, Mr. Robinson
and Major-General Lilburne. In this liberality there was something
more than interested flattery · the Parliament believed that the

revolution had reached its goal, and was anxious to establish its government.[1]

Cromwell was more desirous to do this than any other person could be ; but he understood the difficulty of the undertaking better than any one else. He possessed the two qualities which make men great, and lead them to do great things ; he was at once sensible and bold, under no illusion as to his actual position, and indomitable in his hopes. His power was absolute, but precarious ; acquiesced in as necessary and provisional, not as legitimate and final. Though they had undergone fifteen years of alternate violation and suppression, three institutions still retained their rightfulness in the eyes of the English people : these were—the Parliament, the Crown, and the Law. The intervention of the country in its own government by means of the two Houses ; the hereditary transmission of the royal power ; and that collection of statutes, customs, forms, traditions, and judicial decisions which represented justice, and was called the law,—constituted, according to the public conscience, the legitimate power of the State. Cromwell was so profoundly convinced of this, that the re-establishment of legitimate royalty sometimes even presented itself before his mind, if not as a chance, at least as a doubt ; and he readily encouraged friendly conversation on this topic. Lord Broghill told him one day that he had spent the morning in the city. " Cromwell asked him what news he had heard there. The other answered that he was told he was in treaty with the King, who was to be restored, and to marry his daughter. Cromwell expressing no indignation at this, Lord Broghill said, in the state to which things were brought, he saw not a better expedient ; they might bring him in on what terms they pleased, and Cromwell might retain the same authority he then had, with less trouble. Cromwell answered, 'The King can never forgive his father's blood.' Broghill said, he was one of many that were concerned in that, but he would be alone in the merit of restoring him. Cromwell replied, ' He is so damnably debauched, he would undo us all ;' and so turned to another discourse, without any emotion, which made Broghill conclude that he had often thought of that expedient."[2]

About the same period, the Marquis of Hertford, one of the most honourable of the advisers of Charles I., and who, since the death of that monarch, had lived in retirement on his estates, lost his eldest son, Lord Beauchamp. Cromwell, who eagerly availed

  [1] Commons' Journals, vol. vii. pp. 428, 436, 431, 481—490, 583, 431, 437, 438, 429, 524, 526, 528 ; Burton's Diary, vol. i. pp. 174, 191, 269, 259, 260.
  [2] Burnet's History of His Own Time, vol. i. p. 119.

himself of every opportunity for placing himself in communication with the great royalist nobles, sent Sir Edward Sydenham to assure him of his sympathy and condolence. Lord Hertford returned a suitable acknowledgment of his courtesy. " Some time after this, the Protector sent to invite the Marquis to dine with him. This great nobleman knew not how to waive or excuse it, considering it was in Cromwell's power to ruin him and all his family ; he sent him word that he would wait upon his Highness. Cromwell received him with all imaginable respect ; and after dinner took him by the hand and led him into his withdrawing room, where they two being alone, he told the Marquis he had desired his company that he might have his advice what to do. ' For,' said he, ' I am not able to bear the weight of business that is upon me ; I am weary of it, and you, my lord, are a great and a wise man, and of great experience, and have been much versed in the business of government. Pray advise me what I shall do.' The Marquis was much surprised at this discourse of the Protector, and desired again and again to be excused, telling him he had served King Charles all along, and been of his private council ; and that it was no way consistent with his principles that either the Protector should ask, or he (the Marquis) adventure, to give him any advice. This, notwithstanding, would not satisfy Cromwell ; but he pressed him still, and told him he would receive no excuses nor denials, but bid the Marquis speak freely, and whatsoever he said it should not turn in the least to his prejudice. The Marquis, seeing himself thus pressed, and that he could not avoid giving an answer, said :—" Sir, upon this assurance you have given me, I will declare to your Highness my thoughts, by which you may continue to be great, and establish your name and family for ever. Our young master that is abroad—that is, my master, and the master of us all—restore him to his crowns ; and by doing this you may have what you please.' The Protector, no way disturbed at this, answered very sedately, that he had gone so far that the young gentleman could not forgive. The Marquis replied, that if his Highness pleased, he would undertake with his master for what he had said. The Protector returned answer, that, in his circumstances, he could not trust. Thus they parted, and the Marquis received no prejudice thereby as long as Cromwell lived."[1]

But this was only the toleration of a victor, in a private conversation ; although he allowed men to speak to him of Charles Stuart.

---

[1] Lady Theresa Lewis's Lives from the Clarendon Gallery, vol. iii. pp. 122, 123.

Cromwell thought of himself alone, in connection with the restoration of the monarchy. And he had reason to believe himself entitled to entertain this idea with some confidence ; as his power increased and consolidated itself, the notion that he ought to be and would be king gained ground throughout the country. Petitions were sent from several counties to request him to assume the title and authority of royalty. In the name of religion and good government, the Commonwealth was spoken ill of; and it was remembered that a king had first introduced the Christian faith into the island. It was asserted that, though certain officers were opposed to this very natural transformation of the Protector into a king, the soldiers in general approved of it, and would remain faithful to him. "We must have a king, and will have a king," said many of his partisans; "and the Lord Protector dares not refuse it." And when Waller celebrated the victory of the English fleet before Cadiz, and the arrival of the treasures of Spain in England, it was not by a mere poetic impulse, nor in a strain of unusual flattery, that he said :—

> " His conquering head has no more room for bays—
> Then let it be as the glad nation prays.
> Let the rich ore be forthwith melted down,
> And the State fixed, by making him a crown;
> With ermine clad, and purple, let him hold
> A royal sceptre, made of Spanish gold."[1]

In proportion as this movement of popular opinion became more distinct, and might have led Cromwell to believe himself near the attainment of his object, the less he spoke about it ; he was one of those who, in all decisive conjunctures, prelude action by silence. He was, moreover, well aware that nothing was possible until he had a Parliament which would spontaneously impose the crown upon him. But, towards the end of 1656, when the new assembly which he had caused to be elected quietly consented to its own mutilation, Cromwell believed that the favourable moment had arrived ; he felt himself at length in possession of a Parliament thoroughly servile, and boldly devoted to his cause. Outside the walls of Parliament, the state of the public mind and of political parties seemed equally propitious to his hopes. Among the Cavaliers, many were thoroughly discouraged, and having ceased to believe in the possibility of the King's return, manifested a willingness to content themselves with a restoration of monarchy ; while others, with greater obstinacy and boldness, flattered themselves that, if royalty were once re-established,

---

[1] Burton's Diary, vol. i. pp. cxli., 384, vol. ii. pp. 2, 141, 220; Waller's oetical Works, p. 63.

the country would not endure to see the crown on any head but
that of the legitimate king; and they therefore hoped that Cromwell would raise himself to the throne, feeling confident that he
would speedily fall from it again. The chief desire of the Presbyterians had been for the triumph of their religious system in the
Church, and of constitutional government in the State : Cromwell
treated their clergy with favour, sustained their preachings, and
granted them the greater number of benefices; in religious matters,
they undoubtedly enjoyed the predominance ; if Cromwell, therefore, on becoming king, could be induced to act in conformity with
legal order, and to govern in concert with the Parliament, why
should not the nation acquiesce in a change of monarch, which
could not fail in the end, to serve the cause of its religious faith and
its political liberties? The sectaries, Independents, Anabaptists,
Millenarians, and Quakers, were more opposed to every prospect of
monarchy ; many of them, however, were beginning to grow tired
of their unfruitful political efforts, and to care only to secure the
free exercise of their belief and worship : Cromwell granted them
this, to as great an extent as the general intolerance would permit,
and more, assuredly, than any other ruler would have done. Finally,
he had governed for three years as an absolute master: he had
succeeded in all his undertakings : the last blows which he had
struck proved that his audacity was boundless; and most men,
whether friends, enemies, or neutral, were inclined to believe that
his good fortune would be equally unlimited, and to watch his progress with confidence or resignation.

Instinctively aware of this disposition of the public mind, Cromwell began once more to discuss the great question with his
confidants. Among these were men of very various origin, and
enjoying very unequal degrees of intimacy : the royalist Lord
Broghill, a warrior, a courtier, and intriguer, who delighted to share
in the fortune of a great man ; the Presbyterian Pierrepoint, a man
of judicious and liberal mind, ready to support and advise any
government which he thought would conduce to the welfare of his
country ; the jurisconsults, Whitelocke, Widdrington, Glynn, St.
John, and Lenthall, ready to serve the existing powers with zeal,
provided that they were not required to make any personal sacrifice
in its cause ; and the man who, of all others, possessed the greatest
amount of Cromwell's confidence, Thurloe, who directed his secret
police, both in England and on the Continent, and conducted his
private correspondence, both on public and family affairs; a shrewd,
active, and discreet servant, without any pretension either to independence or to glory, which rendered him as convenient as he was

useful to his master. To these different confidants, even to Thurloe himself, Cromwell gave no distinct explanation of his designs. Though naturally as impetuous as untruthful, age and experience had taught him to practise greater reserve; but by exciting, by his conversations, sometimes their curiosity, and sometimes their zeal, he daily urged them further forward on the road which was to conduct him to his object, whilst he always remained in a position either to arrest their progress or to deny that he had given them any encouragement in their designs.

Rumours of this policy soon spread, not only through England, but also over the Continent. In France, especially, the fact was neither novel nor unexpected. During the previous year a citizen of Paris, who noted down contemporary events with considerable care, and who was moreover a great enemy of the English revolutionaries and of Cromwell, wrote in his journal, " A singular report has been spread through Paris during the present month. It was said that Cromwell, not content with that sovereign authority which he has arrogated to himself over England, Scotland, and Ireland, under the title of Protector of those three nations, secretly aspired to retain it under the name of king; and that, with a view to secure the approbation of all Christendom to his project, he had sent two English Catholics to Rome, who were negotiating underhand with his Holiness on his behalf, and endeavouring to persuade him that, by giving his consent to the ambitious design of this usurper, he would assuredly bring again within the pale of the church that infinite number of souls who recognise his authority and his new establishment over them. Time will show us whether this illustrious impostor was capable of so fine a thought, and whether from so wicked a beginning, so great a blessing can accrue to all these parricidal islanders."[1]

Parliament had scarcely assembled when M. de Bordeaux, the French ambassador at London, wrote thus to M. de Brienne:— "The Protector granted me, this evening, the audience which I had requested. . . . I left him, persuaded, both by his words and by the expression of his countenance, that the internal affairs of England occupy his mind more than her external relations; and his conduct during the last few days makes it evident that he is either in great alarm or has a great design on foot."[2] A month

---

[1] The journal, which extends from 1648 to 1657, is contained among the MSS. of the Bibliothèque Impériale at Paris, Supplément Français, No. 1238 bis. It consists of five volumes.

[2] Letter from M. de Bordeaux to M. de Brienne, September 21st, 1656; in the Archives des Affaires Étrangères de France.

afterwards he added:—"The Protector still professes a desire to make no changes; nevertheless, public rumour will have it that the Parliament intends to make some innovation in his favour, after the means for continuing the war with the King of Spain have been resolved upon."[1] At the beginning of December, 1656, he wrote:— "It was the common belief that the Parliament would to-day discuss the succession, and that, notwithstanding the apparent opposition of some officers of the army, it would be resolved upon. I learn, however, that nothing was said on the subject this morning. Some assert that the proposition is postponed until after all other business shall have been concluded; others that the repugnance of the officers of the army has deferred it for a still longer period; and though it is most probable that the Protector must eventually succeed in his design, I should, nevertheless, feel a difficulty in speaking of it so boldly as Colonel Lockhart does; and he would never have gone so far if he had regulated his speeches by those of his master."[2] Lastly, towards the end of the same month, he thus wrote:—"Some affirm that the report of a descent of the King of Great Britain upon Scotland has been spread, in order to give greater plausibility to a proposition which is to be made one of these days in favour of the family of the Protector. The matter has already been treated several times indirectly, and the officers of the army have always appeared opposed to it; but it seems that now a resolution has been taken to speak of it openly. On the day before yesterday, most of the members expected that it would have been brought forward, and the delay which has taken place leads to the belief that the minds of the army are not yet well-disposed towards it. Nevertheless, the most common opinion is that they will agree to it, and that they affect this repugnance only in order to maintain their credit among the inferior officers, who cannot relish the establishment of a perfect monarchy. The gentlemen and lawyers, of whom that body (the Parliament) is composed, and many other persons of all conditions in England, desire it; those even who are attached to the royal family believe that it will be to its advantage for the quarrel to stand only between it and the Protector's family. Nevertheless, if he were to survive for any length of time the settlement to which I allude, his children might probably retain his authority."[3]

When matters had been brought to this point, either by his

---

[1] Letter from M. de Bordeaux to M. de Brienne, October 26th, 1656; in the Archives des Affaires Étrangères de France.

[2] The same to the same, December 11th, 1656; ibid.

[3] The same to the same, end of December, 1656; ibid.

machinations or by the natural course of events, Cromwell boldly entered the field, and his first attack was directed against that very Parliament which was to make him king. It was little to have mutilated and humiliated it; it was necessary to display to England, in the strongest possible light, the formidably vicious character of that assembly, which, notwithstanding its abasement, still regarded itself as the depository of the national sovereignty, and by which all the powers of the State, without distinction or limit, were sometimes unlawfully assumed and carried into tyrannical exercise. The House itself furnished Cromwell with an opportunity for making this danger evident to the eyes of the country. A sectary, named James Naylor, who had been first a soldier, and afterwards a Quaker, and who was one of the insanest of lunatics, pretended that Christ had descended once more upon earth and become incarnate in him; and on this pretext, he indulged in all sorts of the most extravagant and licentious manifestations and actions. Fanatical women and vagabonds of every description followed him wherever he went, singing his praises, and almost offering him worship. He was arrested at Bristol, and brought to London, where the House of Commons, instead of sending him before the ordinary judges, appointed a committee to report on his case, summoned him to its bar, and decided upon trying him itself. It was less a question of liberty of conscience than a renewal of the conflict between the old spirit of cruel severity and the rising spirit of moderation, in regard to the punishment of blasphemy and other offences against the Christian faith. The affair occupied ten sittings. The House maintained that it possessed the right of life and death as fully as the three combined powers of the old Parliament had done, and the fanatics were anxious to make full use of this power. "This man, in short, makes himself God; our God is here supplanted. Should we not be as jealous of God's honour as we are of our own? Wherefore do you sit in that chair but to bear witness of the truth? My ears did tingle and my heart tremble to hear the report. Let the blasphemer be stoned! I humbly beseech you make no delay in it. I cannot hold my peace lest my conscience dog me to my chamber, to my curtains, to my grave!" Such were the speeches of a great number of members, some of whom, as for instance, Skippon, Butler, Downing, and Drake, were men of considerable importance; and if several officers, of whom Desborough was one, and some of the lawyers, including Whitelocke, had not spoken on the subject, this blaspheming maniac would probably have been hanged without further trial; for out of a hundred and seventy-eight who voted, eighty-two members, among whom was Richard Cromwell himself, were in favour of putting him to death. Naylor was condemned to be set in the pillory, to have his tongue bored through with a hot iron, to be whipped by the hangman through the streets, and to be confined in prison, with hard labour, as long as Parliament should please.[1] Cromwell was careful not to interfere with this sentence, such interposition would have offended public feeling, which was aroused against the blasphemer. But another public feeling was also aroused against this violation of the common law—against the assumption of judicial power by the House—suppressing the jury, the judges, and all the formalities of legal procedure, and thus depriving the English of the dearest guarantees of their liberties. Cromwell seized eagerly upon this opportunity, and at the very moment of the execution of the sentence, he wrote thus to the Speaker of the Parliament :—

"Right trusty and well-beloved, we greet you well. Having taken notice of a judgment lately given by yourselves against one James Naylor: Although we detest and abhor the giving or occasioning the least countenance to persons of such opinions and practices, or who are under the guilt of the crimes commonly imputed to the said person ; yet we, being intrusted in the present government, on behalf of the people of these nations ; and not knowing how far such proceedings, entered into wholly without us, may extend in the consequence of it,—Do desire that the House will let us know the grounds and reasons whereupon they have proceeded."[2]

The House was embarrassed ; it was unwilling either to enter into open conflict with the Protector, or to abandon the jurisdiction which it had arrogated to itself; its only answer was to reject a proposition which was made to it, on the 27th of December, for postponing the complete execution of Naylor's sentence; and on the very next day, that part of the punishment which remained to be inflicted, was carried into effect.[3] This mattered little to Cromwell ; he had exposed the vices of the republican constitution, and charged the Parliament alone with the most flagrant of those violations of the law which he had himself so frequently committed ; whilst, at the same time, without making any compromising advance to the fanatical sectaries, he cleared himself, in their eyes, of all

---

[1] Journals of the House of Commons, vol. vii. pp. 418—469; State Trials, vol. v. cols. 801—842 ; Burton's Diary, vol. i. pp. 24—167.

[2] Cromwell to Sir Thomas Widdrington, December 25th, 1656; in his Letters and Speeches, vol. iii. p. 265.

[3] Commons' Journals, vol. vii. p. 470; Burton's Diary, vol. i. pp. 260—264.

connection with the rigorous punishment which one of their number had just undergone.

After this exposure of the Parliament, Cromwell's next care was to humiliate and compromise the army, or at least those of the leaders of the army whose influence or ill-will he feared. Under the pretext of providing for the maintenance of the militia, Desborough brought forward a bill, on the 25th of December, 1656, for continuing the tax of a tenth part of their revenue upon members of the royalist party alone, which had been imposed during the previous year. The real object of this bill was to amnesty the Major-generals, who had, each in his own district, arbitrarily imposed this tax, and thus at once to sanction the tax, and the military authority which had already levied it. There was every reason to believe that this bill had been brought forward with Cromwell's consent; for he alone, in 1655, had appointed the Major-generals, and given them all their instructions. Indeed, when the bill was first mentioned in the House, Thurloe had given it his support; but, to the great astonishment of all parties, when the debate began, one of Cromwell's sons-in-law, John Claypole, the husband of his favourite daughter, Elizabeth, opened the discussion by saying: " The bill consists of two parts : 1. Decimations, and the continuance of them ; 2. Indemnity to such persons as have acted in it. For the first, I cannot see how it can stand, unless you violate your articles and the Act of Oblivion ; for, by the bill, you punish men wholly for an offence before committed. It lies altogether upon retrospection. It will be hard to convict men upon this bill, and you will not surely lay this tax upon men till conviction. It ought to be considered whether you will entail this upon their posterity; whether the children shall be punished for the father's offence. I like the second part of it, that is, indemnity ; but I hope that will be provided for in another bill. I did but only start this debate, and leave it to others who are better able to speak to it. My opinion is, upon the whole matter, that this bill ought to be rejected ; and that is my humble motion."[1]

The anger of the Major-generals was extreme ; they found themselves betrayed by the very man from whom they held their mission ; and he exposed them to all the hatred which they had incurred by carrying out the arbitrary measures which he had commanded. Lambert, Desborough, Whalley, Butler, and their friends

---

[1] Burton's Parliamentary Diary, vol. i. pp. 310, 311, 230—243 ; Commons' Journals, vol. vii. p. 475 ; Thurloe's State Papers, vol. v. p. 786.

warmly supported the bill. Encouraged by the example of Claypole, the lawyers and courtiers persisted in opposing it. The
debate became violent and personal. One day, Major-General
Butler having spoken harshly of the Cavaliers, Harry Cromwell,
the Protector's cousin, said in reply : " Many gentlemen do say and
think it just that, because some of the Cavaliers have done amiss,
therefore all should be punished : by the same argument, because
some of the Major-generals have done amiss, which I offer to prove,
therefore all of them deserve to be punished." The Major-generals
cried out at this ; and one of them, Kelsey, demanded that Harry
Cromwell should be required to name those whom he intended to
inculpate. Up started Harry, and begged the House to give him
leave to name them ; "and offered to prove unwarrantable actions
done by them." This set the House on fire ; " but," says the
member who relates this incident, " this fire was put out by the
grave water-carriers." As he left the House, some of the friends of
the Major-generals threatened Harry Cromwell with the Protector's
anger ; so Harry went to Whitehall that very evening, and repeated
to his cousin all that he had said in the House, adding, that he had
brought " his black book and papers to make good what he said."
Cromwell treated the whole matter as a joke, and, taking from his
shoulders a rich scarlet cloak which he wore that day, he gave it,
with his gloves, to Harry, " who," says the narrator of the story,
" strutted with his new cloak and gloves in the House this day, to
the great satisfaction and delight of some, and trouble of others. It
was a pretty passage of his Highness."[1]

Jocular and sarcastic, with more heartiness than good taste,
Cromwell took almost as much pleasure in tricking his adversaries
as in conquering them, and he was, on this occasion most assuredly,
amused at their surprise and anger at finding themselves thus
braved and duped. He foresaw that some of the Major-generals
would oppose his cherished plan, and he was more desirous to discredit than to exasperate them. It exhibited a want of his ordinary
prudence, for he did not believe he could make himself king without the assistance of a majority of the most influential of his old
comrades ; but one idea alone now filled his mind ; to make himself
independent of, and superior to, both the Parliament and the army ;
to offer himself to the country as the only refuge from their
excesses, and thus to found the final triumph of his fortune upon
the merited unpopularity of his own instruments.

[1] Thurloe's State Papers, vol. vi. pp. 20, 21 ; Burton's Parliamentary Diary,
vol. i. p. 369 ; Mark Noble's Memoirs of the Protectoral House of Cromwell,
vol. i. pp. 67—79.

While his friends were thus divided, his enemies came to his aid, and most efficiently promoted his design. Charles II., who was then residing at Bruges, was collecting some few companies of soldiers, had received a supply of money from Spain, and seemed, in short, to be preparing an expedition for his restoration to his kingdom. His ally, the republican Sexby, had recently returned to Flanders, after having spent several months in England; he demanded only a thousand infantry and five hundred horse, and promised that, as soon as he had landed in Kent, he would bring to pass a republican insurrection against Cromwell, which would become a royalist rebellion as soon as the Protector was overthrown. Sexby reckoned on assassination as the most effectual means of overthrowing Cromwell; and he had left in London one of his old comrades in war and conspiracy, Miles Sindercombe, a brave soldier and zealous republican, rather a freethinker than a Christian sectary, who, with four or five accomplices, spent his time in devising means, and watching for opportunities, of killing the Protector. On his departure from London, Sexby had given Sindercombe five hundred pounds, and was to have sent him a further sum · by his own confession, it was the former ambassador of Spain to England, Don Alonzo de Cardenas, who had concerted this plot with him at Brussels, and had furnished him with the means of carrying it into execution.[1]

On the 19th of January, 1657, Thurloe got up in his place in Parliament, and solemnly revealed the whole plot, announcing that Sindercombe and two of his accomplices had been arrested, giving full details, reading lengthy depositions, and hinting at perils still more dark and destructive, such as a general insurrection of the Cavaliers, and an invasion of England by the combined forces of Charles Stuart and the Spaniards. Whether sincere or affected, the emotion caused by this statement was profound; it was voted that a solemn service should be celebrated in the three kingdoms to give thanks to God for the discovery of the plot; and it was proposed that a committee should be appointed to learn from the Protector when it would be convenient for him to grant audience to the House, and receive its congratulations upon his deliverance. " I would have something else added," said Mr. Ashe, an obscure member, " which, in my opinion, would tend very much to the preservation of himself and us, and to the quieting of all the designs

---

[1] Clarendon's History of the Rebellion, vol. vii. p. 278 ; Clarendon's State Papers, vol. iii. pp. 315, 321, 324, 327, 338; Thurloe's State Papers, vol. iv pp. 1, 2, 33, 182, 560; Godwin's History of the Commonwealth, vol. iv. pp. 278, 333.

of our enemies;—that his Highness would be pleased to take upon him the government according to the ancient constitution. Both our liberties and peace, and the preservation and privilege of his Highness would then be founded upon an old and sure foundation."

The general emotion was now succeeded by violent excitement. "I understand not," said Mr. Robinson, "what that gentleman's motion means, who talks of an old constitution, so I cannot tell how we should debate upon it. The old constitution is Charles Stuart's interest. I hope we are not calling him in again." "The gentleman that moved this," said Mr. Highland, "was one of those that was for the pulling down of what he would now set up again. That was King, Lords, and Commons; a constitution which we have pulled down with our blood and treasure. Will you make the Lord Protector the greatest hypocrite in the world, to make him sit in that place, which God has borne testimony sufficiently against? Are you now going to set up kingly government, which, for these thousand years, has persecuted the people of God? Do you expect a better consequence? I beseech you consider of it! What a crime it is to offer such a motion as this! Do you expect a thanksgiving day upon this? I desire that this motion may die as abominable; and I beseech you, that such a thing as this may never receive footing here."[1]

Thus violently attacked, Mr. Ashe's motion was, nevertheless, defended, but with considerable timidity and embarrassment. It was, at length, by general consent, allowed to drop as not being in order, but it was not altogether rejected. Burton says, "I have not seen so hot a debate vanish so strangely, like an *ignis fatuus*."[2]

This was not the first occasion, however, upon which the Parliament had heard such a proposition. Some time before, Colonel William Jephson, in the course of debate, had distinctly proposed to make Cromwell king; but his proposition was not entertained for a moment, and fell to the ground almost unnoticed. A few days after, he dined at Whitehall, and Cromwell gently reproved him for it, telling him, "that he wondered what he could mean by such a proposition." Jephson replied, "that whilst he was permitted the honour of sitting in that House, he must desire the liberty to discharge his conscience, though his opinion should happen to displease." Whereupon, Cromwell, clapping him on the shoulder, said, "Get thee gone for a mad fellow as thou art!" "But," says Ludlow, "it soon appeared with what madness he was

---

[1] Commons' Journals, vol. vii. p. 481; Clarendon's State Papers, vol. iii. p. 320; Burton's Parliamentary Diary, vol. i. pp. 356—361.

[2] Burton's Parliamentary Diary, p. 366.

possessed ; for he immediately obtained a foot company for his son, then a scholar at Oxford, and a troop of horse for himself."[1]

These preliminaries were significant, but futile ; they disclosed the object without making any advance towards it. Meanwhile, circumstances grew urgent; the bill which Desborough had brought forward to screen the Major-generals was rejected, and it became clear that Cromwell was preparing to dispense with their services; Sindercombe was found guilty by the jury, and poisoned himself in the Tower, on the evening before the day fixed for his execution. Dark suspicions were awakened.[2] It was necessary to escape from this state of restless expectancy, which threatened to prove fatal, if it were allowed to remain unproductive. A decisive proposition was prepared, and Whitelocke was requested to submit it to the Parliament; he declined, but promised to support it when brought forward.[3] He was one of those men who wish events to precede them, and prefer to account for servile complaisance rather than for bold forwardness. Alderman Sir Christopher Pack, one of the representatives of the city of London, undertook to make the proposition. Cromwell had recently made him a knight, and, as one of the Commissioners of the Excise, he had sundry accounts to render, which caused him no slight embarrassment. On the 23rd of February, 1656, as soon as the House met, he rose, and, presenting a long paper to the House, requested permission to read it. "It was something come to his hands," he said, " tending to the settlement of the nation, and of liberty and property." The storm broke out immediately, for no one could mistake the object of the proposition. The republicans, both soldiers and civilians, opposed the reading of the paper, declared that it was an unparliamentary proceeding, overwhelmed Pack with questions and reproaches, and eventually carried their violence so far as to drag him from his seat, near the Speaker's chair, to the bar of the House. But the Protector's partisans, and nearly all the lawyers, resolutely supported both the proposition and its author. On the question being put, the reading of the paper was ordered, by 144 votes against 54 ; it was accordingly read at once, and a resolution was passed that the debate upon it should begin on the next day.[4]

The paper was entitled — "The humble address and remonstrance of the knights, citizens, and burgesses, now assembled in

---

[1] Ludlow's Memoirs, p. 246.
[2] February 13, 1657; State Trials, vol. v. cols. 850, 851.
[3] Whitelocke's Memorials, p. 656.
[4] Journals of the House of Commons, vol. vii. p. 490; Ludlow's Memoirs, pp. 246, 247.

the Parliament of this Commonwealth ;" it restored the monarchy, and invited the Protector to assume the title of King, and also to point out his successor.

On the following day, the 24th of February, Thurloe wrote to Monk, who was then governor of Scotland : "Yesterday we fell into a great debate in Parliament. One of the aldermen who serve for the city of London brought in a paper called a *Remonstrance*, desiring my Lord Protector to assume kingly power, and to call future Parliaments, consisting of two Houses." And, after having explained to Monk the various articles of the scheme, Thurloe thus concluded :—" I have written most fully to you in these particulars, because you might satisfy any others who may have scruples about this business. I do assure you it ariseth from the Parliament only ; his Highness knew nothing of the preambles until they were brought into the House, and no man knows whether, if they be passed, but that his Highness will reject them. It is certain he will, if the security of the good people and cause be not provided for therein to the full. It is good that you inform yourself concerning the posture of the army with you ; lest some unquiet spirit or other will take this or any other occasion to put the army into discontent by false reports."[1]

This notice was opportune, for on the 27th of February, the very day on which the Parliament was celebrating a solemn fast, in order to obtain light from above in reference to the great debate on which it was about to enter, a hundred officers, led by several of the Major-generals, Lambert, Desborough, Fleetwood, Whalley, and Goffe, waited upon Cromwell, and entreated him not to accept the title of King : "because," said Colonel Mills, who acted as their spokesman, "it was not pleasing to his army, and was matter of scandal to the people of God, and of great rejoicing to the enemy ; and that it was also hazardous to his own person, and of great danger to the three nations, as such an assumption made way for Charles Stuart to come in again."

Cromwell immediately replied : " **The first man that told me of** it was he who is the mouth of the officers now present. For my part I have never been in any cabal about the same. Time was when you boggled not at the word *King*, for the Instrument by which the Government now stands, was presented to me with that title in it, as some here present could witness ; and I refused to

---

[1] This letter from Thurloe to Monk, as far at least as I am aware, has remained hitherto unpublished. I am indebted for it to the kindness of Dr. Travers Twiss, by whom it was discovered among the manuscripts in Littlecott Castle.

accept of the title. But how it comes to pass that you now startle at the title, you best know. For my part, I love the title,—a mere feather in a hat,—as little as you do. You have made me your drudge, upon all occasions : to dissolve the Long Parliament, who had contracted evil enough by long sitting ; to call a Parliament, or Convention, of your naming, who met, and what did they ?— fly at liberty and property ; insomuch as if one man had twelve cows, they held that another who wanted cows ought to take share with his neighbour. Who could have said anything was their own, if these men had gone on ? After their dissolution, how was I pressed by you for the rooting out of the ministry ; nay, rather than fail, to starve them out. A Parliament was afterwards called ; they sat five months ; it is true we hardly heard of them in all that time. They took the Instrument into debate, and they must needs be dissolved ; and yet, stood not the Instrument in need of mending ? Was not the case hard with me, to be put upon to swear to that which was so hard to be kept ? Some time after that, you thought it was necessary to have Major-generals ; and the first rise to that motion (the late general insurrections) was justifiable ; and you Major-generals did your parts well. You might have gone on. Who bid you go to the House with a bill, and there receive a foil ? After you had exercised this power a while, impatient were you till a Parliament was called. I gave my vote against it ; but you were confident, by your own strength and interest, to get men chosen to your heart's desire. How you have failed therein, and how much the country hath been disobliged, is well known. It is time to come to a settlement, and lay aside arbitrary proceedings, so unacceptable to the nation ; and by the proceedings of this Parliament, you see they stand in need of a check, or balancing power ; for the case of James Naylor might happen to be your own case. By their judicial power they fall upon life and member ; and doth the Instrument enable me to control it ?"[1]

The facts mentioned by Cromwell were embarrassing, his ideas were striking and unexpected, and his voice still possessed great influence over his old companions. Many grew feebler in their resistance, among others three of the Major-generals, Whalley, Goffe, and Berry. A compromise was made. It was agreed that the question of title should remain in suspense until the end of the debate, and that no clause of the bill should be considered definitive

---

[1] Burton's Parliamentary Diary, vol. i. pp. 382 –384; Cromwell's Letters and Speeches, vol. iii. pp. 268, 269.

or obligatory, until the whole had been resolved upon. On these conditions, the officers consented that the Parliament should in future consist of two Houses, admitted the right of Cromwell to appoint his successor, and pledged themselves to allow the debate to pursue its course without interruption.

The debate extended from the 23rd of February to the 30th of March, 1657, and occupied twenty-four sittings, seven of which, contrary to the usages of the House, continued during the whole of the day, both before and after noon. The few details which have been transmitted to us regarding it, seem to indicate that, though the discussions were long and animated, they were not disturbed by any manifestations of violence. Only when, after having discussed the entire project, the House returned to the first article, which proposed the re-establishment of the monarchy, and which had been purposely left in suspense, it was directed that the doors should be closed, and that no member should be allowed to absent himself without a special permission. Many, doubtless, would have preferred to escape from the necessity of taking part in so embarrassing a question. A hundred and eighty-five members voted, sixty-two against, and a hundred and twenty-three in favour of, the article, which was adopted in these terms: "That your Highness will be pleased to assume the name, style, title, dignity, and office of King of England, Scotland, and Ireland, and the respective dominions and territories thereunto belonging; and to exercise the same according to the laws of these nations." And, with a view to make the form of the document comply at once with monarchical usages, instead of being called an "Address and Remonstrance," it was entitled the "Humble Petition and Advice."[1]

We have no reason to believe that, during this debate, the country was either violently agitated, or paid any very passionate attention to it. The newspapers of the time, which were either rigidly censured or roughly intimidated, allude to it with curt and dry reserve, generally in some such terms as these: "On the 25th of March, the House came to a resolution of great concernment, of which you may expect an account hereafter."[2] Justly wearied and distrustful, the population cared little who were its masters, or about changes in which they alone seemed to be interested. Passion as well as action in the matter was concentrated around the Government itself, among its servants and opponents; and even in this sphere, notwithstanding the ardour of the struggle, great doubt and

[1] Journals of the House of Commons, vol. vii. pp. 496—514.
[2] Public Intelligencer, March 30, 1657; Mercurius Politicus, April 2, 1657; Godwin's History of the Commonwealth, vol. iv. p. 355.

reserve prevailed.   On the 3rd of March, Thurloe wrote thus to
Henry Cromwell: "His Highness spake to the officers in very plain,
yet loving and kind, expressions, and, as I hear, very much to their
satisfaction ; but yet I am not able to say what the issue of affairs
will be.   I do not like the complexion and constitution of things.
Settlement, I fear, is not in some men's minds, nor ever will be.   I
trust those who would be glad to see it, will be taught to submit
themselves to the all-wise disposing hand of God."[1]   And almost
at the same time,[2] Henry Cromwell wrote to Thurloe from Dublin :
"I bless the Lord to see his Highness hath such an interest in the
affections of so far the major part of the Parliament, as that they
should express so much satisfaction in his exercise of the present
power, as to think it the concernment and good of the nation to
entrust him with more.   .   .   .   .   As for the matter and merit of
the proposals themselves, I say in general that I do not like them
the worse, because some of the great ones could no better digest
them ; for since they cannot allow of what a Parliament of their
own modelling hath done, I look upon them as persons very unapt
to be quiet, nor able to endure any settlement whatsoever.   And,
therefore, I think that the depraved appetites of such sick minds
ought the less to be valued.   .   .   .   And I am so far from a
tender sense of their dissatisfaction, that I rather esteem it a provi-
dential opportunity to pull out those thorns, which are like to be
troublesome in the sides of his Highness.   .   .   .   .   The Lord
give him to see how much safer it is to rely upon persons of estate,
interest, integrity, and wisdom, than upon such as have so amply
discovered their envy and ambition, and whose faculty it is, by continuing of confusion, to support themselves.   As for myself, for
this also, as for all other things, I will more and more endeavour to
resign my own will unto His providence, unto whom I commit you."[3]
   What a remarkable example is this of prudent tranquillity on
the part of two men so deeply interested in the event, and who
were writing to each other with the most intimate freedom !
   As soon as it had reached the conclusion of its labours, on the
27th of March, the House appointed a deputation to inquire of the
Protector upon what day he would grant it audience for the
purpose of presenting to him the bill.   Four days after, on the 31st
of March, at about eleven o'clock, Cromwell, surrounded by the
principal officers of his government, received the Parliament at
Whitehall, in that same Banqueting Hall through which, eight

[1] Thurloe's State Papers, vol. vi. p. 93.
[2] On the 4th of March, 1657.
[3] Thurloe's State Papers, vol. vi. pp. 93, 94.

years before, Charles had passed, between a double line of soldiers, on his way to the scaffold. "May it please your Highness," said Sir Thomas Widdrington, the Speaker of the House, "I am commanded by the Parliament of England, Scotland, and Ireland, and in their name, to present this humble Petition and Advice to your Highness. I am sensible that I speak before a great person, the exactness of whose judgment ought to scatter and chase away all unnecessary speeches, as the sun doth the vapours. I am a servant, however, and a man not to vent my own conceits, but to declare the things which I have in command from the Parliament. I am not unlike a gardener, who gathers flowers in his master's garden, and out of them composeth a nosegay. I shall offer nothing but what I have collected in the garden of the Parliament."

Widdrington then gave a detailed analysis of the eighteen articles of the petition. The restoration of kingship, and of a second House of Parliament under the name of the Other House; the mode of election or nomination of the various members of the Parliament thus formed; the fixation of a permanent public revenue; and the exclusive domination of the Protestant religion, with a "provision for tender consciences;"—these were its principal recommendations, all of which he supported, with more art than taste, by quotations from the most heterogeneous authorities—Abraham and Aristotle, the Bible and Magna Charta, the doctrines of Christianity, and the legal traditions of England. "I have now done," he said, "with the several pieces of the government, but not with the articles. There remaineth yet one. The Parliament hath so good an apprehension of this frame of government in all the articles of it, that it is their humble desire that you may be pleased to accept of them all. They are bound up in one link or chain; or, like a building well knit and cemented, if one stone be taken out, it loosens the whole. The rejection of one may make all the rest unsuitable and impracticable. They are all offered to you, with the same heart and affection, and we hope they will be received by you in the same manner. They are all the children of one mother—the Parliament, and we expect from your Highness an adoption of them all · *Aut nihil aut totum dabit*."[1]

Cromwell immediately replied: "This frame of government, Mr. Speaker, which it hath pleased the Parliament by your hand to offer to me,—truly I should have a very brazen forehead if it did not beget in me a great deal of consternation of spirit;

[1] Burton's Parliamentary Diary, vol. i. pp. 397—413.

it being of so high and great importance, as by your opening of it, and by the reading of it, is manifest to all men ; the welfare, the peace and settlement of three nations, and all that rich treasure of the best people in the world, being involved therein. I say this consideration alone ought to beget in me the greatest reverence and fear of God, that ever possessed a man in this world. . . . I have lived the latter part of my age in—if I may say so—the fire ; in the midst of troubles. But all the things that have befallen me since I was first engaged in the affairs of this Commonwealth, if they could be supposed to be all brought into such a narrow com-pass that I could take a view of them at once, truly I do not think they would so move, nor do I think they ought so to move, my heart and spirit with that fear and reverence of God that becomes a Christian, as this thing that hath now been offered by you to me ! . . . And should I give any resolution in this matter suddenly, without seeking to have an answer put into my heart, and into my mouth, by Him that hath been my God and my guide hitherto, —it would give you very little cause of comfort in such a choice as you have made, in such a business as this, because it would savour more to be of the flesh, to proceed from lust, to arise from argu-ments of self. And if,—whatsoever the issue of this matter be,— it should have such motives in me, and such a rise in me, it may prove even a curse to you, and to these three nations—who, I verily believe, have intended well in this business, and have had those honest and sincere aims towards the glory of God, the good of his people, the rights of the nation. . . . I have therefore but this one word to say to you, that, seeing you have made pro-gress in this business, and completed the work on your part, I may have some short time to ask counsel of God, and of my own heart. And I hope that neither the humour of any weak or unwise people, nor yet the desire of any who may be lusting after things that are not good, shall steer me to give other than such an answer as may be ingenuous and thankful,—thankfully acknow-ledging your care and integrity ;—and such an answer as shall be for the good of those that I presume you and I serve, and are made for serving. And truly I may say this also, that, as the thing will deserve deliberation, the utmost deliberation and consideration on my part, so I shall think myself bound to give as speedy an answer to these things as I can."[1]

What were the thoughts which passed through the minds of

[1] Burton's Parliamentary Diary, vol. i. pp. 419—110 ; Cromwell's Letters and Speeches, vol. iii. pp. 269—272.

Cromwell and his audience when this conference came to an end, we cannot tell. Three days after, on the 3rd of April, he wrote to request the Parliament to appoint commissioners to receive his answer; and, on the same day, at three o'clock in the afternoon, a very large committee, consisting of eighty-two members, proceeded to Whitehall. " My Lords," said Cromwell to them, " I am heartily sorry that I did not make this desire of mine known to the Parliament sooner. The reason was because some infirmity of body hath seized upon me these two last days, yesterday and Wednesday. I have, as well as I could, taken consideration of the things contained in the paper which was presented to me by the Parliament on Tuesday last; and sought of God that I might return such an answer as might become me, and be worthy of the Parliament. I must needs bear this testimony to them, that they have been zealous of the two greatest concernments that God hath in the world. The one is that of religion, and of the preservation of the professors of it, to give them all due and just liberty. . . . The other is the civil liberty and interest of the nation. . . . These are things I must acknowledge Christian and honourable; and they are provided for by you like Christian men, and also men of honour,—like yourselves, Englishmen. And upon these two interests, if God shall account me worthy, I shall live and die. . . . Now give me leave to say, and to say it seriously, that you have one or two considerations that do stick with me. The one is, you have named me by another title than I now bear. You do necessitate my answer to be categorical; and you have made me without a liberty of choice, save as to all. I question not your wisdom in doing so: I think myself obliged to acquiesce in your determination, knowing you are men of wisdom, and considering the trust you are under. It is a duty not to question the reason of anything you have done. I should be very brutish, did I not acknowledge the exceeding high honour and respect you have had for me in this paper: . . . and by you I return the Parliament this my grateful acknowledgment. But I must needs say, that that may be fit for you to offer, which may not be fit for me to undertake. And as I should reckon it a very great presumption were I to ask the reason of your doing any one thing in this paper,—so you will not take it unkindly if I beg of you this addition to the Parliament's favour, love, and indulgence unto me, that it be taken in tender part if I give such an answer as I find it in my heart to give in this business, without urging many reasons for it, save such as are most obvious, and most to my advantage in answering, namely, that I am not able for such a trust and charge; . . . seeing the way is hedged up so as it is to me, that I cannot accept the things offered, unless I accept all, I have not been able to find it my duty to God and to you to undertake this charge under that title. The most I said in commendation of the instrument may be retorted on me, as thus: 'Are there such good things provided for? will you refuse to accept them because of such an ingredient?' Nothing must make a man's conscience a servant. And really and sincerely it is my conscience that guides me to this answer; and if the Parliament be so resolved, 'for the whole paper or none of it,' it will not be fit for me to use any inducement to you to alter their resolution. This is all I have to say. I desire it may, and do not doubt but it will, be with candour and ingenuity represented unto them by you."[1]

The Parliament fully perceived all the perplexities and obscurities of this answer; they were used to discern and follow Cromwell's secret desire through the labyrinth of his conduct and language. A vote was passed "that this House doth adhere to their humble Petition and Advice:" a committee was appointed to prepare a written statement of their reasons for such adherence: and, after the report of this committee had been read and approved, it was determined that Commissioners should be sent to inquire of the Protector on what day it would be convenient to him to receive the House, that the Speaker might read to him "the paper containing the reasons, and deliver the same to his Highness, if he desired it."[2]

This new interview took place on Wednesday, the 8th of April. No official report has been preserved, either of the explanation of the reasons of the Parliament, or of Cromwell's answer; but the newspapers of the time give us to understand that the Protector's refusal was less peremptory than it had been on the previous occasion: he pleaded his infirmities and disabilities, and said that since the Parliament had thought proper to persevere in their proposal, all that was left him was to ask further counsel on the subject; and from whom could he seek it, but from the Parliament itself? He therefore desired to be informed a little more particularly of the motives of their determination; and requested permission to state his own doubts, fears, and scruples. He was ready to render a reason of his own apprehensions, which haply might be overruled by better apprehensions; and he hoped that, when they both thoroughly understood the grounds of these things, something would be fixed on that might equally fit what was due from the Parliament and from

[1] Burton's Parliamentary Diary, vol. i. pp. 417—420; Cromwell's Letters and Speeches, vol. iii. pp. 273—276.
[2] Journals of the House of Commons, vol. vii. pp. 519—521.

himself, and might be adapted to the best advantage of the whole nation.[1]

It is evident that, on this occasion, the newspapers did not break through their usual reserve without the permission of the Protector, and that he allowed them to do so only because he thought it wise to submit this great question to the decision of the country.

On the following day, the Parliament voted, "That a Committee be appointed to wait upon his Highness, the Lord Protector, in reference to what his Highness did yesterday propose in his speech; and that this Committee have power to receive from his Highness his doubts and scruples, touching any of the particulars contained in the humble Petition and Advice formerly presented; and in answer thereunto, to offer to his Highness reasons for his satisfaction, and for the maintenance of the resolutions of this House; and such particulars as they cannot satisfy his Highness in, that they report the same to the Parliament."[2]

A solemn discussion thus began between Cromwell and the Parliament, which had undertaken to convince the Protector that he ought not to refuse to be King. A hundred Commissioners, including nearly all the important men in the House, and the great majority of whom were Cromwell's friends, were appointed to undertake this task.

At this very moment, however, a band of religious fanatics were bestirring themselves in London, for the establishment of a monarchy, which, they said, was the only legitimate monarchy,—that of Jesus Christ. These sectaries were called, and they called themselves, Fifth-monarchy-men. All other laws but the law of God, as revealed in the Holy Scriptures, and all other power but that of Christ, represented by the assembly of saints, were to be abolished by them. On the 9th of April, a score of them, under the command of Thomas Venner, a wine-cooper, met at Shoreditch, "booted and spurred," say the newspapers of the time, to proceed from thence to a general place of rendezvous; but a squadron of cavalry occupied the ground before them, and took them all prisoners. In a field near the place appointed for the general meeting, the soldiers found a large supply of arms, a quantity of pamphlets intended for distribution, and a standard "bearing a red lion *couchant*, with this motto: 'Who shall rouse him up?'" Some men of greater importance, such as Vice-Admiral Lawson, Colonels Okey and Danvers,

[1] Mercurius Politicus, April 9; Godwin's History of the Commonwealth, vol. iv. p. 359.

[2] Journals of the House of Commons, vol. vii. p. 521.

and even Major-General Harrison and Colonel Rich, who had been recently liberated from imprisonment, were compromised, either by their own acts, or by the words of the sectaries, and were also arrested. Two days after, Thurloe, by the Protector's command, gave an account to the Parliament of the plot, and of the measures taken to defeat it. Like an experienced politician, he did not attempt to exaggerate the danger, but declared that "the number and quality of the persons, who had resolved to begin this attempt, were truly very inconsiderable, and indeed despicable." He connected this movement, however, and not unreasonably, with the general state of parties and of minds; and he gave full details regarding the secret organisation of these sectaries, and their relations with all the disaffected politicians of the day. The Parliament understood and realised Thurloe's intention. A vote of thanks to him was immediately proposed and adopted; and the Speaker officially addressed him in these words: "Mr. Secretary, I am commanded to return you hearty thanks, in the name of the Parliament, for your great care and pains in discovering this business, and the great services done by you to the Commonwealth, and to the Parliament, both in this and many other particulars." At the same time, the Commissioners who had already been appointed to wait on the Protector, were directed to inform him "That the Parliament hath received the report from Mr. Secretary, and are very sensible of the great importance of it; and have ordered to take the same into consideration on Monday next."[1]

Under these auspices began, on the 11th of April, between the Commissioners of the Parliament and the Protector, those conferences which were to decide whether or not Cromwell should be made King.

It is an undignified and unpleasing thing to behold a comedy perseveringly played by serious men in a serious matter. Cromwell and the Parliament were both aware beforehand, of what was wanting to the government of England; they were both of them convinced that the restoration of the royal power could alone impart to it a regular and stable character. They employed a month in conversations and argumentations, just as if there had been any necessity for such mutual persuasion. In reality, the Parliament did not address themselves to Cromwell, nor did Cromwell reply to the Parliament; both parties spoke to the public outside Whitehall —to the opposing, but moderate republicans whom they hoped to

[1] Journals of the House of Commons, vol. vii. pp. 521, 522; Thurloe's State Papers, vol. vi. pp. 184—186.

gain over to their views—and to the entire country, in order to persuade it to adopt their desire for a new royalty, and to compel all the old parties to accede to it.[1]

Some embarrassment was manifested at the commencement of the first interview. Who should speak first? Ought the Commissioners to begin by explaining the motives of the petition, or ought the Protector to open the matter by stating his objections? On both sides there was a desire to feel the way, and to bring the other party to an explanation. Such a feeling is common during the final period of revolutions, when nearly all men, even the bravest, become sceptical and prudent, and strive either to elude or to diminish their responsibility. As it was easy to foresee, however, the Protector's desire prevailed. Whitelocke began the conference, and, on the first day, Cromwell did hardly anything but listen to the Commissioners of the Parliament. During the course of the five conferences which took place, between the 11th and 21st of April, nine of them spoke in succession, and all of them developed very nearly the same ideas. The lawyers, and especially Whitelocke and Glynn, were learned and judicious, but subtle and diffuse. Lord Broghill, in his triple character of warrior, courtier, and politician, was more precise and practical; he summed up, in these terms, his own reasonings and the arguments of his colleagues :—

" First. I humbly conceive that the title of king is that which the law takes notice of as the title of supreme magistrate, and no other ; and that the old foundations that are good, are better than any new ones, though equally good in their own nature. What is confirmed by time and experience carries along with it the best trial, and the most satisfactory stamp and authority.

" Secondly. It was considered, too, that it was much better that the supreme magistrate should be fitted to the laws that are in being, than that those laws should be fitted unto him.

" Thirdly. The people legally assembled in Parliament, having considered of what title was best for the supreme magistrate, did, after a solemn debate thereof, pitch upon that of king; it being that by which the people knew their duty to him, and he the duty of his office towards them, and both by old and known laws.

" Fourthly. There are hardly any who own government at all in these nations, but think themselves obliged to obey the old laws, or those which your Highness and the Parliament shall enact;

---

[1] A detailed narrative of these conferences will be found in a pamphlet entitled, " Monarchy asserted to be the best, most ancient, and legal form of government," published in 1660, and reprinted in the great Somers' Collection of Tracts, vol. vi. pp. 316—412.

so that if the supreme magistrate of these three nations be entitled king, all those who reverence the old laws will obediently and cheerfully accept of him, as that which is settled upon the establishment they own; and all that own the present authority will do the like, because grafted by it; by which none can rest unsatisfied that think it a duty to obey former authorities or the present.

" Fifthly. The former authorities know no supreme magistrate but by the title of king, and this present authority desires to know him by no other; which, if refused, might it not too much heighten our enemies, who may bolster up their faint hopes with saying to one another, and to those who assist them, that their chief is not only under that title which all past Parliaments have approved, but under that title which even this Parliament doth approve likewise; and that our head is not known by the former laws, and has refused to be known by that appellation which even the Parliament, that he himself hath called, doth desire to know him by?

"Sixthly. By your Highness bearing the title of king, all those that obey and serve you are secured by a law made long before any of our differences had a being—in the 11 of Hen. VII.—where a full provision is made for the safety of those that shall serve whoever is king. It is by that law that hitherto our enemies have pleaded indemnity, and by your assuming what is now desired, that law, which hitherto they pretended for their disobedience, ties them, even by their own profession and principles, to obedience; and I hope taking off all pretences from so numerous a party, may not be a thing unworthy of consideration. That law seems very rational, for it doth not provide for any particular family or person, but for the peace and safety of the people, by obeying whoever is in that office and bears that title. The end of all government is to give the people justice and safety, and the best means to obtain that end is to settle a supreme magistrate. It would, therefore, seem very irrational that the people, having obtained the end, should decline that end only to follow the means which are but conducing to that end. So that if the title and office of king be vested in your Highness, and the people thereby enjoy their rights and peace, it would be little less than madness for any of them to cast off those blessings, only in order to obtain the same end under another person.

" Seventhly. There is at present but a divorce between the pretending king and the imperial crown of these nations, and we know that persons divorced may marry again; but if the person be married to another, it cuts off all hope. These may be some of those reasons which invited the Parliament to make that desire, and to give that advice to your Highness, of assuming the title of king. There is another, and a very strong one, which is, that now they have actually given you that advice—and the advices of the Parliament are things which always ought, and therefore I am confident will, carry with them very great force and authority. Nor doth this advice come singly, but accompanied with many other excellent things in reference to our civil and spiritual liberties, which your Highness hath borne a just and signal testimony to. It is also a Parliament who have given unquestionable proofs of their affection to your Highness, and who, if listened to in this particular, will be thereby encouraged to give you more." [1]

Cromwell listened to these exhortations with evident satisfaction, but at the same time with great perturbation of mind. He was not a man of simple and fixed ideas, nor did he go straight forward to his object ; he wandered on all sides as he proceeded, making sure of his ground in every direction, and plunging into all sorts of indirect and even contrary paths. Whilst the Commissioners were speaking to him, his vivid imagination brought rapidly before his eyes all the inmost recesses and most various aspects of his position, as well as all the near and remote, probable or possible, consequences of the act which he was deliberating. He spoke several times, at greater length and with more diffuseness than even the lawyers, adopting and giving utterance to any reflections, recollections, allusions, or presentiments, just as they occurred to him ; talking incoherently and obscurely, sometimes from impetuosity, and sometimes intentionally ; now and then throwing out a few rays of light, but more frequently giving the very reverse of his real thoughts, like a man fully determined not to afford any positive clue to his intentions, and at the same time quite sure of being able, when he pleased, to produce a fixed resolution from the labyrinth of his mind. " If your arguments," he said to the Commissioners, " come upon me to enforce upon me the ground of necessity, why then I have no room to answer, for what must be, must be." He then summed up, in clear and striking language, all that the lawyers had said, with a view to prove that kingship was, in fact, a necessary title and office, so interwoven with the fundamental laws of England that they could not be properly executed without its authority. " But," continued Cromwell, " if a remedy or expedient may be found that this title and office are not necessary, they are not in

[1] Somers' Tracts, vol. vi. pp. 363, 364.

evitable grounds; and if not necessary and concluding, why then they will hang upon the reason of expediency or conveniency. . . . Truly, though kingship be not a title, but a name of office that runs through the law, yet it is not so *ratione nominis*, but from what is signified; it is a name of office plainly implying a supreme authority; and if it be so, why then I would suppose that whatsoever name hath been, or shall be, the name in which the supreme authority shall act—if it had been those four or five letters, or whatever else it had been—that signification goes to the thing and not to the name. I think the authority that could christen it with such a name could have called it by another name; . . . and it is known to you all that the supreme authority hath twice gone in another name and under another title than king, namely, under the *Custodes Libertatis Angliæ*,[1] and since I exercised the place (of Protector). And truly I may say that almost universal obedience hath been given by all ranks and sorts of men to both. . . . And as for my own part, I profess I think I may say, since the beginning of that change—though I should be loath to speak anything vainly—but since the beginning of that change to this day, I do not think there hath been a freer procedure of the laws, not even in those days called, and not unworthily, the 'halcyon days of peace,' from the twentieth of Elizabeth to King James and King Charles's time. . . . And if more of my lords the judges were here than now are, they could tell us, perhaps, somewhat further.

. . . .

" I am a man standing in the place I am in; which place I undertook not so much out of hope of doing any good, as out of a desire to prevent mischief and evil, which I did see was imminent on the nation. I say, we were running headlong into confusion and disorder, and would necessarily have run into blood; and I was passive to those that desired me to undertake the place which I now have. . . . . If you do not all of you, I am sure some of you do, and it behoves me to say that I do, know my calling from the first to this day. I was a person who, from my first employment, was suddenly preferred, and lifted up from lesser trusts to greater; from my first being a captain of a troop of horse; and I did labour as well as I could to discharge my trust; and God blessed me therein as it pleased Him. And I did truly and plainly, and in a

---

[1] This was the name substituted for that of King, in 1649 (when the Commonwealth was first established), at the head of the decrees of the courts of justice, and of all similar documents: it referred particularly to the Commissioners of the Great Seal, as guardians of the public liberties, by and under the authority of the Parliament.

way of foolish simplicity, as it was judged by very great and wise men, and good men too,—desire to make my instruments help me in that work. And I will deal plainly with you: I had a very worthy friend then; and he was a very noble person, and I know his memory is very grateful to all—Mr. John Hampden. At my first going out into this engagement, I saw our men were beaten at every hand; and I desired him that he would make some additions to my Lord Essex's army, of some new regiments; and I told him I would be serviceable to him in bringing such men in, as I thought had a spirit that would do something in the work. This is very true that I tell you: God knows I lie not. 'Your troops,' said I, 'are most of them old decayed serving-men and tapsters, and such kind of fellows; and,' said I, 'their troops are gentlemen's sons, younger sons, and persons of quality· do you think that the spirits of such mean and base fellows will ever be able to encounter gentlemen, that have honour, and courage, and resolution in them?' Truly I did represent to him in this manner conscientiously: and truly I did tell him: 'You must get men of a spirit—and take it not ill what I say: I know you will not,—of a spirit that is likely to go on as far as gentlemen will go: or else you will be beaten still.' I told him so; I did truly. He was a wise and worthy person; and he did think that I talked a good notion, but an impracticable one. I told him I could *do* somewhat in it; and truly I must needs say this to you,—impute it to what you please,—I raised such men as had the fear of God before them, as made some conscience of what they did; and from that day forward, I must say to you, they were never beaten, and wherever they were engaged against the enemy, they beat continually. . . . .

"I will be bold to apply this to our present purpose, because it is my all! . . . I tell you there are such men in this nation; godly men of the same spirit, men that will not be beaten down by a worldly or carnal spirit, while they keep their integrity. And I deal plainly and faithfully with you when I say: I cannot think that God would bless an undertaking of anything (kingship or whatever else), which would, justly and with cause, grieve *them*. True, they may be troubled without cause;—and I must be a slave if I should comply with any such humour as that. But I say there are honest men and faithful men, true to the great things of the Government, namely, the liberty of the people, giving them what is due to them, and protecting this interest, . . who very generally do not swallow this title. And though really it is no part of their goodness to be unwilling to submit to what a Parliament shall settle over them, yet I must say, it is my duty and my conscience to beg of you that there may be no hard things put upon me ; things, I mean, hard to *them*, which they cannot swallow. . . . .

" Truly the providence of God hath laid aside this title of king providentially *de facto ;* and that not by sudden humour or passion : but it hath been by issue of as great deliberation as ever was in a nation. It hath been by issue of ten or twelve years of civil war, wherein much blood hath been shed. I will not dispute the justice of it when it was done ; nor need I tell you what my opinion is, in the case were it *de novo* to be done. But if it be at all disputable ; and a man comes and finds that God, in his severity, hath not only eradicated a whole family, and thrust them out of the land, for reasons best known to Himself, but also hath made the issue and close of that to be the very eradication of a name or title. It was not done by me, nor by them that tendered me the government I now act in ; it was done by the Long Parliament. . . .

" Truly, as I have often said to the Parliament itself, so I may now say to you, who are a very considerable representation of the Parliament, I am hugely taken with the word *settlement*—with the thing, and with the notion of it. And, indeed, I think he is not worthy to live in England who is not ! No : I will do my part, so far as I am able, to expel that man out of the nation who desireth not that, in the general, we come to a settlement : because, indeed, it is the great misery and unhappiness of a nation to be without such. . . . . And truly I have said, and I say it again, that I think this present proposed form of settlement doth tend to the making of the nation enjoy the things we have all along declared for. . . . . And this it is makes me in love with this paper ; and with all the things in it ; and with the additions I have now to tender you thereto ; and with *settlement* above all things in the world !—except only that, where I left you last time ; for that I think we have debated. I have heard your mind, and you have heard mine as to that ; I have told you my heart and judgment ; and the Lord bring forth His own issue." [1]

Cromwell then turned to the Petition itself, and examined its different dispositions, one after the other—especially those which related to the conditions of eligibility to a seat in Parliament, to the mode of examining into the qualification of members, to the nomination of members of the Other House, of the judges and of all the officers of State, and to the fixation of the public revenue ;

---

[1] Somers' Tracts, vol. vi. pp. 365—373 ; Cromwell's Letters and Speeches, vol. iii. pp. 296—315.

and on each of these points he indicated the modifications which he
desired to introduce, nearly all of which were judicious, and
dictated by a clear understanding of the conditions of public order,
and the necessities of power. He also insisted, either from real
conviction, or in compliance with a popular feeling, which was
especially powerful and current among the party which he was
desirous to gain over, upon reform of the civil laws, and a reformation of manners,—complacently developing the salutary effects of a
simple course of procedure in the affairs of common life, and of the
exercise of vigorous discipline in the national morality. He then
handed to the Commissioners a written copy of his observations
and propositions. "And so," he said, "I have done with what I
had to offer you,—I think I have, truly, for my part. And when I
shall understand where it lies on me to do farther; and when I
shall understand your pleasure in these things a little farther; and
when you will be pleased to let me hear farther of your thoughts in
these things, *then* I suppose I shall be in a condition to discharge
myself, as God shall put in my mind. And I speak not this to
evade; but I speak in the fear and reverence of God. And I
shall plainly and clearly, I say,—when you shall have been pleased
among yourselves to take consideration of these things, that I may
hear what your thoughts are of them; I do not say that as a
condition to anything, but I shall then be free, and honest, and
plain, to discharge myself of what, in the whole, and upon the
whole, may reasonably be expected from me, and what God shall
set me free to answer you in."[1]

Two days afterwards, on the 23rd of April, the Commissioners,
by the mouth of Whitelocke, made their report to the House respecting these conferences. During the course of the affair, they
had several times reported progress, and the House, with wise dis-
cretion, had done all in its power to support them, without embarrassing them in the negotiation. When it was informed, by its
Commissioners, of all Cromwell's fluctuations and obscurities, and of
the impossibility of obtaining a distinct answer from him, it manifested at first some displeasure. It was quite willing to help the
Protector to make himself king, but it did not wish to appear to be
making him king in spite of himself, and thus to take upon itself
alone the entire responsibility of the re-establishment of monarchy.
It entered at once, however, upon the examination of the modifications which Cromwell wished to introduce into the plan of govern-

---

[1] Somers' Tracts, vol. vi. pp. 389—400; Cromwell's Letters and Speeches,
vol. iii. pp. 327—365.

ment recommended by the Petition. The discussion on this point was longer and more animated than any one had anticipated; even among the friends of the Protector, two classes of men, if not two parties, found themselves in presence in the Parliament—old partisans of monarchy, who had accepted the Commonwealth only from necessity, and against their will; and wearied, but not converted republicans, who acquiesced in a return to monarchical government only from the same cause, and with the same dissatisfaction. Upon every question, these two tendencies were manifested and came into collision—the one party being anxious to save at least some fragments of the shipwrecked Commonwealth, and the others eagerly seizing upon this opportunity of restoring to monarchical power all its former force and vitality. Those among them, moreover, who had taken an active part in the deeds of violence and spoliation committed by the republicans, began already to feel apprehensive of the consequences to which this monarchical reaction might lead, and at every step demanded effectual guarantees for the safety of their persons and their fortunes. Complicated and heated by all these causes, the debate was prolonged from the 23rd to the 30th of April, and occupied five long sittings, the last of which extended from eight o'clock in the morning to half-past eight in the evening, without any adjournment for dinner—"the first instance I have met with of such a sitting," says Thomas Burton, in his Diary.[1]

Cromwell was still more anxious and active than the House. Independently of his hesitation, whether real or affected, he wished the discussion to be protracted, and the question incessantly brought forward and discussed before the public, either in order to convince it, or to alarm it by the prospect of fresh catastrophes; a most powerful means of conviction, and one which the leaders of revolutions turn to enormous account. He ordered a report of these conferences with the Commissioners of the Parliament, to be printed and circulated; and the principal newspapers published the speeches which he had made. He attracted near his person, under a thousand pretexts, the officers of the army, whether known or unknown, favourable or opposed to his plans, and he made every effort to secure, if not their co-operation, at least their neutrality. Even with his most intimate confidants, on whose assistance he could rely, he took the most assiduous pains to keep up their confidence and zeal. "The Protector," says Whitelocke, "often advised about this and other great businesses with the Lord Broghill, Pierrepoint,

<hr>
[1] Burton's Parliamentary Diary, vol. ii. pp. 23—94; Journals of the House of Commons, vol. vii. pp. 523—529.

myself, Sir Charles Wolseley, and Thurloe, and would be shut up three or four hours together in private discourse, and none were admitted to come in to him. He would sometimes be very cheerful with us, and laying aside his greatness, he would be exceeding familiar with us, and, by way of diversion, would make verses with us, and every one must try his fancy. He commonly called for tobacco, pipes, and a candle, and would now and then take tobacco himself. Then he would fall again to his serious and great business, and advise with us in those affairs · and this he did often with us."[1]

It was the general belief that he had fully determined to succeed, and that his success was certain. "I have seen letters," wrote Colonel Titus to Sir Edward Hyde, on the 10th of April, 1657, "from the Presbyterian party, that say all things in order to the making Cromwell king go on without any opposition; that though the republican party in the House and army at first talked very high, yet now they are submissive enough, and begin to distrust their own strength to make good any opposition."[2] Sir Francis Russell, whose daughter was the wife of Henry Cromwell, wrote thus to his son-in-law, on the 27th of April: "I do in this (I think) desire to take leave of your lordship, for my next is likely to be to the Duke of York. Your father begins to come out of the clouds, and it appears to us that he will take the kingly power upon him. That great noise which was made about this business not long since is almost over, and I cannot think there will be the least combustion about it. This day I have had some discourse with your father about this great business. He is very cheerful, and his troubled thoughts seem to be over."[3]

Cromwell's habitual intimates were not so confident: "Certainly," wrote Thurloe to Henry Cromwell, on the 21st of April, 1657, "his Highness hath very great difficulties in his own mind, although he hath had the clearest call that ever man had; and for aught I see, the Parliament will not be persuaded that there can be any settlement any other way. . . . Many of the soldiers are not only content, but are very well satisfied with this change. Some indeed grumble, but that's the most, for aught I can perceive. And surely whatever resolutions his Highness takes, they will be his own, there being nothing from without that should be any constraint upon him, either to take or refuse it. . The truth is, his carriage

[1] Whitelocke's Memorials, p. 656.
[2] Clarendon's State Papers, vol. iii. p. 335.
[3] Forster's Statesmen of the Commonwealth, vol. v. p. 353; Burton's Parliamentary Diary, vol. ii. p. 118.

in this debate was such that it gave great hopes to some, that he would at last comply with the Parliament; but that time must show—for the present, we can but guess."[1]

These, however, were only the doubts of an old politician, and the anxieties of an interested servant. The public did not share in them; it believed firmly in the fixity of Cromwell's resolution, and the certainty of his success; some even went so far as to say that "a crown was actually made, and brought to Whitehall," in readiness for the coronation;[2] and Cromwell, in his confidential moments, confirmed these public rumours, for he even went so far as to say, after his third conference with the Parliament's Commissioners, that he was satisfied in his private judgment that it was f[.] for him to take upon him the title of king."[3]

On the 30th of April, the debate on the amendments to the Petition came to an end. The Parliament requested of the Protector an audience, that it might present to him the amended document. The interview was a brief and cold one. Cromwell received the Petition from the hands of Whitelocke, cast his eyes over the last phrases, and contented himself with saying, hurriedly and in a low tone, "that the papers would ask some consideration, therefore he could not then appoint the time, but he would acquaint the House when he had considered of the time, and that in as short a time as might be, or as he could."[4]

It was of little consequence to him that most of his amendments to the Petition had been adopted; the difficulty did not lie there, nor in the Parliament. Notwithstanding his persevering labour, he had not succeeded in gaining over some of the most popular leaders of the army; they persisted in their opposition, either from envy, personal dignity, republican fidelity, sectarian fanaticism, or resentment of his conduct towards the Major-generals. Some of them, Cromwell's near relations,—such as Fleetwood, his son-in-law, and Desborough, his brother-in-law,—grounded their resistance on their family interest, as they were convinced that the restoration of the monarchy would turn to the advantage of Charles Stuart. With the general mass of the nation, Cromwell had had no better success; they offered no resistance, but made no movement to promote the realisation of his design: he had not succeeded in leading them to

[1] Thurloe's State Papers, vol. vi. p. 219.
[2] Forster's Statesmen of the Commonwealth, vol. v. p. 354; Welwood's Memoirs, p. 116.
[3] Whitelocke's Memorials, p. 656.
[4] Burton's Parliamentary Diary, vol. ii. p. 101; Commons' Journals, vol. vii. p. 529.

regard it as important and useful to themselves: so they looked on the undertaking with indifferent curiosity, as an affair of personal ambition and political partisanship. The people of England felt instinctively convinced that their condition would be but slightly changed by it, and that even if the proposed alteration were effected, it would not restore to them the two things which they held most dear—a true King and a true Parliament. It is impossible to rekindle at will trustful enthusiasm in the heart of a people; and the ablest often fail to persuade the very men whom they may frequently have deceived.

But Cromwell never renounced an intention. He could not bring himself to believe that this resistance in his own family was invincible. On the 5th of May, he requested the Commissioners of the Parliament to wait upon him on the next day in the afternoon: and on that same day, he invited himself to dinner at the house of his brother-in-law, Desborough, and took his son-in-law, Fleetwood, with him. At table, with his usual gay familiarity, he joked about kingship, repeating his favourite phrase "that it was but a feather in a man's cap, and he therefore wondered that men would not please the children, and permit them to enjoy their rattle." But Fleetwood and Desborough remained serious and unconvinced. They assured him "that there was more in this matter than he perceived; that those who put him upon it were no enemies to Charles Stuart; and that if he accepted of it, he would infallibly draw ruin on himself and friends." "You are a couple of scrupulous fellows," said Cromwell, laughing; and he left them, determined to go forward, in spite of their opposition.[1] On the following day, he announced to the Commissioners of the Parliament, who waited on him in obedience to his instructions, that, on the next day, he would receive the whole House at Westminster Hall, in the Painted Chamber, and that he would then give his final answer to the Petition. The place appointed for this audience seemed to indicate that he had resolved to become king. Ordinarily he received the Parliament in the palace of Whitehall, in which he resided; on great occasions only, such as the opening of the session, or when any important event was in contemplation, he repaired to the Painted Chamber in Westminster Hall, and sent a message from thence to invite the Parliament to come to him.[2] But on the 7th of May, at about eleven o'clock in the morning, when the House had met, and was momently expecting to receive this message,

---

[1] Ludlow's Memoirs, p. 249.
- [2] Godwin's History of the Commonwealth, vol. iv. p. 305

Lenthall, one of the Commissioners, announced that, that very morning, the Protector had sent to inform as many of the members as could be found, that he desired that the audience of the whole House might be deferred until the next day, and that the Commissioners would meet him again in the evening, at five o'clock, for he had something to say to them.[1] The reason of this postponement was this : while walking in St. James's Park on the previous evening, Cromwell had met Desborough, and had either plainly declared to him, or given him to understand, that he had made up his mind to accept the crown. Desborough, who became daily more strenuous in his opposition, replied, " That he then gave the cause and Cromwell's family also for lost ; and that though he was resolved never to act against him, yet he would not act for him after that time." Upon which they separated, the one in fresh perplexity, and the other in great irritation. On his return home, Desborough found Colonel Pride, the man who, on the 6th of December, 1648, had, by his general's order, driven the whole Presbyterian party out of the House of Commons : he had recently been knighted by Cromwell, and he was now one of the intractable republicans. " Cromwell is determined to accept the crown," said Desborough. " He shall not," answered Pride. " Why," said Desborough, " how wilt thou hinder it ? " " Get me a petition drawn," said Pride, " and I will prevent it." They went together at once to Dr. Owen, one of Cromwell's favourite preachers, and Vice-Chancellor of the University of Oxford : the divine was of the same opinion as the officers, and willingly drew up the petition which they required.[2] Cromwell doubtless received some information of this, and hence his delay in giving audience to the Parliament. He did not even grant an interview to the Commissioners on that evening, although he had specially invited them to meet him. They had been waiting at Whitehall for more than two hours, when, a Barbary horse having been brought into the garden for him to see, he had occasion to pass through the room where they were in attendance. He " excused himself slightly," says Ludlow, for having made them wait so long, and begged them to return on the following morning.[3] They did return : and either while they were with the Protector, or as they were on their way to give an account to the Parliament of their interview, some officers arrived at the door of the House, and demanded admittance to present a petition. On being brought to the bar, one of them, named Colonel Mason,

[1] Journals of the House of Commons, vol. vii. p. 531.
[2] Ludlow's Memoirs, pp. 248, 249.
[3] Journals of the House of Commons, vol. vii. p. 531.

presented the petition which Dr. Owen had drawn up, and which
had been signed by two colonels, seven lieutenant-colonels, eight
majors, and sixteen captains. The officers withdrew : their petition
was read. It was to this effect : "That they had hazarded their
lives against monarchy, and were still ready so to do, in defence of
the liberties of the nation ; and that, having observed in some men
great endeavours to bring the nation again under their old servitude,
by pressing their general to take upon him the title and government
of a king, in order to destroy him, and weaken the hands of those
who were faithful to the public,—they therefore humbly desired that
the Parliament would discountenance all such persons and endeavours,
and continue steadfast to the old cause, for the preservation of which
they, for their parts, were most ready to lay down their lives."[1]

The House, in embarrassment, hesitated and waited. Cromwell,
who received instant information of this occurrence, sent for Fleetwood, and complained bitterly that he had allowed such a petition
to be presented : " he could and ought to have prevented it, for he
knew well that he (Cromwell) was resolved not to accept the
crown without the consent of the army." He therefore requested
Fleetwood to hasten at once to the House, to prevent them from
doing anything further in the matter; and he sent to the Commissioners to invite the House, in his name, to meet him on that very
day, at Whitehall, to receive his definitive answer. Fleetwood
obeyed; the Commissioners and the whole House obeyed ; and, as soon
as they were assembled in the Banqueting-hall, Cromwell came in.

" Mr. Speaker," he said, " I come hither to answer that that
was in your last paper to your Committee you sent to me—which
was in relation to the desires that were offered me by the House in
that they called their Petition.

" I confess that business hath put the House, the Parliament,
to a great deal of trouble, and spent much time. I am very sorry
for that. It hath cost me some trouble, and some thoughts : and
because I have been the unhappy occasion of the expense of so
much time, I shall spend little of it now.

" I have, the best I can, revolved the whole business in my
thoughts : and I have said so much already in testimony to the
whole, I think I shall not need to repeat what I have said. I think
it is an Act of Government which, in the aims of it, seeks the
settling of the nation on a good foot, in relation to civil rights and
liberties, which are the rights of the nation. And I hope I shall

[1] Ludlow's Memoirs, p. 249; Journals of the House of Commons, vol. vii.
p. 531; Godwin's History of the Commonwealth, vol. iv. pp. 365–367.

never be found one of them that go about to rob the nation of those
rights; but always to serve it what I can to the attaining of them.
It has also been exceedingly well provided there for the safety and
security of honest men, in that great natural and religious liberty,
which is liberty of conscience. These are the great fundamentals,
and I must bear my testimony to them—as I have done, and shall
do still—so long as God lets me live in this world: that the intentions and the things are very honourable and honest, and the pro-
duct worthy of a Parliament.

"I have only had the unhappiness, both in my conferences with
your committees, and in the best thoughts I could take to myself,
not to be convinced of the necessity of that thing which hath so
often been insisted on by you, to wit, the title of King, as in itself
so necessary as it seems to be apprehended by you. And yet I do,
with all honour and respect, testify that, *cæteris paribus*, no private
judgment is to be in the balance with the judgment of Parliament. But in things that respect particular persons, every man
who is to give an account to God of his actions must in some
measure be able to prove his own work, and to have an approbation
in his own conscience of that which he is to do or to forbear. And
whilst you are granting others liberties, surely you will not deny
me this—it being not only a liberty, but a duty, and such a duty as
I cannot without sinning forbear,—to examine my own heart, and
thoughts, and judgment, in every work which I am to set my hand
to, or to appear in or for.

"I must confess, therefore, that I have truly thought, and I do
still think, that if I should do anything on this account to answer
your expectation, at the best I should do it doubtingly. And
certainly whatsoever is so, is not of faith. And whatsoever is not
of faith, is sin to him that doth it.

"I, lying under this consideration, think it my duty—only I
could have wished I had done it sooner, for the sake of the House,
who have laid such infinite obligations on me; I wish I had done
it sooner for your sake, and for saving time and trouble; and for
the Committee's sake, to whom I must acknowledge I have been
unreasonably troublesome—but truly this is my answer, that
(although I think the Act of Government doth consist of very
excellent parts, in all but that one thing, of the title as to me) I
should not be an honest man, if I did not tell you that I cannot
accept of the government, nor undertake the trouble and charge of
it—as to which I have a little more experimented than everybody,
what troubles and difficulties do befall men under such trusts, and
in such undertakings—I say I am persuaded to return this answer

to you: that I cannot undertake this government with the title of King. And that is mine answer to this great and weighty business."[1]

The House withdrew in silence, and postponed all further deliberation on the subject to the 13th of May. Six weeks were passed in insipid debates, which were uninteresting even to those who took part in them. The title of Lord-Protector was substituted for that of King, in the Petition and Advice ;[2] and Major-General Jephson ironically proposed that the four letters which formed the word *King*, should be expunged from the alphabet, as many persons " were so out of love with them."[3] It was also demanded that certain conditions should be attached to the appointment of members of the Other House. This was a subject of great anxiety to the old republican party; they feared that many of the old nobility might be invited to sit in this new House; and, in order to exclude them altogether, or at least to humiliate before admitting them, it was proposed that they should be required to approve of the execution of the late king, of the expulsion of his family, and of the abolition of the House of Lords.[4] It was also discussed whether the Protectorate, thus modified in its constitution, would be a new government; and whether it would be necessary for the Protector and the members of the two Houses to take a new oath.[5] These debates were marked by greater obstinacy than animation; the House was impatient to dissolve. "I move," said Lenthall, on the 26th of May, "that all private business may be laid aside. The weather grows hot. I hope we shall not sit all summer. I would have public business, as moneys and the like, and the clamours for the public faith, attended to." "I second the motion," said Sir Thomas Wroth, "that all private business be laid aside, and that we go to those affairs that are most public. It is all that the people are like to have for their moneys. They are likely to pay well for it."[6] When these various questions had been resolved, on the 25th of May, 1657, the House met once more, to present the Protector with the Humble Petition and Advice, in its modified form; a sergeant came to acquaint the House that " his Highness was in the House of Lords, waiting to

[1] Cromwell's Letters and Speeches, vol. iii. pp. 367, 370; Ludlow's Memoirs, p. 250.
[2] May 22, 1657 ; Burton's Diary, vol. ii. p. 119.
[3] May 27, 1657 ; ibid. vol. ii. p. 140.
[4] June 24, 1657 ; Burton's Diary, vol. ii. pp. 298—300.
[5] June 23, 24, 1657 ; Commons' Journals, vol. vii. pp. 570—574 ; Burton's Diary, vol. ii. pp. 280, 284, 295.
[6] May 26, 1657 ; Burton's Diary, vol. ii. pp. 124, 125.

receive them." This misnomer was received in profound silence
but it was excused as a mistake on the part of the sergeant, who
had been directed to request the House to attend the Protector in
the Painted Chamber.[1] They proceeded thither at once. "I
desire to offer a word or two unto you," said Cromwell, "which
shall be but a word. I did well bethink myself before I came
hither to-day, that I came not as to a triumph, but with the most
serious thoughts that ever I had in all my life, to undertake one of
the greatest tasks that ever was laid upon the back of a human
creature." He dwelt upon the idea with melancholy firmness,
declaring himself incapable of efficiently discharging his duty,
without the support of the Almighty, and the co-operation of the
Parliament, which, he said, had already shown great forwardness
and readiness to assist him, but which still had much to do " for
the good of these nations, and the carrying on of this government."
" I do heartily and earnestly desire," he said, in conclusion, " that
God may crown your work, and bless you, that, in your own time,
and with what speed you judge fit, these things may be provided
for." He then gave his formal consent to the new constitution of
the Protectorate, and returned to Whitehall.[2]

Whilst, under an air of pious indifference to the disappointment
he had experienced, Cromwell was still giving utterance to his
unextinguishable hopes, a pamphlet, entitled " Killing no Murder,"
was widely circulated in all directions. It opened with a dedication
" To his Highness, Oliver Cromwell," in these terms: " My
intention is to procure your Highness that justice that nobody yet
does you, and to let the people see, the longer they defer it, the
greater injury they do both themselves and you. To your Highness
justly belongs the honour of dying for the people; and it cannot
but be an unspeakable consolation to you, in the last moments of
your life, to consider with how much benefit to the world you are
likely to leave it. It is then only, my Lord, the titles you now
usurp will be truly yours; you will then be, indeed, the deliverer
of your country, and free it from a bondage little inferior to that
from which Moses delivered his. You will then be that true
reformer which you would now be thought; religion shall then be
restored, liberty asserted, and Parliaments have those privileges
they have fought for. All this we hope from your Highness's
happy expiration. To hasten this great good, is the chief end of

[1] May 25, 1657; Burton's Diary, vol. ii. p. 129.
[2] Commons' Journals, vol. vii. pp. 539, 540. By a singular omission, this
speech is not included in Mr. Carlyle's Collection of Cromwell's Letters and
Speeches. It should be Speech XV. vol. iii. p. 374.

my writing this paper; and if it have the effects I hope it will, your Highness will quickly be out of the reach of men's malice, and your enemies will only be able to wound you in your memory, which strokes you will not feel." Widely circulated and eagerly read, this publication inspired the friends of the Protector with great alarm. "It is the most dangerous pamphlet that ever has been printed in these times," wrote Morland to Pell, on the 1st of June, 1657; "and I think the devil himself could not have shown more rancour, malice, and wickedness than is in it." The indefatigable deviser of all these projects of assassination and revolt,— Colonel Sexby, was, there is reason to believe, the author of this pamphlet; but he had reckoned too rashly on his ability to instigate assassins, and on his adroitness to escape Cromwell's police; he was detected in London, arrested, and sent to the Tower, in July, 1657; and in January, 1658, he died in imprisonment; declaring, sometimes with pride, and sometimes with sorrow, that he had originated Sindercombe's plot, and written the celebrated pamphlet.[1]

Amidst this hostile agitation, on the 26th of June, 1657, an estrade was erected in Westminster Hall. The royal chair of Scotland, brought for the purpose from Westminster Abbey, was placed upon it, beneath "a prince-like canopy of state." In front of the chair, but a little below it, stood a table "covered with pink-coloured velvet of Genoa, fringed with fringe of gold." On this table were the Bible, sword, and sceptre of the Commonwealth. Before the table, on a chair, sat Sir Thomas Widdrington, the Speaker of the Parliament. At some distance were seats, "built scaffold-wise, like an amphitheatre," for the members of both Houses of Parliament. Below, places were reserved for the aldermen of the city of London, and other spectators.

At about two o'clock, Cromwell entered the hall, preceded and followed by a numerous and brilliant company. The members, or lords of the Other House, walked immediately behind him; and after them came the knights, citizens, and burgesses, elected to sit in Parliament for the counties, cities, and boroughs of the Com-

[1] Harleian Miscellany, vol. iv. pp. 289—305 ; Thurloe's State Papers, vol. vi. pp. 485, 560 ; Burton's Diary, vol. ii. pp. 312—314 ; Godwin's History of the Commonwealth, vol. iv. p. 390. This pamphlet has frequently been attributed to Colonel Silas Titus, a Presbyterian Royalist, who, after the Restoration, claimed its authorship, and was probably indebted to this assertion for his appointment as groom of the bedchamber to Charles II. But an attentive examination of the circumstances and evidence relating to the case leads me to think, with Mr. Godwin, that Sexby was the real author of " Killing no Murder."

monwealth.   In the midst of loud acclamations, Cromwell sat down in the chair of state.   On his left stood the Lord Mayor of London, and the Dutch Ambassador; and on his right the French Ambassador, and Robert, Earl of Warwick, who, during the procession, had borne the sword before him.   The Speaker, in the name of the Parliament, then presented to Cromwell "a rich and costly robe of purple velvet, lined with ermines ; a Bible, ornamented with bosses and clasps, richly gilt; a rich and costly sword, and a sceptre of massy gold."   He made a speech upon these four emblems, then took the Bible, and administered to Cromwell the following oath :—

"I do in the presence and by the name of God Almighty, promise and swear, that, to the utmost of my power, I will uphold and maintain the true, reformed, Protestant, Christian religion, in the purity thereof, as it is contained in the Holy Scriptures of the Old and New Testament : and encourage the profession and professors of the same ;—and that, to the utmost of my power, I will endeavour, as chief magistrate of these three nations, the maintenance and preservation of the just rights and privileges of the people thereof; and shall, in all things, according to my best knowledge and power, govern the people of these nations according to law."

Cromwell took the oath.   Dr. Manton delivered a prayer.   The heralds, by loud sound of trumpet, proclaimed his Highness, Oliver Cromwell, Protector of England, Scotland, and Ireland, and the dominions and territories thereunto belonging.   To which the people replied with shouts,—"Long live his Highness! huzza!" Cromwell rose, bowed to the assembly, came down from the estrade, and, with his retinue, returned in procession to Whitehall.   The members of Parliament returned to the House, and adjourned to the 20th of January following.[1]

Thus was inaugurated, for the second time, the Protectorate of Cromwell, as established by the new constitution which had been agreed upon by Cromwell and the Parliament.   The two Houses were restored.   The government was concentrated in the hands of the Protector.   He had the right of appointing his successor. The State was no longer a Commonwealth ; it only required hereditary succession, and the title of king, to make it a monarchy.

Cromwell had formally refused that title.   To all appearance, his honour was unscathed ; neither had he suffered any diminution

---

[1] Old Parliamentary History, vol. xxi. pp. 148, 152—159 ; Commons' Journals, vol. vii. pp. 577, 578; Burton's Diary, vol. ii. pp. 511—515; Whitelocke, pp. 662—664 ; Cromwelliana, pp. 165—167.

of his power. The House, though abandoned by him after he had instigated it to act as it had done, either did not desire, or did not dare, to manifest any resentment. All disturbance in the army ceased; satisfied, but not intoxicated, with their success, the opposing officers now rallied round the Protector; he continued powerful and formidable as ever. Yet he had received a severe blow. His enemies taxed him with irresolution and pusillanimity. "The Major-generals and officers of the army," wrote Mr. Broderick to Sir Edward Hyde, on the 7th of May, 1657, "laugh at his hopes, and despise him for his fears; in the opinions of the impartial, he is a wild and wanton lavisher of his good fortune."[1] His most intimate friends were surprised and grieved to find him hesitate and draw back, after having gone so far. "Every wise man without doors," wrote Thurloe to Henry Cromwell, on the 29th of April, 1657, "wonders at the delay. If this Parliament settle us not, there is no hopes to have any settlement by a Parliament; none will be ever brought to spend so much time about it, or to do half that this hath done."[2] Evidently, in the opinion of his contemporaries, Cromwell was lessened by his conduct in this matter; he had attempted more than he had been able to accomplish,—he had formed a desire, and abandoned it. When a man is placed in so high a position, and on so slippery an ascent, he must either mount constantly higher, or remain perfectly motionless; if he pauses in his attempt to mount, he will inevitably come down.

But Cromwell understood how to submit quietly to repulses which he was determined not to accept as defeats; and ever confident in the return of good fortune, his only thought was, as soon as it became necessary, to prepare for, and await its coming. He began his new work with an act of vengeance, which seemed bold, though it really was easy. Among the adversaries who had opposed his elevation to royalty, Lambert had been one of the most ardent and active; and his hostility would have been singular after the services which Cromwell and he had mutually rendered each other, if presumption and vanity were not enough to explain all inconsistencies. Lambert had promoted Cromwell's advancement so long as he fancied he would hold his position for life only, and that he, Lambert, might also one day become Lord Protector. It is one of the most pernicious consequences of the revolutionary success of a great man, that it makes every ambitious fool aspire to similar fortune. Lambert could not endure the idea of Cromwell's

[1] Clarendon's State Papers, vol. iii. p. 339; Clarendon's History of the Rebellion, vol. vii. pp. 192, 193.
[2] Thurloe's State Papers, vol. vi. p. 243.

power becoming hereditary, as it would deprive him of what he regarded as his future position. Either voluntarily, and from ill-humour, or because he had not been invited, he was not present at the banquet which Cromwell gave to the members of Parliament, and chief officers of the army, after the proclamation of the new Protectorate ; and when the day arrived on which the oath of fidelity was to be taken to the Protector, Lambert still remained absent. Cromwell sent for him. " I am well assured," he told him, " that your refusal does not proceed from dislike of this new authority ; for you may remember, that at the first, you did yourself press me to accept the title of king ; and, therefore, if you are now dissatisfied with the present posture of affairs, I desire you to surrender your commission." " As I had no suspicion," replied Lambert, " that it would be now demanded of me, I did not bring it ; but if you please to send for it, you can have it." Two days after this, Cromwell deprived him of all his employments ; but careful to degrade while disgracing him, and in order still to retain some hold upon him, he allowed him a pension of two thousand pounds a-year ; and Lambert, who had the meanness to accept it, went to reside obscurely at his country-house at Wimbledon, where he spent his time in cultivating flowers, and watching an opportunity for taking his revenge.[1]

Whilst he thus rid himself of a troublesome enemy, death delivered Cromwell from a stern witness. In the early part of August, 1657, Admiral Blake returned to England on board his flag-ship, the *St. George*, after having, on the 20th of April preceding, gained over the Spaniards, in the bay of Teneriffe, the most perilous and splendid of his victories. When within sight of Plymouth, Blake, worn out by wounds, illness, and devoted attention to the hard duties of a winter campaign, at the head of a disabled fleet, breathed his last at the moment when the sight of the white coasts of his native land gladdened his dying gaze ; and the same signals that announced his return, also announced that he had ceased to exist. His death was a source of public grief to England ; Cromwell took a melancholy pleasure in paying the utmost honours to the remains of the republican hero, who had spent his life in rendering his country illustrious, by serving a power which he disliked. As the body was conveyed along the Thames to Greenwich, all the ships in the

[1] Ludlow's Memoirs, p. 251 ; Memoirs of Colonel Hutchinson, p. 361 ; Life of Cromwell, p. 358 ; Mark Noble's Memoirs of the Protectoral House of Cromwell, vol. i. p. 366 ; Clarendon's History of the Rebellion, vol. vii. pp. 192—210 ; Godwin's History of the Commonwealth, vol. iv, pp. 415—418.

river lowered their sails in sign of mourning; and the corpse lay in state for several days, on the very spot where now stands the noble hospital for British seamen   On the 4th of September, Blake's obsequies were celebrated in Westminster Abbey, with all the honours with which official pomp and popular sympathy can surround a tomb.[1]

The new Protectorate was, to Cromwell, only another step towards the object to which he aspired; but it was an important step: he found himself at length in presence of a Parliament which was well-disposed towards him, as well as monarchical both in its constitution and sentiments.   He had now to form that other House, which had just been restored in principle, and to prepare for the second session of the Parliament thus remodelled. This naturally furnished him with an opportunity for rallying men of importance to his government, and obtaining the support of some true royalists for his future royalty. He sought for means of accomplishing this design, in his own family as well as throughout the country. Of his four daughters, two, Mary and Frances, remained unmarried; both were young and attractive in manners and appearance: Mary was witty, sensible, active, and high-spirited, fond of excitement and power, ardently devoted to the interests of her family, and a zealous supporter of the views of her father, to whom, it is said, her features bore some resemblance; Frances was pretty, sprightly, gay, tender-hearted, and easily impressionable. A young man of high rank, Thomas Bellasis, Viscount Faulconbridge, returned at about this time from his travels on the Continent, and, as he passed through Paris, he had expressed the most favourable sentiments with regard to the Protector. "He is a person of extraordinary parts," wrote Lockhart to Thurloe, on the 21st of March, 1657, "and hath all those qualities in a high measure that can fit one for his Highness's and the country's service. He seemed to be much troubled for a report he heard, that the enemy gave him out to be a Catholic, and did purge himself from having any inclinations that way. He is of opinion that the intended settlement will be very acceptable to all the nobility and gentry of the country, save a few, who may be biassed by the interests of their relations." Cromwell gladly welcomed his overtures of friendship, and on the 18th of November, 1657, his daughter Mary married Lord Faulconbridge. Frances, his youngest daughter, had at one time seemed destined to a loftier alliance;

[1] Dixon's Life of Blake; pp. 361—365; Whitelocke, pp. 664, 665; Clarendon's History of the Rebellion, vol. vii. p. 215; Godwin's History of the Commonwealth, vol. iv. pp. 418—421.

Lord Broghill had conceived the idea of marrying her to Charles II., and effecting his restoration on these terms: it is even stated that Charles had signified his willingness to accept such a proposal, and that Lady Dysart (who, according to some authorities, was too intimate a friend of the Protector) had mentioned the matter to the Protectress, who had endeavoured, unsuccessfully, to induce her husband to consent to the match. "You are a fool," said Cromwell to his wife; "Charles Stuart can never forgive me his father's death, and if he can, he is unworthy of the crown." Failing the King of England, it was proposed that the Lady Frances should wed a French prince, the Duke d'Enghien, eldest son of the Prince of Condé; and a sovereignty, won in the Spanish Netherlands, was to be the price of this alliance. But this idea also fell to the ground, and Cromwell was thinking of marrying his daughter to a wealthy gentleman of Gloucestershire, when he was led to believe, by domestic gossip, that one of his own chaplains, Mr. Jeremy White, a young man of pleasing manners, and "a top wit of his court," was secretly paying his addresses to Lady Frances, who was far from discouraging his attentions. Entering his daughter's room suddenly one day, the Protector caught White on his knees, kissing the lady's hand. "What is the meaning of this?" he demanded. "May it please your Highness," replied White, with great presence of mind, pointing to one of the lady's maids who happened to be in the room, "I have a long time courted that young gentlewoman, and cannot prevail; I was therefore humbly praying her ladyship to intercede for me." "How now, hussey!" said Cromwell, to the young woman; "why do you refuse the honour Mr. White would do you? He is my friend, and I expect you should treat him as such." "If Mr. White intends me that honour," answered the woman, with a very low courtesy, "I shall not be against him." "Say'st thou so, my lass?" said Cromwell; "call Goodwin! this business shall be done presently, before I go out of the room." Goodwin, the chaplain, arrived; White had gone too far to recede, and he was married on the spot to the young woman, on whom Cromwell bestowed a fitting portion. A short time afterwards, on the 11th of November, 1657, Lady Frances married Robert Rich, grandson of the Earl of Warwick, and heir to that nobleman's influence and estates. Although Lord Warwick was his particular friend, the Protector at the outset placed some difficulties in the way of this marriage, in reference to pecuniary settlements; but the anxiety of Lady Frances herself soon overcame his opposition. "I must tell you privately," wrote Mary Cromwell to her brother Henry, "that they are so far engaged, as the match cannot be broken off."[1] The Protector was certainly well pleased with the marriage, for it was celebrated with great pomp; and in the private festivities at Whitehall, he indulged in demonstrations of gaiety which were more indicative of his joy than of his good taste.[2]

Having thus established his daughters as members of the old aristocracy of the country, his next care was to seek among the ranks of the peerage for the means of strengthening and adorning the second House of Parliament which he had to form; in this he was guided rather by an instinctive acquaintance with the great conditions of government, than by vanity; he was anxious to secure for his power the adherence of men whose names were consecrated by time, and celebrated in the history of their country. Of the members of the old House of Lords, seven only consented to receive his writs of summons to sit in the new House. Its other members were, nine great civil functionaries, fifteen general officers, among whom were some of the humblest soldiers of fortune, who had risen to eminence in the civil war, a number of country gentle-men and substantial citizens of local importance, and the most notable of the actors who had figured in the last Parliament of the Revolution; in all, sixty-three persons, without counting eight of the superior judges, who sat as assistants. The Protector had great difficulty in forming this list: he sometimes met with great hesita-tion, and sometimes with troublesome readiness, on the part of those whom he considered eligible for the office. "The difficulty proves great," wrote Thurloe to Henry Cromwell, on the 1st of December, 1657, "between those who are fit and not willing to serve, and those who are willing, and expect it, and are not fit." One of the most violent leaders of the opposition, Sir Arthur Haslerig, was nominated, but it was thought doubtful whether he would accept the appointment. "I pray write to him," said Lenthall, who was also one of the new lords, "and desire him by no means to omit taking his place in that House; and assure him from me, that all that do so shall themselves and their heirs be for ever peers of England." At length, on the 10th of December, 1657, at the latest period

---

[1] This letter, according to Thurloe's State Papers, vol. vi. p. 146, is dated on the 23rd of June, 1656. I am inclined to believe that this date is incorrect, and should be 1657; as I cannot understand why, under the circumstances, the marriage should have been postponed from the 23rd of June, 1656, to the 11th of November, 1657.

[2] Thurloe's State Papers, vol. v. p. 146, vol. vi. pp. 104, 125, 134, 573, 628; Noble's Memoirs of the Protectoral House of Cromwell, vol. i. pp. 123—157, 311—319, vol. ii. pp. 388—402; Cromwelliana, p. 169; Forster's Statesmen of the Commonwealth, vol. iv. pp. 184—186, vol. v. pp. 365—369; Godwin's History of the Commonwealth, vol. iv. pp. 421, 422.

allowed by the Protectoral Constitution, the list was published; the writs of summons, which neither granted nor denied a hereditary character to the new peerage, were addressed to the members who had been nominated; and, on the 20th of January, 1658, the two Houses of Parliament met, one in the ordinary room of the House of Commons, and the other in the old House of Lords.[1]

The session was opened with significant formalities. The usher of the black rod came to inform the Commons that his Highness the Lord Protector was waiting to receive them in the House of Lords. They proceeded thither, and Cromwell addressed them in the old form:—"My Lords, and Gentlemen of the House of Commons," just as the King had done under the monarchy. His speech was brief and unremarkable; he merely alluded to the prosperous state of the country, which at length enjoyed those civil and religious liberties for which it had fought so manfully during ten years. "I have not liberty to speak much unto you," he said, "for I have some infirmities upon me;" and he therefore had deputed Nathaniel Fiennes, the chief Commissioner of the Great Seal, to enter into further particulars. Fiennes began his speech in this manner:—"It is a signal and remarkable Providence that we see this day, in this place, a chief magistrate, and two Houses of Parliament. Jacob, speaking to his son Joseph, said—'I had not thought to have seen thy face, and lo! God hath showed me thy seed also;' meaning his two sons, Ephraim and Manasseh. And may not many amongst us well say—some years since we had not thought to have seen a chief magistrate again among us; and lo! God hath shown us a chief magistrate in his two Houses of Parliament. Now, may the good God make them like Ephraim and Manasseh, that the three nations may be blessed in them, saying, God make thee like those two Houses of Parliament, which, like Leah and Rachael, did build the house of Israel." Fiennes spoke for more than an hour, giving a diffuse, subtle, and tedious, though really judicious and opportune, commentary on the merits of the new monarchical and parliamentary constitution of the Protectorate, on the dangers which threatened it, and on the course which it would behove the two Houses and the country to adopt, in order to avert those dangers; then turning to the Protector, he thus addressed him:—"Sir, whatever you are or shall be, whatever you have done or shall do, and whatever abilities you are or shall be endowed with, are not from nor for yourself, but from and for God, and for the good of men, and especially of God's people among

[1] Old Parliamentary History, vol. xxi. pp. 105–160; Thurloe's State Papers, vol. vi. pp. 647, 648; Ludlow's Memoirs, p. 252.

men.   .   .   Wherefore, having our eyes fixed on that kingdom which is above, let us bend our course that way, with our
faces thitherward, discharging every one his duty, in his place,
diligently and faithfully, and finishing the work which God hath
appointed us to do in this life, that in the life to come, we
may hear that sweet and blessed voice directed unto us : ' *Come,
good and faithful servants, enter into your Master's joy.*' "[1]

Notwithstanding the solemn hopefulness of their language,
the Protector and his Chancellor were, in reality, sorrowful ;
and they had reason to be so. By all minds, the future was
regarded as more obscure and uncertain than ever : it was
evident that Cromwell had not abandoned the idea of making
himself king ;—would he ever be able to overcome the obstacles
which had so recently frustrated his purpose ? His failing health
gave fresh courage to his enemies, and filled his friends with apprehension : even his most devoted adherents hesitated to attach themselves more closely to his fortune. Of the seven noblemen whom he
had summoned to the new House of Lords, one alone, Lord Eure, took
his seat ; the other six did not appear ; even Lord Warwick declared
that " he could not sit in the same assembly with Hewson, the cob-
bler, and Pride, the drayman." In order to fill his Upper House
with suitable persons, the Protector had removed from the House of
Commons some of the ablest and most influential leaders of his
party. And not only did his adversaries remain in that assembly,
but those even who had been violently excluded from their seats, at
the opening of the Parliament, now presented themselves for admission. He was unable again to exclude them, for they offered to
take the oath required by the new constitution ; and the Protector's
friends, eager to avail themselves of this opportunity to wipe off the
disgrace to which they had formerly submitted, loudly rejected all
idea of a second exclusion. On the very first day of the session,
six commissioners were stationed at the door of the House, to
receive the oaths of the members as they arrived, and nearly all
those who had been excluded, in September, 1656, now made no
objection to be sworn. Great curiosity was felt as to what would be
done by Sir Arthur Haslerig, whom the Protector had appointed a
member of the Other House : he did not appear in answer to the
summons, and remained for some days in concealment ; but, on the
25th of December, he presented himself unexpectedly at the door of
the House of Commons, and demanded to be sworn. Some diffi-

[1] Cromwell's Letters and Speeches, vol. iii. pp. 392—399; Old Parliamentary History, vol. xxi. pp. 169—191; Comr   ' Journals, vol. vii. pp
578—587.

culty was made about admitting him ; he was, it was urged, a
member of the Other House ; but Sir Arthur peremptorily insisted
on his right : " I have been elected by the people to sit in this
House," he said.   " I shall heartily take the oath.   I will be faithful to my Lord Protector's person.   I will murder no man."   He
was eventually admitted, and took his place at once at the head of
the opposition.[1]

The conflict had already commenced.   On the 22nd of January,
1658, two days after the opening of the session, two messengers
came from the House of Lords to invite the Commons to unite with
them in an humble address to his Highness, to appoint a day for
public prayer and fasting throughout the country.   A great clamour
immediately arose.   " You have no message to receive from them
as Lords," exclaimed several members : " they are at last but a
swarm from you ; you have resolved they shall be another House,
but not Lords ; it looks like children, that because they can pronounce A, they must say also B."   No one ventured to remonstrate
with this indignation ; yet it was judged advisable to take time to
reflect ; and the House merely replied that it would send a speedy
answer by its own messengers.[2]

Cromwell at once felt the full force of this incident ; the republican and alone sovereign Commons were in revolt against the restoration of the three powers of the ancient monarchy ; the new constitution of the Protectorate was attacked for its renewal of the past,
and for its future tendencies.   On the 25th of January, 1658, the
Protector summoned the two Houses to attend him in the Banqueting
Hall at Whitehall ; and there, during more than an hour, he dis-
coursed to them on the external and internal dangers which
threatened England.   Abroad, throughout all Europe, Protestantism
was violently attacked, and in imminent danger ; in Germany, Italy,
and Switzerland, the House of Austria and the Pope still retained,
or were regaining, the ascendency ; the most faithful Protestant
ally of England, the King of Sweden, had been defeated in Poland,
and was at war with his neighbour, the King of Denmark.   " But
it may be said," he continued, " this is a great way off, what is it to
us ?   If it be nothing to you, let it be nothing to you !   I have told
you it is somewhat to you.   It concerns all your religions, and all
the good interests of England. . . .   This complex design
against the Protestant interest is a design against your very being.

---

[1] Commons' Journals, vol. vii. p. 578; Burton's Diary, vol. ii. pp. 316, 346;
Ludlow's Memoirs, pp. 252, 253; Cromwell's Letters and Speeches, vol. iii.
pp. 391, 401, 402.
[2] Commons' Journals, vol. vii. p. 581; Burton's Diary, vol. ii. pp. 330—844.

If they can shut us out of the Baltic Sea, and make themselves masters of that, where is your trade? where are your materials to preserve your shipping? Where will you be able to challenge any right by sea, or justify yourselves against a foreign invasion of your own soil? You have accounted yourselves happy in being environed with a great ditch from all the world beside. Truly, you will not be able to keep your ditch, nor your shipping, unless you turn your ships and shipping into troops of horse and companies of foot, and fight to defend yourselves on *terra firma*. . Your allies, the Dutch, have professed a principle which, thanks be to God, we never knew. They will sell arms to their enemies, and lend their ships to their enemies. I dare assure you of it; and I think if your Exchange here in London were resorted to, it would let you know, as clearly as you can desire to know, that they have let sloops on hire to transport upon you four thousand foot and a thousand horse, upon the pretended interest of that young man that was the late king's son. . . .

"If this be the condition of your affairs abroad, I pray a little consider what is the estate of your affairs at home. . . . Is not this nation miserably divided into sects.—if I may call them sects, whether sects upon a religious account or upon a civil account? And what is that which possesseth every sect? That every sect may be uppermost, and may get the power into their hands. . .

"We have had now six years of peace,—of peace and the Gospel,—after an interruption of ten years' war. Let us have one heart and soul; one mind to maintain the honest and just rights of this nation. . . . Having said this, I have discharged my duty to God and to you. While I live, and am able, I shall be ready to stand and fall with you in this cause. I have taken my oath to govern according to the laws that are now made; and I trust I shall fully answer it. I took my oath to be faithful to the interest of these nations—to be faithful to the government: and, I trust, by the grace of God, as I have taken my oath to serve the Commonwealth upon such an account, I shall—I must!—see it done according to the articles of government, that every just interest may be preserved, that a godly ministry may be upheld, and not affronted by seducing and seduced spirits; that all men may be preserved in their just rights, whether civil or spiritual; upon this account did I take oath, and swear to this government; and so, having declared my heart and mind to you in this, I have no more to say, but to pray, God Almighty bless you."[1]

[1] Cromwell's Letters and Speeches, vol. iii. pp. 402—425; Commons' Journals, vol. vii. pp. 587—589; Burton's Diary, vol. ii. pp. 351—371.

Views so sensible and resolute should have produced a deep impression, but they were confusedly and tediously expressed; Cromwell, indeed, had frequently said the same things already, and although true, they were trite, for he had made too much use of them. Confidence, moreover, was not felt in the speaker; even those who thought that Cromwell was right, doubted him while listening to him, and were unwilling to trust him. In his words, too, there breathed an air of fatigue which greatly weakened their influence. They were far from producing the effect intended: on their return to the House after this conference, the Commons resumed, with redoubled asperity, their debate regarding the House of Lords. The question was not allowed to remain a simple question of practical policy and present utility; it was made, at the same time, historical and speculative; the Long Parliament, the old House of Lords, the Episcopal Church, the national sovereignty, indeed, the whole of the revolution and civil war, were introduced as topics in the discussion. "We must lay things bare and naked," said Mr. Scott, on the 29th of January, 1658. "The Lords would not join in the trial of the King. We were either to lay all the blood of ten years' war upon ourselves, or upon some other object. We called the King of England to our bar, and arraigned him. He was for his obstinacy and guilt condemned and executed; and so let all the enemies of God perish! Upon this, the Lords' House adjourned, and never met; and hereby came a farewell of all those peers; and it was hoped the people of England should never again have a negative upon them." Sir Arthur Haslerig was not less violent than Scott. "Well it is," he exclaimed, "for Pym, Strode, and Hampden, my fellow-traitors, impeached by the King—they are dead! Yet I am glad I am alive to say this at this day. You know how useless and pernicious the House of Lords was. The saint-like army, who were not mercenary, were sensible of those grievances. The Lords willingly laid down their lives; and the army desired they might have a decent interment; which was done accordingly. And shall we now rake them up, after they have so long lain in the grave? Will it not be infamous all the nation over? Shall we be a grand jury again? There is not a man in this House but has sworn against it. Why do we keep out the Cavaliers?" This vehemence on the part of the republican revolutionaries gave rise to equally strong language on the other side. "The Lords are a House of Parliament," said Colonel Shapcott, on the 30th of January; "it is clear, nothing can be clearer; and if so, it was never known that two Houses of Commons were in England. You cannot own them to be a House of Parliament, unless you call them a House of Lords."

* The title *Other House* signifies nothing," said Mr. Nanfan, " it is absurd and repugnant ; for when you come to these doors, then you are the other House to them." " Some say," exclaimed Major Beake, on the 2nd of February, " set not up a King or a House of Lords, for God hath poured contempt upon them. Let me retort upon such persons : God has also poured contempt upon a Commonwealth. Was there so much as one drop of blood when it went out ? Nay ; I am confident it did extinguish with the least noise that ever Commonwealth did." " We are a free Parliament," said Mr. Gewen, " and I move we draw up a bill to invest his Highness with the title and dignity of King—Providence having cast it upon him."[1]

During five days, the House was a constant scene of similar violence and recrimination. On the one hand, was revolutionary obstinacy assuming and believing itself to be republican heroism, and endeavouring to link the destiny of the country, at any cost and for ever, with its own fate ; on the other hand, was the rough, or sceptical, zeal of the soldiers and lawyers who were engaged in the service of a master whose success they had long shared, and whose decline they were beginning to foresee. In this conflict, the sincerer and more contagious earnestness of the old revolutionists prevailed ; the House of Commons decidedly refused to recognise the House of Lords under that title ; and on the 3rd of February, 1658, it voted that it would send its answer to the *Other House* by its own messengers.[2]

On the following day, the 4th of February, a little before noon, without having consulted or communicated with any one, the Protector, attended only by a few guards, proceeded to the House of Lords, and summoned the House of Commons to attend him. His speech was short and severe. He had hoped, he said, that God would make the meeting of that Parliament a blessing ; and he believed that the Petition and Advice adopted by the House, had established the government on a fixed basis, or he would not have accepted the Protectorate. " I did tell you," he continued, " that I would not undertake it, unless there might be some other persons to interpose between me and the House of Commons, and prevent tumultuary and popular spirits. It was granted I should name another House. I named it of men of your own rank and quality, who shall meet you wherever you go, and shake hands with you ; and who will not only be a balance unto you, but to me and to

[1] Commons' Journals, vol. vii. pp. 588 — 599 ; Burton's Diary, vol. ii. pp. 387, 406, 407, 402, 401, 416, 421.

[2] Commons' Journals, vol. vii. p. 591 ; Burton's Diary, vol. ii. p. 441.

themselves. . . . If there had been in you any intention of settlement, you would have settled upon this basis. . . . Yet, instead of owning this actual settlement, some must have I know not what; and you have not only disjointed yourselves, but the whole nation. . . . And this at a time when the King of Scots hath an army at the water's side, ready to be shipped for England! . . . And what is like to come upon this, but present blood and confusion? And if this be the end of your sitting, and this be your carriage, I think it high time that an end be put to your sitting. And I do dissolve this Parliament. And let God be judge between you and me!" "Amen!" answered some of the opposition members, in audible indignation.[1]

This hasty measure produced very great excitement throughout the country, and alarmed even the intimate friends of Cromwell himself: it appeared that, like Charles I., he was determined to break with every Parliament, and that no Parliament could exist while he held the reins of government. Some of his most trusted confidants, Fleetwood, Whitelocke, and even Thurloe, had endeavoured, it is said, to dissuade him from this step; they would have been glad to rest quietly in the comfortable positions he had provided for them; and they were tired of the new dangers and efforts to which he seemed disposed once more to condemn them. Cromwell was more ardently desirous than any of them, that the government should be firmly and finally established; but in his view, the only stable and definitive settlement was monarchy, with its inseparable conditions of strength and duration; his great mind and soaring ambition could be contented with nothing less; and in spite of all obstacles and delays, he steadily pursued his object, equally unable to abandon all hope of attaining it, and to pause in his endeavours so long as it was not within his grasp. He had just made an important advance; the system of two Houses of Parliament had once more become the legal and constitutional order of the country: he was resolved to maintain his conquest. Around him the revolutionary spirit was in a ferment of irritation and alarm at this restoration of monarchical institutions, which threatened it with irretrievable defeat; the Anabaptists, the Levellers, the religious and political sectaries of every denomination, were preparing petitions to protest against these retrograde innovations, and to demand the inauguration of a true Commonwealth, without either Protector or House of Lords. The

[1] Commons' Journals, vol. vii. p. 592; Cromwell's Letters and Speeches, vol. iii. pp. 427—432; Burton's Diary, vol. ii. pp. 462—470; Thurloe's State Papers, vol. vi. pp. 778, 781.

opposition members in the Parliament, Haslerig and Scott among others, were the chief support of these hopes and intrigues—which were powerless so long as they could proceed only by seditious means, but which became formidable when, from connivance or want of courage, they found exponents and advocates in the legally-constituted authorities of the country. Cromwell was resolved, at all risks, to strike his enemies a decisive blow: when the factious Parliament had ceased to exist, he would easily be able to control the revolutionary mob; and at no distant period, he hoped to have another Parliament, more intelligent or more docile, which would enable him to take the last step towards his cherished goal.[1]

Two days after the dissolution, he assembled a great council of his officers at Whitehall, and explained to them the reasons of his conduct: an invasion and insurrection were, he said, imminent. Charles Stuart was leagued with the Spaniards, the Spaniards with the Cavaliers, the Cavaliers with the Levellers and all the factious spirits in England; civil war and anarchy were about to recommence, and the whole fruit of the labours and victories of the army would be lost to the country and to themselves. These were the evils which he had been anxious to prevent by dismissing a Parliament which fostered and encouraged them by its own opposition and disorders. Besides, he had only maintained the Instrument of Government which that very Parliament had voted and sworn to observe, and to which he had himself sworn fidelity. Were the army and its leaders resolved to maintain it with him? Were they willing to defend public peace, religion, and liberty, as well as their own rights and property? or would they allow England and their families to relapse into confusion and bloodshed? His words were greeted with great enthusiasm; nearly all present declared that they were ready to stand and fall—to live and die with him. Cromwell was never satisfied with appearances, and skilfully pushed his advantage: he had noticed that some of the officers had remained gloomy and silent; he addressed them personally, singling out Packer and Gladman among others, the first of whom was major in his own regiment, and asked them what they would do? They replied that they were ready to fight against Charles Stuart and his adherents, but that they could not engage against they knew not whom, and for they knew not what. Cromwell did not press them further; but, a few days after, by a sweeping measure of purifica-

---

[1] Thurloe's State Papers, vol. vi. pp. 709, 775, 796; Old Parliamentary History, vol. xxi. pp. 205, 206; Cromwell's Letters and Speeches, vol. iii. p. 432; Godwin's History of the Commonwealth, vol. iv. pp. 192—195.

tion, he removed from the ranks of the army all those officers who had appeared to be ill-disposed or wavering in their allegiance to him. Packer, among others, was deprived of his commission : " I had served him fourteen years, ever since he was captain of a troop of horse, till he came to this power," said that blunt and honest republican, after Cromwell's death ; " I had commanded a regiment seven years , yet, without any trial or appeal, with the breath of his nostrils, I was outed ; and lost not only my place, but a dear friend to boot. Five captains under my command—all men of integrity, courage, and valour—were outed with me, because they could not say that was a House of Lords."[1]

In such a posture of affairs, and to such malcontents, Lambert, in his solitude and disgrace at Wimbledon, was a leader naturally pointed out by the circumstances of the time. They went to him, and he received them with open arms. The more impetuous had devised a plot " to come with a petition to Cromwell, and, while he was reading it, to cast him out of a window at Whitehall that looked upon the Thames, and then to set up Lambert in his place." Colonel Hutchinson happened to be in London at the time, and became aware of this design ; not that the conspirators took him into their confidence, but they inadvertently let fall some remarks in his presence, which aroused his suspicions, and led him to make further inquiries. Hutchinson, who may be regarded as the type of a Christian gentleman and sincere republican, had, ever since the expulsion of the Long Parliament, retired from the army and from political life ; he detested the tyranny of Cromwell, but he regarded with still greater detestation the pretensions of the subaltern factionists who aspired to succeed him. " Cromwell," says Mrs. Hutchinson, " was gallant and great ; Lambert had nothing but an unworthy pride, most insolent in prosperity, and as abject and base in adversity." Hutchinson went to Fleetwood, and without mentioning any names, advised him to warn Cromwell against petitioners, who might entertain designs against his life. Having given this caution, he was about to leave London, when Cromwell sent for him, " with great earnestness and haste, and the colonel went to him." The Protector " received him with open arms and the kindest embraces that could be given, thanking him for the advertisement he had sent him by Fleetwood, and using all his art to get out of the colonel the knowledge of the persons engaged in

[1] Thurloe's State Papers, vol. vi. pp. 780, 793 ; Cromwell's Letters and Speeches, vol. iii. p. 433; Burton's Diary, vol. iii. pp. 105—107; Godwin's History of the Commonwealth, vol. iv. p. 406, Old Parliamentary History vol. xxi. p. 205.

the conspiracy against him." Hutchinson, however, would give him no names. " But, dear colonel," said Cromwell, " why will you not come in and act among us?" Hutchinson told him plainly, " because he liked not any of his ways since he broke up the Parliament, as they would inevitably lead to the destruction of the whole Parliament party and cause, and to the restitution of all former tyranny and bondage." Cromwell listened to him with patient attention, affirmed that his intentions were good, and attempted to justify his conduct; then, leading him to the end of the gallery in which they had been walking, he embraced him in presence of a group of his courtiers, who were standing there, and said aloud to him : " Well, colonel, satisfied or dissatisfied, you shall be one of us, for we can no longer exempt a person so able and faithful from the public service, and you shall be satisfied in all honest things."[1]

When he had secured the officers of the army, Cromwell assembled the aldermen of the city of London, and explained to them the reasons which had induced him to dissolve the Parliament, endeavouring to alarm them for the security of the capital and the prosperity of their trade.[2] He was fully alive to the necessity of retaining the support of this powerful corporation; for, latterly, with a view to acquire influence in city matters, many royalists had bound their sons apprentices to London tradesmen; and opposition to the Protector was making rapid progress in the metropolis.

It was the general belief that, in all these demonstrations, Cromwell greatly exaggerated the dangers by which public tranquillity and his government were threatened. His constant success, the unwavering fidelity of the bulk of the army, the submission which he met with in every quarter, and the numerous examples which occurred of defection and servility, on the part of both royalists and republicans, created an erroneous impression with regard to the real state of the country. Indomitable in their hopes as in their animosities, the hostile parties seemed to gain fresh vigour after every defeat; and as soon as they found the Protector at variance with the Parliament which had proposed to make him king, a plot, more serious than any of those with which he had hitherto had to contend, was formed against him. Notwithstanding the parsimony of the Court of Madrid and his own idleness, Charles II. had at length collected a small body of troops along the coast of the Spanish Netherlands, and had hired transports to

---

[1] Memoirs of Colonel Hutchinson, pp. 373—376.
[2] Old Parliamentary History, vol. xxi. pp. 206—208 ; Clarendon's History of the Rebellion, vol. vii. pp. 222, 223.

convey them to England. Rumours of an impending invasion began to assume some consistency; the royalists in England ardently encouraged the idea, promising to rise *en masse*, and secure Gloucester, Bristol, Shrewsbury, and Windsor, as soon as the king should set foot on English soil. Nor were the royalists alone in their entreaties and promises; several Anabaptist congregations sent a messenger to Charles II. with a long address, in which they gave humble but manly expression to their disappointments, repentance, desires, and hopes, and formally offered the king their arms and lives to restore him to his throne. Charles hesitated, though not without some feeling of shame, to involve himself once more, in reliance on these promises, in dangers from which he had formerly so miraculously escaped. One of his most trusted counsellors, the Marquis of Ormonde, relieved him from his dilemma by offering to go to London for the purpose of observing the state of affairs, and estimating the strength of their party on the spot, so as to be able to judge whether the moment had really arrived for the king to unfurl his banner in person. Hyde, who was less confident than even Charles himself, opposed Ormonde's journey, "as an unreasonable adventure upon an improbable design." Ormonde, nevertheless, set out in January, 1658; and, under all sorts of disguises, and by constantly changing his place of concealment, he contrived to spend a month in London, where he had frequent interviews with all the leading conspirators of all origins and conditions; and he returned to the Continent, convinced that an immediate invasion would have no chance of success, and that the king ought not to risk it; but that the Protector was tottering—that he was regarded with passionate hatred by large numbers of people—that the plots formed against him were serious —that he, Ormonde, had promised to return to England, to aid the insurrection in the western counties,—and that the moment would perhaps soon arrive for the king himself to attempt some decisive enterprise.[1]

Ormonde spoke truly; no sooner had he left England, than the spirit of insurrection daily became more active and wide-spread. In the north, in Yorkshire, Sir Henry Slingsby, who for two years had been detained a prisoner in Hull, had intrigued with certain officers of the garrison to deliver up the town to Charles II., who would probably land there. In the south, in Sussex, John Mordaunt, a younger son of the Earl of Peterborough, was striving to rally the

---

[1] Clarendon's History of the Rebellion, vol. vii. pp. 237—243; Carte's Life of Ormonde, vol. ii. pp. 175—179; Carte's Ormonde Letters, vol. ii pp. 118—130.

gentlemen in his neighbourhood to the royal cause, and had succeeded so well in his attempt, that the son of one of the judges of
Charles I., Mr. Stapley, had consented to receive from Charles II.
a commission to raise, for his service, a squadron of cavalry, of
which he would take the command when the occasion arrived. In
the western and midland counties, similar intrigues were pursued
with similar success; Levellers and Cavaliers, republicans and
royalists, old members of Cromwell's Council of State, and Anabaptist preachers, were engaged in the work; the most unexpected
combinations were effected, and manifestoes, varying in expression,
but identical in object, were prepared. Even in London, under
Cromwell's own eyes, the conspirators carried their audacity so far
as to fix the day and hour on which they were, some to occupy the
principal positions in the city, others to seize the Lord Mayor and
civic authorities, and others to set fire to the Tower, and gain
possession of it whilst the conflagration absorbed the attention and
efforts of the garrison.

But the vigilance of Cromwell's police had not been exhausted
by long use, and it was present and active wherever danger was to
be apprehended. At Hull, two of the officers to whom Sir Henry
Slingsby had confided his plan, had listened to his proposals with
the sanction of their superiors, in order that they might afterwards
give evidence against him. On being informed that Mr. Stapley
had entered into negotiations with Charles Stuart, Cromwell sent
for him, and threw him into consternation by reminding him, with
menacing but friendly earnestness, of his father's opinions and
actions; and he finally obtained from him a detailed confession
of the designs in which he had taken part, and the names of the
persons who had been the means of involving him therein. While
Ormonde was in London, the Protector said one day to Lord
Broghill, "An old friend of yours is just come to town." "Who
is that?" inquired Broghill. "The Marquis of Ormonde," replied
Cromwell. Lord Broghill protested that he was wholly ignorant
of the matter. "I know that very well," answered the Protector,
"but he lodges in such a place; and, if you have a mind to save
your old acquaintance, let him know that I am informed where he
is, and what he is doing." Cromwell had in his service Sir Richard
Willis, one of the leading members of the Sealed Knot, a small
secret Committee which had the management of the affairs of
Charles II. in England. Willis had sold himself to the Protector
on condition that he should communicate only with Cromwell himself, and should never be obliged to give evidence against any one.
It was principally with Willis that Ormonde had communicated

during his stay in London; and to purge himself of his meanness, to some extent, in his own eyes, he had urged the Marquis to leave London almost at the very time that the Protector himself sent him the same salutary advice by Lord Broghill. Cromwell was always glad to deal thus generously with those enemies whom he honoured without greatly fearing; but he nevertheless persevered in his stern and relentless policy towards all others. In all parts of England, the conspirators were thrown into dismay by numerous and unexpected arrests; royalists, republicans, and Anabaptists were all treated alike; Sir William Compton and Colonel John Russell, both members of the Sealed Knot—Hugh Courtney and John Rogers, two sectarian preachers, who had been active in the dispersion of seditious pamphlets—Portman, who had been secretary to Admiral Blake—Carew and Harrison, who had but recently been liberated from prison, and many other persons, then famous but now perfectly forgotten, were suddenly seized and committed to the Tower. And in London, on the 15th of May, 1658, the day fixed for the great insurrection, as the conspirators were betaking themselves to their posts, they learned that their leaders had been arrested in the house where they were met in secret conclave: all the guards had been doubled, the militia had been called out, and Colonel Barkstead, the Lieutenant of the Tower, marched into the very centre of the city with a strong body of troops, and five pieces of artillery. About forty conspirators and as many apprentices were arrested in the streets. This great plot, so general and comprehensive in its character, was everywhere frustrated and suppressed, either before it could break out, or at the moment of its explosion.[1]

Then were renewed those melancholy scenes of political trials, condemnations, and executions which England, during eighteen years, had so frequently been compelled to witness. There was some difference of opinion in the Protector's council, regarding the jurisdiction by which the prisoners should be tried: from respect for the laws of the country, or with a view prudently to separate themselves from a tyranny so earnestly and universally attacked, Whitelocke and some others demanded that they should be brought before a jury. But Cromwell wished to make sure that his enemies would be punished. By virtue of an act of the Parliament

---

[1] Clarendon's History of the Rebellion, vol. vii. pp. 242—245, 324—328; Clarendon's State Papers, vol. iii. pp. 3-8—402; Thurloe's State Papers, vol. vi. pp. 781, 786, vol. vii. pp. 25, 27, 77, 78, 82, 86, 88, 89, 141, 148; Whitelocke, p. 673; Carte's Ormonde Letters, vol. ii. pp. 118—134; Godwin's History of the Commonwealth, vol. iv. pp. 492—527.

which he had just dissolved, he erected, on the 27th of April, 1658, another High Court of Justice, composed of a hundred and thirty members of his own selection, and presided over by Lord Lisle, one of the Judges of Charles I. Stern regicides, irretrievably-compromised revolutionaries, disciplined officers, and tried servants, formed this Court, which, however, contained a few more impartial members; among others Whitelocke himself, who had the courage and prudence not to take his seat. During the period from the 25th of May to the 1st of July, fifteen of the principal conspirators were brought successively before this tribunal, and impeached by the learned Sergeant Maynard, in the name of the Protector. Sir Henry Slingsby, Dr. Hewett, an episcopal divine of deservedly high reputation, and John Mordaunt, were the first placed at the bar. Mordaunt was a very young man, and but lately married; the earnest and intelligent activity of his wife, the confidential advice of some of his judges who were anxious to provide friends for future emergencies, a note which was secretly conveyed to him in court, and the voluntary or purchased absence of an indispensable witness, saved him: he was acquitted. Sir Henry Slingsby and Dr. Hewett were less fortunate; they boldly questioned the competency of the Court. "I desire to be tried by a jury," said Slingsby; "you are my enemies; I see among you many of those who sequestrated and sold my estates. . . . I have not violated your laws, for I never have submitted to them." Dr. Hewett's language was less haughty, but equally firm. "I shall be very loth," he said, "to do anything to save my life and forfeit a good conscience. I am looked upon in a double capacity—as a clergyman, and as a commonwealth's man—and I shall not, for my private interest, give up the privileges of those that are equal freemen with myself;" and he so boldly maintained his point against the Attorney-General and the President of the Court, that Lord Lisle at last told him: "I must take you off; you have been required—often required, to answer; and having refused, in the name of the Court, I require the Clerk to record it. Officer, take away your prisoner." "My Lord," remonstrated Hewett—— "Take him away, take him away," repeated the judges. He was accordingly removed, and condemned to death, as Slingsby had been already. But, when the time drew near for his execution, the Protector had to resist the tears and entreaties of his own family. Sir Henry Slingsby was uncle to Lord Faulconbridge, who had married Lady Mary Cromwell; and after the official celebration of their nuptials at Hampton Court, by one of Cromwell's chaplains, Dr. Hewett had performed the ceremony a second time; for the Protector's daughters would not

have believed themselves lawfully married unless a priest of the
Episcopal Church had blessed their union; and Cromwell had
given his consent, "in compliance," he said, "with the importunity
and folly of his daughter." Moreover, Dr. Hewett secretly celebrated the Anglican form of worship in his own house, and Lady
Claypole, Cromwell's favourite daughter, regularly attended this
service. Not that she was, as has been stated, a royalist at heart,
and favourable to the restoration of Charles Stuart; on the contrary, she was tenderly attached to her father, trembled for his
safety, and rejoiced at his success. Soon after the plot of Slingsby
and Hewett was discovered, on the 12th of June, 1658, she wrote
to her sister-in-law : " Truly the Lord has been very gracious to us,
in delivering my father out of the hands of his enemies, which we
all have reason to be sensible of in a very particular manner; for
certainly not only his family would have been ruined, but, in all
probability, the whole nation would have been involved in blood."
But although she remained true to her father, Lady Claypole was
generous and affectionate, and gave far greater heed to the dictates
of her heart than to the requirements of political necessity. In
concert with her sister, she made zealous efforts to obtain Dr.
Hewett's pardon. Cromwell was extremely attached to his
daughter; but he believed severity indispensable, and his own
robust and hardy constitution did not allow him to estimate the
effect which a strong painful emotion might produce on a delicate,
sensitive, and sickly frame. He peremptorily refused. Hewett
and Slingsby were beheaded in the Tower, on the 8th of June.
Three weeks after, the High Court passed sentence of death on six
other conspirators, three of whom were hanged, drawn, and quartered with all the barbarous ceremonies ordained by the laws of the
time, to strike terror into all accomplices and beholders.[1]

For the moment, his object was attained; hatred was held in
check by fear; plots ceased; the conspirators either concealed
themselves, or fled. Cromwell took no great pains to discover them;
he even allowed his High Court of Justice to rest from its labours,
and committed to a jury the task of trying the insignificant
prisoners whom he had still in his hands. Once again, his enemies
had failed; but he was too clear-sighted and strong-minded to delude

[1] Whitelocke, p. 673; Clarendon's History of the Rebellion, vol. vii.
pp. 246, 251, 253; State Trials, vol. v. cols. 871—936; Thurloe's State
Papers, vol. vii. pp. 40, 65, 98, 111, 121, 150, 162; Ludlow's Memoirs, p. 256;
Noble's Memoirs of the Protectoral House of Cromwell, vol. i. pp. 138, 143,
314; Godwin's History of the Commonwealth, vol. iv. pp. 517—527; Forster's
Statesmen of the Commonwealth, vol. v. pp. 379—382.

himself as to the extent of his success : he did not attempt to slight the danger from which he had escaped ; though safe for the present, and possibly for some time to come, he felt that peril was always imminent. The war between him and the implacable enemies arrayed against him, was a war to the death, and the chances were too unequal ; they might murder him on any day, but he was constantly under the necessity of renewing his victories over their conspiracies against him. The consciousness of this position, which daily impressed itself more strongly on his mind, led him to adopt incessant and most vigilant precautions for his own safety ; he wore a steel shirt under his clothes ; whenever he went out, his carriage was filled with attendants, a numerous escort accompanied him, and he proceeded at full speed, " frequently diverging from the road to the right or left, and generally returning by a different route." In his residence at Whitehall, he reserved several bedchambers to his own use, each of which was provided with a secret door. He selected from different cavalry regiments a hundred and sixty men, all of whom were well known to him, gave them the pay of officers, divided them into eight troops of twenty men each, and ordered that two of these bodies, in rotation, should always be on duty near his person. And ever ready to expose himself to danger in order to make sure that he was faithfully served, he frequently made the round of the sentries at Whitehall, and changed the guard himself. When he gave audience, which he constantly found it necessary to do, for he depended greatly on his personal influence, " he sternly watched the eyes and gestures of those who addressed him." He was ever ready to form sudden suspicions, and to take extreme precautions : one night, he went to confer secretly with Thurloe on a matter of great importance, and all at once he perceived Thurloe's clerk, Samuel Morland, sleeping on a desk in a corner of the room ; fearing that he might have overheard them, Cromwell drew a dagger, and was about to despatch him, if " Thurloe had not, with great entreaties, prevailed on him to desist, assuring him Morland had sat up two nights together, and was certainly fast asleep." This constant anxiety for his safety was repugnant to the character of Cromwell, whose self-regard, though all-absorbing, was averse to gloomy precaution or reserve ; even in his falsehood and artifices, he was naturally free and open, and loved to be engaged in proceedings which betokened hardihood and confidence. But he was governed by an evident necessity, and he admitted it without illusion or compromise ; and watched over his life with the same ardour which he had displayed in achieving his greatness.[1]

[1] Ludlow's Memoirs, p. 257 ; Burnet's History of His Own Time, vol. i.

F F

He must assuredly have been moved by mingled feelings of displeasure and pride, when he cast his eyes on the other side of the Channel, and compared his perilous and precarious position at home with the power and glory which he had won for his country and himself in foreign lands. It was at the very moment when he was so earnestly struggling against plots in England, that he obtained his most brilliant successes on the Continent. He had not been slow to perceive that, in order to wage an effectual warfare against Spain, his treaty of peace and commerce with France would not be sufficient, and he had readily met the proposals of Mazarin for a closer and more active alliance. In the month of August, 1656, proposals had been made for the levying, in England, of four thousand men for the service of the King of France against the Spaniards. The negotiation was tedious and difficult, and incessantly interrupted by mutual feelings of distrust; sometimes Cromwell suddenly drew back, on discovering traces of Mazarin's constant though secret labours to prepare the way for peace with the Court of Madrid; sometimes the visit of one of the secretaries of Cardenas to London, led Mazarin, in his turn, to dread a reconciliation between England and Spain. In his long conversations with Lockhart, the Cardinal would vaguely hint at the great and indefinite advantages which the Protector might derive from an intimate connection with France; and Lockhart, though not his dupe, carefully treasured these insinuations in his mind, and communicated them to Cromwell with complacent satisfaction. In spite of all their distrust and reticence, the two negotiators were evidently pleased with each other, and gradually coalesced, without, however, overstepping their design on either side. At length, on the 23rd of March, 1657, the negotiation was brought to a conclusion, and a treaty of offensive alliance was signed at Paris between France and England: Cromwell promised that a body of six thousand English troops, backed by a fleet which would always be ready to victual and support them along the coast, should join the French army of twenty thousand strong, to carry on the war in the Spanish Netherlands, and more particularly to besiege Gravelines, Mardyke, and Dunkirk, the last of which three towns was to remain in the hands of the English. The pay and expenses of this auxiliary force were to be divided between the King of France and the Protector. The conclusion of this treaty gave the liveliest satisfaction to both courts, and Cromwell soon after testified his pleasure by warmly recom-

pp. 120, 121; Bates's Elenchus Motuum Nuperorum, part ii. p. 399; Welwood's Memoirs, p. 94; Oldmixon's History of the Stuarts, p. 494; Forster's Statesmen of the Commonwealth, vol. v. pp. 386—384.

mending to Mazarin's favour the French ambassador in London, M. de Bordeaux, whose shrewd sense and diplomatic ability had mainly contributed to this fortunate result. The death of M. de Bellièvre, on the 15th of March, 1657, created a vacancy in the office of First President of the Parliament of Paris, and Cromwell, as it would appear, had even gone so far as to request this appointment, for Bordeaux apologised to the Cardinal on the subject, and said that the post of President à *mortier* would realise his most sanguine expectations. Cromwell's recommendation was excessive, and consequently failed; M. de Lamoignon was appointed First President of the Parliament of Paris. Mazarin had no idea of paying so dearly for a success, after his object had been achieved.[1]

About six weeks after the conclusion of the treaty, on the 13th and 14th of May, 1657, the English troops, under the command of Sir John Reynolds, disembarked at Boulogne. Both the court and the army, Mazarin and Turenne, were impatiently awaiting them, and received them with great marks of satisfaction: administrative measures, imperfect and inefficient, indeed, but at that time of rare occurrence, were adopted to insure their proper treatment. They were regiments formed and trained in the long struggles of the civil war, accustomed to the strictest discipline, of unblemished morals and determined bravery: some of them, at their departure from England, and the others at their arrival at Boulogne, had been newly armed and equipped. Louis XIV. came in person to see them, and passed them in review. "Sire," said Lockhart to him, "the Protector has enjoined both officers and soldiers to display the same zeal in the service of your Majesty, as in his own;" and the young king replied, that he "was transported to receive so noble a testimony of the affection of a prince, whom he had always considered as the greatest and happiest in Europe." The English lost no time in joining Turenne's army, and engaging in the campaign; but misunderstandings and complaints soon succeeded mutual contentment: the soldiers were astonished to find the villages deserted by their inhabitants when they arrived;—they were not properly supplied with provisions,—many of them fell ill, and some of them sent home pieces of the bread which was served out to them, to show how inferior it was to English bread. The officers shared in the ill-humour of the

---

[1] Thurloe's State Papers, vol. v. pp. 318, 369, vol. vi. pp. 115, 116, 126, 618; Dumont's Corps Diplomatique, vol. vi. part ii. pp. 178, 224; Garden's Histoire Générale des Traités de Paix, vol. ii. pp. 10—12; Godwin's History of the Commonwealth, vol. iv. pp. 532—542; Correspondence of M. de Bordeaux with M. de Brienne and Cardinal Mazarin.

soldiers, and Cromwell himself became ere long dissatisfied; the campaign was protracted, and yet the special promises of the treaty, that is to say, the sieges of Gravelines, Mardyke, and Dunkirk, had not been accomplished or even attempted; the English auxiliaries were employed in the interior of the country, on expeditions which interested the Court of France alone, and which, when successful, were productive of no advantage to England. Lockhart protested and complained in vain; on the 31st of August, 1657, Cromwell wrote to him:—" I have no doubt either of your diligence or ability to serve us in so great a business, but I am deeply sensible that the French are very much short with us in ingenuousness and performance. And that which increaseth our sense of this is the resolution we had, rather to overdo than to be behindhand in anything of our treaty. And although we never were so foolish as to apprehend that the French and their interests were the same with ours in all things, yet, as to the Spaniard, who hath been known, in all ages, to be the most implacable enemy that France hath,—we never could doubt, before we made our treaty, that, going upon such grounds, we should have been failed towards as we are. To talk of giving us garrisons, which are inland, as caution for future action; to talk of what will be done next campaign,—are but parcels of words for children. If they will give us garrisons, let them give us Calais, Dieppe, and Boulogne. . . . I pray you, tell the Cardinal, from me, that I think, if France desires to maintain its ground, much more to get ground upon the Spaniard, the performance of his treaty with us will better do it than any other design he hath. . . . If this will not be listened to, I desire that things may be considered of, to give us satisfaction for the great expense we have been at with our naval forces and otherwise; and that consideration may be had how our men may be put into a position to be returned to us:—whom we hope we shall employ to a better purpose than to have them continue where they are."[1]

This language did not fail to produce its effect. Mazarin easily allowed himself to fall into the embarrassments of a complicated position and a crafty policy; but he also understood how to escape from his embarrassments as soon as they became real dangers. The French army was ordered to abandon its operations in the interior of the country, and to draw nearer the coast; Mardyke was besieged and taken on the 3rd of October, and delivered provisionally into the hands of the English. Turenne then marched against

[1] Thurloe's State Papers, vol. vi. pp. 220, 287, 400, 618; The Perfect Politician, pp. 232, 327; Godwin's History of the Commonwealth, vol. iv. pp. 512—515; Bordeaux to Brienne, August 23, 1657.

Gravelines, but the Spaniards opened the sluices, inundated the environs of the town, and rendered a near approach impossible. Cromwell insisted that siege should immediately be laid to Dunkirk, and offered to send an additional two thousand men to assist in the enterprise. Turenne thought an immediate attempt would be unadvisable, and put an end to the campaign. Cromwell submitted without great reluctance; he had now regained some confidence in Mazarin's intentions, and he bowed to the high military authority of Turenne. On the 28th of March, 1658, the treaty of offensive alliance was renewed for a year, on the same terms; and when the campaign was re-opened, in the spring of 1658, Cromwell demanded their immediate performance. Turenne advanced towards the coast, " without knowing," he says, " whether we could besiege Dunkirk, for to attack that place before having taken Furnes, Bergues, and Gravelines, which are in its neighbourhood, was to be besieged at the same time that we were besieging. But his lordship the Cardinal desired that we should march into Flanders, and M. de Turenne also wished honestly to show the English that we were doing all in our power for the execution of the treaty." The two new regiments that Cromwell had promised, arrived: Lockhart took the command of the English troops, with General Morgan, a valiant officer formed in the school of Cromwell and Monk, as his lieutenant. Dunkirk was invested on the 25th of May, 1658. Louis XIV. and Mazarin came to Calais in order to watch the siege. The Marquis of Leyden defended the town. At Brussels, neither Don John, nor the Marquis of Carracena, was willing to believe that the place was in danger. At once haughty and indolent, they condemned the advice which Condé was constantly giving them to act, now with vigilant activity, and now with prudent reserve: they would not suffer any one to disturb them at their siesta because some unexpected event had occurred, nor would they tolerate any doubt of their success when they were once up and on horseback. They hastened to the defence of Dunkirk, leaving behind them their artillery and a portion of their cavalry. Condé entreated them to remain within their intrenchments until these arrived; but Don John wished, on the contrary, to advance along the Dunes, and march to meet the French army. " Surely you cannot think of doing so," said Condé; " the ground is favourable to infantry only, and the French infantry are more numerous and veteran than your own." " I am persuaded," answered Don John, " that they will not even dare to look the army of his Catholic Majesty in the face." " Ah," exclaimed Condé, " you don't know M. de Turenne! He is not a man to allow you to commit blunders with impunity." Don

John persisted, and began to march along the Dunes. On the
following day, the 13th of June, Condé, becoming more and more
convinced of their danger, renewed his efforts to induce him to turn
back. "Turn back," cried Don John; "if the French dare to
fight, that day will be the most glorious that ever shone on the
armies of his Catholic Majesty." "Very glorious, indeed," replied
Condé, "but to make it so, you must retreat and wait." Turenne
put an end to this discord in the enemy's camp: having determined
to give battle, at daybreak on the 14th of June, he sent notice of his
intention to the English general, by one of his officers, who was
directed at the same time to explain to Lockhart the plan and
motives of the commander-in-chief. "Very good," said Lockhart,
"I shall obey M. de Turenne's orders, and he may explain his
reasons after the battle, if he pleases." The contrast is striking between the manly discipline of English good sense, and the wanton
blindness of Spanish pride. Condé was not mistaken ; the issue of
a battle, fought under such auspices, could not be doubtful. "My
lord," he said to the young Duke of Gloucester, who was serving in
the Spanish army with his brother the Duke of York, "have you
ever seen a battle fought ?" "No, Prince," was the answer. "Well,
then," rejoined Condé, "you will presently see one lost." The
Spaniards were, in fact, utterly defeated, after four hours' hard fighting, during which the English regiments carried, with distinguished
bravery, but great loss, the most difficult and best-defended post of
the enemy. All the officers of Lockhart's regiment, with the exception of two, were either killed or wounded. The Duke of York,
with his small band of English and Irish royalists who fought under
the Spanish flag, contested the palm of bravery in hand-to-hand encounters with their republican countrymen. Turenne and Condé,
each of whom, to use the expression of the Duke of York, had done,
in his own camp, "all that it was possible to do, both as a general
and as a soldier," worthily supported their allies. Before the day
was over, the Spanish army retreated in confusion, leaving four
thousand prisoners in the hands of the victors. "The enemies
have encountered us," wrote Turenne to his wife that evening,
"and they are defeated. God be praised ! I have been rather
fatigued all day, so I wish you good night, and I shall go to bed."
Ten days after, on the 23rd of June, 1658, the garrison of Dunkirk
was reduced to extremities ; the old governor, the Marquis of
Leyden, had been mortally wounded in a sortie; the place surrendered ; and two days later, on the 25th of June, Louis XIV.
entered the town, which was immediately placed in the hands of the
English. "Although the Court and army," wrote Lockhart to

Thurloe. " are even mad to see themselves part with what they call so delicate a bit, yet the Cardinal is still constant to his promises, and seems to be as glad, in the general, to give this place to his Highness, as I can be to receive it. The King is also exceedingly obliging and civil, and hath more true worth in him than I could have imagined."[1]

Cromwell had not waited until Dunkirk was taken, to manifest to Louis XIV. his proud satisfaction at the alliance which united them. As soon as he became aware that the King and Mazarin were at Calais, he sent his son-in-law, Lord Faulconbridge, as an ambassador extraordinary, to compliment them in his name. Two ships-of-war and three smaller vessels were assigned to convoy the ambassador, his equipages, and suite of more than a hundred and fifty gentlemen. A violent tempest scattered the little fleet off Calais; and to his great disappointment, Lord Faulconbridge landed with a very small retinue, on the 29th of May, 1658, within sight of the King, Queen, and Court, who were in a tent on the quay. The Count de Charost, the governor of the town, came to meet him with eight or ten carriages, and conducted him to the lodging which had been prepared for him, and at the doors of which the King's own Swiss guards stood as sentries. Lord Faulconbridge brought letters to the King and Cardinal from the Protector, in which he insisted on the speedy reduction of Dunkirk, "that den of pirates." They both received him, in public and in private, with the greatest official honours and the most familiar marks of friendship. Louis XIV. walked with him for more than an hour in his garden, tête-à-tête, and uncovered. Mazarin, after a long interview, attended him to the door of his carriage—" a ceremony," writes Lord Faulconbridge, " which he dispenses with, not only to all others, but even to the King himself." Louis XIV. presented the ambassador with his portrait, in a rich frame, and gave him a magnificent sword for the Protector. Mazarin also sent Cromwell a handsome piece of tapestry. It is the policy and pleasure of ancient courts to heap favours on any great parvenu whose friendships they need to gain. Louis XIV. and his Cardinal-minister did not rest satisfied with giving this splendid reception to the Protector's

---

[1] Thurloe's State Papers, vol. vi. pp. 489, 524, 525, 537; vol. vii. pp. 52 69, 146, 148, 151, 173, 174, 175, 178, 192; Histoire et Mémoires du Vicomte de Turenne, vol. i. pp. 360—375; vol. ii. pp. 158—166; Desormeaux, Histoire de Louis II., Prince de Condé, vol. iv. pp. 118—141; Œuvres de Louis XIV., Mémoires Historiques, vol. i. pp. 167—174; Memoirs of James II., vol. i., p. 468; Clarendon's History of the Rebellion, vol. vii. pp. 279—286; Godwin's History of the Commonwealth, vol. iv. pp. 516—548; Echard's History of England, vol. ii. p. 821.

ambassador: a few days after his return home, they also sent an extraordinary ambassador to London, the Duke de Créqui, accompanied by young Mancini, the nephew of Mazarin, and bearing two letters addressed to Cromwell personally from the King and Cardinal. "Monsieur le Protecteur," wrote Louis XIV., "as I have feelingly appreciated the testimonies of your affection conveyed to me by Viscount Faulconbridge, your son-in-law, I have been unable to rest satisfied with having replied to them by his means, and I have desired to give you more express marks of my affection by sending to you my cousin, the Duke de Créqui, first gentleman of my bed-chamber, whom I have ordered to acquaint you particularly of the esteem in which I hold your person, and how greatly I value your friendship. I have also charged him to express to you the joy I felt at the glorious success achieved by our arms on that fortunate day, the 14th of this month, and how confidently that victory, and the vigour with which Dunkirk continues to be pressed, lead me to hope for the reduction of that place in a few days: to which end I shall not cease to apply myself with the same care as I have devoted to it ever since the commencement of the siege. And although I have informed my cousin, the Duke de Créqui, of my intentions, as well as of the details of this affair, that he may communicate them to you, I cannot omit to tell you in this letter that the Lord Lockhart, your ambassador to me, greatly distinguished himself by his valour and conduct in this encounter, and that the troops which you sent me, following his example, gave extraordinary proofs of generosity and courage. For the rest, I promise myself that you will, as I beseech you, place entire confidence in what my cousin will tell you on my part, and most of all that you will believe that there is nothing that I desire more than to prove to you by my actions how dear your interests are to me."

Cromwell met these splendid demonstrations with great magnificence. Another of his sons-in-law, Fleetwood, went to Dover to receive the Duke de Créqui, with a train of twenty carriages, each drawn by six horses, and an escort of two hundred horse soldiers, who, with drawn swords, accompanied the French ambassador wherever he went. On his arrival in London, the Duke de Créqui was treated as Lord Faulconbridge had been at Calais: at his public reception, Cromwell rose from his chair, and advanced two steps to meet him, and afterwards seated him on his right hand, while his son Richard sat on his left. At his departure, the ambassador received costly presents for his masters and himself; among others, six cases of pure Cornwall tin,—a solid gift, which Cromwell sent to Mazarin with familiar and somewhat contemptuous confidence, knowing him to be more avaricious than vain.[1]

In the midst of such success, won with so much vigour, and manifested with such pomp—on beholding the keys of Dunkirk delivered into his hands by France, to be kept by him for England—Cromwell began once more to think and to hope that a Parliament would sanction, support, and perpetuate his power. His most confidential advisers, and particularly Thurloe, never ceased to urge him to summon another Representative; notwithstanding all their master's triumphs, they were painfully conscious of the daily embarrassments of his government; they wanted both confidence and money. "We are so out at the heels here, that I know not what we shall do for money. . . . We are forced to go a-begging to particular aldermen of London, for five or six thousand pounds to send to Dunkirk, and I fear we shall be delayed. . . . We spend as little of the State's money upon any but public occasions as ever any did; but the truth is, our expenses and occasions are extraordinary, and we cannot with safety retrench them. . . How our needs are to be supplied, I confess I know not, without the help of a Parliament!" Thus wrote Fleetwood and Thurloe to Henry Cromwell, whom they carefully kept acquainted with the state of affairs in London. On the other hand, the Protector was assured that the feelings of the remonstrant officers had undergone a change; that he would no longer meet with the same opposition from the army, and that he might boldly accept the crown which the Parliament would not fail to offer him. His friends even went so far as to assert, that some of the most illustrious and unyielding of the republican leaders, Rich, Ludlow, and Vane himself, were now disposed to prove more compliant. Cromwell listened to all these statements, but came to no decision. "If you ask," wrote Thurloe to Henry Cromwell, on the 27th of April, 1658, "what are the difficulties of coming to those resolutions, I answer, I know none but the fears in some honest men that they will settle us upon some foundations: and the doubts of some others that, if those fears still prevail and disappoint us of a settlement, a Parliament will then ruin us." Cromwell resolved to sound the intentions of some of the most important men; and he appointed a committee of nine members to

[1] Thurloe's State Papers, vol. vii. pp. 151, 158, 192; Clarendon's History of the Rebellion, vol. vii. p. 286; Noble's Memoirs of the Protectoral House of Cromwell, vol. ii. pp. 391—393; Godwin's History of the Commonwealth, vol. iv. pp. 546—550; Larrey's Histoire de France sous Louis XIV., vol. iii. pp. 36—41.

report upon what was to be done, in the next Parliament, to defend
the Government against the attacks of the Cavaliers and old
republicans.   Fiennes, Fleetwood, Pickering, Desborough, Whalley,
Goffe, Philip Jones, Cooper, and Thurloe, five officers and four
civilians, constituted this committee.   After spending more than a
month in deliberation, the majority voted, " that it was indifferent
whether succession in the government were by election or hereditary ;" but, out of complaisance to the dissidents, they added, " that
it was desirable to have it continued elective, that is, that the chief
magistrate should always name his successor."   When this childishly
futile resolution was submitted to him, " his Highness," says
Thurloe, " finding he can have no advice from those he most
expected it from, saith he will take his own resolutions, and that he
cannot any longer satisfy himself to sit still, and make himself
guilty of the loss of all the honest party, and of the nation itself.
And truly," adds Thurloe, " I have long wished that his Highness
would proceed according to his own satisfaction, and not so much
consider others, who truly are to be indulged in everything but
where the being of the nation is concerned.   His Highness is now
at Hampton Court, and will continue there for some time, as well
for his own health as to be near my Lady Elizabeth, who hath been
of late very dangerously ill, but now is somewhat better.[1]

It was, in fact, the case that, for some months, Cromwell had
devoted neither all his time nor all his energy to the duties of his
government and the designs of his ambition.   Throughout his
career, the interests and destiny of his family and children had been
a source of deep anxiety to him.   Feeling no ambitious ardour or
paternal illusion with regard to them, he did not allow himself to
overrate their talents or merits, and treated their affairs as an
affectionate and prudent father, rather than as a powerful sovereign
desirous to shed the lustre of his high position over all his relatives.
Aware of the natural indolence and political indifference of his
eldest son Richard, he allowed him to live with his father-in-law,
Mr. Major, at Hursley Manor, like a quiet country gentleman ; and
he did not intrust the government of Ireland to his second son
Henry, until he had made trial of his capabilities ; and then he
promoted him by slow degrees, and under modest titles.   When he
became Protector, he resolved to have a court ; but the austerity
of his party, the military character of his government, and the
manners, tastes, and jealousies of most of his adherents, confined it

[1] Thurloe's State Papers, vol. vii. pp. 71, 84, 99, 100, 144, 269, 295 ;
Burnet's History of His Own Time, vol. i. p. 129 ; Godwin's History of the
Commonwealth, vol. iv. pp 552—568.

within very narrow limits. Cromwell's own family was the centre and chief element of his court. His wife, Elizabeth Bourchier, was but little calculated to shine in it; she was a simple and timid person, less ambitious than interested, anxious about her future fate, careful to secure resources for every contingency, and jealous of her husband, who, though he lived on good terms with her, furnished her more than once with just cause for complaint. Lady Dysart, who afterwards became Duchess of Lauderdale, Lady Lambert, and perhaps others, whose names are not so certainly known, had been, or still were, on terms of intimacy with Cromwell, which, though carefully kept secret, had not completely escaped detection : he is said to have had several natural children ; and the conjugal suspicions of Lady Elizabeth were so active, that she is even said to have fixed them on Queen Christina of Sweden, who, after her abdication, announced her intention to visit England. It was more on his children, than on his wife, that the Protector relied for the direction of his court. He summoned his son Richard to London, and obtained his election as a member of Parliament, a Privy Councillor, and Chancellor of the University of Oxford. His son-in-law, John Claypole, was a man of elegant tastes, and, like Richard Cromwell, was on friendly terms with a great many Cavaliers. After the marriage of his two younger daughters with Lord Faulconbridge and Mr. Rich, Cromwell had about him four young and wealthy families, desirous to enjoy life, and to share their enjoyments with all who came near them in rank and fortune. The Protector himself was fond of social amusements and brilliant assemblies ; he was also passionately fond of music, and took delight in surrounding himself with musicians, and in listening to their performances. His court became, under the direction of his daughters, numerous and gay. One alone of them, the widow of Ireton and wife of Fleetwood, was a zealous and austere republican, who took but little part in their festivities, and deplored the monarchical and worldly tendencies which prevailed in the household as well as in the policy of the Protector.[1]

In the midst of his public labours, Cromwell exulted in the enjoyment of this domestic prosperity. Family afflictions had not, however, been altogether spared him : in July, 1648, during the course of the civil war, he had lost his eldest son, a young captain, of nineteen years of age, who bore the name of Oliver, and who was killed in a skirmish with the Scots. Until ten years after his

[1] Noble's Memoirs of the Protectoral House of Cromwell, vol. i. pp. 124—128, 135, 159—162, vol. ii. pp. 376—378; Cromwell's Letters and Speeches, vol. i. pp. 64, 92, vol. iii. pp. 260, 295, 382.

death, we find no allusion to the fate of this young man; but in
1658, the fidelity of paternal love in Cromwell's heart found
audible expression; hearing some one read a passage from St. Paul's
Epistle to the Philippians, "This Scripture," he said, "did once
save my life, when my eldest son, poor Oliver, died, which went
dagger to my heart, indeed it did." In 1654, Cromwell lost his
mother, Elizabeth Stuart, a woman of much sense and virtue, for
whom he never ceased to entertain and manifest the utmost respect.
She regarded her son's good fortune with distrust, and could not be
induced to share it without feelings of modesty and regret.   He
found it very difficult to persuade her to take up her abode in
Whitehall; and she lived in a state of constant disquietude, always
expecting some sudden catastrophe, and exclaiming, whenever she
heard the sound of a musket, that her son was shot.   At her death
she expressed her wish to be buried without pomp in a small
country church; but Cromwell ordered that she should be interred,
with great magnificence, in Henry the Seventh's Chapel, in Westminster Abbey.   For four years, from 1654 to 1658, his family was
visited by no misfortune; it continued to enjoy unmixed happiness
and prosperity.   But during the winter of 1658, death entered it
with unusual severity; three months after her marriage, his
daughter Frances lost her husband, Robert Rich, at the early age
of twenty-three; and three months later, Mr. Rich's grandfather,
the Earl of Warwick, the most intimate of Cromwell's friends
among the nobility, and a man who had never failed to serve him
with useful advice and true devotion, followed his grandson to the
tomb.   Cromwell felt these losses keenly; the one was premature,
the other warned him of the approach of old age, and the irreparable
voids which it creates.   But ere many weeks had passed, he had to
endure a still heavier blow.   His beloved daughter, Lady Claypole,
had long been weak and invalid; and he had sent her to reside at
Hampton Court Palace, that she might have the benefit of country
air and complete tranquillity.   Finding that her illness increased, he
went to reside there himself, that he might watch over her with
tender and constant care.   She possessed, in his mind, great and
peculiar attractions; she was a person of noble and delicate sentiments, of an elegant and cultivated mind, faithful to her friends,
generous to her enemies, and tenderly attached to her father, of
whom she felt at once proud and anxious, and who rejoiced greatly
in her affection.   When fatigued, as he often was, not only by the
men who surrounded him, but by his own agitated thoughts, Cromwell took pleasure in seeking repose in the society of a person so
entirely a stranger to the brutal conflicts and violent actions which

had occupied, and still continued to occupy, his life. But this pleasure was now changed into bitter sorrow; the complicated internal disease of Lady Claypole grew rapidly worse; she became subject to convulsion-fits, during which she gave utterance, in her father's presence, sometimes to her own cruel sufferings, and sometimes to the grief and pious anxiety which she felt regarding himself. Sitting constantly by his daughter's bedside, Cromwell had need of all his self-control to endure these painful impressions. On the 6th of August, 1658, Lady Claypole died. The Protector took a melancholy pleasure in surrounding his daughter's coffin with all the pomp which he could command; her body was conveyed to the Painted Chamber at Westminster, where it lay in state for twenty-four hours; after which it was taken to Henry the Seventh's Chapel, and solemnly interred in a special vault, among the tombs of the kings.[1]

When Lady Claypole fell ill, Cromwell himself was not in good health. Although he had successfully resisted the attacks of fever, which he had suffered during his campaigns in Scotland and Ireland, his strong constitution had been shaken by them: he was subject to many painful maladies, which might at any time prove exceedingly dangerous; gout, gravel, affections of the liver and loins, and want of sleep, were his habitual enemies. When he had any attack which prevented his attending to business, he grew impatient, and ordered his physicians to set him right again at any cost. At the time when Lady Claypole's illness assumed a dangerous character, he was suffering from an attack of gout; while giving audience to the Dutch ambassador, Nieuport, on the 30th of July, he felt so unwell, that he broke off the interview, and adjourned the business to the following week. Three days before, on the 27th of July, Thurloe wrote to Henry Cromwell: "His Highness's constant residence at Hampton Court, and the sickness of my Lady Elizabeth, which is a great affliction to him, hath hindered the consideration of public matters, so that very little or nothing hath been done therein for these fourteen days." After the death of Lady Claypole, the Protector made an effort to resume his labours: he held his council; he reviewed some troops; he terminated a commercial negotiation with Sweden; he grew alarmed at the sudden arrival of Ludlow in London, and ordered Fleetwood to make sure that he entertained no evil designs. But an intermittent fever broke out with great violence; he was obliged to remain

[1] Cromwell's Letters and Speeches, vol. iii. pp. 448—452; Thurloe's State Papers, vol. vii. p. 320; Noble's Memoirs of the Protectoral House of Cromwell, vol. i. pp. 84—90, 132, 134, 137—142, vol. ii. pp. 399—402; Godwin's History of the Commonwealth, vol. iv. pp. 527—530.

in bed, and his physicians believed him to be in great danger. About the 20th of August, however. the fever ceased; he left his bed, and resumed his former occupations. George Fox, the Quaker, who was always sure to meet with a friendly reception from him, went to Hampton Court, and requested to speak with him "about the sufferings of Friends." "I met him riding into Hampton Court Park," says Fox; "and before I came to him, as he rode at the head of his life-guards, I saw and felt a waft of death go forth against him; and when I came to him, he looked like a dead man. After I had laid the sufferings of Friends before him, and had warned him according as I was moved to speak to him, he bade me come to his house; and, the next day, I went up to Hampton Court to speak farther with him. But when I came, Harvey, who was one that waited on him, told me the doctors were not willing that I should speak with him. So I passed away, and never saw him more."[1]

The fever had greatly increased; his physicians prescribed change of air, and recommended him to leave Hampton Court for London. He returned to Whitehall on the 24th of August, 1658. and from that moment, notwithstanding some few intervals of respite, the disease and danger became more and more urgent. Cromwell ceased to attend to public business, and seemed not even to think of it. In his own soul, however, he had not yet given up all hope of life, and future worldly achievements. Having heard his physicians whisper that his pulse was intermittent, the words filled him with alarm: he turned pale, a cold perspiration covered his face, and, requesting to be placed in bed, he sent for a secretary, and executed his private will. On the following morning, one of his physicians entered his room. "Why do you look so sad?" said Cromwell to him. "How can I look otherwise," replied the physician, "when I have the responsibility of your life upon me?" "You doctors think I shall die," returned Cromwell; and he took the hand of his wife, who was sitting by his bedside, and said to her, "I tell thee I shall not die of this bout; I am sure I shall not." Observing the surprise of his physician at these words, he added: "Do not think that I am mad; I tell you the truth; I know it from better authority than any which you can have from Galen or Hippocrates. It is the answer of God himself to our prayers; not to mine alone, but those of others, who have a more intimate interest in Him than I have. Therefore, take courage; banish sor-

[1] Thurloe's State Papers, vol. vii. pp. 294, 299, 301, 320, 365; Fox's Journal, vol. i. pp. 485, 486; Cromwell's Letters and Speeches, vol. iii. pp. 452, 453; Clarendon's History of the Rebellion, vol. vii. p. 292.

row from your eyes, and treat me as you would treat a mere servant. You can do much by your science; but nature can do more than all the doctors in the world, and God is infinitely more powerful than nature." Finding him so strangely excited after an almost sleepless night, the physician ordered that he should be kept perfectly quiet, and left the room. As he was going away, he met one of his colleagues, and said to him, "I fear our patient is well nigh deranged," and he repeated what he had heard. "Are you so far a stranger here," replied the other, "that you do not know what took place last night? The Protector's chaplains, and all their friends the saints, engaged in prayers for his safety, in different parts of the palace, and they all heard the voice of God, saying, 'He will recover!' so they are all certain of it."[1]

Not in Whitehall only, but in a multitude of churches and houses in London, fervent prayers were offered for the Protector's recovery; prayers at once sincere and interested,—dictated alike by sympathy and fear. Independently of the men who were attached to his person and government, and whose fortune was dependent on his own, Cromwell was, to all those revolutionists and sectaries, whom republican fanaticism had not rendered his enemies, the representative of their cause, and the defender of their civil and religious liberties. What would be their fate if he should die? Under what yoke would they next fall? And their prayers were not, to them, cold and empty forms;—they had firm faith in their access to God, and they presumptuously believed that he revealed to them His designs. "O Lord," exclaimed Goodwin, one of the Protector's chaplains, "we pray not for his recovery,—that thou hast granted already; what we now beg is his speedy recovery." The politicians were not so sanguine,—and yet they too had great hopes. "Never," wrote Thurloe to Henry Cromwell, on the 30th of August, 1658, "was there a greater stock of prayers going for any man than for him; and truly, there is a general consternation upon the spirits of all men, good and bad, fearing what may be the event of it, should it please God to take his Highness at this time: and God, having prepared the heart to pray, I trust He will incline His ear to hear."[2]

Cromwell was far from getting better; his fits became far more violent and frequent; and when they were over, he was left in a state of profound despondency. His family and his confidants

---

[1] Bates's Elenchus Motuum Nuperorum, part ii. pp. 413—415; Heath's Chronicle, pp. 736, 737.

[2] Thurloe's State Papers, vol. vii. pp. 364, 366, 367, 369; Neal's History of the Puritans, vol. iv. p. 180; Ludlow's Memoirs, p. 259.

were agitated by the utmost anxiety regarding the future. Who was to be his successor? By the terms of the Instrument of Government, he was himself to appoint him. After he fell ill, and before he left Hampton Court to return to London, Cromwell had given some thought to the matter, and had directed John Barrington, one of his secretaries, to fetch from his study-table at Whitehall, a sealed paper, in the form of a letter directed to Thurloe, in which, immediately after the second constitution of the Protectorate, he had nominated his successor, without communicating the secret to any other person. This paper could not be found, and Cromwell said no more about it. When his death seemed to be imminent, his children and sons-in-law, Lord Faulconbridge among others, urged Thurloe, the Protector's only real confidant, to put some question to him on this subject. Thurloe promised to do so, but delayed performing his promise. He had no certain knowledge of his master's intentions;—Cromwell had kept them perfectly secret, as he was unwilling to deprive any of those who aspired to succeed him, of the hope of doing so. Some persons affirmed that his choice would not rest on either of his sons, but on his son-in-law, Fleetwood, who was more popular with the army and with the republicans. Under these doubtful circumstances, Thurloe hesitated to undertake to demand a positive answer from the Protector, as he was unwilling to incur the enmity of any of the aspirants.[1]

In these perplexities of those who surrounded him, Cromwell took no part; worldly affairs, political questions, even the interests of those persons who were dearest to him, retreated and disappeared in proportion as he drew nearer to the grave; his soul fell back upon itself, and, as it advanced towards the mysteries of the eternal future, it came in contact with other thoughts and other perplexities than those which agitated the mourners around his bed. Cromwell's religious faith had exercised but little influence over his conduct; the necessities, combinations, and passions of this world had more generally swayed him, and he had yielded to their mastery with cynical recklessness,—as he was determined to succeed, to become great, and to rule at any cost. The Christian had disappeared beneath the revolutionary politician and despot; but though it had disappeared, it had not altogether perished: Christian faith had survived in his soul, though overladen by so many falsehoods and crimes; and when the final trial arrived, it re-asserted its power; and, to use the fine expression of Archbishop Tillotson, "Cromwell's religious enthusiasm gained the victory over his hy-

---

[1] Thurloe's State Papers, vol. vii. pp. 303, 306.

pocrisy." On the 2nd of September, Cromwell, who had been delirious, had a lucid interval of some duration. His chaplains were standing around his bed. "Tell me," he said to one of them,[1] "is it possible to fall from grace?" "It is not possible," replied the minister. "Then," exclaimed the dying man, "I am safe; for I know that I was once in grace." He then turned round, and prayed aloud "Lord," he said, "though I am a miserable and wretched creature, I am in covenant with Thee through grace; and ! may, I will, come to Thee, for thy people! Thou hast made me, though very unworthy, a mean instrument to do them some good, and Thee service; and many of them have set too high a value upon me, though others wish, and would be glad of my death; but, Lord, however Thou do dispose of me, continue and go on to do good for them. Give them consistency of judgment, one heart, and mutual love; and go on to deliver them, and with the work of reformation; and make the name of Christ glorious in the world. Teach those who look too much on Thy instruments to depend more upon Thyself. Pardon such as desire to trample upon the dust of a poor worm, for they are Thy people too; and pardon the folly of this short prayer, even for Jesus Christ's sake. Amen."[2]

This pious exercise was followed by a kind of stupor, which continued until evening. As the night closed in, Cromwell became greatly agitated; he spoke in low and broken tones, terminating neither his ideas nor his words. "Truly God is good," he said, "indeed he is . . . he will not . . . he will not leave me . . . I would be willing to live to be farther serviceable to God and His people . . . but my work is done . . . yet God will be with His people." One of his attendants offered him something to drink, and besought him to endeavour to sleep. "It is not my design," he answered, "to drink or sleep, but my design is to make what haste I can to be gone." Day dawned at length: it was the 3rd of September, his FORTUNATE DAY, as he had often called it—the anniversary of his victories at Dunbar and Worcester.

---

[1] To Dr. Goodwin, according to some authorities; or Dr. Sterry, according to others.

[2] Baxter's Life, part i. p. 98; Neal's History of the Puritans, vol. iv. p. 181; Cromwell's Letters and Speeches, vol. iii. pp. 453—457. Most of these details are derived from a pamphlet entitled, "A Collection of several passages concerning his late Highness Oliver Cromwell in the time of his Sickness; written by one that was then groom of his bedchamber." This pamphlet is attributed by some to Maidstone, who was at that time Steward of Cromwell's household; and by others (as I think, with greater probability) to Underwood, one of the grooms of his bedchamber, who was sent to Henry Cromwell in Ireland with the sad intelligence. Thurloe's State Papers, vol. vii. pp. 374, 375; Harris's Life of Cromwell, pp. 484—486; Biographia Britannica, vol. iii. p. 1572.

By a singular coincidence, the night which had just ended had been very stormy—a violent tempest had caused many disasters both on land and sea; Cromwell had relapsed into a state of utter insensibility, from which he did not again recover. Between three and four o'clock in the afternoon, as he lay still unconscious, he heaved a deep sigh; the attendants drew near his bed; he had just expired.[1]

At the news of his death, a general shudder, arising from very different feelings, ran through all England. Cavaliers and Republicans, Episcopalians and Presbyterians, Levellers and Anabaptists—all Cromwell's enemies breathed freely, like ransomed prisoners; but they did not stir. More than this; they repressed their joy, in presence of the imposing grief of the army, and the restless disquietude of the people. Both officers and soldiers proved themselves devoted to their dead general; and the public at large, having lost their master, inquired with anxiety how they were to obtain a new government. Demonstrations of family grief and official sorrow alone appeared. The first were sincere, and the second, from a regard to propriety no less than from policy, were manifested with great splendour, as though they would secure the future by the magnificence of their homage to the past. "The bearer of this letter," wrote Lord Faulconbridge to Henry Cromwell, on the 7th of September, "brings your lordship the sad news of our general loss, in your incomparable father's death, by which · these poor nations are deprived of the greatest personage and instrument of happiness, not only our own, but indeed any other age ever produced. The preceding night, and not before, in presence of four or five of the council, he declared my Lord Richard his successor; . . . and some three hours after his decease, (a time spent only in framing the draft—not in any doubtful dispute,) was your Lordship's brother, his now Highness, declared Protector of these nations, with full consent of council, soldiers, and city. . . . All the time his late Highness was drawing on to his end, the consternation and astonishment of people was inexpressible; their hearts seemed sunk within them. And if this abroad of the family, your Lordship may imagine what it was in her Highness, and other near relations. My poor wife, I know not what in the earth to do with her; when seemingly quieted, she bursts out again into passion, that tears her very heart in pieces; nor can I blame her, considering what she has lost." The same messenger also conveyed to Henry Cromwell a letter from Thurloe, in which he states: "It hath

[1] Thurloe's State Papers, vol. vii. p. 372; Forster's Statesmen of the Commonwealth, vol. v. pp. 389—392; Heath's Chronicle, pp. 736, 737; Cromwelliana, p. 177.

pleased God hitherto to give his Highness, your brother, a very easy
and peaceable entrance upon his government. There is not a dog
that wags his tongue, so great a calm are we in." In the midst of
this calm, the pious enthusiasts who had surrounded Cromwell's
death-bed, alone raised their voices, saying to his weeping friends and
servants : " Cease to weep ; you have more reason to rejoice. He
was your protector here ; he will prove a still more powerful protector
now that he is with Christ, at the right hand of the Father."[1]

More than two months after these exhibitions of domestic grief
and enthusiasm, on the 23rd of November, 1658, the obsequies of
the Protector were celebrated in Westminster Abbey, with a pomp
which far exceeded all that had ever yet been displayed in England
at the funerals of kings. Although the body had been embalmed,
its rapid decomposition had rendered it necessary to bury it without
ceremony a few days after his death. On the 26th of September, a
magnificent catafalque was erected at Somerset House, in the fourth
of a suite of rooms hung with black velvet; and the effigy of the
Protector lay there for more than six weeks, exposed to the gaze of
an immense crowd of people, who daily thronged to behold it. In
regulating the order of these ceremonies, not only had national
recollections been consulted, but the learning of men versed in the
study of royal pageants, as illustrated by the practice of the great
continental monarchies. One of these, Mr. Kinnersley, suggested
the obsequies of the most Catholic of kings, Philip II. of Spain,
as most worthy to be imitated in the interment of the Protector of
European Protestantism. His suggestion was adopted ; and at an
interval of sixty years,[2] Philip II. and Cromwell, at the solemn
moment of their appearance before God, received, amidst the same
funereal splendour, the same testimonies of the pious respect of the
nations they had governed.[3]

Cromwell died in the plenitude of his power and greatness. He
had succeeded beyond all expectation, far more than any other of
those men has succeeded, who, by their genius, have raised themselves, as he had done, to supreme authority; for he had attempted
and accomplished, with equal success, the most opposite designs.
During eighteen years that he had been an ever-victorious actor on
the world's stage, he had alternately sown disorder and established

[1] Thurloe's State Papers, vol. vii. pp. 374, 375 ; Ludlow's Memoirs, p. 259 ;
Continuation of Baker's Chronicle, p. 690.
[2] Philip II. died just sixty years, day for day, before Cromwell, on the 13|3
of September, 1598.
[3] Old Parliamentary History, vol. xxi. pp. 238—245; Cromwelliana, pp.
178—181; Ludlow's Memoirs, p. 260.

order, effected and punished revolution, overthrown and restored government, in his country. At every moment, under all circumstances, he had distinguished with admirable sagacity the dominant interests and passions of the time, so as to make them the instruments of his own rule,—careless whether he belied his antecedent conduct, so long as he triumphed in concert with the popular instinct, and explaining the inconsistencies of his conduct by the ascendant unity of his power. He is, perhaps, the only example which history affords of one man having governed the most opposite events, and proved sufficient for the most various destinies. And in the course of his violent and changeful career, incessantly exposed to all kinds of enemies and conspiracies, Cromwell experienced this crowning favour of fortune, that his life was never actually attacked; the sovereign against whom Killing had been declared to be No Murder, never found himself face to face with an assassin. The world has never known another example of success at once so constant and so various, or of fortune so invariably favourable, in the midst of such manifold conflicts and perils.

Yet Cromwell's death-bed was clouded with gloom. He was unwilling not only to die, but also, and most of all, to die without having attained his real and final object. However great his egotism may have been, his soul was too great to rest satisfied with the highest fortune, if it were merely personal, and, like himself, of ephemeral earthly duration. Weary of the ruin he had caused, it was his cherished wish to restore to his country a regular and stable government—the only government which was suited to its wants, a monarchy under the control of Parliament. And at the same time, with an ambition which extended beyond the grave, under the influence of that thirst for permanence which is the stamp of true greatness, he aspired to leave his name and race in possession of the throne. He failed in both designs: his crimes had raised up obstacles against him, which neither his prudent genius nor his persevering will could surmount; and though covered, as far as he was himself concerned, with power and glory, he died with his dearest hopes frustrated, and leaving behind him, as his successors, the two enemies whom he had so ardently combated—anarchy and the Stuarts.

God does not grant to those great men, who have laid the foundations of their greatness amidst disorder and revolution, the power of regulating at their pleasure, and for succeeding ages, the government of nations.

THE END.

PRINTED BY WILLIAM CLOWES AND SONS, LIMITED, LONDON AND BECCLES.   S & H

www.ingramcontent.com/pod-product-compliance
Lightning Source LLC
Chambersburg PA
CBHW020856130726
47900CB00014B/833